Table of

Introduction ....
What Lies Beneath by Adaline 5
Dark Flame by Aisling Elizabeth 19
The Right Time by Amy Davies 34
The Tourist by Anna Edwards 48
Crimson Army by Annalee Adams 59
Pursuing Lilly by Annie Charme 75
Sugarplum by B Crowhurst 91
Sunshine and the Vamp by Bailey Grayson 104
Finding Bob by Belinda E Edwards 120
Red Zone by Carol Kerry-Green 135
Angels Rest by Cassidy Reyne 146
Bound Desires by CC Gedling 160
A Soul So Fierce and Furry by Chloë L. Blyth 175
David by Chris Turnbull 188
Here There Be Tygers by Clare London 203
Twinkle Toes by Colette Davison 219
The Queen by David E. Gordon 235
Scattering Elephants by Eleanor Lloyd-Jones 248
Three's Company by Elle M Thomas 263
More Than Men: The Lost Diaries by Gemini Black 276
Ravenswood After Dark by Harley Raige 290
A Special Place Wedding by Helen C Kelly 303
Don of Avery by J.D. Groom 316
Tangles of Desire by Karen Nappa 332
Yours in the Next Life by Laura Rush 348
Hidden Identity (ClubHS #3) by Lisa M. Miller 360
Dealer's Arrival by Liz Cain 373
A Hard Sell by Lucy Felthouse 387
Champion by M.F. Moody 402
Forged by Shadows by Maddison Cole 419
The Creaking Bough by Marie Anne Cope 435
Two Days by Marie Anne Cope 444

Falling for the Scammer by Martina Dale 451
A Night to Remember by Mia Kun 465
Raven Seer Beginnings by Paula Acton 479
Monstrous Grave by Rainelyn 487
The Betrayal by Ruby Bloom 496
Notorious Legacy #1 by Sophie Dyer 509
Secret Project by Stephanie Hurst (Title TBA) 524
The Viking City Murders by Marie Moore 539
The Waiter by Suzanne Lissaman 558
A Shot in Time by T.S. Simons 573
Thank You for Reading 590

Copyright © VARIOUS AUTHORS 2024

The moral right of THE AUTHORS to be identified as authors of this Work has been asserted by them in accordance with the Copyright, Designs and Patents Act of 1988.

All rights reserved.

No part of this publication may be reproduced, stored in a retrieval system, or transmitted in any form or by any means, electronic, mechanical, photocopying, recording or otherwise, without the prior permission of the copyright owner. You must not circulate this book without the authority to do so.

All characters in this book are fictitious, and any resemblance to actual persons living or dead is purely coincidental.

Cover design, typesetting, arrangement and introduction by
Sarah Michelle Lynch

Introduction

Dear Reader,

This is a showcase of work from various authors we are hosting this year at "Authors at the Armouries" Book Festival and Signing.

Our event is multi-genre so within this collection you will discover contemporary romance (some stories steamier than others; some darker than others). Not to mention thriller, PNR, fantasy and sci-fi.

AATA prides itself on bringing new and emerging talent, as well as established talent, to the masses and this annual is just one way in which we do that. And a big bonus of it is that this anthology also will raise money for charity. This year's charity is the RSPCA and you may even find a couple of stories in this book that feature the kind of loveable animal friends that many of us within the book community couldn't imagine life without.

Happy reading!

With much love,

Sarah Michelle Lynch (event organiser) x

AATA 2024: THE ANNUAL

A Multi-Genre Anthology

Various Authors

What Lies Beneath by Adaline Winters

A Ruthless Creatures Prequel to Beneath Your Beautiful

Content Warning

What Lies Beneath features stalking, controlling behavior, sexual scenes, physical assault, and domestic violence. 18+ only

Beauty Is in the Eye of the Beholder.

~ Honor ~
New Year's Eve
One year after marriage.

My heart races, a galloping deer looking to escape the beast stalking it in the darkness. I don't run. It never ends well. Instead, I await Gideon on the edge of the enormous bed, with my eyes trained to the floor and my spine ramrod straight. He enjoys letting the fear build until my limbs shake. I pluck at a loose strand on the white silk dressing gown shielding my body and work through the steps of meditation. Breathe. Funny how people make millions teaching us to do something we are naturally born to. My deep breaths are hindered, getting stuck part way down. Instead, I entertain myself with fantasies of stabbing Gideon with the steak knife he cut into his beef wellington with last night. My mouth waters. How long has it been since I tasted steak?

The door to our bedroom swings open, and all my clever breathing techniques evaporate as his shoes tap on the hardwood floor. They pause in front of me, and the hair on the nape of my neck lifts. I've become intimate with the many pairs of shoes he owns, given they are the first thing I see each day.

A finger curves under my chin and tilts my head back. My gaze locks onto the startling baby blues the city has declared their savior. Gideon Lowell is now the district attorney for New York. Powerful, untouchable, and wicked. A dangerous combination.

His blonde hair is styled back, one lock seemingly escaping onto his forehead. But nothing about Gideon is accidental. He's disarming, dressed in a classic tailored black suit and white shirt. The bow tie hangs undone around his neck, a job he considers important for his wife.

I don't doubt that my husband covets me, but there is a difference between love and obsession. The beauticians did my makeup and styled my long ice-blonde hair into an elegant updo based on Gideon's instructions. His excuse for such control is the dress he's had made for me as a surprise, so only he would know what matches. They made noises of approval, like he was Prince Charming. It astounds me how people gloss over the obvious facts and cling to the fairytale. Anyone looking close enough would see the cracks covering my facade. I am breaking piece by piece.

"You look stunning," he utters.

My brain processes his relaxed shoulders, his steady breathing, and the calmness in his eyes. The beast he houses is not in control.

"Thank you. You look handsome." My words are clear. I've learned to not whisper or stutter.

He hums in the back of his throat. "Stand, Honor."

I hide the wince as I comply. He tilts his head as he undoes the knot at my waist and slides the gown off my shoulders. His fingers trail over my naked breasts, pebbling my nipples. His hands curve around the leather clinched around my abdomen.

His jaw tics as his hands fail to touch as they circle the dip in my waist. "Almost there. Let's tighten this up a little. Turn around and hold the bedpost."

Ice inches down my spine as I spin and clutch the wooden post. "I think we can get this into its final position tonight, baby. Giving you the perfect body to show off."

"Thank you." He's training my body into what he considers ideal—all for my benefit, of course—and he expects me to be eternally grateful for it. Secretly, I dream of wearing sweats while eating pizza.

His fingers sweep the length of my spine, following the cold sensation. He undoes the heavy-duty laces holding the steel-lined leather in place. "Deep breath in, baby, hold it, then release slowly."

Ha. Deep breath, what a joke. I drag in the air, spiced with his expensive cologne. As I exhale, my grip tightens on the bedpost, and he yanks. My body lifts in the air, but gravity doesn't help his cause.

Bones click behind me as he snaps his neck, an action which always heralds suffering. Mine, not his. I glance over my shoulder as he lifts his foot and braces it against my bare ass.

"Again," he snaps.

As I exhale, he yanks on the laces and pushes against my butt to keep me in place. The leather tightens, and bile rushes up my throat. I swallow the burning liquid.

"Once more."

Tears spring in my eyes, but no sound leaves my throat as he pulls the waist trainer into its ultimate position. He breathes heavily behind me as he secures the laces. He kisses along my shoulder as his fingers touch over my stomach.

"Perfect," he utters against my ear. For now. "Come look at yourself in the mirror, Honor."

He guides me to the gilded full-length mirror hanging opposite the bed. My mismatched eyes blink at the body shape he's created. If it keeps him happy, then the pain is worth it. He curves one hand around my throat and puts pressure on my lower stomach with the other, so his erection presses against my ass. He towers over my five-foot three height, at almost six foot.

"You'll need to wear it continuously with only an hour or two breaks for the next month to ensure you maintain this shape. After that we can start reducing it. It also helps you maintain control over your diet."

Diet? What a joke. My stomach is clamped inside a vise—that's control. Rage burns before I douse it. Luckily, he's too busy examining my body to notice. "I can't wait to fuck you like this later."

"Me too." Gideon's expectation of a wife. He loves me, therefore has rights to my body at any time. These were his words the first time I woke to him moving inside of me. When I said I do, I gave up my right to consent. It's bullshit. I know this deep down. But going against the city's knight of virtue and warrior of justice isn't an easy feat. It takes time, planning, and courage.

He drags his teeth over his bottom lip, and my stomach flops. That's a bad sign.

He turns and strides into the dressing room. "Stay here."

Where would I go? The only places I can escape are inside my mind, but he doesn't tolerate disconnection. I must be aware of everything he does, every move he makes, and every demand he makes.

He reappears with a large square black velvet box in one hand and a dress bag in the other. He hooks the bag on the top of the mirror and unzips it. A stunning black velvet floor-length gown spills out of the bag. He runs his hand along the material. The V in the neckline will plunge between my breasts, but not deep enough to reveal the trainer.

"It's gorgeous, Gideon."

"Only the best, as I show my wife off to the city's elite tonight."

He snaps open the box, revealing a complex set of rose gold chains and three clips. I swallow as my eyes rise to his.

He places the box on the floor and lifts the jewelry. "This part goes around your throat."

His arms brush my shoulders as he secures the snug thin chain around my neck. His eyes blaze with possessiveness. "Fold your hands behind your back." I do so, weaving my fingers together and clenching them tight. His hands graze my breasts, and he dips his head and sucks on my left nipple hard, causing me to hiss. He lets it go with a pop before he lifts one of the chains.

"These go here." He pinches my erect nipple and snaps the metal clip onto the end, applying pressure until he's happy with the tightness. My hands clench tighter to temper the scream in my throat. He repeats it with my other nipple, then he gives the chains a tug.

My breath stutters. He glances at my face in warning. "Do they hurt?"

What do you think, asshole? I nod.

"Words, Honor."

"Yes."

He drops to his knees, and I squeeze my eyes closed. There's a third clip. No prizes for guessing where that's going.

His mouth closes around my clit and he draws it into his mouth, encouraging the sensitive bundle to swell.

"Look at me," he demands. My eyes fly open, and he grins. "Watch in the mirror." He shifts, giving me a full view of his actions. He scissors his fingers on either side of my clit, exposing it. "Brace yourself, baby."

My hand cramps as I squeeze my fingers. The last clip is attached to the central chain, and it tugs as he pulls it. He snaps it on, and I double over as sharp pain lances between my legs. My hands land on his shoulders.

He places his hands over mine and rises to his feet, forcing me to stand straight. The position pulls the chains taught. He finishes fixing a few more decorative chains disguising the whole thing like sexy jewelry.

"These have little metal teeth that grip tighter the more you tug them." He demonstrates by giving a small pull on the central chain. "This way, you'll feel my touch every moment tonight. The longer they remain on, the more restricted your blood flow, and the more pain you'll feel when they come off. I'll be inside of you when that happens."

Of course, he can't pass up feeling the evidence of my pain. He unhooks the gown from the hanger and helps me into it. He grins over my shoulder at the result. The pretty chains look like they are part of the dress's design, while the waist clings to my figure, showing off the shape he's created.

He selects a pair of heels, completing the outfit. He stands behind me, once again trailing his hand between my breasts and catching the chains. My eyes prickle. The burning pressure is already too much, and the throbbing between my legs builds. How is this going to feel hours from now?

"Don't ruin your makeup," he snaps. I close my eyes and will away the tears. "Last thing. Your allowance for the night is three canapes of your choice and a glass of champagne. I don't want you vomiting later when I take you."

It's more than some nights. I guess we can't have our guests suspicious of the fact that their golden boy is, in fact, the worst of monsters.

I thought if I loved him harder, deeper, it would change. I would become worthy of the man I first met. I was wrong.

Now I stand on the precipice of our one-year anniversary, a shell of the woman I once was. Gutted by his words, hands, emotions, and control. But there's a place deep inside of me, one he cannot reach, that clings to a thin ray of light. I just have to be brave enough to grasp it, for there is no salvation in the vast darkness, and I am not ready to go without a fight.

Get ready to hunt, husband. I'm about to test your resolve.

Love, Honor, Betray.

~ Honor ~

July 1st

Six months after marriage.

I burst into the house, full of excitement, my heels clicking on the marble floor as I search for my husband in this mansion I'm lucky enough to call home. White roses sit in a vase in the hallway, an apology for me having to miss my company retreat last week. Always white roses from the prince of New York. They are pure, ethereal, perfect. At least, that's what Gideon believes. I prefer explosions of color—pinks, purples, and yellows. Life should be lived to the fullest, grasping each and every magical moment.

Six blissful months we've been wed. I promised to love, honor, and obey, and in return, he promised to cherish. Gideon is a complicated man, one I've barely scratched the surface of. But that's no problem, as I have a lifetime to unravel him.

"Gideon," I call out. He's not fond of me raising my voice, but I'm too wound up to search each room in this vast place.

"I'm in my office," he responds. I move past the dining room, set with silverware ready for our evening meal. I wonder if I could persuade him to get takeout, just this once in celebration. I burst into his office. He leans his elbows on his heavyset walnut desk, his oceanic eyes tracking me. He's always watching, like a hunter.

"I got the job," I declare.

He frowns. "What job?"

I flop into the high back leather chair opposite him and drop my purse on the floor as I toe off my expensive heels while wiggling my toes. "The promotion. I didn't tell you, as I didn't want to disappoint you if I wasn't successful."

He stares at me, and I stare back, unsure of his mood. "I see. Will this job demand more of your time?"

"There will be some traveling involved, yes. But I've practically been doing the job already."

"No."

I blink. "What do you mean, no?"

"I've just made DA, Honor. I need you here, supporting me as my wife, not jetting around the country, making a spectacle of yourself as a woman in a man's world."

My fists clench. We don't argue. We don't shout. We rarely disagree. "I already accepted."

He quirks a brow and leans back as he studies me. "In fact, you'll be needed here full time."

I jerk back. "No, Gideon. I can't be fulfilled picking out curtain fabric, choosing weekly menus, and tending to the rose bushes."

He flicks his fingers. "We have people for those roles. I need my *wife*, here, present, not exhausted from jet lag and dealing with meaningless tasks."

Meaningless? I work in the energy industry. "That's not your decision."

He hums in the back of his throat as his gaze narrows. He rises from his chair, a six-foot golden adonis that the media are obsessed with. He's the crime-fighting superhero, cleaning up the streets of the city. He stalks around the desk and circles the room behind me. The hairs on my nape rise. He comes closer, and his warm lips skim my ear. "Did I mishear your defiance, Mrs. Lowell?" he utters.

My eyes flutter closed, and I shake my head. Gideon wields his lethal tongue like a weapon—whether through spoken word or by the things it can do to my body.

"The deal is done," I say. "Wicked promises won't change it."

He sighs against my throat. My shoulders sag. Good—he's seen reason. The metal clang of a belt buckle being undone fills the room. Here? Now? He's insatiable.

Leather loops around my neck, and he yanks it tight. My hands fly up and grip the belt as the pressure cuts off my air. My legs kick out as panic overtakes me. What is he doing?

He leans over me, keeping the unyielding grip on the belt around my throat. He picks up his cell phone and presses a button. It rings three times, then my boss's voice croaks through the line. "Mr. Lowell, how can I help you?" Frederick asks.

My head tips back, and I glare at Gideon as I shake my head. *Don't you fucking dare.* "My wife won't be taking you up on your offer of promotion, which you failed to inform me about."

"Mr. Lowell, that is your wife's decis—"

"Are you still waiting on the planning permission?" Gideon drawls.

Oh, no. My mouth opens to protest, but nothing comes out. Not a whimper, not a breath, not a protest. Black spots dance across my vision as the silence stretches.

"Yes," Frederick eventually snaps.

"Then consider this my wife's notice of termination of employment. I will send a driver for her personal belongings tomorrow." He stabs the phone and drops it back onto the desk. His gaze trails down my heaving chest, a fire burning in his eyes as he watches me struggle.

"There. That wasn't so hard, baby," he says as he loosens the belt. I gasp, tears spilling down my hot cheeks. He yanks hard, pulling me to the floor, and my knees bounce on the hardwood, making me cry out. He hooks his thumb inside of my mouth, and I briefly consider biting the fucking thing off, but his ice-cold gaze makes me pause. The veil has lifted, and the man I'm seeing now is the real Gideon. It's terrifying. "Get used to being on your knees, Honor. It's time for your punishment. I won't tolerate defiance. If I'm lenient now, it will only escalate. I do this because I love you; a little pain and discomfort now for a lifetime of happiness. That's worth it."

The notion of obeying one's spouse—specifically the wife obeying the husband—is antiquated. They're meant to cherish us in return, but on balance, it's a poor deal. I just want the man I fell for to keep his promises of loving me unconditionally. Now he's betrayed that love. He's betrayed me.

The world is full of monsters, ruthless creatures that covet light until they suffocate it with their darkness. The trick is to hold on tight to the goodness in your soul. Nurture it, feed it the fire of betrayal, and when the time is right, wield it like the sharpest blade.

Your Soul to Take.

~ Gideon ~

Six months before marriage.

Everything is in place. Now, all I need is my wife to be. She's late. Again. No matter, she won't be in that job for long. Her place is by my side, and once I secure her hand tonight, she will understand that I'm all she needs.

The door opens, and I sink to one knee. It's the one and only time I will ever bow or beg, but I'm a traditionalist. She's a vision in the cream sheath dress I had delivered to her apartment and those nude heels. She's taken the time to do her hair and makeup how I like it.

"Gideon?" she mutters as she stalls in front of me.

I pop open the small black velvet box, displaying the classy three-carat diamond set in a bed of sapphires. It reflects the unique color of her eyes.

"Yes," she says.

I smirk. "I haven't asked you yet."

She goes to her knees in front of me, cups my face, and gives me one of those greedy kisses that I live for. I pluck the ring from the box and grab her left hand, sliding it onto her ring finger without breaking contact. My hands cup her ass, and I encourage her to wrap her legs around my waist as I rise and carry her to the dining room. The maid appears with the starters, but I glare at her, and she makes a hasty retreat.

I lay Honor onto the unset end of the dining table and spread her out to look at her as I begin unbuttoning my shirt. She's stunning, but I can make her better. Perfection is not something many can achieve. With a little gentle guidance, Honor can represent the flawlessness I exude. We will be the power couple the city aspires to.

I peel her matching cream silk panties down her toned thighs and stuff them in my pants pocket before grasping her knees and pinning them to the table. My mouth descends on her core, and she gasps as my tongue enters her tight channel. Her hands thread into my hair as she arches her spine. I grab them and pin them to the table, unwilling to be controlled or directed. She will take exactly what I give her—no more, no less. I drag her to the edge of an orgasm before tearing my mouth away and unzipping my pants. I sheath myself inside her in one hard thrust. She cries out at the intrusion, but I don't give her a second to adjust.

Her body, mind, and soul is forever mine now. Until death do us part.

A Wet Dream

~ Honor ~

The night they met.

It's a glorious evening, and I'm high on a life full of laughter, friendship, and good food as I rush toward my apartment. A shiver runs down my spine as the evening air turns muggy. I giggle as a splash of cool rain beats against my overheated skin makes me giggle. My heeled feet pause on the sidewalk as a town car races past and splashes me from head to toe, soaking my short flirty red summer dress. I suck in a shocked breath before spewing a string of colorful curses with a grin on my face. My mischievous father would be proud, and my tight-laced mother mortified.

The car skids to a halt, blurry red lights winking at me as it reverses inch by inch until it blocks the road. They couldn't have heard me, right?

AATA 2024: THE ANNUAL

I dart my gaze up and down the street. This isn't like the smut books I love. If some masked dude exits this car, I am running, and I do not wish to be chased. Morally gray is all good and well between the pages, but that's where it needs to stay.

Left or right? I turn right as the car door opens and a huge black umbrella snaps out, shielding the person from view. My feet freeze, and my heart pounds in my chest. My fingertips tingle as adrenaline floods my body. If they're after a fight, I'll damn well give it to them.

The umbrella lifts, and a real-life Prince Charming steps forward, shielding us both. He displaces the rain like a god in a storm, as if the elements are his to command, and the world his to rearrange.

"Are you okay?" His voice is cultured, smooth, lulling.

I blink the water off my eyelashes as he examines me from head to toe. It's not slimy but assessing. Be still my beating heart. Did I stumble upon the rare breed of gentleman in New York? According to my best friend, they are the things of myth and legend. *Sucks to be a nonbeliever right now, huh, Jen?* I'm a closet romantic, and my manifesting has paid off. Unless he's a murderer.

"You're shivering. Here, hold this." He hands me the handle of the umbrella, our fingers brushing causing little tingles to zip up my arm. He shrugs off his long dress coat before wrapping it around my shoulders and enclosing me in his warmth. Damn, he smells good. What is that? Woodsy, smoky, with a hint of vanilla. I inhale again like a lunatic.

"I'll give you a lift home." He wraps an arm around my waist and ushers me toward the car. My survival instincts kick in, and I dig my heels in as I shake my head.

"Thank you, but it's just a little water."

"You'll catch a cold."

"It's a common misconception that being cold gives you a virus. Also, colds don't kill twenty-something-year-old healthy women."

He throws his head back and laughs, making my lips twitch. "Beautiful, funny, and smart. You get more intriguing with every word, Miss...?"

"Honor." Wait, no. I shouldn't be giving out my name to gorgeous strangers. Did he call me beautiful and smart? That's a sure-fire way to win my heart.

"Honor." My name graces his lips, and I'm on the verge of begging him to say it again so I can watch the way his plush mouth forms the syllables. I wonder if his lips are as soft as they look? "I insist."

I shrug out of his coat. He shakes his head and tucks it around me tighter. "I can walk. It's only a few blocks from here."

He raises his brow. "Worried I'm going to kidnap you?"

My lips twitch. "And the murder. Let's not forget the endgame."

He runs a hand over his jaw. "If I was going to kidnap you, Honor, and have you at my mercy, you wouldn't be screaming in fear."

My lips twitch. Oh, he's a little cocky under that smooth exterior. I kinda like it. "Really?"

"Alas, you are not on the menu tonight as I have a meeting to get to after I've dropped you safe and sound at home. Plus, you are the sort of woman who deserves to be wined, dined, and wooed."

Who says wooed? I relent for a split second. Murderers don't drive around in town cars, right? I shake my head and whip his coat off before handing it back to him. He sighs.

"Take the umbrella at least."

I laugh as I spin in a circle in the pouring rain. "Why? The weather is glorious."

I disappear into the night, a carefree soul, not knowing I've incited a monster to stalk the freedom I took for granted.

~ *Gideon* ~

I watch this stunning creature disappear into the night, waltzing through the rain like she has the world at her feet. She could, with my help. She radiates goodness like an angel. I drum my fingers against the open door of the town car and debate following her. Would she turn me away? There's a wildness to her, something only a man can tame.

I climb into the car and pull the door closed. I need to bide my time, play this right. Going after her tonight won't give me the life I deserve.

The driver pulls away, and we make the short drive to the governor's city apartment. After exiting the elevator, he greets me with a smile, still dressed in an impeccable suit despite the late hour. Men like us don't sleep much.

"Gideon, glad you could make it," he says with a firm handshake. Terry Garcia is a fifty-four-year-old man, with a beautiful wife who he's had two children with. He keeps his mistress in an apartment just below this one. Marriage and mistresses have never appealed to me.

He guides me to the L-shaped sofa and offers me a whiskey before pouring himself one and settling on the chair across from me.

"The DA is retiring," he says, cutting straight to the point.

"Is the assistant not up to par?" I ask carefully as a shot of excitement runs through me. This is it, what I've been working toward.

"She's not ready."

"I see."

"But like a politician, it would be better if his successor had a stable relationship, a home life people can get behind. You keep your nose clean, Gideon, but your position would be strengthened by having the right woman at your side."

Actually, I keep my private life just that—private. I highly doubt Terry would class my tastes as clean. My mind flicks to Honor, soaked and dancing in the rain wearing that short red dress. "I understand."

We chat about his vision for the city while I make plans to ensnare a wild woman and bring her to heel.

As I make my way down to the garage, I drop a message to one of my tech team. I give him a few blocks radius and ask him to hunt for a twenty to thirty-year-old woman living in that area with the first name of Honor. People leave a digital footprint that is easily traceable with the right tools.

By the time the car pulls into my driveway, I have her address, place of work, where she buys her morning coffee, and even what store she buys her underwear from.

Game on, Honor. Prepare to be hunted, caught, and tamed.

~ *Honor* ~

Coffee, pants, work. Wait. No, pants, coffee, then work. Don't want to give Harry at The Daily Grind an eyeful because I forgot pants. Although it might mean extra foam on my mocha with a shot of vanilla.

The sun is shining and the world is good as I rush into the cafe. I check my purse for my phone and wallet as I join the line. I rustle around the random crinkled receipts dating back months and pens I've swiped from various places, coming up short for my wallet. I'm sure I packed it. Wait, no. It's on the dining table. I'm an idiot. I glance at my watch, but I don't have time to make it back to my apartment. This day is going to suck big time. I'm nursing a headache from too much tequila, and now my caffeine fix is being withheld. There's always Barry's instant granules... I shudder.

"Is that from the cold you caught?" a familiar male voice drawls.

My head pops up, and my gaze collides with gorgeous sky-blue eyes. He's here. How?

"It's you." I look around the cafe. He's never been here before. I don't think.

"It's me."

I don't even know his name, and now he's invading my space in this city of eight point five million people. It's not a coincidence, and it's not fate. This man hunted me down in one night. Who does that?

I drag my bottom lip between my teeth, and his eyes drop to the motion. The heat from his gaze licks at my spine. Oh, he's trouble with a capital T. Maybe I'm in the mood for a little trouble.

"I need to go," I mutter, backing up straight into another customer. "Watch it, bitch," the guy behind me snaps.

Excuse me, what? My cheeks flush in embarrassment, and I prepare to turn around and give this asshole a piece of my mind. But my Prince Charming grips my arm and tugs me forward. My nose brushes his crisp expensive white shirt. There's that smell again. *Fucking hell.*

"Apologize," he commands.

"She backed into me.".

"Are you injured? Did this small woman damage your ego?"

Ha. This *small* woman has a mean right hook.

"Look, I was just waiting in line for my coffee."

I glance to the side, everyone has paused their morning madness to watch the drama unfold. Being the center of attention makes me itch.

"I don't care if you are taking a shit on the sidewalk at noon. Apologize to the lady, pay for her coffee, and then leave and never come back to this establishment again."

"It's fine," I mutter, trying to diffuse this situation.

"No, it's not fine."

"Not happening, dude," the idiot behind me replies.

Harry moves down the counter. "Her coffee is eight dollars. Pay up or get out." A real spectacle now.

"You're fucking joking."

Enough. I spin around, and I'm met with a slim middle-aged man wearing oil-stained overalls and looking like he uses said oil to slick his lanky hair back. His beady eyes narrow, and he sneers. "Going to stop hiding behind these men like a little bitch?" he snarls.

My hand fists, and my arm rises. A hand snaps out over my shoulder and then he's on the floor, his nose spurting blood over the black and white tiles. I blink and turn back around.

"Why did you do that? You'll get in trouble."

"Not likely," he rumbles, pulling me in front of him and away from the bleeding asshole on the floor.

Harry slides my order over with a wink. "Nobody saw a thing, Mr. Lowell."

Who? "I don't have my purse," I mutter, confused.

"Already paid for." Harry smiles as he tends to the next customer. My Prince Charming scoops up my coffee alongside his own and urges me around the guy on the floor. Is this some alternate reality?

We spill onto the busy sidewalk. I eyeball the coffee in his hands.

"Are you stalking me?"

"Stalking is illegal. I'm persistent, Honor."

"I don't even know your name."

"Gideon."

"And you somehow tracked me to my regular café, but you aren't stalking me?"

"No, I tracked you to your home address but thought you would freak out if I showed up on your doorstep."

My mouth pops open before I slam it closed. "Because this is less creepy? Are you holding my coffee hostage? Or do I need to beg for it?"

His eyes flare as his lips twitch. "I'm not above being floored by a beautiful smart woman begging me."

"Figure of speech. There will be no begging."

He offers me the cup, and when my hand wraps around it, he grasps my elbow and pulls me closer. My breath stutters.

His gaze burrows into my soul. "I know what I want, and I am single-minded in

my determination to get it."

"And what is it you want?" I whisper.

He tucks a lock of my wild hair behind my ear, sending shivers racing down my spine. "You."

Perhaps this was my first clue. Gideon Lowell wasn't the savior of our fine city... but the demon who feasted on your soul one sliver at a time until all that remained was an empty shell.

The hunt is on, and I'm the ultimate prey.

⊙≈⊙

Eager to find out what happens next?
Beneath Your Beautiful is a full length standalone dark romance novel featuring a grumpy bodyguard and a sassy heroine.
Please check the content warnings.

Dark Flame by Aisling Elizabeth

A Sample from Book One of Dark Heath University Series

One ~ Ember

I looked around the stuffy dark wood panelled office before allowing my eyes to settle on the equally stuffy greying haired man sitting behind the desk in front of me. He was droning on in a monotonous tone about what a wonderful experience I was going to have here at Dark Heath University. I held back the derisive snort that I wanted to expel and settled for trying to stifle a yawn.

"Miss Woods?" The man, or Headteacher Grovins, as he introduced himself, glared at me. "I don't think you understand the severity of the situation here." I rolled my eyes, which was met with another glare. I understood all too well how fucked up this all was. That I was sitting in a Headteacher's office at twenty-three years old was only the beginning of the shit stain turn that my life had taken. I tried to force a smile on my face but had a feeling it came out more of a grimace.

"I am sorry headteacher Grovins," I said in the politest tone that my mother would have been proud of. A flash of grief hit me at the thought of my mother, but I pushed forward.

"I understand completely. Excuse me if I appear dismissive, it has been quite the week." The headteacher's stern expression slipped slightly, before setting back into the frown that seemed to be a permanent feature. But I saw sympathy for the briefest of moments. I much preferred the frown.

"Yes well," he said, "I know that you have had a significant shock to your reality."

That was an understatement. A week ago my biggest concern was trying to figure out how to pay the costs of my mum's funeral on my minimum wage cafe job, and still be able to afford to eat. But at least the world was normal. Since then I found out that there was a whole hidden world of all the supernatural creatures that I had only read about in books, and I was actually a witch. Add to that little revelation that I was apparently breaking some supernatural law by unknowingly practising magic and was arrested and sentenced to death for these crimes. Yep, I would say that would be considered a significant shock to my reality.

"I do hope that you consider yourself lucky to be afforded the opportunity to immerse yourself into the heritage that was taken from you," the headteacher said, his voice softening a bit. "You could consider this a silver lining, so to speak." I grimaced again at his words.

"Sure," I said, "I would probably do that if I had the choice. But I don't really do I?" The frown deepened on Grovins face. Oops, I guess that was the wrong thing to say.

"Miss Woods," he snapped, "I understand that this is a difficult situation, but you are very lucky to be a student at such a prestigious school. I rather think that you should consider that luck and make the best of this."

I took a deep breath and rubbed my temple. I felt like I was getting a headache. I knew he was right. The alternative was to lose my life, and despite what I thought about the idea of being forced to go back to school, it would only be for a few years, and then my life would be my own again. That was if I graduated. That was one condition of my probation. I had to learn how to be a witch, or something. It was the law to get a licence to practise magic in this whole new world and apparently it was normal for witches and sorcerers, that's right there are sorcerers as well, to attend a magic university from the age of twenty-one. That meant I was two years behind already. Two years and an entire lifetime of knowledge behind, more like.

"I'm sorry," I whispered, I knew I could be a bit of a brat when I was stressed, but I also knew it wasn't this guy's fault either. "I'm just exhausted. Those cells that I have been in all week don't exactly have five-star hotel quality." Or one star, I thought to myself. My request to return home before coming to this place had been denied, and I was kept in the Shadow Council, which I was told was the name of the supernatural officials, cells. I was brought here today in an armoured van with Council guard, or whatever they were called. I was marched into this office by two of the guards, past all the other students, like the low life criminal I apparently was.

"I understand your discomfort, and will allow you to retire to your room soon," Grovins said. "But first I have to go over some important rules." He looked down at the papers that had been handed to him by one of the guards.

"Miss Ember Woods," he started reading. "You have been convicted of crimes against the shadow world as a rogue witch. You were found to be practising magic without a licence and the original sentence was death." Yep, I thought. I remember all too well what the extremely pale Judge said last week. I could still feel the heavy sick feeling in my stomach when he said it, which was funny considering my thoughts in the weeks before.

"Due to the circumstances that have occurred," Grovins carried on, "You have been given the opportunity to correct the error and, through a rich and excellent education, obtain the adequate knowledge and licence to be considered a valued member of our society as a legally practising witch. Should you not demonstrate the required knowledge to achieve your licence by the required time, then the original sentence of death will be carried out." He stopped and looked at me. I could tell that he was as uncomfortable about this as I was. He looked back down at the paper with a cough.

"The conditions of your parole are set forth as follows. One, you must remain on Dark Heath University campus at all times, unless you have an approved chaperone or you have a family obligation." Well that was easy, my mum was my only family and since she was now dead, there weren't really any other obligations. "You will put your full effort into your studies and maintain your grades to an acceptable level, as agreed by the headteacher of the establishment." Grovins stopped and looked at me again. I gave him a weak smile, and he coughed again.

"I erm," he said, his voice softening again. "I am planning for a one-on-one mentor to help you with your studies." I smiled again. At least he was trying to help. He looked back down at the paper and then rubbed his eyes, before placing it back in the brown folder.

"I felt that despite your heritage, being thrust into the Grand accommodations that you might be more comfortable in a more relaxed setting," he said, "at least to begin with. You are sharing a room with one of our loveliest students, who has agreed to show you the ropes and help you settle in." I was starting to feel like I was missing some information.

"I'm sorry?" I asked, "Heritage? Grand? Should I understand what these mean?" The headteacher looked at me like I had grown an extra head. He was about to speak when there was a sharp knock at the door behind me. Grovins looked up at the door and forced the frown back on his face.

"Come in," he called.

The door opened, and a well-dressed woman walked in. Her perfectly styled bun, subtle makeup and elegant skirt suit screamed authority. I recognised her from my court hearing last week. She had been sitting in the back of the courtroom. The judge had delivered my sentence and then a clerk had whispered something in his ear that caused him to look up behind me. Seeing the not so carefully concealed shock look on his face made me turn around. It was this woman that had caused the reaction. She nodded to the judge and then looked directly at me before standing up and walking out of the room. That was when the judge had changed my sentence to the mandatory attendance at Dark Heath University.

The woman smiled at headteacher Grovins as she sat down in the chair next to me. She looked at me with a small smile and a nod.

"Priestess Heathwood," Grovins said. I could tell he was excited to have this woman in his office, so she must have been someone important. "How lovely to see you."

"Thank you for taking the time to see me, Headteacher," the woman said. Her voice was lighter than I expected and had a familiar sound to it that sent a twinge to my heart. I studied her face intently, a strange feeling in my stomach as I felt like she felt more familiar than just seeing her the week before. She watched me with a smile.

"I can see that you are an intelligent girl," she said to me and my heart fluttered again.

"Who are you?" I asked and Grovins practically choked on thin air. I looked over at him as the woman chuckled.

"Miss Woods," he scolded once he could breathe again. "This is Mirriam Heathwood." I looked between the two and shrugged. Like that meant something to me. "She is the Grand High Priestess of the Shadow Council," Grovins continued. Oh, so I guess she was someone important. The woman reached out to grab my hand. I looked down at her hand and then back up at her smiling face.

"More importantly dear," she said with a tone that I recognised almost instantly, "I am your grandmother."

Two ~ Ember

"I'm sorry, what did you say?" I asked. I pulled my hand out from under her grasp and saw a flicker of what looked like hurt before she smiled again.

"Miss Woods, please," the headteacher said, and I turned to look at him. "I must ask that you address our Grand High Priestess with respect."

"Miss Heathwood," the woman said, and I looked back at her. She was watching the headteacher and from the way he squirmed I guessed he wasn't happy about it. She turned back to me with a smile.

"Her name is Ember Heathwood."

"No, it isn't," I said, shaking my head. "Maybe you have mistaken me for someone else." Even as I said it I knew I was kidding myself. I could tell by the way she smiled and the crinkle and sparkle of her eyes that she was telling the truth. It was like I was looking at an older version of my mother. It was so clear that it hurt my heart.

"Your mother was called Enid, was she not?" the woman, or priestess or whatever asked. I nodded in confirmation and she smiled. I knew she was humouring me and that we both knew the truth.

"Her full name was Enid Mirriam Heathwood, and she was the next in line to be the Grand High Priestess." I felt a sting of betrayal for my mother. I had asked about family when I was younger. I knew it wasn't normal for us to have nobody, but any mention of family and my mum would change the subject or get angry. After a while I stopped asking.

"Why didn't I know about you?" I asked, and the woman, or I guess my grandmother, shook her head. A sad look crossed her face, and I felt the hurt along with it.

"I don't know, child," she said. "Your mother disappeared just twenty-four years ago. We searched of course but she was an excellently skilled witch and knew how to cover her tracks. Last week was the first I heard of her and of you."

"Twenty-four years?" I asked, looking down in thought. "So she was pregnant with me." I looked back up at her. "Do you know who my father is then?" My grandmother shook her head.

"I am sorry dear," she said. "I didn't even know she was intimate with anyone. I certainly didn't know she was pregnant." I felt deflated. Why would my mum hide all this from me?

My grandmother obviously saw my sadness because she reached out again and took my hand. I looked up at her and she smiled brightly.

"I am sure we will get answers when the Goddess deems so," she said. "But for now I am thrilled to meet you and look forward to getting to know you well." I forced a smile on my face. I felt uncomfortable and like I had a million questions going around in my head.

"Well, yes," the headteacher said with a cough. "I will of course have the records changed immediately, Priestess." My grandmother smiled at him and nodded. She squeezed my hand and stood up.

"I am aware that you have had quite the eventful week dear one," she said. "I will leave you in the hands of headteacher Grovins and look forward to seeing you at the family dinner."

"Family dinner?" I asked.

"Yes, we have a Heathwood family dinner once a month," she said. "I have no doubt that you will meet your cousin Amelia before then, but I will introduce you to the rest of our family next week." Oh. Suddenly everything seemed way too overwhelming. Rest of the family? Cousin? I felt my chest tightening and the beginnings of a panic attack coming on. My grandmother looked at me with concern as I tried to even my breath.

"Oh dear," she said and knelt down beside me. "My poor sweet child. You really are your mother's daughter." She looked up at the headteacher as she took my hand. "Get me a glass of water." I was vaguely aware of him rushing around but I was also trying not to lose control. I had been suffering from panic attacks, as a part of my depression and anxiety, since I was a child. I knew a few techniques to calm myself down, but they didn't always work.

I felt something cool on my forehead and was vaguely aware of what felt like a rush of light flowing through my body before I felt like I could breathe again. My vision cleared up, and I saw my Grandmother was holding her hand to my head and mumbling something under her breath. She smiled as I relaxed and stopped what she was doing. She took a glass of water from a worried-looking headteacher and handed it to me, holding my shaking hands and helping me guide the glass to my mouth.

Once I had taken a few sips I pushed against the glass, and she took it from me.

"Are you feeling better?" she asked, and I nodded.

"Yes, thank you," I said. Although I felt sweaty and shaky, I didn't feel like I was going to pass out so it was an improvement.

"I'm sorry," I said again. "I have panic attacks sometimes." My grandmother nodded.

"And depression?" she asked, and I narrowed my eyes.

"How did you know?"

"Because your mother was the same," she said. "Did she have you on medication?"

"Yes, but I haven't had any in the last week," I said with a nod. I had tried to tell the guards at the Shadow Council that I needed my medication, but my requests fell on deaf ears. Being in withdrawals was made worse with all that had happened, starting with my mum dying. My grandmother nodded and turned to the headteacher.

"Please see that she has everything she needs as soon as possible," she said with a stern look. The headteacher nodded quickly. My Grandmother looked back at me and smiled.

"Get some rest child and please do not worry about our dinner, or the Grand dinners," she said and smiled as my eyes widened. "Don't worry, you have the support of your family now." She leaned down, and I felt as she kissed my cheek. She looked at the headteacher once again before turning and walking out of the room.

I turned back to the headteacher. He looked back at me uncomfortably and smiled weakly.

"Grand dinners?" I asked, and he grimaced.

"The Grand families have a monthly dinner as well," he said. "I know it seems a lot but I am sure that your new roommate will guide you through everything. She is a lovely young lady." I could tell he was trying to be dismissive and change the subject so I let it go. The headteacher reached for his phone and pressed a button.

"Could you send Rose in please," he said and let go of the button. He smiled at me briefly before setting his face back into the stern scowl that I saw when I first met him. There was a light knock at the door and he called for the person to enter. I turned to see a young woman walk into the room. She was dressed in a sage green tailored dress that set the green in her eyes a light and her honey blond hair was tied back in a low ponytail. She glanced at me briefly before looking at the headteacher. I could tell she had quite the nervous energy about her as she came and sat down in the vacant seat.

"Miss Heathwood, this is Rose Newman," the headteacher said, and I saw her eyes widen at my new last name. I guess it made an impact. "Miss Newman will help you settle into the school, and I am sure that she will answer any questions that you have." The woman hesitated before smiling at me.

"I am so happy to meet you," she blurted out. "I was told that I would be getting a new roommate and some extra duties, I had no idea that it would be a Heathwood. I didn't even know there was another Heathwood." I smiled as she rambled on. I could tell I was going to like this girl a lot. The headteacher coughed which prompted Rose to look between us in horror.

"Oh my gosh, I am so sorry," she said. "I just get a little excited when I meet new people." The headteacher coughed again, and she clasped her hand to her mouth. I couldn't stop the chuckle that escaped me. She really was a breath of fresh air.

"Yes, well," the headteacher said, obviously he wasn't so entertained by Rose. "I am sure that you will take good care of our new student, Rose." Rose nodded her head, with her hand still clasped to her mouth. The headteacher turned to me and smiled.

"I will ensure that we find you a mentor as soon as possible, and come and see me at any time," the headteacher said. I was sure that it wasn't a sentiment that he gave often, so I smiled at him.

"Other than that, welcome to Dark Heath University."

"Thank you Headteacher Grovins," I said in my politest tone and stood up. We were clearly dismissed but Rose was still looking between us.

"Want to show me our new room?" I asked her and she blushed as she realised I was waiting for her.

"Of course, yes," she blurted and stood up quickly. I nodded to the headteacher who was trying to hide an amused smirk and turned and followed Rose out of the room. We headed out through the outer office and into the wood panelled hallway. I let out a relieved sigh as I closed the door and Rose giggled.

"He can be quite intimidating," she said, and I smiled.

"This whole place is intimidating," I replied with a nod. Rose gave me a sympathetic smile.

"It's not so bad, once you get used to it," she said and pointed down the hallway. "We will go through the main courtyard to Citrine Hall, that is where our room is."

She started heading in the direction she was pointing and I followed her. We soon came to two big doors and Rose pushed one open and light flooded into the hallway. I looked around as I followed her through the door and into a mostly open area. There were so many students though. Most in little groups, and most ignoring us as we made our way through the centre. I noticed a few glances and whispers as we passed some groups. I tried to ignore it, knowing that it was probably the excitement of someone new. Then I stopped dead as I saw someone that I recognised. Rose stopped and looked at me and then toward where I was staring. I felt my heart speed up as I took in the obviously muscular body that the black t-shirt made no attempt to hide. Tattoos descended his arms, and I knew from memory how they continued under the t-shirt and into an expansive and beautiful back piece. I smiled as he looked up at me, but my smile faded as his eyes widened and his face hardened into a glare.

"What's wrong?" Rose asked. "Do you know Jackson?" I tore my eyes away from the hateful glare and looked at Rose. I nodded and looked back just in time to see him storming through another set of doors.

"I thought I did," I said, with a tremor in my voice. I thought I knew him very well, or at least for one amazing night.

Three ~ Jackson

The doors of the school entrance slammed against the wall, causing a couple of students to jump at the noise, but I didn't care as I stormed past them. I headed around the corner to the student car park and looked towards my private space. My new black Audi sat exactly where I left it. I unlocked it as I walked up and got in the car, slamming the door after me. I started the car and gunned the engine before peeling out of the space.

I was halfway down the school drive when my phone went off in my pocket. I glanced at the dashboard and saw the screen tell me that Alex was calling.

"What?" I snapped as I hit the answer button on my steering wheel.

"Dude," Alex's voice floated through the car speakers, "Where the fuck did you go?"

"I'm on my way home," I said, and I heard him groan. Alex wasn't just my best friend, he was also my warrior guard. He was still in training but his dad was the Warrior Commander for the Shadow Council so it made sense that Alex got paired with me. He was probably pissed off that I left without saying anything.

But that was nothing compared to how pissed off I was right now. Just thinking about seeing that traitorous bitch again was enough to send another flood of rage flooding through my body.

"Why are you going home?" Alex asked, pulling me from my rage.

"Because I need to have a conversation with my father," I said and Alex groaned again.

"I'll get some whisky in," he said with a sigh before cutting off the call. If I wasn't so furious I would probably appreciate his knowledge of my need for alcohol after I got back to school. Talking to my father was a ball ache, and I avoided it whenever I could. Except for now when I wanted to know what the fuck was going on.

My family home was only a twenty-minute drive from school but I got there a lot quicker. I jumped out of the car, not bothering to close the door and stalked in through the double door entrance of the hideous place that I grew up in. I headed straight for my father's office, not even stopping when I heard my step mum calling my name. I threw the doors open and my eyes immediately fell on my father as he sat on the phone behind his large ostentatious oak desk.

"What in the fuck!" I snarled before he had time to even look up. I saw the shock briefly in his eyes before the disapproving mask settled back again on his face.

"I'll have to call you back, Stephen," he said into the phone. "It appears I have a surprise visit from my son." He glared at me as he said it. Part of me wanted to shrink back, but I held my place and returned his glare. He hung up the phone and looked up at me with a tight smile on his face.

"And what do I owe the pleasure, son?" he snipped, his voice edged with anger.

"I just saw her at school," I said. "Why the fuck is that bitch at my school?"

"You are going to have to narrow down on who you are talking about. I am sure that there are many at the school who would fit that description," my father said.

"The one who should be dead right now," I snarled. "*Her* daughter." The last part left a bitter taste in my mouth. The last thing I wanted to deal with was the woman who ruined my family and my life. The fact that her daughter tricked me a couple of weeks ago left more of a murderous rage in me.

"Oh, I assume you mean Miss Heathwood." My father stood up from his desk and walked over to his bar. I watched as he poured a drink into a crystal cut glass and drank it down before pouring another.

"Yeah, her," I said. "She should be waiting for her death in Blackwell Prison right now."

"Yes, well, things didn't quite go the usual route with her arrest," my father said as he sat down on his leather sofa.

"Why the fuck not?" I growled.

"Because her grandmother got word of her existence and pulled her own set of strings at the Council," he replied, in almost a bored tone.

"And who is the bastard that I have to beat the fuck out of for telling her?" My father raised his eyebrow at me in obvious amusement.

"That would be me, son," he said and my jaw dropped.

"Why the fuck would you do that?" I growled after I could form the words. Other than myself, my father would have the biggest reason to have her life ended. After all, it was his wife that suffered for her mother's actions.

My father waved off my rage with his hand and took another drink.

"I informed Mirriam Heathwood of her granddaughter's existence due to the incompetence of the people who led the interrogation," he said. "They couldn't even get her to admit to being a witch. The bloody girl insisted she had no clue of the supernatural world."

"Well, that's bullshit," I snapped. "I met her in Paragon." My father huffed at my response. He already knew how I had met her. It should have been enough to convict her since Paragon was a supernatural only club.

"Well, apparently her friend being human was enough to cause doubt in the evidence," my father replied.

"But she was convicted, right?" I asked, and he nodded.

"Yes, but if she had gone to Blackwell, then we wouldn't have been able to get the information we need to clear your mother." My father looked up at me. "That is top priority, isn't it, son?"

"You know it is," I said through gritted teeth. "So what do we do now?" My father stood up and walked over to the bar again. I watched as he placed his glass on the counter and turned and looked at me. There was a glint in his eyes that I hated. It told me I wouldn't like what he said next.

"You, my son, are going to get the information we need from her," he said and my eyes widened. He didn't really think what I thought he was thinking. "Get close to her. Charm her. All we need is for her to admit her and her mother's involvement and we can get a scan." I grimaced at his words. Not only because the last thing I wanted to do was to see that bitch alive, but to actually be nice to her as well, I wasn't sure I had the stomach or the serenity for that. The thought that it would end in a council scan though actually excited me. The scans were the most painful form of interrogation, but they provided all the evidence we would need. The only issue is that the prisoner rarely survived them so they were only when deemed the last resort.

"I'm not sure I can do it," I said and my father sneered at me.

"You aren't a little boy anymore," he snapped, "Stop acting like one."

I was about to respond when the doors to the office burst open and something hit me at speed.

"Jacky," my sister squealed as she wrapped her arms around me. "Mum said you were here. Why didn't you come and see me?" I grinned at my little sister Aria and hugged her back.

"Hey kid," I said, and she pulled a face at me.

"I'm not a kid," she declared, "I'm twenty years old for fuck's sake."

"Language," my father snapped and Aria rolled her eyes at him before turning back to me. She might have been twenty, but she looked like a little blond hair and blue eyed innocent doll. I was not looking forward to her joining Dark Heath next year. I was already anticipating having to put several douchebags in their place.

"So why are you here?" she asked. "I thought term started today." I nodded in response.

"It does, I was just there." I looked up at my father. "I just had some business with dad that's all."

"Business that is settled now," my father said with a pointed look. I resisted the urge to glare at him and nodded my head. I knew he was right, but I wasn't happy about it.

"Oh good," Aria said happily, "Do you want to stay for lunch?" I shook my head.

"I can't," I said to her disappointed expression, "Anyway, why aren't you off at Oxford already?" Aria screwed her face up. I knew she hated being at Oxford, and hated that father had insisted on her doing Economics. I took it in my stride, after all the plan was for me to take over as the Grand Priest for the Sorcerers when my father stepped down. But Aria was more of an artistic kind and wanted to do something in the creative field. Father was having none of it though. Despite her hatred of the subject, Aria, like myself, excelled at her studies. I knew she was excited to move to Dark Heath where she could work on her witch abilities at least.

"I don't start till next week," she said. "I'm travelling down at the weekend to get settled in." Then her face lit up. "Maybe I could come and spend a few days at Dark Heath with you?" she asked hopefully. I didn't even have a chance to answer before my father decided.

"No, I don't think that would be wise, sweetheart," he said. "Jackson is going to be very busy getting settled in himself, isn't that right son?" I nodded as my sister's face fell again.

"Let me at least walk you to your car," she said. I nodded goodbye to my father and turned to leave the office.

"Son?" my father called, and I looked round at him. "Just remember what we talked about." I clenched my fists as the thought of getting close to that bitch sent anger racing through me again. But I nodded stiffly before turning and following Aria out of the office. I said a quick goodbye to my step mum, Clara, and headed out to my car.

"Jackson, is everything okay?" Aria asked as I gave her a hug.

"Not yet," I said truthfully, "But it will be." I forced a smile on my face, even though she knew it was fake. I climbed into the car and started the engine. Aria waved as I pulled away from the house and down the driveway. I wasn't happy about what my father wanted me to do. I knew one thing though. I wasn't going to be all nice to that bitch. I was going to make her regret the day she met me.

※

Dark Flame is available for preorder now, and will be released 30th September 2024.

The Right Time by Amy Davies

One

Sitting my ten-month-old daughter Bella on my hip, I walk the short way to a coffee shop where I am meeting my best friends sister. Someone I am honoured to have in my life.

My feelings for Norah Hartley, has been suppressed for fucking years.

Her brother, Ian has always known my feelings for her but something always got in the fucking way of me telling her how I feel, but today is the day and nothing will stop me.

"Dada," I smile down at my daughter, seeing a toothy smile looking back at me.

She is my whole world.

When I found out that I was going to be a father, I was over the moon, but what I didn't count on was the two other men turning up at my house telling me that they could be her father also. It turned out that the woman I was married to was cheating on me, and had been for fucking years.

So I filed for divorce, did a paternity test and thankfully, Bella was mine. We later found out that my ex-wife decided that she was only with me for my money as I own a lucrative company with my brothers. She asked for money; a lot of fucking money and I would get my daughter.

I hated her to my core for suggesting such a thing but we designed a contract that she would leave with the amount I gave her and never contact us again. I had full parental responsibility for Bella.

Thankfully, that all came to fruition today after months or back and forth with my ex, and the courts.

I kiss her head, that is covered by a pink beanie with two fluffy pom-poms, that covers her dark hair, letting her baby smell sooth me and my fraying nerves.

I knew Norah better than any man that she dated on and off over the years. There was always a part of me that blamed her for my marriage to my ex-wife, even though I know my thoughts on that are irrational. So I learned to deal with my feelings, and worked it out in my head that it was my fault, not Norah's.

It was when I had come home from travelling and found out that Norah was engaged to some prick from a town over, I went off the rails and ended up marrying Bella's mum. I tried to make it work, tried to give her everything and convince myself that I was in love with her, but shit hit the fan quickly, but I never like failing at something.

Her cheating was the catalyst I needed.

"Ah, there is my Bella-bear." I hear Norah's voice as we step inside.

Her ink black-curly hair, makes her stand out in the crowd, and I can't stop the smile that fills my face when I spot her. We walk towards her, I take in her casual outfit fit for our cold November month.

In ankle boots with a heel, jeans that fit her just right, a belt that I got her for her birthday and seeing that on her body does stupid things to my own. I spy the green cropped cardigan that she has buttoned up but has it off her shoulder, showing off the grey camisole top with lace that frames her cleavage.

I love the fact that she is also wearing the necklace that I got her one year for Christmas.

As soon as we are close enough she stands, holding her hands out. Flexing her fingers.

"Gimmie, gimmie, gimmie. I need Auntie Norah hugs."

"What am I chopped liver?" I fake hurt, sitting in the seat across from her.

She pokes her tongue out at me and very erotic images pop into my head on her on her knees, with my thick cock in her mouth. Stretching her lips, her dark red lipstick leaving marks on my shaft.

Shaking the thoughts off for now, I focus on the two most important girls in my life, besides my mum.

"So how have things been? You have been a little distant lately" she says to me but her main focus is on Bella.

I watch them before I answer. Seeing her with my daughter, treating her like she is her own flesh and blood makes my anger spike a little after Bella's biological mum didn't give two fucks about her.

Norah was made to be a mother.

She is caring, loving and will do anything for anyone. She works and helps out at the animal shelter. Thanks to working there she has collected two dogs and once upon a time she had four cats but now she only has the one. A little ginger fucker that hates me.

"Shane." She says my name bringing me back into the coffee shop.

What I wouldn't give to hear her screaming my name as she is laid out under me, as I fuck her into the bed, or having her use my cock as she rides me to find her orgasm.

"Things have been good. We got a new contract so that has been taking up a lot of time. It is a good thing that we turned that spare room at the office into a nursey-slash-playroom for this little miss." I tug on Bella's foot making her giggle.

That sound clutches at my heart with the promise to never leave.

"You are not just a pretty face with a body most women drool over, Shane." She winks at me.

Leaning in, I lower my voice. "You think I am pretty, hot and drool worthy enough to make woman pant after me, sweetheart?"

Our gazes lock, and the sound from the coffee shop fades away, and it is just the tow of us here. I have never spoken to her like this before, we have always kept thinks friendly, polite.

"Do I make you pant after me, Norah?" my voice deep.

The little action of her licking her lips draws my gaze to her mouth and my cock thickens in my jeans. Her eyes dilate, and her chest heaves. If she wasn't sitting here with my daughter in her lap and we were not in a public place, I would bend her over this table and fuck her hard, making her mine.

"Here you go." A voice snaps us out of our lusty fog and I blink, smiling up at the young girl setting our coffees down on the table.

Norah blinks, her cheeks pink from her blush. She busies herself with Bella, and I don't miss seeing her looking at me from the corner of her eye.

Fuck me, I want her.

"Can you come to my place tonight. We need to have a talk."

With a nod, she goes back to feeding Bella some of her cookie, making sure that she doesn't choke.

She will make a fucking fantastic mum to my girl.

Two

Slowly stepping out of Bella's room, I gently close the door praying to the nursey Gods, that the door clicking does not wake her.

Once I have successfully, extracted myself from her room without any Special Ops training, I fist pump the air, then head to my room for a quick shower. I need to wash the day for me, before Norah comes over.

Making sure that I shave my pubic area because if I am lucky, I can get Norah to take a chance on me. I do not want her to have a mouthful of hair when she swallows my dick for the first time.

Been there with a chick and it was not fucking fun. Shaved pussy for me all day long.

Once I am showered and shaved, I walk back into my bedroom, dry off and dressing in a simple pair of jeans and a long sleeve V-neck top, leaving my feet bare, since I am not leaving my cottage, that my grandparents left me in their will. When I got divorced I sold the house that I hated but my ex-wife wanted it, and I had the cottage renovated to suit both Bella and me.

Padding into my kitchen, I set the baby monitor on the counter top and check the lasagna that is in the oven, it is Norah's favourite comfort food and on a freezing cold day like today, it seemed perfect. Just over an hour ago the snow started, fingers crossed it stick and traps Norah here with me and Bella for the night.

At least that will give me more time to woo her. Fuck, do women like to be wooed?

Liking how the meal is cooking, I add some garlic knots onto the oven shelf to head up, because again it is one of Norah's all-time delights.

There is a light tap on the front door, and I smile to myself, because she is not banging as she knows it is Bella's bedtime.

Closing the oven, I walk to the front door and pull it open.

Norah stands there with her big black coat wrapped around her shivering body.

"Get in here" I tug her inside and she lets out a squeal.

"Shit, it is so warm in here." Her voice quakes from the cold.

Helping her out of her coat, I breathe her in, letting the sweet strawberry scent invade my senses. "You smell good."

She tenses, but says nothing as I turn, putting her coat the hook by the door, then turn back to her, taking her in as she stands before me. Dressed in heeled ankle boots, black tights, a leather skirt that stops mid-thigh and a white knitted jumper.

Her dark hair is curled, some up and some hanging over her shoulders.

Standing looking at her each other, no words pass between us, but you can feel the sexual tension floating around us. Her eyes widen a fraction, as she watches me watching her, her eyes dilate and I smirk seeing that she is effected by me as I am her.

"Bella-bear sleeping?" I nod.

"Out like a night. We have all the night to ourselves."

"Why?" she blurts out.

"Why, what?" I grin.

I know what she is asking but I need her to talk to me. This quite Norah is not what I am used too. Norah and I have always had this fun banter that we have been careful not to cross the line with any flirting but fuck me, that line will be wiped away tonight.

"Why did you invite me here, Shane? We have spent many times alone together but I am getting the vibe off you that tonight is different. Are you sick? Are you seeing someone knew?" she rushes out.

Chuckling, I step to her, leaning in to kiss her cheek, then letting my lips brush against the shell of her ear. "This time it is different."

Stepping back I smile at the shocked look on her face.

"Come on, I made your favourite. Let's eat, then we can talk."

I turn. leaving her standing there looking at me like I just told her that I am the King of England. She follows behind me but knowing my friend like I do, she will not leave it there, and there is no way that she will allow us to eat before I tell her why I wanted her here tonight.

"You can't do that shit, Shane. Why is it different?"

Told you.

"Sit." I point to the small dining table.

She listens thankfully while I dish out the food.

"Oh, god that smells good." She murmurs. "You make the best lasagne, Shane."

I smile over my shoulder. "I learned from the best." I wink.

Her and Ian's mum loved cooking and when I would go over there for tea after school, I would help her, so I picked up a few things. Norah smiles warmly at me remembering the fond memories of our childhood.

I place her plate in front of her, before taking a seat next to her and digging into my food. She moans and sighs as the flavours bursting onto her taste buds.

Norah is a foodie, always has been. I love that about her, she is never one to shy away from eating what she wants. That is what keeps her sexy curves on her body, that makes my mouth water.

My cock twitches hearing her moan, as she bites into a garlic knot.

"You really have to stop moaning like that, baby." I growl, my food abandoned.

Her eyes widen in shock at my words but more so that I used an endearment that I have never used on her before. Her folk hits the plate, her mouth dropping open and closed every few seconds before she blinks and looks be dead in the eyes.

"You had better start fucking talking, Shane. No more games, why am I here?" her voice firm but I hear the quiver in her tone.

Sighing, I climb to my feet, ignoring her questioning look and go to collect the letter from my solicitor and hand it to her.

"What is this?"

"Are you done?" I nod to the food, she nods her head. "Open it."

I clear away our plates, then leans against the kitchen counter, folding my arms and crossing my ankles, watching her eyes scan the letter in her hand. Her lips move as she reads each word silently.

Her eyes suddenly widen in shock, her head snapping up to look at me. I smile and nod.

"Is this real?" I nod. "Holy shit, Shane. This is amazing. Fucking huge."

"It is."

Looking back to the papers like she needs to reread to confirm what she is reading.

"You are finally divorced and free of that money grabbing skank."

"I am. She also took money for Bella. Walked away, giving me full parental responsibility of our girl."

Her face darkens as I explain what my ex-wife have done.

"She wanted money for Bella-bear?" Her growly voice makes my cock twitch.

I love seeing this side to her, so protective, a mama bear. I chuckle to myself at the nickname because it matches what she calls Bella.

"We can hate on her all we want but at the end of the day, babe, she is gone and Bella is here with us. She is fucking gone, and that is all I care about." stepping back to the table, I stand before her, offering her my hands.

She looks between me and the offered limp, her worried look makes me think she will not take it.

Three

After a few seconds, she slips her hand in mine and I tug her to her feet, then lead her into the living room, where the log fire is blazing behind the safety guard, and the small lamp gives the room a romantic ambience feel to it.

We sit on the soft couch, that has many scatter cushions thanks to my mum's design. Apparently it is not a house unless you have a fuck tone of cushions.

She sits on the corner, whole I sit next to her, but bring my bent leg up so it is pressed against her thigh. My arm settles across the back of the couch, keeping me close to her. I want more than anything to lean in and kiss her plump lips but we need to talk first. I have known for years how she feels about me but I need to know that she wants this right now, before I let anything deep happen.

"How do you feel about being free of her finally?" she asks me.

"Lighter. Like I can finally be me. I had so much rage for her when she asked for money for Bella, but I spoke to my solicitor, and your folks for advice."

"My parents know?" she gawks at me.

"Baby, they are a huge part of my life, so yeah, I asked them, since I have no parents to ask. My brother helped me out too."

"Ian knew also?" I nod to her question.

My parents died when I was sixteen, in a small plane crash. Me and my brothers, went to live with our grandparents and we had a great childhood with them.

"So why not say anything to me? I thought we were close enough, that you would want to share this with me," I can hear the hurt in her voice and it makes my stomach tighten.

Taking her hand in mine, I look her in the eye.

"I wanted to tell you alone, just the two of us because I have something I want to come clean about. Plus, I wanted to do this." I lean in pressing my lips to hers.

Her body goes stocks till for all of three seconds, then she is kissing me back. I part her lips with my tongue, devouring her mouth with mine. Pouring every emotion I have felt for her over the last many years.

Her hands to my face holding me in place like she is scared that I will pull back and tell her that this was a mistake, but I could never regret kissing her like this.

It is all consuming.

Hot and frenzied.

All too fucking soon she pulls back breaking the kissing, looking at me with dark desired eyes, her lips red and plump, perfect for wrapping around my cock.

Fuck, mate, give her a chance to breathe before you want to cut her air off with you cock.

My inner sensible side calls out to me while the other side is ready to lay her out for us.

"Shane," she stops. "What was that?" her voice is low filled with lust and it makes my cock twitch.

"That was me finally manning the fuck up and taking what I have always wanted but it was never the right time."

"And now is the time?" she asks.

"Yeah." She frowns.

Shaking her head, she pushes to her feet, then starts pacing back and forth in front on the window.

My gut tightens, my palms become clammy.

Did I read her wrong all of these years?

I sit forward on the couch, resting my elbows on my knees while my hands scrub back and forth over my bowed head.

She says nothing, her steps falter every few seconds like she is going to say something but she doesn't.

With each passing minute, she keeps quiet the pain in my tightening stomach gets worse, to a point that I feel sick as fuck. I hate that she is not speaking, this is not like her, Norah is the one that will speak her mind, the one that will put you in your place if you step out of line.

"Norah, say something." I look up at her.

She sighs, stopping at the side of the room that is closest to the front door. Not one bit do I like her that close to the one thing that is stopping her from running.

"Why now, Shane? Shit, we have been friends for years and you have never let on that you like me that way. Yeah, we have flirted but never crossed that line." Her eyes widen. "Is this some sort of move to get a new mum for Bella?" I stare at her with disbelief that she would think that.

My shock wears off, anger taking over.

"You think that little of me. We have been friends for fucking years. Jesus Christ, Norah" I push to my feet, the need to move itching at my skin.

I run my hands through my hair a few times letting her words bounce around my head, the pain and anger swirling in my blood at what she is accusing me of.

Needing to cool off I walk into the kitchen, and busy myself with cleaning up from earlier. All I could think about was spending some quality with Norah and making it known how I feel about her, but she just fucked with that.

Do I want her to me a mum figure in Bella's life? Hell, yes. She is a great role model and a perfect person to be a mum to my daughter but that is not the reason that I made my move now.

It hurts that she thought that of me.

I have no idea how long I stand in my kitchen, watching some light snow flakes drop from the night sky, but I feel her when she steps into the room.

"I think I should go." Her voice is low, showing her pain and it packs punch to my stomach but I can't find it in me to turn and face her, to tell her that we can forget about what was just said and move forward.

I nod.

I hear her sniff, then the sound of the front door opening and closing gently behind her. Even though she did it quiet so not to wake up Bella, that gentle click is like a bomb going off in my chest.

Fuck me, how the hell did we get here?

Four

It has been a week since I have seen or heard from Norah. Ian told me that she has been busy with work and taken some extra shifts to help others out,

Typical Norah

I miss her.

Her witty banter, the way she makes fun of shit I do but all in good taste.

Sighing I run my fingers through my hair, noting that I need it cut, but that will have to wait until my baby girl is feeling better from her ear infection, she is not a happy bunny right now.

Once she is down for a nap, I decided to take a page from her book and nap too, because shit I am shattered from little to no sleep.

I stir from my sleep, my ears focusing on any sound but the house is silent.

Scrubbing my hands over my face to swipe the sleep away, I sling my legs over the bed and go to relieve my full bladder, before going to check on Bella.

After splashing some cold water on my face, I pull on a pair of joggers before leaving my room.

Reaching Bella's room I find it empty, panic rises in me, my heart races, then I hear low singing. Running to my living room, with my heart trying to beat me there in fear, I come to a skidding stop, seeing Norah in the oversized chair with a sleeping Bella on her chest.

"Hi," she whispers.

Her eyes showing her unease.

My heart stops in my chest seeing them like this.

"Hey. What are you doing here?" my voice is till thick with sleep so it sounds harsher than normal.

She flinches a little, my stomach clenches.

"Shit, I didn't mean it like that." I step closer, sitting on the edge of the couch.

"I know. I came to see you, to clear the air. Not long after I stepped inside I heard her whimpering and I remembered my mum saying she was unwell. You were passed out so I decided to take care of her while you caught up on your rest."

I nod with a gentle smile, my heart falling more for this woman.

"Thanks."

"Let me lay her down and we can talk."

She gets up and takes Bella to her room, before coming back, and stopping in front of the fire so she is facing me, with an unsure look on her face and I fucking hate it.

"Before you speak, let me get this out, okay." I nod.

"I am sorry for what went down the last time I was here. It all came as a shock to me, Shane, I had no clue what the fuck to say to you. We have been friends for years, and yeah we have had banter but never crossed into flirting territory. Then all of a sudden you were kissing me, frying my brain. It was overwhelming. I was turned on, nervous, scared and that is not me," she grins. "Well not the last two." I chuckle.

"I should have gave you an exploration before I kissed you. If I had known that you didn't feel the same way I wouldn't have done it. I am sorry, Norah" I sigh.

She pulls a face, making me cough to cover my laugh.

"*Don't feel the same way*?" she scoffs. "Are you fucking crazy, blind and stupid, Shane?"

"Um, I don't think so, but I am a guy." I push to my feet stepping to her, leaving very little room between us.

She looks me in the eyes, her hands coming to rest on my chest.

"I have always liked you, Shane. Always wanted you but it was never the right time for us."

I don't reply, just slam my mouth on hers.

Her little gasp gives me access to her mouth, slipping my tongue inside to toy with hers. My hands slip around her waist pulling her flush to my body, needing to feel her against me, as my mouth devours hers, my kisses showing her what I want.

I move is over to the couch, pulling at her clothes, while she does the same with mine. We are frenzied, and the heat between us build like I have never felt before with other women.

"I need you. I know we need to talk but, baby, I need to feel you wrapped around my cock. Tell me I can have you."

"Yes. Fuck me, Shane."

"Can I take you bare, or do we need a condom? I am clean I got tested after her."

"I am on the pill and clean, now fuck me like you have always wanted too." Her voice is low and husky, the sound going straight to my hard cock.

We strip naked, I lay her down on the couch, dropping to me knees and feasting on her sweet, dripping cunt. Licking her pussy, her flavour hits my taste buds making my cock leak with need for her.

For years I have wanted this and fuck me I plan on keeping her for as long as she will have me.

"Oh, shit, Shane, yes suck my clit," I do as my woman asks, adding two fingers into her dripping cunt, and pump making her feel good, but deny her an orgasm.

"I want you to come on my cock the first time, baby." I lift up, settling between her thighs and line my cock while my mouth devours hers.

"In me, please." She begs and I give my girl what she wants.

I slam into her, making her cry out.

Her hands go to my arse pulling me in deeper, and I fuck in and out of her. My body tingle with desire for this woman. The one that I have been lusting over for fucking years and now here she is beneath me, withering in arousal with my cock buried deep, marking her on the inside.

"Yes. Yes" she chants in a husky voice.

"Get there, baby, my balls are going to explode. You feel too damn good."

My balls slap against her arse, the sound of her juices fills the air with our heavy breathing. Her is soaking wet, my cock is slipping in and out of her with ease, she is that wet for me.

Lifting myself up, I move one hand between us finding her clit swollen and throbbing for my though, pressing on his she gasps, her eyes widen as they focus on me.

"Yes, baby, there is it. Come for me, Norah Give it to me," my hips bump harder, as I rub her nub.

"Yes. Yes. Oh shit, oh shit. I'm coming."

I watch her face as her pussy clamps down open my cock strangling the life out of it but I wouldn't want it any other way.

"Fuck yes." I growl, as I come with her pussy pulling my cum from my body.

My hips keep bucking, as I fill her with my cum. Images of her round with my baby flash in my head but I push it down, that is way to fucking soon.

Dropping my head to her chest, her arms go around my back holding me to her, sweat covers the both of us but right now neither of us fucking care. My cum starts to leak from her but again we do not move, this is where I want to fucking be right now.

"I always knew you would be good at this." She murmurs, I head comes up do I can look her in the eyes.

She is smiling lazily and I love that I put that look there.

"So you have dreamed of taking my cock, baby?" I wink at her making her giggle and I moan as her pussy flutters around my semi-hard dick.

She slaps my bicep, then her hand lingers, her fingers tracing the tattoo that I have there. A serious look crosses her face, while she is looking at it, before she brings her gaze to mine.

"Tell me this is real? That you are not going to regret it in the morning." I can hear the uncertainty in her voice.

Kissing her lips, I pour as much feeling into it as I can to convince her along with my words that I want this and more.

"Baby, you are it for me. I will only regret that time that we have lost."

Her smile makes my heart flutter.

"Good, because I am right there with you, Shane. You and Bella are everything to me."

I kiss her again, my body dropping back down on her but not crushing her. We kiss, and my cock hardens again, so my hips move needing to make love to her this time.

"Oh, shit, I love you, Shane."

"Good, baby, because I love you too."

I make love to her, two more times through the night, thankfully Bella slept through the night, the worst of her ear infection passing.

We have gone down so many different paths in our lifetime, dealt with many obstacles during our friendship, but here with Norah is what I have always wanted.

Now is the right time for us.

THE END

The Tourist by Anna Edwards

Foreword

Six people auctioned to the highest bidder.
Six lives were destroyed forever.
All because of Richard Armstrong.
The Tourist.
The Sister.
The Nephew.
The Princess.
The Debt.
The Nobody.
He's dead now, but they're still in hell.
Can they be saved?
Do they have any hope?
Or is it too late?

One ~ Chloe
Six Months Ago

"I can't believe it's been so long since we last did this," I announce before taking a sip of the sweet cocktail made with vodka, orange juice, and cranberry that Serena, my best friend, just handed me.

"I know. You work far too hard these days," Serena teases.

It's been a year since I was last in Las Vegas. My journalist apprenticeship in London has consumed me, but it's all been worth it. Last week, I was given a full-time position at the magazine I've been working for as a trainee. I'm now employed in the women's section, focusing on current issues that affect females. I'm halfway through my first article on the oppression of women in some Middle Eastern countries, focusing on those who've been able to find their voice, freedom, and a career after years of silence under harsh regimes.

"But it does mean I'll finally see my name in print when my article comes out," I retort.

"And we'll cut it out and frame it."

We clink our cocktail glasses together. The night is starting out, like any other in Vegas, with bright lights, pulsating music, and an air of excitement that electrifies the atmosphere.

Serena and I are dolled up in high heels and short black dresses. We've curled our hair and put on lots of makeup—silver eyeshadow for me, to accentuate my blue eyes, and gold for Serena, to complement her darker features from her Mexican ancestry.

We're ready to paint the town red.

We've already made enough memories to last a lifetime, having been friends since we started elementary school together, but there's always room for more. We'll be old and gray before we stop adding to our list of fun nights out.

Serena's my best friend, despite our very different upbringings. I was born to Tim and Patricia Benson in suburban London. My mother was a stay-at-home mom, and my father, who's now retired, was a doctor. He specialized in plastic surgery, not the type concerned with bigger tits and asses or smaller hips and stomachs, but the type focused on reconstructing physical deformities and burns injuries.

When I was three, we moved to America for my father's work. He was offered an opportunity of a lifetime, and he couldn't turn it down. It's surprising how much in demand his specialist skills were in Las Vegas!

Last year, my parents moved back to England after my father took early retirement. I wasn't sure if I should go with them, but when I got the offer of an apprenticeship with the magazine in London, the decision was made for me. Saying goodbye to my best friend was hard, but Serena and I vowed to talk daily, and we've kept that promise.

My best friend's start in life was very different from mine. At first, my parents were reluctant to encourage our friendship because she's a member of a well-known cartel family. However, once they saw the way her relatives helped the local community, they changed their minds. Serena's family own several hotels in Las Vegas, and although they do some dodgy dealings, which I know nothing about and never want to, they are a good family, on the whole, who protect their own and those close to them.

Serena's father, Carlos, and her mother, Lucia, were both killed in a plane crash when my friend was fifteen years old. After Serena's father died, her brother, Diego, took on the family empire. I've known Diego almost as long as I've known his sister. He's handsome with dark features, and if he wasn't so intimidating, I might find him attractive. He scares the life out of me, though, especially when his brows furrow together in a scowl when he's chastising Serena for taking risks. He adores his sister, but I know he constantly worries about her safety, and at times, he finds her reckless behavior frustrating.

My best friend doesn't need to work, so instead, she helps the less fortunate citizens of Las Vegas. With the assistance of some of the other cartel wives and daughters, she runs clothing and food banks and shelters where the homeless can get a shower and a decent night's sleep. Many are reluctant to use the facilities she offers, though, because of the stigma attached to being poor in such a wealthy, thriving city. Ironically, it's often the gambling and readily available alcohol and drugs that's caused their downfall in the first place.

For all that glitters in the city that never sleeps, there's also a darker side, especially since Covid.

"Have you finished your drink, yet?" Serena asks as she sips the last of her cocktail through a straw.

I shake my head, laughing. "I can't keep up with you."

"That's because you've been living with all those stiff upper lip Brits for the last year." She playfully sticks her tongue out at me.

"How rude!" I shake my head, and with a wave of my hand, I call over our private waiter.

We're currently in the VIP section of one of the night clubs belonging to Serena's family. As special guests, our every whim is catered to, even if it's a request for a greasy kebab from Downtown, later on. The club is in the basement of the casino the family also owns. It's a massive place and very easy to get lost in. There are restaurants, theaters, hotel suites, and so much more all under one roof.

The only drawback to it being owned by Serena's family is the security detail stopping anyone from approaching us. With the presence of Diego's guards, there's no chance of me getting any sex tonight. Not that I'm seriously looking for it. It usually ends in a less than satisfactory experience because I have the worst taste in men.

Serena is Catholic and has chosen to save herself for her husband, but even if she was interested in finding a man, I secretly think her brother would kill anyone who dared to look at her. He's a bit protective, hence all the guards. I mean, seven big, burly men for two tiny women is a bit excessive.

"Three shots of xtra Añejo tequila, please," I order.

Even though this particular brand is expensive, we always drink it when we're out.

The waiter lines our drinks up, and without a momentary pause, Serena takes the first shot down in one then sucks on a piece of lime.

"It's so smooth," Serena purrs as she pops the chewed lime into one of the empty glasses.

"It's because the agave plants are grown in the fertile, rich soil of the Mexican highlands and lowlands," I recite the facts she's told me so many times before. "It's the land your ancestors are from, and they always age their tequila for at least three years."

Rolling her eyes, she waves at the waiter. "Another one just to shut her up," she orders with a groan.

"Not for me, thank you. Maybe later." I chuckle.

Serena leans into me, and we cuddle together on the plush leather sofa.

"I'm so glad you're here, Chloe. I've missed you," she tells me. "I know we talk every day, but it's not the same. I was wondering about asking Diego if I could move to London for a while and maybe help some of the homeless people there. I know London has a big problem as well."

"I would love that!" I exclaim excitedly, tucking a stray strand of my blonde hair behind my ear. "We could get an apartment together. I could move out of my parents' house." I'm so sick of being told at twenty-four years old to clean my room and ensure my washing is put away.

"That's a must, then. I'll ask Diego to get us a place somewhere fashionable. Where are the best stores? We'll need to live near them. Maybe I could find myself a handsome prince to marry. Where do they hang out in London?"

I know Serena isn't joking about this. She would love to marry into the royal family. She's always dreamed of being a princess.

"I think you'll find they have even more security than you. I don't think you'll get anywhere near them."

She pouts at me. "What is it with the British royalty and Americans, anyway? At least I'm not a divorcee."

I let out a booming laugh and throw my head back.

The guard behind us shuffles forward to check that nothing is wrong with me.

I grab Serena's hand. "Come on, let's dance. We can hit the slot machines afterward. It feels like forever since I played on one."

"You are such a geek. I don't know how you can be bothered to spend hours and hours pulling on a lever when you never win anything."

"I win the occasional dollar." I pout sulkily.

We both get to our feet, but Henri, the head of the security detail, blocks our path.

"Where are you two going?" he asks, his voice stern and brows furrowed, as if we're naughty schoolgirls who need to be supervised.

"We're going to dance and then play on the slot machines. If that's all right with *you*..." Serena responds with an eye roll.

Henri motions for a couple of guards, Joe and Sal, to accompany us.

"You two stay with the girls. Don't let them out of your sight," he instructs.

They both nod their acceptance of the assigned task and follow Serena and me as we make our way onto the dance floor. We lose ourselves in the music for the next half an hour, dancing madly to cheesy classics such as 'Walk like an Egyptian', 'Barbie Girl', and 'Livin' la Vida Loca'.

We perform all the moves and shout out the words in all the right places. We've always been crazy like this; it's what drew us to each other on the first day of kindergarten. We performed 'I'm a little teapot' and were the only two who would do it. The rest, as they say, is history.

"I need to use the restroom," Serena whispers in my ear at the end of 'Macarena'.

"Let's go."

As the opening bars of 'Dancing Queen' start up, we make our way off the dance floor, and after telling our two male guards to wait outside, we head into the opulent restroom of the casino.

We use the facilities and then come out to wash our hands.

"I'm so sick of being followed around all the time," Serena slides her ass up onto the counter. "I swear Diego has gotten worse lately. I've always had Henri for protection, but seven men following me around is crazy. I feel like I can't breathe without them asking me why I'm doing it. I need a break from it all. It's one of the reasons I want to come to London."

I dry my hands on a freshly laundered cotton towel.

"And you don't think Diego will send guards with you?" I question.

I'm also feeling the oppression of her security after being able to walk around freely for the past twelve months. Even though the guards aren't there to judge you, it's impossible to fully relax and enjoy yourself when there's someone always watching. Despite the tequila shots, I'm not letting my hair down as much as I'd like.

"Probably." Serena slides off the marble counter. "Come on. I've had enough. Let's lose the guards and have some fun." I shake my head, knowing it's a bad idea. "We won't leave the casino," my friend promises. "I want to be safe, but I'd prefer not to be followed around. I want to enjoy a drink without someone staring at me."

"Okay, but how do you plan on doing it?"

"We'll head to the main gaming floor and lose the guards there. When I say go, follow me."

We leave the restroom and find the two guards still looming large outside the door, scaring away anyone who wants to enter.

"Go," Serena shouts, and we run as fast as we can through the casino and into an empty back corridor. The guards are quickly and easily lost, and when we realize we've managed to escape, we collapse into each other's arms, laughing like mad women.

"That was so much fun," I chuckle as Serena, in a fit of giggles, collapses into my arms.

"Diego is going to be so pissed at me, but why does he get to have all the fun and I have none." Serena stands upright, composing herself. "Let's go finish partying!"

Before we can react, even to scream, we are surrounded by a group of masked men. These aren't our bodyguards. Their faces, shrouded in darkness, are scary. I can only assume their intentions are sinister. Panic grips me as strong arms drag us out of the rear exit to the casino and into a waiting car.

This wasn't part of the plan.

This wasn't supposed to happen to us.

The screeching of tires echoes in my ears as the car speeds away from the curb, and when we leave the bright lights of the Strip behind, I know there's no turning back.

We are at the mercy of forces beyond our control, and I fear what lies ahead.

Two ~ Diego

I pace back and forth in the dusty warehouse, which is used for one thing only—revenge. My mind is consumed by fury. The air crackles with tension as I clench my fists so tightly the whites of my knuckles show. The man in front of me, crouching on the floor in the fetal position, has dared to betray me. I will not stand for it.

My day started like any other, balls deep in a warm pussy, but things have gone rapidly downhill since then. I've a great deal of power and influence in the bustling cityscape of Las Vegas, so most people know not to mess with me or my business. That doesn't stop the occasional idiot, like the one in front of me, from trying to test me.

When I learned of this man's betrayal, I was fueled by righteous indignation and searched for him with relentless determination. I eventually tracked him down to a seedy brothel and brought him here, to my warehouse on the outskirts of the city. It's a place where his screams won't be heard. In addition to his treachery, he brought a rapid halt to my early morning sexual escapades, so he's going to suffer doubly for that.

"Did you really think you'd get away with it?" I stare him in the eye, looking for any signs of remorse or even guilt at what he's done. But there's none.

He's lied to me and sold information to a rival of mine, which has cost me money and dented my reputation.

"It wasn't about getting away with it," the man responds disparagingly. When he was brought into the warehouse, he was crying like a baby, but he seems to have found some bravado since then. "It was about seeing you lose money."

He spits in my face.

Without even so much as a growl of disgust at the slight, I wipe the saliva away, breathe in deeply, and then, in a fit of rage, I unleash my fury upon the man. Every blow I land on his body is a symphony of retribution for his audacity to show such disrespect to me.

Eventually, I stop. The man is now lying curled up at my feet. The wounds I've inflicted on his face are bleeding, and he's groaning in pain. As I stare at him, my mind begins to race with thoughts of the torture that awaits him.

"String him up," I order, and the other men in the room, loyal bodyguards who've been with me for many years, immediately do as I command. "I'm looking forward to trying out this new punishment. It's guaranteed to get the information we need from this piece of shit."

Strappado is a medieval torture method I recently read about in an old book an English historian friend of mine sent me, and I've been looking forward to using it on someone.

Walking over to the sink, situated in one corner of the warehouse, I wash my hands and dry them on a soft, black towel while I watch what's happening to the man. His hands are bound with rope behind his back, and a chain, hanging down from the ceiling, is attached to the bindings around his wrists.

When the man's lifted off the floor, using the chain, he screams as the muscles and ligaments in his arms are strained. Once he's suspended high above us, my men look to me for my next order. With a wave of my finger, the chain is released, and the man is dropped suddenly from height. When he's a few feet above the concrete floor, the men pull on the chain and he comes to an abrupt halt.

I've never seen this torture method used before, but I know he'll have experienced a painful and damaging jerk to his joints as his arms take the full weight of his body. If done right, it will have dislocated his shoulders, and from the loud screams of agony filling the room, I know it's worked.

I motion for him to be raised again.

"Who did you sell my secrets to?" I demand, holding my hand in the air, ready to indicate another sudden drop to my men.

"Go to Hell!" the man screams.

Beads of sweat are now mixing with the blood on his face and dripping down onto what was once a white T-shirt.

"Are you sure that's all you want to tell me? Next time you drop, it will break bones and pull your arms out of their sockets. You'll be crippled for life. That is, if I decide to let you live."

"I'm not telling you anything. We both know I'm a dead man anyway, so do whatever you want."

I wave my finger, signaling to my men to drop him again. His blood-curdling screams ring out around the warehouse, along with the loud snapping of bones. I revel in the punishment. No one betrays me and gets away with it.

"Raise him up again," I order.

But before I can exact the punishment for a third time, my sanctuary is breached by the sound of urgent voices and footsteps. I'm distracted when the door to the warehouse opens, and Henri, the head of Serena's security detail, walks in. His face is ashen white.

My eyes narrow as I regard him, my anger simmering beneath the surface. This is a complete turnaround from the excitement of a few moments earlier. I don't need to be told to know my guards have failed me.

"What is it?" My voice is cold and commanding in stark contrast with the chaos swirling inside me.

Henri steps forward, his voice hesitant but resolute. "Forgive the interruption, sir, but there has been a development. It's Serena and her friend. They...they're missing."

My heart tightens at the mention of my sister's name. My parents died in a plane crash over the Grand Canyon a few years ago, and Serena is the only family I have left. She's my cherished sibling, and I've sworn to protect her at all costs. I've also known Chloe for a long time, so her safety's important to me, as well.

Serena and her best friend are like chalk and cheese together—one being fair and the other dark. Chloe has always captivated me with her blonde hair and blue eyes, but as my sister's friend, she's strictly off limits. Now, they're both missing and presumably in danger.

"Tell me everything," I demand, my tone brooking no prevarication.

Henri relays the dreadful details, explaining how Serena and Chloe had slipped away from his security detail. Their movements were captured by the watchful eyes of surveillance cameras in the casino. The footage, from the live feed, shows masked men descending on the girls before the guards had a chance to catch up to them at the rear of the premises.

The kidnappers' identities were shrouded in mystery as they spirited away my sister and her friend to gods-knows-where. It was only later, as my men searched for clues, that the number plate of the vehicle used was traced back to the man behind nearly all the missing girls in Las Vegas.

Richard Armstrong, my archenemy and family's nemesis, has my sister and her friend.

Rage boils within my veins, a storm threatening to consume me. My sister, my flesh and blood, has been taken from me by a man who frequently challenges my authority and traffics women as sex slaves. I will move heaven and earth to bring Serena and Chloe back home safely.

"Set up a search party," I command to those around me, my voice a thunderous decree that none of them would dare question. "I want every available resource dedicated to finding them. And bring me the guards who who were responsible for my sister's safety." I address my last comment to Henri. He knows the consequences of failure, the price to be paid for allowing harm to befall those under his protection. "They will all answer for their negligence."

Next, I turn to the head of my security, Ramon. His expression is grim as he acknowledges my orders. He's been holding the strung-up man in the air, and without a moment's hesitation, he drops him onto the concrete floor. I don't even hear the man's screams of agony. Fearful of what's happened to my sister, the pounding in my head overrides everything else.

I watch as everyone hurriedly leaves the warehouse. Their footsteps echo in the silence that follows until a groan draws my attention back to the battered man writhing on the floor. I no longer care about what he's done or why he's done it. I retrieve my Glock from my jacket, cock it, and execute him with a single bullet to the skull.

Alone, I allow myself a moment of vulnerability, my facade of strength crumbling in the face of uncertainty. I grab hold of the crucifix around my neck and say a silent prayer for my sister and her friend. But then, with steely resolve, I push aside my doubts and fears and focus instead on the task at hand.

Time is of the essence, and I won't rest until Serena and Chloe are safe. I'll hunt down those responsible. I'll track them to the ends of the earth if I have to, and when I find them, they'll pay dearly for their crimes.

No one takes what's mine to protect and lives to tell the tale.

Afterword

Coming soon is the 'SOLD' series...
Available 6th August 2024 on all platforms.

Crimson Army by Annalee Adams

One ~ Willa

"If your ass weren't as hot damn sexy, I'd have kicked it by now!"

I growled. "Wait up! You're not being fair!"

"Then shift Princess, it's not that hard!"

"Like hell it isn't Ethan, you show me how to and I'll happily oblige."

He laughed as his wolf ran faster through the Elder Vale. My mortal legs slogged after him, cumbersome and concrete. Shit. It's not that easy at all! He's such an asshole at times.

"You do know I can hear you, don't you?" he bellowed through the mind link.

"That's the point!" I yelled, huffing and puffing. The ground is hard beneath my feet.

Ethan ran back, his jet-black wolf enjoyed running circles around me.

I stopped, leaned against a tree and crossed my arms, pouting. "I quit!" I huffed, red-faced and angry about the whole situation.

Ethan slowed to a stop, his body shook and piece by piece he shifted into the magnificent muscular man I knew and loved. Toned, tanned and tantalising he strode over to me, smirked and lifted my chin, proceeding to kiss the pout right off my face.

Grinning he pulled back, standing there for a moment as I watched his eyes scan over my body, taking in every piece of me from my head to my toes. Ethan growled a raw primal growl. Biting my bottom lip, I felt his urge to take me right there and then. My body trembled in anticipation, his eyes hungry and lustful. He looked as though his need for me had overgrown his appetite.

Before I could pull him closer, his hand gripped my waist. "Willa," he said, his inner wolf growling under his breath. Caged against the tree he span me around, his cock hard, standing to attention. Lips crashed against the back of my neck, tasting me, biting my mark, urging for more. The urgency of his hunger was paramount, and as I felt his erection pressed up against me, I groaned, legs buckling under me. His muscular arms held me up, and kisses caressed my neckline. I ached for him, wet and ready. Biting down on my lip, I curled into his embrace. My hands grasping at him as our eyes met. Lips touched, tongues searched deep, sucking and tasting one another, groaning as he lifted me, mounting me onto him.

The intensity of his cock inside, made the warmth of our love rush through me. His mouth was at my neck again, sweet kisses planted there as my body slid onto his. Trembling I cried out, his hands devouring my breasts, his mouth sucking my mark, biting down as both pain and pleasure rushed through me.

Placing me on the floor he growled, pushing in deeper, harder still. My insides melted; fingernails clawed at his back. I needed him, more of him, faster, harder, deeper inside. Sliding up and down he quickened his pace, growling. I cried out, panting. "Hot damn Princess... I can smell your fucking arousal." Gripping him hard, and pulling him closer, I groaned, my body shaking as he pushed faster. Everything became quicker as I bit down, curbing the euphoric screams inside of me. With that bite Ethan arched upright, I released and we both cried out together, reaching our crescendo as the world began to shine all that brighter.

Out of breath, Ethan fell off of me. I snuggled into him; my leg wrapped around his.

"I could do this type of training any day," I said, smirking.

He laughed, kissed my forehead and sat up, pulling me up with him. "Oh, so that was your plan, was it? Distract me long enough so I forget about the training ah?"

I smirked. "Why heavens no!"

He stood up, pulled out a pair of jeans and a top from his bag and threw it over to me. "Come on Princess, we've got work to do!"

I caught the bag, groaned and fell back to the floor, snuggling against the soft texture of the meadow.

He laughed, bent down and slid his arms under my very naked body, lifting me. "Get changed, or I'll carry you back home like this."

I pouted. "But wouldn't everyone see me then?"

He grinned. "Yes."

"And you're happy with that then. The whole pack seeing your mate, naked?"

His face dropped. He clearly hadn't thought this through. I smirked. "Well, err... no. Damn it." He huffed, putting me down. Taking the bag from me, he pulled out top, and slid it up and over my head. I obliged, kissing him afterwards.

"Don't you prefer to get changed this way?" I asked him. He growled, pulling out underwear and jeans. "Now shall I put that on, or would you like to?" Ethan's eyes met my own, hunger sat beneath his gaze, his wolf yearning for more. He gripped the pants tight, bent down placing butterfly kisses down the line of my stomach, to my hips, his hands gripping my buttocks, pulling me towards him. Tongue sliding over my clitoris. I groaned, arched up, legs buckling. His arms steadied me, soothing me slowly down to the floor. Lips kissing my thigh, tongue circling over the lower lips, teasing me, making me want more.

I pulled at the grass, fingers clawing out for him. Tangled in his soft black curls I pulled, his head raising as his eyes met my own. One by one his fingers found their way inside me, watching as I bit my lip, sliding myself down onto them even more. Moments later he pulled away, the wetness between my legs enticing him further. With his button unhooked, jeans pulled down his cock was hard and ready once again. Growling he mounted me, pushing in deep. Up and down, faster and faster. Curling my legs around his buttocks he hit deeper, harder still. There was nothing in the world that could prepare me, as his face began to change. While pounding deep inside of me, the wolf in him was fighting to take over, fighting to take me as his own.

Ethan roared out, his teeth salivating at the sight of me. I cried out in ecstasy. His clawed hands held my own above my head. Still mid-change, Ethan roared again, fighting his wolf for custody of his body. Nails digging in his back I pulled him closer, my animal instincts unearthing deep within. Sex between us had turned into a fight of willpower. The intensity of the pleasure, the need to be connected deeper than ever before, changed me and pushed me. Ethan yelled as my hands shifted to claws. My body began to change as each of our bodies arched through the force of our climax, and as we both reached euphoria, we gave in to the change. Ethan's jet-black wolf stood over my crimson-red wolf, our bodies intertwined as I stood up, freeing myself from his shadow. Standing beside him, he nuzzled his snout into my neck, jumping around, wanting to play. I laughed inside as I joyfully accepted, chasing him through the woods, and tackling each other to the ground.

This was our first time together as wolves. It was not what I expected. Not what I'd believed it to be. Instead, Ethan's wolf was a playful beast, he enjoyed the chase, the fun and the games. He also enjoyed the calm, as we lay beside the lake, taking in the beautiful scenery before us. I hadn't been back to this lake since those wolves attacked me, but to see it now, and to see it with the person I love by my side, is to see it in a whole new light.

By far, it was the most beautiful I'd ever seen it. It enchanted me so. Ethan grumbled as he stretched out, resting under the afternoon sun. I lay there on my front, my snout resting on my paws. Every so often I'd turn and see Ethan drifting off to sleep, his mind and body finally relaxed enough to let go. He'd been so protective of me since the palace. So fearful of the fact Hela could send her army at any time. But there was one reason I wasn't living a life of worry and fear, and that was because I had faith. Faith in the fact that my brothers were right. Faith in the prophecy of the red wolf leading an army against the black crystal queen, and belief in the fact that the red wolf in the prophesy, was in fact, me.

Two ~ Ethan

New Haven Castle was breathtaking. Even after living here for months now, I would still catch Willa mesmerised by the gothic architecture. It always reminded me of something you'd expect to see in Count Dracula's castle, not in a home fit for a wolf king and his family. I smirked. But it's what Father wanted, and how it was designed many moons ago. To be perfectly honest, I'm not one for home décor, but Willa has that creative eye.

I finished dressing and sat down at the mahogany desk in Father's office.

"Aaden!" I yelled. Aaden was my next most trustworthy pack member since my brothers Nic and Alaric were still in London. I stared down at the map of New Haven on the desk.

The door flung open. "Yes, Alpha?"

"Has Arwen raised the protective shield around the whole town or just the castle grounds?"

"The castle grounds Alpha."

I pursed my lips. "Can she not bring in the town too?"

He shook his head. "Damn it, I'd planned to take Willa to town for a birthday surprise."

Aaden's eyes widened. "Of course, how long do we have before it's her true birthday?"

"Less than a week."

He scratched his head and sat down beside the desk. "How about a party in the Elder Vale?"

I sat down. She might like that... but then she would expect it. We always go there.

"No, it needs to be something different, unique. It is her eighteenth after all."

Aaden nodded. "Why don't you contact her friend from her old town? Juliet, was it?"

My eyes widened. "Yes," I said, standing back up. "Yes, that's a brilliant idea!" I slammed my hand down on the table and smiled. "Now where's the phone." Alaric pointed behind me at the old phone Father had finally agreed to install a few years back. It was a little dusty. I believe it was only Willa who used it. Well up until we had one installed in our bedroom for her.

Aaden grinned, "Right I'll leave you to your planning then." He stood up and walked out, closing the office door behind him.

Yes. Planning... that's what I'll do. Now where the heck is Willa's black book? I searched around the desk, opened every drawer and still couldn't find the damn thing. Sitting down in a huff I tapped my fingers on the desk. The jolt of the perfect idea slipped into my mind. "Of course!" I yelled, rushing out of the room, and skidding down the corridor to our bedroom. Willa was out in the gardens with Cleo, I had plenty of time to plan this thing.

Sitting at her vanity table, I opened the drawer and there it was, her old dilapidated black book. The oracle of all things Willa. Inside I flicked through to the phone numbers section and found Juliet's number. Dialling the numbers felt strange. I couldn't remember the last time I'd used a phone.

"Hello," a soft voice spoke. I was taken aback. I'd expected the harshness of her stepmother ringing through my ears. "Hello?" a more impatient, yet softly spoken voice said.

"Is that Juliet?"

"Yes, who is it?"

"Juliet, it's Willa's husband Ethan."

"Oh my, Ethan James Bane? The very Prince himself?"

I coughed. "Err, yes."

"Well heavens, what can I do for you?"

I smirked. She was a comical this one.

"Well, I am planning a party for Willa's eighteenth birthday."

"Huh. It's not her eighteenth until the summer..."

I chuckled. "Yes, well... we found her brothers."

"You're shitting me?"

"I'm what? I can assure you there is no shit involved in this plan."

Juliet laughed. "The comical type I see? I can see why Willa likes you."

"Oh, so you've spoken about me?"

She laughed. "It's mostly all she talks about."

I smiled. "Well, how would you like to come to our home for Willa's eighteenth?"

"EEK!"

I pulled the phone away from my ear. "Is that a, yes?"

"I would love to! Can Valentina and Angelo come too?"

"They're the twins, right?"

"Yes."

"Then of course they can."

"Yay!" she shouted. "So, when and where is this big bonanza?"

"Well, it will be next Saturday. But that's also why I'm phoning you... where would you suggest I hold it?"

"Don't you want to hold it at the castle?"

"No, I wanted somewhere special."

"What about Elder Vale?"

"No. We always go there... where else do you think she would love?"

"Hmm... well there's only one other place, especially if you don't want to hold it in the library..."

I laughed. "No, she would just sit there reading books all night."

Juliet laughed. "True. Then there's only one other place."

"Go on..."

"A beach party!"

My eyes widened. "Yes. Now that would be perfect. She has mentioned she loves the beach."

"We used to have a few bonfires on the beach when we snuck out past curfew."

I laughed. "Brilliant. The beach it is then! So, I will send a car for the three of you Saturday morning. But this is all a surprise, so can I rely on the fact that you won't tell Willa anything?"

"Of course, Prince Ethan, you can trust me."

I chuckled. "That's perfect then. But there's one more thing Juliet."

"Yes?"

"I'm just Ethan. There's no need for the formalities."

She laughed, "That's fine then, just Ethan. I look forward to meeting you on Saturday."

I hung up the phone after saying goodbye and sat back at the vanity table, placing Willa's black book exactly where I found it.

There was a knock at the door. Alaric entered followed by Darius.

Darius nodded and stood leaning against the bedpost. If only he realised that he was leaning against the very bedpost that his little sister and I fucked against from time to time. I smirked.

"What's up?" Darius asked.

"Ah, yes. So, I hear Willa invited you to live with us?"

Darius's brow furrowed. "Yes. We decided it would be good to be near her, to help protect her. She has a prophecy to fulfil after all."

I nodded. "Indeed. So, I agree, you should all stay with us. However, you and I have a history." Darius nodded, lowering his head to the floor. "It is a history that has caused my family a great deal of pain."

"Yes, I expect it did."

"But even though I can never forget what happened with Layla. I can, for the benefit of my mate, put it aside." Darius looked up, puzzled. "You are, after all, our family now. We must work together no matter our past grievances."

"Really?" he asked, his voice a higher pitch than normal.

"Really," I said, then walked over to him and held out my hand to shake his.

He smiled, no, in fact, he grinned. "Family," he said, smiling. He ignored my hand and pulled me in tight for a big, brutish hug. I groaned as he crushed me, and just as Willa walked in.

"Now is this something I should be worried about?" she asked, smirking.

Darius let go, and I coughed a little, regaining my breath. I held up my hand as she walked over concerned. "No. No, we're all good."

Darius grinned. "Your husband said we're all family now," Willa smirked.

"He did, did he?" I nodded. "Well, that's a relief," she said. "Now that we're all under the same roof, things will be easier."

Darius nodded, and then monkey scrubbed her head. "It will," he said. "Now we can keep on top of your training."

Willa groaned. I laughed. Well, if anything good came out of it, it was to see Willa with her big brother again and for us all to be one big dysfunctional happy family.

Three ~ Willa

The room felt cold and silent after Darius left. "Ethan, what's wrong?" I asked, my brow furrowed as he puzzled over something.

Ethan smiled and bowed his head. Standing up, he walked over, making his way towards me. The space between us dwindled as his muscular arms wrapped themselves around my body, bringing me into his chest. His hot, heavy, safe chest. "Nothing princess, I was thinking back to when Darius and I played together as mere children."

My heart sank. They had lost so much time over the years. All over a misunderstanding, one which caused the death of little Layla. "Are you okay with my brothers living here?" I asked, uncertain of his reply.

He sighed, smiled and brought his finger to my chin, lifting it so our eyes met. Sweet ocean-blue eyes swirled before me, dreamy and sensual. He gazed down at me. "Yes. Yes, I am. I need to learn to move on from what happened. They're my family now. You all are. We must make it work."

I leaned up and kissed him softly. "Thank you."

The sensation of warmth slivered through my body; my thoughts succumbed to my needs. I ached for him. His instinct was to protect me, to make me happy, and as mates, we were both in tune that way. Both of us connected like never before. Leaning into him, my head cushioned on his chest, the aroma of the forest enticed me further. Biting my lower lip I took a few deep breaths, he too did the same. Each of us began to taste the other's sexuality as it encased the air, the scent of arousal escaping us.

Hot heavy breaths fell on me. Strong hands curled under my legs as Ethan bent down, carrying me to our bed. Satin sheets sculpted my frame as I sunk into the softness of our devotion.

Planting delicate kisses on my lips, and down to my neck. Hands sliding over my breasts, one by one my buttons opened. Ethan growled, looking deep into my eyes. His raw primal urge taking him over. I gripped his back, pulled off his shirt and cradled my legs around his body. Moving up and down he groaned.

Pulling his hair, I needed him close, gripping his head to my neck as I sucked on his mark, lips embracing the bite as my teeth shifted and canines dug deep releasing his essence into me. Ethan growled louder. Pulling back I released, tasting my bloodied lips. He rose, pulled off my jeans and unzipped his own. Moments later we were in the throes of passion, grinding our way to a crescendo of symphonic proportions. He was mine and I was his. Faster and harder we moved. His cock filled me, satisfying my womanly needs as I gripped his buttocks, rocking back and forth. Kissing hard we came, reaching euphoria together. Screams and groans betrayed us, the whole castle would have heard our bedroom antics, especially with their enhanced wolf hearing. I smirked as he rolled off me, pulling me in for a hot sweaty cuddle.

"What?" he grinned, kissing my forehead.

"I expect the whole castle heard us."

He smirked and nodded. "I expect they did."

Lying back, we breathed, taking a few moments to catch our breath. Ethan raised himself onto his side. "So, what do you have planned for today?" he asked.

I groaned, "More training."

He laughed, pulled me up to stand and kissed me hard. "Well don't let them train you too hard princess," he grinned, slapping my bottom as I walked over to the en-suite shower.

"Oi, hands off the merchandise," I said, chuckling, then disappearing to shower and redress.

⁂

When I had finished, I dried off and changed into a new pair of jeans and a t-shirt, leaving the bathroom while towel-drying my hair. I heard voices as I appeared, and there was my husband, my life-long lover, sitting in a pair of satin pyjama bottoms, his hunky-tanned chest exposed. He was sat at his desk, talking to Aaden and Xander. Aaden was casually sat in the chair beside the desk, his hand resting on the arm, head leaned into his hand. He looked tired, his spiked blond hair, a little less spiked than the last time I saw it. He nodded to me. Xander was stood up, leaning against the wardrobe facing Ethan - he hadn't noticed me walk in.

Ethan looked up from his paperwork and smiled. Xander continued talking, something about the army and changing mortals. I believe he mentioned something about the death pits.

"What death pits?" I asked, creeping up behind Xander. He jumped.

"Whoa! Don't you have a bell, Luna!"

Ethan snarled, and Xander jumped again, forgetting his place. I laughed. "So, what are the death pits?" I asked, as I walked over to my handsome husband and sat on his lap. He wrapped his arms around my waist.

Xander huffed. "They are a necessity my Luna, only a few humans will survive the change."

I frowned. "When you say a few, what do you mean?"

Ethan stroked my hair. "He means not everyone survives. Those who are old and vulnerable will most likely perish before their first shift. Children can sometimes be too young and underdeveloped to handle such a change."

I sighed, and he continued. "But, with Hela waging war, this is the only way we can give any of them a fighting chance... we simply do not have the numbers she does."

Nodding, I said, "We should secure the children somewhere until they are old enough, maybe bring them here? Then we can keep them safe."

"This isn't a creche my Luna," Xander scoffed. I scowled at him and he changed his tone. "What I meant was, can't they stay with their parents?"

Ethan nodded. "They can, if their parents survive. But if they don't then they would need re-homing."

I sighed, walking over and perching on my mate's lap. "I can help with that."

He smiled, brushing my hair behind my ear. "Just remember princess. By changing them, we are at least giving them a fighting chance. Otherwise, they would be lambs to the slaughter."

I bit my bottom lip. "I know. But it doesn't make it any less easy."

He nodded, rested his hand on my thigh and squeezed it.

Aaden sat forward in his chair. "We will give every human the choice first Luna, we will not take away their free will."

"Yes, but if they don't choose the shift, then won't they be prey to any new wolves? We are predators after all."

Xander grinned and Aaden sighed. "Yes, but that is their choice."

"Someone from the packs will have to stay behind to control the new wolves."

"No," Ethan said. "The new wolves will have to be re-homed here. They will need training."

I smiled. "Good plan."

"Speaking of training, my little slacker," Ethan said. "Shouldn't you have started half an hour ago?"

I grinned. "I would have done it if you didn't keep me so busy."

Xander smirked, "Oh yes, the whole castle heard you two being busy earlier."

"XANDER!" Ethan boomed. Xander flushed and lowered his head in submission.

"He's fine Ethan," I said, smirking. "I did say we were overtly loud!"

Ethan nodded and smiled, kissing me. "Anyway, as you said, I have training to do. Now please be good in my absence," I grinned.

Ethan snarled then blew me a kiss as I upped and walked out the door.

Four ~ Willa

Walking out of the castle grounds and passing Darkwater Lake, I smiled. It was a cool spring day, and the bluebells had started to curtain the entrance to Elder Vale. I pulled my dark red coat tighter, fastening the belt buckle to keep the wind at bay. I was a shifter now; my body ran on the hotter side of normal. That meant that the slightest cool breeze had my hair standing on end. Goose pimples were my new normality, as were the teeth chattering and consistent shivering. The strange thing though, is that no matter how tightly I wrapped my coat, I never truly felt warm enough. It seemed that by having a higher body temperature you felt the cold even more so. Ethan didn't though. I'd never seen him shiver once. I guess he was used to it, used to the acrid changes in the weather around us. I'd like to say it's one of Hela's witches messing with my mind, but the whole place was covered by one of Arwen's protective shields. There was no way any magic was getting through those walls. At least I hoped there wasn't

Arwen was powerful, granted. But not as powerful as the first witch, the original; Edwina. She was after all the one who cast the love spell causing Ethan to fall head over heels in love with Danica Daventry. No one saw past that. Well, not until I arrived on the scene. Jeez, I remember being the third wheel like it was yesterday. The hot-headed asshole of a husband, the she-devil temptress taking my lover by storm. There was no way little ol' me could have survived all that. If it wasn't for our mate bond, Ethan would have been trapped by Danica's side for all eternity.

Who would have thought though, that he could love me? I know it sounds pathetic. But really though, he was the most handsome hot-headed asshole I'd ever seen, and he chose me! Clearly, though I chose him. After all, I wasn't the type of person to bend over and take it willingly. I smirked. Well, not unless it was an enjoyable experience at least!

I know I'm worth more than I make out. Heck, I'm supposed to be this almighty prophecy chick with a flaming red wolf. Even when I changed the other day, I still couldn't believe it. I had laid there staring into the lake, looking at my reflection as the ripples carried my flames away. Yet still, somehow, I think it's a fluke. Maybe that's what the training is for. Maybe I need to learn to be the leader they all want and need. But I do think I'm likely to get them killed, no matter how confident I appear to be. I sighed, walking into the clearing. I could hear my brothers chatting up ahead. Yes… I sighed, perhaps I'm the villain in this story. The prophetic princess leads her army to its death. That's one for the history books.

"WILLA!" Stefan yelled. His dark curls bounced as he ran over. I feigned a smile. What the heck had got into me? "What's with your face?"

"Huh?"

"It's long and drawn, boring and sad."

I laughed. "Well, thanks, brother!"

Darius walked up and slapped him on the back. Stefan fell forward into me. I steadied him. "What's Stefan said now?" he asked, frowning.

Stefan pouted. "Nothing, she's having a grump."

"I am not!" I said. Okay, so I was. Why the heck my emotions were all out of sync I had no idea!

Darius laughed. "Well let's take that mood of yours and channel it into training."

I nodded and we walked over to my other brothers. Adam was sitting next to Stylan chatting about the forthcoming war. They both looked up and waved. Harper and Stefan started brawling in the corner by the old oak tree, determined to beat each other to a pulp. "Err?"

Darius shook his head. "HARPER, STEFAN, pack it in!"

Harper looked up and dropped his brother from the headlock he had him in. He nodded to me, and Stefan raised his hand from the puddle he'd landed on the forest floor.

"BROTHERS!" Darius yelled. Stylan stirred and looked over, smiling at me.

They all stopped what they were doing and huddled around me, asking a thousand and one questions. "Have you shifted yet? Have you heard anything from Hela? Did you hear back from Nic and Alaric? Did they find Lorena in London? What's it like being married to that dick?" I smirked at that one.

Holding up my hands I pushed my way out of their group hug. "I need to breathe you know!" I said, smirking.

Stefan laughed. "She's in a mood brothers, don't push your luck."

I rolled my eyes at him. He was an asshole at times too. To be fair... I think all men are. Maybe that's why I like them so much. I shrugged, sat down on the log and watched as Darius introduced the first moves, I needed to learn in fighting.

"Right, your turn," he said, ushering me to stand up.

I nodded, took a deep breath and walked forward. He threw the first punch. I dodged it in the nick of time. "Whoa!" I said, backing off.

My brothers sat down and watched, talking amongst themselves. Darius smiled, stepped forward and kicked at my feet. "Remember to position your feet correctly," he said, showing me two different foot positions; how to strike and how to defend. He made it look easy. It was a simple combination of bouncing from one foot to the other, moving around to make you harder to hit, then using your arms to block, your fists to strike. It may have looked simple to start with... but the many combinations of stances appeared to turn into a dance. I guess in some respects it was; a dance of bravery and stupidity, a dance of life and death. But throughout the whole hour of training, my mind would not settle. Why did I even need to learn this? Why wouldn't I just turn into a wolf and be done with it?

Darius stopped dancing about and looked at me. "What's wrong?"

I took a deep breath throughout all my panting. "Why do I need to know this?"

His brow furrowed. "To defend yourself, Willa," he said, asking as though he were questioning it himself.

"But surely if I'm a wolf, I won't need to know how to punch?"

Stefan coughed and laughed behind me. I turned around and snarled at him. He held up his hands and smirked.

"Because Willa, you can't always turn into a wolf."

"But if you teach me then I can."

"Yes. But what happens if Hela has her witch army beside her and they prevent us from shifting?"

I took a step back. "Huh? They can do that?"

He nodded. "Yes, there are many things they can do."

I sighed. "So, what's the point in creating a wolf army if they won't be able to change into wolves?"

"She has a point," Stefan said.

Darius sighed. "Because we need to take the witches out first. That way Hela is defenceless and she and her army will only have their brute strength left to take us on."

"So, how do we do that?"

He laughed. "That's for you to decide Willa. You were born to lead the army, so that is what you will do."

"Shit."

Everyone laughed. I shrugged off my concerns and continued training. Darius was right, I had to learn everything I could to win this war, and not just fight or shift. But I had to learn strategy, tactics, and even propaganda. If I could change the minds of the supernaturals who lived outside of Hela's court, perhaps they could join the fight as well. Perhaps somehow and with some kind of magic of our own, perhaps we could stand a chance and win this thing.

To be continued in *Crimson Army*, book 2 of The Fire Wolf Prophecies by Annalee Adams

Pursuing Lilly by Annie Charme

One ~ Shane

"Hey, trouble." I walk into Lilly's small home with a bag of tools I've borrowed from Kane.

"Thank you for helping me. I didn't want to ask Kane with everything he has going on." She closes the front door behind me and walks ahead, holding her satin dressing gown at the front as she leads me into her kitchen. The afternoon light pouring through the window shines on her long black hair.

"You working the night shift last night?" I set the bag of tools on the floor as she fills the kettle. I've missed her at the bar, assumed she's had extra shifts at the hospital.

"I was at home studying late." The satin fabric shows off every delicious curve of her ass. I shouldn't be looking at my ex-wife's little sister's ass, and I certainly shouldn't be thinking about all the things I want to do with said ass, but the older and curvier she gets, my resolve weakens.

"Coffee?" She lifts two mugs from the cupboard, then spoons in instant coffee without me even giving her so much as a nod. She knows me well enough to know I'll say yes. Anything to prolong my time here.

"Want to show me the damage while we wait for the kettle to boil?" I lift the bag of tools from the floor.

She turns around, holding her dressing gown over her camisole and shorts. Her full breasts hang low, telling me she's not wearing her usual push-up bra. "It's in my bedroom. I'll show you."

A slither of thigh with black ink peeks through the gap in her dressing gown as she shows me up the stairs, her ass bouncing under the satin with each step, daring me to take a bite.

She pushes against her bedroom door, letting it swing open. Black lily patterned wallpaper lines the main wall, framing her huge pewter headboard above a super king size bed.

"The leg broke and the slat." She lifts the bottom of the duvet where the mattress slopes towards the floor.

I grind my back teeth. Visions of what she was doing to break the bed, and more importantly, who she was doing them with, cloud my mind.

She moves a ring light to the corner of the room, next to her dressing table, giving me more space to manoeuvre.

"What's that for?" I nod towards the ring light with a mobile phone holder in the centre. The blood in my veins bubbles at thoughts of someone filming her while they do things to her I can only dream of.

Her mouth parts. She looks between me and the ring light. "I do makeup tutorials online." She waves to the dressing table covered in various products.

Exhaling, I relax and kneel to inspect the bed slats.

"And before you go all big brother on me, I know what you're thinking and you're wrong. No man's been here. I broke the bed while I was standing on the edge to reach the top cupboard." She points to the built-in wardrobe a few feet away.

A chuckle escapes, more a sigh of relief. "I wasn't thinking anything."

"It was written all over your face." She folds her arms over her chest. "I've no time for another man. But don't tell Kane that."

I raise an eyebrow and look up at her from my knelt position, like I'm worshipping the ground she walks on. "Are you still holding out for him?" I hate to break it to her, but that ship sailed the minute his ex's daughter showed up on his doorstep.

Kane's been my right-hand man since we were at school together. I know him better than anyone, and I know he tried to be the man Lilly deserved, but he's tormented by his past. If anyone can help him, it's Violet, his deceased ex's kid. Though she's not a kid anymore. She's a curvy woman with violet hair and a bratty attitude to keep him on his toes.

Lilly rolls her eyes. "He was..." She sighs. "Emotionally unavailable. That little brat's done me a favour."

I smirk. Kane's got his hands full. "Sounds like you're jealous."

"I'm sorry. I'm sure she's nice enough. And I'm not jealous. I don't understand why I wasn't enough for him, but he prioritises this girl who arrives out of the blue."

Hearing her say she's not enough twists my insides. I stand and place my palms on either side of her shoulders. "You're enough for any man. Kane has his own demons to fight. It's nothing to do with you. He still carries the guilt of what happened twenty years ago, and he thinks it's his duty to take care of his ex's girl."

She bites on her bottom lip as she nods in agreement. The plump pink skin bulges between the gap in her front teeth. She wore braces throughout high school to close the gap. They worked a little and pulled her teeth inline, but they never closed the gap completely and I'm glad. It's what makes her unique, that and the beauty spot on her left cheek above her dimple when she smiles.

"What are you looking at? Do I have something on my face?" She wipes a hand over her lips and cheek. It's then I realise I'm all dopey eyed, staring at her like a fucking idiot.

"Sorry I was miles away." My hands burn on her shoulders, itching to pull her closer to me. Before I give in to my body's demands, I dive back down and inspect the bed again. "I've some wood in the car. You need to replace two slats."

A pink plastic tub holds up the bed where the leg's broken. I lift the frame with one hand and reach for the box with the other.

"Oh. Let me get that." Electricity shoots the length of my arm as our fingers touch. The lid catches on the frame as she slides it from under the bed, revealing her stash of toys.

My eyes widen, taking in the sheer number of them.

Her face reddens. She scrambles for the lid which has fallen off underneath the bed.

I lift out a red rose shaped toy and can't contain my smile.

She swipes it from my grasp like I've just been caught with my hand in the cookie jar. And these cookies are so, so tempting.

"You're a busy girl." Our eyes lock.

Her cheeks match the colour of her red dressing gown. The flush against her black glossy hair is breathtaking.

"I'm an overworked and underpaid twenty-seven-year-old singleton. A girl's gotta have some pleasures in life." She reaches again for the pink lid, but I grab it before she does.

"I wouldn't have thought you'd be short on offers."

"In all honesty, I'd sooner do it myself. Dick is over-rated."

"Maybe you haven't found the right dick." I rest the lid on top of the box before I prove my cock's better than anything in here.

"They're all the same." She sighs as she stands, then the front door handle clicks at the bottom of the stairs. A voice I know all too well hollers up the staircase. Hairs prickle all over my skin.

"Lils?" Fern, my ex-wife shouts.

Two ~ Lilly

"Coming," I yell, then wince, scrunching my face at Shane. She's the last person he wants to encounter. It's been eight years since their divorce. There's no feelings between them, but I can cut the frosty atmosphere with a knife every time they're in the same bar, let alone in a room together.

And now he's in my house.

My bedroom of all places.

I look down at Shane nestled at my feet. If she were to walk in here, she'd probably get the wrong idea.

I mouth sorry to Shane, grabbing a pair of leggings and a baggy tee, and quickly change in the bathroom.

The kettle bubbles as I rush downstairs. My older sister's already in the kitchen pouring herself a brew.

"Auntie Lils." Harry runs to me, holding a police car in his hand. "Look at my new hot wheel."

I take it from him, inspecting the metal car with fake enthusiasm. "That's cool."

Harry makes shapes along my shaggy rug in the dining area.

"What do I owe the pleasure?"

"Can't a sister simply visit for a catch up?"

I smile. "Yes, but with you, it's usually when you want something."

"Can you watch Harry for me this afternoon?"

"There it is."

"I'm going on a date. I was going to send him to the childminders, but he wanted to stay with his cool aunt." She gives me a smile, and of course, I agree. Being a single mum must be tough so I give her a break.

Footsteps echo down the hall.

Fern's eyes widen in fear. Her body freezes. "Is someone here?"

"Yes, but don't freak out."

The front door clicks. I peer down the hall from the kitchen doorway as Shane walks out to his car. Fern absentmindedly places her mug on the worktop and steps towards the opening. "Is that?"

"I..." She freezes in the hallway as Shane returns with two planks of wood and a saw under his arms.

"Hey Fern, how's it going?"

"Good," she squeaks.

Shane walks up the stairs all nonchalant.

Fern turns back to me with pinched brows. "Why is my ex husband in your house and walking upstairs?"

"He's fixing my bed."

Her eyebrow rises, practically lifting off her head. "Who broke the bed?"

"Not him, if that's your assumption." I open the cupboard, making myself look busy.

"Why isn't your boyfriend fixing your bed?"

"Er. Maybe because I don't have one."

Her brow wrinkles. "What happened with Kane?"

"Argh. Why does everyone keep talking as though we were married off? He was never my boyfriend. We were..." I search the room for little ears. When Harry is out of earshot, I whisper, "We were fuck buddies at best. Nothing more."

"Kane wasn't the same after that night." Fern sips her drink again, her eyes staring off into the distance as if thinking back to twenty years ago. I was just a child, but I remember hearing about what happened. The whole town talked about it for months.

"Lilly, do you have a pencil? I need to mark the wood." Shane stands in the doorway of my hall and kitchen with his hands in his combat trouser pockets.

Harry approaches with his car in hand. "Are you Auntie Lilly's boyfriend?"

Shane glances at Fern. All the colour drains from her face, as if transferring to mine as my cheeks heat.

"Shane's just a friend," I say. "In fact, he's a policeman. Show him your car."

Shane's eyes sadden as he gazes at Fern and my nephew, but he crouches down to the six-year-old's height and gives him a bright smile. "What you got there, buddy?"

Harry steps closer and gives Shane his car.

"Oh, wow." Shane holds it up at eye level. "It's a 2016 BMW M2."

"Are you really a policeman?"

"Sure am, bud." He hands the car back to Harry.

"I'm going to be one when I'm big. And I'm gonna catch all the baddies."

"You'd make a great cop, kid." He ruffles his messy brown hair and stands, giving Fern a sad smile.

Harry rushes back to the living room, where the TV blares Paw Patrol.

"Thanks for being nice to him," Fern says, all wide-eyed at Shane in a white tee that clings to his pecs, the skull tattoo chewing on a bullet that covers his torso visible through the fabric.

"Of course." He runs a hand through his black curly hair, cut short, but long enough to run my fingers through and bunch in my fist. Not that I've thought about doing that... much.

"Right. Pencil." I open a drawer in the kitchen and pull out an old pencil.

"Thanks." Shane turns around and heads back upstairs.

My sister closes the door and whispers, "Is he still single?"

"Don't you have a date?" I fold my arms over my chest.

"Yes, if I text you 'I'm a celebrity', you get me outta there. Call me and tell me Harry's sick or something, okay?"

I roll my eyes. "Sure. You still owe me for getting you out of the last one."

She shivers. "His teeth fell out during dinner. I didn't know whether to laugh or cry. You're a nurse. You're used to taking care of old people. I'm not." She wanders into the living room. "Harry, I'm going now."

Harry jumps from the sofa and squeezes his mum's thighs.

"Be good for your aunt, okay?" She kisses his head, then lets him go. She grabs her bag from the worktop. "Love you, sis." She pulls the keys from her bag as she walks out the door.

I lean against the wall with a sigh of relief. The last thing I wanted was her seeing my toy box as well. Which reminds me I need to deal with it before Harry wanders upstairs. Shane's probably had a good look and laugh.

With heated cheeks, I climb the stairs. "How's it going?"

He lifts his head as he slots a new slat in place. "Almost done. I've attached a piece of wood and fixed the broken leg."

"Thank you." I search the area for my pink box.

"I put your toys back under the bed in case the little one came up. Or worse, your sister." He chuckles. "Though maybe she could use one or two, she seemed a little uptight."

"I think you have that effect on her." I gaze around my room, not wanting to look him in the eye.

He stands, stepping closer. "Do I have that effect on you, too? You've gone quiet. And red."

The heat from his gaze ignites a fire in my belly. He's so close I can smell his scent. Minty aftershave, cigarettes and something musky that's just him, sending me delirious.

"Cat got your tongue?" He dips his head a little so our eyes lock. He's not much taller than my five foot nine inches when he bends to look at me.

"Just my brother-in-law seeing my toy collection. That would render anyone speechless."

He grins at me with his chipped front tooth. Anyone else might find it unattractive, but it makes me incredibly hot, especially as it happened during a fight at the Black Crow when he and Kane were defending me against a pack of bikers. The words, 'keep your hands off *our* property' ring in my head each time Shane smiles. I was as much his as I was Kanes. I've always been his to protect. His trouble, as he calls me.

Shane's head moves closer to my face. He whispers in my ear, "Ex brother-in-law." His breath on my neck sends a flurry of goose bumps over my skin.

I'm so turned on my clit is tingling, my nipples pebble. Every hair on my body stands to attention.

"I'll fix the other slat, then get out of your hair."

"Thank you." Without thinking, I lift on my toes slightly and peck his cheek. The scruff on his jaw scratches at my skin. The scent of him sends me dizzy. I grab a hold of his biceps before I topple.

Large, strong hands slide around my waist. He pulls me close with a groan vibrating in his chest. My body shudders against him. The only thing between us is a growing bulge beneath his combats.

"Lilly," he growls inches from my face. His eyes darkening. I've never seen him like this. The loyal German shepherd that is my brother-in-law is replaced by a ravenous jackal who's set his sights on his next meal. Hopefully, my aching pussy.

"Aunty Lil?" Harry shouts, breaking me from Shane's gaze. We break apart. For a minute there, I'd forgot Harry was here. I was dickmatised. It's been too long since I had any action, I'm practically throwing myself at my brother-in-law. Or ex brother-in-law as he put it. It makes no difference. My sister would never forgive me if anything were to happen between us. No matter how much I want it.

"I'm up here, sweetie." I spin on my heel and step to the landing. "Do you want anything?" I ask Shane.

He says, "No." But when I turn my head back to gaze into his eyes, they convey a different answer, full of everything he wants in his dark, deep brown pools of desire, taking my breath away.

Three ~ Shane

My fingers fly over the black keys of my iMac like a man possessed. It's been an eventful day on the job. A drug bust left me furious and I still haven't calmed down.

With clammy palms, I run my fingers through my hair in frustration. The small office at my home becomes stifling, despite the cool autumn chill outside.

Since I saw Lilly's body with her black flowered bedroom wall behind her on some fucking pervert's computer screen during the raid today, I've been desperate to get on my computer and find her account, along with every picture there is of her on the internet, and erase it from every motherfuckers drive.

Waiting for the image I took on my phone to upload, I glance out the window on the first floor. Orange leaves swirl in the wind, matching my scrambled mind. My ex-wife's little sister shouldn't be on a dealer's screen.

The girl with braces and pigtails has grown into a woman. Her soft bountiful curves covered in lace are enough to turn a man to sin. It's not the first time I've noticed and it won't be the last, but damnit, I don't want every scumbag in the Lake District seeing her body, much less anyone around the world.

Smoke curls from the cigarette butt in the ashtray. I clench my fist, then release and clench again. The search for her image on the internet is taking a fucking age. She doesn't have her face on the photo, but I'd know those thick thighs anywhere and her black flower tattoos climbing up her leg.

The computer beeps, distracting me from my phone and the image of her on my screen. Several matches pop up, filling the monitor of her from every angle, always sitting on the corner of her bed with the black wallpaper behind her.

I recall fixing her bed where the leg was broken. And the ring light she said was for makeup tutorials. Fucking makeup tutorials. I should've known then. Should've looked into it more, but I never in my wildest dreams thought my sister-in-law would put herself in this position, though she's always been trouble.

Clicking through the matching images found, I check the metadata and trace it back to her account. "Fuck's sake." My voice echoes off the four walls in the box bedroom that's my office. A room more like a teenage gaming lair, but lately all I've done is use it to track down my enemies with the help of Dom and Dan's skills.

Finally, I find the account. @nurseinfullbloom. It sounds more like a fucking garden centre than an account for adult content creation. With my fingers flying over the keyboard again, I subscribe to her account under my pseudonym. @black_shad0w.

Once I'm subscribed to her highest tier, I've access to an album of photos and videos that date back to the summer. My shoulders relax a little when I see the feet fetish stuff. A seed of hope sprouts in my chest, hoping this is just a channel for her to create feet content and earn a few quid on the side.

I scroll through an assortment of weird and crazy videos of her replying to messages asking for strange kinks like popping balloons, eating cake and other snacks. The further I go, leading up to the present day, the more sexual and daring she gets. If I wasn't so damn mad, I'd get off, but even my cock is infuriated.

The next video, however, grabs both our attention. My balls draw up tight. Wide eyed, I watch her glorious tits bounce in a white cotton bra. Hard nipples chafe under the fabric as she bounces on a large teddy, the fur from its head between her thighs, hiding most of her white cotton knickers.

No wonder she broke the fucking bed, bouncing like she's on a bouncy castle. Her moans fill the room, jolting me back to reality, and I click the cross in the corner of the screen. I shouldn't be looking at my sister-in-law like this. I shouldn't be picturing her bouncing on my cock. Or imagining what her stiff nipples will feel like against my tongue. And I certainly shouldn't be wondering how much mess she's making in her knickers or what she tastes like.

I close my eyes to stop looking at the screen, but she's still in my head, calling my name when I make her come.

I'm finished.

Fuck. I'll never be able to look at her the same way again. My little sister. *Who you want to fuck.* The voice in my head couldn't be more wrong.

I don't want to fuck her.

I want to ravish her, eat her pussy, and make her beg for my cock. I want to feel those thick thighs wrapped tightly around my waist; her painted red nails digging into my shoulders while I rip her apart.

A notification pops up on my screen.

@nurseinfullbloom Live at 9pm.

"Over my dead body," I growl and light up another cigarette. I'll be damned if I sit back and let every fucker jerk off to her.

Four ~ Shane

I'm counting down the seconds to her live, every muscle in my body tense with dread. Or is it anticipation?

Three dots appear on the monitor. I hold my breath. Lilly fills the screen. Her tits bursting out of a naughty nurse costume two sizes too small.

Plump red lips wrap around a pink lollipop as she smooths a hand over a long blonde wig, hiding her ebony locks. Her other hand pushes up a pair of black-framed fake glasses. It's a disguise.

She pops the lolly from her mouth. "Hello, boys." Her sultry tone gets my cock's attention.

I huff. Bloody pointless disguise when she has her bedroom wall in the background for all to see. Not to mention the lily tattoo climbing up her thick thigh on full display. She may as well just tell everyone her fucking name and give out her address while she's at it.

She wriggles on the edge of the bed, her breasts jiggling, threatening to burst out at any minute. The only thing holding them in place is a zip on her white uniform straining at her cleavage.

With a click of the mouse, I zone in on the valley of her tits. A deep crevice begging to be explored, and I want to explore it with my tongue.

Down, boy. Now isn't the time to play. We're on a fucking mission. This is nothing more than surveillance. Since she lied through the gap in her teeth about the ring light, here we are. I have to extract any information I can about what kind of trouble she's in.

Of course, she could just like this. Get off on it even. In which case, I have a bigger problem than I initially thought. She might never be mine, but I'm not sharing her. I was okay when she was sleeping with my mate. I trust Kane with my life, and I trusted him with her. But I don't trust any of these motherfuckers filling up the side chat.

Lilly answers messages in a seductive way, playing with the zipper on her extremely tight dress.

More messages fill the chat. There must be fifty subs on tonight.

'You're such a tease.'

'Where's your toys tonight?'

'Lick the lolly, sweetheart.'

'Daddy's good girl.'

I snarl as I read each one. Bile rising in my throat.

She keeps her knees together. Her touching thighs make it difficult to see what she's wearing under her costume.

Holding the lolly an inch from her lips, her tongue darts out to lick the tip. She moans. Her bottom shuffles on the edge of the bed I fixed a few days ago.

"Makeup tutorials, my fucking arse," I mutter under my breath.

More messages appear in the chat.

'Touch yourself.'

'Lift the dress. Be a good girl for Daddy.'

'Such a naughty nurse.'

'Lick the tip, baby. Just like that.'

I taste the acid on my tongue. My chest burning with rage, my stomach on fire with desire and my balls sweating with the heat of that fucking tongue, but I refuse to jerk off.

I'm no better than these dirty fuckers. I'd give my right arm for a night with her, but I'm here to protect her and keep her out of trouble. It's what I've done for the past twenty years since I've known the lass.

And it's what I'll always do. Even when she doesn't realise she needs protecting from herself.

When she stopped seeing Kane, a slither of hope creeped in that maybe I could be more than a brother-in-law.

She'd never go for it, though. I'm no fool. She cares for her sister too much. It's one of the many things I love about her. Between her and her fucking sister, I'm screwed, and not in the way I want.

"Who wants to watch me make this lolly disappear?" Lilly says as she fondles it with her tongue, the bright pink staining the surface. "I'll be a good girl for you, daddy."

"The fuck you will," I growl. With swift fingers, I get to work. My training in the Special Reconnaissance Regiment has never been put to better use. That and the incognito software my mate, Dom, installed for me. In minutes, I'm infiltrating her IP address. It helps that I fitted her security system last year.

The lolly slips down the valley of her breasts. My fingers slow on the keyboard, hoping that's all she meant when she said she was going to make it disappear.

Her tongue teasing the gap between her teeth. "You want to find the lolly for me?" She leans towards the camera, giving me a bird's-eye view of the landscape down there. It's dark, deep, and fucking tropical.

My dick twitches again, but I'm too incensed to care.

With a tug on the zip, she exposes more of her chest. "You boys want more?" She exposes another inch. "How's that?" The stick of the lollypop protrudes between the two hills. Like a mast on the land I'm going to claim.

With another pull on her zip, the front of her chest is set free, her pebbled nipples barely covered by the fabric of her dress. With a bounce on the bed, the lolly drops to her lap. "Oops, there it is." She lifts it with her fingers, and licks it again before running it over her exposed skin.

"You want me to make it disappear again? I wonder where it could go this time?" Her mouth lifts in the corner. She slips it inside her dress as if fondling her nipple with the sticky end. A moan escapes her lips, but I can tell it's all for show. She's in the wrong bloody profession. She could be an actress with this performance.

The subs all text in unison, wanting her to remove the dress.

She swipes her hair over her shoulder. "I am getting a little hot and sticky. Maybe I'll just slide this off." She tugs at the fabric on her shoulder.

My heart stops. Without thinking, my fingers fly over the keyboard at robotic speed as I type in a private chat for only the host to see.

Text: 'You move that dress one more inch, and I'll shut down this party.'

Her brow furrows. She squints through the fake lens of her glasses. Her mouth parts. She doesn't acknowledge it, but I can tell she's read it. For the first time since she started this charade, she's flustered. Her fingers tap the screen.

I huff out a silent chuckle. She's blocked me. At least she thinks she's blocked me, but I'm hacked into her account, still seeing everything.

As if brushing off a fly, she continues with her seduction, inching the fabric of her dress down again. She drops the shoulder, holding the lolly over her nipple. And I drop her subs.

She gasps. "Where did everybody go?" Her finger frantically taps the screen.

My eyes fix on her nipple, playing peekaboo behind the fucking lollipop. I thought I could relax once everyone else was off the feed, but now it's just the two of us—or three if you include her rosy pebble winking at me—I'm wound up like a Jack-in-the-box, my dick ready to burst free at any minute, hoping to be acquainted with her nipple.

I unblock myself and type into the chat. 'I hate to say I told you so.'

She covers her breast. The lolly's forgotten as it drops to the floor. "Who?" She swallows, shaking her head in disbelief. "What do you want?"

"I want you to keep your clothes on," I growl through gritted teeth, willing my dick to calm the fuck down. I check the voice distorter is on, so she can't tell it's me.

Her beautiful face reddens, her nostrils flare. She's mad. "If you want people to keep their clothes on, you're on the wrong platform," she spits out. "What have you done with all my subscribers?"

"From now on, I'm your only sub." I lean close to the screen as if leaning closer to her. "You won't be getting your tits out for the lads again, lass. Not on my watch. Never. You hear me?"

She juts her chin out, lifts her head high with a huff. "Are you going to pay me for my exclusive time?" Her arms fold over her chest. "That's five grand a month. Are you going to pay that?"

"No."

"Then I guess this conversation is over. I'll let you see yourself out. And I'll be sure to report you."

I chuckle. "It's a good thing I like your smart mouth." She's clever trying to bargain for more money. But I've done my homework. "You had one hundred and sixteen subs at £14.99 each. That's £1738.84. I'll pay you £2000, but first you tell me why you need the money so bad that you feel you have to get your tits out."

"Why does there have to be a reason? Can't a woman enjoy expressing her sexuality?" Her nipple pops out again as she battles with the dress, wrestling with it to get her arm back in the sleeve.

"You can express your sexuality all you want." There's a rawness in my voice. "With me," I add.

She doesn't miss the longing and desperate need in my tone. Her ruby lips part as she sucks in a breath. "You said you want me to keep my clothes on."

"For now."

"So, what do you want to do?"

"Just talk."

"You want to pay me two grand to just talk?" Her brow furrows. "I'm not a therapist. I suggest you seek medical treatment elsewhere."

"I don't need a therapist. I need a nurse."

She pushes her glasses up, her lip pinches between the gap in her teeth as she chews on the plump skin.

"And yes, I'll pay you. Send me your bank details through the app. I'll pay you one thousand up front and one thousand at the end of the month. You cancel your subs. You don't talk to anyone else or send anyone any pictures or videos of you. The only person who gets to see you from now on is me. Got it?"

"Yes, Daddy," she says in a sarcastic voice.

"I'm not your daddy," I growl. "But you can call me sir."

Her chest rises with a gasp. A flush paints her chest, creeping up her neck. She liked that domineering tone.

I wonder what else she'll respond to. "Do we have a deal?"

She nibbles her plump lip again with those two front teeth I want to feel scraping along my shaft.

I shake the thought before I get ahead of myself. This is purely recon. Find out what's going on with her and help her out. "Well?" I say, growing impatient.

"All right. Yes."

"Yes, what?"

"Yes, sir."

"Good girl." I relax back in the leather chair, getting myself comfortable. My dick softens when the lad realises he's not coming out to play. Not tonight, anyway. But I don't know how long I can keep him at bay when my little sister-in-law wants to express her sexuality.

I always said she was trouble.

For more Shane and Lilly, you can pre order their story Pursuing Lilly. *In the meantime you can read* Taming Violet *and* Protecting Poppy, *featuring Shane and Lilly in the Sinful Secrets Series. All books are standalone, but part of a shared world.*

Sugarplum by B Crowhurst

Prologue
One Year Earlier...

It's just gone midnight and the club is still in full festive swing. *I'm far too old and far too sober for this shit.* Every year I offer to be designated driver on our Christmas work do and every year I regret it. So far, this year's has been more civilised than most but the night is still young apparently...unlike me.

Our small team of five enjoyed a meal at the local bistro earlier and have since gone on to hit several bars and clubs. The girls seem hell bent on trying every cocktail on every menu while me and Josh trail along behind them like some sort of senior citizens security service. Josh is the only other man in our office and therefore my source of sanity. The girls are great but they can get a bit much sometimes. It's nice to have someone to talk football and sink a beer with. Josh is drinking tonight but has only had a few so is still capable of decent conversation. We're sat in a booth in the club people watching, one of my favourite past times. The girls have gone off to dance somewhere. Lord only knows how they can even stand let alone dance after what they've consumed tonight.

The thumping beat of the music and the strobe lighting is making even me feel sick and I've only had fruit juice all night! The group of people in front of us moves away bringing the girls back into view. There she is, my Sugarplum Fairy. Except she's not mine at all. Never has been, never will be. She's dancing with Maya and Jules totally oblivious to the world around her. Swaying her hips to the music with her arms in the air. She's wearing a short dress entirely covered in silver sequins, shimmying around like some sort of sexy goddamn disco ball. I watch her dancing, mesmerised by her as always. It's never been any different. She walks in a room and I stop seeing everyone else. It certainly makes for an interesting working day. I don't know why I keep putting myself through this perpetual torture.

"Are you ever going to do anything about that?" Josh shouting in my ear above the music brings me out of my Sophie trance.

"About what?" I yell back, still not taking my eyes off of Sophie's sashaying backside.

"Come on mate, you might think you have the rest of the world fooled but you know she has you by the heart and the balls. Isn't it high time you did something about it?" Josh smirks as he takes a swig of his beer.

"I don't know what you're talking about." I lie. "And even if I did, she's so far off limits she might as well be in outer space."

"You're a glutton for punishment my friend. Surely there are no repercussions worse than this painful pining shit you put yourself through on a daily basis." Josh chuckles and shakes his head.

"I do not pine." I shoot back sulkily.

"Whatever you need to tell yourself." Josh says as the girls make their way back to the booth.

They're all giggling and talking at once as they stagger about so it's hard to tell what on earth they're saying but they start to pull Josh and I up by our arms.

"Come on you two, dance with us! You're not ready to retire yet!" Maya laughs as her and Sophie pull an arm each.

Jules tugs Josh until we are both on our feet and being forcibly led to the dance floor. We roll our eyes at each other. The girls are so wasted. They know dancing is not our thing.

The girls dance round us giggling and laughing. I shuffle my feet to the beat trying to hide just how ridiculously out of place I feel. Being this close to Sophie while she wiggles and thrusts around is doing unfortunate things to my manhood. She has absolutely no idea the affect she has on me but if she continues to grind that sweet arse of hers against my groin then she's about to be in for a shock.

I take a step back from her and swing her round to face me before that happens. She smiles as she drapes her arms round my shoulders. *Well that backfired.*

"Having fun yet Mr Grinch?" she shouts as she presses closer against me to try and reach my ear. Even with heels on I'm almost a foot taller than her. I can feel her breasts push against my chest as she continues her mindless dancing. *Heaven help me.*

"If you're having fun then I'm happy Sugarplum." I tell her as I attempt to unwrap her arms from my neck. I need to get some distance between her and the raging bull in my pants. Whoever said erections come fewer and further between as you age clearly has never spent time with Sophie Plumstead.

Sophie stops dancing and puts her hands on her hips pouting at me. "I keep telling you not to call me that at work."

I chuckle at her mock tantrum. She reminds me of when she was little, she used to do the exact same thing back then.

"We're not at work." I point out.

"But our work friends are here and they are seriously not going to take me seriously as a serious boss if you keep calling me Sugarplum!" she protests.

I laugh out loud at her. How many times can someone use the word serious is one drunken sentence?

"Come on Miss Serious Boss Lady, I think it's time we got you home." I put my arm across her shoulders to steady her as she starts to stagger and sway.

"Oh, come on Adrian, I'm having so much fun! Don't be such a party pooper!" She whines as she sticks out her bottom lip.

"Sugarplum I'm trying to save you from a date with your toilet pan. Right now, you're about one drink away from being very well acquainted with it by morning." I start to lead her towards the exit and the others follow.

"Hmm you may be onto something there." She slurs and clings onto my collar as she tries to walk in a straight line but fails miserably.

It's about an hour later by the time we've said our goodbyes and I've managed to get Sophie in the car and drive her home. She slumps against my shoulder as I unlock her front door; a task that is far beyond her capabilities at this point. Once we're inside, she kicks her ridiculously high heels off and shrinks several inches. She flops onto her sofa in the most unladylike fashion and closes her eyes.

"Soph you need to sleep this off. Your brother is going to kill me for letting you get this drunk. Come on, let's get you into bed." I bend down and scoop her up like a baby.

"Well, that's the best damn offer I've had all night.' She whispers as she tucks her head under my chin and drifts in and out of sleep. I try not to let her words even register in my brain. *She's just drunk and rambling.* I tell myself over and over. *She doesn't know what she's saying.*

When I reach her bedroom, I pull back the covers and gently lay her down on the bed. Her eyes are closed and she's breathing deeply. I doubt she will remember getting home in the morning but the banging headache is sure to remind her. I pull the covers over her and start to tuck her in.

"Adrian?" she mumbles quietly and reaches for my hand with her eyes still closed.

"Yeah Sugarplum?" I stroke her hair as I finish tucking her in, convinced she's not really awake.

"I wish you'd never married your bitch of an ex-wife instead of me." She rolls over and snuggles into the duvet as sleep claims her, leaving me stunned.

What. The. Fuck? Sophie thinks of me like another brother, this is not how things work between us. I can only assume this is nothing but drunken nonsense. She won't even remember this in the morning.

I kiss her on the forehead as she sleeps before I leave her. "Me too darling, me too." I whisper.

I head downstairs and put a box of Paracetamol on the kitchen counter with a large glass of water for when she wakes up before leaving her house. I lock the door and cross the street to my car. I take one last glance at Sophie's bedroom window before driving home. Back to reality. Back to a world where Sophie can never be mine.

One ~ Sophie

Christmas – the most wonderful time of the year. The season of joy and magic. At least that's what I tell my clients anyway. Having been single for Christmas since forever it's actually my own personal hell but I don't tell them that. Misery doesn't sell, magic does.

I run a successful events company with my business partner Adrian and making magic is what we do. Actually, to be more accurate I create the magic, Adrian crunches the numbers. It works. We both stick to what we're good at and cross over somewhere in the middle.

Christmas starts early for us and goes on for months. It takes a lot of prep to pull off the kind of events we do for such big-name clients. Of course, on top of Christmas the usual events carry on still such as weddings, charity balls, award ceremonies etc. To say December is tiring would be an understatement.

Today is the first of December and we are dressing the venue for a high-profile wedding. The soon to be happy couple are two of London's top models and anyone who's anyone is on the guest list. We were hired by the venue to turn their ballroom into a Roman Colosseum at the client's request.

Josh is busy installing the last enormous column at the far side of the room while Jules and I swag the doorways with garlands of lush, green foliage.

"Miss Plumstead, just to let you know the bride and groom are due to arrive any minute now for their rehearsal. As I mentioned on the phone, they are more than happy for you to continue working through the rehearsal as we are all on a tight deadline." The hotel events manager reminds me.

"Please, call me Sophie. Thank you, that's great. I promise you won't even know we're here."

I'm all smiles and dimples while she is deadly serious and professional to a fault. She arches one perfectly plucked brow and nods at me before disappearing off again back to her desk.

"Oh and the clients have requested to meet you after the rehearsal to thank you." She says turning back to me momentarily.

"Soph, how many more garlands do we have in the box?" Jules asks me through my earpiece. We often use headsets for big venues to save us from keep running around looking for each other or shouting.

"Two. We're almost done."

"Great, so that's one for the exit on the left and one for the groom's side archway." She replies a little out of breath. *All this up and down ladders is exhausting!*

I grab my last garland and leave one in the box for Jules. Making my way to the ladder that's already in position I throw the garland over my shoulder and start to climb.

There is noise and commotion in the corridor outside so I assume they have arrived. I start the meticulous task of pinning the heavy garland in place and stick the spare pins to my t-shirt while I work.

"Psst Soph." Jules hisses through my earpiece. "Don't look now but the groom is wearing a toga...and I'm pretty sure there's nothing underneath it."

I giggle as I try not to lose my balance. "Is he good looking?"

"What do you think? He's a model!"

I can see Jules from across the other side of the room getting animated with her arms as she talks to me.

"Just look busy." She adds

"I am busy." I take three more pins and poke them in my t-shirt as I position the garland in place.

I can see in my peripheral that the bride and groom are now walking across the room followed by their entourage. My ladder is just to the left of where the rehearsal will take place so I try to focus on the task in hand and not look down. *I am nothing if not professional.* If I say it to myself enough times, it might actually come true.

After several minutes of pretending not to be aware of what's happening below, temptation gets the better of me. *Just a quick look won't hurt.*

I crane my neck to see through the leaves and catch a glimpse of the bride. She looks stunning in her ivory Roman Goddess gown. *I thought it was bad luck to see the bride's dress before the ceremony?* I lean a little further forward to search for the groom.

Holy mother of mayhem!! Jules is right. Not only is he drop dead gorgeous but he's also wearing the thinnest fabric known to man and there is not a lot left to the imagination!

Before I realise what's happening, I've over stretched on the ladder and it starts to topple.

"Aaaaahhh!" I fall through the air and land with a thump in a heap of organza and leaves right in the middle of their rehearsal.

As I fight my way out of the pile of materials I've landed in, I become painfully aware of the group of people all circled round me in shock. All wondering what on earth just crash landed into their rehearsal.

"Rico and Bella, let me introduce you to Sophie, your designer and decorator." says the sarcastic little witch in charge.

Please, let an enormous black hole open up right here and swallow me whole.

"Hello there." I smile awkwardly and give a little wave. The heat coming from my embarrassed cheeks could start a small fire.

Could this day get any worse?

When we get back to the office after that monumental cock-up, all I want to do is put the kettle on and hide at my desk.

Josh and Jules have done nothing but make fun of me the entire way back. Jules is still laughing hysterically as we walk through the door.

"What's all the laughter about?" Adrian asks.

He's leaning against the front desk wearing a light grey suit. His slightly greying hair only adding to the look of sophistication he effortlessly pulls off. Under normal circumstances, the sound of his voice would make me feel a hundred times better but I don't relish the thought of him finding out about my little mishap earlier. *Which is about to happen in approximately three seconds.*

"Oh, nothing major. Just Sophie falling off a ladder at the sight of a penis." Jules can hardly contain her laughter.

Adrian looks quite rightly confused. "Why was there a penis?"

"The groom had his knob out during the rehearsal and Sophie fell off her ladder trying to look at it." Josh offers his version of events. *So not helping.*

Jules and Josh once again fall about the office laughing.

"Wait, hold on. Rewind a sec. What kind of a wedding was this?!"

I can feel the heat creeping up my cheeks as Adrian's eyes ping pong between me and the laughing pair of lunatics on the other side of the office.

"Umm, it really wasn't quite like that. I'll explain it to you later. Tea?" I offer, in hopes of deflecting Adrian's attention elsewhere.

He follows me into our office and closes the door.

"Did you hurt yourself Sugarplum?" he asks, seeming genuinely concerned.

Adrian's nickname for me goes back to my ballerina days. When I was about seven years old, I was a sugarplum fairy in a performance of the nutcracker. Adrian and my brother who were seventeen at the time, came to watch and the name just stuck. Since we became business partners though, he is under strict instructions never to utter it in front of the staff.

"I don't think so." I say giving myself a quick once over inspection. "Although I did hit my shoulder pretty hard."

"Let me take a look." Gently Adrian sweeps my long, blonde hair off my shoulder, setting off a string of fireworks as he goes.

The thing about Adrian is, I've been head over heels in love with him for as long as I can remember. Unfortunately for me, he still sees me as the little girl in the pink tutu and probably always will. I've gotten used to it over the years. It's something I've learned to live with, that's always there in the background like a dull ache. It doesn't bother me anymore; I know he will never see me that way and I manage to shelve my feelings most of the time. *But dammit it's not easy when his fingertips are brushing across my shoulder and I can feel his breath against the back of my neck.*

"Looks like you have a bruise coming." He says gently. "Maybe you should spend less time ogling stray penises. It seems rather dangerous." I can't tell if he's joking or cross with me for hurting myself. He's always been over-protective just like James but he holds his cards much closer to his chest than my brother.

"It wasn't quite how they're making out; you know." I'm so embarrassed at the memory of the scantily clad groom helping me to my feet.

"You don't have to explain yourself to me Sugarplum, just as long as you're safe." He ruffles my hair before putting distance between us, reaffirming what I already know – that he sees me as nothing more than a younger sister.

Ugh! Who needs a man anyway, right?!

Two ~ Sophie

Toast or cereal? My usual morning dilemma. I don't particularly fancy either but apparently ice cream is not considered a suitable breakfast. *Cereal it is.* I pour an extra big bowl as I have a full diary today so who knows when I'll get lunch.

Just as I'm about to sit down to my uninspiring breakfast, the doorbell rings. *There's only one person that could be this time of the morning; Luke.* Sure enough, I open the door to see my regular delivery man standing in the doorway in all his tanned gloriousness. *Seriously, who is that bronzed in December?* Luke has been covering our area for the past few weeks and is an outrageous flirt. *Not that I mind, the man looks like he just walked off the set of Baywatch except in postal uniform.* It's a wonder he ever finishes his round on time with all the sweet-talking he does.

"Good morning beautiful. Just the three parcels for you this morning. Did you run out of things to buy?" he hands me my small stack of parcels and grins at me cheekily.

"Morning Luke. Yes, I've almost finished my Christmas shopping actually."

"Well then it's about time you started spending some money on yourself, otherwise I won't have a good reason to knock on your door in the mornings."

I'm pretty certain he gives these lines to all the women he delivers to but it makes me smile all the same.

"Hmm maybe I'll treat myself to something new for the festive season. It's not like anyone else will." I joke, not meaning to sound quite as pathetic and desperate as I just did.

"You never know beautiful, you never know." He winks at me before he turns and heads off down the street to the next house.

When I arrive at the office, Adrian is already sat at his desk typing away on one of his many spreadsheets. We both like to arrive early and discuss the day ahead before the rest of the rabble arrives. I love my team, I picked each and every one of them carefully for their individual talents but put us all together and we are rather rowdy.

"How's my favourite Sugarplum this morning?" Adrian asks looking up from his computer. He greets me the same way almost every morning. Today he is wearing a navy suit with a cream shirt. His dark hair and short beard are flecked with silver which only adds to his attractiveness. Adrian hates it, he has major age issues but I think he only gets hotter the older he gets.

"Hungry. I got distracted by some Christmas shopping that arrived and by time I opened it all my cereal was soggy. That's the worst!"

"Ah indeed, say no more. I'll order us some coffees and pastries from across the road. A hungry Sophie is a dangerous creature."

I choose to ignore his dig at me and instead switch my computer on while he phones through our order. *Today's going to be a good day. We're interviewing all day and I have a good feeling about some of the candidates.*

Seven hours later and I'm losing the will to live.

"Please tell me we are almost at the end of the shortlist?" I beg Adrian as he draws a fat red line through the latest interviewee's resume.

We have been interviewing all day for a new Marketing Assistant and to say the calibre of prospective applicants was abysmal, would be kind.

"Just one more Sugarplum. Get yourself another one of those frothy, frappe, coffee, mocha things you like and slap on your happy face one more time."

"Uuughhhh" I groan and rest my head on the desk dramatically.

"As soon as we're done, I promise I'll take you home and order you Chinese food while we go through the options." he offers with a handsome, warm smile.

"Options? You can't seriously be considering hiring one of those buffoons?"

"I think you're being a tad dramatic Soph. Some of them were very highly qualified." He says casually leaning back in his chair.

"But boring as hell Adrian! I don't want people like that on my team. I need people with creative spark and a sense of fun!"

Just as Adrian is about to open his mouth, Michaela quietly knocks on the door.

"Your last candidate is here Sophie. Shall I show Mr Reynolds in?"

No time for more coffee then.

"Please do. Thank you, Michaela."

As I'm busy shuffling the papers on my desk to neaten them up in walks one of the most gorgeous men I've seen in a long time. *Well, hello handsome. You certainly have my full attention.* I immediately stop what I'm doing and smooth out my suit jacket before offering him my hand.

"Lovely to meet you Mr Reynolds, thanks for joining us today." I say overenthusiastically as I shake his hand.

"Please, call me Sean." He says as he shakes Adrian's hand too. *That voice.*

Adrian clears his throat bringing me out of my swoony daydream.

"Well Sean, I'm Adrian, I handle the financial side of things and this is Sophie the Managing Director. Please take a seat."

Adrian shoots me an unimpressed look across the table and takes his seat.

"Why don't you start by telling us a little bit about yourself?" I suggest to Sean.

He starts to talk about his qualifications and education whilst Adrian is busily scribbling down notes. I on the other hand, haven't listened to a single word Sean has said. Instead, I've been focused entirely on watching the way his lips move and his fingers slide up and down his pen while he answers the question.

Suddenly I realise Sean has stopped talking and Adrian has stopped writing. *Geez Soph, concentrate. How long have they been waiting for you to ask the next question?*

"That's great. Thank you. Could you tell us in more detail about the previous positions you've been in?" As soon as the words leave my mouth, I realise the double meaning behind what I just said and get flustered.

"In marketing I mean." I add hurriedly. I can feel my cheeks burning.

He smiles at me and tries not to laugh but I can see the glimmer of humour in his eyes.

"I know what you meant."

Sean launches into an impressive speech about his previous experiences and thankfully the rest of the interview goes off without a hitch. I even manage to concentrate and make some notes myself.

After Michaela sees Sean out, I turn to Adrian with a huge grin on my face.

"No." He says bluntly. "Just no."

We've known each other so long he knows what I'm going to say before I even say it.

"But why not? He was very well qualified."

"Name me one qualification he had." Adrian folds his arms across his chest and smirks at me.

"Erm you know... The marketing ones."

Adrian throws his head back and laughs his deep laugh. He has a laugh that envelops you like a warm hug.

"You didn't hear a word that idiot had to say, you were too busy drooling over him." He shakes his head in amusement.

"That's not true. I think he would fit in perfectly here. I want to hire him."

"Hmm fit perfectly where exactly?" Adrian raises one eyebrow as he rubs his silvering stubble.

"Adrian!" I ball up a piece of paper and throw it at him, pretending to be shocked. *As if I hadn't already thought of several places Sean would fit just nicely.*

"Please?" I pull out the big doe-eyed routine. We only mess around like this when it's just the two of us. The staff would never take me seriously at all if we behaved like this in front of them.

Adrian lets out a defeated sigh, knowing he's lost. I always win eventually with Adrian. He hasn't been able to say no to me since I was little.

"This is a mistake Sugarplum. You mark my words. That guy is trouble."

Sunshine and the Vamp by Bailey Grayson

Morozov Family: Book One

Blurb

Best intentions can go suck it.

I walked into a dark alley with the best of intentions and look where that got me. Drugged, kidnapped and thrown into a world I didn't even know existed.

Now I'm being held captive by a hot as sin vampire, whilst trying not to be killed by his wife and, oh yeah, he's the leader of the Russian Mob and I'm suddenly a target. Go me.

Safe to say, I'm not sure I'll do anything for anyone ever again.

Follow Benji as he learns about vampires, the Russian mob and tries to dodge a knife wielding soon-to-be ex wife. There are curse words, graphic sexual scenes and lots of blood (hey, it's a book about vampires...). Recommended for 18+ only.

This is the opening of a brand new world I'm hoping to write later in the year. It's dark PNR, set in a Mafia world with grumpy vampire men and the rays of sunshine that love them despite all their flaws. Expect violence, sass, drama and lots of blood.

One ~ Benji

I never thought this was how I was going to die. I was just trying to save someone who didn't even stay long enough to say thank you. The asshole just scrambled to his feet and fled the dark alley that smelled of stale piss and week old sashimi, leaving me staring at a barrel of a gun and trying really hard not to piss my pants. I wasn't sure I was going to succeed with that one.

"Do you know how long it took me to find that guy?" came the menacing growl from the shadows.

Shit. I was really gonna die. "I'm s-sorry."

The man grunted.

"I just heard the scream. I was passing and I just wanted to help."

"Help?"

"Yes," I squealed. I probably should be concerned with how high my voice was going, but I guess it wasn't quite as high on my priority list as the fucking gun in my face! "I know it's cliché. There's a dark alley and a scream and we all know the guy is going to die but I didn't think it'd actually happen. Guess it's a cliché for a reason."

"Cliché?"

"An expression that's overused and not original. Like—"

"I know what a cliché is," the man snapped and stepped closer, bringing him out of the shadows and into what little light there was.

And holy fuck.

The guy was too pretty to be a murderer. His eyes were a beautiful shade of blue, like the ocean bathed in sunlight, and his face was all angles with a jaw sharp enough to cut glass. Damn, I think I'd lose a finger tracing those lines. The only thing that took away from how pretty he was, was that there was no expression on his face. Nothing to give away what he was thinking, which was weird given the amount of anger I'd heard in his voice already. What kind of person had no emotion—

Wait.

A psychopath.

Fuck.

Fucking fuckity fuck.

"What are you staring at?" he asked gruffly, his voice thick and low.

"You." I blinked. Wait... "The gun. I meant the gun." Fuck, I was an idiot. An idiot who was about to die.

His dark brows lowered over those gorgeous eyes and his face went from cold and expressionless to very pissed off. Maybe he wasn't a psychopath. Perhaps he was just crazy. Hang on, wouldn't that be worse? A psycho could probably be reasoned with, crazy was just crazy.

He stepped closer, and, naturally, I stepped back but he kept following until I was stopped by the wall behind me.

He stared at me for the longest time, his gaze dark and assessing. And god, it was quiet. And I was nervous. And shit, I could feel word vomit about to explode from my mouth.

"Please don't kill me. I don't want to die. I was just trying to help and I didn't mean to interrupt. I'll just pretend I didn't see anything. I mean, who am I gonna tell. There's only old Mrs. Mickles who lives next door who has loads of cats and—"

A hand slammed over my face cutting off the tirade of shit spewing from my mouth.

The mystery murder man grunted. "You talk too much."

Only when I was nervous. And about to die apparently.

"I'm not going to kill you," he said. My shoulders sagged and some of the tension left my shoulders. "But I can't leave you here."

Oh, shit.

"I'm sorry for this."

Panic started to rise again. I tried to say 'For what?' but it came out as a high pitched muffle against the man's hand – which was soft and smelled like sandalwood and bergamot and something darker which was all him but I hadn't noticed that. Not at all.

Then, before I could blink, the man had moved, there was a sharp sting in my neck and the world went fuzzy.

Who was going to feed Mrs. Mickles' cats when she went on a cruise now that I was dead?

I came around, my head throbbing and my mouth feeling like it'd been stuffed with cotton wool. My eyes felt glued shut, refusing to cooperate. Judging by the smell, that was probably a good thing. There was a definite metallic tang to the air that was assaulting my senses and that didn't help my panic abate.

I couldn't hear much. Just the faint humming of an AC unit. Probably why it felt like the arctic in here. I was only in a long-sleeved Henley as the days were mild enough not to need a jacket now we were heading into summer. I went to rub my arms but found they were tied down. I groaned as the rest of my limbs started to wake up. Pins and needles exploded in my feet, and I winced as I picked my head up and finally opened my eyes.

"Welcome back."

I flinched. Well, as much as I could considering I was tied to a chair. It was the guy from the alley, the one who was too pretty to be a psycho. Not that I could see him. I couldn't see anything beyond the ring of light I was sitting in.

"Where am I?" I asked, my mouth dry and my words sluggish.

"What's your name?" he replied, completely ignoring my question.

I licked my dry lips. The guy probably already knew; I'd had my wallet on me and now I couldn't feel it in my back pocket. I guess that could also be from the fact that my ass was numb. How long had I been sitting here? "My name is Benjamin Barrett but I go by Benji."

Footsteps echoed around the room as the mystery man stepped forwards out of the shadows. He was tall, or maybe that was a trick of the light, but he definitely looked taller than me and I was six foot. He squatted in front of me, his face just as cold as I remembered.

"Charlie Kent."

Huh? "I don't—"

"Do you know him?"

"No." I shook my head and regretted it. "Did you drug me?"

"Yes. Do you know who I am?"

"No. Have you forgotten?"

A low growl rose from his throat. Probably wise not to antagonise the crazy guy who'd kidnapped me.

"Sorry," I said quickly. "My thoughts don't seem to be… organised. Wait, you drugged me?"

"Yes. I already answered that." He cocked his head to one side, his gaze assessing.

"Why?"

"Would you have come willingly if I'd asked?"

"Probably not."

The guy continued to study me in silence. It was weird, like he was waiting for something, or for me to *do* something, but what, I didn't know. He just watched me, those impossibly blue eyes tracking every movement, hell, every frantic breath that escaped my lips. There was no doubt that I was looking at someone that was way beyond an ordinary person.

"What are you going to do with me?" I asked, my voice barely above a whisper. He'd said he wasn't going to kill me, but maybe death was going to be better than any alternative this guy could think of.

A long slender finger reached out and brushed a damp lock from my forehead. "I haven't decided yet."

I swallowed, the sound a loud gulp in the empty room. "Who are you?"

The smile that spread across his face was unsettling. "Damyr Morozov."

Morozov. I knew that name, but I couldn't quite grasp why. Stupid drugs. Making everything foggy and—

Damyr traced his finger between my brows. "The drugs will wear off soon."

I hoped so because I could barely string a sentence together. It didn't help that he was still touching me. Which was doing something to me, and my dick was starting to take notice. On a normal day I'd probably ask him out, but this was as far from normal as possible. And besides, he'd kidnapped me and tied me to a fucking chair. I mean, who did he think he was?

Well, shit.

Damyr let out a low chuckle, but it was anything but warm. "Figured it out, pretty boy?"

Morozov. Current ruling family of the *Bratva*. "Russian mob."

His nose wrinkled in disgust, and it made him look cute. "I don't like the word 'mob'. It makes it sound sleazy."

"Oh, I'm sorry. I didn't take the mobster etiquette class."

He looked at me curiously. "There's no such thing. You're being sarcastic."

I rolled my eyes at him. Who was this guy?

His hand shot out and grabbed my chin, his nails sharp against my skin. "If you worked for me, you'd lose your eyes for that."

I gulped, my throat brushing against his hand. Damyr's eyes dropped to my neck, his eyes darkening as he leant closer. He forced my head to the side and brought his nose to the spot just below my ear. My heart fucking raced.

He hummed, the sound low and predatory. Throaty.

Aaand there went my dick again.

"Wh-what are you doing?"

When Damyr pulled back his eyes burned like fire. "You have no idea what world you've wandered into."

Two ~ Damyr

The moment I saw him in the alley I knew I wasn't ever going to let him go. The boy was beautiful. Lips that pouted, desperate to be kissed and, fuck, did I want to taste them. His Cupid's bow was a thing of perfection, plump and arched and I wanted to bite it. I think that was the only reason he was still alive. And those eyes that were so delicious and dark. I could stare into them forever.

Have you ever looked at a thing and just wanted it. Knowing that you'd probably break it because you wanted to find out how it worked. But that was the fun. Uncovering the secrets that made it work.

I wanted to break Benjamin. I wanted to know what made him tick.

I traced my finger over that perfect Cupid's bow and felt his sharp intake of breath against my skin. He was so alive. So fragile.

Not like me. I was anything but.

"What are you doing to my face? It's rude to just touch someone, you know."

"You talk too much, Benjamin."

"It's Benji," he snapped, making me smile. No one spoke to me like he did. I kind of liked it. Everyone was too scared of me. That's how I liked things, but there was something intriguing about this boy.

"Will anyone miss you, Benjamin?"

He stilled, his eyes wide with something. But not fear. That emotion I recognised easily. This one...

"Ex-fucking-scuse me?! What kind of person says that? Look, I was being a decent human being and trying to rescue someone. I thought I was doing the right thing. That doesn't give you the right to drug me and take me off the street. Just because you're some high and mighty mobster, doesn't mean you can swan around doing whatever the fuck you'd want. In fact—"

I gripped his chin again, halting the tirade falling from that beautiful mouth. "Pretty boy, I'm not just some mobster."

"I don't give a shit. If you're not going to kill me, you need to let me go. And stop calling me pretty boy."

"I'm not letting you go," I said simply. And I wasn't. Something inside me was saying this boy was *mine*. And it was a part of me that had been quiet for so long I thought the monster had been sated. But no. There it was. Churning in my gut. Demanding to keep the boy. To hide him away from the world so no one else could take him.

"Why?" he asked, his voice a little breathless, his heartbeat a little fast.

I traced that plump bottom lip with my thumb. "Have you ever looked at something and just wanted it?"

Benjamin froze for a moment before bursting into a laugh, so rich and deep that it almost took my breath away. Which was impressive since I didn't breathe anymore.

"I'm sorry," he said through a chuckle, tears leaking from his eyes. "That's the most ridiculous thing I've heard. What are you? Twelve? I'm not a toy or a possession. Now untie me or—"

"Or what?" I interrupted with a grin, almost giddy with excitement as to what was going to come out of his mouth next. "Are you going to gut me? Pluck out my eyes? Break my knees?"

"Those are all oddly specific," he muttered. "No. I'm not a violent person. I don't think. But I've never been in this position before so there's no knowing what I might be capable of."

"Curious to find out?" I asked with a raised brow.

He shook his head but there was a lack of conviction to it. Interesting. My pretty ray of sunshine might want to indulge in something a little darker. That was definitely food for thought.

"Are you hungry?" I asked. Benjamin had been down here a while, and, for some reason, drugging him had left a sour taste in my mouth. I didn't feel regret, but something had me wanting to make it up to him.

"No," he replied defiantly right before his stomach let out an angry growl. I almost chuckled. "Okay, fine. Yes, I'm hungry. What time is it anyway?"

"A little past 3am."

"The fuck?! I've been out for five hours?"

His indignation was almost charming. "Yes."

"No wonder my ass is numb. And you're only now offering me food?"

"So it would seem."

"Are you going to bring it to me or are you going to cut me loose?" he asked haughtily.

I pulled a knife from the back of my belt and went to break the cable ties.

"I'm sorry," Benjamin squeaked. "I didn't mean it. Please don't kill me."

I sighed. "Are you going to do this every time I pull out a sharp instrument? I'm not going to kill you, Benjamin."

I cut through the ties around his wrists and ankles, enjoying the marks they'd left behind on his skin.

"That's better," he grumbled as he rubbed his wrists to help his circulation. He stood and stretched, and I caught a glimpse of abs as his t-shirt rose above his hips. He looked solidly built and I had a sudden urge to strip him bare and taste every inch of his skin.

"Follow me," I said, my mouth suddenly drier than the desert.

"Why won't you kill me?" Benjamin asked, his voice tinged with curiosity, as he trailed behind me through the basement corridors.

"Why, do you want me to? It could be arranged." Very easily actually. I wasn't the leader of the *Bratva* for no reason. I had connections. I could make it look like Benjamin had never even existed.

"Of course not," he snapped. "It just seems to be more effort to keep me."

"You wouldn't think that if you knew what I wanted to do with you."

"Wh-what?"

I was starting to enjoy turning him into a stammering mess, even if it was starting to annoy me that he didn't believe I'd keep my word. I turned to face him, and he halted in his tracks. "Benjamin, if there is one thing you can trust about me, it's that I'm a man of my word. No harm will come to you under my roof. You're under my protection and I will keep you safe."

"But why? I don't understand. I'm not anything special."

"I meant what I said before. I know you laughed, but I'm not wired like you. If I see something I want, I take it."

He took a hesitant step backwards. "But that's not normal."

I shrugged. "Never said I was." Then I turned and continued towards the kitchen. I left it up to him if he wanted to follow or not. I didn't need to worry about him escaping the house. There was no way out unless I let him free.

And that wasn't going to happen anytime soon.

Three ~ Benji

Holy fuck. He really was a psychopath. What had I gotten myself into?

I watched Damyr retreat down the corridor and tried not to look at how delectable his ass was in the tailored black trousers he wore, but failed miserably. Jesus fuck, the guy was hot. Why couldn't he be hideous and smell funny? That would make this so much easier. I'd certainly be less confused. I mean the guy kidnapped me! I shouldn't be thinking about anything other than escaping. Although, the blasé way the guy just swanned off gave me enough indication that escape was most likely impossible.

And I *was* hungry...

My feet had started moving before I even registered that I was catching up with Damyr. I followed him into a massive, state-of-the-art kitchen. There were gleaming marble worktops and shiny appliances.

"Damn," I muttered.

"I never use it," Damyr confessed.

"What?! That's sacrilege. This kitchen was made to be cooked in. Just think of all the food you could eat." I was shocked that he let this amazing space go to waste. You could fit my entire apartment in this kitchen and all I had at home was a little stove and enough countertop space to slice an onion.

"I take it you like to cook?" Damyr asked.

"Yes." When I got the time, which was usually never. It reminded me of my childhood, of the Sunday's I'd spend with my nan in the kitchen cooking the roast. My parents had died in a car crash when I was young, leaving my nan to raise me. But then she had died in my early teens leaving me to suffer the foster system. There were some good foster parents, and some not so good ones. But I had to be thankful apparently because I was older, and most people wanted to adopt babies or younger kids.

"You're sad," Damyr said, suddenly appearing in front of me.

I hadn't noticed he'd moved. Had I been that zoned out?

"I don't like it. I prefer the..." he waved his hand in front of my face as if trying to summon the word just by looking at me. "...sunshine."

I raised a brow. "Sunshine?"

"Yes. Sunshine. I think this is the best word for you."

I scoffed. "Nobody has ever called me sunshine before."

Damyr peered deep into my eyes, almost as if he was trying to locate my very soul. "There is a light in you that I can't seem to look away from. You draw me in. I don't think you realise quite how powerful that is. Especially for someone like me."

Wow did this guy have a way with words. Talk about sweeping a guy off his feet. "Um, thank you."

"You're welcome. Now, let me feed you." He pointed to the barstool on the other side of the breakfast bar. "Sit."

I did as he said, still unsure of what was really happening here. I glanced around the room, noting the large windows with blackout blinds, the hallway that disappeared somewhere and I wondered whether I could escape. The worrying thing was that I wasn't sure I wanted to. I mean, he hadn't been all bad... who was I kidding. He'd drugged me and kidnapped me, but he *was* now cooking for me... wouldn't that balance some of the bad deeds out? Suppose it depended on how good the food was.

"Tell me about yourself, Benjamin."

I both hated and loved that he called me Benjamin. There was something formal and uptight about the way my name sounded in his mouth, a hint of an accent long since buried, and it caused a shiver to run up my spine when he said those syllables.

"Um, there's not much to tell. Only child, orphaned. I work in marketing, and I have a little apartment that I bought all by myself. I like Asian food best, my favourite movie is *The Princess Bride* and I hope one day to find the love of my life."

"So no one special at the moment?" Damyr asked, a little too quickly.

"No," I said, trying hard to keep the grin off my face. "Subtle, Damyr. Subtle."

He huffed a breath and turned back to cooking something.

"If you don't use this kitchen, how do you know how to cook?"

"I'm older than I look," he said as he continued to work, chopping vegetables with a precision that was a little unsettling actually. "And I'm rich. I have a chef."

I rolled my eyes. At least he was matter of fact about it and didn't flaunt it in my face. "I figured. What with the big basement, super-sized kitchen, long corridors leading to more and more rooms."

"Are you poking fun at me?" he asked with a deep scowl, but it was hard to be intimidated by him when he was also holding a wooden spoon covered in tomato sauce.

I pinched my finger and thumb together. "Maybe a little."

He grunted but went back to his task and before too long, he was plating up the most delicious looking penne al'arrabbiata I'd ever seen. "God, that smells good."

He placed a dish in front of me, then sat on the stool beside me.

"Are you not eating any?"

Damyr shook his head. "I ate earlier."

"Seems a lot of effort to go to for just me. I'd have been happy with a slice of toast."

"It's no trouble and I wanted to... um..."

"Apologise?"

"Yes. That."

I chuckled. "Don't say sorry often then?"

He straightened his back, and a sneer curled his lips. "I do not need to."

"I can imagine," I mumbled before finally taking a bite of the delicious smelling pasta.

Holy moly.

Flavour exploded along my tastebuds. Tomatoes and spices and fuck me, that was so good. A guttural moan passed my lips as I swallowed the food.

"Fuck," Damyr mumbled under his breath.

I shot my eyes over to his and watched the blue darken to a colour as rich and deep as the darkest night. Keeping his eyes fixed on mine, he leaned forward and pressed his lips against mine. It was a quick firm press, hot with a tease of his tongue against my bottom lip and then it was over.

And still his eyes held mine. Unblinkingly. Like there was a wolf lurking behind the blue. I knew I should be afraid. I mean, he might eat me, but that didn't make me want to run away. Nope. It was the most thrilling feeling I'd felt in a very long time.

"I don't want you to be afraid of me," Damyr said softly.

"Why?" I asked, my brows knitting together. I still didn't understand what he saw in me that made him so... possessive.

"Because I want you," he replied simply.

"For what?"

"Many things," he said, brushing his lips against mine again. "But they can wait. You need to know about me and that goes into far more dangerous territory than the *Bratva*."

"Like what?"

"May I kiss you again?"

"No."

Damyr pouted and it would be cute if the guy wasn't talking in riddles. "Fine. Then eat your dinner."

"Fine. But you need to tell me what you mean. Or I'm leaving."

He snorted and folded his arms across his chest. I didn't notice how the white fabric stretched across his ridiculously well-defined muscles. Not one little bit. It was definitely the food making my mouth water.

"I won't let you leave. I'm keeping you."

"Why?" I asked around another mouthful of pasta.

"To keep you safe. Protect you."

"From what?"

"People like me."

"You sound crazy." I rubbed my forehead, trying to stave off the headache that I knew was on its way.

"I'm not crazy. And that word can be quite hurtful."

"Sorry," I said, reaching for his hand before I could think too hard about it.

"Please, don't try and leave," he said with the biggest, saddest eyes and gripped my hand back. "I won't be able to protect you if you leave."

I snorted at him. "Are you trying to manipulate me?"

"Yes, is it working?"

Yeah, it kind of was. I took a deep breath and thought about what I could feel. There was a connection here, something that I couldn't deny. Something that I'd never felt in all my twenty-eight years. Was I really going to pass up whatever this was, even if the guy was a little... unusual?

"Fine," I said on a sigh. "But you tell me the darkest, biggest secret you have right now or I'm walking."

"I'm a vampire."

Four ~ Damyr

There. I said the words. And he was still here. Perhaps that was shock though. He was looking a little pale.

"Benjamin?"

"A vampire?"

I nodded. "Yes."

He went quiet again. Perhaps I should find him some water. I went to stand but his hand shot out and grabbed my arm.

"Prove it."

"What?"

"Prove to me that you are what you say you are and—"

There was an audible *snick* as my fangs popped out and Benjamin gasped.

"Are they real?"

"Yesh," I replied. Stupid fucking lisp. I hated talking with my fangs out. It made me sound like a... well, I don't know what, but I didn't like it. But for him, I didn't mind as much as I normally would.

He reached his hand out toward me. "May I?"

"Yes. But be careful," I said as his fingers were a hair's breadth from my lips, "I bite."

His finger brushed my bottom lip and I had the most visceral reaction to his touch. It was all consuming, like a fire that erupted in my veins and knew the only way to be quenched was through his touch. But I didn't want to scare him, so I sat completely still and let him explore my mouth.

I also might have enjoyed it a little bit.

"I can't feel a groove or anything. They are actually your teeth, aren't they?"

I nodded, but the movement brought his finger in contact with the razor sharp point of my fang. He hissed right before the most gorgeous taste blossomed over my tongue. It was like honey and chocolate and sex and something that was all Benjamin. I could feast on him forever and never find my fill. He moaned as my tongue wrapped around his finger and the sound went straight to my cock. It pressed painfully against the zipper of my pants and I suddenly wanted more.

I released his finger from the warmth of my mouth and loved how short and sharp his breaths were. How frantic his heart raced. It called to the predator in me. It made me want to tell him to run, just so I could catch him.

There was a moment caught in time where I could see every thought cross his beautiful face. Indecision. Curiosity. Lust.

It was the final one that won out because he flung himself forwards and pressed his lips against mine. Fuck. They were as soft as I'd imagined, just as plump and sweet as I'd hoped.

There was a frantic rush about him as he scrambled onto my lap, thrusting his hands into my hair. I didn't even care that he was ruining it. I just wanted him to pull harder, to get rid of his clothes. There were so many clothes.

I grabbed his hips and pulled him closer, moaning sinfully as his hard cock brushed against mine. Fucking hell. I was going to come in my trousers if I didn't slow—

Benjamin was ripped away from me, his cry of pain sending a jolt through me I'd never expected to feel.

It took a second for my eyes to focus on the scene in front of me. Benjamin was on the floor with an angry looking, red-soled stiletto shoed woman pressing her heel into his neck.

Fury and rage like nothing I'd ever felt before made my skin crawl and my fangs ache.

"Who the fuck is this?" the woman spat, pushing her heel harder into his throat.

"None of your business!" I roared. "Now let him go!"

"Tell me who he is! Who dares touch what's mine?" she screamed.

"Damyr, who is she?" Benjamin asked, his voice hoarse.

I looked at the woman who'd stormed into my home. I really needed to revoke her invitation and get my keys back. "My wife."

AATA 2024: THE ANNUAL

To be continued...
Find out what happens next in Sunshine and the Vamp. Coming 2025

Finding Bob by Belinda E Edwards

I wanted to introduce you to Tessa March and DS Richard Stone, two characters from my Hursts Bridge series. As this anthology is raising funds for the RSPCA, it seemed like a good fit. This scene is from Spring Explosions, which isn't completed yet. It is an important scene for me, so I am quite sure it will make the final version of the book in some form. This is your chance to read it as it exists now.

Tessa had only drunk one glass of wine at dinner, but a thunderstorm had started, and she was finding it hard to focus on her drive home. She liked a storm, but she felt they were best viewed from the warmth of her room, curled up on her bed with a good book.

Over the meal tonight, there had been a lot of questions about Dan. *He is a great friend and always has been. I love it when he holds my hand, and his kisses are so gentle, just like when we were fifteen, but I'm not fifteen anymore.* Tessa was a woman now, something she felt particularly in the presence of DS Richard Stone. That hard face didn't fool her now she'd seen a glimpse of his smile. A smile that created a fire inside her. When she closed her eyes at night, it was the moody policeman she saw, not Daniel.

The rhythm of the windscreen wipers was hypnotic at the end of a long day. Tessa forced herself to concentrate on the road as a runner came towards her. Visibility was low, and she needed to focus to avoid him. *Who would go out running in this weather?*

The tall, angular runner made her think of Richard Stone again. This time, the thought brought with it a vision of him in a running vest and shorts, dripping wet. As she got closer, she realised it was possibly the man himself. *Look straight ahead, Tessa. Do not stare at him.*

From her right, a streak of grey wool shot across the road in front of her. She hit the brakes hard, and the back end of her car slid around, leaving her facing a very shocked and very wet-looking Richard Stone. He crouched down to a dirty bundle of grey at his feet.

Her headlights lit up the two on the grass. Tessa froze, her knuckles white as she gripped the steering wheel. Eventually, she threw open her door and, on shaky legs, approached Rick and the dog, who lay at his feet.

"I didn't see him. Is he OK?"

Rick didn't look up. Instead, he scowled down at the dog. *What have I done? Was I too distracted by seeing him ... and so much of him? Tessa's eyes drifted to Rick's powerful thighs.*

"You did amazing to miss him, actually. It's like he had a death wish."

"Is he hurt? Does he have a tag?" She pulled her coat tighter around her dress, which was getting soaked.

"He doesn't even have a collar. Don't worry, he was definitely already limping. You know, I think this is the stray we've been looking for."

"You're sure I didn't hit him?" Tessa felt sick at the thought she could've killed the small dog because she'd been distracted by this man.

"No idea how, but no, you didn't hit him. Are you OK?" He lifted those icy blue eyes to hers.

"Why are you looking for him? You can't put him in jail. He's injured." Tessa got ready to fight to protect this dog.

"He's been going through bins and scaring chickens. I suppose we can't leave him here."

"I can't have pets in my flat..." Before she could say more, Rick scooped up the wet dog and pulled him into his chest. "I'll take him home, see how hurt he is, and if I think he needs it, I'll get him to the vet." *Wow, I wasn't expecting that. Tessa needed to do something to help.*

"How far is it? Let me give you a lift." He shook his head, but she persisted. "If you do need to take him to a vet, you'll want someone to hold him while you drive." Tessa held open the passenger door to her car.

He looked about to argue the point, but in the end, he quietly got into the car, still holding the dog to his chest. Tessa closed the door and skipped around to the driver's side. Once inside, she turned on the engine and looked at Rick.

"Where to?"

"Back the way you came until you come to a lane on your right. I'm just down there."

Tessa gingerly turned her Mini around in the tight space and took the lane. *Goodness, it's even darker down this lane and so narrow. Where on earth does he live?* She drove cautiously into the darkness.

"Don't worry. No one else is going to be driving the other way," he croaked.

Eventually, a row of four cottages she'd never seen before came into view.

Rick cleared his throat. "This is me at the end cottage."

A light shone above the first door, and as the car came to a halt, more lights flickered to life.

As Tessa pulled on the handbrake, she finally found her voice.

"Stay there. I'll come and open that for you."

"Thanks."

Tessa held her breath as he hugged the dog to his body, squinting into the driving rain. They both hesitated outside the cottage. Rick's face twisted.

"Could you get this door too, please?" he asked. "I leave it locked on the keypad when I'm running; it saves me carrying keys."

"Sure, what do I do?"

"Punch in two zero zero nine and then the enter button. Then, just open it."

Tessa followed his instructions and held the door for him. He carried the dog swiftly into the kitchen, gently lowering it to the floor. It stood shivering and hunched. Tessa pushed the wet hair from her face with her shaking hands.

"You're wet. I'll grab some towels. I won't be a minute."

Whilst he was gone, she sat down next to the dog. Tenderly stroking his head, Tessa spoke softly to him. She looked around the kitchen. The cabinets and appliances were new, but the walls showed a history of different wall coverings. The floor had bare boards, like the hall they'd entered through. Even the window appeared to have been replaced as the rain lashed against it.

The gentle movements soothed both Tessa and the dog. When she reached as far as his back leg, he mouthed her hand in protest. She whispered softly to the dog to let him know he was safe now. *I wonder what his name is. He needs a name.*

Rick returned with a pile of towels, passing the top one to her.

"Here, you look like you need one, too." *Way to go, Stoneface, help a girl feel good about herself.*

"He does have something wrong with that leg. He isn't keen on letting me near it."

"OK, but I really should shower and get dry. If you want to get off, I won't keep you. It's late, and you probably want to go home." *Oh! Tessa bit her lip.*

"I thought I'd wait to look at his leg until there were two of us and he'd relaxed a little." Rick scowled. "Please, I'd like to stay and see if he is alright. He's clearly scared." He stared at her, not giving anything away. She tried again. "And I won't sleep if I think he may be in pain because I hit him. I wonder where his family is?"

He let out a long breath, and his eyes softened. "If you are going to sit down there, have this cushion; that floor is hard and cold!" Then he put on the kettle and pulled out two mugs. "I'll get showered. Feel free to make a hot drink if you get fed up sitting down there with the mutt." He left the room without looking back.

"Don't listen to him, Bob. It's not your fault if you are wet and a bit whiffy. Me and Uncle Rick will soon have you sorted and back with your family."

Tessa talked incessantly, stroking and murmuring to the dog. She had an urge to do something practical. According to her friend Michelle, Tessa used it as her way of handling any crisis.

She could hear the shower running, and the idea of a naked Rick wasn't helping to settle her emotions after the near miss on the road. Seeing him dripping wet in just shorts and a torn T-shirt had been hard enough.

If she hadn't already been thinking about the man who had brought her breakfast last week, she was certainly thinking about him now. When he reappeared, she was relieved to see him fully dressed in tracksuit bottoms and a well-worn sweatshirt.

"Coffee?"

"I prefer tea."

At that moment, cracks of thunder and lightning happened almost instantaneously; the dog changed shape, immediately cowering into Tessa's chest, shaking and whimpering.

"Wow, that was so close," Tessa said. "I can see this is going to be a long night. You'd better make that a coffee. This poor dog clearly hates this sort of weather."

"Who doesn't? I can't say I like thunderstorms."

"Says the man who was out running in it." Rick looked at his feet.

"Yeah, well, it's been a rough day. Running helps me think and find some headspace; it's something about the rhythm of it," he shrugged. "I don't know; it works for me."

"So why were you out in it, Bob?" She dropped her eyes to the dog. "Something brought us all together on that lane." She looked up at Rick. "Perhaps we were supposed to save Bob." Rick coughed and spooned instant coffee into mugs.

"Just why are you calling him Bob?"

"I don't know. He looks like a Bob, don't you think? First, I thought Bobby, you know, because he's grey, but then he looks like he's had such a hard life. So, I thought, Bob, he looks like a Bob, so until we find out what his name is, why don't we call him Bob?" Tessa closed her eyes. *I'm babbling again. He must think I'm crazy.*

"I'll give you that. Calling him Bob seems simple enough, and when we're talking about our dog, he has a name." Rick blushed.

Tessa raised an eyebrow. *Did he just say, 'our dog'?* He turned away from her, back to the kettle. Tessa's head dropped back, hitting the wall. *What a day!*

Rick made the drinks and carried them over.

"How are you both doing now?" His voice had softened, and it helped Tessa feel better.

"I hoped he'd relax and trust me more, but I don't see that happening soon. I think we need a plan."

"OK. Like what?"

"Can you get a bowl of water to clean his leg? Then maybe if we could take him to a room with curtains and put on a TV or some music, it would help to mask the noises of a storm."

"OK, water coming up. The room with curtains might be a bit harder. I haven't been here long, and interiors aren't my strength. With no neighbours ... Let's just say it hasn't been a top priority."

"So, you have no rooms with curtains?" She looked around her, and from what she could see, the place was almost bare.

"Just my bedroom."

Tessa's eyes widened. "Really! Is there a spare bedroom?"

"Yes."

"Does it have curtains?"

"Do you know, I haven't looked. Honestly, I don't spend much time here, just come home and crash. I've been working on the downstairs. I started in the kitchen, but I haven't got far."

"I see." Her eyes danced from the new appliances to the history-baring walls.

Rick filled a bowl with water. "This is a little hot. Shall I add some cold?"

"Sure. Now, come down here and see if Bob remembers that he likes you."

Rick cautiously sat on the floor opposite Tessa and reached out his long arms. The dog only huddled closer to Tessa.

"Hey, come here, Bob. Come on, Bob, I'm not going to hurt you. Come here, Bob." Rick encouraged. With a stern gaze fixed on Tessa, he growled. "Do you think he knows his name is Bob?"

Tessa smiled, half laughing. "Hey Bob," she said, gently pushing the dog towards him, "go see Uncle Rick."

Rick scowled.

"He must be starving. Do you have anything for him to eat?" Rick stood up and opened the cupboard before checking the fridge. There wasn't much, just some cheese, milk, eggs, and some salad that had seen better days.

"Oh, cheese and eggs," declared Tessa. "Dogs love cheese, so that could work as a bribe, but maybe a spot of scrambled egg will fill his tummy nicely."

Rick was about to agree with the plan when another flash of lightning hit, followed by a long rumble of thunder. It shook the panes of glass in the window behind Tessa. Bob retreated into her chest some more.

"It looks like we should sort the room first. Let me check the spare room. I'll get some cushions and blankets in there; if not, maybe we have to use my bedroom." Rick could hear her talking to the dog as he made his way upstairs. *Enough with the 'Uncle Rick'. Still, the job needs doing, and you know that sometimes you can soften your voice.* His boss had given him a lecture on changing his tone, explaining that his tough cop attitude might work in London, but it wouldn't help him in Hursts Bridge. Somehow, he needed to prove he could listen to advice, and that he wasn't the hot head he'd been labelled.

Rick couldn't remember looking in the spare room since the day he arrived. He'd bought this cottage without seeing it before his hurried departure from London. Sadly, he only found a single dining chair and an old chest. The room had nothing on the floor and certainly no curtains.

"I'm sorry the spare room is not going to work. My room has blackout curtains. I can do something in there if you like?"

Tessa had begun to clean Bob's legs. She screwed up her face.

"Look, I need to move. Can you take over from me, and I'll sort the food out? Have you eaten? I ate with the girls at Autumn's house, but I don't want to give the dog your dinner."

"OK." Rick sat on the floor at Tessa's side and gently lifted Bob and his towel between his legs. "I planned something fairly instant out of the freezer." *How sad is my life? She is out for dinner with friends, and I am having frozen lasagne.*

Tessa eased herself up and stretched. Rick watched her uncurl her body. Her T-shirt rose as she lifted her hands above her head, showing him a tempting inch of skin at the top of her jeans. Rick gulped; fortunately, Bob sat firmly in place on his lap, hiding his body's reaction to her. More lightning stopped his thoughts.

"Why don't we get Bob settled upstairs, and then we can sort the food."

"If you like," Tessa shrugged.

Rick stood, lifting Bob to his chest. He led the way up the steep stairs. Tessa followed behind with the bowl and towels. There were no carpets, simply bare boards in the hall and up the stairs. His bedroom was more comfortable.

He gently laid Bob on the floor and passed her pillows and blankets. As he closed the thick curtains, Tessa made a nest on the floor and sat down; Bob instantly took up his spot between her legs. Rick smiled.

"Looks like I'm sorting food then. Are you alright down there?"

"We'll be fine, won't we, Bob?" She lowered her voice. "Have you got some noise? Music? Anything to cut out the sounds of the storm."

"The radio OK?"

"Sure." Voices and music from the radio filled the room.

In the kitchen, he found frozen pizza. He put that in the oven, setting the timer. Looking out at the weather, he pulled his hand down his face. What a mess.

Isn't my world complicated enough? Just when I realise I must live without women, along comes the biggest crush of my painful teenage existence to test me. Who would want my father as their granddad? Elliot Stone's life choices ruined my life. I will not let them destroy the life of my family, my kids. WOW, back up there, Mate! Wife and kids?

Having a family wasn't something he'd ever aspired to. It had never entered his brain. So why think about it now? He groaned. *Because Tessa March is in my bedroom talking to a dog, referring to me as Uncle Rick. What else?... Oh yes, and she is upset... And, of course, you want to fix that...*

Rick phoned the police station about the dog. Sergeant Williams explained they normally held strays in the old outside lock-up until the morning when the dog warden came. She would take the dog to the vet. Any young and healthy dogs go to a re-homing centre, whilst ill or old dogs are kept for just seven days in case anyone is looking.

"Sorry, sir. This one had been causing havoc locally for over two weeks, so I've already checked. There are no missing dogs that match his description." *Bob's future doesn't look good.*

"Thanks, Joe. Is there anything else that can be done?" Rick sighed, wondering how he could tell Tessa about Bob's probable fate. She was upset already, and he couldn't face telling her the cruel choices ahead for the dog.

"Sometimes the people who find the dog keep it for seven days. If anyone comes forward, they return the dog to the owner. We have a list of folks who'll foster lost dogs somewhere. I can look." At last, some hope for poor Bob.

"Please do that, Joe. I don't want to be the one to tell her that Bob could be put down."

"Sorry, sir, what was that?"

"Nothing, sergeant. Get back to me with anything you think will help. In the meantime, the dog is with me."

Cursing to himself yet again, Rick scrambled some eggs and cut cheese into small cubes.

Maybe it was the rain rattling the windows or this girl taking the time to reassure the scruffiest dog he'd ever seen he was safe. She'd even named the awful-looking thing. Maybe it was just because it was her. The jumbled thoughts and emotions confused him. After last year, Rick didn't think he would ever feel emotions again. He'd tried hard enough to turn off these feelings, so why was his body fizzing?

When he couldn't put it off any longer, he reluctantly carried the food to Bob, and Tessa took it from him.

"Did I hear you talking to someone?" Tessa asked, biting her lip. Rick looked at her face; he was good at reading people, but she confused him. Not ready to tell her Bob's possible fate, he adjusted his expression and tried to find a smile.

"Only the station. I rang to let them know I had the dog in case anyone was looking. I said I'd drop him at the vet tomorrow. That way, we're sure he is OK."

"And were they?"

"Who?"

"Bob's family? Were they looking for him?"

"No."

"Oh," Tessa didn't hide her disappointment, "he looks like he's been on the streets for weeks, doesn't he?"

"Yes, I think he has."

Tessa slowly fed Bob the scrambled eggs, cooing and whispering to him all the time. Rick watched her, fascinated by how gentle she seemed.

"I am going to need your help when I look at his leg." Tessa looked up at Rick with her sea-green eyes.

He nodded his head and croaked out, "Yes." He cleared his throat. "What do you want me to do?"

"One of us needs to hold him whilst the other parts his fur to look for open wounds or something. Which would you like to do?" Rick's mouth twisted as he pondered his answer.

"I am pretty sure you would be best at both those things, but I guess Bob would prefer if you hold him, and I'll check out the leg,"

When Bob had finished the egg, he curled back into Tessa, finally looking comfortable.

"OK, let's do this," Tessa said, taking a firmer grip on Bob and ensuring his head was away from his leg. Rick sat down next to Tessa and then got up to fetch the lamp from the side of the bed. "I need the extra light if I'm going to make sure I miss nothing."

"Good idea. OK, use a flannel and wipe away as much dirt as possible." Tessa seemed calmer now, and Rick felt relieved. He needed to get this right; he didn't want to scare the dog, and he certainly didn't want to scare Tessa. All the time trying not to think about the fact they were in his bedroom. *Focus, Rick, Focus.*

Rick tried squatting next to Tessa's legs, but it wasn't working. In the end, he sat on the floor facing her, his legs crossing hers. The heat where they touched made it harder to concentrate. "Sorry, I just need to get closer." *Does she feel it? Is she blushing? Don't be stupid.*

"I get it." Tessa's face still puzzled him. He looked carefully through the wool-like fur on the dog's hind leg, searching diligently for any sign of what might trouble him.

"I can't see anything," he shrugged, moving backwards. "I don't know if that is good or bad. What do you think?" he asked, seeking reassurance.

"I guess neither of us are experts, but he seems calmer now, even if the storm outside doesn't. I don't think we need to wake a vet up tonight. The morning might be better when he's rested."

Bob nuzzled back into Tessa, and the weather seemed to get worse. Thunder and lightning had subsided, but rain relentlessly lashed against the windows of Rick's bedroom.

"Time to eat. I put a pizza in the oven. I know you said you'd eaten, but you're welcome to a slice or three. What about another coffee?"

"I should be getting home, but maybe a cup of tea whilst we see if he'll settle."

"Sure."

Back in the kitchen, Rick knew that Tessa had to go home at some point, but teenage Rick was still trying to understand that Tessa March was here. Being so close to her, watching her with the dog, the way she whispered and calmed him, wasn't helping him create a distance between them.

Rick was sure Tessa was seeing Daniel Harris, her boyfriend from school. He also knew he couldn't offer Tessa anything. Thoughts of her were already invading his brain far too often, making it harder for him to concentrate on his job.

The smell of burning cheese brought him back to tonight's problem. *What am I going to do about this damn dog? It's not looking good for Bob. He won't survive if there isn't someone to take him on.*

Rick took the pizza and hot drinks upstairs. He craved the bottle of beer he'd promised himself after work. But now he had precious time to get to know Tessa better and for her to get to know him. Maybe they could be friends? If he were stuck in this far too-quiet town, he would need some distractions.

He'd enjoyed the friendship of his last partner in London. Cassy had talked to him and helped him understand the world from a woman's point of view. She'd taught him how to cook and tried to help him work out what clothes to wear. *I think I was one long project for her, but it was a project that ended her life.* No, Tessa was better off without him. He couldn't let her life end like Cassy's.

Back in the bedroom, the stern-faced police officer had returned.

"Don't let me keep you. I can take it from here. You must want to get home." It came out more dismissive than he meant. Rick closed his eyes to avoid seeing her reaction to this coldness.

"I guess so. My bed is calling me. It's been a long day followed by a busy evening and then this excitement. Bob seems more settled, and I haven't heard any thunder for a while." *Good, she is on the same page.*

"I thought I could just drink my tea and see if he would settle without me beside him." It sounded like a question, but Rick was keen to rip off the Band-Aid. The part of him that wanted her to stay, was ready to suggest they get into his bed, and he could hold her. His logical brain said the longer she stayed, the harder he would find it when she left.

"Don't you have someone waiting at home for you?" Rick wasn't sure which part of him was asking. He held his breath, anticipating her reply.

"No, I live alone. I'd just be going back to an empty flat, no one to miss me." *Oh!*

"Not even Daniel Harris?" *Stop poking. You really don't want to hear the answer.*

"Dan? No. I haven't seen him in ten years until, well, the day after the explosion."

"Really?" Rick tried to work that out. Was the timing significant? A coincidence? Was the universe laughing at his expense? *Hey, look, here is another girl you care about. Watch what cruel ways we can take her away from you.*

"Sure, we've been out on a few dates, and I guess we're still working out what that means. But no, we don't live together."

Tessa carefully arranged Bob down on the floor in a nest of blankets and cushions and looked for a place to sit herself.

"You sit on the bed, and I'll get a chair from the other room." Tessa looked at the bed, shrugged her shoulders, and climbed on with tea in hand. Rick returned with the dining chair from the spare bedroom and found her settled there, back against the headboard and legs stretched out, crossed at the ankles. Tessa wasn't especially tall, but to Rick, her legs appeared to go on forever. She'd removed her boots, and her feet wiggled in multicoloured socks.

"Can I tempt you to some pizza? I took it out of the freezer myself." The friendly Rick seeped out, and that coaxed a smile from Tessa. Rick swallowed.

"OK, it smells wonderful." Her smile widened, and he became transfixed.

Rick reached out to her with the plate of pizza and then edged back to sit on the dining chair as he watched her take a first bite. The cheese pulling out in long strings made her giggle, adding to his distraction. Rick's empty stomach growled and churned. He became hopelessly lost as her tongue attempted to catch the stray cheese. As he backed up, he missed sitting squarely on the chair, and it overbalanced, leaving him to hit the floor with a thump and the old chair splintered around him. It knocked the wind out of him and the pizza plate from his hand.

Bob woke and dashed towards the food. Tessa dropped her slice and rushed to stop the dog from eating Rick's dinner. And Rick? Well, he sat where he fell, thinking, what next?

Tessa laughed, Bob was awake and now back to shaking and leaning into her.

"Are you OK? I hope that wasn't a family piece," she said, trying to stifle her laugh.

"My body is fine. My ego, I'm not so sure about." He tried to smile.

"What happened?"

"It's an old chair. I found it in the spare room earlier. I should have checked out better, I guess." *I can't say I was too busy watching you tackle melted cheese with that tongue to watch what I was doing.*

"Come sit with me. There's plenty of space." She patted the mattress at her side.

Rick lifted an eyebrow. Was he about to make another silly decision?

"No, I'm sitting here now. I might as well stay."

"In that case, I won't stay long. I'll just get Bob calm again."

And she did. Tessa settled the dog and drank her tea as Rick watched from the floor, finally eating his pizza. She waited until he'd eaten a couple of slices to say, "I'll go home now if you think you can cope. Will you let me know what the vet says?"

"Of course. Thank you for all your help."

Bob didn't stir this time as Tessa quietly left the room, and Rick followed her downstairs and to the door.

"Thanks again for the lift home and the help with Bob."

"No, thank goodness you were there. I couldn't have coped if I thought I'd hit him or if he'd run off, and I didn't know if he was OK."

"I'll ring you at the shop tomorrow."

"Goodnight, DS Stone."

Rick held open the door and said, "Please, call me Rick."

"Goodnight, Rick," she touched his arm and looked up into his eyes. "Look after Bob. He deserves a break. I think he has had a rough life." Rick's skin burned under her touch.

"Goodnight, Tessa." Unsure how he didn't pull her into his arms, he stood rooted to the spot, his hands thrust firmly into his pockets, as his eyes followed her, climbing into the dark green Mini and driving away. Slowly, he closed the door and took himself upstairs to look at Bob. The grimy dog lay in the nest Tessa had meticulously prepared for him, his breathing steady and peaceful now. Rick couldn't help but feel jealous of all those words she'd whispered affectionately to the dog.

The remains of his pizza sat cold on the plate, but Rick no longer felt hungry. He slipped back to the kitchen, poured himself a large scotch, and wandered back to get into the bed that Tessa had been sitting on such a brief time ago.

Walking into his room, he could smell wet dog. He could also smell the delicate fragrance of orange blossom, a scent that reminded him of Cassy and now of Tessa. That would not help him forget tonight or that night not so long ago when he lost his best friend in the back of a police car.

He sat down on the floor next to the dog and sipped his whisky.

VARIOUS AUTHORS

"So, Bob, do you think either of us has any hope with a girl like Tessa March?"

⚜

To be continued...

Red Zone by Carol Kerry-Green

Julie replaced the washing-up bowl under sink along with the rubber gloves she had been using. Glancing around she picked up the tea cloth and wiped the sink dry. She smiled, satisfied that she had been able to return the kitchen to the way it had been that morning before she had started cooking.

Outside the kitchen window, she could see Karim and Emily playing on the swings and trampoline in the garden, with Peter, Emily's grandfather keeping watch over them. It was good to hear the childish laughter that floated towards her on the evening air. The two dogs Remus and Romulus lolled beneath Peter's chair, enjoying the late evening sunshine.

Turning she made her way into the living room and smiled at her husband John. He had his maps spread out over the dining table, now that they had finished eating. His notepad was open, and he was jotting down directions and suggestions for routes.

Julie wandered around the living room looking at the photos on the wall and the knickknacks on shelves and the mantlepiece. The collection of Schwartz glass reminded her of the one her sister had had. She moved over to the cupboard in the alcove and opening the doors, spent a few happy minutes rummaging through its contents. She picked up a pair of knitting needles, she could knit, but wasn't very good at it. Further down she found a crochet hook. This was more like it, the yarn in the cupboard was thick and warm, which was good they'd be needing hats and scarves soon as autumn turned to winter.

Just then, John's modified crystal radio came to life and she strained to hear the message.

"Red Zone, Red Zone, fliers moving east. Yellow Zone, Yellow Zone, all clear. Green Zone, Green Zone, crawlers heading west clearing the area. Blue Zone, Blue Zone, fliers heading back northwards."

They were in the Yellow Zone nearly at the border with the Red Zone. Hopefully, they'd have an undisturbed night's sleep, though she didn't hold out that much hope. John looked up and grimaced as he updated his notebook and checked his maps once more. Julie got up from where she had been kneeling in front of the cupboard, the light had faded, and there was not enough left to begin to crochet this evening.

Peter came in then with the children and the dogs, The dogs immediately went to John and flopped down on the floor next to him.

Julie smiled as Karim opened his arms to her and she picked him up. He was about five years old and rarely spoke. She'd asked him and Emily to call her Nana, and that was about the only word he said. She knew English wasn't his first language, but he didn't even try to speak in his native tongue. He laughed and giggled with Emily when they played though, so she thought it was probably psychological.

"Time for their bath, then bedtime." Peter said holding his hand out for Karim. "There should just be enough hot water left, I've banked down the Aga and it will be cold soon."

She nodded. Julie had never used an Aga before, but Peter's grandmother had had one, and he knew how to light it and get it working so she could cook them a hot meal. The bonus had been that it was attached to a back boiler and had provided hot water. They had all taken turns having a shower, a luxury she had almost forgotten about.

"Do you need a hand?" She asked Peter.

"No, it's fine, I've got this. I'll put them to bed afterwards, then be back down for a while."

She nodded and settled on the sofa next to John, who had lit one of the few candles they had left. They'd have to restock soon. She'd check the kitchen in the morning in case there were any hidden in drawers or under the sink - people used to keep them for emergencies if the lights went out, so there might be some here. She yawned.

"Tired?" John asked pulling her close.

"It's been a long day, but nice." She pecked his lips. "It was great to be able to use a proper kitchen again and find supplies in the cupboards. We can take some of the tins with us when we move on, the kids will enjoy the spaghetti hoops."

He nodded, his head falling to the back of the sofa. Sounds of childish squeals could be heard from the bathroom above them and a faint smile touched his lips.

"I'm going to go down and check on Bertha, make sure she has enough feed in her nosebag."

"Okay, make sure her blanket is on securely."

He touched her shoulder as he got up, of course, he'd make sure she was covered properly, they needed Bertha. John would make sure she was looked after.

⁂

Peter entered the living room just as Julie was tidying up. She smiled at him, "Kids go down, okay?"

"Yes, they wanted a story. They're asleep now, not sure how long for though."

Julie nodded, none of them slept much. Having to be on guard all the time got a bit wearing after a while.

John came in and shucked off his anorak, "Bertha's all settled for the night. Gave her a couple of apples from next door's garden, no point in them going to waste."

"If we can gather enough before we leave, I'll see if I can make a pie," Julie snuggled up to John as he joined her on the sofa once more. She'd been able to bake bread today, the Aga had got a good workout and she silently thanked the family who used to live in the house for keeping it in good condition.

They spent the next few minutes discussing their next move. John showing them his maps and the disused railway track shown on the old

OS map. It had been turned into a walking track but was wide enough for Bertha and their wagon. Talk turned to places they had been and places they had still hoped to see one day. There wasn't much communication outside of the country, they knew the fliers and crawlers were all over the world, and that people were fighting back where they could. The few of them that were left that was.

"I'm going to bed," Julie yawned getting up and kissing John. She squeezed Peter's shoulder on her way by.

Upstairs she entered the main bedroom and was happy to see that Peter had begun setting up their sleeping quarters for the night. There was a large brass bedstead in the middle of the room and it was covered in a lovely crocheted Afghan. Julie fingered it and decided it was coming with them when they moved on.

Under the bed, duvets and pillows were piled up to create a comfortable resting place. The two children lay in the middle covered by a light blanket. Julie folded the Afghan at the bottom beneath the children's feet and pulled down the sides of their 'tent'. The heavy lead lined canvas was hard to work with, but she got it into place. Changing into a t-shirt and track pants she crawled in next to the children.

"Nana?" Karim's brown eyes met hers and she settled in and pulled him into a cuddle, he giggled a bit when she tickled him.

Emily lay watching them. "Tell us a story?" she demanded.

Julie told them about Peter Rabbit and Squirrel Nutkin, trying to remember the old Beatrix Potter stories she used to tell her daughter, when she was little. Karim and Emily drifted off to sleep again as Peter slipped in next to Emily. He pulled down the canvas at his side and secured it firmly all around, using the bricks Julie passed him to secure it in place.

Only a few more minutes and John crawled in behind Julie. Doing the same on his side, the ever-present crystal radio on the pillow next to his head. The dogs settled in with them at the bottom of their makeshift bed, getting comfortable on the Afghan Julie had left there. Shortly they were ensconced in the darkness, no light from outside filtered in, there were no street lights to reflect through the windows, and the only sounds from outside were that of foxes crying into the night. Julie closed her eyes, comforted by John's presence and fell asleep.

Julie turned over and snuggled in with John, it was still late but she was awake, her mind processing what needed doing the next day. John squeezed her hand letting her know he was awake as well.

"Okay?" He whispered.

"Yes, just sorting out what to do tomorrow."

"Try to sleep some more if you can."

Julie closed her eyes and began to drift off again when the crystal radio resting on the pillow by John burst into life once more. John moved the single earpiece closer so she could hear as well.

"Red Zone, Red Zone, all clear. Yellow Zone, Yellow Zone, fliers moving in east to west. Green Zone, Green Zone, fliers heading east out of the area. Blue Zone, Blue Zone, all clear."

"Heading our way," John said. He moved to the edge of their temporary tent and began checking that there were no holes in the canvas covering. On the other side of the children, Peter started doing the same. Fliers and Crawlers both were attracted by body heat. It had taken a while to figure that one out. Once they'd worked that out calls had gone out to let as many people know as possible, to find something, any kind of material that would block body heat from being detected.

John and Julie like many of their colleagues used lead-lined canvas, as long as there were no gaps, the fliers and crawlers couldn't detect them.

The children stirred, knowing something was going on, and the adults strained their ears to listen for the fliers. They emitted a constant drone as they flew overhead alerting humans to their presence. They were always listening as their grandparents had done for the drone of V1 rockets over their homes at the end of the 2nd World War.

"They may not come this way." Julie stated comforting Karim as he tried to burrow into her seeking safety.

Just as the words left her mouth though, they heard the droning and listened to the fliers as they got closer. Just then a bomb went off as one of the fliers let go of its deadly cargo, they all jumped but stayed still. It wasn't too near them, maybe a couple of miles?

Then the whole house shook as a bomb was detonated closer to them, maybe even only a few streets away. Julie and Peter rocked the children who were screaming and crying now, trying to keep them from hysterics. The shaking of the house didn't last long and they listened as the fliers droned on overhead, no more bombs were dropped.

Peter offered the children a drink of cocoa from the flask he kept near them and both of them drank and they began to calm down. He whispered another story to them and they closed their eyes, but Julie wasn't sure if any of them would get back to sleep that night.

"We'll have to go look tomorrow," John said. "That last one was near, there may be someone injured."

"Peter and I will go," Julie replied. "You'll need to get the wagon and Bertha ready. It's time to move on."

After breakfast the next morning, Julie and Peter ventured out of the house. The morning bulletin from the crystal radio had declared that Yellow Zone was free, at least for the moment. They weren't taking chances, but if there was someone alive then they needed to help.

The deserted streets were quiet, with only some bird song to break the silence. No barking dogs. Julie was glad for that, she loved their dogs, but they had come across feral dogs a couple of trips before. John had been badly bitten before Romulus and Remus had chased them off.

A couple of streets over from where they were staying, Peter smelt burning and they headed off in that direction. Where two 1930s semi-detached houses had been was now a hole in the ground. They'd found where the bomb had landed.

"Hello!" Julie called. "Anyone here?"

They listened but didn't hear anything to begin with. Then Julie heard it, a slight scratching. She moved closer to the bomb crater but realised it was coming from the house next door which had been damaged but was still standing.

"Can you move?" Julie shouted.

"Yes," a quiet voice came back. "Who are you?"

"My name's Julie and this is Peter. We're heading back to the shelters. I work with my husband, John to find and take people to the shelters."

"Oh," the voice was female and a moment later, a tall lanky girl moved out from behind the fence separating the two driveways. She looked a bit shaken up and as though she hadn't had anything to eat for a while, but Julie couldn't see any obvious injuries.

"What's your name?" She asked the girl.

"Jhodi."

"Hi, Jhodi. Would you like to come with us?"

"I don't know... Mam said not to trust anyone."

"I know your mum meant well love, but things have changed. There're fewer and fewer people left out of the shelters; this is our last trip for the season. Once winter gets here..." She broke off and watched Jhodi as she thought of her invitation.

"I don't want to be on my own anymore," she spoke quietly and Julie could see the tears running down her face. She held open her arms and Jhodi lunged at her crying into her shoulder. Julie held her close. "It's okay, it's okay, I've got you."

They took the route along the old railway line that John had found on his map. Moving closer to the Red Zone where the shelters they used were, London. The city had been the capital city and because of its deep tunnels where trains had once run, they were being used as shelters.

Shelters had been set up throughout the country, in mines, caves and old underground tunnels. Anywhere were people could hide from the invaders underground and be safe.

"Nearly there," John assured Julie. She smiled at him and looked back at Peter and the kids in the back of the wagon.

Jhodi was quiet, she hadn't said much, just settling in and hanging on. Julie hadn't been able to pry her story out of her yet. There would be help for her when they got to the shelters in the underground.

They stopped for the night and tethered Bertha further along the route, around a corner. Out here, in the open, it was harder to keep her safe, but they hung her lead-lined blanket in place and hoped she'd be okay. Peter made sure she had plenty to eat.

"Here you go, love." Julie handed a hunk of bread and some spaghetti hoops in a bowl to Karim then did the same for Emily. Jhodi looked interested and Julie handed her some as well.

"Hungry?" she asked her. Jhodi just nodded and dove into the food as if she hadn't eaten for weeks. For all Julie knew she probably hadn't.

That night they set up their sleeping quarters in the wagon. The lead-lined canvas covered the whole wagon and kept them as safe as it could. Julie snuggled into John, listening to the crystal radio.

"Fliers heading into Green Zone. Crawlers coming from Red Zone to Yellow Zone."

Jhodi started crying and Julie tried to comfort her.

"They'll get us!" She screamed as she struggled to get out of the wagon.

"Jhodi no." Julie said pulling the girl towards her. "Stay here, it's safer."

She settled down again sobbing into the pillow and Julie held her close. Wondering what had happened to the young girl. She drifted off to sleep with John's arm around her.

A couple of hours later she heard screaming coming from outside. John was already awake and checking on them all.

"Jhodi's missing," he said.

Julie could only nod in the darkness. Everyone else was awake by now and wondering what was going on.

Carefully John pulled aside the canvas of the wagon, swallowing harshly when he saw what was happening. The moon was full that night and he could see Jhodi standing on the old track before them. In front of her one of the blind crawlers was heading straight for her. Its feelers on the top of its head were rotating around as it zeroed in to the heat given off by the scared girl.

John went to go after her, but Julie pulled him back. "It's too late." She swallowed. "It knows she's there; you go out there and it'll get you too."

John just nodded, and they watched in horror as the crawler headed for Jhodi who was screaming incoherently and began running. She ran away from the wagon back the way they'd come. The crawler followed her and they watched in horror as it rolled over her and consumed her.

Julie burrowed her head in John's shoulder and he gulped and closed the canvas tight again. They could only hope it continued the way it was going, that it didn't turn around. With the narrowness of the track, it would crawl right over them. Lead canvas or not, they wouldn't survive that.

They all held their breaths, and after a few moments, John dared to open the canvas again. He sighed in relief. The crawler was gone and there was no sign of Jhodi left.

No one got any more sleep that night.

Two days later they arrived in what had been London. It had been one of the most heavily bombed places and crawlers had gone through it day after day without cease for months. Now though it was eerily quiet as they moved through the streets. Rubble still strewn all over the place.

They were headed for the old tube station at Kings Cross where their shelters were. They should make it before nightfall. Julie kept an eye out, occasionally there were scavengers about, not all of them friendly.

"Nana?" Karim asked, holding his arms out to her. He looked scared.

"It's okay Karim. We'll soon be safe."

He didn't say anything, just snuggled against her. His large brown eyes taking in everything around them.

Emily on the other hand was practically bounding in her seat. All they'd told her was that the shelters were underground in London, but she'd been told that the young King George lived underground in London and she'd become excited at the idea of meeting him.

"Will we see the king?" she asked.

"Not this time, lovey," Peter answered his granddaughter. "He's safe under Buckingham Palace with Princess Charlotte and Prince Louis."

She nodded. "Maybe another time then." She answered.

Julie remembered the announcement stating that King Charles and the Prince and Princess of Wales had been killed in the bombing when the fliers had first appeared. The children had managed to escape, and young George had become king. Not that it meant anything now, but people liked to know that some part of the royal family had survived.

"Nearly there," John smiled at her. They were now passing the bombed-out British Library, and Julie could see people moving in the rubble. They were trying to rescue as many books as they could. Some people had complained about that, but others agreed that they would need the knowledge contained in those books sooner or later.

With a grateful sigh, John turned through the arch of what had once been St Pancras Station. As it was daylight, there were more people about and they were greeted happily as they made their way down the spiral ramp to the underground.

Changes had had to be made and people were still working to make the shelters as comfortable as they could. John, Julie and the others climbed from the wagon. Leon, one of the grooms who worked in the underground stable came and took Bertha away for a well-earned rest.

"Mama!" Julie smiled as her daughter Millie rushed into her arms.

"Hi, sweetheart." She greeted her. They'd managed to send an encrypted message via the small radio giving a rough idea of when they'd be back.

"Come meet Peter and the children."

Millie moved with her. She was in her twenties now and part of the rescue committee tasked with settling newcomers into the shelters.

Karim clung to Julie, not wanting to let go of a familiar face, but Millie persuaded him and he eventually went with her.

Exhausted Julie followed John through the underground tunnels until they came to the place they called home. Julie opened the canvas doorway and pinned it back to let in what fresh air there was.

"Glad to be home?" John asked.

She could only nod as they got ready for bed. Laying in John's arms, she thought of Jhodi, wishing there had been more that they could have done to help the young girl. But knowing if they'd have left the wagon, they'd have joined her in death.

"We did what we could." John assured her, knowing where her thoughts had gone.

The crystal radio that hung beside their bed began its nightly check-in.

"Red Zone, Red Zone, all clear. Yellow Zone, yellow zone fliers heading west. Green zone, green zone, all clear. Blue Zone, Blue Zone crawlers heading east."

"Do you think..." Julie hesitated.

"Do I think what?" John asked rolling over.

"I was being silly," she replied, tears in her eyes. "Of course it will never go back to normal. Not now, how could it?"

He held her close as she cried. Cried for Jhodi, cried for all the people they'd lost. John wiped her tears away and kissed her.

"We're alive love," he said. "As long as we're alive, we'll win out in the end."

Julie nodded and rolled over to get comfortable. This was their life now and she had to remember that. Tomorrow they'd go back to their jobs with the rescue committee, until heading out again once weather got warmer. Checking to see if there were any more survivors.

Every time they risked their lives and went out, they found someone to save. It was their contribution to the weird world they found themselves living in.

Closing her eyes with a sigh, Julie allowed sleep to overtake her. Tomorrow would come soon enough.

Angels Rest by Cassidy Reyne

Note from the Author

These are the first two chapters of a brand new Small Town romance series, of which I hope to release book one next year. *Angels Rest* is a working title only, and it will change once all four books have been written.

Happy Reading!

One

"Damn it! Stupid piece of crap." Kristoff Hawkins grumbled, slamming his palm on the messy desk.

"Now, now, dear." An older woman stood in the doorway to his office, arching a brow at his outburst.

"Aww. Come on, Maggie," Kit whined. "There's something wrong with the website" — he pointed at the screen where a text box was filled with jumbled words in various fonts and colors — "and I've just spent two hours trying to figure out what it is. All I've managed to do is make it worse." He scratched his head. "At least the online booking and check out system still works."

Maggie tutted and smiled indulgently, shaking her head at his frustration. She worked for Kit at the small inn he'd taken over from his parents when they retired. With only twenty bedrooms, they were rarely rushed off their feet, but she helped out wherever she could. In the mornings, you'd find her serving breakfast, organizing the rooms needing to be cleaned, and checking guests out.

She'd started working for his parents over ten years ago, and he'd inherited her when he took over. She was a Godsend, and he didn't know what he'd do without her. Websites, however, were not her forte, as far as he knew, at least.

She harrumphed. "I've told you many times that you need to hire a web designer to set up the site properly from scratch, and who can teach you to maintain it afterward."

"Yeah." Kit sighed. "You're right. But they cost a lot of money, and I need all the spare cash I can lay my hands on to renovate the upstairs."

Maggie stepped into his tiny office, which had once been a cleaning closet, and peered at the computer.

"Now, see, if you highlight all that gibberish, change the font back to what it should be, and the size as well, and then re-write the information, it's the same as on the brochure we give out to guests. Click the little cog in the corner, select default, and then apply all."

Kit did as she suggested and stared in surprise when it all looked like it had before he started messing with it.

"Yes! Finally!" He fist-pumped and then twisted in the chair to look at her. "How did you know all that? I mean about the font and the size?"

Maggie smirked cheekily. "I may be a little older than you, but I have grandchildren, and I listen when they tell me things."

She winked, swiveled on her heel, and ambled back to the reception area.

<hr />

It was June, and the inn was fully booked for the entire week. Bookings had been steady all year, but summer was naturally their busiest season. Most guests came to hike, fish, or just to enjoy the quaint little town with its selection of various shops, the library, café, diner, and bar. A few miles down the road was the bigger town of Spirit Falls, but it didn't have the charm and ambiance of Angels Rest.

As a kid, the tiny municipality with its lack of anything to do other than outdoor activities used to drive Kit nuts, especially when he started high school and wanted to be like all the other teenagers. But after spending twelve years in the Marines, the gentle solitude, slow pace of life, and childhood friends had worked their magic on him. Now he couldn't imagine living anywhere else.

When the little hotel went up for sale after its owner passed away, the only interest had been from property developers who wanted to build condominiums and turn the town into a health resort. All the residents had been in an uproar, and his parents had decided on the spot to buy it for themselves and run it the way it had always been run.

His mom had been a middle grade teacher, and his dad had been an attorney in Spirit Falls, but he had been thinking about slowing down and enjoying a little more freedom. It hadn't quite worked out that way after buying the property, but they enjoyed running their own business and no longer having to commute. They still worked long hours, but it was all to their and Kit's benefit, no one else's.

His dad had added a second floor soon after they bought the place but had never really used it for more than storage. When Kit took over, he'd seen the potential of the space and was slowly renovating into a large room that could be used for weddings and other events all year round.

At the far end, a hallway led to an additional suite of rooms he'd built over what had once been a garage for several cars, and he was turning them into an apartment for himself to live in. Currently, his living quarters consisted of a small studio space in the old garage. It was a combined bedroom, kitchen, and living room with no closet space and bad insulation.

Kit had been busy all day, running around fixing broken door handles, a leaky faucet, taking in deliveries, paying bills, and making sure the guests had everything they needed. He'd done it all with a smile, and now his jaw was aching with rarely used muscles. He wasn't a natural smiler. In fact, his default setting was grouchy and surly, which wasn't the best when dealing with paying guests.

He'd always been the quiet one, especially in elementary school, the one no one noticed, the kid with his nose in a book. It wasn't because he loved reading so much, or because he had no friends. No, he used the books to hide his lack of self-confidence and that he was painfully shy, for which the other school kids would sometimes bully him mercilessly. Thankfully, he had a small group of close friends who'd stand up for him whenever the bullying started.

The shyness wasn't so bad when talking to other boys, but as he entered his teenage years and started noticing girls as not just friends, he got tongue-tied, blushed, and wanted the ground to swallow him up. He couldn't explain it, or maybe it was more that he didn't want to think of the real reason why.

It didn't improve as he got older. Quite the opposite, since he started to avoid speaking with girls at all costs. He only had a prom date because one of his buddies insisted he asked out a friend of his who had just broken up with her boyfriend. Kit had felt sick with nerves for weeks beforehand, but Sarah had been sweet, funny, and very patient with him. They'd ended up having a great night, and it had given him some hope that one day, he'd get over the shyness.

Academically, school had been easy for Kit, too easy, and he often got bored when he wasn't challenged enough. It could easily have led to him hanging out with the wrong people, but his PE teacher in high school during his sophomore year, an ex-army man, had recognized the situation and taken Kit under his wing.

Together with a few of Kit's friends — Cruz, Eden, and Ro included — they'd constructed an obstacle course in the woods, complete with a small cabin kitted out with a boxing ring, some gym equipment donated by a parent, a kitchenette, and a table and chairs, where they spent a lot of their free time getting fit, learning new skills, talking about life, and keeping out of trouble.

The teacher had regaled them with stories from his life in the army — those that he could share, at least — and Kit had been fascinated. The camaraderie, rigorous training, responsibilities, and discipline appealed to him even then, and the day after his eighteenth birthday, he signed up to join the Marines.

His parents couldn't understand why he wanted to serve but supported him nonetheless. They were proud of him and were there every step of the way. His mom had cried sad tears every time he deployed and happy tears when he returned. His dad rarely said much, but hugged him tight each time. Kit had had many reasons for signing up. He wanted to serve his country, feel as if he'd contributed something to the world, and challenge himself to be the best he could be.

Seventeen years later, his time in the Marines had helped him with his self-confidence, but the shyness was still there. It wasn't too bad when dealing with the guests as he could put his professional mask on and didn't have to get personal with any of them. He'd smile, greet them, say goodbye, or give them whatever information they were after. That was easy. Ish. Actually getting to know someone new, on the other hand, was nearly impossible, and something he avoided like the plague.

Kit's retirement from active service coincided with his parents wanting to retire to a warmer climate since the weather played havoc with his dad's arthritis, and it had seemed like the perfect solution.

His original plan had been to take over the inn, get his bearings, and adjust to civilian life after so many years in the military, and then sell the lodge or put a manager in place while he moved to a city for the buzz and vibrant atmosphere. To his great surprise, he'd quickly settled back into life in the rural community and soon felt as if he'd never left.

Even though his self-confidence had soared as his military training progressed, leaving the Marines had meant leaving some of that behind as well. It had worried him and had been one of the reasons he'd thought he wanted to be in a big city. Now, he was glad his parents had made him come back here. They obviously knew something he didn't, and he'd settled in to his new life with minimal effort. After losing the tight-knit group of buddies the military had provided him with, he'd felt a little lost and worried he'd struggle to find it again, but he had friends here, real friends, and running the inn had reminded him of that.

He was single, owned his own business, had no financial worries, and had rediscovered his love for hiking and nature photography. So what if he sometimes dreamed of finding a woman he could love, who loved him back, and who wanted to build a life with him here? Marriage and kids would be great, but he'd have to look outside of town for that, something he was far from ready for.

His cell buzzed in his desk drawer, and he put down the stack of bills he'd been sorting through to answer.

"Hey, Cruz. How's it going?" he asked after swiping across the screen to answer, having seen the caller ID on the display.

"I'm good, bro. Gingerbread house doing okay?" Cruz Hamilton, the town's sheriff, let loose his rumbling laughter.

Cruz had once likened the lodge, when it was decorated for Christmas and covered in snow, to the fairytale gingerbread house, and the moniker had stuck.

A chuckle bubbled in Kit's chest. "Fully booked this week, and it looks as if it'll carry on for the rest of the season."

"That's great. For you, I mean. For me, not quite so much." Cruz sighed. "A busy summer always means more fights at the bar, people getting lost on the trails, and more cars being broken into. But I guess it's better than the town dying out if businesses have to close because of no trade."

"You're right," Kit agreed. "Which is why I'm happy to have every room booked out for the rest of the month."

"Listen, you're still up for meeting at the bar tomorrow night, right?" Cruz asked.

Kit waved goodnight to the newlyweds staying in the honeymoon suite before he replied, "Yeah, sure. It's just the usual, right?"

"Of course. Devin was asking as he'll have come off a twelve-hour shift and wants to kick back and decompress before he goes home to sleep.

"I don't know how he does it." Kit chuckled. "Running into burning buildings, I mean. You have to be fucking crazy for that kind of thing."

Cruz snorted. "Says the dude who ran straight into danger every day of the week in the backends of hell. And you did it voluntarily!"

"That's different," he argued. "It's war, and you just get on with it. Besides, Devin chooses to fight fires on a daily basis."

"I couldn't do it, dude, so I'm glad someone is willing to. And Devin is crazy, that's why he does it." Cruz was being sincere.

Kit knew Cruz loved his job as the sheriff and had had his fair share of dangerous situations, but it was nothing like being a member of the armed forces on deployment.

They said goodbye and hung up, and Kit returned to the stack of bills he'd been paying. It was getting late in the evening, and he'd still not eaten dinner. The thought of the leftover pizza in his fridge upstairs made his stomach growl.

The sound of light footfalls coming down the hallway from where the rooms were caught his attention, and he ventured out into the reception area in case whichever guest it was needed something from him.

The woman from room seven gave him a slight nod and a small smile.

"Heading out, Mrs. Montgomery?" he asked, internally cringing at the stupid question.

Of course, she was going out. That's why she had her coat on and was about to leave the building.

The woman stopped, and once again, Kit found something profoundly sad about her. He couldn't pinpoint what it was as she was very friendly and always smiled. She was exactly the kind of woman he'd normally avoid — about his age, pretty, with a bright smile and beautiful eyes — because he'd stumble his over words, knock something over, and go beet red for no reason. Not with her, though. He felt totally at ease around her but sensed this deep melancholy surrounding her like a cloak.

"Yes, I am. I'm only taking a short walk for some fresh air. And please, call me Alina."

Kit smiled and nodded. "Alina, then. Make sure you stay where it's lit. It's easy to get lost around here."

"I will," Alina replied. "Have a good night." She gave him a tentative smile and a brief waggle with her fingers.

Kit returned her wave and watched as Alina exited through the huge wooden front door with the thick glass pane. He followed her with his gaze as she strolled down the lane in the warm glow from the lamp posts. As the lane bent around a clump of trees, she disappeared from his sight, and he returned to his bill paying. He dropped into the chair and pulled the small pile of papers toward him again. He felt ridiculous and sighed but couldn't shake the feeling he'd never see Alina Montgomery again.

Two

"Damn it! Stupid piece of shit! How could he do that to me? With my best friend of all people!" Allegra Gilbert pounded her fist against the steering wheel of her little electric BMW.

She hated the car, but Elijah had insisted on it being a European make, and he'd demanded it be electric. She had to drive a foreign car, and it had to be electric because that's what all his friends' wives drove. Allegra had grudgingly agreed. At least she hadn't had to pay for it.

"Where the hell am I going? This isn't the way to LA. Shit, I've taken a wrong turn somewhere." According to the road signs, she was now heading north instead of west. She'd left Las Vegas an hour ago and must have gotten on the interstate in the wrong direction. It didn't matter. As long as no one knew where she was going, especially not Elijah or Carmen, she didn't care where she ended up. She just had to get away.

The day after tomorrow was her wedding day. Or it should have been her wedding day had she not come home early from her appointment with the manicurist that day. The salon had called her to say they could fit her in the afternoon instead of the last appointment of the day, and she'd jumped at the chance. Her best friend and maid of honor was the one who'd made her the appointment as a small gift to help her relax before the big day. Now she knew why.

It had been only a little after three when her nails were done, and she'd decided to go straight home instead of back to her little office next to the library off Main Street in Sun Canyon, a few miles east of the Strip. That turned out to be a big mistake, or not, depending on how you looked at it. If she hadn't gone home, maybe she would have never found out that her fiancé was banging her friend. It wasn't the first time either, it seemed.

It was pitch black outside, the only lights those from cars in the oncoming lane. She had no idea where she was going, just that she was putting some distance between herself and Elijah. The lonely, dark ride toward… somewhere gave her a lot of time to think.

Looking back, she wondered if she'd been blind to all the signs that Eli wasn't totally committed to their relationship. All the times he'd suddenly had to work late, or had to go on unexpected business trips, had they been big red flags waving in her face, and she'd ignored them? Was she that desperate to cling onto him and what she thought they'd had?

With the music up loud, she kept going, heading north-east. She figured she'd stop for the night in a motel along the highway somewhere, but for the moment, she didn't want to stop driving. The music filled her ears but couldn't quite stop her mind from churning. The scene that had met her when she walked into their bedroom was burned into the back of her eyelids.

After parking in the driveway, she'd let herself into the house, stopping in the hallway only to drop her keys into the bowl on the table, and put her briefcase on the floor next to it, before heading up to the bedroom to change. She hadn't reflected on the noises coming from upstairs, thinking it was the neighbor's kids screaming, as usual.

Pushing the door open, the first thing she saw was Carmen, on top of Eli, *her fiancé*, bouncing up and down hard, screaming his name. Eli's face had been contorted with lust, sweat dripping from his temples, and his hands gripping Carmen's tits so hard he had to have been leaving marks.

The gasp that flew from her lips had barely registered with either of them, so she'd put two fingers in her mouth and let out a piercing whistle. If she hadn't been so furious, the expressions on their faces would have been funny. As it was, all she could do was order them both out of the house. Eli had tried to apologize, to say it wasn't what she thought it was, but Allegra had laughed in his face and said even a dead person could work out what was going on.

A large neon sign advertising a nearby motel came into view, but she kept going. Her brain wasn't in any fit state to switch off and let her sleep. Her body was buzzing with adrenaline and caffeine from the extra strong coffee in the thermos sitting in the cup holder. To distract herself, she changed her playlist to one with some country pop where guys with cowboy hats sang about lost love, and women lamented the one who got away. Maybe it wasn't the best music to listen to, but it helped her relax and take her mind off her bastard ex-fiancé and former best friend.

Several hours later, as the skies began to lighten, she pulled into a small lay-by where the car would be shielded from the road and switched off the ignition. The silence was deafening but also welcoming. Leaning her head against the neck rest, she closed her eyes and tried to transport herself to a happy place.

The sound of a car revving its engine pulled her out of her dreamlike state, and she noticed to her surprise that the sun was well above the horizon. She must have fallen asleep without realizing. Cursing herself for being careless, she rubbed the sleep out of her eyes and took a swig of water from the bottle on the passenger seat. Glancing at the date on the dash, her brows knitted with dismay. It was the day before what should have been her wedding. The thought made her stomach sour.

After she'd kicked Elijah and Carmen out of the house, she'd pulled out her phone and cancelled the entire wedding. All the invited guests got the same email, explaining exactly what had happened and that she'd be going away for a while. She didn't care that she was exposing Eli's dirty little secret and hung him out to dry. He deserved it, and so did Carmen. Heartbreak, devastation, and embarrassment had fueled her craving for revenge.

The one thing she and Eli had always said they wanted from a relationship was honesty and openness. Guess that was a one-sided thing as far as he was concerned. She'd loved him. Or at least thought she'd loved him. Now she wasn't so sure if she was more pissed about the betrayal or about having lost her future husband.

She'd packed a bag with the essentials and thrown it in the trunk of her car where she kept her easel, painting supplies, and several canvases. She never went anywhere without them as she didn't know when she'd find an opportunity to create. Painting was her passion. She loved both photography and watercolor painting, and often combined the two.

Taking a moment to get her bearings, she looked around, but saw only the barren desert landscape of southern Utah. According to her GPS, she'd left Nevada, briefly crossed into Arizona, and entered Utah without even realizing. Taking a deep breath, she turned the engine back on, noting she'd need to stop to recharge soon, and carried on driving.

Her cell buzzed angrily for the millionth time in its holder on the dash, and for the millionth time, she declined the call and refocused on the road. It had been a steady stream of messages and calls all day from her mom, her sister, Eli's mom, Eli, and even Carmen. Why the hell Carmen and Eli would call her she couldn't figure out. She'd been clear enough yesterday when she said she didn't want to speak to either of them ever again. Her mom was furious with her, she knew that much, as the one thing Constance Gilbert hated most was anything that made her family look less than perfect.

Allegra had always had to be the perfect child, daughter, student, girlfriend, fiancée, and anything else she'd ever attempted in her life. Mediocre was a word that didn't exist in Constance's vocabulary, which meant it wasn't allowed to exist for anyone in her family either.

Her dad had been the counterweight to her mom's quest for perfection and without him, Allegra's childhood would have been miserable. He was the one who helped clean up her messes while gently teaching her a life lesson, and who supported her without question whenever she came to him for help. He was her lodestone and her rock. He was also the one person who hadn't tried to reach her, knowing he'd be her first call as soon as she'd gotten her head straight.

Her sister Miranda was only three years older, but they hadn't been close since Miranda started high school, and Allegra suddenly became the annoying little sister who was only good for teasing and used as a scapegoat for when things broke or went missing. Things were better between them now, but Miranda had moved to Texas when she met her husband, so they rarely saw each other and only talked sporadically.

Miranda had only come to Las Vegas for the wedding after much berating by their mom. She'd said she had too much work, her husband was too busy, their son had soccer practice, and any other thing she could think of. In the end, she'd reluctantly agreed to come, but only if she wasn't involved in any way, could leave right after the reception, and her husband and Allegra's nephew didn't have to come. Allegra had shrugged and said she didn't care one way or the other. Why worry about someone who clearly didn't want to be there even if it was your only sister?

<hr>

The low, rugged, scrub-filled ridges of Nevada had long since given way to lush pine forests and tall, green hillsides. After skirting the northwestern edge of Arizona and bisecting Utah, she was now heading northeast through Colorado. She'd eventually hit Denver and then enter either Nebraska or Kansas if she didn't stop in Colorado. With every mile she put behind her, she felt a little calmer, but her heart was still clenched in a tight grip. It was probably something she'd have to put up with for a while longer. At least until she'd exorcised the sight of Carmen riding Eli's cock out of her head for good.

The hills turned into craggy mountains the farther north she drove. The display on the dash told her she'd traveled nearly five-hundred miles in the last ten hours, with a couple of hours' sleep thrown in and a couple of brief stops to recharge the car. She needed to find a place to stay for a few nights while she decided on her next steps. According to the virtual map on the heads-up-display, the next larger town was Spirit Falls.

It had sounded like a nice place, so when she rolled down Main Street and saw the boxy looking buildings, cluster of generic shops and restaurants, she was disappointed. She almost drove past the small shopping mall when she spotted the electric vehicle charging sign and abruptly turned into the lot. She bounced with joy on her seat when it also turned out to be a free charging station, as long as she spent a minimum of thirty bucks in one of the stores.

She parked in the designated bay, managed to plug the car in after some fumbling with the adapter and cable, and then entered the store to spend her dollars so she would get her ticket with a code to scan into the machine. She spotted a Walgreens right inside the doors, and headed there to stock up on the toiletries and makeup she'd forgotten in her haste to pack.

She took her time finding what she needed since the car would take at least half an hour to charge. She still found the time it took to recharge annoying compared to the speed and ease of filling up a tank of gas. But as it was better for the environment and she could charge it at home, she'd accepted it when Eli purchased the car. Luckily, he'd put it in her name and not his.

He'd also never gotten around to installing the app that could track it, and he needed to be sitting in the car and enter a code generated by the car's navigation system to set it up, so he couldn't see where she was.

On her way back to the car, she'd bought an armful of sandwiches, snacks, and drinks as she still didn't know where she was going or how long it would take to get to wherever that was. Right now, it felt as if she could carry on forever, but that was ridiculous.

The next place that had a nice name and actually looked like a nice place when she drove through it would be the place where she stopped for a few days. As long as it had somewhere she could stay, of course. With that decision firmly planted in her mind, she got in the car and headed back onto the highway.

It took her another hour before weariness began to set in, so when she saw a sign for somewhere called Angels Rest, she figured it was meant to be. Not that she was an angel in any way, but she definitely needed a rest. If it was good enough for angels, it was good enough for her.

The road had wound its way between the mountains with tall pine trees on either side for such a long time that when it suddenly opened out and a bridge appeared before her, she stomped on the brakes, the car coming to a screeching halt. She stared at the sight before her. The long bridge stretched out over a deep chasm, the tall structures on either end reaching high in the sky, with thick cables stretching in graceful curves from one to the other. Their shape from a distance reminded her of wings. Angel wings.

Maybe that's where the name comes from.

Glancing behind her, she was glad she was alone on the road. It gave her the chance to cross the bridge at a snail's pace, catching glimpses of the churning river below. It was both captivating and slightly daunting to find herself suspended in the air with nothing beneath her, or so it felt.

Once she reached the other side, a strange calm filled her head, soothing the calamity still bouncing around in there, and the claws that had held a tight grip on her heart loosened, allowing it to resume its normal, steady rhythm.

She followed the road around a bend, unsure of what she'd find when she reached the town, but before she got there, a large wooden sign carved with the name Angel Lake Lodge caught her attention. Pulling onto the path leading off the main road, she held her breath, hoping she was right in thinking it was a hotel of some kind. When the building came into view, she wasn't disappointed. A large, timber-framed lodge stood on a small slope with another sign welcoming guests to the inn. A round, graveled area in front offered plenty of space for guests to pull up and unload their cars, and to the side was a generously-sized parking lot with a small assortment of vehicles, mainly SUVs, which she assumed belonged to the guests staying here.

A tall, broad-shouldered man with light brown hair came around the corner of the building. He cast a long glance at her car before yanking open the tall front door and going inside. The sight of his chiseled jaw, straight nose, powerful arms, and long legs sent heat shooting through her body.

She stared after him. A tingle of excitement lingered in her belly, but she ignored it and put it down to exhaustion and emotional distress. Besides, she wasn't here to be attracted to every stranger she came into contact with. All men could go to hell for the time being as far as she was concerned.

What was more important was that she felt as if she'd reached her destination, that she belonged here. It was weird. A warm sensation of familiarity spread through her core. If she hadn't been a hundred percent certain she'd never been to Colorado, let alone this tiny little town, she'd have sworn she knew the area intimately. It felt a little like she'd returned after a long time away. Either she was going insane from the stress of the last twenty-four hours, or she was having an otherworldly experience, but she felt as if she'd come home.

Bound Desires by CC Gedling

Desire Genie Series

About the Story

For a decade, my best friend and I enjoyed Shibari, but after he died, I lost not only him but the practice I held dear. After a disastrous attempt, I finally found a trusted rigger. They call him the Desire Genie. He helps bring people's desires to life. But will he help me reawaken mine?

Author Note

This short story does not contain sexual scenes. This was done out of respect for the range of readers of this anthology and because it is a common misconception that BDSM scenes must always involve sexual acts. That said, the rest of the Desire Genie series has plenty!

The book uses British English

Content Warnings: Grief. BDSM. Rope bondage and suspension.

One ~ Angie

The taxi pulled away from the edge of the stone steps, and the wind whipped at the ends of my newly dyed hair. Butterflies fluttered through my belly as I turned towards the imposing Georgian mansion I'd only seen pictures of until today.

This day was a new beginning: a funeral and a rebirth in one.

If you can handle it, a savage little voice reminded me.

I climbed the steps, bouncing my wheeled suitcase up each, and rang the buzzer. The buzzer's modern brushed chrome contrasted with the intricate woodwork of the oak door and the old sandstone columns.

"How may I help you?" a cheerful voice came through the speakers.

"It's Angie, here to see Gene."

"Pull the door and head to the check-in desk." The door buzzed electronically, and I depressed the handle with a sweaty hand and headed inside.

The interior loomed impressively upwards, with a double-height ceiling and a split staircase rising behind the reception desk. An open fire crackled in the hearth next to some comfy-looking couches and armchairs. Various doors off the main entrance were closed, but the closest opened into a lounge bar beyond. *Classy place.*

I headed for the person I presumed the cheerful voice belonged to. Her name tag read "Celeste." She smiled, taking my details as I leaned against the counter.

"This is the key to your pod. Leave your suitcase here, and we will take it to your room."

"Thank you." I rolled the case to the side and took the fob.

"Gene will meet you shortly. Please take a seat. Would you like a glass of water?"

"Yes, please." I licked my dry lips and walked to one of the sofas.

The soft leather enveloped me like a warm hug. I crossed my legs and bounced my top foot as the nerves returned full force.

Celeste came over with a glass of iced water with a slice of lemon, and I took it with a slight tremor and thanked her. It calmed my nerves somewhat that they didn't offer guests caffeine or alcohol before a rope scene.

A rope scene.

The butterflies now exploded in my stomach and a buzz tingled under my skin. Was I truly ready this time?

"You must be Angie."

My head snapped up at the deep voice. It belonged to a gorgeous man.

"Don't get up," he said as I scrambled forward.

I sank back into my seat, my heart pounding. He was wearing a white short-sleeved button-down shirt and deep purple slacks. Vibrant tattoos decorated his arms. I spotted dunes, a lamp, and the smoky base of a genie before they snaked away under his sleeves. Wow! They weren't lying on the forums when they said he was hot. His dark hair and tall frame created an imposing effect. I'd only chatted with him via text, so seeing him in real life was an experience.

"How was your trip?" he asked, his gaze steady as he sat opposite.

"The train was packed, but I managed to snag a seat."

"I thought you might prefer to swing from one of those hand grips." He raised an eyebrow, which gave him a mischievous look.

"It's not as satisfying on a train packed with sweaty commuters." I grinned at him, relaxing with his teasing.

"True." He nodded at my glass. "Shall we head upstairs?"

"Sure!" I tripped over myself in my haste to get up.

Gene stabilised me with his hand. "Take a breath." His calm, authoritative tone helped me gulp in a breath.

"I'm sorry. I'm just nervous."

"We will go through everything, but remember, if we need to stop the scene, we will. Nothing is more important than your safety and comfort. Well... relative comfort." He grinned again.

I snorted this time because Shibari was many things, but "comfortable" wasn't necessarily one of them.

Two ~ Angie

I followed him up the stairs and thought about what he said. My heartbeat sped up again, and I reminisced about my first attempt with rope after losing Miles. It was a total disaster, and I prayed for another chance.

Gene led me down a plushly carpeted corridor adorned with erotic art. I paused at one particularly beautiful piece depicting a Shibari scene. A mixture of coloured ropes displayed the sub stunningly. The look on her face made my breathing hitch. That was what I wanted again. I needed it at a soul-deep level and resolved to fight for it.

"I love that picture," Gene said, pausing beside me.

"Did you rig them?"

"No, that was our Master of Ropes. He's since moved away. He was an incredible rigger, and we all learned a lot from him."

I nodded and continued to follow him up the corridor. We stopped in front of a door with an intricate symbol, and Gene opened the door.

I sucked in another breath at the scene inside. From the ceiling, chains suspended a bamboo pole above a thick mat in the middle of the room – muted shades of green and brown created a calming effect. The only furniture was a couch and a side table.

"There is a bathroom through there." Gene indicated the only other door.

I nodded as he steered me toward the couch and took a seat.

"How are you feeling?" he asked me as we sat down.

"Nervous but determined. The picture out there reminded me of how good it can be. I want to get that back."

"If we don't achieve that in this session, that is okay, too."

"I know," I said, frustration welling me up. "But I want this back in my life. M-Miles..." I choked over his name, my heart heavy in my chest. "He would have wanted this for me."

"If he was the man you told me about, he would understand."

I nodded, and he would. Although, he might have spanked my arse for being so silly.

"Listen, Angie. Losing someone as important to you as Miles and having the experience you did when you tried to return to the scene would make anyone hesitant. But it says a lot about your courage that you are here to try again."

Something warmed inside me. Gene was like Miles, who always knew the right words to boost my confidence.

"I just miss him so much." I swallowed over the restriction in my throat.

Miles wasn't my lover. He was my best friend. We discovered the kink scene together, and we were only ever platonic friends, but our bond was really strong.

"How long was he your rigger for?" Gene asked.

"Ten years." I closed my eyes and smiled despite my deep sorrow. "When he decided to learn Shibari, I agreed to be his willing victim."

"I'm pretty sure the term is a rope bunny." Gene chuckled.

"No, you don't understand. I was literally a victim. That dope didn't have the first clue." I choked on a laugh. "I'm surprised he didn't give me nerve damage. After I threatened to call time on his experimenting, he found a proper mentor, and we never looked back." A wave of profound loneliness washed through me. "It got me through my degree and through starting my career."

As a clinical pharmacist, my job was high-pressured, and rope gave me a sense of freedom. But ever since Miles died two years ago, I'd lost the practice.

"I didn't just lose my best friend; I lost a connection to myself."

Gene nodded. It might sound stupid to those outside the scene, but that was how I felt.

"Were you able to identify any factors behind what went wrong when you tried again?"

I closed my eyes. "I didn't trust her, and I wasn't ready."

It took me a while to understand why my first attempt to return to Shibari a year ago went wrong. In our initial messages, Gene had asked me to delve deeper and identify the root cause, if possible, to avoid triggers.

"Don't get me wrong, Olivia was an experienced rigger at the club we used to attend. However, I think she skipped the safety steps, assuming I knew what I was doing. While I knew how to bottom, I didn't know her well enough.

"Miles and I had worked together for ten years, and he still had me check in. I can't blame her fully. I didn't communicate my fears either, but it put me on edge immediately. All of my grief had been building, and I spiralled. A panic attack hit me mid-suspension. I couldn't breathe, and it felt like an eternity before she let me down." I shuddered, remembering the utter terror.

"Did she cut the ropes?"

"No. I remember needing to get out, and the chest harness felt too tight. She tried to calm me down, but I couldn't pull myself back."

Gene nodded. "Will you notice the signs of panic creeping up on you this time?"

"I noticed them last time, but I was too worried to voice them. Mentally, I was in a terrible state and clinging to the idea that Shibari could fix my grief. I've had a lot of therapy since then, and I'm in a better place now. The grief hasn't gone, and it still hits me, but I'm functioning again."

Gene smiled. "Thank you for sharing those with me. We don't skip safety discussions here. Are you ready to discuss them?"

"Yes, Sir," I said, rolling my shoulders back.

He grabbed two iPads from the side table and handed one to me.

"Please review the limits questionnaire you filled in for me and tell me if anything has changed. Then we will run through things."

We lapsed into silence as I skimmed the extensive questions. Everything had stayed the same since our initial online discussions. I had heard about Gene and that they called him the Desire Genie because he fulfilled people's deepest desires. My desire was a little more complex than most, mixed with trauma and grief. His reputation for impeccable attention to safety, consent, and clear communication made me contact him.

"It's all fine." I placed the iPad on my lap.

"Do you have any old injuries or current soreness?"

"No, Sir."

"I've only given you the Shibari questionnaire as you aren't playing downstairs in the main club. We will remain in this room until the scene concludes. No one will be allowed in unless I call a moderator for emergency assistance."

"I understand, Sir." I nodded.

"Are you happy with the traffic light system?"

"Yes, Sir. Red for stop, yellow for pause, and green for proceed."

"Good. Give me a yellow if you begin to panic or if anything feels too tight."

"Yes, Sir." My chest loosened a little.

"Do I have your consent to touch you to check the rope tension, your temperature, and grip?"

"Yes, Sir."

This scene would not be sexual, just like my scenes with Miles. I had experienced sex during Shibari with other members of our club occasionally, but it was the subspace I craved, not a sexual release.

Although, the man sat opposite me could tempt a nun.

Gene ran through a long list of safety questions. He outlined every part of the process, and as each point on his checklist was complete, it bolstered my confidence in him, and I relaxed further. It was the right choice to choose this man.

"What was your favourite suspension position?"

I thought for a moment. A technicolour of positions and ties flashed through my memory.

"Probably a classic upward-facing like the one outside. Because working at a computer or hunching over trays of pills all day made the backward bend harsh but beneficial afterwards."

"Good. Tell me, do you tend to slip deep into subspace? While I'll try not to disturb you, I must check in. What should I expect?"

"For me, subspace is more like soaring. I'm here but not here. I could always answer Miles, but he said it took me a few moments to reply. Like the light was on, but no one was home."

Gene chuckled. "Okay. Are you ready?"

Was I ready? I touched base with myself and found a sense of calm and ease.

"Yes, Sir," I answered with confidence this time.

Three ~ Angie

"Would you like to use the bathroom before we start?" Gene asked.

"Yes." I was thankful for his thoughtfulness as my full bladder reminded me that peeing myself while dangling from the ceiling wasn't how I wanted to rejoin the rope scene.

"Take your shoes and socks off."

Gene had told me to come dressed in clothes that I was happy to be tied up in, so I was already wearing soft leggings, a T-shirt, and my wireless sports bra.

I emerged from the toilet and saw that Gene had clipped a ligature knife to his belt and pulled out a selection of jute ropes. The natural brown ropes made me smile. After a few years, Miles had moved onto colourful nylon ropes because he liked a splash of colour.

"What's the smile for?" Gene asked.

"The rope reminds me of our early days. Miles was passionate about learning every facet of the craft. I think I've tried every Shibari position known to man. He would fanboy over your bamboo, though. Most of the time, we used a suspension ring, carabiner, and climbing strap combo."

"Then I'm honoured to rig you today."

I smiled, blinking back tears. This was about honouring Miles and our connection.

"We will start with a chest harness and then move on to the hip harness. As you know, we don't need a hip harness for this suspension, but I want to give you some grounding."

"Thank you, Sir."

"One last thing. Please squeeze my fingers." He held out two fingers, and I gripped his warm digits.

Good rope tops checked for circulation regularly, and the familiar action settled me.

"Please join me for ten deep breaths," Gene said, bringing me to the mat.

The inhalations came easily to me as he counted us through the inhalations.

"Are you ready to begin?" he asked as my eyes flicked open.

"Yes, Sir." Anticipation slithered through me.

"Give me a colour."

"Green, Sir."

"Hands together in prayer position, elbows tucked in."

Mentally, I handed my control over to Gene, and he began wrapping the rope around my torso and arms. The familiar tugging and pressure lulled me into a meditative state. Each pass infused me with warmth, and as the knots tightened, my mind emptied of concerns.

"Colour?" Gene asked as he passed the rope over to my back again, walking around me.

"Green, Sir." I exhaled and let my eyes close, sinking into the calming sensation of the harness.

The tugs and nips of the rope, accompanied by Gene's steady breathing, helped me centre, anchoring me in my body as my mind began to float.

"Squeeze my fingers." Gene's deep voice was calm and close to my ear.

I gripped him within the confines of my bindings.

"Good. I'm moving on to the hip harness."

I basked in familiar sensations as he wrapped the rope around my pelvis, and Gene tightened the knots.

"Colour?" Gene asked again, touching my skin in a few places and getting me to clench his fingers again.

I popped my eyes open. "Green, Sir."

It was surreal to slip back into the familiar and sensual feeling. I watched as Gene prepared the rope for the suspension.

"I'm going to connect you to the rig now."

His knots were beautiful. Although the edges of my vision were fuzzy, the rope fibres and knots were in sharp focus. Gene connected the ropes to the front of my chest harness and then to the bamboo pole above.

"I'm going to bring you up to tiptoes." He flexed, and the harness pulled tight.

My breathing hitched, but instead of panic, joy flooded me. Intoxicated with relief, I knew at that moment I could fly again.

"Colour?" Gene paused.

"Green, Sir. Thank you." A single tear slid down my cheek.

He tied the rope off and rechecked my skin and grip. I inhaled and dropped my head back on the exhale. Blood rushed to my brain and pounded in my ears.

"I'll tie your left thigh now."

I leaned into the feeling of suspension as he pulled the rope and hoisted my leg. My other leg balanced on tiptoes, poised to soar.

"Colour?"

"Green, Sir." The pulse was thick in my ears.

"I'll do the ankle now." He lifted my remaining leg, and I swung forward.

The momentum made me smile despite the pressure on my arms and left thigh, which took most of my weight. Like always, the discomfort transformed into a sense of exhilaration, and my thoughts became floaty and fuzzy.

I became aware Gene had spoken as his hand touched my shoulder. "Colour, Angie?"

A moan escaped my throat. "Green, Sir."

The insulated confidence I'd missed for so long flooded through me.

"Would you like some momentum?" His voice penetrated my scattered mind.

"Yes, Sir."

He nudged me forward. The movement created a slight breeze, lifting the strands of my hair. I swung, and intense pleasure infused me as I soared back into being me.

Four ~ Gene

She swung gently, her face and neck flushed and her deep-red hair swaying. Her flesh blanched prettily under the pressure of the bindings. They say that for some, Shibari mimicked the feeling of the womb. Indeed, the subspace achieved through rope work was the deepest type in my experience.

A lightness entered my chest, knowing that my ropes had created that euphoric effect in her. The satisfaction I drew from bringing people's desires to life and the power and trust subs gifted me was unparalleled.

I observed Angie for any signs of panic. Her experience with the other rigger was a disaster. One that might have been avoided through more transparent communication and a proper check in. For that to compound Angie's grief of losing her rope-top and best friend must have made it hard to recover. I smiled, proud of Angie for trying again.

I checked her skin temperature in various vital spots and coaxed her to grip my fingers. Her friend Miles wasn't wrong that she went deep with Shibari. She was present but slow to react.

The timer I set told me she had another fifteen minutes, providing the checks were satisfactory. Angie had experience with much longer suspensions with her previous rigger, but we had negotiated a timeframe we both felt comfortable with. We also left off a blindfold because the first time rigging someone, you needed every facet of their body language. Over the years, I'd grown very attuned to minor shifts in subs.

I grabbed a bottle of water from the side and surveyed the scene. Rope work was incredible in its ability to display the beauty of the human body. Contrary to popular belief, it didn't have to include sex, whether penetrative or not. Nor did it have to involve impact play. Many scenes weren't sexual at all. Erotic, maybe, but not overtly sexual.

Rigging wasn't my strongest skill, but the myth that had sprung up around the title of the Desire Genie had become part of my identity. I'd spent a large section of my life learning human psychology, and early on, I became fascinated by the theories behind sexual desire and kink. Something that had begun as research became a rabbit hole from which I never returned. Then, a joke made by a friend turned into something that fulfilled a fundamental part of my personality. The mission of my role as Desire Genie, helping people fulfil their desires, was my purpose.

I checked Angie and continued to watch her for signs of distress.

The timer beeped, and I stretched my neck.

"I'm going to bring you down now, Angie," I told her.

Her eyelids fluttered, but she gave no other sign she heard me. Her unconscious mind was in the driving seat as the endorphins pumped through her. After gifting me control, I would need to help her return from subspace.

Releasing the suspension on her legs first, I allowed her to become upright and for the blood to drain back. I cradled the back of her head, supporting its weight.

"Give me a colour."

She blinked her eyes open, but they were unfocused.

"Green," she eventually replied.

I'd forgive her for not saying "Sir."

"Wiggle your toes for me. Can you feel them?"

"Yes, Sir." Her voice was stronger as she came back to me.

"I will let you down slowly," I said as I untied the main line and winched her down slowly, with a hand around her back.

She sat on the mat with a lovely smile as I released the ropes from the main line.

"I'm going to release your hands now. Wiggle your fingers for me."

As I began untying the knots, she flexed her hands. Her breathing was deep and slow, and tears rolled down her cheeks.

"He would be proud of you."

A sob hitched as the last rope fell away.

"Would you like me to hold you?" I asked.

"Y-yes," she choked out.

I gathered her up in my arms and brought her onto my lap. Her sobs racked her body, but this wasn't panic. It was grief – pure and unadulterated. Trying to calm the storm was pointless. You had to wait it out.

Gradually, she came back to herself and rubbed her drenched cheeks.

"Thank you for that." Her voice was croaky from tears. "You don't know what you've given me back."

"I'm glad I could help. Can you stand? I've got you a bottle of water and a glucose tablet."

She stretched her limbs and neck out as I helped her up. Though a little wobbly-legged, we made it to the couch. I gave her space to process, and we remained silent for some minutes.

"For a while, I was angry at him for dying. It was irrational, but when that passed, it was like life had lost its colour. I finally feel like the spring has arrived after a long winter. He would paddle my arse if he had seen me these past two years."

I chuckled.

"I'm so glad we did this."

"I'll help you find a rope top if you like?" I offered.

"You would?" She blinked red-ringed eyes up at me.

"I could ask around, and then we could set up a three-way video call. We'll chat with them and help you find a good fit."

"Thank you, that would be amazing. As much as I'd love to join here, the 350-mile round trip is inhibitory."

"That's fair enough. How are you feeling?"

"Achy, happy." She smiled.

"Would you like to go to your pod?"

"Yes, please."

I helped her up and watched for signs of shakiness, but she seemed steady. We walked down the corridor to her room. The pods were designed specifically for individuals to decompress after a scene or a night in the club. The elements in the room aided recovery from an intense session and enhanced feelings of safety. They were tiny boxrooms filled with soft furnishings, from hammocks to floor beds covered in cushions or giant bean bags. This one had a floor bed, and the material sashes created a low-ceilinged crawl space.

"Would you like me to stay?"

"I think I'd like to be alone."

Angie had already told me she often liked to recover alone in the quiet, which was why I suggested a pod.

"Of course. There's cream on the counter for any sore areas." I pointed to the bathroom door.

She settled herself onto a large cushion and sighed, relaxing into it. My chest filled with the satisfaction of seeing her previous tension wholly gone.

༺ ༻

Five ~ Angie

Part of my brain knew where I was, and as Gene said goodbye, I answered. The other part remained a million miles away, where it had retreated to a sheltered place. As I relaxed into the comfortable pillow mountain, my body almost felt like it remained swaying in the bindings, with my limbs tightly encased.

Gradually, those two realities merged, and the overwhelming urge to cry didn't hit me again. The crashing grief I experienced when Gene had released my binding did not reappear, and the sadness that had closed over my throat like an iron fist didn't either. The frustration that had warred inside me since I lost Miles seemed dull, and the absence of despair filled me with relief. It was a sweet balm as if the turbulent emotions had washed me clean.

I smoothed a hand over the silky pillowcase, feeling a lightness in my chest. The familiar soreness in my limbs, as if I'd done a heavy workout, filled me with gratitude for Gene. I would always miss Miles fiercely, but this session healed something deep inside me. It had allowed me to return to being myself.

Eventually, I padded to the small bathroom connected to the tiny plush space. The time read eight in the evening, and although the club provided food on request, I hadn't pre-ordered anything. I often couldn't eat much after an intense session, so I grabbed a protein bar from my bag. After munching on it, I changed into my pyjamas, brushed my teeth, and returned to the bed-of-fluff, which I'd named it in my head. I wasn't sure I would want to leave tomorrow.

A cathartic feeling of exhaustion swept over me, and I nestled down. A little zing of excitement flared at the thought of searching for a new rope top, knowing Gene would help me find someone. He really was the Desire Genie.

Afterword

Thank you for reading this short story. If you or anyone close to you has experienced grief and is struggling in the UK, the charity Cruse Bereavement Support offers counselling: https://www.cruse.org.uk

Acknowledgements

Thanks to my alpha readers, Nicole and Noor, and my sensitivity readers, Logan and Katie, who helped me keep the kink authentic. Shout out to TheDuchy, an excellent web-based and community resource for learning more about safe rope practice.

VARIOUS AUTHORS

My extra eyes, Monika. And to my editors, Katie of Spice Me Up Editing and Chloe of Chloe L Proofreader.

A Soul So Fierce and Furry by Chloë L. Blyth

A tale of new beginnings, fur in surprising places, and violent urges.
So many violent urges.

One

If actions speak louder than words, then you're screaming, and I'm deaf.

What are we even doing here? I came on this trip to reconnect, to rediscover the man I fell in love with all those years ago. Instead, all I've done is follow you around beautiful landscapes, watching as you leave me behind and take selfies for your followers. I don't belong here. With you, or in Scotland. Which isn't to say it isn't beautiful, you're both beautiful (I think you know that). But I don't like who I am when I'm with you.

I used to laugh you know, really laugh. Do you remember that? And when I fell, you would catch me. Literally. You would see the hazard before I did. Do you remember when I nearly killed myself trying to step out of that hotel bath? I was operating in blur-vision (no glasses) and completely mis-judged the height of the bath I needed to step out of. I would have faceplanted onto stone tiles if you hadn't caught me. Back then, you always caught me. Now, it's like you're waiting for me to fall and deliberately looking the other way.

I can't keep up with you on these hikes, I'm not a gym bunny like you. I prefer to stay at home and read or do paint-by-numbers. There's nothing more soothing to me than paint-by-numbers. Unless I run out of a particular colour. Gosh, those people in Customer Services probably see me a little differently to everyone else. Polite, people-pleasing, kind Lucy can get a little fiery over a lack of red paint. But seriously, do they not test the kits to ensure there's enough of each colour?

I suppose it's good for me to be out here in the fresh air, panting like a dog. I do need to exercise more. But you know what I'm like, I'm accident prone. I'm yet to find a hobby that doesn't result in bruises at the very least. I even hurt myself doing yoga. Yoga. Who the hell hurts themselves moving gracefully from position to position on a 24 by 68-inch mat? Me, that's who. And that's not even taking into account the internal damage I'm sure I caused myself by holding in wind for a full 60 minutes. They don't warn you about that, do they? I've never been so uncomfortable!

My quads are on fire, this walk is the steepest we've done on this trip by far. I'm sure the views will be worth it, and your followers will absolutely love your photos, but can't we slow down the pace? This isn't a timed event!

I shout in your general direction, but you don't even glance over your shoulder. Perhaps you can't hear me. Yeah, right. I pause beside a tree to catch my breath. We really need to talk. This isn't a couple's holiday, this is a 'you' holiday. I was a fool to think it would be any different. Our whole lives are 'the Scott show' now. You're desperate to be famous, transforming yourself into everything that's popular, and I'm in the background, clinging on to the person you used to be.

Tugging my socks up over my latest blister, I prepare to resume walking. Who knew walking in nature could stir up such strong emotions? It must be a side effect of the pain.

I usually push negativity aside and focus on the good points. *He took me out to dinner* I tell my colleagues, *it was lovely, that new place in town*. I don't mention that he was on his phone the entire time, frown lines deeper than potholes, and didn't even let me choose what I had to eat – because he needed to see what the crab linguine looked like, never mind that I'm the one who had to eat it. And I don't even like seafood. I was up at 1am searching the cupboards for a snack to stop my stomach rumbling until breakfast.

I need to get moving, I can't even see him anymore. I'd hate to get lost here, the trees are tall and uninviting, and the rushing River Affric only adds to my fears. Water is not my friend. But I'll get to that later.

I push myself away from the tree I'm leaning against and continue uphill, my legs complaining with each step. Why didn't he warn me that today's route would be this hard? He could have left me back at the hotel. He knows I'm not as fit as he is, he knows I'm inexperienced at hiking. Is this his way of making me lose a few pounds?

I focus on my breathing as I attempt to increase my pace. In for four, out for four. The ground is uneven with tree-roots creating trip hazards everywhere, but I've got this. I can do this. I am a strong, independent woman. I don't need a man to look after me. I can –

Oh shoot, I'm falling.

My feet come out from under me, and I throw my hands forwards as I fall towards the ground and close my eyes, bracing for impact. I expect to feel the harsh scrape of the ground beneath my palms but instead I feel fur, and I hear a yelp. My eyes open and I start to push myself up but before I can fully stand, I see two amber eyes looking back at me, I feel a sharp bite on my forearm, and I tumble back to the ground. A grey-haired wolf-cub runs away into the trees, away from the path. I sit and stare at my arm.

It hurts. Oh, it really hurts. There's blood, and teeth marks. Oh my God, I'm going to die!

"What's all the noise about, Luce?" Scott finally comes to see what's taking me so long. He looks angry, like I'm wasting his time over something trivial like a twisted ankle.

"It bit me! A little wolf bit me!" I wail, holding my arm out to him.

"Don't be absurd, there aren't any wild wolves in Scotland," he says as if I'm an idiot, not even bothering to look at the bitemark. There are teeth holes for God's sake, I've clearly been bitten!

"Well, what do you think it was then?" I ask, standing up. He shrugs, so I repeat. "It was a baby wolf, a wolf-cub if that's what they're called. I tripped over him, and he bit me!"

"That does sound like something you'd do. Are you okay to continue?" he asks, looking back up the path.

"Do I *look* like I'm okay to continue? I'm in *pain*, Scott! It hurts! Can't you put me in front of your Insta-goals for once in your life? Sacrifice the perfect photo for your girlfriend who has just been bitten by a wolf?" I snap, the pain clearly giving me a backbone.

"But we're so close to the top," he mumbles, avoiding eye contact.

"Scott, if you don't help me down this bloody hill and out of this godforsaken nature reserve and get me to a doctor, I'll... I'll..."

"You'll what?" he asks with a smirk.

"I don't know, but it'll be bad."

I never could threaten people properly.

Two

"You'll live," the doctor proclaims with a smile, having cleaned my wound thoroughly, closed the worst bits with sticky strips, wrapped it up, and given me an injection in case of rabies. "I'll prescribe you a course of antibiotics, just to be safe."

"Thank you. I can't believe there are wild wolves here!" I tell him, smiling with vindication. Apparently, the local council decided to release a pack of European grey wolves into the wild around Glen Affric in hopes of controlling the number of red deer.

"Well, they usually steer clear of humans. I suppose as you stumbled across a young one, perhaps he had lost the pack." I nod in agreement. Of course I'd be the one to stumble across a wolf, I could stumble across anything, even when paying my very best attention. "That said, I'm sure the council would appreciate it if you don't tell too many people about what happened. They faced a lot of opposition against re-introducing wolves into the eco-system. It would be a shame to have to remove them for such a silly incident."

"Oh, I was hoping to get a slot on morning TV," I joke. That would be my worst nightmare. The doctor chuckles, lines reaching from his eyes to the edge of his auburn hair.

"Well Lucy, it was lovely to meet you. I hope Scotland hasn't left too bad an impression on you and you'll come back again someday. But perhaps, stay out of the woods next time?" he steps towards the door, indicating it's time for me to leave. I push myself off the examination bed I've been sat on and immediately regret it as my right arm gives way through the pain. I grimace. "I would probably avoid putting any weight on it until it starts to heal, okay?"

I nod, pushing my lips together and fighting back tears.

I find Scott in the waiting room, flicking through an old edition of Muscle and Health magazine.

"All good?" he asks.

"Yeah, just need to pick up some antibiotics from the pharmacy to make sure it doesn't get infected." He rolls his eyes.

"Fine."

"You know this wouldn't have happened if you hadn't left me behind."

"Why, because I'm supposed to catch you every time you fall?" he asks snidely; I don't like his tone.

"Basically, yes. If you were walking with me, I wouldn't have been so out of breath, trying to push myself to keep up, that I tripped and fell onto a sleeping wolf!"

I enter the double doors to the pharmacy. Scott hates arguing in public.

"A baby wolf. It's a tiny bite. And you trip over everything!" he retorts quietly. I give my name, and the pharmacist asks me to wait to the side. "I bet it doesn't even hurt."

"Are you kidding me right now?"

"I'm just saying, if anyone was going to fall over a wolf, it'd be you."

"So that makes it okay then? Because the more you fall, the less it hurts? Because when your boyfriend invites you on a holiday to Scotland, you should expect to spend your time following him up and down footpaths out of breath and then eating dinner with zero conversation as he picks out the best photos to share online? It's funny because that isn't what I had in mind, but I don't know why I expected it to be any different."

"Oh, come on Lucy, don't be like that. You knew there'd be a lot of walking, I told you all the places I wanted to see."

"Right, and it always has to be about you, doesn't it? What about me? What about what I wanted to do? What about what I wanted from this trip?"

"What did you want, Luce? I don't know because you didn't tell me. You never tell me what you want, am I supposed to read your mind?"

"Oh, that's hilarious. Just because you're not around most of the time, and when you are you never listen because you're always on your phone, doesn't mean that I'm not talking. Just because you can't hear me!"

"So, tell me now then," Scott says, looking around to ensure we don't have an audience. "What do you want Lucy?"

"I want you! I want to go back to how things used to be, when you actually gave a crap about me. When you wanted to spend time with me, when you wanted to look after me. When you made me laugh. When I didn't cry myself to sleep in the dark." My eyes start to water.

"That's a low blow. You know I care about you."

"Do you?" I ask a little louder. "Because you don't act like it."

"And you don't cry yourself to sleep in the dark."

He narrows his eyes at me and mine instantly retract their tears in anger.

"How would you know, you're too busy snoring to notice!"

"Erm, Miss Bartlett?" the pharmacist calls. I hurry over. "I need to confirm your date of birth, first line of your address, and postcode." I tell him my details, accept the small paper bag, and walk out of the door without looking back to see if Scott is following.

How dare he? This is probably the most real conversation we've had in months, and it terrifies me. I'm hundreds of miles from home and I've been bitten by a wolf. What I need right now is a supportive boyfriend to look after me and make me feel better, not pull my heart out and stamp it into the mud. What am I going to do? Think, Lucy. Think! If this is it, what are you going to do? How are you going to get home, and where are you going to live? What if Scott refuses to move out?

"Lucy, wait!" he calls from behind. Why should I? He could catch up with me if he wanted to. Why should I stop? I've spent the last three days following him around. It's his turn, even if I don't have a clue where I'm going and my bite stings like someone's rubbing salt and vinegar crisps into it. He has no idea of the pain I'm in. I'd like to see him get bitten by a wolf and have to walk miles back to the car because his boyfriend wouldn't carry him! (Okay, I may have taken that a little far, but seriously, he could have carried me. I was in pain! What if I'd broken my leg? Would he have made me walk on that, too?)

"Stop walking away from me. We need to talk!"

I stop and turn around.

"No kidding."

"I'm sorry you're upset, I'm sorry this hasn't been the trip you were hoping for, but I had no idea you didn't want to go on all those walks with me. I thought you were enjoying it too!"

I frown at him.

"Really? Which part of me examining my blisters each night and sticking plasters all over my feet and ankles each morning made you think I was enjoying myself the most?" he doesn't answer. "Oh, that's right, you didn't know about that because you were at the gym. Or was it the sauna?"

"You know my fitness routine is important to me. I can't just stop for a week!"

"I used to be important to you too! And er, what about all the walking? Is that not exercise? Does that not count?"

"No, I need to do weights too. Weights are most important."

"Oh right, sure." I shake my head dismissively. I know I'm being a bitch, but it's about time. I've put up with this for years now. I've witnessed his transformation, both physically and mentally. He used to be slim, he used to have a softer belly, and smaller shoulders. He used to be *nice*.

"Stop it, Luce. Just stop it. Let's both calm down, go for a nice meal, and talk about this like adults."

"Sure, and what will I be having for your Insta-worthy dinner tonight?"

"Excuse me?"

"Where do you want to tag us? What's the latest trend we need to try?"

"I'm trying to be nice."

I reach out for his arm with my good hand, and look up into his eyes, "Oh my goodness, are you okay?" I ask, my voice dripping with sarcasm.

He grabs my hand and throws it away.

"I can't talk to you when you're being like this," he says, walking away. "You can find your own way back to the hotel."

Sure I can, I can find my own way back to England, too. I don't even need my passport. Just a set of wheels... and maybe a driver because my arm hurts way too much to steer and I'm not one of those people who can comfortably drive one-handed. I'm a two hands on the wheel kind of girl, not always 10 and 2, but always on the wheel.

Three

3 weeks later

Why is it that when you want someone to fight for you, they don't, but when you've given up and the ship has sailed, that's when you find a wet-faced mopey loser at your front door? And why do I always fall for the wet-eyed apology?

When he finally showed me emotion, when he showed me that he does want me in his life, that being without me makes him miserable, that's when I forgave him. Again. So now we're back home, and he's trying, in his way. Things haven't gone back the way they were before we went away and I discovered my backbone, we're better; we're on sort of good terms. I'm just a bit irritable, and it has a lot to do with the lack of caffeine in my system.

I do not know what is going on with me, but ever since I came back from Scotland, I haven't been able to stand coffee. But I usually need it to function, it's been the one stable thing in my life since I was a teenager. Two cups a day, minimum. The first within minutes of waking, and preferably with a good book. I take it black because I like to taste the bitterness as it powers me up for the day. For my second and any subsequent cups I'll add a little milk, but it's always dark and devilish.

I'm really good at my job, but I do believe that is partially due to my caffeine consumption. I am alert, on the ball. I do not drop the ball. I am on it like a car bonnet as they say. Do they say? I don't know, I haven't had my coffee! I thought caffeine was supposed to make you jittery, not withdrawal from it! The smell of coffee now makes me wince, and the taste is like sour milk. (Not that I've ever tried sour milk, the clue is usually the lump that plops out as you pour...)

"Aren't you going to kiss me goodbye?" asks Scott, dressed ready for work. He's an estate agent by day, so he's dressed in a suit and ready to say anything to get that commission. I look from him to his travel mug. I bet he's already sipped it.

I stand up to give him a quick peck and try not to react to the coffee taste. Once he's gone, I settle back into my armchair. I've got time to read another chapter or three before I need to get ready. I'm going in late today to make up for staying late at work last night. I'd rather be paid overtime, but beggars can't be choosers and all that.

I work for a magazine, it's a hybrid position. I get to write a few articles when my pitches are approved, I have an advertising goal to meet for each issue, and I help with literally everything. If we need to have a photoshoot, I'm the one booking the venue and calling the photographer. If we need NDA's, I'm sending them out. If it's someone's birthday and we need cake: me too. According to my job title, I'm a PA to the editor, but I don't think that paints a very accurate picture. I do a lot more than support Agatha Sparks (Aggy as I call her behind her back). She's a strong, opinionated businesswoman, and I live in her shadow making sure nothing goes wrong. We bonded over black coffee on the day of my interview, so now I'm the only one she trusts to make her a drink. Ordinarily, that would be great (an excuse to make myself one at the same time), but not anymore.

No, not anymore.

Arriving at work, I dump my bag at my desk and make my way to the kitchen.

"Are you feeling okay? You look a bit pale," says Hugo-not-the-boss, my colleague and part-time nemesis. He wishes he was Agatha's assistant, and he worships her like a goddess.

"I'm fine, thank you. Just a bit tired."

"Not making one for yourself?" he tilts his head in surprise as I retrieve only Agatha's special mug from the cupboard.

"No, not today, I'm, uh, cutting back on caffeine," I tell him. His eyes light up.

"You're not pregnant, are you? Oh my, is it morning sickness that's given you that deathly pallor?" he asks with glee. He would love me to take maternity leave and let him swoop in and steal my job.

"No," I say with a smile. "Still haven't changed my mind about kids, but thanks for your concern."

"Well in that case, you should probably see a doctor, because you're not looking so great. And cover your arm up, Agatha doesn't want to see... whatever that is," he wrinkles his nose at my wolf bite. I'll admit, it doesn't look great. But keeping it uncovered makes it easier for me to scratch. Which of course I know I shouldn't be doing but if you knew how blooming itchy that thing is, you'd do the same. It's like there are little bugs crawling under my skin.

I unroll my shirt sleeve and carry Agatha's coffee into her office, trying not to breathe.

"Nothing for you again, Lucy?" she observes.

"No, I'm having a bit of a cleanse," I reply weakly. Nobody is falling for my bullshit. The sooner I get back on the coffee wagon, the better. I'm making people nervous.

"Well, don't deprive yourself for too long, it's making you pale," she comments before signalling that I should take a seat. Great, she's got a 'project' for me today. I was hoping to just get on and sell ad space today. I'm really not feeling up for a challenge.

"You went to Scotland recently, yes?" I nod. "We need a story, something a little different, something to appeal to the younger readers. Something 'fun,'" she says the word with distaste.

"Okay." I wait for her to continue. I can write an article, but I'm not the best at 'fun' either. I might be fifteen years her junior, but that doesn't mean I'm 'hip and with the kids.' I like a book in bed much more than a nightclub and a hangover.

"We were thinking something along the lines of, 'what's under a Scot's kilt?' but, and here's the clever part, that can also be a pun, because your boyfriend is called Scott, correct? We just need a silly relationship piece aimed at twenty-somethings with some kind of connection to travel in Scotland and a theme of keeping the spark alive as you grow up together. It sounds perfect for you. You have been together for a few years now, correct?"

"Yes, five." I answer.

"So you'll do it? I need the article by Friday."

"Of course," I say, hiding my disappointment. An article about young love and growing up together? About traveling and keeping the spark alive? What do I know about any of those things? We broke up the last time we travelled, and our relationship is only just hanging on by a thread even now. In my experience, relationships are exhausting. But hell, I can pretend.

"That's all," she says, looking up meaningfully. I stand and hurry out of the door so fast, my arm hits the doorframe. Ow!

"So, I heard you get to write about your boyfriend, huh? Perks of being the editor's PA?" Briana (or 'Brian' as I like to call her in my head) nudges me in the corridor as I cradle my arm. She doesn't know about the bite, but seriously? Ouch.

"Yep," I say with a fake smile.

"Well, good luck!" she replies, equally fake, before strutting away in her heels.

She wants the article. She *always* wants the article. But the one thing I have that she doesn't, is a boyfriend, even if he is a shitty one. He is trying though, and he has been a lot better this time around. There haven't been any more 'crab linguine' type incidents. Then again, there haven't been many meals out at all... he's started eating with mates after the gym rather than with me. Which is fine, I guess. I didn't like waiting for him anyway.

Briana has been jealous of my relationship with Scott ever since they met at the work Christmas party two years ago. I saw the way she was looking at him, and I'm ashamed to admit, it made me act a little less 'nice' than usual. There may have been an accidental spillage on our table that caused her to go home early. But what can I say, accidents happen, and I'm particularly prone to them, as everyone knows.

I sit back down at my desk. Now I just need to come up with an article to appease my boss and fool my peers whom I am so unlike, it's almost criminal. How many twenty-five-year-olds do you know who paint by numbers on a Friday night whilst their partner is at the gym? It's a good job I can spin a good tale because I'm going to have to get creative with this one. Right after I find some paracetamol because my recurring headache is back. I suspect it's caused by the caffeine withdrawal, but who knows. I remove my glasses and rub the bridge of my nose and then my temples.

I never normally get headaches, and I've never gone off coffee before. I know I snapped at Hugo about not being pregnant, but I also couldn't stand the smell of cauliflower last night and whilst I know that's not a particularly pleasant smell anyway (a bit too much like farts), my reaction was extreme. I threw up in the bathroom and had to throw the cauliflower cheese away, all the way to the outside bin so I couldn't smell it anymore. And I love cauliflower cheese. I ended up eating sausages and microwave rice. Scott and I have been intimate, so maybe I should do a test, just to rule it out. I'm OCD about when I take my pills, but on the off chance the world is playing a cruel trick on me, I should probably find out before I drown my sorrows in pinot grigio. Or, maybe a baby would get us back on track. Ha.

If there's one thing I'm certain about right now, it's that I'm not ready to have children. I am quite happy not dealing with sleepless nights and crying babies and 'poonamis'! And older kids are just as bad, I barely made it through high school unscathed myself, I don't want to be guiding anyone through what they have to go through today. Never mind the homework. My home is where I relax and read and paint. There are no formulas or equations to solve, no –

"Samosa?" Hugo shoves a plate under my nose. "They're leftover from the Indian shoot. They're good!" I cover my nose and mouth with my hand and run towards the toilets.

Four

"Oh, thank goodness it's only you!" says Stacie as I hurry into a cubicle and throw up this morning's cereal. "Are you okay? Do you need me to hold your hair back?"

I return to the sinks and wash my face and rinse my mouth out.

"I've been better," I joke, finally looking at her before reaching for a paper towel. She looks terrible too; she's clearly been crying.

"Are you okay?" I return the question.

"I've been better," she laughs, wiping her eyes.

"Do you want to talk about it?"

"Do you?" she raises her eyebrows.

"What time do you finish?" I ask, looking around the room. It looks clean, apart from the vomit splatters I've most likely just left down the toilet I used.

"About two hours ago. I just can't bring myself to leave. It's... Oh, it's..." she hiccups and struggles to hold back tears. I reach out and put my arms around her.

"It's okay, I'll take an early lunch. Shall we go to the café and talk?"

She nods and allows me to guide her out of the room. I'll tidy her mop bucket away for her later.

TO BE CONTINUED...

I hope you enjoyed this exclusive extract from my new paranormal (werewolf) romance, due out in Autumn 2024.

David by Chris Turnbull

One

The Mediterranean Sea was tumultuous as I clung to my weathered suitcase on the small boat. The struggle to maintain balance intensified as the wooden deck grew slippery beneath me, buffeted by the rain and effortlessly tossed by the vast waves.

'Hold on tight,' urged one of the crew over the harsh wind. He, too, grappled with the challenge of staying upright as he moved towards the front of the boat.

The compact vessel teemed with individuals from various walks of life, spanning the elderly to young families. We all gathered closely, seeking refuge from the pouring rain and striving to stay warm amid the early spring downpour. Dawn gradually unfolded around us, revealing the dark waters through the persistent rain.

A petite horn atop the Captain's cabin sounded, prompting the assembled passengers to simultaneously look up. Land was finally discernible in the distance, and a palpable shift in atmosphere accompanied the collective smiles and tightened embraces.

As the boat accelerated towards the shore, the rain gradually relented. I strained to catch a glimpse of the eagerly anticipated shoreline, peering around a sizable man with the hope of witnessing the excitement that now animated everyone on board.

It was a cool spring morning when I arrived in Florence, weary from a lengthy journey. Though I hailed from this city, my early departure at the age of two left me with no recollections. Almost two decades later, with my mother no longer by my side, I felt compelled to return to the place of my birth and chase the aspirations that had lingered in my dreams.

Before me, Florence unfolded like a captivating mosaic, adorned with red-tiled roofs and sunlit buildings, teeming with life, culture, and promise. As I navigated the lively streets, a mix of excitement and apprehension pulsed through my heart. A stranger in a foreign land, the weight of the unknown pressed down on me.

In an almost trance state, I wandered through the streets, marvelling at the artistic wonders that surrounded me. The cobblestone pathways resonated with the footsteps of merchants, artists, and aristocrats, all seemingly breathing in the essence of art and inspiration. Florence, a city where dreams took flight, talent was revered, and the very streets embodied a living canvas.

I had set out on a perilous quest for work, driven by the tales of opportunities in this magnificent city. The idea of an apprenticeship, the age-old tradition where a young aspirant could learn the craft from a master, had taken root in my mind. I yearned to become a skilled artist, to breathe life into my artistic aspirations, and to escape the mundanity of rural life. My mother had always disapproved of my desire to follow the artistic lifestyle, and instead pushed me towards a more solid profession, but now she is gone it is time to for fill my own dreams.

With no money after the boat fare, I spent my initial nights sleeping rough, urgently seeking work.

During my brief stay I couldn't help but notice a buzz of excitement surrounding a particular young artist in his twenties. His name was uttered with reverence on every street corner, his work praised as if divine. My curiosity led me to investigate further.

Rumours guided me to a modest workshop tucked away in a quiet alley. The entrance, unassuming and almost hidden, opened to the intoxicating scent of fresh clay and the rhythmic chiselling of stone. The space served as an art sanctuary, with dust-covered sculptures bearing witness to the craftsman's mastery.

In the heart of the workshop, the artist, hands strong and skilled, moulded clay into a figure brimming with life. His deep, contemplative eyes and wise lines on his face bespoke a creativity beyond his years. His captivating aura held me in thrall as I entered.

He glanced up, meeting my eyes with a keen, appraising gaze. 'Who are you, and what brings you here?' he inquired, his voice carrying the weight of authority.

Swallowing hard, I mustered the words, 'My name is Lorenzo, a newcomer to Florence seeking work. I've heard of your talent and come to inquire if you are taking on an apprentice?'

The artist regarded me thoughtfully as he walked towards me, as if assessing the raw material from which a masterpiece might emerge. 'Lorenzo, you say?' he mused. 'Well, young man, my name is Michelangelo.' He paused for a moment as he looked me up and down with curiosity. 'My last assistant left a couple of months ago. An apprentice you wish to be? Let's start with assistant for now, and if you prove capable, we can discuss that apprenticeship.'

Two

In the days that followed my first meeting with Michelangelo, I became a frequent visitor to the small workshop tucked away in the heart of Florence. Every morning, I arrived with a heart filled with both anticipation and trepidation, ready to immerse myself in the world of art that Michelangelo had so graciously opened up to me.

As the sun cast its golden glow across the city, Michelangelo would already be at work, his hands caressing the rough surface of a stone sculpture. He greeted me with a nod, his dedication to his craft evident in the intensity with which he carved and chiselled. I would watch in awe as he coaxed life from the unyielding marble, his every movement a testament to his mastery.

'Come, Lorenzo,' he beckoned one morning. 'I see that you are eager to learn. I shall teach you the art of sculpting.' His voice was soft but carried a sense of authority that compelled me to listen closely.

With an eagerness born of genuine passion, I joined him at the sculpting table. He showed me how to hold the chisel and mallet, guiding my hands as I tentatively struck the stone. I could feel the vibrations travel up my arms and into my core, as if I were connecting with the very essence of the material. Michelangelo's touch was gentle yet firm, a paradox that mirrored his character.

In the afternoon, he generously provided me with marble offcuts and granted permission to practice shaping them. Additionally, he lent me some of his old tools for the task. While I recognized that I was far from achieving the elegance he effortlessly displayed, the straightforward assignment infused me with a remarkable adrenaline rush.

As the days turned into weeks, Michelangelo and I got to know each other better. He shared stories of his youth, his struggles, and his relentless pursuit of perfection. He was a man of few words, but when he spoke, it was with a deep sense of purpose.

One afternoon, after a gruelling session of carving, Michelangelo wiped the sweat from his brow and looked at me with a glint of mischief in his eyes. 'I think it's time I show you the rest of this place," he said. "There is more to learn about art than just what happens in the studio.'

We climbed a narrow, creaking staircase that led to a modest apartment just above the workshop. Michelangelo pushed open the door, revealing a cosy living space filled with books, paintings, and sculptures. It was a sanctuary of creativity, a place where the art extended beyond the studio walls.

'This is where I sketch my inspirations,' he explained, gesturing to the paintings and drawings that adorned the walls. 'Here, I study the human form, anatomy, and the works of great masters. It is essential for an artist to understand the world, both within and without.'

I nodded in agreement, taking in the wealth of knowledge and inspiration that surrounded us. It was a privilege to be welcomed into this inner sanctum of art.

As our tour continued, Michelangelo led me down a narrow corridor and stopped in front of a small, unassuming door. He pushed it open to reveal a compact room with a single window that allowed a shaft of sunlight to pierce the shadows. 'This, Lorenzo, will be your space. A humble abode, but it is here that you will rest, dream, and absorb the art that we create together. Should you work late, you are welcome to stay here instead of travelling through the city in the dead of night.'

My heart swelled with gratitude, and I couldn't help but feel a profound sense of belonging. 'Thank you, Maestro,' I whispered, overwhelmed by the generosity and trust he had bestowed upon me. It was at that moment that I confessed to him my living arrangements. I had not yet found a place to live in these weeks, and had been sleeping by the river, just a short walk away.

With a nod and a small smile, Michelangelo told me that the room was mine. He didn't seem surprised by my revelation of being homeless.

Spring and summer passed by so quickly that I can hardly remember it at all. I just remember the heat in the studio being unbearable on those particularly blistering days.

Three

The arrival of winter brought a different kind of magic to Michelangelo's studio. While the chill gripped Florence and the city wrapped itself in a quiet blanket of snow, the artistic flames within our small enclave burned brighter than ever. It was during those cold months that I delved into the world of drawing and painting, my hands trading the chisel and mallet for brushes and pencils.

Under Michelangelo's guidance, I began to discover the power of lines and shadows, of capturing life on a canvas. He patiently taught me the intricacies of sketching, emphasizing the importance of observing the world around us. Our mornings were dedicated to sketching studies of the human form, practicing anatomy and proportion, while the afternoons were reserved for painting, as we explored the nuances of colour, light, and shadow.

With every stroke of the brush, Michelangelo's wisdom infused my work. He was a demanding teacher, never satisfied with mediocrity, and his exacting standards pushed me to the limits of my abilities. Yet, each critique and correction served as a stepping stone towards mastery.

As the days grew longer and the promise of spring whispered in the air, Michelangelo unveiled his plan for the upcoming season. 'Lorenzo,' he said, his eyes bright with excitement, 'I have been invited to showcase my sculptures and paintings in an art exhibition that will gather the finest artists of Florence. It is an opportunity to display our talents, and I intend to make a mark.'

His words ignited a fire of anticipation in me. To contribute to the preparations for such a prestigious event was a privilege beyond measure. Michelangelo's determination was unwavering, and he expected nothing less than perfection from each of his creations.

We spent weeks perfecting his sculptures, making every chisel mark count. The marble dust filled the air like a fine mist, and the sculptures themselves seemed to come to life under our touch.

The paintings, too, demanded our attention. We chose the most vibrant pigments and delved into the world of chiaroscuro, seeking to capture the essence of life on canvas. Each brushstroke was a testament to the passion and vision of our master.

As the days melted into weeks and the colours of spring began to bloom, Michelangelo and I toiled tirelessly, driven by a shared commitment to excellence. The studio became a whirlwind of creativity, with the anticipation of the art show hanging over us like a tapestry of destiny.

'Lorenzo I want you to choose one of your own paintings for the show. Your art is coming on spectacularly and people deserve to see it.' I could find the words to thank him enough. Having one of my pieces shown was such an honour, I would have to work even harder to make sure I had something suitable.

The winter had transformed me from a wide-eyed novice into an artist in my own right, and I was grateful for Michelangelo's patient mentorship. With every stroke of the brush, every touch of the chisel, I felt a deeper connection to my Maestro and to the world of art that had become my home. As the spring exhibition approached, I couldn't help but wonder how our art would be received, especially the piece with only my name upon it.

Four

VARIOUS AUTHORS

The evening of the art show arrived, and the atmosphere in Florence was charged with anticipation. The exhibition was to be held in a grand gallery, where artists from all corners of the city had gathered to display their works. The name on everyone's lips was Michelangelo, and the weight of expectation seemed to hang in the air as we made our way into the event.

Michelangelo's creations were displayed with an aura of reverence, commanding the attention of all who entered the gallery. The sculptures, the paintings, each piece seemed to exude life, embodying the very essence of art itself. The room buzzed with admiration, and the visitors spoke in hushed tones, their voices filled with awe.

As we stood together, watching the crowd's reaction, Michelangelo's eyes glimmered with pride. He had every reason to be proud, for his work had left an indelible mark on all those in attendance. Although other artists were being featured at the event, it was clear that Michelangelo had been given the largest of the rooms.

My own painting, which was hung in the gallery just before that of Michelangelo's, was a painting of my employer himself. I had captured him working on a small sculpture, surrounded by many more in his workshop. Even now, looking at the paining I could smell the dusty sweaty workspace.

The highlight of the evening came when a group of influential city officials approached Michelangelo, their faces lit with admiration. They spoke of a grand project, a vision to honour Florence with a statue that would grace the city square for all to see. They proposed that Michelangelo be the one to create this masterpiece. It was an offer that left him visibly overwhelmed.

I was stood beside Michelangelo as he accepted the offer, his mind racing with plans for the project evident in his eyes. The news of this offer quick spread around the gallery, and the whispers grew louder, their voices filled with respect and reverence for the artist who had been chosen for such a prestigious task.

As the evening continued and the celebratory atmosphere grew, we found ourselves drawn into the merriment of the occasion. We shared laughter, wine, and the camaraderie of fellow artists, celebrating

Michelangelo's well-deserved triumph. In the midst of the revelry, a spark of connection blossomed between us, a connection that had been growing silently but steadily.

As the night wore on and the wine flowed more freely, I could see the hesitant barriers that Michelangelo would often hide behind, began to soften. It was late when we finally left the celebrations, walking home together through the dark streets.

I don't recall what we talked about on the walk home, but it was clear how happy he was with the evening. Arriving back, I had not realised the barriers between Michelangelo and myself beginning to blur. In a moment of shared elation, a celebratory kiss was exchanged, a fleeting connection between two souls who had become entwined in the tapestry of art, friendship, and something deeper.

The kiss hung in the air, a silent acknowledgment of a bond that defied definition. Our gazes locked for a moment, and then, with a mixture of emotions, we retreated to our separate bedrooms, leaving the night's revelations to linger in the quiet darkness.

Five

The following morning, I stepped into the studio, anticipating a certain tension after the unexpected kiss. However, as I entered, Michelangelo was already engrossed in his work, barely lifting his gaze from the marble as I entered the workshop. The awkwardness I feared hung in the air, and I grappled with whether I should address it or let the incident fade into the background. The apprenticeship I had longed for was everything to me, and I couldn't help but worry if that moment of impulsiveness had jeopardized it.

Throughout the morning, we worked side by side in silence. Questions and uncertainties swirled in my mind. Was I expected to say something, or should I pretend as though the kiss had never occurred? The weight of uncertainty clung to me, and I wondered if our professional relationship could withstand the unexpected intimacy.

By the afternoon, however, the atmosphere shifted, and conversation flowed as naturally as before. Michelangelo made no mention of the kiss, and the routine of our work settled back into its familiar rhythm. A part of me felt a twinge of disappointment that the incident wasn't acknowledged, but the importance of my apprenticeship took precedence.

It wasn't until Michelangelo's stern voice broke the comfortable silence that I realized the gravity of his next artistic endeavour. 'Lorenzo,' he began, 'I've been contemplating the creation of the sculpture for the city. Before any work on marble can begin, I will need to spend time sketching the male form and conceptualizing the final sculpture.'

Intrigued by his passion, I listened intently, eager to contribute. 'How can I assist?' I asked.

Michelangelo paced the room, his mind abuzz with ideas. 'I require a model,' he explained, 'someone whose physique embodies the essence of strength, grace, and perfection. I need a living, breathing representation to guide my hands in shaping David with unparalleled detail.'

The weight of Michelangelo's request settled upon me. After a brief moment of contemplation, I offered myself as a temporary solution. 'If it would aid your vision, I would be pleased to help. While I may not possess the idealized physique, I'm willing to lend myself for the lesser sketches, perhaps for the hands, until we can find somebody perfect.'

A contemplative silence filled the room as Michelangelo studied my earnest expression. A faint smile played on his lips. 'Lorenzo, your willingness to contribute to the creative process is commendable. If you are comfortable with the idea, I would appreciate having you as the model for the time being.'

I nodded, a mixture of excitement and nervousness coursing through me. 'It would be an honour, maestro.'

'Well I suppose there's no time like the present.'

Anticipation coursed through me as I followed him to a corner of the studio where a small table was set with parchment, quills, and ink. The air seemed charged with creative energy as Michelangelo carefully prepared his tools.

'Your hands,' he remarked, looking at me with a discerning gaze, 'they possess a certain character and strength that I believe will convey the essence I seek for David's hands.'

The scratching of the quill against parchment echoed through the studio, and I marvelled at Michelangelo's ability to transform simple lines into a three dimensional sketch of my own hands. His eyes, filled with an artist's focus, never wavered from the task at hand. It was as if the world around us faded away, leaving only the dance between the artist and his subject.

As Michelangelo completed the sketch, he stepped back to admire his work. A satisfied smile played on his lips, and he looked at me with gratitude. 'Lorenzo, you have lent your hands to the birth of David, and for that, I am grateful. This is just the beginning of the journey in bringing this chef-d'oeuvre to life.'

Six

In the days that followed our initial sketching of my hand, our collaboration deepened and expanded. Michelangelo's desire for perfection, his relentless pursuit of capturing the essence of the human form, led us to embark on a series of sittings. Each session focused on a different aspect of the human body.

The quiet of the studio became our sanctuary, a place where time seemed to stand still, and the world outside faded into insignificance. In this cocoon of creativity, we explored the subtleties and intricacies of my body. Every session was a journey of trust and discovery, a shared venture that felt like a secret we alone held.

He moved onto sketching my feet, Michelangelo's hands gently cradling each one as he sketched the curves of my arches and the graceful lines of my toes. With each touch of his pencil, I could feel a subtle connection forming, an intimacy that went beyond the ordinary boundaries of friendship.

The ears followed, with Michelangelo's eyes studying the delicate contours and the intricate folds. He rendered every detail with a precision that mirrored the dedication he had for his sculptures. I could feel his breath against my face as he memorized the details of my ear.

The sketches of my eyes were perhaps the most revealing of all. As Michelangelo focused on them, I felt his gaze pierce through the windows to my soul. His eyes met mine with a depth of understanding and connection that transcended words. It was as though, through the art, he was exploring the very core of my being.

Finally, the sittings for my mouth were a testament to the sensuality and desire that had quietly simmered between us. As his pencil traced the contours of my lips, the memory of our shared kiss hung in the air, a reminder of a connection that had never truly faded.

The sketches were completed with meticulous care, and Michelangelo's eyes lingered on his work, as though he was committing it to memory. With a soft exhale, he finally broke the silence. 'Lorenzo,' he whispered, his voice trembling with a mixture of vulnerability and longing, 'you are a work of art in your own right.'

I remained silent, taken aback by this unexpected compliment. Michelangelo didn't wait for a response; instead, he gently placed down his sketchbook and ascended to bed for the evening.

Seven

The sketches of my features had become my favourite part of the day. It had now been weeks since my first sitting, and I confess I had yet to even begin looking for a model to take over. He must have known this, yet he never once asked me to get on with it.

As our collaboration continued, it was only a matter of time before we arrived at the most intimate subject matter of all—the sketching of my torso. The anticipation of the session had been building within me, a mixture of excitement and trepidation.

The day of the sitting arrived, and as I disrobed and took my position, the atmosphere in the studio grew charged with a palpable intensity. The afternoon sun filtered through the window, casting a warm, honeyed light upon my bare skin. Michelangelo's eyes were upon me; a gaze I couldn't read.

As he sketched, I could feel his intense scrutiny, his pencil capturing the contours of my chest and abdomen. His hands moved with a slow and deliberate grace, tracing every line and curve with a precision that mirrored the dedication he had for his sculpting. The intensity of his focus seemed to draw me in, like a moth to a flame.

And then it happened. In the midst of the sketch, as Michelangelo worked to perfect the lines of my torso, his hand left the canvas and found its place on my chest. The touch was electric, igniting a fire of desire that had been simmering within me for far too long. I looked into his eyes, and the unspoken longing that had bound us seemed to demand action.

In that moment, we kissed—passionately, desperately, as though it were the culmination of every unspoken desire and longing we had ever felt. The studio seemed to dissolve around us, and all that existed was the warmth of our embrace, the taste of his lips on mine, and the feeling of his hands on my body.

The world spun with a dizzying intensity, and time seemed to blur as we lost ourselves in the depths of our desire. It was a moment of surrender, an acknowledgment of a connection that could no longer be denied.

When I awoke the next morning, I found myself in Michelangelo's bed. The memories of the night before flooded back, and I felt a mixture of anxiety and anticipation. I turned to face him, but he was not in the bed next to me. I looked around to see him sitting on a stool in the corner of the room, a sketchpad in his hands. He had been drawing me, laid there naked on his bed. He gave a gentle smile in acknowledgement, before continuing with his drawing. He must have been there a while as he had sketched the whole of me and the bed in considerable detail.

To my relief, Michelangelo did not act weird about our shared intimacy. He looked at me with a mixture of affection and understanding, as though he had finally come to terms with his own desires and longings.

My apprenticeship continued, as did our collaboration of sketches.

Eight

Two years had passed since that fateful day when Michelangelo and I had first crossed the boundary from mentorship and friendship into an intimate and passionate relationship. During that time, our connection had deepened in ways I could have never imagined. Our love was a secret that only a select few knew, hidden beneath the surface of our shared world of art.

Our intimacy had become woven into the fabric of our creative collaboration. As we worked on numerous paintings, sculptures, and art exhibitions together, our passion for one another fuelled our artistic pursuits. The studio had transformed into a place where our desires and creativity flowed freely, each project a reflection of the love we shared.

One of the most significant undertakings during those two years was Michelangelo's grand sculpture for the Florence square. The project had begun to take shape, the colossal block of marble had finally arrived and his attention was now completely fixed on it every day.

Despite my own artistic pursuits, I frequently found myself mesmerized, observing Michelangelo at work on the massive marble. After many weeks, the form had yet to resemble a person, and I understood that his pursuit of perfection would see him toiling over this colossal piece for years to come. The sculpture demanded his unwavering dedication, and the weight of his artistic legacy pressed heavily upon him.

The day arrived when I had to bid farewell. My apprenticeship had reached its conclusion, and the time had come for me to venture out on my own. Michelangelo had been immersed in the marble for approximately six months, and it still bore only a vague semblance to a person. Recognizing that he needed the space to complete his magnum opus and that I needed to explore new artistic horizons, the parting was inevitable.

We both knew that the day of my departure would eventually arrive, but neither of us anticipated it so soon. The farewell proved more challenging than either of us could have imagined. The final kiss he bestowed upon me seemed to carry a weight that would endure for eternity.

Though I left behind much of my artwork, some of which I had managed to sell in the square to help fund my journey, there was one piece

I couldn't bear to part with. It was the very first painting I created of Michelangelo, capturing him sculpting shirtless in his studio—the same piece I had proudly displayed during that initial show I attended.

❦

Nine

Ten years soon passed since that bittersweet day when I had left Florence. I had watched the city disappear into the horizon, knowing that the love we had shared would forever be a part of my heart.

Over those years, I ventured far and wide, refining my artistic skills and exploring realms beyond Florence. Despite the physical separation, my connection with Michelangelo remained an unwavering wellspring of inspiration. His mentorship, influence, and the tender intimacy we once shared had etched an enduring mark on the canvas of my life.

The longing to see the completed statue of David, had never waned. I yearned to behold the sculpture that had been the labour of Michelangelo's passion for so long, knowing that I had played such a small role in its creation. With anticipation weighing heavily on my heart, I returned to Florence, the city where our artistic journey had commenced.

Approaching the square, the imposing figure of David came into view. I was speechless by the sheer scale of it. Bathed in the golden embrace of sunlight, the marble statue stood as a testament to Michelangelo's genius. The precision in the proportions, the fluid lines, and the purpose evident in the sculpted figure left me breathless.

However, it was when my gaze met the eyes of the statue that I was truly moved. There, in the gaze of David, I saw a reflection of myself, a resemblance that left me jaw hanging in disbelief. The eyes seemed to hold my gaze, an unspoken connection that transcended the boundaries of time and space. It was then I realised much more the of statue resembled me, from the ears, mouth, hands and even feet. True it was not a statue of me, but he had clearly used the sketches as his inspiration on some of the finer details.

It felt as though Michelangelo had not only captured the physical form but also the essence of our intimacy. The statue became a celebration of the male form—my form—a lasting testament to the love, intimacy, and shared passion that once bound us.

My brief return to Florence stirred memories of the artist who had indelibly shaped my life. I longed to see Michelangelo once more, to hear his voice, to tell him how much I adored his statue, but it was not to be. Learning he was in Rome on a commission, dashed my hopes of a reunion during my visit. Our paths did not cross, leaving me with the bittersweet yearning for what could have been.

I spent only a week in Florence, and each day I visited David. Reflecting on the memories from the studio where it was crafted brought a smile to my face daily. On my last morning in the city, I made a point to pay one last visit. With a lingering gaze at the sculpture, I quietly expressed my gratitude to Michelangelo, the master artist who had not only fashioned a masterpiece but also etched an enduring chapter into the story of my life.

The End

Here There Be Tygers by Clare London

The three of us ran for the huge, glass-windowed Palm House like scampering squirrels, as the wind and the rain whipped up speed at our heels. One skinny twenty-five-year-old with curly auburn hair that frizzed in the wet, who wished he'd worn his raincoat instead of being too vain to wear anything heavier than his new spring jacket, plus two shrieking, giggling, six-year-old twins. The gravel path cutting across Kew Gardens' lawn scrunched and squelched beneath the kids' Wellington boots, and the scattered leaves threatened to send me arse over tit if I took a careless step, but I hurried us all along. The storm clouds had appeared from almost nowhere on what had been a lovely, bright February day—that's the volatility of the English weather for you—and we were making a dash for the nearest cover.

"Uncky Dunk!" Emma blinked hard against the rain, gasping my nickname in her soft little voice, and hanging tightly onto my hand. "Are there tigers inside?"

"No way, Em, don't panic. Sid, come back here!"

I was simultaneously keeping her balanced while I watched out for her twin, leaping over puddles with the triumphant cry of an Olympic high jumper, although his feet slipped in and out of his hand-me-down wellies. His rain-hood had fallen back onto his shoulders, and his messy fair hair was turning dark with the rain.

My sister Cathy, their mum, was gonna kill me if they came down with a cold, just as she went into the last weeks of her current pregnancy.

"Here we are, kids." I hustled them up to the door of the oversized greenhouse, with Sid shaking his head like a dog come out of the sea, showering our coats.

"Uncky Dunk, I'm drowned-ing!" Emma snorted a trail of raindrops off the end of her little red nose, and when Sid stuck his tongue out at her, we all started giggling. But I closed the door behind us with relief.

The indoor temperature was much warmer, and the huge palms and grasses loomed all around, swamping us in a world of rich, green foliage. I gazed at the twins' bright eyes and damp cheeks as they hopped from one foot to the other, wide-eyed at the new place I'd brought them to.

"Jungle!" Sid cried.

"You said, no tigers." Emma frowned, her hand tightening again on mine.

"Giant ones, gonna eat us up!" Sid yelled louder, while even Emma's little wail rose to a shriek, making me wince.

"No tigers here, we're still in London." I made shushing motions at Sid which, of course, he ignored. Half of me wondered why I'd never brought them here before, while the other half wondered if it wasn't the daftest bloody decision I'd made this century. Sid was already straining to get out of my grip and climb up on the benching that ran along the path. "Em, these are just some of the plants you'd see in a jungle. It's like we can move around the world, but all in one room."

"No aeroplane?" Emma said softly.

I smiled at her. "No, we stay right here. What do you want to see first?"

"All of it," she breathed.

The twins were so dear to me, even at their most mischievous. Now we were out of the wind and the wet, I was thrilled with joining in their games. It was way too easy when you got to adulthood to find discomfort and frustration in everything, rather than fun.

I'd been pretty miserable since Eddy dumped me at Christmas for a perky elf—not a real one, of course, just a bossy little twink in a green costume at a themed bar, while I was marking classwork from my primary school pupils, and Eddy obviously didn't even consider waiting in with me which, to be honest, had been the case for months, way before Christmas... anyway, that was all over now. I wasn't going to get distracted by regrets or what-ifs. *No more moping!* I'd announced this morning to Cathy, who'd waddled over to hug me. She'd never liked Eddy—and had said so, a couple of times or hundreds more—and she'd always been fond of *I told you so*. I was relieved the pregnancy stopped her poking me in the ribs like she used to when we were kids.

And, of course, there was nothing like a couple of lively kids to help you get over yourself. How could you dwell on a crappy ex-boyfriend, the cost-of-living crisis, and the looming spectre of two more bags-full of holiday marking, when you had the company of delightful little—

"That tree did a wee on me," Sid announced, fiercely rubbing the top of his head.

I bit back a sigh. "It's only moisture from the leaves. They need to keep the temperature humid for the plants to feel at home."

Emma was tugging on my hand so I brushed off Sid's head—pretending I felt the massive bucketful of water he claimed had dropped on him—and turned them both towards the 'Americas' area. The Palm House wasn't very full; I suspected most of the visitors had taken refuge from the sudden downpour in the cosy café. Unfortunately, we'd been too far away from there, and the Palm House was nearer.

Shame, because I could have murdered a slice of cake and a mug of thick, hot chocolate.

The path took a circular and cross route around the greenhouse, and we set off clockwise. I could hear the murmur of voices on the parallel side of the loop, and the tap and shuffle of feet, so I knew there were other visitors here, but I couldn't see anyone in particular through the undergrowth. Trunks were thick and tall, and the palm fronds swung out over our heads, as the rain beat outside at the arched windows.

"One of the palms broke through the roof a few years ago," I said. I'd opened my phone to find facts the twins would enjoy best. Cathy would tease me I never left off my teaching hat, but there were always new and exciting things to learn.

"Did they chop it down?" Sid huffed and mimicked hefting a huge axe.

I laughed. "Yes, I think so. But there are plenty of other ones left. Shall we try and guess how high some of them go?" Cathy had looked so grateful when I offered to take the twins out for the day, I was determined they'd have a good time. "If we go farther up here, we can see the oldest pot plant in the world!"

"How old?" Sid asked, pedantic angel that he was.

"Older than Dad?" Emma asked innocently.

To my surprise, I thought I heard a chuckle. I glanced around quickly, while also yanking Sid away from climbing on the nearest exposed roots, but I couldn't see anyone nearby.

"Bananas!" Sid grumbled. "I wanna get to the bananas!"

"They're not for us to eat, Sid, they're for research purposes."

His little arm shot out in a triumphant point. "Reeeeaaallly? Even those—?"

"—yes, *really*, especially not the pink hairy ones," I said, as firmly as I could.

This time I definitely heard another chuckle. I looked around again, but all I could see were palm fronds, twisted brown trunks, and a mass of shiny, leafy vines. We hadn't moved far from the entrance, and I watched as another couple of visitors ducked in, laughing and shaking rain off their umbrellas. But there was no one else on our path.

When the trees rustled on the other side of the foliage, I peered through the thick leaves. Was that a person striding past? The glimpse of a bearded face between two massive bamboo shoots? Heavy boots on the other path? The laugh had sounded male and had a very nice tone to it. It raised goose bumps on my arms and stirred a warm feeling in my gut that had nothing to do with the temperature. It sounded friendly, not scornful. Deep. *Sexy*.

Looked like my melodrama was running away with me! And, of course, the chuckle wasn't in response to anything we'd said—the timing was coincidence. *Right*. It had been a trick of the acoustics in here...

"Tiger in the bushes!" crowed Sid from somewhere behind me. He'd slipped my grip and clambered back up on the seating that ran around the planted areas.

Emma was trying to climb up after him, but she wasn't as agile. "It's gonna eeeeat meeeee!" she wailed. How did she manage to make such short words four syllables long?

I grabbed one twin with each hand and pulled them back onto the path. "I told you, there are no tigers," I said sternly. "Maybe the occasional lizard, but you like those, don't you? And there are birds—"

"Birds?" Both little heads dropped back to gaze eagerly at the ceiling.

Trying not to laugh, I took a calming breath. "Listen, you two. I need better behaviour from you, or we'll have to leave. Do you hear me? No shouting, no touching the plants, no climbing. Do I have your promises?"

Sid scowled. Em offered a ridiculously innocent gaze. I continued to look stern.

"Yes, Uncky Dunk," they chorused at last.

"And no running off," I suddenly thought to add.

"Not even from the tiger?" Emma said.

"It's prob'ly a friendly one." Sid shrugged, careless.

"How many times?" I tried to keep my calm. "There are no—"

"There!" she insisted, pointing past me. "Tiger stripes!"

I looked back and, for a moment, I saw a flash of orange and black passing through the bamboo stalks, a shockingly bright contrast among the mottled undergrowth. Not a tiger—of course it wasn't, I mean, in Kew Gardens?—instead, it looked like a tall, well-built man in a brightly-striped hiking jacket on the opposite path.

"It's just another visitor, Em," I said. "A person, not an animal."

As I stared, the jacket snuck in and out of view like a zoetrope, one of those slotted devices you wind up, and the whizzing slots make static photos look like they're moving. Though this man *was* moving, he was real, he wasn't a picture. Broad shoulders, firm stride. My heart started beating faster for some unknown reason. It was like the excitement of following the sunset through the window of a fast-moving car, but the high hedges kept obscuring the view...

Don't be daft, Duncan! Why was I still obsessing on those previous chuckles?

And then the man moved completely out of view and there was no more orange-and-black to be seen.

I felt strangely, deeply, disappointed.

We meandered along the path, visiting the Asian and African areas. The twins were still lively but not as unruly now, more used to the unusual sights and sounds. We made "oooh" noises at the huge arches that braced the greenhouse, and took lots of photos of the ancient pot plant—I must remember to tell Nathan his kids thought he was born in the 1770s—and all the bananas for Sid to show his schoolmates.

"And the plant like a pineapple!"

"And the rubbery ones!"

They kept me busy. Outside, the rain was easing off, but the kids were happy to keep going around. I was eager too—and not because of the bananas.

The mystery jacket was really tantalising. We never seemed to catch up with the wearer. Among all the rich natural colours, the striped fabric flashed in and out of view, like Emma's imaginary tiger, stalking the jungle. How daft was that thought? But I couldn't stop watching for another sighting.

A couple of times, I caught a glimpse of his face. Not the whole of it, but enough to see bright, brown eyes. I was convinced by now he was the chuckler. The hiking gear made him look a real outdoors-man. Maybe he was a famous producer, scoping a location for a new action movie. Or a famous explorer, doing research on his next expedition to a land where these plants were indigenous.

Melodrama, Duncan! But even if he wasn't famous, I was intrigued.

Just once, I could have sworn he caught my gaze in return. Deliberately, I mean. There was a brief gap in the cocoa palms, while Emma sat for a while to get her breath back, and Sid did a weird ballet dance around a pile of fallen leaves. The man paused, his face in full view. He looked several years older than me, with tanned skin, a smart beard, and a generous mouth. It opened, as if he was about to speak. But then

Sid grabbed my hand to come and see the purple plants growing up a crooked tree.

When I had a chance to look back, the mystery man had moved on again.

Funny thing, though... he wasn't walking at his own pace anymore. Instead, he kept up with ours, moving in the same direction. He was probably getting plenty of opportunity to read all the explanatory notices, because he didn't have two lively kids who were starting to get fractious now and were trying to push each other up against the low-hanging bamboo tree fans so the raindrops dribbled down the other's neck—anyway, he wasn't *following* us. I was getting fanciful again.

Maybe not, said my quick-beating heart.

When Emma started to whimper a little, I sat us down on the benching and unwrapped the emergency sandwiches Cathy had insisted I take with us.

"Didn't Eddy want to come today?" Sid asked.

I tried not to roll my eyes. "It's nothing personal, chum. Eddy and I... we're not boyfriends anymore."

"Mum'll be pleased," Sid muttered in that not-properly-secretive way that small children have.

"What?" I frowned.

"Dad said he'd block his knock off," Emma murmured.

"Knock his block off," I corrected instinctively.

"—if he messed you about anymore."

Oh. I was torn between gratitude that my family had my back, and dejection about my woeful love life.

"You can bring a new boyfriend next time, Uncky Dunk," Em said, patting my arm with the crust of her cheese sandwich, and tutting softly like the time I comforted her when she fell off the swing.

I nodded. *I wish*.

"What's that pink flower?" Sid gestured at the information board across the pathway.

"It's a very rare flower that grows in Madagascar." The twins were like information sponges sometimes, it made me so proud of them! "It's called a periwinkle."

There was a moment's silence, then they both burst into insane giggles, sending sandwich crumbs all down their coats.

"What?" I protested.

"Winkle! Winkle!" Emma snorted.

"It's what Germy Lincoln—"

"Jeremy Lincoln," I corrected, knowing I didn't stand a chance of them ever using the poor kid's proper name.

"—calls his willy!" Sid finished with glee.

It took every bit of willpower I had, but I bit back my own laughter. "Well, this plant is serious, it can be used in medicine to help people with leukaemia. It's all explained on the visitors' board. Listen for a minute."

Sid grumbled while I read the notes aloud. He wasn't the greatest fan of schoolwork, especially not in the holidays. But Emma leaned against me and sighed happily.

"You're very clever, Uncky Dunk."

I smiled down at the tousled top of her head. "Oh, I don't know about that. One day, Em, you'll be able to read all these words too. I'm not anything special."

"Yes, you are. 'Course I'll read them myself one day." She peered up at me, shaking her head in pity that I was so dim. "But you read them to me *now*. That's the best. You're very good, and you look after us like… like *treasure*."

I thought I heard a gasp from the other side of the greenery and my head jerked up. Was that the orange-and-black coat again? A figure stood directly opposite us, stock still, between a coffee plant and something furry and fringed I hadn't bothered to read the label for.

"The friendly tiger!" cried Emma and leapt off the seat beside me.

"Me first!" yelled Sid and followed her.

༺❀༻

They shot off around the corner like little terriers, clad in shiny yellow macs. I clambered after them, still shoving my litter into my backpack, muttering "sorry" to anyone I dashed past—

And I came abruptly up against the tiger jacket. The *man* in the tiger jacket. The *very attractive*, strongly-built, salt-and-pepper-haired man in the tiger.... Anyway, *rambling, Duncan*. He was smiling, the skin beside his eyes crinkling delightfully, and actually, it was light brown hair with sexy strands of grey threaded through—

My lust-filled thoughts washed over me, from head to toe.

"Hey." His hand rested on my chest, holding my flight, but in the very best way. A firm, muscular, handsome... hand. My God, *he* was handsome, not only his hand. Could he feel my heart doing backflips?

"Are you okay?"

"I am now. Oh, shoot. I mean, as long as I haven't hurt you?"

He raised an eyebrow, and kindly didn't laugh at me for implying my skinny little limbs would have injured his gorgeous studly sturdiness. Behind me, I could hear the twins squabbling over a twig on the path. They'd temporarily forgotten both me and the maybe-tiger.

Mr Tiger cleared his throat. "I was hoping I'd catch up with you on some circuit or other. Eventually."

"Oh, it's not that big a room." My involuntary laugh was more of an ugly snort. Wow, you'd never know I had a university education. *Mortifying*.

He flushed, but handsomely, of course. "Sure. But we've been chasing each other around for a while, and... well, our paths didn't look like they were ever going to meet."

"I saw your coat. A lot." I couldn't hold back my grin. "But never..." *More of you*, I wanted to say. "Are you an explorer? God, sorry, that's stupid—"

"No," he interrupted gently. "Not stupid. But, unfortunately not."

"It's the jacket and... the boots." I glanced at his very expensive-looking hiking boots. I was suddenly, horribly aware of my spring jacket, my skinny jeans and muddy shoes, and my old football shirt which was clinging to my chest by now, due to the humidity.

To my surprise, when I looked back up, I caught Mr Tiger looking at the clingy shirt too.

"I'm breaking in the damn boots," he said with that rich chuckle I'd heard and liked so much. "Ready for a sponsored walk I'm doing at East-er. Part of my before-turning-forty bucket list." He grimaced, and even that looked hot. "I confess, they're killing me today."

"Well, you look pretty fit." Shit, my filter had taken a total holiday.

He chuckled again. "So do you." Then he flushed deeper. "Oh my God, I can't believe I said that. Cheesy. And *rude*."

I touched his arm without thinking. "It's okay. It was a compliment, I think."

His smile bloomed. "It most certainly was."

Sid yelped a protest over something, then both twins laughed and went back to squabbling. *Thank you, kids*, I prayed silently. *Give me a little adult moment here.*

"It looks like you have your hands full. Lively, but lovely children." There was a wistful look on Mr Tiger's face. "It's wonderful you enjoy their company, and connect with them so well—"

"They're not mine," I blurted out.

"I... sorry?"

"They're my sister's. My niece and nephew. Cathy, my sister, she's expecting again and I—I'm taking the twins out during the school holidays, to give her a break."

Mr Tiger nodded, not fazed by my stuttering. "You know, it's said that six-year-olds laugh on average three hundred times a day. Adults only fifteen to a hundred. We can learn a lot from that."

What *I* learned was that he looked like he needed to laugh a lot more.

"Sorry, I haven't even introduced myself." He held out a hand. "Mike Shaw."

"Dunk," I said without thinking. *Ugh.* "I mean, Duncan. Duncan Harrington. The kids call me Uncky Dunk, it's a nickname, and it sometimes drives me mad. But they mean it fondly, so I shouldn't complain." Because, actually, I loved the kids' silly names, and their teasing, and the way Emma still got words mixed up. But... "Shit. I'm rambling, I do that. I get flustered, I open my mouth before I think, and my filter seems to shut right down."

"I like it," Mike said.

"Er... you do?"

"It's friendly." He paused a moment. "And *honest*. I don't want to sound like a stalker or anything, but I've really enjoyed listening to the way you interact with the children. They obviously love you."

Well. That made a pleasant change from Eddy's "can't you keep your pretty mouth shut for half a minute at a time, Duncan?" which I'd heard way too often in the months before we broke up.

"I've offended you." Mike sighed. "I do sound like a stalker, don't I?"

I grinned again. "No way. But I've been gabbling on while we've been walking around, to keep the kids amused, I suppose. It's more than a bit embarrassing."

"Please, Duncan. Don't be embarrassed. I'm the one who's ambushing you with probably inappropriately comments—"

"No," I said quickly. "I like it. Your…"

"Honesty?" Mike gave a wry smile. And we both laughed.

"Uncky Dunk, look!"

We turned at Sid's sudden call, to find him waving a sodden sock in front of Emma's nose. "I stepped on the leaves and now my foot's all wet!"

It was a rare treat, wandering the Palm House with Mike beside me. I let the twins have a little more freedom, now they'd proved they could (mostly) be trusted to behave, and they were currently at the other end of the path, listening, rapt, to one of the staff explaining how the greenhouse was built. I paused to watch them, and Mike stopped too.

"So, the sponsored walk?" I asked. "Will it be up Everest?"

He laughed, a warm belly laugh this time, warming me better than that hot chocolate I'd missed. "No, north Wales. It's in aid of the local children's hospital. I run a bistro up the Kew Road, and my business partner has a sick child who's had a lot of medical care. We wanted to support the treatments they offer. Kew Gardens is my nearest green space and I always loved coming here. I thought it'd be a good place to train, to build up my stamina. I'd prefer better weather, though."

He smiled, but his troubled expression made me want to put an arm around him. "I've worked in a restaurant, when I was a student," I said. "It's not an easy job."

He blinked hard. "Yes. And it's been very difficult recently. My partner's understandably taken a lot of time off. And it's stressful for everyone who knows and works with him. We're all worrying about his little one." He sighed. "So, does that mean I look as worn out as I feel?"

I smiled back, his shoulder bumped mine, and my gut was ambushed by butterflies. "Of course not."

"I haven't had time for fun in a long while," he continued. "In fact, this is the first time I've come out to the Gardens since Christmas. Bob and I used to take lunches here whenever we could."

"You will again, I'm sure," I said gently. "In the meantime, you've been hijacked by a chatty kid and his even chattier little relatives."

"No hijack. Not at all. The chatting has..." He shook his head, looking pleased. "It's lightened the load. Got me out of myself. And you're not a kid, far from it. *Oh*. Unless I've misjudged..."

"I'm not still a student," I said quickly. Was he worried he was flirting with someone too young? "I'm twenty-five. I'm a primary school teacher. Totally legal." *Oh, Duncan, what the hell?* "I mean, I'm not sure why I phrased it like that, I mean I can do adult stuff." *Yeah, double right down, you berk.* Mike's mouth was twitching. "I mean, I have a job, I have a flat, for God's sake. I'm legal for all kinds of..." And that was that. Words deserted me, in my squidgy pile of deep embarrassment.

Mike took pity on me. "You mean for drinking?"

"Uh. Yes. That."

"And eating?" His eyes twinkled.

"I... well, of course."

"Then if you have any more free time during this spring break, maybe I could introduce you to my bistro. Treat you to a meal."

Should I double-check, was I still being fanciful...?

"On my own?"

Oh yes, he pinked up *really* handsomely. "No. I hoped you'd be with me. We could have dinner together. I'm single, and you—um."

I cut off another moment of panic from him. "I am, too." As I was sure the twins would tell him, if they found Uncky Dunk, the guy with the woeful love life, making a date. "That'd be great. And you must let me know how to sponsor you. The hospital is a fabulous place."

"You haven't—?"

"No, not me." I kept my voice low in case the twins suddenly came running. "But the twins were premature, a difficult birth, and Em's development has been slower and quieter than her brother's. The hospital staff have been wonderful, helping and supporting Cathy and Nathan all the way."

To my delight, Mike reached out and took my hand. It was nice to find a man who didn't mind showing some affection in public. Eddy had spent most of our outdoor dates keeping social distancing in place, long after the government lifted official restrictions.

"May I say something inappropriate again, Duncan?"

I nodded. Hey, he hadn't stepped wrong so far.

"You've made this day special for me. You made me smile, from the first moment I met you. *Heard* you."

Oh. Was I grinning like an idiot?

"I confess it's been a complete surprise to me, and I don't want to make a fool of myself, but I'm really looking forward to getting to know you better. If, that is, you feel, even a little, the same way—"

"Totally," I said swiftly. "I do. Fully. Whatever."

Yes, this was fast, but in the best possible way. And before I could gabble on and make an even bigger fool of myself, I checked there was no one approaching on our pathway, dipped my head away from an overhanging fan of damp palm leaves, and kissed his cheek.

It was like some cheesy romcom! He moved at the same time, and instead of his cheek, I got his mouth. It was warm, soft, and felt like a perfect fit. I thought *why not?* and I didn't pull back for a satisfyingly, deliciously long moment.

"Whoa," Mike said softly. It looked like he was bending in for another go but, from the corner of my eye, I could see movement at the end of the pathway. I rested my hand on his arm.

"Easy, tiger," I murmured.

Mike looked immediately apologetic. "Too fast?"

I grinned. He wouldn't get the joke... not yet. "Oh, no way. Absolutely the right speed." And as the twins came hurtling towards us. Mike slipped his hand into mine.

Yes, I was *so* pleased to find a man who didn't mind public affection!

The twins arrived with giggles and gasps and pattering Wellington boots on the path. The soggy socks didn't seem to have held Sid back from having fun. They paused, stopped wriggling, and stared at us. Two small faces, so similar but with their own special features, two sets of bright eyes, tousled hair, and little mouths in Os.

"Are you Uncky Dunk's new boyfriend?" Sid asked.

"Sid!"

"'Cos you can be," he continued blithely.

"We're okay with it," Emma all but whispered at his side.

"Right. Thanks for that, kids," I said, assuming they'd never get the sarcasm. Though Sid's eyebrows went up under his still-damp fringe, maybe at my tone rather than the words.

"I'm hoping so," Mike said. He didn't seem at all fazed by them. In fact, his eyes softened and his cheeks pinked again with pleasure at their welcome.

Emma tugged at my sleeve, with an intense frown in Mike's direction, "Is he a friendly tiger?"

Mike looked puzzled; I tried to bite back my laugh.

"It's your coat," I explained to him. "It's orange and black, and looks like stripes through the palm leaves."

Emma tugged again, demanding in a splendidly clear stage whisper, "But will he look after you, Uncky Dunk? Like, when we're at school and can't do the job."

"Oh, Em, darling, it's not like that with grown-ups—"

"Excuse me butting in," Mike said firmly, "but actually, Duncan, it *is* the same with adults. Or at least, it should be." He turned to the twins, and his smile twinkled in his eyes. "If your uncle and I start dating regularly, I will definitely commit to looking after him. I trust you when you say he's a very good man..."

Oh God, I was blushing again.

"...and we'll be happy to check in with you now and then, so you can see how it's going."

We will?

"You see," Sid said, with a little wobble in his voice. "Uncky Dunk d'serves better than Eddy, who was a bast—"

"No!" I clapped a hand over Sid's mouth. That sounded too like my protective sister's words for comfort, though I wholeheartedly agreed with the sentiment. "I don't know where you heard all that."

"Mum and Dad talk really loudly in the kitchen sometimes," Sid said helpfully, "especially when the baby's kicking a lot."

Sid was very perceptive for one so young. He'd be either a politician or a scam artist when he grew up. Whereas Emma... her first instinct had been to protect me. Though maybe not through a career in a caring profession, but more possibly a despot on the way into battle. Carrying a machete.

"I understand," Mike said gravely to Sid. "All we can do for the ones we love is to be there if we're needed."

Sid nodded with a strangely mature look on his little face and turned to Emma. "He's clever, like Uncky Dunk," he said. "He's a kipper, Em."

"*Keeper*," I moaned under my breath.

But how sweet had that been, the respectful way Mike treated Sid and Emma? It was always my belief that children were adults-in-training, not some alien species. I squeezed Mike's hand.

"I think it's time for me to get the twins home. Imaginations are running riot."

"They certainly are." His smile was all for me, and the flicker in his warm, sympathetic eyes seemed to be heating up. Was he remembering that kiss? That damp, clumsy, accidental, totally gorgeous, hope-to-repeat-it-soon kiss? My goosebumps were back in force. I wasn't going to rush into anything, but I could certainly anticipate more delicious—

"Ice cream!" Sid yelled and started jumping up and down.

Mike laughed and squeezed my hand back. "I'll walk you to your car," he said. "I can't risk losing you now."

His palm was warm and protective around mine.

I wondered, had I been ensnared by a predatory tiger? Maybe not.

But maybe by something just as fierce and exciting.

Twinkle Toes by Colette Davison

A Don't Hold Back Bonus Scene

~ Garrett ~

Garrett rotated his arms to keep them warm while his training partner, Reece, took his turn on the rings under the supervision of their coach, Douglas. The atmosphere in the gymnasium was one of focus. It stank of sweat too. Training was hard work. Garrett and Reece had been part of the British team at the Olympics in Japan, and now they had their sights fixed firmly on the Commonwealth Games.

Garrett's attention was divided. He was supposed to be watching Reece, but his gaze kept travelling to the pommel horse, where Ryder was training. Ryder was an American gymnast who competed for the US team and trained in the UK, where Lennie, his coach, was from. His and Garrett's relationship had got off to a rocky start, which had been entirely Garrett's fault. Luckily for him, Ryder had given him more chances than he'd deserved, and they'd gone from rivals to boyfriends.

The US Championships were looming, but Ryder's training performance lacked its usual sparkle. He'd been thinking about quitting competing since the Olympics. He'd told Garrett and Lennie he was tired. He'd worked hard to do well at the Olympics while battling an eating disorder. But was giving up what he really wanted? If it were, Garrett would respect it, but until Ryder had made his decision, Garrett wanted to help his partner find joy in gymnastics again. But how could he do that?

They spent long hours in the gym, often focusing on one routine or even one element of a routine, doing it over and over again until they'd perfected it. He loved it. He hungered for it, but he could understand why the sport had lost its shine for Ryder since he'd achieved his dreams. What his boyfriend needed was to have some fun. Garrett was certain he and Reece would benefit from letting loose too.

The music for one of the women's floor routines interrupted his train of thought. He grinned as an idea formed in his mind.

Ryder finished his pommel horse routine, dismounted, and walked to Lennie. After a short chat, he wandered across the floor to the steps that led to the changing rooms.

"Toilet break," Garrett said.

Douglas nodded to acknowledge Garrett's statement without taking his eyes off Reece. Garrett jogged across to Lennie, who was waiting by the pommel horse. It was safe to assume that Ryder would only be gone for a few minutes.

"Do you know what your gymnast needs today?" Garrett asked Lennie.

Lennie folded his arms. "What?"

"To have some fun."

"What would you suggest, Coach Garrett?"

Garrett snorted. He was no coach, although that would likely be his retirement plan. "A friendly competition."

Lennie side-eyed him.

"Give us one hour to develop a women's floor routine and then decide which of us is the best."

"*Us?*"

"Ryder, Reece, and I."

"Does Reece know about this plan of yours?"

"No, but he'll be up for it."

Lennie quirked an eyebrow. "I suppose taking the morning off serious training won't harm any of you. But you have to get Douglas's agreement."

"I can do that." Garrett grinned and hurried over to his coach.

"I thought you were going to the toilet. Not having a chit-chat with a rival coach," Douglas said.

"Ryder and I won't be competing against each other until Worlds."

Douglas rolled his eyes. "What were you and Lennie talking about?"

"I convinced him to let me borrow his gymnast for fun."

"Fun?"

"Yes, and now I need to convince you to let Reece and me have fun."

"Fun?" Reece grabbed a towel and dabbed his face and neck.

"Is there an echo in here?" Garrett asked.

Reece grinned. "I'm up for some fun."

"I knew you would be. Fancy spending the next hour devising a women's floor routine?"

Reece scratched his jaw. "Are you serious?"

"Yes."

"It doesn't sound like something you'd enjoy."

"It's not about me." Garrett glanced at the pommel horse and pointed at Ryder, who had returned.

"Ah. That makes more sense."

"Sounds like a waste of time," Douglas said.

"Please, Coach. I want to help Ryder find his love for the sport again. After everything he did for me—" He hung his head and scuffed the matting with his toe. If not for Ryder, he'd have bombed at the Olympics and likely been dropped from the British team.

Douglas sighed. "Fine. But once you're done prancing, I want you focused on *your* training. Understood?"

"Understood," Garrett and Reece said in unison.

"I'll go get Ryder."

Garrett couldn't help but grin as he approached his boyfriend from behind. He wrapped his arms around him and kissed his cheek.

"We're not meant to do that when we're trainin'." Ryder leant against Garrett's chest despite his protest.

Garrett loved his boyfriend's thick Texan twang. "We're on a break."

"We are?"

"Yes. Aren't we?" Garrett asked Lennie.

"Yes. One hour."

"Umm, that's a long break. What gives?" Ryder asked.

"We're not going to be sitting around doing nothing," Garrett said.

"We're not?"

"No. We're going to devise a floor routine."

Ryder stroked Garrett's arm. "We already have floor routines. Mine's pretty darn good."

"And mine's shabby, is it?"

Ryder chuckled. "I didn't say that. You said that."

"You're distracting me."

"I'm good at that."

Garrett kissed Ryder's jaw. "Yes, you are."

Lennie cleared his throat. They weren't supposed to display affection publicly during training.

"Right, sorry. Floor routines. Set to music. Women's rules," Garrett said.

Ryder frowned. "Uh…"

"One hour. Best routine wins. You'd better bring it, Ryder Anderson. Don't hold back."

Ryder snorted. "And what will I win when I whoop your ass, Garrett Kidd?"

Garrett chewed the inside of his cheek. He hadn't thought of a prize. "The winner gets bragging rights. Come on, Ry. It'll be fun."

"And you're okay with this?" Ryder asked Lennie.

Lennie nodded.

"Okay. I'm in." Ryder spun away from Garrett.

"Where are you going?"

"To work on my routine. I can't have you spyin' on me, can I? One hour?"

Garrett smiled. "One hour. Bring it."

"Oh, I'll be bringin' it. Don't you worry."

Garrett watched Ryder go. Would this silly competition be enough to reignite the fire in Ryder's heart for gymnastics? Garrett hoped so.

He retrieved his phone from his kit bag, sat in the changing room, and sent a text message to Reece's boyfriend, Alex. A few months ago, Garrett wouldn't have dreamt of contacting Alex. In fact, he'd actively avoided spending time with Alex and Reece. It was stupid, but he'd been a jealous idiot, and his thoughts had been clouded by anger.

Garrett: Could you come to the gym in an hour? We're doing a daft competition. I think you'd enjoy watching it.

Alex was a reporter for a local newspaper. He'd done articles on Garrett and Reece when they'd gone to Worlds and again when they'd gone to the Olympics. He was a talented writer. At one point, he'd been a gymnast, but he'd given it up in secondary school. He didn't have the fire for the sport that Garrett and Reece did.

Alex: I can get there. Does Reece know I'm coming?

Garrett: No. That's half the fun.

Alex: Now I'm curious. I'll see you soon.

Garrett switched apps on his phone and looked up the rules for women's floor routines. He'd watched the women compete plenty of times—it was expected that they'd cheer their teammates on—but he'd never paid close attention to the rules. The women performed to music, and their routine was composed of acrobatic and dance elements. Contrary to the men's, which lacked the artistic component. The women had to include at least two leaps, another requirement the men didn't have. Spins were common. Like the men, they had to have tumbles. He was strong at those.

Next, he watched routines on YouTube to get some ideas, picked some music, and returned to the floor.

Ryder was nowhere to be seen. Reece was working with two of the junior women, who were cackling while he attempted a leap. Garrett couldn't concentrate on his friend. He had to work on his routine. He couldn't hand either of his friends a win, which meant he had to put his all into devising and performing a routine, no matter how daft he felt doing it.

As the hour wore on, Garrett realised two things. First, the women's skills were one hell of a lot harder than he'd anticipated. Second, he couldn't produce even a half-decent routine. He couldn't learn how to do leaps, expand his limited repertoire of spins, or incorporate dance in an hour, so he would embrace the hilarity, look like a prat, and hopefully make Ryder smile and laugh. Would he have done something like this before he'd met Ryder? Not a chance. His boyfriend brought out the best in him.

Douglas clapped his hands, bringing the gym to a standstill. "Right, then. It's time for the competition of the century. Who will win? Who will fall flat on their face? Gather round to find out."

Garrett groaned as everyone came and sat close to the floor mats. Was this Douglas's way of punishing him for slacking off real training for an hour? Thankfully, it was during school time, so there weren't too many people to witness him make a fool of himself.

"Howdy," Ryder whispered from behind Garrett.

Garrett pressed his hand to his heart. "F—" He caught himself just in time. "Where did you come from?"

Ryder tapped the side of his nose and grinned.

"What's Alex doing here?" Reece asked.

Alex stood at the gymnasium's entrance, taking his shoes off so he could step onto the mat.

"No idea," Garrett said.

"Yeah, right. You called him, didn't you?"

"No." Garrett pinched his lips together.

"Liar."

"I didn't call him. I texted him."

Reece play-punched his friend in the arm and then walked to his fiancé. He embraced and kissed Alex.

"Is there something in the water today? You all seem to have forgotten the no fraternising rules," Lennie said.

"I'm not a gymnast," Alex said.

"No, but your boyfriend is." Douglas gave Reece a pointed glare.

Reece replied with an innocent smile and joined Garrett and Ryder.

"Who's going first?" Douglas asked.

Garrett stepped forward. "I will."

Ryder arched a brow.

"I might as well get it over and done with."

"Aww, and there was me thinking you were goin' to show us how it's done."

"Don't worry. I'm going to bring it."

Ryder grinned. "I'm lookin' forward to it."

Garrett wanted to kiss Ryder, but he'd already pushed the 'no fraternising during practice' rule too many times. Instead, he hooked his phone up to the PA system and asked one of the younger gymnasts to press Play for him once he was ready to begin his hastily put-together routine.

He was used to starting in a corner, ready to do his first tumbling pass, so starting a little farther into the mat was strange. He took a deep breath. *Embrace the hilarity. Don't aim for perfection. Make Ryder smile.* He grimaced. He'd probably be the laughingstock at the gym for the next few weeks, but so be it. He tilted his hips and adopted what he hoped was a sassy pose. Someone wolf-whistled at him. He didn't look to see who.

His music started to play.

Embrace the hilarity.

He could do that. Couldn't he?

He chasséd to the corner, swinging his arms from side to side as he wiggled his hips. Laughter filled the air. He did a half jump, facing along the diagonal, and ended with a roundoff with a double twist, which was part of his actual routine. With a grin, he improvised some dance steps in the corner. They involved lots of hip wiggling and striking poses. The audience was in stitches. It felt good to let loose and have fun. Much like the time when he and Ryder had gone to crazy golf for the first time together. He hadn't cared about winning then, and he didn't care about winning now.

He did another tumble pass and tried to replicate a leap-run-leap-with-splits combo he'd seen in one of the videos, pointing his fingers and toes and fluttering his lashes as he did it. He alternated between serious tumble passes and dancing and twists. It was fun, although he couldn't do anything too risky. Douglas would go mad if he hurt himself larking about. The most ambitious new skill he tried was a free cartwheel. He could put his hands down if he needed to. Not that he did. Completing the skill gave him a momentary burst of pride and confidence, though he doubted his execution was as elegant as the women.

By the time he was done and saluting Douglas, he was exhausted but happy. He burst out laughing as the audience applauded him.

"My turn." Reece squeezed his shoulder as they passed.

Garrett sat beside his boyfriend. Reece's routine was hilarious. He pranced and preened and made a total tit of himself, smiling all the time.

Ryder put his hand over Garrett's and leant his head on Garrett's shoulder. "I'm proud of you."

"Me? Why?"

"I was worried you were goin' to take this too seriously and try to win."

"Hey, I brought it."

Ryder laughed. "You did. You had fun."

"Did I make you smile?"

"And laugh until my sides hurt."

Garrett kissed Ryder's temple. "Good. That's what I was hoping for."

When Reece finished, Garrett clapped until his palms hurt.

Ryder bounced to his feet. "My turn."

"Did you even practice?" Garrett asked. "I didn't see you in the gym."

Ryder winked and jogged onto the mat. Garrett watched, mesmerised, as his boyfriend did the silliest floor routine he'd ever seen. He looked gorgeous, even when he stepped out of a spin and fell trying to do a backwards walkover. Garrett hadn't even attempted the walkovers. Backflip? No problem. Frontflip? Easy peasy. Walkovers? No way. Best of all, excitement made Ryder's bright blue eyes blaze.

"How did I do?" Ryder asked as he returned to Garrett.

Garrett embraced him. "You were amazing."

"Hardly."

"You're always amazing." He kissed the tip of Ryder's nose.

"You're biased."

"Hopelessly."

To hell with the 'no fraternising during practice' rules. Garrett kissed Ryder long and slow.

"Ahem," Douglas said. "We're ready to announce the winner."

Garrett held Ryder's hand. Win or lose, it didn't matter. They'd had fun.

"I bet I won," Reece said. He and Alex had joined them.

"Cocky much," Garrett teased. "Alex, who do you think's going to win?"

Alex held his hands up. "I'm staying out of this."

Reece nudged him. "You're meant to say I was the best."

"This is why I'm not getting involved." Alex pretended to zip his lips shut.

"Maybe we all won," Ryder said.

"There's always one winner," Garrett said.

"In a real competition, sure. But we were havin' fun."

Douglas cleared his throat. "May I have your attention, please? The winner is—"

Their audience hammered their hands on the mats like a drumroll.

"Garrett."

Garrett blinked.

Ryder laughed. "He said your name. Step forward and bask in your moment of glory."

"Me? But—" He shook his head.

"Congrats. You deserved the win." Reece patted him on the back.

"It's true," Ryder said.

Douglas held Garrett's hand up as he received another round of applause. "Have a ten-minute break, and then let's get back to it."

"Yes, Coach." Garrett laced his fingers through Ryder's.

They went upstairs to the viewing gallery with Reece and Alex and sat at a table with their water bottles.

"How did you convince Douglas to let you fool around like that?" Alex asked.

"It was all Garrett's doing," Reece said.

Garrett shrugged. "We all needed some downtime. I still can't believe I won." Was it because he was the least likely of the three to let himself go and be silly?

"You deserved it," Ryder said.

"Your routine was great," Reece said.

Garrett smiled. "Alex, can I ask you something?"

"Sure."

"When you quit gymnastics, how did you know it was the right decision?"

Alex puffed his cheeks out.

Reece pinched his brows together. "You're not thinking of quitting, are you?"

Garrett shook his head. At the same time, he caught Ryder's eye. His boyfriend replied with a soft smile.

"I didn't know for sure. Not right away," Alex replied.

"When did you know?"

"During the first competition you and Reece went to without me."

"You were there," Reece said.

"Well, yes, I watched. But it was the first one I didn't compete in. I didn't miss it. I was happy being in the audience."

Ryder stared at the table.

"Did you ever regret it?" Garrett asked.

"No," Alex replied.

Reece tugged Alex to him and kissed his hair. "Come on. Let's get some fresh air."

"Is that code for let's go to the car park and make out?" Garrett asked.

Reece gave him the finger.

"That was real subtle," Ryder said once they were alone.

"Sorry."

"Naw, don't be sorry. It was interesting to hear what Alex had to say. Did you suggest that crazy competition because I'm thinking about quittin'?"

"Yes. I wanted you to remember how fun gymnastics can be. Did it work?"

Ryder straddled Garrett's lap and rested his forehead against his boyfriend's. "Yes."

"Are you still thinking about quitting?"

"Yeah, at some point. It's a lot. Concentrating on winning and on stayin' well. But not today or tomorrow."

It was so good to hear Ryder say that. Garrett stroked his nape and kissed him.

"Thank you for comin' up with such a crazy idea and making me laugh," Ryder said.

"Still tired?"

"A little less after today. Thank you. I'll bring it at the US Championships, y'know."

"I know. I'll be there to watch."

Ryder smiled. "It helps me to know I have you and Lennie in my corner, watchin' out for me and spurring me on." He cupped Garrett's jaw. "I love you, Gar the Great."

Garrett groaned, but secretly he loved the crazy nickname.

Ryder gasped. "Although after today, I think I need to start callin' you Twinkle Toes."

"You wouldn't dare."

"Yes, I would. Which do you think is catchier?"

"Neither."

"I know. I can call you Gar the Great when it's just you and me, and Twinkle Toes in front of everyone else." He grinned.

"Please tell me you're joking."

"Half joking. You'll always be Gar the Great to me." He kissed Garrett.

Garrett made a grumbling noise, but he wasn't really annoyed.

Ryder stood. "We'd best get back onto the floor. We've got competitions to train for, Twinkle Toes."

"I'm going to tickle you for calling me that."

"Only if you can catch me." Laughing, Ryder darted away from him and out the door. The light had returned to his eyes, which made the day's silliness worth it.

~ Ryder ~

Unlike the other gymnasts, Ryder always showered at home. These days, home was with Garrett, in an apartment in a converted school building. It was small, quirky, and theirs.

After showering, Ryder spent some time on a goofy, secret project, which he held behind his back as he joined Garrett on the mezzanine level. Garrett was stretched out on the couch with the TV remote in his hand, channel-hopping. His T-shirt was pulled up slightly, revealing a sliver of skin. Garrett was the sexiest guy alive. However, he missed Garrett's resting scowly face, which he seldom saw now that his boyfriend was focused on getting past his anger issues.

"Nothing on?" Ryder asked.

Garrett turned the TV off. "No. Not that it matters now you're here."

Ryder raised his eyebrows.

Garrett held his hand out and wriggled his fingers. Then he frowned. "What have you got behind your back?"

"Who? Me? Nothin'."

Garrett narrowed his eyes and pressed his lips together, blanching them. His expression would have been sterner if his lips hadn't curled into an amused smile at the corners. "Yes, you. Do I need to tickle you?"

Ryder laughed. "Nope." He perched on the edge of the sofa and leant down to peck his boyfriend's lips. He laid it on Garrett's chest.

Garrett picked it up and stared at it. "What is it?"

"A gold medal for bein' the best boyfriend in the world."

Garrett widened his eyes. "I'm flattered." He shuffled up so Ryder could lie beside him, facing him.

"It's true. I know I could be hard work—"

Garrett silenced Ryder with a kiss. "You're not hard work."

Ryder rolled his eyes. "That's not true, and you know it."

"You have more good days than bad days. I'm here for you no matter what kind of day it is."

"I know, and it means a lot. Today was a good day, even before your crazy idea. That made it a great day." He stroked Garrett's face.

"I'm glad. I'm here for you, Ry. Good and bad."

"I know."

He did his best to be there for Garrett too. It wasn't always possible. His eating disorder was mostly under control, but some days were terrible for no reason. On those days, he could barely keep himself above water, let alone be an emotional life buoy for anyone else.

"Y'know, somethin' Alex said got me thinking."

"What?"

"He knew he'd made the right decision to quit gymnastics when he didn't miss it."

Garrett sucked in a breath.

"When I took two weeks off after the Olympics, I missed it somethin' fierce."

"You did?"

"Yeah. Almost as much as I missed you."

"Something tells me you missed gymnastics more."

"Naw, don't say that. I love you, Gar the Great. Sure, gymnastics was my whole life until I fell for you. Well, gymnastics and therapy. But y'know what I mean."

Garrett stroked Ryder's cheek. "I do. It was the same for me. It was all-consuming. It's why I got so angry when I didn't do as well as I'd hoped at Worlds. I'm sorry I took that anger out on you."

Ryder tapped Garrett's nose. "You've got to stop apologising. I forgave you."

"So you've decided not to quit?"

"Not yet. I will. Probably sooner than you. But if today taught me anythin', it's that I still love it. I still need it. I'd miss not goin' into the gym every day. Which means you're stuck with having to train alongside the competition every day."

"I can handle that." Garrett pulled Ryder closer.

"Sure?"

"Absolutely positive." He kissed Ryder softly.

Ryder pressed into the kiss. He sometimes had trouble with other aspects of their physical relationship but never with kissing. He loved kissing Garrett, adoring how close he felt to his boyfriend. Most of all, he loved how patient Garrett was with him, never pushing for more than he could give in the moment.

"We should get a poster for the wall that says 'Eat, Breathe, and Sleep Gymnastics,'" Ryder said.

"Or we could get new hobbies."

Ryder gasped. "New hobbies? You mean there are things to do except gymnastics and kissin'?"

"Loon. You know there are."

"You might have to educate me."

"Bowling."

Ryder clicked his fingers. "Oh, shoot, I forgot to bring my bowling shoes and ball home from Texas."

"You don't have bowling shoes or a bowling ball."

"Are you sure about that?"

"Yes."

Ryder laughed. "You might be right. What other hobbies are there?"

"We wouldn't be the first Olympians to take up knitting."

"I could knit you a jockstrap."

Garrett scowled.

"No?"

"No."

Ryder picked up the paper gold medal. "D'you think I've got a future in medal design?"

Garrett pressed his lips together.

"You're right. That's not a hobby. Gardening?"

"We don't have a garden."

"True."

It was a downside of living in an apartment. Ryder's home back in Texas had a huge yard. Not that his dad had ever done much besides mowing the lawn every couple of weeks. When he was younger, his mom had grown flowers in pots, but she'd ended up too busy taking Ryder to training and competitions to keep looking after them. Then he'd got sick, and all her energy had gone into helping him get well.

"What's on your mind?" Garrett asked softly.

"Huh?"

"You had your thinking face on."

Ryder wrinkled his nose. "I don't have a thinking face."

"Of course you do. Everyone does. Yours is cute." Garrett kissed Ryder's forehead. "But it was your slightly sad thinking face. Tell me what's wrong."

"I was thinking about everythin' my parents gave up so I could do gymnastics."

"Probably lots. But I bet they're proud of everything you've achieved."

Ryder smiled. "Yeah, they are. We're meant to be thinking of new hobbies." He stifled a yawn with his hand.

"I'm not sure we'd have the energy for a new hobby until after we quit."

"Probably not."

"We'd probably forget we even had a new hobby."

"What makes you say that?"

"We've forgotten that we're gymnasts and need fuel."

Ryder dipped his gaze. "Oh. Right. Yeah."

"I can cook."

He shook his head sharply. "It's okay. I've got it. You go back to channel-hopping. I'll call you when the food's ready." He stood.

Garrett caught hold of his hand and threaded their fingers together. "Let's cook together."

Ryder smiled. He had the best boyfriend. Trust Garrett to know cooking would be a chore for him. If only he could relinquish the task to Garrett. But he couldn't. Not yet. Even on a good day, he needed to control what he ate. He yanked Garrett to his feet a little too hard. They overbalanced. Garrett wrapped his arms around Ryder and steadied them both.

"I've got you, Ry," he whispered.

Ryder pressed his face against Garrett's shoulder and returned his boyfriend's embrace. "Thank you."

"We might not have a garden, but we could grow herbs on the windowsill."

"That would be fun." It was always nicer to cook with fresh herbs than dried ones.

"We could decorate the pots with faces and give all the herbs names."

Ryder snort-laughed. "I like this side of you, Gar the Great."

"What side?"

"The silly side. I hope I get to see more of it."

Garrett put his fingers underneath Ryder's chin and tilted his face so their gazes locked. "It's here to stay, I promise. I'll do anything to make you smile."

"You don't have to do anythin' special to make my smile. Just be you."

They kissed and cuddled for far longer than they should have, considering they needed to make food, and it was getting late. But being close to Garrett was exactly what Ryder needed.

"Time to cook," Garrett said decisively.

Ryder pulled away. "Race you downstairs, Twinkle Toes." He darted away and jogged down the open staircase as fast as he dared.

Garrett caught up with him in their tiny kitchen space, pinned him against the cupboards, and kissed him. "How long are you going to call me Twinkle Toes?"

Ryder shrugged. "Is forever long enough?"

"I'm going to have to come up with an annoying nickname for you."

"Naw, I'm too cute for that."

Garrett sighed. "It's true. You are far too cute." He rested his forehead against Ryder's and stroked him behind his ear. "I love you, Ry."

"I love you too, Twinkle Toes."

"No."

"Gar the Great?"

"Better."

If you enjoyed this story, please check out the *Chasing Gold* series:
Hold Me Up: Reese and Alex's story
Don't Hold Back: Garrett and Ryder's story

The Queen by David E. Gordon

Finn paused at the mirror making sure that his bow tie was straight and even on both sides. Finn smiled remembering what Claudia would have said - *you scrub up nice. And stop fidgeting.* She would have loved this kind of an event - classical music, fancy gowns and tuxedos, and for her charity - while Finn definitely would have preferred staying home watching his sports team play. It had been five years and Finn still asked himself what would Claudia do or say. He turned towards the entrance to the ballroom, a flash of long red hair making him pause. His first thought was of Claudia but Finn knew that couldn't be. She was gone and not as in moved to Florida, as in permanently. Finn felt the tug at his heart which quickly moved to his eyes and sucked in a breath to clear the tears. Dammit! Just when he thought he might be over losing her.

As he entered the ballroom he glanced around trying to prove to himself that he had in fact seen a redhead. He made his way to the bar and took in the rainbow of glittering gowns and black tuxedos. He asked for a scotch, neat and taking his glass made his way to a nearby high top table. Finn talked to several guests as the crowd started to grow around the room when he saw her cross the dance floor. Finn could see her long red hair swinging across her back as she... sashayed through the crowd. She glided as if her legs were not moving, the slit along the side of her dress showed the black lace at the top of her stockings and a splash of color from a tattoo above the lace and when she turned away from him the backless dress revealed more colors from a large tattoo but her hair covered most of it. Finn tried to extricate himself from the group but it felt like they were holding his arms and feet so he couldn't move. Timothy was beside him as always and after about an hour whispered "its time" in his ear then led him towards the front of the room. Slowly the voices quieted to complete silence, so he held up a hand as the room now faced him completely.

"Good evening. Welcome to the fifth annual Claudia Foundation gala. I would like to thank you for joining us and for your already large commitments. As you know, my wife Claudia died five years ago from an incredibly rare brain disease. Before she passed we discussed starting a children's foundation. Once she got sick we shifted to focus on children's brain diseases. And now because of all of you we have already raised almost fifty million dollars. And this year we should be close to sixty million. I cannot put into words what this means to me so I have invited a group of kids from St. Thomas Children's Hospital." Finn paused while the kids moved to stand with him. "Please give the kids some space but they are here to answer any questions. Thank you for all you do for the foundation."

As he started to move through the crowd he saw the redhead standing to the far side of the room. He made his way to the bar but kept getting stopped by different people and was surprised when the redhead suddenly appeared at his side and then held out a glass of scotch for him. Finn gave her his best smile and mouthed *thanks* but she was already backing away from him. He nodded to Timothy who made his way to her and they exchanged words. Finn finally managed to pull away from the crowd and moved quickly to Timothy only to find that he had lost sight of the woman. Again. Finn didn't see her for the rest of the night and no-one seemed to know who she was or where she went. Even though Timothy had spoken with her, he had not gotten her name. This event was by invitation only so it was surprising that no one seemed to know who she was. Finn had to stay late and by the time he was ready to go he was fighting back a yawn. There was an SUV waiting for him and his driver held the door open. He slid into the backseat and as the vehicle pulled away he closed his eyes. Finn suddenly became aware of someone else in the backseat and as he started to reach for a light she whispered "don't".

"What do you want? If you are thinking of anything ridiculous like a ransom my driver is retired military."

In the dim light from the dashboard he watched as she turned to face him. "Don't be silly Mr. McMasters. Your driver is with me." She surprised him by turning on a small reading light which allowed Finn to see how beautiful she really was. She crossed her legs and once again he could see the black lace at the top of her stockings and the color from a tattoo that he still couldn't make out. The black dress she wore shifted and fell away revealing most of her legs and he could see when the v-neck sagged open that she was not wearing anything underneath. Her skin was a caramel color and looked flawless, her mouth had formed into a smile that reached all the way to her emerald green eyes. Her long red hair was now gathered and lay across her shoulder.

Finn saw a wicked grin spread even wider as she whispered. "Can I have my clothes back?"

He laughed "well you are the one who snuck into my SUV".

"True. But we need to talk."

He decided to see how much she was flirting and reached out running the back of his hand across her cheek, down her neck to her shoulder. He pushed the shoulder strap off and let it fall down her arm. "Talk is over rated." She didn't flinch and he realized he didn't even know her name. "Can I at least know your name?"

She raked her foot along his lower leg and he realized that she was not wearing shoes. "Isabell." He shifted closer and kissed her cheek. Finn could almost taste the beauty and sensuality that seemed to ooze from every pore. He brushed his lips along her jawline moving them to her neck. As Isabell shifted he kissed his way to her shoulder then kissed around to the other side of her neck. He caressed her shoulder with his hand and pushed the other shoulder strap down her arm. As they kissed her mouth opened and he slowly lowered the top of her dress revealing her firm breasts and hard nipples. She sucked in a breath when he took one between his teeth and nibbled. There was something about Isabell. Something more than just a sensuality. He almost felt weak as he tasted more and more of her skin, now kissing lower. Finn pushed her dress up her thighs and as she lifted off the car seat, to her waist. He kissed the soft bare skin above the stockings moving his mouth inward and finding a small triangle of silk covering her body. Finn's hunger for her knew no bounds and moving between her legs he pulled her panties to the side and dragged his tongue across her heated flesh. Hearing her moan he thrust his tongue inside until she growled for him to finish it. Finn devoured her body until she rose up off the car seat and her body rocked as the orgasm struck. He grabbed her body as she thrust against his mouth, her orgasm rolling through her like the waves of an ocean.

As her body settled Finn kissed his way up to her mouth as she quickly undid his pants. Before Finn knew it she had pushed him back against the car door and lowered her body down around him. The sensation as she began to ride him was almost overwhelming and he reached around fondling and stroking her body. Finn pulled her back against his chest kissing her neck, and holding her steady as he thrust in and out of her. He could feel another orgasm roll through her body and kept pushing until he finally couldn't take it any more and then exploded deep inside. His explosion pushed Isabell over the edge one more time and he could feel her orgasm gush all over his crotch. She slowly extricated herself from his body and then turned into his arms and kissed him deeply and passionately. After they caught their breath she shifted back to her side of the car. Finn watched as she removed her now torn panties then pulled her dress back into place. She was almost as sexy getting dressed as she had been naked.

Finn was torn between the passion and desire that had erupted between them and celebrating Claudia's foundation and life. He almost spoke sheepishly. "Do you want us to drive you some where?"

"We should go to your house so we can talk. This was not the reason for... I am going to be direct Mr. McMasters and I would like you to keep an open mind."

"Please call me Finn."

Isabell nodded "I came to see you because I felt you were finally ready to hear this. It has to do with Claudia. We were friends for many years and I know what really killed her."

Finn felt every fiber in his body tighten and hissed through clenched teeth. "Be very careful with what you say next. I knew my wife since college and she has never mentioned you or anyone like you."

"I am sorry but I lost contact with Claudia. I heard in the news that she was sick and I was able to reconnect with her. As you know she preferred to stay out of the spotlight. You are going to have a lot of questions. I am going to need you to... well... trust me." Finn nodded and handed her a bottle of water. "Claudia and I grew up together. When we were just becoming women Claudia was promised to a Clan Laird who was an evil man. She brought me into the castle so she had a friend, and confidant. Unfortunately, he was an evil man and he took advantage of both of us. Claudia had trouble getting pregnant and he beat her constantly. And when he got tired of beating her he would hit me. After six months Claudia and I would stay away from him so he turned to other women. One summer a distant nephew came to visit and when the nephew found out the Laird was abusive he killed him. The nephew became Laird simply because there was no one else. For several years he kept both Claudia and myself as lovers, although neither of us were able to get pregnant. We were just turning twenty-one and one night the... um... the three of us... Something happened that night and it changed our lives."

Isabell paused and took a drink while Finn continued watching her. "I'm not sure I am following you. All of this happened before college? Claudia never mentioned having issues with getting pregnant."

"Finn... this happened five hundred years ago. The nephew was a vampire."

His mouth dropped open and eyes as big as saucers. "What?? That's not possible. Wait... you said was? I thought vampires were immortal. Assuming they are even real."

"Trust me its very possible. We are immortal unless someone takes our head. Which is how Dimitar - the nephew - ruled the clan, making sure no one got close enough to kill him. He surrounded himself with his most trusted men. It happened one day while out in the garden. The three of us were resting after... Dimitar started to get flushed and shaking uncontrollably. After a few moments he seemed okay so we started back to the castle, and then he just collapsed. We got him back to the castle but he never woke up, two weeks later he stopped breathing. With Dimitar gone we had no protector and the new Laird was not going to put up with our... loving each other more than as sisters. We heard he was going to put us to death, but were able to escape before he could take action. We managed to move around enough that people never knew how old we really were. In the sixteen-hundreds we made our way here to the colonies. Eventually we decided to split up for safety and we were never able to find each other. Until Claudia got sick."

"You... you're serious? And you think they went after Claudia? Why?" He leaned forward and tapped Max on the shoulder. "Are you hearing this story? What do you think?"

Max - the driver - turned to face him and smiled. "Yes sir. I've been working for Miss Claudia since... well... for years. Since she... they left Scotland."

Finn stared at Max then finally drew his eyes back to Isabell. "Are you saying you are a vampire also? All three... both of you? I thought... doesn't sunlight bother you?"

Isabell reached over and took his hand in hers. "Finn I know this is a lot to take in. Yes, I think that person came after Claudia. We thought we had left that life and lived and loved mortals trying to live normally. Over the years we have learned how to fake aging - with makeup and such. We spoke quite a bit before... she passed. She told me she wanted to grow old with you." She looked out the window and Finn could see her eyes were wet. "And no to sunlight. Different vampire clans or regions are affected by it."

"Why are you telling me this now? Wasn't there anything... Claudia? Maybe if you had said something? I have the money and means."

Before Isabell could answer Max pulled the SUV up to the house. Finn led Isabell into the study and poured himself a double scotch, then poured one for Isabell. He downed the scotch in one gulp and poured another. She sat down on the couch and Finn saw her revealing dress felt a stirring deep inside. It was almost enough for him to forget this crazy talk and take her right here. She must have noticed because she smiled and he saw something in her eyes. Finn turned his back to the room and walked over to the desk knowing he needed to hear more before anything else could happen. Finn took a deep breath, closed his eyes for a moment then told Isabell to continue.

He kept his back to the room not sure if he could face Isabell. "After our first conversation I talked to Claudia often before she passed. We both knew there was nothing we could do. Instead... she asked me to look after you. And when you were ready, I should explain this to you. But..." Finn felt her hands on his shoulders. "Don't turn Finn. I can't look... The truth is that Claudia and I have always had a deep, soulful connection. And now I have fallen for you. You don't have to turn for me see the look of disbelief on your face. I have been working in your offices for the past four years. You know me as Martha - your sixty year old executive admin."

"Martha? That's not possible. Hell... I need a damn drink!" Isabell giggled and lifted his hand with the half full glass and he felt her resting her head against his back. "Why now? What do we do now?"

"Finn there is a lot you have to learn about me, Max, and the others. We think the man that attacked Claudia did so to get to you and was hoping to take her place in your life. And if I am right, he used his... skills to get inside her head and make her sick. Over the years we have perfected changing our appearance which is why only saw me as Martha."

"Take her place? You have to know I am straight." Isabell wrapped her arms around his waist and leaned against his back.

"Yeah I know." Finn could almost hear the blush in her voice. "You hired a new Vice President of Strategic Planning. Luc De'Ardent. I believe he is the man we have been looking for. We have to be very careful as we don't think he has any idea who we really are."

Finn took a drink, put the glass down, then turned and wrapped an arm around her waist. "What does he want from me? He must also know I am straight."

Isabell rose up on her toes then gently caressed his cheek before kissing Finn. He could see the answer in her eyes. He wrapped both arms around her kissing her deeply and as she pressed her body against his the feelings he was developing for her became almost overwhelming. Isabell sensed the change in him almost before he did and rested her head on his chest. "Maybe I should have Max drive you home." She looked up at him and grinned before stepping out of his arms and stopped against a leather chair. She crossed her arms in front of her chest and slowly lowered the shoulder straps of her dress. As she let her hands drop to her sides the straps slid lower followed by the dress. Finn watched as it slid down to her ankles revealing her gorgeous body, the curves accentuated by the dark leather behind her.

She giggled "that's one option. I'm assuming you have a shower somewhere in this place?" Finn watched as she turned her back on him and as she walked towards the door stepped out of her heels. "Maybe you could help wash my back?"

Finn shook his head telling himself it was crazy to fall for... her. He realized that he was actually starting to believe her. He cocked his head for a moment, wondering how many of them looked like that?! He moved after her stripping off his shirt and stepping out of his shoes. As he turned into the hallway he laughed, seeing her heading up the stairs called out "left at the top, end of the hallway". He stood watching as her legs moved, her bum shifting from side to side in an invitation he knew he could not turn down. He moved quickly up the stairs and as he moved through the bedroom's double doors he stripped off his pants and briefs. He walked into the bathroom as he heard the shower come on. Finn leaned against the door watching Isabell as she pulled the glass door of the shower closed, she turned on the water and he could feel his body stiffening as he watched her stretch her arms up letting the water cascade over her chest. He joined her in the shower sliding his arms around her stomach as he pressed his lips against her neck. He pulled her into his arms, his body pressing against hers then moved back to the bench in the shower. Isabell knelt over his lap before lowering herself down around him. Both of them groaning as she leaned back taking him completely inside. Finn kissed her neck and chest before thrusting up into her. They began to move together, the heat of the shower and the sex making their bodies slick with sweat. After several long minutes his entire body stiffened as his orgasm took hold. He held her hips as he exploded inside of her then lifted her body to his mouth until her orgasm rocked and rolled through her body.

They slowly stood up and moved under the multiple shower heads holding each other as they let the water wash over them. He picked up the soap and thoroughly washed her body, taking her through another orgasm. When she finally settled down she picked up the soap and did the same for him. The water was still hot after Finn had another orgasm and then thy got dried off and went to bed. As Isabell lay against him he slid his arm down her back pulling her even closer. He kissed her softly on the mouth, her body curling against his as if it was made to fit. They took their time kissing and caressing each other, making love slowly and passionately. They stopped and started several times, bringing each other to the edge of orgasms before finally giving in. This time it was more intense and gratifying when they reached the eclipse together. He held Isabell to his chest and kissed her softly, brushing her hair back from her face and smiled.

"I think you need another shower."

She purred against his chest. "I don't want to get up."

In the morning, the sun shone brightly through the light curtains and Finn grinned seeing their clothes folded neatly on the bench at the edge of the bed. He realized Isabell was gone but smiled when she stepped out of the bathroom. She wore a large, fluffy bathrobe and held one out for him. She sat on the side of the bed and kissed him softly. "Finn..."

Before she could continue Max knocked and quickly entered the bedroom. He walked straight to Isabell holding out his phone. "My Queen, we need to get you out of here. He can't see you here."

Finn placed my hand on hers. "Go... I will take care of Luc for now. We can talk about how to finish him when we have more time."

Isabell dropped the robe and took the clothes from Max. As she pulled on shorts and a t-shirt Finn sat with large eyes taking in the gigantic dragon tattoo covering most of her back. The wings spanned from her left shoulder down to the bottom right side of her back. The color was amazing and the fire breathing mouth was in the upper right corner. The tail wrapped around its body several times flashing its bards. The artwork was so precise it almost looked like the dragon would come to life. Sliding to the edge of the bed he stopped her hands from pulling the shorts higher. He ran my fingers across another tattoo - this was a gleaming silver dagger with a black leather handle running through a black and gray skull with red roses on both sides of the skull. "Isabell... what does this one mean?"

Max stepped closer holding out a robe for Finn. Isabell turned and gently caressed his cheek. "Finn, we still have a lot to talk about. We have to save this fight to another day. When I am more... prepared. I promise we will talk later. In the office."

They were all surprised when the door burst open and Luc stood there. He slammed the door closed then glared at Max before turning to Isabell. Finn slipped on the robe and stood as tall as he could. Luc looked very different than the man who worked for him in the executive suite. He wore black slacks and a black button down shirt. The shirt was open several buttons showing a large medallion and was pulled tightly across his barrel chest and muscled arms. He bared his teeth at Finn and snarled. He glared at Isabell, his eyes blazing red. "BITCH! I should have known you would be here! Now we can finish this once and for all!"

Max growled and took a half step then charged at Luc. "You will respect the Queen!" Finn was shocked at the speed Max was moving and when he slammed his shoulder into Luc's check it sounded like a truck hitting a wall. Max carried Luc backwards through the closed double doors tearing the hinges from the frame and the wood splintering all around them. Finn started to step forward but Isabell put her hand out stopping him. He could feel the strength in her light touch and noticed that her body seemed a lot more muscular and toned. He watched through the doorway as the men pounded at each other, their fists flying like jackhammers. This wasn't a simple bar fight, these two men were throwing punches hard enough to break through the drywall when they missed. And when they connected it sounded like a hammer pounding in a nail. They grunted, snarled, and growled at each. He watched as Max caught Luc with several rabbit punches to the chest, stomach, and jaw so swiftly that it lifted him off his feet crashing him into the far wall. Max went after him throwing punch after punch until Luc seemed to sink to the floor like a broken doll.

Max's chest heaved as he caught his breath and in the sudden silence Finn could hear Luc snarl. "Not bad for a minion." He started to rise and Max went into a defensive position as Luc started to hit back. Each time he connected it seemed like Max was getting smaller, as if each punch was taking years away from him. Isabell spoke softly "stay" then moved to the desk in the corner. She grabbed an ornamental samurai sword off the wall and strode towards the hallway. She slowly removed the sheath, dropping it on the floor. She stood taller than possible and he could hear her hiss "this ends now". Finn started to tell her it was an ornamental sword and probably not even steel. He watched as she gripped the handle with both hands and there was a flash of light off the blade. Finn noticed an etching along the blade that he had never noticed before and watched as she swung it left, then right, then straight ahead. Max was now fighting back against Luc's pounding and as Finn stepped to the edge of the bed he could see the Max was slowing, but was also getting Luc to turn his back to the doorway.

Luc suddenly realized that Isabell was standing there and threw a punch straight into Max's chest. Finn stared as Max doubled over gasping to catch his breath. Luc spun on Isabell moving quickly to avoid the blade as it swung sideways towards him. As he swung a fist towards Isabell she leaped forward, tossed the blade to Max who caught it easily and thrust it through the back of Luc's neck. Max and Isabell moved easily as if this had been rehearsed many times over the years, perhaps they had. Finn stared as the blade came all the way through his windpipe just as Luc caught Isabell on the side of the head sending her flying back into the bedroom. At the same time Luc's eyes bulged out in shock as he felt the blade, the blood pouring from the wound as it drained from his face. As Luc's knees buckled Max swung the blade to the left slicing out the side, then he turned it over and quickly sliced back through taking his head completely off. In an odd way it seemed like Finn could still see a desire to fight in Luc's eyes, even as the head rolled across the bedroom floor. Max stood there holding the blade ready to swing again as if there was a chance Luc could still attack.

Finn moved quickly to Isabell, who's eyes were fluttering open. He knelt down and gently held her head in his arms. "Talk to me Isabell. Say something." Max put the sword on the desk, then left the room. A few moments later he was back and Finn looked away as he gathered the head in a bag. Isabell smiled softly "your robe is open." They both laughed even as Finn stood up and carried Isabell to the bed laying her down gently then started to step away. "Stay." This time the words were spoken softly and as he sat down beside her he caressed her hair and face. He heard a commotion behind him and turning saw there were a couple of other men helping Max clean up. "We can talk later, lay with me?" Finn lay down beside her, pulling the covers up and was surprised when a woman walked in carrying a tray of coffee and juice. She was incredibly beautiful with short dark hair and the body of a goddess. They sipped coffee and juice while Isabell rested her head against Finn's shoulder. There seemed to be an army of people removing all of the debris and remains. Several others started cleaning as much as they could from the carpet and walls. Max finally came back and cleaned off the samurai sword before replacing it carefully in its holder.

In the morning while they lay in bed Isabell spoke softly. "Do you want to ask or listen?" He shrugged so she started. "Luc was one of Dimitar's most trusted advisors, his true right hand. When Dimitar died Luc should have been next in line, but instead a vampire named Normond took over. Over the next six months Normond proved to be more evil than anyone, and if someone tried to leave or stand up to him they were killed. Immediately, publicly, and in as gruesome as possible. Luc knew he had no choice and became his right hand man. Claudia, Max and myself finally managed to escape with a small group of my loyal followers. We managed to evade Luc and his people for months. One night we slipped back into the castle and killed Normond. I became the Queen, but couldn't publicly lead the clan so that fell to Max. I gave Luc a simple choice - die or go back to his homeland and never return. He chose to leave taking a group of his loyal followers with him. For years we lived in peace and harmony. I married a human and even bore him a child. The child was mostly human, but with some of my vampire blood flowing through him. I finally had to leave with Claudia, Max and about a dozen followers. We moved all over the world, growing our clan and wealth. I never saw the child or my husband again, but over the years Max has followed the family. They were a prominent family and over the past hundred years have become incredibly wealthy.

"About twenty years ago, a doctor who is a member of our clan, was able to do some research and found a poison that could have been given to the target over many months and slowly ate away at his brain until it killed Dimitar. Only someone from our time could have known about it and if used properly can have healing properties. He also found a connection to Luc and we spent many years following his movements. When Claudia started to get sick we saw the connection and there was still no cure. We also learned that Luc had come here to start building an opportunity to get to you. Claudia was... was..." she swiped at a tear.

"I don't know what to say... but why me?"

"Finn... you have great wealth and a global organization. Luc's business and wealth was dwindling due to bad investments and worse habits. And... perhaps to get to me. We think he found out that you are... my only living heir. At this point there is very little of my blood in you."

"We are related? Directly? But we... you... why did you seduce me?"

He felt her tears on his chest and he wiped them away. "Yes - from five hundred years ago but not directly enough. I didn't intend to seduce you. I definitely did not intend on falling in love with you. When Claudia got sick she asked me to watch over you. The rest of our clan was spread around the country but we have been bringing them closer. I had hoped we could have this discussion sooner... I really didn't plan on us. I have lived for many years by distancing myself from people, passion, and love. I was just going to warn you, not tell you how much I love you."

"I am falling for you too. And in the car... holy hell. One kiss of your skin and I was surprised to feel that I couldn't stop. I had to have you."

"Maybe we should go to the office. And talk about this later."

Finn grinned and pulled her t-shirt up over her head then tossed it aside. "Is that all you ever want to do is talk?"

The End

Scattering Elephants by Eleanor Lloyd-Jones

One

Blinking heavily with pursed lips, Billy dropped his eyes to the fretboard of his guitar, concentrating on his fingers as they danced the length of it to the sound of the roaring crowd below. He flicked his head up, droplets of sweat flying through the air from the ends of his hair, and nodded at the patrons who bounced along to his rhythm.

Hitting his pedal with the toe of his boot, he looped the drum beat, taking the opportunity to turn his back to the audience—to break away from the unnerving way that all he had left behind seemed to shine back at him in the eyes of the nameless strangers in the crowd. His breath caught in his chest and Billy squeezed his eyes tightly shut, trying to ignore the ringing in his ears—trying to regain control.

What's happening?

The chorus was creeping up on him, but he still couldn't breathe.

Get a grip.

With his guitar limp by his side, he reached backwards over his shoulder, grabbing the material of his T-shirt, yanking the damn thing off and throwing it to the side of the stage as he took a moment to steady his heaving chest.

Come on, Bill. Come on.

He swiped a bottle of beer from the top of the amp, glugging down as much as he could before slinging his guitar strap back over his head, spinning to face his fans and launching into the final chorus with professional precision.

This time, he strode across the stage—back and forth, back and forth—his naked torso slick with sweat, the contours of his muscles flexing with his movements and the tendons and sinews of his forearms twitching as he thrashed his pain out with each strum of the strings.

Never standing still.

Never giving his past a chance to capture him again until his set was done.

Adrenaline was the best drug, and performing gave him a rush like no other. When he was on stage, he felt free, alive. Night after night, he entertained, warming up the masses for Eboracum Rain and filling his new fans with a feeling only live music could gift. Every night, he would run backstage filled with a euphoric high that carried him through to the morning.

But not tonight...

Another roar from the crowd pushed him off the stage, shaking his guitar high in the air to say thank you to the people who were out there dragging his dream a little closer each time he played.

He had craved acceptance for so long, and now he had it from these strangers who seemed to love him. It was what kept him going—what kept him moving from venue to venue, stage to stage, bigger crowd to bigger crowd, touring the whole of the south of England.

He'd been accepted not as Billy, the son of a drunk; not Billy the carer; but Billy the independent man who'd needed to put his life back together.

And with this acceptance, he was reassured that he'd done exactly the right thing in leaving York. He'd left to find himself, to figure out who he was and how he was supposed to function in the world. He'd spent so long shouldering every other fucker, Eve included, and he'd needed to cut loose.

This was his time, his time to shine, and he was fucking shining.

But despite the good, the positive and the love he had for his new life, he was still so full of her: every day, every night, every waking minute. His mind constantly reeled with memories of her face, of the way he'd left her broken and alone, and how he had run away.

Tonight he had allowed his guilt to consume him.

As he shoved past the band through the doors at the end of the corridor and into the alleyway, he doubled over, retching with his hands on his thighs. Billy dragged air into his lungs, causing them to erupt and leaving him coughing and spluttering. He squeezed his eyes tightly shut and wiped his mouth with the heel of his hand before standing, turning around and planting his palms flat against the brick wall in front of him, his head hanging between his shoulders.

Eventually, his breathing returned to normal and as he stood to his full height, Billy threw a punch at the wall, an angry grunt escaping from the back of his throat before he re-entered the building. He moved quickly past Matt, pushing his hand away as he tried to grab hold of him.

"What's the deal, Bill?"

Slumping into the plastic chair in the dressing room, he pulled out a pack of Camels, snatching at a cigarette with his teeth and sitting forwards to light it. "Nothing."

Dylan sneered from the corner of the room. "Bull."

Billy's eyes flicked over to the drummer of the band, who wasn't known for expressing his opinions verbally.

"I said it's nothing. Shouldn't you be getting ready to go on anyway?"

An arm reached out to hand him a beer, and Billy shook his head, standing and shrugging into his jacket. He couldn't bring himself to go back out there to watch his friends do their set, so he picked up his guitar and walked towards the door. "I'll be in the van."

Entering the alleyway again, he trudged slowly, kicking at broken glass, before reaching the transit that acted as their tour bus.

Digging around in his pocket for the key, he unlocked the door and hauled himself up and inside, moving to the back where he sat and leaned wearily against the cool metal.

What had happened tonight?

He'd been doing this for three years now—every night different, every night something unexpected—but tonight it had been as though someone had reached into his body and squeezed his heart until it had given up. He thought of Eve every day, but tonight a soul destroying pain had grabbed him by the throat up there and shaken him until he couldn't breathe.

He had put his best foot forwards on his journey to heal himself, leaving everyone else behind him until he was sure he was able to be who he was meant to be—for himself and for anyone else who needed him in his future—but tonight had seemed and felt different. Tonight it had been as if the steps forward he had made to get his life in order had taken a wrong turn.

"Yeah, we're in Bradley's." Billy trapped his phone between his raised shoulder and his ear as he dug around in his pockets to find cash to pay the barman, mouthing an apology at him for keeping him waiting. "Well, we can meet you there, can't we?" His eyes squinted as he tried to hear Matt's voice above the humdrum of the pub and grabbing the two full pint glasses, he turned and weaved his way through the crowd. "Right, that's fine. Later."

As the call disconnected, and with his phone still stuck to his face, Billy reached the table Dobbo was waiting at, and he grinned.

"There we go, mate."

The two of them clinked glasses and sat in silence for a moment, downing large mouthfuls of cold liquid, almost synchronised in movement as they reached up and wiped froth from their top lips with the backs of their sleeves.

"Still drinking then?" Dobbo approached the question with a little caution in his voice.

Glancing at him, Billy shrugged, trying hard to disguise the guilt that chugged around in his stomach for countless reasons. "Part of the scene, isn't it."

Dobbo gave him a curt nod. He was reluctant to press any further, his visit being about their friendship and forgetting about real life for a while. He dropped the matter immediately.

"So." Dobbo took another sip of beer and slapped his hand down on the table. "Come on then. Tell me this news."

Billy ran his thumb under his nose before leaning back in his seat, a small smile tugging at the corner of his mouth before he spoke. "I'm playing Glastonbury, mate."

Dobbo almost spat his mouthful of beer across the table. "You're fucking what?"

"Don't get too excited. It's only the BBC Introducing Stage. I'm not headlining just yet."

"I don't give a shit! That's fucking awesome! So you can get me free tickets and backstage passes, right? Who even is headlining this year?"

Billy laughed. "Top secret. As is this news. You can't tell anyone, not even Mo. I'm not meant to be leaking info. And it's really not a big deal. I've not even made Radio One yet."

"Don't be so modest. It's fucking immense. But Mum's the word." He pulled an imaginary zip across his mouth and sat back in his seat, shaking his head with a grin. "Unbelievable. Who'da thunk it, eh?" Draining his pint, he stood. "Next round is on me. Lap it up while I'm offering because you're buying all the rounds forever when you hit the big time," he joked before jostling his way to the bar.

"What's on the cards? I haven't come all the way down to old London Town to sit in a stuffy little hole like this all night, I hope."

Billy laughed. It was a good feeling having his friend by his side, even though he had been a huge part of his life up north—the life he was trying so hard to shake. He'd missed their easy banter, not having seen him for a good few months, and he was determined to relax and put everything aside for the evening—to put aside all of the strangeness from the week before that had continued to climb on his back and wrestle with him night after night.

"We'll have another couple in here and then we're meeting the band at a club they've been given tickets for."

"Sounds good." They sat together through another two pints, avoiding all talk of home—of Eve—as was usual when they saw each other, and Billy remained silent about the details of his recently troubled mind.

Arriving outside the club an hour later, the two of them met up with the band and were ushered in by burly bouncers once they'd shown their VIP tickets.

The bass of the music thumped along their veins as they entered the main room, dance tunes eating up any other sound in the place so that conversation was near impossible.

The group of young men walked towards the back of the club—careful not to bump into male bodies and gently placing their hands in the smalls of female backs in order to squeeze past them—and immediately caught the attention of heavily-lashed eyes and pouting lips from every corner of the large room.

Dobbo didn't notice them: his eyes were fixed on the tops of heads. He scanned the perimeter of the dance floor, taking in the neon lights and dark silhouettes that writhed and flung themselves around to the sound of synthesisers and auto-tuned voices as he manoeuvred his way through. Matt and the lads smiled their best smiles at the girls who were watching their every move, but Billy locked eyes with every one of them, searching for that feeling he was desperate to re-discover—a feeling he'd mourned every day recently and the same feeling that had ripped him apart on stage the week before.

It was unfathomable.

He had gone for so long focusing only on himself, on his need to become the Billy he'd lost along the way. He couldn't put a finger on why he suddenly craved that almost helpless feeling so much when it had nearly floored him with pain and emotion. Yet he continued to search for it, to grasp at anything that made him feel more than the beat of the music, the adrenaline high, the euphoria of being the centre of attention.

He followed the gang to the VIP area where they sat down, immediately swamped by topless waitresses, who delighted in leaning over them to take their orders, another pair of tuxedo-clad heavies watching every move that the punters made.

"Bloody hell." Dobbo stretched over the arm of his chair, his mouth close to Billy's ear. "Tits everywhere."

Billy gave him a smirk and moved his eyes for the fourth time away from the big-breasted woman, who kept giving him the eye as she asked him what he wanted to drink. He ordered a beer from her quickly then turned back to face Dobbo. "I can't stay here all night."

"What?" Dobo scrunched his face up.

Billy raised his voice. "I can't stay around here all night. It's just..." He gestured towards the waitresses and cocked his eyebrow. "Not really my scene."

Dobbo laughed and shook his head. "No, mate. Not mine either, but we get free drinks for the next two hours, so I'm not about to complain."

He had a point, and Billy sank into his seat, his legs stretched out in front of him, conceding defeat for the time being.

The pair settled into easy banter, albeit stilted due to the noise levels, and the drinks continued to flow. They watched as other groups of guests entered the cordoned off area, their names ticked off the coveted list, and Billy soon relaxed and forgot about how uncomfortable he was.

"So where are you from?" A blue-eyed blonde plonked herself next to him, her ripped jeans and untamed, long, platinum hair pulling his attention away from the bottom of his glass.

He glanced up at her, his eyes flicking over her features momentarily before he cleared his throat and answered. "What are you doing here?"

Libby reminded him a little of Kate Moss in the way she was effortlessly beautiful and how she looked good in anything she wore. She shrugged out of her leather jacket, revealing a worn Rolling Stones gig T-shirt, and slung it across an empty stool, making herself comfortable beside him. "You didn't answer my calls last week."

Billy continued to watch her, enjoying the confident air that she exuded, completely transfixed by the way she always seemed comfortable in her own skin.

"I'm erm..." He let out an amused laugh and shook his head a little, dropping it between his shoulders. "I've been busy."

She smiled and nodded. "Thought that might be the case. I could see you're not busy now so thought I'd take my chances."

Billy eyed her with his usual interest. "How did you know I was going to be here?"

She picked up his pint and took a sip from it. "I have my means."

Glancing at her long, slim fingers—her nails chewed to within an inch of their lives—he replied. "Of course you do."

He spent the next hour with his mouth close to Libby's ear, his own finely tuned to the gravelly sound of her voice and with his senses filled with her floral scent. Each time their eyes met, something inside of him would ignite, and for a split second he wondered if this was what he had been waiting for. Had he been too blind to pick up on it, too drunk, too stupid, too self-involved? As they sat in the dark corner of the club, they discussed music and how it had swallowed them both whole, while a strange and increasingly familiar chemical reaction that grew from a shared passion took hold of him like a burning flame. They talked about how the excitement of performing kept them dream-chasing. His eyes caught her blue ones in a silent exchange of mutual attraction and lust, the magnetic pull of their shared enthusiasm creating a bubble of compatibility. Billy's gaze roamed across her collarbone that lay bare above her low-necked T-shirt; he chewed the inside of his cheek as his gaze flitted across his features; and he clenched his teeth to relieve the ache as he watched, transfixed, the way she combed her fingers through her hair to brush it back from her face while she talked.

She was beautiful.

She made him feel good.

Was that enough?

Was this it?

Dobbo sat beside Matt and the boys, joining in with their chatter, but kept glancing over at the pair who seemed completely lost to anyone else in the room. He scrutinised them, their body language speaking volumes and their eye contact uncomfortable to watch.

"Who's that?" He leaned back in his chair, gesturing over towards Billy with his beer bottle before taking a generous swig.

Jason shrugged. "Libby. She's become a bit of a regular."

Flicking his eyes back over to his friend, Dobbo observed the intensity that their discussion held. It was strange to see Billy so tuned in to another woman—it was an alien sight—but he wondered if this was the turning point he'd been anticipating, the shift he had hoped for.

For a long time after Billy left, there had been no one. Whenever Dobbo had made the trip to see him, he'd almost been able to see Billy's broken heart through his chest. So much had weighed his friend down back then, and if he were to be truthful, he was glad to see the change in him—to see he was finally moving past the whole thing.

He'd watched Eve begin to heal and move on, too, but had been worried Billy would try to rekindle things with her instead of laying his past to rest. Dobbo was fond of Eve, but too much time had passed—too much irreparable damage had been done back then in York for it to be even remotely healthy for either of them to step backwards and try to fight for something he was sure had died along with Billy's father.

Billy stood and pulled on his jacket. "Are you coming then?"

"Coming where?"

"Libby's invited us to her house party." Billy flicked his head to the right of him. "Thought it might be fun." The corner of his mouth lifted into a half-smile and Dobbo shrugged, not wanting to abandon his friend.

"Guess so. Thanks, Libby." He glanced across at her and threw his thumb back over his shoulder. "The lads invited, too?"

She winked at him. "Sure. The more the merrier."

Billy followed Libby out of the VIP area and down the steps, his heart racing with anticipation and an alcohol-fuelled confidence that he was becoming more than familiar with. Her slim figure led the band of friends out into the cool night air, and it wasn't long before they were piling through the front door of a large Victorian terrace that swarmed with strangers, beer bottles swinging by their sides or their limbs tangled together on large sofas and armchairs that littered every room.

"Help yourselves to drinks in there," Libby shouted above the dull bass of the music, pointing into the large kitchen—the hub of the party. She high-fived a couple of lads and grinned at some equally beautiful girls, whose bodies were slumped against the wall in drunken ecstasy as they allowed pairs of roaming hands to explore greedily beneath their clothes.

There was a distinct smell of weed and the musky scent of student life in the air, and as Billy took in his surroundings, Libby took his hand and led him down the hallway, his easy compliance watched carefully by Dobbo.

Two

Stumbling bleary-eyed and naked into the bathroom in the early hours of the morning, Billy stood in front of the toilet as he emptied his bladder. Pulling the handle down on the cistern, he watched the water flush away the last remaining evidence of his evening before shuffling back to the bedroom he'd woken up in. He sat down on the edge of the bed, his elbows on his knees and his head in his hands, glancing to the floor to locate his clothes and boots but stopping as an arm snaked around his waist from behind, a long, tanned and naked leg hooking itself over his thigh.

Libby's husky voice reached his ear. "Don't leave yet. It's Saturday."

He took a moment to school his facial expression into something a little more welcoming than the one he knew he was wearing—the alcohol cloak he'd worn last night slipping away and revealing the turmoil he'd been trying to hide.

Turning his body, he faced the blonde beauty whose tousled, just-been-fucked hair and come-to-bed eyes had his dick remembering exactly how the remainder of his night had panned out, images of hot sex with her flooding his consciousness.

She reached out and pulled him to her by the back of his neck until he was lying beside her, her full lips pressing against his. She found his hand with her own and before he had a chance to resist, she pulled it under the duvet, dragging his fingers down the naked, velvet-like skin of her stomach and through the wet heat between her thighs, a soft moan leaving the back of her throat as her hips lifted from the bed.

"See what you do to me?" Her breathy whisper against his mouth had him releasing his own guttural moan, the physical attraction he always felt in her presence pooling at the pit of his stomach. She guided his fingers deeper—his thumb brushing the most sensitive part of her—pulling his hips to hers as her tongue danced with his in a lazy morning kiss.

He'd slept with his fair share of women during his time away—groupies desperate for attention, usually—and often after a skinful of beer when his head had switched off and his dick had switched on. All of it was mindless, none of it satisfying other than in a physical sense.

But there was something different about this girl that seemed to amplify each time he saw her, and she'd been the first girl he'd looked twice at since arriving in London.

When he'd left York, his love for Eve had been as strong as it ever had, yet loving her had been the most complicated part of his existence. It was all-consuming, and it had remained that way for months. He'd continued to struggle every day to forgive himself for letting her go in her hour of need, but those last few weeks after Eve had returned from her mother's house had buried into his skin like a parasite, his father's death and the accident punctuating everything like a huge fucking exclamation mark.

They'd tried so hard to carry on as normal, but normal hadn't existed anymore. Grief had eaten him alive, stealing his ability to be strong, and strength had been what Eve had needed back then.

He hadn't been able to be strong for her.

He hadn't been able to be strong for himself.

Not then.

And now?

Now, it was three years down the line and he hadn't spoken to her since the morning of his father's funeral.

Now, there was Libby.

There was much about her that was so far removed from Eve and her life that being around her meant he felt free. Libby was confident, uncomplicated, without a history, and when he was with her, he felt a little lighter and a little emptier instead of being full to the brim with unsquashable emotion.

The previous evening had been one filled with chatter that hadn't involved hurt or heartache, and the sex had been devoid of feeling.

Leaving his home and the only girl he had ever loved, he'd not really been sure what the future would hold for him, but Libby had begun to occupy his hours of loneliness with her bright optimism and her carefree outlook on life. She was filling a hole, keeping his head above water in so many ways. His heart would slow to a normal pace when she was around, his brain ceasing to be fuzzy with hurt and guilt, and he felt able to let go. He let go of everything whenever they were together, and it felt good. It felt liberating to be reckless and to not berate himself for all of his short fallings.

Whenever he was with Libby, he felt like the weight of his past lifted, and it felt good.

However, there was always a flip side, and the flip side of feeling good was him feeling heavier than he had ever felt once the glow wore off.

Like now, when reality struck him like a wrecking ball: she in fact wasn't Eve and therefore didn't compare.

He pushed his thoughts away, and after they'd satisfied each other for another hour, Billy made his way downstairs and sat on the moth-eaten sofa in the living room with a hot drink.

"Morning, Romeo." Dobbo's mocking tone sliced through Billy's headache like a knife through butter as he continued to stare into the bottom of his coffee cup, refusing to rise to the taunt. A slap of a hand on his shoulder had him jolting from his thoughts, and he turned to see his friend's expression much less judgemental than he'd expected. There was a certain amount of understanding in his eyes as he sat down next to his friend, and Billy pulled his lips into a tight smile.

"What time is it? My battery is dead."

Dobbo glanced at his phone. "Nearly half ten. We got plans for the day?"

Draining the last of his drink, Billy shook his head. "Nothing in particular. Only plans to get out of here and have a shower. Fancy seeing some sights?"

Before replying, Dobbo scrubbed his hands down his face. "I rather fancy spending some time seeing inside that head of yours, buddy. You seem a little... distracted."

Billy's head kicked up and he turned to look at him. He was his best friend. If he couldn't open up to him, who could he talk to?

He inhaled deeply and averted his eyes, staring ahead of him. "Dude, I'm a mess. I'm not sure you really want that tour."

"I mean, I get it. She's fucking gorgeous, but I have the feeling she's just a plaster...a temporary patch for—"

"Don't. Don't make this into something it's not. This has nothing to do with Eve." Billy ran his thumb underneath his nose and stood, shoving his hands into his pockets as he walked over to the window. Truth was, it had everything to do with Eve. She was all he'd been able to focus on all week, and spending the night with Libby had been a subconscious attempt to get rid of those thoughts, he was sure of it.

He took a deep breath. "How is she?"

There was so much silence. It was the first time she'd been brought up in conversation, and Billy waited patiently as Dobbo gathered his thoughts.

"She's okay, I think. I haven't seen much of her since—"

"What?" Billy flicked his eyes to his friend, his brow furrowing. "Since what? What's happened?"

Dobbo rubbed his hand across his chin and grimaced. "Um..."

"Fuck's sake, Dobs. What? Is she okay?" Billy clenched his back teeth, his heart thumping wildly. "What the hell has happened?"

Inhaling deeply and blowing the air back out again just as noisily, Dobbo squinted up at him. "She's with someone. She's in, erm, in a relationship."

Billy stopped dead, his eyes never leaving Dobbo's. His mind emptied of everything he had been trying to push away in recent days, and all he could think of were the words he'd just heard.

She was in a relationship.

She was with someone else.

Someone else.

Eve was with someone else.

He crouched down and scrubbed his hands up and down his face, his brows rising. "Wow."

"Sorry, mate. I didn't want to, y'know..." Dobbo sighed. "We haven't been discussing her, so I thought you wouldn't be interested in knowing."

He wasn't interested. Was he? Either way, the news had seared him from the inside out.

"How long?"

Dobbo twisted his mouth to the side. "A year. Maybe? Bit longer?"

A fucking year. They'd kept this from him for a year.

Billy rubbed the heel of his hand on his breastbone in an attempt to ease the ache in his heart. He'd often wondered how one's body could react so violently and so instantly to trauma or upset, like how you could wake up with that feeling in the pit of your stomach when you were anticipating a difficult day ahead.

A year.

A whole year.

She'd spent a whole twelve months getting to know someone else as intimately as she'd known him. Twelve months—even longer than they'd been together.

Well, that was that.

Dobbo sat silently, watching the news spread through Billy's whole body.

"I mean. That's good, right?" Billy's eyes pleaded with his friend to agree with him, to take this feeling of despair away from him so he could make peace with it somehow. "Means she's happy. Right?"

Dobbo sniffed and nodded gently. "Yeah. I think she is. Like I said, I haven't seen her for a while. She's still in York, but she moved across to Southbank after uni finished last year. I think she lives there with Jamie."

Billy lifted his head quickly, his eyes wide. "Jamie. That's his name, huh?"

"Yeah."

"Have you met him?" His questions were firing out of his mouth faster than he could process them.

Holding him in his gaze for what felt like an eternity before he cleared his throat, Dobbo nodded. "Um, yeah. I, erm... I met him a bit ago. Seems decent enough. Don't know him really."

Decent? He'd better be fucking decent. He'd better be the best goddamned thing that has ever happened to her.

"Good." Billy stood and pushed his hand through his hair before grabbing his jacket from the arm of the sofa. "Good. Okay. Let's get out of here, huh? Let's go nuts."

Standing and shrugging into his coat, Dobbo nodded, but his mind was reeling. Billy had Libby. So why was he acting like his world had just caved in? He had been hopeful that his friend was over all the crap from three years ago, but seeing that look in his eyes, he wasn't so sure.

"Fuck's sake." The words came out as a quiet breath, and he followed Billy out of the living room, into the hallway and towards the front door.

"Hey, handsome." Libby appeared at the top of the stairs, scantily clad in an oversized T-shirt and bed socks. "Where are you disappearing off to?"

Billy continued to walk towards the front door.

"Billy."

Dobbo shrugged as Libby rolled her eyes and ran down the stairs to catch up with them. She jumped on Billy's back as he reached the door, wrapping her arms and legs around him.

Stopping, he sighed, turning his head over his shoulder to look at her. "I'll call you later. Just got some shit to deal with."

She slid down and moved to stand in front of him, cupping him through his jeans and pushing her mouth against his in a kiss that Dobbo could only describe as pornographic.

"You've always got shit to deal with. Don't let me down, Taylor. I'll be waiting for you in my bed tonight."

Billy closed his eyes and clenched his back teeth as she shimmied away from them, winking at Dobbo as she passed, who whistled through his teeth.

"Lucky son of a bitch, that's all I can say."

Billy pulled the front door open and stepped into the cold morning air, immediately reaching for his cigarettes. He leaned against the wall of the house and shielded the flame from the Zippo that he carried everywhere, his eyes lingering on the inscription for a moment.

Follow your heart... I'll be right behind you following it, too.

Full story coming soon...

Three's Company by Elle M Thomas

An Erotic Short Story

"Hey there, baby cakes, how was it?" Daryl calls as I close the front door behind me.

"Shit." My answer is a serious understatement because it didn't feel as though even one area of my life was currently positive. Turning into the lounge, my flat mate is sitting with his girlfriend, Mila, the two of them looking the picture of happiness.

"Hi, Mila." I smile as I take in her appearance, freshly showered, and wearing the shortest of cotton shorts and a vest, but clearly no bra judging by the way her boobs are moving freely and her nipples look as though they might take someone's eye out.

I chide myself for being jealous of the way she's draped over Daryl, especially as they have obviously already been shagging. My jealousy is for the shagging rather than her personally because she is one of the nicest people I have ever met and I genuinely like her. She is exactly the sort of person I would hand pick for my friend, and there has never been anything remotely romantic with me and Daryl.

"Was he not your type?" Mila asks, referring to my date, first date, another first date. The last in an ever-growing list of disastrous dates.

"No, he was," I begin and allow a small, short smile as I recall my date. "He was tall, dark, and handsome, just like his profile picture. He was funny, charming and clearly after a one-night stand."

"Oh." Both Daryl and Mila say as they pull apart.

"I mean, don't get me wrong I want to have sex, in fact I am gagging for it. It has been a year since I had sex with another human being and I miss it." I drop into the space they've made for me, nestled between them, none of us bothered by the directness of my admission. "But not like that. Why would I go to the trouble of joining an online dating agency if all I wanted was a quick shag? I could go to a pub or a club and do that." I sigh, sad as well as frustrated now.

"You deserve better than a line of slime balls, baby cakes." There's anger in Daryl's voice that makes me smile a little, just knowing he cares about me as much as I care for him means I don't hate every man on the planet.

"Maybe I should just do it." I feel their heavy gazes from either side. "Next date, if I fancy them, shag them, scratch my itch, and then give myself another year to meet a real person." My musings aren't really serious, well, they might be, a little bit.

I am shocked when Daryl turns to me, his hand firmly gripping my chin as he turns me to face him. His expression is dark and his voice raised. "Don't you fucking dare. If you do, I am going to be beyond pissed off with you, and I'll... whatever, just forget that idea right now. I don't like you doing the online dating never mind shagging them, and not because you're a woman or anything like that, but you deserve to be treated with respect and sleeping with you should be something that is valued. You should not be a notch on anyone's bedpost, not ever."

I'm unsure what to say, and with his hand still holding my face, I look at him, simply staring into his dark brown eyes and allow him to continue to speak.

"Oh, and forget clubs and pubs to pick someone up, too... we'll sort it," he says a little softer, then pulls me in for a hug while Mila seems to be stroking circles on my back and patting my leg.

I awkwardly release myself from between them. I love Daryl, but he can be a little overprotective and overbearing. I don't think he has ever really approved of anyone I've dated and as much as he is this way because he cares and wants me to be happy and safe, sometimes, like tonight, it's a little too much.

Mila, possibly sensing I am becoming overwhelmed, puts her arm around my shoulders and pulls me in for a friendly hug. "Ooh, you're so tense."

"Come on, let me give you a massage," Daryl offers. As much as I think going to bed would be the best option, I don't want him to think I am being off with him. Especially not after his threat of whatever it was, and his weird, angry, bossy mood change just a few seconds before.

He spreads his legs and taps his inner thigh to indicate that I should position myself between them, which I do. This is not the first shoulder massage I have had from him and I hope not the last as he has very talented fingers.

Gently at first, his fingers get to work rubbing and kneading the taut muscles across my shoulders, then his touch gets firmer, working the tight knots, forcing them to loosen up, making me cry out in discomfort while I attempt to pull away. It hurts, but I know that's due to the tension I am holding and will feel the benefit of it once it's done. I enjoy a massage, but I prefer a relaxing one; fragrant oils filling my senses while warm, lubricated hands glide over my skin making me feel lax, warm, and usually sleepy.

My earlier moans of protest become more appreciative as the stress across my shoulders begins to ease. With my eyes closed, I can almost forget that I am sat on the lounge floor between my best friend's thighs. Instead, I imagine myself lying face down, on a bed, maybe in a spa or at the beach. Somewhere hot, the heat of the sun warming my skin as much as the hands skimming across my flesh. Hands moving down my back, my hips, my legs, covering my sides as well as my back, bringing my whole body to life before reversing the journey up my body, perhaps diverting as my legs spread slightly, allowing the oiled fingers to explore..

A loud mewl brings me out of what was ultimately a fantasy playing in my head. Shit! This little scenario is all the more shocking because it has Daryl front and centre, touching me in a way I have never imagined before.

Looking around, I realise that my friend and his girlfriend are watching me, meaning they're fully aware of the effect Daryl's hands were having on me.

Leaping to my feet, I spin to face them, my face burning with embarrassment and quite clumsily make excuses to go to bed but offer a final thought as I attempt to gather my equilibrium. "If I can't bang my matches online, and you're banning clubs and pubs, I might as well join a convent because I may actually be turning into a born again virgin."

Mila laughs, and in turn I laugh, too, slightly less angsty and awkward until Daryl speaks again.

"Good. Virginity looks good on you."

When I wake up, I see it's just after midnight, meaning I haven't been asleep that long. I quickly roll over and will my mind not to become too alert or else I will never get back to sleep. A noise startles me. It's quickly followed by another. I figure that is what woke me and potentially what is going to be the cause of any insomnia I now suffer. The sounds continue, getting louder, and with a grimace they become all too familiar. Daryl and Mila are having sex. Could this night get any worse? Turning down the chance of a quick bunk up with my date seems even more of a mistake now. I recall how angry Daryl became at the idea of me having any kind of hook up. I'm not sure I have ever heard him speak with such firmness before. He often speaks with that authority at work but never at home and never directed at me. I ignore the burn in my tummy, coiling and spreading lower as I replay his words. *Don't you fucking dare. If you do, I am going to be beyond pissed off with you, and I'll . . .* What had he been about to say? What had been the threat he'd cut off? And why am I now imagining how my best friend's kiss and touch might feel?

"Oh God!" Mila cries making me groan and then she begins to pant and moan.

That is just what I don't need to hear, sex. People having sex with another person rather than a vibrator or their own hand.

"All me, Mila," Daryl tells her as she begins to mewl like a cat calling. "And don't ever fucking forget it." Unless I am mistaken, his voice is a growl and if that doesn't have me squeezing my thighs together.

In other circumstances I would laugh, but tonight I might cry instead. I don't ever recall being so sexually frustrated. My body is tightly wound and the pent up urges and desire are messing with my head if I am thinking of Daryl in any way other than a platonic one. If it was anyone else besides Daryl and Mila, I'd swear they were doing this on purpose, to be cruel, but they wouldn't, I know that. Although they do seem to be especially loud tonight.

My own hand creeps beneath my pyjama bottoms, finding me wet. Greedy for relief, my fingers dips inside me before using my own arousal to easily move to my clit. The sound of Mila's moaning and cries serves an aphrodisiac, as does the sound of Daryl's dirty talk.

"I'm going to make you beg me to fuck this pussy, and you're going to, aren't you?"

Biting into my own lip prevents me from responding, unlike Mila who is as on board with the plan as I appear to be.

"Whose pussy is this?"

Fuck me! What has gotten into Daryl tonight? Has he forgotten I am home and the walls are thin?

"Yours," Mila whines.

"Too fucking right it is. And whose arse is this?"

My fingers still. I had not been expecting that. In fairness, none of what is happening had been expected, but definitely not that. I'm unsure if I miss Mila's response because the next voice I hear is Daryl's.

"Are you going to be a good girl and take my cock in your arse?"

I stifle my own moans, desperate to feel someone inside me, touching me, kissing me, holding me. Even Daryl, I tell myself before a louder voice in my head shocks me, *only Daryl*.

Mila begins to chant, "Yes, yes, I'm going to come."

She's not the only one judging by the speed with which my fingers are moving now as I try to push all thoughts of my best friend from my head because thinking of him in that way would end in tears, especially since he doesn't see me that way.

"Yes, babe," Daryl tells her. "Fucking do it, come for me."

Oh God! I am going to come thinking of Daryl.

"I love you," Mila says and Daryl reciprocates.

Just like that I am pulling my hand from my clothing and getting out of bed, hearing their declaration of love in the aftermath of her climax from their love making has just turned me off, even if the burn between my thighs when I stand disputes that.

My plan is to go into the kitchen and grab a drink before going back to my room and watching something on catch up, with earphones in, but you know what they say about best laid plans.

As I am about to pass Daryl's room, I notice that the door is unusually open. I should walk straight past, I intend to, but the sound of Mila moaning again draws me in and as I attempt to position myself out of sight, I witness my friend's naked girlfriend sprawled out on his bed, thrashing around in the midst of the orgasm she had warned Daryl of a few seconds before. My pussy clenches and I swear I feel moisture pooling in my shorts. I cross my legs, hoping for some kind of relief but all that does is make my clit pulse and for a second, I think I might come.

Spreading my legs, I see Daryl leaning over Mila. One hand is between her thighs and he has a finger, maybe a couple inside of her, and is also stroking her clit from his position between her lewdly spread thighs and now that he is hovering over her, he takes one of her nipples into his mouth as she rides out the remainder of her climax. My glance flits between the sight of the other woman's pleasure and Daryl's rock hard cock that his free hand is stroking. I have never thought of Daryl in sexual terms, not really, but if I had, I may not have done him justice.

"Do you want my cock inside you, fucking you and making you come again?"

I all but answer in the affirmative but it's not me he's speaking to. I am beyond jealous now; my nipples are pressing hard against the fabric of my thin pyjama top, I can feel how swollen my clit is and my earlier wetness has increased, to the extent that my shorts are stuck to me and embarrassingly, all I can think about is going back to my room, getting several of my toys out and making myself come to the backdrop of the fantasy of Mila and Daryl.

My own arousal distracts me from anything else until I realise that Mila is quiet and calm again and as I return my full attention back towards the bed, there are four eyes focused on me.

What should I do? Run, hide, apologise? I am running through countless options when Mila speaks.

"Hey there, what took you so long?"

"What?" I stammer.

"Come in, we've been waiting." Mila grins.

"I erm . . ."

"Luce, come in, if you want," Daryl says. "We'd like you to, but only if you want to."

"With you, both of you?" I ask nervously and disbelievingly.

"Mmm," Daryl confirms. "You need something we can give you; it doesn't need to be weird."

I am staring, wildly, but as I am about to protest that no matter what else this might be, it will definitely be weird, it might just be the weirdest situation I have ever been in.

My objection sticks in my throat when Daryl gets off the bed and begins to stride towards me and I see him in all his naked glory, and how glorious he is. I can't stop looking at his cock that is erect, glistening, and resting against his belly. It is big and beautiful, perfectly nestled in a thatch of dark hair that reduces to reveal large balls hanging, begging to be cupped and stroked.

"Daryl," I whisper but have already moved closer, crossing the threshold.

He comes to a standstill before me and then leans down to kiss me, lips on lips for a brief moment, but as his tongue licks across the seam of mine, I open up, welcoming him inside. The feeling of a body behind me startles me until I feel Mila's breath on my neck while Daryl's tongue continues to explore my mouth. The hands from behind are pushing beneath my pyjama top, stroking the skin of my belly and slowly they move up until they reach the underside of my breasts.

I remember messing around with a girl once before, years ago when I was about seventeen and at a party. It was fun, although boys are my thing really.

Daryl breaks our kiss and smiles down at me, "You don't have to do this, if you don't want to..."

I cut him off by turning to face Mila and after removing my pyjama top, I cup her face to pull her in for a deep and lustful kiss. Girls kiss differently to boys, their lips are softer and their tongues are less forceful but nice, gentler.

Daryl is behind me now and is wrapping himself around me. He has one hand running up my belly while the other one is pushing my trousers down until I am stepping out of them. Both hands work in unison now until they each hold a breast; cupping, holding, weighing and teasing before eventually honing in on my nipples that are aching and swollen.

My groan of pain and pleasure is lost in a gasp that's caught in Mila's mouth. As Daryl teases and torments me into a frenzy, Mila is taking control of our kiss. So much for girls being less forceful, gentler. I can feel Daryl's erection rubbing and poking me which only makes me even more frantic, so much so that I think I might actually come without being touched below the waist.

"Luce," Daryl whispers against my neck and sensing he might be about to stop, I break the kiss and desperately reply.

"Don't stop. I want this."

"Then get on the fucking bed and show yourself to me."

I would never have expected kind, sweet Daryl to speak this way, certainly not to me, even if I now knew he was dominant with Mila. By contrast, I had never considered myself to be in any way submissive, but here I am making my way to the bed and settling in the middle of it.

The blood was hammering through my veins, nerves and excitement mingling as Mila and Daryl come to stand beside me as I lay my arms at my side, leaving an unobstructed view of my breasts as I spread my legs.

"Look how fucking wet you are." Daryl drops onto the bed between my splayed thighs.

Immediately I close them, but only a little before his hands move to push them back open, maybe wider than before.

"Whose pussy is this?"

Recalling him asking Mila the same question, I already know the answer. "Yours."

He grins. "Too fucking right, so don't ever hide it from me or I will tie your legs apart and fuck you until you remember who it belongs to."

The moan that leaves my lips makes him smile more, but his eyes are fixed on my pussy that may have just leaked arousal all over the bed.

"How long were you at the door, watching?" Mila asks, coming to lie on the bed next to me.

"I saw you come, and Daryl touched himself. I heard you before that."

Mila reaches forward and turns my face to hers. "We're going to make you feel so good, okay?" She smiles at my nod. "I have been desperate to touch you since the first time I set eyes on you, but Daryl didn't think you'd want to share."

"I do," I cry, unsure if I know what I want right now.

"There's no pressure," Daryl tells me, his voice softer than a few seconds ago, reminding me of the friend I know so well.

My nod is for Daryl this time.

Mila pulls my mouth to hers and kisses me again, her tongue quickly making its way into my mouth, distracting me from the dip of the bed on the other side.

Hands cover my body and although they blur at times, the smaller softer ones are easy to distinguish from the larger firmer ones that are currently skimming down my body, not stopping until one of them is nestled between my thighs.

I'm not entirely sure how it happens but we all end up in a big hug in the middle of the bed. Daryl is lying behind me, my back to his front and Mila is in front, chest to chest, and it feels divine. Mila's lips seem to be attached to my own, her kisses leaving me equally desperate as I am breathless, the caressing and touching of my breasts as relentless as her kisses. She introduces pinches and rolls of my nipples and as they become firmer with each touch, my mewls become louder and more frantic.

"Oh God!" I cry as Daryl pulls my knee up and I feel his erection prodding my entrance.

"What is it with you girls that you keep giving God the credit for my work here?" he asks with a laugh against my ear that sees me reaching behind to grab his hip in an attempt to pull him closer, to pull him in. "Soon, baby cakes, condom first." Daryl moves as far as the top drawer of his bedside cabinet where I know he keeps his condom stash.

It's a matter of seconds before he is positioned behind me again, sheathed and ready.

"Daryl," I moan as he edges closer still, but he simply kisses my ear, kisses, licks and then nips it as his hand runs over my hip and travels lower until he applies pressure to my mound, making me buck against him.

My desperation is no secret to anyone in this room, although, right now, the fact that I am hanging onto my composure by a thread may not be apparent. Mila releases my mouth and is scooting down a little where she suckles against one of my breasts while her hands work the other one.

I am a mass of sensation right now, my breasts are being tormented in the most glorious way and there seem to be hands everywhere, including my own that are reaching forward and behind to pull my lovers closer, preventing them from stopping what they're doing. My moans are getting louder, deeper, and more desperate with every touch, thought and breath.

Daryl still hasn't entered me and I am just about ready to beg when I feel something rimming my sopping wet entrance. I want to push back onto it but all of the hands holding me prevent that.

"Please," I plead and am relieved to feel a finger enter me fully, then it is withdrawn and a second is added. "Thank you, oh God!" I whine as sensations begin to ricochet through my body.

Another hand is between my thighs, possibly Mila as this one feels smaller, more delicate. Who it belongs to doesn't bother me at all because it is gently stroking my clit and edging me towards release.

"You need to come, baby?" Daryl asks, his words only exciting me further.

"Mmm," I manage to reply as I try to focus on the feelings I am chasing and dreaming of.

Mila immediately begins to increase the suction and pinching on my nipples at the same time as her other hand picks up speed, rubbing and circling my clit. All the time Daryl is driving his fingers in and out of me, making sure he is stroking all my special places as he does so and then with a final nip at my neck, I am coming undone in the most spectacular style.

I can hear my own garbled words, cries and screams as I shake and tremble with the intensity of my climax. My sex is contracting around Daryl's fingers while my clit throbs beneath Mila's touch.

I can barely catch my breath as they each continue to work me, intent on drawing every last ounce of pleasure from me until I am unsure whether this is all one orgasm or whether this is a multiple affair, but whatever it is, it is like nothing I have ever known.

Eventually I stop crying and calling and quickly become aware of my neighbours who must have heard me and will be in no doubt about what has just occurred.

The sensations that were previously giving me pleasure are bordering on the painful now, my flesh is over-sensitised, but as I try to pull away only my breasts are unhanded.

"It hurts," I whine as Mila continues to manipulate my clit.

"Ssh," she soothes as she moves back up so that we are eye to eye again. "It's going to feel good," she assures me and a split second later I feel a glorious burn warming my sex, somewhere between pleasure and pain. I never knew pain like this existed, pain that I want to feel again.

As I begin to embrace it and allow it to wash over and absorb me, Daryl moves a little lower and replaces his finger with his cock. The way it stretches and fills me only intensifies the burn Mila started and I can already feel another orgasm beginning to build.

"Oh, Lucy," he whispers hoarsely. "You feel so fucking good."

I feel a sense of panic that as his girlfriend, Mila is about to flip out because not only is her boyfriend fucking me, he's telling me and her how good it feels. She seems to recognise my worry and leans in to kiss me, pausing with her lips against mine.

"Don't think about it, enjoy it," she says as she runs a hand through my hair to gently cradle my head.

"But…" I begin but she cuts me off, which is for the best really as I was unsure what I was going to say next; 'but he's your boyfriend', 'but you haven't come', 'but this is all going to be very complicated in the morning'. Any of those would have been options, but right now she is stemming any words with her kiss.

Instinctively, I allow her entry to my mouth with her tongue and meekly lap against her tongue that is replicating fucking, somehow perfectly in time with Daryl whose thrusts are becoming harder and faster. Mila's still playing and teasing my clit that I can feel is engorged.

I am at the eye of a tidal storm.

"Come on, baby," Daryl seems to demand as he drives into me, "Come for me, while I fuck you."

I feel the crash of the wave as I tip over the edge. With more crying and screaming, I am unsure where I start and Daryl and Mila end. We are all fused together in a gigantic ball of frenzied arousal and release and then everything slows, becomes less fraught and erratic as we all come down.

There's an awkwardness settling in my chest as I realise the enormity of what has just occurred.

Daryl is my best friend and we have never come close to having sex before. His girlfriend is Mila and they are in a serious relationship and then there is me, literally and metaphorically wedged between them now.

Daryl is moving, heading for the bathroom where I assume he discards the condom and Mila is getting into bed. I have no clue what to do or what to say so quickly get up and gather my clothes and am preparing to leave when Daryl returns.

My nakedness causes embarrassment now, to me at least, not him, he smiles as he eyes me up and down.

"Get into bed," he says flatly and I am deciding whether I should run to my room and lock the door.

I attempt to sidestep him but he moves.

"Lucy, get into bed," he says again but points at the space next to Mila, "Unless you want to go back to your room and we can all pretend this didn't happen, that it was a dream."

I look back at Mila who is throwing the covers back, inviting me in.

"What about in the morning?" I ask, although my question really is so much more than that.

"Well," Daryl begins as he steps closer and strokes a hand over my cheek. "I need a brief recharge and then I was hoping you ladies would like to ride me, one on my dick and the other on my face."

"Oh," I say, and could kick myself for that alone.

"Lucy," Mila calls. "We've done this before, with someone we knew, but it's cool, we're cool with whatever you want to do. Like Daryl said we can forget, pretend, whatever."

Looking between the two of them I know they mean every word and I don't know if this will last beyond tonight or if it's something I would want to do on an ongoing basis, but for tonight, I clearly want it as I am already taking up a position in the middle of Daryl's bed and he is climbing in behind me leaving me sandwiched between him and Mila once more.

THE END

More Than Men: The Lost Diaries by Gemini Black

The following pages are excerpts from a diary found in an abandoned lab facility following intel from a group of escaped victims. Their experiences were harrowing to say the least, so continue with caution.

Day 12

If you're reading these pages, I'm probably dead. We all are, me and my friends that is. My name is Jasper and my friends are Ben, Darryl, Spencer and Cole. The year is 2014, but I have no idea of the month. We are being held at a facility somewhere in Europe by a group of men calling themselves KJ-51. We are human guinea pigs for a large-scale criminal experiment. Time is running out for us.

It's day twelve in this godforsaken hell hole. Well, twelve days that I've been aware of. I have no idea how long we've actually been here as we were drugged for an unknown amount of time. Judging by my weight loss and facial hair, it was a while.

Every day is the same and yet somehow different. It's always torturous and unbearable, they just find new ways to make it so. At least they're creative, I'll give them that much. I haven't seen the others for a few days now. I haven't even heard their screams. I don't know what's worse, hearing their pain or hearing nothing at all. The silence makes my overactive brain concoct all sorts of reasons as to why I haven't seen or heard them. If they've killed them, I'll find a way to end my own life. They're the only thing keeping me going. If they're all dead then there's no way these fuckers are getting what they need from me. They can get screwed.

I tried to ask one of the lab technicians yesterday but they never speak directly to us, they're not allowed. This place is fucking weird, the people who run it are more robotic and monstrous than the so called 'super beings' they're trying to create. They're like some sort of sick cult, all brainwashed to believe that what they're doing serves some sort of greater purpose for the good of humanity.

It's so hard to get my head around what's happened, even for a brain like mine. One minute we were out drinking in this bar, having the time of our lives on holiday and the next thing we know we're chained to beds in what can only be described as Frankenstein's laboratory on crack. I found this old notebook yesterday under the cupboard in my cell and managed to swipe a pen from one of the technician's pockets. I'm hoping that writing my thoughts down might go some way to keeping me sane and helping me to process.

As far as I can tell, I'm the only one so far who's no longer restrained. I caught on fast that if I comply then my treatment is slightly less barbaric. Sadly, the others are slower to adapt and far more stubborn. Darryl has been sedated more often than not. He knocked out three agents and two technicians within the first eight hours of waking up so they injected him with something and he was out for several days.

That was when we were all still in one long room in a row of hospital beds. They quickly realised that keeping us together was going to be bad news for them and split us up. For a few days I could hear them screaming in pain and shouting out for help. I even heard them cry. There's nothing quite as desperate as the sound of grown men crying. Especially when

those men are the closest thing you have to brothers. Now I hear nothing. I don't know what I hate more.

There are people that love us back in the real world. We will be missed and being looked for. My hope is fading though, whoever these KJ-51 people are, they are not amateurs and it will not be easy to find us. That's if there's anything left of us worth finding by the time they're done.

Day 13 (that I know of)

I saw Spencer today. He looked like shit. It was only for a moment as he was being dragged past my cell door. He couldn't even stand on his own, his head was flopping around to one side and he was soaking wet. He was trying to shout out but nothing of any sense was coming out. I wanted to bang on the door and tell the agents what sadistic fucks they are but I resisted. That wouldn't be smart. The smart thing to do is let them keep believing that I don't pose them a threat. Then when the time is right, and I've got things all figured out, then I'll make my move and they won't see me coming.

The problem is, I now know that being smart is what fucking landed us here in the first place. This is all my fault. Each day we get played a video that is supposed to teach us more about why we are here and what our purpose will be. Today's video sucked. We were chosen, selected, cherry picked, whatever the fuck you want to call it, based on certain characteristics. Characteristics they discovered we had when we took part in drug trials for booze money. Our pre-existing skills or attributes are what landed us here and they plan on evolving and enhancing them to a superhuman level. What. The. Actual. Fuck.

Apparently, according to today's educational home video, they hit the jackpot when they came across us. My exceptional IQ was what they really wanted, I was the prize. They just happened to strike gold when it turned out I'm friends with a precision shooter, a body language expert and an absolute man mountain. For whatever reason, Ben doesn't seem to have anything they want or need but unfortunately for him, they decided to take him anyway until they decide what to do with him. Poor bugger, he's just collateral damage because he happened to have the wrong friends. These people make me sick.

∞§∞

Day 15

So much for me playing the smart game and biding my time. Two days ago I saw red and flipped out, stabbing an agent in the neck with a needle that was meant for me. I got put in 'the box' for two days and nights as punishment, (hence my lack of diary entries). I didn't know the box existed until I was thrown in it. It's literally just that, a small metal box that they have to fold you up and stuff you into like a pretzel to make you fit before slamming the lid shut. The only light comes from the five tiny breathing holes they so kindly drilled in the top. No one comes to check on you. There's no sound, no light, no food or water and no fucking toilet. It's just you and the box. So when nature calls, no fucker answers. You can imagine the stench by the time they let you out. I've never experienced humiliation and degradation like it.

Day 16

I actually ate a proper meal today. It was such an unfamiliar feeling that it made my stomach hurt. They put me in shackles and took me to a small makeshift dining hall that had a long metal table and benches on either side. The others were brought in too but we weren't allowed to speak to each other. Cole tried and got a cattle prod in the back for his efforts. Watching the closest thing I have to brothers being treated like farm animals both sickens and saddens me.

They sat us down at the table and chained us together by our wrists and feet before presenting us with huge plates of piping hot food. It smelled so good that you could hear the echo of our stomachs growling bounce around the room. Spencer refused to eat at first, convinced it must be a trick and that we'd be poisoned but he soon caved into the hunger when he saw the rest of us very much still alive and enjoying a decent meal.

I watched each of my closest friends in turn as we ate in silence. Every one of them resembling a hollow shell of their former selves. All of them dead behind the eyes. I don't understand what kind of mind fuckery this is but I do know that we have to find a way out of this hell hole before it's too late.

Day 17

Maddy McCarthy. Madeline Joanna McCarthy. That's a name I hadn't thought about in a long time, up until I wound up here. The drugs they've got me on give me the most vivid dreams, dreams that make no sense at all but feel as real as this pen in my hand.

Maddy lived next door when I was growing up. We were the same age and went to the same school that everybody did in our village. She was beautiful, she used to skip to school with her blonde hair in two pigtails full of ringlets. As she grew up, she lost her pigtails and gained a figure that turned heads wherever she went. Her long hair would fall down her back in a dead straight, platinum sheet. She was so unreachable she may as well have lived on Mars rather than next door.

I watched her grow up, quietly admiring from the short distance between our two houses. I was never brave enough to actually speak to her and she never seemed to notice I even lived there. That was until the day a boy on a motorbike came tearing through the village, almost ploughing into Maddy and her friends on the way home from school. I saw the whole thing play out from further down the road. The near miss, the screaming, the wall of muddy water that splashed up their uniforms making Maddy drop her algebra assignment into the puddle.

Once the chaos died down and everyone had walked away, I scooped the soggy pages up from the puddle and took them home with me. This was my opportunity, my chance to stand up and be seen. I spent the entire night re-writing her assignment for her, almost certainly raising it up by several grades to what it was before. I left it on her front doorstep with a note the next morning. Later that day Maddy came up to me and kissed me on the cheek in front of the whole cafeteria. No one had ever kissed me before, it was warm and pepperminty and I tried my hardest not to turn red even though most of the school was watching.

Maddy spoke to me often after that, even walking to school with me sometimes. One day out the blue she asked me if I wanted to finger her behind the gym hall to which I awkwardly declined out of sheer panic and ran away. Cole and the others teased me mercilessly for months. They were all so much better at girls than I was. Not much changed on that front. My actions that day, or lack thereof earned me a permanent spot in 'the friend zone' where I remained for the rest of school. So I went back to fantasising from afar like a loser.

I had long since forgotten all this, but these drugs are causing Maddy to make a regular appearance in my dreams. Dreams I have no business having in a disgusting place like this. The kind that leave you rock hard, panting and sweating when you wake up. *Fucking weird.*

Day 20 (?)

I think I've skipped a day. Time has no sense or meaning here, but I'm almost certain I was asleep for longer than a normal night. It's not natural sleep, it's drug induced and my body clock is fucked as a result. I feel groggy and hungover but without the fun prelude.

I dreamt about Maddy again last night. I never saw her naked in real life but boy do I see her naked in my larger than life dreams. The way her tits bounce up and down as she sits on my face will be forever etched in my brain, even if it is only a fantasy. I swear I could still taste her sweet saltiness on my tongue when I woke up this morning. Whatever these fucking drugs are they're giving me, they're messing with my mind.

I also suspect that they're monitoring my brain activity while I sleep. As if waking up with a boner and cum stained boxers isn't humiliating enough, I think they might even have a front row seat to my nightly action. More than once I've noticed sticky residue on my temples when I wake up as if electrodes have been stuck to my head. *Sick fucks. I hope they enjoy the show.* At least in my dreams I'm hung like Cole. Last night Maddy moaned and whimpered as I stretched her tight pussy with my impressive girth. Cole would be proud if I could actually speak to him. He's always been so confident with the ladies, I guess he's never had a reason not to be.

It's weird though, my dreams don't evoke any emotion. Considering that at the time, Maddy meant a great deal to me and I'd spent so much of my youth pining over her, it's odd that these dreams do not stir up any old feelings, but they really don't. It's purely physical. The only driving force is lust and a basic, animalistic need to stick my dick in a woman. I'd never been so impulsive in the real world or so downright disrespectful to use someone that way, but I can't deny it is freeing. Experiencing what it's like to fuck care-free and without expectation or consequence is truly liberating.

I wonder if the real Maddy looks anything like my dream Maddy. She's probably married and got kids by now. While we were busy drinking our way through university, she was on the prowl for an older, rich man who could take care of her. Well, I hope if she found him that he's even half as good at making her scream as I am in my head, she deserves that much at least. With any luck, tonight I'll dream that she's on top again. Those nights are my favourite. I'm painfully aware of how pathetic this sounds as I write it down but it's not as if there's a

whole lot else to look forward to stuck in here. If dream porn is as good as it gets, then so be it.

Day 21

So, the honeymoon period is over. What an absolute fucking joke that the previous three weeks of hell turned out to be nothing more than a settling in session. A sort of 'dipping our toes in' if you will.

Today I experienced a level of physical pain that I have never felt before. One of the agents took me to a room full of computers. It was a test, to see how quickly I could hack various systems. According to 'G', they went easy on me today. *How fucking sweet of them.* Every time I hacked a system before the timer ran out, I was rewarded with a privilege such as added time out of my cell later or half hour in the gym room. Every time I failed, I was shocked by the enormous, heavy-duty dog collar they had clamped round my neck. Needless to say, I got shocked, *a lot*. I'm a damn good hacker, maybe even one of the best but what they were asking of me was next level crazy shit. After the seventh or eighth shock, I passed out with a nosebleed and woke up back in my cell, my face covered in blood. I don't even want to know what tomorrow will bring if today was their idea of easy. I can only imagine what the others are going through.

AATA 2024: THE ANNUAL

<u>Day 25</u>

 I haven't had the energy to write for a few days. Their 'tests' have been taking it out of me, both mentally and physically. I'm not even sure if I was presented with an open door, I'd have the ability to run through it and get out. I guess that's all part of their master plan, to completely break us in every way. We can't fight back or escape if we're broken and weak. *Broken*. That's the perfect word for the way I feel. I can't speak for the others but I can't imagine they're feeling much different.

 Spencer will be raging. He has a filthy temper at the best of times but he does not take kindly at all to people invading his personal space. This will be killing him slowly. Darryl will blame himself. It's not his fault of course but that's how Darryl's mind works. He carries the weight of everyone around with him and feels responsible for things he shouldn't. Ben and Cole are probably fairing the best. They are adaptable and calm under pressure. I'm not suggesting this is a fucking walk in the park for any of us but we're all very different personalities and our reactions to these extreme conditions will be just as varied.

 I want to lay eyes on them all, just for five minutes. I want to know how they're doing. I need to see for myself. I want to -

⁂

<u>Day 26</u>

 I almost got caught writing in here yesterday. I stashed my journal under the floorboards just in time but I got thrown in 'the box' for the night anyway for having a pen. Luckily, I was quick enough to pocket a new one from the technician who let me out this morning.

 I was ushered straight to the shower block after that where I saw Darryl. I say shower block, that makes it sound vaguely humane. It's more of a concrete hole that they shove you in naked and hose you down with jets of freezing cold water while you scream like a pussy. At least that's how it goes for me.

 When I got there today, Darryl was just leaving. He was escorted on either side by two burly guards who he was chained to at the wrists. He was covered in bruises and needle marks. They've clearly been injecting him with something because his veins looked like black vines under his skin. It was as if someone had traced them with a marker pen. He looked at me with haunted, hollow eyes and it crushed my soul. His eye sockets were dark and sunken like he hadn't slept for days. He seemed much bigger too, more bulked up and muscular. The way you might look after excessive steroid abuse.

I need to get us out of here.

Day 27

Just when I think I've found a way of managing the level of horror and pain that goes on here, they switch things up again and blindside me.

Today they took me out of my cell and told me I was moving. I've learnt not to ask such stupid questions as 'why?' and 'where am I going?'. They reveal everything as and when they choose to and not a moment before.

Turns out they were putting the five of us back together again. There will be a method to their madness, I just haven't figured out what it is yet. Each of us has been given a new cell. A small concrete box essentially with a reinforced glass front. Our cells are arranged in a circle off of a small empty room with a single chair in it so we can all see each other. We can hear each other too. There are vents in the walls so the sound travels between the cells. That will be very much by design. There is no such thing as an oversight here.

My circle of friends is a harrowing sight. What once was five young men with bright futures ahead of us, fuelled by ambition and dreams is now a ring of hollow, defeated shells with no hope. Sometimes I lay awake at night and wonder what they will say about us on the news when we're dead. *When* being the operative word. There's no fucking chance we're getting out of here alive. I'm convinced of that. If we do get out it will only be to serve our purpose in their sick fucking masterplan and I want no part in it. I'd rather be dead than become like these monsters.

Darryl looks the worst by far, physically at least. Lord only knows how damaged their minds and souls are. He's barely recognisable any more. Darryl is usually the one we're moaning at before a night out because he's still got his face in the mirror. He'll never leave the house until his hair is styled to perfection and everyone is choking on his aftershave. You'd never guess that looking at him now.

Spencer is painfully thin, I'm going to guess he's refusing to eat. He's a stubborn bastard at the best of times and he'll be grabbing hold of any piece of control he has left. He's always been pale skinned with dark hair. The girls have always liked him, saying he's brooding and

mysterious. Too bad, he's never liked any of them enough to fuck them twice. Spencer's tolerance of people is pretty low. Looking at him now, there's no sign of his moody, roguish charm. He looks like he's been freshly resurrected from the dead.

I have to admire his sheer defiance and determination. Spencer is certainly not everyone's cup of tea, he's an acquired taste and not for the faint of heart. If he were a cocktail he'd be something akin to a Moscow Mule. Bitter, sour and comes with a real kick, but a treat if you can stomach it.

I'm writing about my friends as if they're drinks. I must be slowly sliding into insanity.

Day 28

The circular arrangement of cells revealed its true purpose today when the sadistic bastards keeping us here put a stop to Spencer's hunger strike.

We've been here long enough for them to have gotten under our skin and inside our heads. They know our weaknesses and what buttons they need to press to get what they want. It just so happens that Spencer's weakness is Ben. They've always been close and Spencer protects Ben with a brotherly like ferocity. They must have figured that out.

Ben was strapped to the chair in the centre of our cells in just his boxers and a blindfold. They didn't gag him. They wanted us all to watch and hear his screams. Spencer was brought a huge tray full of food and ordered to eat. He was also told that if he refused, Ben would pay the price.

Spencer resisted at first, until they gave Ben so many lashings across his chest that the floor ran red with his blood.

The rest of us watched from our cells like crazed gorillas in a zoo. We shouted and thumped at the glass, powerless to help either of them. Ben took it like a hero and never once asked Spencer to eat but Spencer caved anyway and gulped down the food in an effort to protect Ben from any further torture. The faster Spencer ate, the slower they whipped Ben. Unfortunately for both of them, Spencer ate so much, so fast that he threw up everywhere, pissing off the agents. Ben suffered the punishment for Spencer's weakness and eventually passed out in the chair. The rest of us watched in horror as the agents left us to it. Ben slumped in the chair in a pool of his own blood and Spencer doubled over on the floor crying and vomiting, clutching at his stomach.

I'd never seen a person break before. Now I've seen two. I'm pretty sure a piece of the rest of us broke along with them. Pieces of men, that's what we are now.

Day 30

Today was a monumental day. A day that will be etched into my brain for the rest of my sorry existence. Today was the day I lost my faith in humanity completely.

All five of us were escorted from our cells at the same time and led through the maze of corridors to a room with a huge projector on the wall. I say led, Spencer and Ben had to be dragged. Ben because he's too weak to hold up his own body weight right now. He lost a lot of blood the other day. And Spencer because he refused to walk. He spat in their faces and locked his knees so they bound his wrists and dragged him like freshly caught game from a hunt.

There's no way we could have prepared ourselves for what they were about to show us. The scraps of hope and determination we had been hanging on to (albeit by a thread) are gone. They turned to dust and fell through our fingertips today. We were each in turn shown video footage of our own funerals. The bastards had told our families we died in a tragic accident whilst away travelling and tied the whole thing up so neatly that no questions were asked.

First it was Darryl's funeral. The room was packed with people, he's a popular guy. His mum sobbed over a black coffin adorned with deep red roses. She did not hold back or hide the depth of her grief. She let her tears flow freely over what she believed to be her son's body. Even when the ceremony ended, she wouldn't leave him. The camera stopped rolling as the celebrant eventually had to ask her to leave. Darryl roared like a wild animal being maimed. He threw his chair at the wall where the harrowing images played. He may as well have been in that coffin as I watched the final flicker of light go out inside him. Eventually the agents who had been watching us from outside the room came in and drugged him back into submission.

Next was Ben's turn. Ben comes from a large family with a whole array of younger siblings, some full, some half, some step. All devastated by their loss. The children took turns to place things on the coffin top, things they thought he might need or miss. His parents wept silently, each with their respective new partners comforting them. Ben's coffin was white and draped in his leather bike jacket. Ben watched in horror as his family said their goodbyes. He didn't have the energy to react. He just shed quiet tears that soaked into his shirt.

Cole's funeral was an entirely different affair. It was as large and outlandish as he is. His close knit family of four laughed and cried as they read funny anecdotes to the gathering of mourners. There were plenty to choose from, Cole's always been somewhat of a clown. His favourite R'n'B tracks were played as his coffin was carried out. Cole watched the footage in silence. He didn't react in any way. Cole's ability to suppress his emotions is so unhealthy.

Spencer's service was very small and intimate. His family are as unsociable as he is. His parents are both work obsessed business types who lack any sort of parental instincts. His younger sister is an odd sort of girl. It was hard to tell from the footage whether she was crying or not as her face was mostly hidden behind a glossy curtain of black hair. It's ironic really that Spencer grew up to be a body language expert when his family have always shown little to no emotion. Maybe that's exactly why.

Spencer hummed with visceral anger as he watched his funeral take place. A low growl rumbled in his throat as he struggled to contain his pain. Eventually he flipped and hurled himself at the glass wall where the agents watched us from. It didn't break of course, it's reinforced but he beat his fists against it until they bled anyway. The agents watched and waited for him to burn himself out. They didn't intervene. They don't fear him in the same way they fear Darryl.

By the time my turn came around I was numb. So traumatised by everything I'd seen so far that I couldn't even watch. I sat with my eyes closed and rocked back and forth on my chair trying to block out what was happening. Because I refused to open my eyes, they turned the volume up instead so I had to listen to my family's sobs in amplified surround sound. *Fuckers.*

I covered my ears as the tears streamed down my face but it did nothing to muffle the sound. The heartbreaking sound of my sister's wobbly voice as she read out loud a poem she wrote for me. It will forever be imprinted in my brain.

He is lost, but one day I'll find him.
He is gone but one day shall return.
He is gone but never forgotten.
He is gone but pieces remain.
He is not gone, he's just not the same.

Nora has no idea how true her words are and how much they resonated with all of us as we sat and listened. She thinks I'm dead. Her poem was written with a spiritual meaning and yet it had a very literal one for the five of us as we sat, each lost in our own thoughts and grief.

Something in the room shifted though. Her words stirred the air and breathed life back into our lungs. Ever so subtly, our heads lifted a little higher and our shoulders fell back a fraction. There was an unmistakable shift in mindset as determination crept back through our veins. No words or exchanges of looks were made, we're not that stupid. We know we're being watched at all times. But each of us felt it and understood it.

We may be broken but we are not beaten. Come what may, we will find a way out of this shit hole or die trying. Never again will we bow to their will. I may have lost my faith in humanity today, but I found it in myself and the others.

We must survive.

This short story is from the start of a prequel to the More Than Men Series. If you're dying to know what happens to Jasper and the others, then check out book 1 in the More Than Men series to continue their story.

Ravenswood After Dark by Harley Raige

This short story follows one of the characters from the Reapers MC, Ravenswood series. This is a snippet of the life of these characters behind closed doors/after dark!

Trigger warning/tropes/shopping list:
Primal kink
Predator/prey
Mild BDSM
Rough Sex
Good girl
Biting
Mild Breath play

~ Cade ~

Pulling into the empty car park and parking up under the cover of the largest tree, I turn off the bike and climb off it, pulling off my helmet, gloves, and jacket. I came by earlier and prepared the site, so now I'm just waiting. I see the lights in the distance before I hear the car. It's my driver, Dawson. He pulls up and gets out of the vehicle. He rounds it, handing me the file containing consent forms, a non-disclosure agreement, medical records, and anything else we should know.

"Is everything in order?"

"Yes, sir." He nods.

I scroll through the paperwork. Everything looks good, and as I see the name, I smile. "Glutton for punishment." I smirk.

"Seems so, sir! Is this four, five? I've lost count." Dawson grins at me.

"Yeah, sure you have. This will be seven." I hand him the file back.

He nods and smiles as he turns and opens the back of the car. Long legs appear, sporting a pair of battered trainers as she climbs out, stepping in front of me.

She's wearing grey sweats that look like they've seen better days, and her long dark brown hair is tied up into a ponytail. She's slimmer than last time but still as beautiful.

She makes eye contact for a split second before dropping her gaze.

"Good girl!" I growl at her.

"My name's Sarah… sir. How can I serve you this evening?"

"I don't care for your name, girl. Undress!"

She unzips the hoodie and slides it off. She's not wearing anything underneath. This isn't her first rodeo, and she knows what to expect. She slips out of her trainers and shucks her bottoms off clearly forgoing the underwear.

I take a step forward and reach my hand across her collarbone, sliding it up to her throat, and squeezing. "You understand the rules?" She nods but never makes eye contact. "That's a good girl!" Her skin flushes as she bites her lip. I lean closer. "You know the safe word?" She nods again. I lean closer still, breathing into her neck, slowly licking up the side of it to her ear as she shudders. I whisper, "Good girl. Now, run!"

Her eyes flick to meet mine, and I smirk at the indecision that flicks across her face before she turns in my grasp and takes off, running into the woods.

Dawson steps back around to the driver's seat. He get. . He will stay in the car as long as this takes. I pick up her clothes, throw them in the back of the car, and walk over to my bike, removing my leathers and boots, sliding off my T-shirt and boxers, and resting them on the bike. I crack my neck and fingers and look at the sky, howling to the moon like the feral creature I am. This is the only warning she will have that I'm coming. I set off running.

There's no better feeling than running through my forest, wind nipping at my skin, dick swinging, fresh air in my face, foliage caressing my heated flesh like a lover's touch, all the while chasing my prey. Well, there is one feeling better, and that's being buried in that prey with my hands round its throat till it begs me to make it come.

I stalk through the undergrowth, tracking every out-of-place leaf, the slight break in twigs, and the shift in the air around me that makes the hairs on my arms stand on end.

The minor disturbance of the soil underfoot tells me it's not running anymore. It's sneaking, calculating. I hear a branch snap and drop to all fours, peering through the ferns. I see its shadow pass between two trees, but it's going in the wrong direction compared to what I had planned. Scrubbing my hand into the dirt, I find a few pebbles and throw them about fifteen feet in front of it, and it turns and bolts in the other direction.

I howl again as I give chase, I can see it darting in and out of the trees and diving behind hedgerows as it tries to evade me, but I'm toying with it now. I stop. Pause. Remain silent as I close my eyes and listen. It's almost like I can hear its heartbeat, feel its breath, and taste the sweat covering its skin.

I tentatively take a few steps in its direction as it stops and pants against a tree, flicking its eyes from side to side. I stalk closer until I can hear the trembling of its body.

"I see you, little doe!" I grin. "Run!"

It sets off running toward the clearing, and I pause for a second. I don't want to catch it too soon. As the footsteps get quieter, I take off jogging in that direction. I can see tracks, a path through the foliage. I sneak toward it, and I can't help the grin spreading across my face.

"I can almost taste you, little doe." I howl to the sky again, but everything goes silent. It's hunkered down somewhere.

Somewhere close, I take a step in the direction I think it would go, but I pause, take a breath, and close my eyes. It must be holding its breath. I don't hear a single sound. Controlling my breath, I take a step forward and close my eyes again, listening to every minute sound, every animal small and large. There's a slight crack. I listen in that direction and then open my eyes. Scanning the area.

My eyes adjust to the moonlight, and I see a gap in the hedge as I stalk toward it. I hear a twig break behind me, sneaky prey trying to evade me. I spin and lunge in that direction. I hear its breath panting now, and I slow and hide behind a tree till I can see it near the edge of the clearing, eyes darting around as it tries to catch its breath.

Watching every step I take, I stalk closer as it takes a step forward, causing a massive crunch from under its feet. It drops to the floor, crouching out of view, but I know it's still there. I stalk closer. I can feel my dick starting to get hard. It seems to only get hard when I'm stalking my prey. Once I can see and almost smell them, I am desperate to taste them.

I lick my lips as I take a step closer. Then another. Its eyes fly in my direction, and it drives up, sprinting as fast as it can away from me. I grin like the sadistic motherfucker that I am as I pause, giving it just enough time to think it's getting away. I'm a total unit, but I'm also fast. I'm like a mountain lion, and this is my playground. I set off after it. I dive for it, smashing my body into it and taking it down, forcing all the air out of its lungs.

I roll it onto its back and climb over its body, securing it with my hand around its throat as I lick all the way up its torso and across its breasts. It grabs my wrist with both hands but doesn't try to stop me as I clamp down, biting on one nipple as it screams out before I bite down on the next. I slide my hand between us, grabbing my dick and slamming inside it. It's soaked as I bottom out. I slam my head back and roar. Fuck, she—I mean, *it*—feels so fucking good. I slam into it again as it screams out. I bite down on its neck, drawing blood, and I suck at it, groaning.

It tastes so good. I slam back into it again as I continue to bite and suck at its neck. It's holding my wrist tight while I grip its throat. I slam into it again as I squeeze, and its eyes start to roll, easing off. I allow it a small amount of breath, which it gasps for, trying to gulp down the fresh air. I tighten my grip again and bite down over its collarbone. It screams as I grin against the broken flesh. Sucking it into my mouth and leaving a massive bruise, I slide my hand up higher and push my thumb under its jaw, turning its head to the side.

Slamming into it again. "I want to taste you, little doe. Can you be trusted?"

"Yes... yes, sir," it whispers. I release its throat and slide my dick out of it, groaning at the lack of warmth. I slide down its body, gripping its thigh and yanking it to the side. I lick from its asshole to its clit before biting down. It screams, lifts its leg, and kicks out, knocking me back. I laugh as it scrambles to get away. Once it's a few steps away, I dive out and grab its leg, bringing it down hard against the floor. I climb over its back. I slam back inside it and bite down on its shoulder, pushing its face into the dirt.

"Do you want to use your safe word, little doe?"

"No!" It snaps.

I slam back into it, slamming its body into the ground. Before pulling back and slapping its perfect round ass... hard."

"Did you just say fucking no? No fucking what?" I slam back into it, pushing it down, and I crawl up its body and bite down on its neck as it screams out.

"No, sir!"

"Good girl," I whisper against its ear as I slam into it again. It tries to move under me, but I'm too strong. "Where do you think you're going, little doe?"

It tries to reply, but I grip tighter, pushing down on its back as I bury myself as deep inside it as physically possible, licking up its back and groaning at the salty taste.

Yanking myself out of it, I drag it up off the floor by the back of its neck and over to the tree in the center of the clearing. This is one of my favourite spots out here, and I've already set up my swing. As I drag it across the ground to the swing, lifting it up, I strap it in.

It's at the perfect height for me to slam my dick into it for as long as I want to, but I fall to my knees as I need to taste it. I remember every inch of its skin from previous times. I remember the delicious smell of its pussy and the delectable taste of its dripping cunt, which is laid out like a Thanksgiving treat for the taking.

I bite down hard on its inner thigh, groaning as I taste its blood again, and I smile against it as I see the scars from the previous times. I like to mark my prey. I like to know they have constant reminders of me. I like to imagine it pleasuring itself and feeling the indentations from my teeth and thinking of me while they get off. I bite down on her clit, and the most exquisite of sounds is ripped from it. It's a cross between a scream and a moan, and it's music to my ears. I grab its hips and swing her into my face, slamming my tongue into her sweet cunt. *Fuck*. I bite at it over and over, yanking at its lips and clit till it's about to come all over my face. Being the asshole that I am, I ease off.

Raising to my feet and standing before it, it gasps and pants at the loss of my mouth, and I grin down at it and spit against its pulsing pussy as it glistens in the moonlight. Its eyes dart around, taking in everything without making eye contact.

"Look at me!" I growl at it. And its eyes fly to mine.

"Sir." It breathes out a breathy moan as I groan. I slide my body over it, sliding a hand up around its throat. Sliding my other hand between its legs and sliding in a thick, calloused finger as it whimpers, swinging against the binds.

I rub my rough thumb across its clit as it bucks against me.

"Do you want me to fuck you into oblivion, or do you fancy your chances at evasion again?"

"Sir?" It groans as it tries to grind itself against my grip on its pussy. Its eyes roll, and it clenches around my thick finger, so I remove my hand, tightening the other around its neck. I lick up its torso and take a nipple into my mouth, sucking hard as it tries to rub against my leg for a release.

"You want to come, little doe?"

"Y...Yes, sir!" it nods without making eye contact.

"Look at me, little doe."

Her eyes slowly rake up my torso, the slight tinge of sweat glistening across my chest, the vast array of multicoloured tattoos that cover the majority of my body twist and turn with my skin as if they have a life of their own.

I slide my fingers into my mouth and slide my hand back down its body. It's fucking beautiful as the moonlight peppers its skin through the trees. I slide my thick finger between its cheeks, pushing against its tight entrance.

It groans and grinds against me, and I grin at it. "Fucked into oblivion it is, little doe."

I force my finger into its ass and push against the resistance. "Let me in, little doe!"

It relaxes against the intrusion, and I groan as my finger slides in, pumping it a few times before I remove it and push my cock in, in its place. I grind my teeth at how tight it is as I force my way in, flexing my fingers tighter around its throat. "I want to own every part of your body, even if it's only for tonight. I want to mark every inch as mine. Do you hear me, little doe?"

"Sir, yes sir, yes, please!" It whimpers as I release its throat and slide my hands over every curve of its body till I reach its hips, pulling out slowly. I push back in till I'm fully seated. Its arms are suspended at a right angle to its body, and I grin.

"Hold on tight, little doe!" I chuckle. "I'm about to ruin you for every other man... again." And with that, I slam myself into its ass as it lets out the most feral scream. I'm relentless as I power forward with every slam of my dick. It screams out. I grip it tighter against its hips, making sure it will feel every fingertip for days. Slamming against it again, I feel my balls start to draw up, and I scream my release half into its ass before pulling out and firing the rest over its naked, suspended body.

Reaching down, I run my fingers through my come seeping out of her and push two fingers back in pushing my come back inside before removing them and sliding them up to its mouth. It gasps and groans around them. I pop them out of its mouth and slide them down to its empty pussy, plunging them in. I push my thumb hard against its clit. It gasps against me as I push another finger in and rub my coarse thumb over her trembling bud.

I squeeze it between my thumb and finger before slamming three fingers back inside it as it gasps and screams for only me to hear as its release is dragged from it. It sags against the binds of the swing. I start to remove its hands from the ties. Its eyes meet mine for a split second before it drops them, and the look of disappointment is clear across its face.

"Oh, don't worry, little doe, I'm not done with you yet." I leave the rest of it strapped in and only free its arms. I want to feel it clawing at my skin when I fuck it again. "I'm not nearly finished with you yet." I slide my hands gently over its wrists and pull them around my neck, adjusting the swing so it's sat up rather than laid down, which drops it down a few inches.

I reach up and ratchet the straps so it's a tad higher. Now I pinch its chin between my thumb and fingers and gaze into its beautiful brown eyes, smirk at it, and pull it forward to claim a kiss.

She gasps before she relaxes into it. I don't usually tend to kiss them, but something about the way she comes undone for me makes me lose my mind, and I just want to taste everything. She bites down on my lip, drawing blood, making me smile and reach up to her throat, squeezing, grinning at her. "Little doe has teeth, duly noted." I grin again and reach between us and start to stimulate her sensitive clit, and she gasps again and then grinds against my hand.

Sliding my dick toward her pussy I tease with just the tip as she tries to swing herself against me. Grinning down at her, I slide slowly inside her till I bottom out, and we both shudder.

I lean over her, lick up her neck, and then bite down, causing a scream to be ripped from her, followed by a growl as she clenches around me.

"Hold on tight, little doe!" I say as I straighten up and slide her back off my dick till I almost slide out before slamming her back against me over and over again. The only sounds to be heard are her feral screams and the sound of my heavy breathing, accompanied by the slapping sound of my balls against her ass, and it's the most beautiful song. I claw at it and submit it to memory as if it's the most beautiful symphony ever created. And it's all for me. I roar my release and sag against her. Wrapped in each other's arms, I relax.

I don't know how long we stay like that before I realize she's drifted off to sleep. I finally let my dick slide out of her.

"Sir?" she mumbles. "Are we done?"

I grin down at her. "Are you ready to be done, little doe?"

I claw at her hips as I draw her away from me before bringing her back to me, impaling her so beautifully. Her nails dig into my shoulders as she clings to me for dear life. Her breath stutters, and she bites down on her lip before screaming out, "Fuck!" as she explodes around me, clamping down so hard on my dick I see stars. I growl my release as deep inside her as I can get.

She sags against the swing as I pant and grin against her neck. I nip and lick at it as my cock softens inside her, but I leave it there, refusing to move. Her arms are wrapped tight around my neck as she struggles for breath against my chest.

She shakes her head against my chest. "Maybe just a little rest?"

I nod and release her from the swing, laying her on the grass beneath. She shudders from the cold as I lay down next to her and scoop her against my chest. "Sleep, little doe. I'm not nearly done with you yet." as her breathing evens out and she drifts into sleep again, I whisper against her temple, "I don't know if I will ever be done with you!"

I wake to the sound of rain, hidden under the tree's canopy, but some raindrops still splatter my skin. I look at the beauty in my arms, who's still sleeping, and slide out from under her, laying her on her back and sliding between her legs. Taking her from the back to the front with the flat of my tongue, I groan. I taste me on her. I lick her thigh, tasting me again. Fuck. Looking down at her, she's covered in bite marks, bruising, and come. Most of all, come, my come, and it makes me want to take her till every inch of her is covered in marks left by me and me alone.

I lick all around her pussy, sucking her clit into my mouth and sliding it between my teeth. She gasps awake, but I continue as she comes around, gripping my hair. She clenches her fist and grinds against my face. Causing me to smile against her before sucking her clit into my mouth again. I slide my hands up her thighs, spreading them as far as I can so I can see her glistening pussy, and I groan into it. "Morning, little doe!"

"Sir." She groans as she grinds against my tongue, digging her fingers into my scalp as she grinds and comes on my face. I lap every drop up while she shakes beneath me, trying to pull me off, but I don't stop till she's delirious as she comes on my face again. Lapping at her, I nip at her clit as her legs shudder.

"Run, little doe!" I grin.

She gasps, sitting up. "Sir?"

"Run... ten... nine..."

She tries to get up, staggering out from under me on shaky legs. I roll over and watch as she stumbles out from under the tree, slipping on the wet ground and gasping.

"Five... four..."

She scrambles to her feet again, trying to sprint across the rain-soaked ground before sliding and skidding to her knees with a grunt, her eyes flick to mine.

"Two... One...!" I howl to the sky as she pushes up and sets off running. I step out from beneath the tree and howl again, spreading my arms and breathing in the air, the fresh scent of rain, the chill of the air. I lock eyes on my target as she reaches the edge of the clearing, looking around at me. I smirk at her and mouth, "Run!" and she does. I roar and take off after her.

The ground is slippier and starting to get muddy, the rains pelting it down. There's a layer of fog forming around the greenery as I bolt after my little doe, I can hear her panting, and her legs are still shaky from the multiple orgasms I gave her. I grin as I take chase.

I hear her footsteps stop and stop myself, just listening to the sounds of the forest. To my right, I hear the faintest crunch, and I spin, taking off in that direction. She hears me coming and screams as she runs, darting through the trees. She's doubling back toward the clearing, and as she breaks the tree line, she slides on the grass, almost stumbling as I gain on her. I launch myself at her, offensive tackling her and twisting onto my back before we land so her back is against my chest. As we stop sliding, I roll us over so I'm on top of her back, and I push her shoulders into the ground. "Cunt or ass?" I bark into her neck.

"Just fuck me, sir!" she moans as she pulls a leg up to the side. I pull back and slam my body over hers, sliding straight into her wet cunt.

"Fuck!" I growl out at the feel of her trembling under me. I put one hand on her back, and the other I grab a handful of her hair, pulling her head back as I slam into her. She screams out again as I crash my hips against her pink full ass cheeks. I pound a few more times before ripping my dick from her, lining it up between her cheeks, and forcing my way inside.

She screams out again as I bottom out, and she shudders around my dick. She slides her hand between us as I ease up so she can reach her clit before I power back into her, trying to force her further into the mud. There's something so feral and primal about being here in the storm naked, pounding into one of the most beautiful women I've ever laid eyes on. I growl as I throw myself onto her back, covering her with my body as I slam into her ass and reach around, squeezing my hand around her throat as she gasps for air. She comes hard around my solid shaft. As I power into her, she clenches hard around me and sends me spiraling over the edge with her.

I pull out, firing my come all over her back before sliding my softening dick into her pussy, then collapsing onto her come-soaked back. I groan into her neck as I slowly slide my soft dick in and out of her, groaning at the sensation as she gasps and writhes underneath me. I reach down and pin her hips as I lean up slightly and start to slowly fuck her into the dirt. Hades only knows how long I fuck her with my soft dick before it starts to stiffen again, and she gasps at the sensation as I harden inside her.

I tug her up to her knees and push down on the back of her neck before grabbing hold of her hips and slamming into her. The rain slams down around us, the steam is coming from our bodies like some kind of mystical fog, and I can't remember ever feeling like this. She is perfect. I lose myself in the feeling of her, and I slam into her repeatedly, chasing another high as she quivers, trembles, and moans, writhing against me.

I roar as I come deep inside her before yanking myself out and sliding my come back inside her with my thick fingers, impaling her with three fingers and my thumb in her ass. She yells out as she pushes back, demanding more from me. I push my fingers in so hard she collapses onto the ground. I pull back, grabbing her thighs and rolling her over before crashing down on top of her. My fingers find their way back inside her as my thumb grinds over her clit, pushing down onto her mud and come-soaked body. I crash my lips to hers as she clenches around me for the final time. Her eyes roll back and flutter closed as I fuck her mouth with my tongue in the same punishing rhythm I do with my fingers in her pussy. She screams out. When she comes, I sag onto the floor at her side, both of us trying to catch our breath as the rain pelts down on us, and all we can do is lay there and try to breathe.

After my heart stops racing and my breathing is less erratic. I drag myself up, leaning down, and pick her up so she's on her knees in front of me. "You did so good, little doe. You're such a good girl for me. Now there's only one place I haven't claimed, so open up that pretty little mouth so I can fuck you in it."

I slide my hand down my tender shaft as I groan, sliding my other hand into her hair. She leans her head back, looking me in the eyes as she steadies herself on my thighs. I tap my dick on her lips as she opens her mouth and hollows her cheek. I push past them.

"Fuck, you take my dick so good, little doe." I tighten my grip as I yank her hair and pull her against me. The tears stream down her cheeks as she gags on my dick, and it's the most beautiful she's ever looked, caked in mud and come, choking on my dick like it's her motherfucking day job.

I lose myself in the feel of her mouth, the feel of her tongue sliding against my shaft, and the tear-stained face, those beautiful eyes red-rimmed and streaming just for me. I pound hard at her face, and she digs her nails into my thighs, never holding me back, though, while I hold her up by her hair as I bruise those beautiful pouty lips of hers.

I growl as I start to come, and she sucks at me harder as I let her have a taste before pulling out and painting her face with the rest. As my come drips down her cheeks with the tears, I pull her to her feet and slam my mouth over hers, kissing her till I lose my mind. She sags against me, and I pull back, sweeping her into my arms, and carry her out of the woods back to the car.

Dawson sees me breach the forest and exits the car with a blanket. I wrap her in it and slide her into the back seat, quietly shutting the door behind her. She's passed out now, so she will probably sleep all the way to the clinic.

"You know what to do!"

Dawson nods as he climbs into the car and takes her to the clinic, where she will get treated, patched up, and cared for. It's the least I can do as it's me that caused it all, and I can't bring myself to feel sorry. I just smile.

I head toward the bike and grab my knife out of my boot. Stalking back to the clearing, I round the tree, my favorite tree in the whole place. As I reach the back side, I run my hand down the rough bark. Over every indentation of every girl's name I carve into it.

I add another tally mark beside Sarah's name and smile at myself. I feel so blessed and spent at this moment, but now I need to get home and clean up. I wonder who will be next and when Sarah will be back, because she will be back.

Thank-you for reading this short story.
This will be part of the book **Ravenswood After Dark** releasing later in 2024-2025

A Special Place Wedding by Helen C Kelly

One ~ Lacy

I was sitting in my office of Especially Yours with my partner Lorraine, finalising everything for my wedding, when in walked James. "Hello Darling, are you all done? I thought I would surprise you tonight."

"We have just finished. I just need to pack up. What have I done to deserve a surprise?"

"You have been working so hard lately and I thought you could do with a treat, and with everything we have coming up, today is the only day left before we get married."

"Come on then, what are you waiting for?"

Laughing, he shook his head. "I wonder? Come on then."

As it was the middle of May, the sun was shining, but it wasn't too hot. Although I didn't quite know what the surprise was, I could guess, as we were walking towards the river—towards my special place—which, in all honesty, should really be called our special place after all this time. It is, after all, the place James made his intentions known about us having a relationship; it is the place where he asked me to move in (although he moved in with me); it is the place we celebrated me concentrating on my business full time, and it is the place where he asked me to marry him.

As we arrived at the bench, I realised, as always, that James had prepared for our arrival; sitting by the side of a bench was our picnic basket. Greengrove was a village in the North of England, and most of the people had lived here since birth. Those that hadn't had moved in at least six years ago; that was the last time a new person came into the village, and that was James's friend David. Everyone seems to know not only everyone, but also everything, so I wouldn't be surprised if James had got someone to drop the basket off just before we'd arrived or if he'd arranged for someone to keep an eye on it, but even if he had dropped it off himself before picking it up, no one would have touched it, because everyone would have known who it belonged to and why.

It was so nice to sit back and do nothing but listen to the peace and quiet of nature. I let my head drop against the back of the bench. Closing my eyes, I could hear the birds tweeting and the river flowing; occasionally you could hear some of the people out on the river shouting to each other, but everything was at a much gentler pace. One of the things I liked about my special place was that it was set back, and no one could really see you here, which had worked out well when I was hiding from the bullies when I was younger. I was worn out; I had been burning the candle at both ends trying to get everything organised before our wedding and our two-week honeymoon. James was organising this, but he wouldn't tell me where we were going.

"You are exhausted!"

"I know; I am just trying to get everything finalised before our wedding so that I don't worry while we are on our honeymoon. Where are we going, again?"

"You know Lorraine has everything covered, so you shouldn't be worried. It's a surprise."

"I know, and I trust Lorraine, but these clients are ones that I have had since I started, and although they know Lorraine, this event is the most important event they have ever asked me to organise for them, as the others were all corporate ones, but this one is personal, as it is their parents' Golden Wedding Anniversary."

"I know, but I also know that you can't do any more. Lacy, darling, you are a perfectionist, and there is nothing wrong with that, but as far as I am concerned, our wedding doesn't need to be perfect. It just needs to have me and you there for it to be perfect; everything else is incidental."

"Thank you, I know, and I came to that realisation this afternoon when, for the fifteenth time, I checked that all the yellows that we were ordering matched in various lights. It was at that point that Lorraine started questioning my sanity, as she started pointing out problems with my rationale; for instance, the lighting in my office is different to the ones in the church and the community centre. The ribbons that are going round the flowers in the church aren't going near the community centre, so why do they need to match exactly? Honestly, that was a bit of a breakthrough."

"I am glad; does that mean I might see you a bit more before the wedding?"

"Well, not really. Tomorrow we both have the appointment with the vicar, then on Friday you have your stag night with the boys and I have my hen night with the girls. Saturday we have your mum's barbeque which she is calling our last barbeque as singletons, Sunday I have my spa day with the girls and you have football with the boys, then next week is busy with wedding things such as picking suits ups, making sure everything is alright at the church and the pub and all the little jobs that needs doing before the family dinner on Friday and then the wedding Saturday."

"Wow. We better take loads of pictures of each other so that we remember what each other looks like; otherwise, when we get to the end of the aisle on Saturday, our first question will be 'who are you?'"

"It won't be that bad, and on the plus side, we will be alright, because we won't be able to argue, because, as you say, we won't see each other."

"Do you know what the girls are doing for your hen night?"

"I think we are starting at Jane's house and taking it from there. We aren't doing anything too racy. Except, of course, the strippers."

"What strippers? I am not sure I agree to strippers."

"You mean you aren't having any?"

"I'd better not; it's not really for me. There's only one woman I want to see with no clothes on, and no one else is allowed to see her with no clothes on. That might make me sound like a caveman, but I don't care."

"That is so sweet, my little caveman, and I feel the same about you. By the way, I don't think there are strippers. Well, I hope there aren't, anyway, because my mum is coming to the hen night, and so is yours and Lily. Although, the more I think about it, the more I wouldn't put it past the three of them to organise it—but I don't think Jane is organising one, because she would be more embarrassed than me."

"Oh no, now you have put the idea of my mum and your mum with a stripper in my mind. I need to get that image out of there, otherwise I will have nightmares."

"Ha ha, poor James. At least I know you aren't going to gatecrash my hen night in case you will find your mum and future mother-in-law in a compromising position with a stripper."

"Will you stop it, please? Anyone would think you don't want me to sleep. How would you like it if I did the same and gave you the vision of your father and my dad and female strippers?"

"Okay, stop it, that's not funny. I really don't need that vision; how could you?"

"See? Now both of us can have nightmares."

"True. Right, no more mention of strippers. Thank you for tonight; I really needed it."

"My pleasure. Come on, we better get home."

Packing up the picnic basket and walking back along the river back to our cottage didn't take long but I felt far more relaxed than I did on the way to the river.

Two ~ Hen Night

On the way to James's pub he walked me to Jane's house ready for my hen night. After dropping me off, he left with David, Jane's partner and his best friend and best man, so that he could go to his stag night. Our parting words to each other were "Don't forget: No Strippers!"

Walking into Jane's kitchen, I saw Jane standing by her workbench, which was covered with bottles of wine and spirit.

"Hi, how are you feeling?"

"I am okay."

"Good. You better grab a drink, because trust me, you will need one before you go in the living room. May has lots of things she wants you to wear, from a bright pink t-shirt to a lovely glittery sash."

"Oh great, is it too late for me and you just to nip out the back and run away?"

"I am afraid so. She saw you and James walking along the road and sent me here as the welcoming party."

"Oh goody. So, what are we doing while I wear my bright pink t-shirt and sash? Please tell me we are staying in."

"Errrmm, nope. After drinks here, we have a minibus taxi taking us into town for dinner. A table is booked for all ten of us at the Italian restaurant you like. Then, we are going to a club where, according to May, we will dance the night away."

"All that sounded good up until you mentioned the word club. You know I am not a club type of person, and, come to think about it, neither are you."

"I know, and trust me, it is not my idea of fun either, but, believe it or not, May took over, and she and your mum are looking forward to it—but that's not the worst."

"I am not sure I want to know."

"You probably don't, but it's best to be prepared."

"Okay, go on then."

"You are not the only one with a t shirt; we all have one. Each one has our position in the wedding party on it."

"I think I need more than one drink to prepare me for this. Why aren't you wearing your t-shirt?"

"Trust me, I was putting it off to the last minute. When I say they are bright, I mean they are bright."

I quickly finished my glass of wine and poured another one. By the sounds of it, I needed a lot of Dutch courage. May was a force to be reckoned with.

"Come on then, let's get this over with."

I walked in arm-in-arm with Jane. Although she'd warned me, nothing could have prepared me to see James's mum May in a neon pink t-shirt with gold wording across the front that said 'Mother of the Groom', let alone seeing my mum (who I have never seen in a t-shirt in my life) wearing a 'Mother of the Bride' one. The other women in the room also wearing t-shirts included Lorraine, Lily who was one of mum and May's friends, and five more girls from school. When I had been at school, I'd thought that they didn't like me, but in the last few years, with Jane and

James' help, our relationships had changed; I had begun to trust that I was wrong, and we have met up a few times. In fact, Debbie and Dawn, who used to hang around with one of my school bullies, had become very close with Jane and me, and we even met up every so often. The others, Joanne, Siobhan and Nichola, all went to the same school as us, and they had each worked in James's pub, so I had gotten to know them quite well. I know as far as a hen night goes, I was hoping for a nice quiet one. so I hadn't expected May to take it to the wild level.

"Here she is, the bride of the moment! Here you go, I have your t shirt, you need to put it on. You and Jane can go and get changed at the same time. Go on, off you go," May said as she pushed me and Jane towards Jane's bedroom.

"Are you sure it's not too late to run away? We could jump out of the window."

"I wish!" Jane replied.

Having put on our t-shirts, I realised they looked worse than I thought they would. I really hoped that no one I knew other than those out with me today would see me in it. It was embarrassing.

"It really does look as bad as I thought it would, doesn't it?" I asked Jane.

"I can't lie; I think you look better in it than I do, but I am glad I have got David, because trust me I wouldn't be finding a boyfriend in this top. It would more likely repel them."

Leaving the safety of the bedroom, we went back into the living room, where I was handed my sash. Just when I didn't think anything could make this t shirt worse, it could: a lovely silver sash. I tried to argue that it was overkill, but that didn't get me very far.

After copious amounts of photos and another glass of wine, it was time to leave the safety of the house into the big wide world. Jane held my hand and whispered, "I am with you all the way, in every painful way."

The meal wasn't too bad, as I had a black jacket and so did Jane, and we both managed to keep them on; we were both faking it till we made it with these t-shirts. If we weren't best friends before we certainly would have bonded by our hatred of these t-shirts now.

Walking into the club was just as I imagined it would be. It was awful. May insisted we weren't allowed our coats, as we would get to hot with all the dancing we were going to be doing, so they had to be left in the cloakroom. We managed to find a big section to sit in, and a few of the group went to the bar to get the drinks. No sooner had the drinks been put on the table than May, Lily and my mum went off to dance, leaving me and Jane just sat there looking at them.

"I don't know whether to die of embarrassment or be proud of them," I shouted to Jane so she could hear me over the music.

"Neither do I."

We were at the club for two hours. My head was beginning to bang along in time with the music. I was not looking forward to the headache I was going to have tomorrow. Throughout those hours, Jane and I just sat at the table, observing and keeping everyone's drinks safe. Intermittently the others came for a rest and to see if we were coming to join them. Then, all of a sudden, May, Lily and mum came towards our table with two boys.

"Oh god, what now?" I said to Jane.

"Girls, let me introduce you to Patrick and Darrell. Me and the ladies are going to have a little chat with them," May said.

Jane whispered, "I think now is the time to die."

She was right, as we had to listen to the three of them teach the boys on decorum and how, 'in their day', boys had behaved in a better manner. I have no idea what they had done, but I am not sure I want to know either. It wasn't long after that when we finally left the club, and I was relieved.

Three ~ Spa Day

Jane had arranged for the bridal party and James's mum to have a spa day the Sunday before the wedding. Me and my mum were at my house, having just eaten breakfast with my dad and James. They were off to watch a football match today with the men, apparently, but I thought more drinking might be involved. The doorbell rang and James went to the door to find that outside was a white limousine with the chauffeur standing with the back door open, ready for me and mum to get in and join my bridesmaid Jane and James's mum, May. On entering the limo, I said to Jane, "I didn't expect the limo, it certainly was a surprise."

"It is still part of the wedding package. Not only that, but you won't feel properly pampered unless you are transported in a limo."

"That's true. What's on today's list?"

"First we have massages, then afternoon tea, followed by a manicure and a pedicure before the limo takes us to the pub."

The trip to the hotel took about an hour. On the way, we all had a glass of champagne. The spa was really relaxing, decorated in white, with orchids not only decorating the wall, but planted in various places around the lobby. We were each shown into our own dressing rooms to get ready for our massages. Before the therapist, Jasmine, started mine, we discussed what type I would like. I decided to have a hot stones massage, as I had never had one before. I was so relaxed after the massage, I decided I needed to do this more often.

Getting dressed into my normal clothes and going through to the room where the afternoon tea would be served, I saw mum and May sitting waiting. They too looked relaxed. As soon as Jane arrived, more glasses of champagne were placed on the table and then two three-tiered stands of plates were placed on the table. This really was more like my idea of a hen party; much better than the chaos of nightclubs and trying to separate May and my Mum from giving boys lectures on decorum. Give me finger sandwiches and cakes any day.

Next up was the manicure and pedicure, where we all sat in a long line with our hands being attended to by one woman and our feet by another. This was certainly the way to live, and after the chaos of the last few days and with the week to come, I needed to stay this relaxed. The four of us talked about our week ahead while our pampering took place around us. It was very easy to just turn our brains off and let our bodies be moved here and there; this hand under the light for the polish to dry, now this one, and so on In no time at all we were back in the limo, on the way to the pub to meet up with boys after their football match and have a big family dinner together.

Four ~ Wedding

The big day had arrived. Jane and I stayed the night before the wedding at my house with Mum and Dad, while James stayed at his mum and dad's house; something he moaned about quite a lot. He couldn't understand why we would worry about seeing each other the night before we got married when we were living together. In the end, it was his mum who finally told him to give up arguing and that we could cope one night apart, especially as, from the next day we were going to spend the rest of our lives together.

After a light breakfast prepared by Mum, me, Mum and Jane had our hair and make-up done, during which time our wedding photographer flittered in and out, taking photographs of us getting ready, and a few staged ones with my mum and dad and Jane, before she left to go to photograph James and his side of the wedding party. Due to our houses not being too far apart, she was going to come back when I was fully dressed in my wedding dress for those pictures too.

Still wearing my silk dressing gown, I turned around and inhaled a sharp breath as I stared at my wedding dress hanging gracefully on the hanger on the wardrobe door. I couldn't believe that the day I'd dreamed of was finally here, and I was getting more nervous by the second. I was beginning to let my worries enter my head. What would happen if I fell going down the aisle? Would James really be there? Will I look stupid? Why, after all this time, had my low self-esteem hit me? I wasn't sure I could do this. I loved James so much, but what if I let him down?

"Lacy, what's wrong? Talk to me," Jane said as she put her hand on my arm to help me sit on the bed. "I can tell you're stressing out about something. Take a deep breath, in and out, and tell me."

"I'm so scared I am going to do something wrong, or what if I let James down? James could do so much better than being with me. I am broken. He has to spend so much time building me up and making me feel like I belong. What if he gets fed up with doing that, and I just become a weight around his neck?"

"Oh Lacy, James loves you more than you will ever know and has done for years , and deep down you know that. You are not broken—well, at least no more broken than anyone else in that church. We all need someone in our corner, even James, and yes, he does build you up, but you build him up too. That's what being in love does to you and being in a partnership is all about. Sometimes you will need more of his strength, and sometimes he will need more of yours. As for doing something wrong, the only thing you need to worry about getting right that James will be upset if you get wrong is saying 'I do', and I know that you want to marry him. You do still want to marry him, don't you?"

"Yes I do, more than anything in the world."

"Well then, that's what is important."

"There is just one more thing I am worried about."

"What's that?"

"I am going to turn into a blubbering mess when I see James, I know I am, and then not only am I going to start everyone else off, but my eyes will look awful for the pictures."

"Now that is a concern that hits every bride, and you should know this, but as you know the best thing about this is that if you lose it, and we all lose it with you, we will all look awful in the pictures, so the pictures will look normal won't they?" She smiled. I laughed. I'd never thought of it that way. The amount of brides I had talked off the edge, and I had never thought of that angle.

Just as I was getting myself together, there was a knock on the door. Jane went to answer the door, and in the doorway stood my dad with a box. Looking at me, he said, "Is everything okay? Have you been crying? Are you alright?"

"Dad, I'm fine. I was just having a funny five minutes worrying about crying during the wedding, and then I started crying."

"Oh, okay, as long as you are sure. Anyway, I have a delivery for you." Handing me a small white box and an envelope, he said, "I will leave you two to get ready."

Opening the white box, inside I found a lovely gold necklace with a drop-down sapphire pendant. "That's lovely. My cousin has excellent taste. Open the card."

Inside the envelope was a card with a picture of my special place and, written on the inside:

To my wonderful fiancée,
I can't believe you ever said yes to me but I am glad that you did.
I missed you last night and I miss you every time we are not near each other.
I can't wait to watch you walk down the aisle to me.
I am glad there isn't long until I can officially call you my wife.
Love you forever and ever
James
XX

Tears filled my eyes as I put down the card on the bed. I looked over at Jane who was crying, Jane wrapped her arms around me and said "I will kill him. I can't believe he has done that to us, we have just had our makeup done. We need to be careful how we wipe our tears, but I have to say, my cousin has just blown it out the water."

"He really has."

With that done, Jane helped me get into my wedding dress and I took off the necklace I was planning on wearing and put on the necklace that James had sent over. No sooner had this been done than there was a knock at the door. Mum opened the door.

"Look at you, darling. You look like a princess."

"Thank you, Mum; you look beautiful."

"Thank you, darling. The photographer has just arrived, and she wants some pictures with me and you before I leave, but I just wanted a couple of minutes with my daughter alone before then."

I looked around the room and Jane had already slipped out.

"I love you. When me and your dad decided to move away from Greengrove, it broke my heart to leave you behind, but May promised me that you would be alright. I know that you have always had all that trouble with Sarah and the effect that it had on you was and still is awful, and it hurt me as a mother to be powerless, as everything we tried to do to stop it never worked. In the end all we could do was hope that we brought up a strong daughter. I am proud to say that we have, and I am so happy that today is your wedding day and that you get to have the man you always wanted. I want you to know that I will always be here for you should you ever need me. I love you so much."

"I love you too, Mum."

We stood there cuddling each other until Jane knocked on the door to warn us that the photographer was on her way up.

The rest of the time went in a bit of a whirlwind, and before I knew it I was on the way to the church on the arms of my dad. Because the church was so close, Dad and I decided to walk to the church, but get the car from the church to the reception after the service; otherwise, we would look like a walking taxi.

Walking down the aisle was a very surreal experience. Anything could have happened beside me or behind me; the only thing I was focussed on was getting to the front of the church, and James who was looking at me from his place as if trying hard not to come and get me. I knew I was smiling from ear to ear as I reached him. I mouthed 'thank you' to him and he winked back as we both looked at the vicar, who started the service.

My worst fears didn't happen in the first part of the day. I didn't trip over going up the aisle, and I didn't burst out crying like an idiot, although I think I heard my mum and May a few times. As we left the church and James said to me, "Hello Mrs Williamson," I realised we had finally done it. I had finally married the love of my life.

The Rolls-Royce took us on a tour of the village, and we had some pictures taken down by the river and at my special place before going to James's pub for our wedding reception. It was a laid-back reception with a buffet and an open bar. I didn't want anyone working too hard, especially my husband, but he wanted the reception to take place there because we had many happy memories there. In the end, it was between there and the community centre, and I honestly preferred my second home.

My dad did, in my opinion, the best father of the bride speech I have ever heard, where he talked about how proud he was of me and how happy he was to hand me over to James because he was proud to have James as a son-in-law. Then we had David's speech, which was funny, and included some pictures that none of us had ever seen before but were very much James. And then there was James's speech, and I couldn't have been prouder to call him my husband than as I was at that moment as he thanked everyone for all their parts in our life. We danced and chatted with our friends and neighbours before it was time to leave on our honeymoon. I still didn't know where we were going.

If you would like to read Lacy and James's story from the beginning, check out A Special Place. This is Book One in the Greengrove series. New Beginnings is Book 2 and Hold Me is Book 3.

Don of Avery by J.D. Groom

This is the working title and excerpt of a future project that I am hoping to release by 2025...

Shoot! I was going to be late and Calvin wasn't the sort of person you crossed. So far, I'd kept my head down trying to stay invisible, but I'd heard things. If you caught his eye and didn't play along, you disappeared quickly.

Crunching into the car park, I took a peek at the clock — five minutes late.

It amazed me how on the outside the building seemed like any other amongst the industrial units, but once you stepped over the threshold, it took on a different vibe entirely. The heavy bass of music vibrated through to your core. The lights and decor were an assault on your eyes, not to mention the activities of the people inside.

Women in different stages of undress were snaking their bodies around poles dotted throughout the main floor, with more performing lap dances on small groups of half-cut men. A girl was leading a man through the 'private' door at the back. I never ventured that way, but I knew what happened on the other side. Not all the girls offered extras, but there were facilities provided if they did. Calvin would take a cut, for room hire.

I felt eyes boring into me from the VIP area, and there he was, the one person I'd hoped wouldn't notice.

Scurrying into the locker room, I'd just placed my bag inside a locker when the sound of the door creaking made me freeze. Releasing a shaky breath, I turned the key before spinning around to find Calvin leaning against the wall, arms folded.

"What time do you call this?" his voice was low and icy, sending a shiver running down my spine at the chill.

"Um, I'm sorry, Calvin. It's only five minutes. I'll make it back at the end." He looked at his watch and then back at me. It was startling how black his eyes appeared.

"Make it fifteen." I nodded as he reached for the door, but before he left he added, "There's a lot we could do in fifteen minutes."

He smirked as he noticed me recoil and then left, leaving me in no doubt what his words implied.

I settled into the job at hand. A few pints here and there, but I was mostly serving spirits. It was business as usual in terms of suggestive remarks from customers, asking when I would be on stage or just generally trying it on, but nothing I couldn't handle. The only issue I had was finding Calvin watching my every move.

"Be careful doll, the boss has eyes for you tonight." Tony, a dark-haired lady in her fifties remarked whilst walking by with a bucket of ice.

Around midnight, like clockwork, Seb claimed his usual stool next to the bar. He'd become a regular in the four months I'd been working there. I didn't know why he chose the strip club as he never seemed much interested in the girls draping themselves around the poles. They had tried on numerous occasions to tempt him into the back rooms, but he would have none of it. Instead, he seemed content to chat and watch me work. On the odd occasion where I needed extra brawn to complete a task or couldn't reach something, he was always there offering to help.

He was gorgeous. A year or two older than me, hailing from the east coast of Spain, Seb's tanned skin and dark, floppy hair would draw any girl. His eyes were his most striking feature. A shimmering powder blue ringed with black and finished perfectly with lashes to be envious of.

Of course I had looked—I wasn't entirely immune—but men were a big no-no in my life. I'd been let down too many times to allow someone to get close.

Tony often commented that Seb was only after one thing when he came to the club, but it was nonsense. He could have his pick of women.

Besides, there was no point hanging around and waiting for the time when I could finally let someone in.

By 2am, the club had quietened, so I joined Seb to enjoy a quick break, my one and only fifteen minutes of downtime.

"Are you working at the coffee shop tomorrow?"

I yawned, trying to cover my mouth with my hand, and shook my head.

"Good, because you look worn out," he said, concern clear in his eyes.

"Gee, thanks! You trying to tell me I look a mess?"

I attempted to pull off a serious face, but gave up as the amused look on his had my lips tugging into a grin.

"Of course not." He placed his hand on my shoulder and gave it a squeeze. "I think you should take care of yourself more. Stop working every hour you can and take time for yourself."

If only he knew that staying still would have the opposite effect.

Averting my gaze from his, I spied Calvin throwing daggers in our direction. I quickly jumped to my feet.

"If anyone wants serving, tell them I'll be a minute."

Seb smiled and nodded before I turned on my heel and pushed through the door behind the bar, leading towards the toilets.

After fluffing up my hair and checking my makeup, I began to exit the bathroom, then was pulled out the rest of the way as a hand clamped around my arm. My back hit the wall so hard I was momentarily winded, and black eyes hovered inches from my face. I froze, my voice trapped somewhere in my throat.

"I've been watching you all night." Calvin blocked my path with one hand against the wall, the other picking up a stray wave of hair and twirling it in his fingers. "I know you've been watching me too."

"Oh, no I-I," I stammered, not sure what my options were.

"Let's skip the teasing and games and get straight to business." His fingers dropped the hair they had been playing with and traced the line of my low cut top towards my cleavage.

My chest was heaving, eyes wide. Not from anticipation but panic. Could he tell and was taking some kind of sick pleasure from it, or did he just not care?

"Hey Avery! I've got the empties you wanted." Seb walked around the corner, a heavy bucket on wheels filled with empty bottles for the recycling rumbling along the ground.

Calvin stopped what he was doing and looked towards Seb, a flash of anger showing in his dark eyes. Using the distraction to my advantage, I quickly slid under Calvin's arm and half walked, half jogged in Seb's direction.

"Th-thank you Seb, I can take it from here." Without looking back, I wheeled the bucket out the fire exit and took a lungful of cool night air.

Seb followed me outside but said nothing. He watched as I threw bottle after bottle into the bin. Now and then there was a satisfying smash breaking through the quiet of the early morning.

"Here, you're shaking." Seb draped his checked shirt over my shoulders. I tried to squeak out a thank you, but what came out was more like a sob. I refused to give Calvin the satisfaction of making me cry, knowing he had power over me, so I took a few breaths and blinked away the tears that had threatened to spill.

"Better?" Seb asked, giving me a nudge with his shoulder. I nodded and slipped my arms through the sleeves of the shirt, wrapping it around my bare stomach. He was only in a vest, showing just how toned his arms were, but the cold didn't seem to bother him.

"How did you know?" I looked up, lifting an eyebrow.

"I saw how he's been watching you all night. Plus, he's a snake." He shrugged. "Not long after you walked out, he followed, and it looked like he was on a mission."

"Well, thank you. I'm not sure what I would've done without you interrupting."

"Are you working tomorrow?" Again, I nodded but this time more slowly. I only hoped that Calvin would look elsewhere and focus on someone else.

There wasn't much left of my shift, so I buckled down and tried to make my way through it quietly. Seb came with me to the locker room, not wanting me to be alone, and even escorted me to my car. It was an old rust bucket, but it got me from A to B. Plus there was a sentimental attachment.

"Now, you take care of yourself." Seb leaned down and gave me a friendly hug. "I'll try to be here tomorrow too."

"Whatever would I do without my knight in shining armour?" I almost regretted saying it before it came out. I didn't want to encourage anything between us, but I wondered what would have happened if he hadn't come to my rescue?

A car pulled around the corner, and Seb eyed it with recognition.

"That's my ride. See you later!"

He sprinted off, and I smiled to myself as I put the key in the lock. My arm and the tartan sleeve caught my attention.

"Wait! I've got..." My voice trailed off as I realised Seb had already gotten in and the taillights of the car were getting farther away.

It was an autumn night. The roads were clear and dry, and even though there wouldn't be any traffic at 3am, it still seemed quicker to go home along the lanes.

It was very rare to meet another car, but on this particular night, there was one coming up from behind me. It seemed to be going fast, the headlights getting bigger in my rear-view mirror. I tried to concentrate on the road ahead, but the car flashed its lights to main beam, almost blinding me in the process.

During the day, I'd have been tempted to find somewhere to pull over and let them pass, but in the pitch black my mind was doing overtime. What if stopping was exactly what they wanted me to do? There were all kinds of stories about women going down country lanes in the dark.

What were you thinking, Avery!?

I pressed on the accelerator, hoping that by going faster it would satisfy the car behind. It didn't.

Moments later, I felt a bump and heard a metallic crunching sound. I immediately gripped the steering wheel harder, knuckles turning white. The panic was rising in my chest, the thumping of my heart at the base of my throat.

The car came at me again, and this time a strangled cry escaped me as I fought to stay in control. Something fell off Connie, but at that moment, it was the last thing on my mind. I begged for another car to appear from the other direction.

There wasn't a lot of the lane left to go. Just two small bends followed by a tree-lined straight, then the canal bridge, before emerging back into civilisation. Connie was only a little Corsa that had seen better times so there was no way I could out drag the car in my mirror. It looked sleek, shiny and fast. Plus the driver seemed to know what they were doing. I was screwed.

As I turned the final corner, darkness stretched before me. My headlights pierced a tunnel between hedges. Trees that were becoming bare of leaves stretched out their branches overhead like arms waving in the breeze. It was serene; calm. That was until the car chasing me made its final move.

The bright lights in my mirror were no longer there. Instead, the car had pulled out and was making its way alongside me. Without warning, there was a heavy nudge from near the fuel cap and Connie lurched to the right.

Trying desperately to gain control, I pulled the wheel in the opposite direction, but it was too much. Connie snapped to the left, and I knew I would spin.

"No, no, no!" I yelled, trying to brake, but before I could do anything, I felt weightless as my poor Connie Corsa became as much a passenger as myself.

My eyes widened at the sight of the gun, but I couldn't hear the muffled voice from the other side of the window. The gun tapped again, and I followed its movements in a hypnotic state. The voice, no voices, were low and indistinct, definitely male.

Why was I here? How did this happen?

It all became clear as someone forced my door open and a gust of fresh morning air washed over me, bringing me to my senses.

"Undo your belt, then place your hands where we can see them!" The man behind the gun growled, waving it in my face. "Now!"

My hands were all fingers and thumbs, and shaking uncontrollably. I gasped for breath as if I was running a marathon and my head was throbbing. Eventually, the clasp gave way, and I lifted my hands, surrendering to my fate.

"P-please d-don't hurt me," I stammered, almost in a whisper. It had been a long time since I had spoken those words, and a tear cascaded down my cheek fighting the memories.

"Do as I say and we may go easier on you. Turn slowly and get out of the car."

My limbs were like jelly as I tried to scoot my legs around and out of the door, the ground crunching below the soles of my boots. It took two attempts to heave myself into a standing position, and even then I had to use the door frame for support.

I could finally take in the body behind the gun. He towered over me with narrowed eyes watching suspiciously, looking smart in a crisp grey suit.

"I-I don't have any money. There's nothing of value. Please don't kill me. Please don't kill me!" My voice was rising, on the verge of hysteria, as the severity of my situation became clear. No passing car would appear. I was on my own.

"Shut it, whore!" His words stung, though the clothes I was wearing didn't help in my defence. "Move."

The gun he held was trained on me the whole time, but he indicated with his elbow and head in the direction of the car they had used to ram me.

I took a tentative step, and then another, trying to test out my legs whilst keeping the movements slow and steady. It was around this time I spotted the owner of the second voice. A dark shadow, he seemed to be rummaging through Connie, on a mission to find something.

"Put your hands on the bonnet." I did as commanded, closing my eyes and saying a silent prayer to a god I didn't know existed.

Please let me come out of this safely. Don't let my last moments in this life be at the hands of these crazed gunmen.

I yelped in surprise as heavy hands were placed on my shoulders and Suits pushed apart my legs with a kick to the ankles. He patted me down roughly, my breathing ragged at the closeness of the man and embarrassment at him touching me without my permission. There weren't a lot of places someone could hide things in hot pants and a cropped top, but there was Seb's shirt...

As if hearing my thoughts, the guy twisted me around so fast I lost my footing and stumbled, having to use the car to break my fall.

"Is this your shirt?" He grunted, piercing me with his eyes and letting me know he wasn't to be messed with.

"No." I shook my head quickly, making my head throb again, and I squeezed my eyes closed until the pain subsided.

The man's hand carefully pinched the fabric of the shirt at the collar and ran it down to the bottom, paying particular attention between each button hole.

He repeated the same motion with the buttons. As the guy's hand reached the bottom his eyes changed, but within a blink he had masked whatever emotion he had shown. He'd found something.

"Whose?" He demanded, obviously not one for small talk as he tugged on the shirt and pulled it off my body.

"Erm... a customer, at the club, The Strip." I shivered and folded my arms across my chest, rubbing where they were now exposed.

"Anything?" He called, eyes still on me but aimed at his pal raiding Connie.

"Clear." A head of black spikes popped out from looking under the bonnet.

"Get a cleaning crew here." The guy in front of me sighed, visibly frustrated as he rubbed a hand across his brow.

Guns, searches, and cleaning crews? Who were these people?

"Any possessions in there?" He was still firm, but his tone had softened slightly.

"My bag." I responded after a moment's hesitation.

Suits led me back to Connie and indicated for me to retrieve my bag. I could hear the other guy mumbling into his phone, looking in through the passenger side, and for a moment, our eyes met. A stunning blue with a slight twinkle. He gave me a cocky smile and winked as he ended the call.

"What will the boss say about this one?" he called to Suits. "I'm sure I could have fun with her before…"

He lifted his right hand, fingers pointing at me like a gun, and mouthed 'boom'. I jumped and gasped, snatching my bag from the passenger footwell where it had landed after the accident, and retreated to the man with the actual gun. Black Spikes' amused laugh followed me.

"Ric." Suits warned, obviously not amused, and turned to face me. "I'm sorry for his behaviour. He thinks he's God's gift to women."

I scowled at this 'Ric' as he neared us and turned my attention back to Suits.

"What will happen now?" I scanned the wreck that was Connie, pieces of bodywork and glass spread across the road. "And what about my car?"

"Now, we will take you to our boss to decide on the next step. As for the car, the cleanup team will be here shortly, and it will be like this never happened."

Of course I didn't want to go with these men, but did I have any choice? The way they carried themselves and the ease with which they waved guns around definitely wasn't a comfort. If they could make a car accident disappear, I knew they could make a twenty-year-old woman with no family and few friends vanish without a trace.

Like a condemned woman, I followed the men back to their sleek black machine and slid onto the back seat as Ric flashed me another grin.

"Enjoy the ride." I rolled my eyes as he shut the door. After a short exchange between the men, Suits climbed into the driver's seat and we drove away, leaving Ric with Connie.

The road was smooth as we drove towards the canal bridge and out into the suburbs. The car was a different class to the ride I was used to. The leather seats were soft and squishy, and the whole interior confirmed that it must have cost a fortune.

I noticed a set of eyes watching me from the mirror and instantly shifted in my seat, trying to make myself as small as possible.

"You might as well get comfy, it'll take about half an hour."

I nodded and turned my gaze out the window before digging for more information.

"So, where are you taking me?" There was silence for so long I didn't think he would answer, but then he cleared his throat.

"A tower in Leeds. My boss owns it. He'll ask you a few questions about the guy whose shirt you were wearing, then you'll probably be free to go."

"As easy as that?" It seemed too good to be true. They'd obviously gone to a lot of trouble—if you included the stalking, guns, and car ramming—so were they really likely to just ask me a few questions and then send me on my way without a second thought?

"That's why it's only a probably. Boss will decide whether you know too much."

"And if I do? Know too much I mean. What's stopping me from going to the police?"

The guy shrugged and grinned, only this one wasn't in humour. "You should be careful shooting your mouth off. Boss won't hesitate to put a bullet in you."

My body went rigid at the thought, but it only confirmed my earlier suspicions.

"You want to go to the police? That's fine, but you need to know most of them are all too willing to turn a blind eye."

I sat back and leaned my head against the window. It wasn't throbbing so much, but the cool glass was helping to soothe what was likely to become a large bruise.

The sky was turning grey, the darker outlines of clouds beginning to show. Street lights were still twinkling away, and in the following hours, people would wake up and start their day just like any other. Just like I had the previous morning.

I must have fallen asleep as a strange juddering rippled through the car, and upon opening my eyes, I was momentarily blinded by light. The underground car park quickly registered, and so did the lines of fancy cars, all mostly black.

We pulled straight into a space near a fire exit and an elevator. In next to no time, Suits walked around my side of the car and opened the door for me.

"As we walk through the building, try to act like everything is normal. Talk to as few people as possible and don't draw attention to yourself." He helped me out of the car but opened his jacket slightly to show the gun tucked into his belt as if to prove a point.

Slipping the strap of my bag over my head, I pulled back my shoulders and straightened up. If I was to face the man who allowed his men to treat me this way, I would not come across as a meek, scared girl. I'd done that too many times before.

We walked to the elevator and went up just one floor. The doors slid open effortlessly and revealed a bright reception area with marble floors and modern chandeliers.

A security officer sitting at a small desk near the main doors looked up briefly but continued with whatever he was doing, obviously not surprised or alarmed.

There was a larger reception desk with a hotel logo on the front where a woman sat filing her nails. I presumed she wasn't used to much traffic at this hour in the morning.

Suits slipped his arm around my shoulder, making me tense, but kept us moving. He guided me past the woman, who didn't even acknowledge us, to a wall with three more elevators.

On pressing the up button, a set of doors opened immediately, and I was, again, guided into the mirrored box.

"I can walk without help!" I muttered, shrugging out of his hold as he pressed the number twenty-three followed by some kind of code.

There was no reaction from him as the doors closed and we zoomed upwards, my stomach doing a little flip. Instead, he took on a bouncer style position in front of me, with his hands clasped together, blocking my route to the doors. I'm not sure what he was expecting me to do, perhaps pry the doors open and try to jump out, but his brown eyes stayed glued on me.

I could hear a heavy beat before the elevator came to a stop. Just like in the reception area, I was met with a crisp, bright and modern entrance hall, but the music was too loud for this hour. Immediately in front of me was a set of double doors, and beyond it I could only assume was a full scale house party.

My chaperone moved forward, and I followed. But before entering, he stopped and looked me up and down, deciding his next move.

"Stay here, and don't think of running." He hissed before opening the door just enough to slide through and close it behind himself.

I looked to the left, and the corridor seemed to end with what I presumed was a kitchen. The door was only open slightly, but I could just make out shiny black cupboards and glinting chrome. The right corridor was a mirror image, only I couldn't tell what was behind that door.

I should have turned around and run, made a break for it and tried to escape, but something told me it would have been in vain. In an apartment of this high a standard, I probably would have been lucky to get to the elevator doors, let alone in it and down to the ground floor. No, I was better off facing my fate, even if I didn't know what that was.

The music behind the wood faded, and the door opened, making my heart skip a beat. Suits stepped back and cocked his head to the side, the international code for 'get in here', and I took a steadying breath before stepping into the room.

This was it. Live or die. Life or death. My entire life in the hands of someone I'd never met but could only assume was a monster.

The first thing to grab my attention was the wall of windows overlooking the city, a streak of orange becoming visible in the dull sky as dawn was fast approaching. Then I noticed all the faces pointed in my direction, my own turning crimson at being the centre of attention.

There were a few people sitting on a stone-coloured sofa. Opposite was another on which a man sat surrounded by several girls in a scene that wouldn't have been out of place at The Strip.

"Gio, you didn't tell me she was here to join the party." The man on the sofa shooed a girl off his lap and sat forward, sounding amused but not taking his eyes off of me. "As you can see, I already have enough entertainment for tonight."

I crossed my arms and scowled back at him as a girl draped an arm over his shoulder, staking a claim. He turned his eyes towards her, and she immediately removed it.

"I'm not a stripper, and I don't want any part of... this."

"Could you blame a man for being a little confused." I was again reminded of my scantily clad body.

"I'm sure you know from Suits what happened tonight." I gestured towards my escort, which seemed to tickle the guy on the sofa.

"Gio."

"Whatever. I don't know why I'm here other than 'his boss' would want to talk."

"Go!" he commanded.

His tone surprised me, but then I realised it was meant for the girls as they dragged themselves from their various positions, sauntering past me into the entrance hall. Suits followed, presumably to make sure they left, and I instantly felt exposed as Sofa Guy walked towards me, a pensive look across his beautiful features. Did I say beautiful?

I mean, yeah, he was good looking. His dark, ruffled hair framed his light eyes perfectly, and a 5 o'clock shadow adorned his chin and top lip. Judging by his tanned skin and overall look, I would have guessed at a Spanish or Italian heritage.

Aware of my scrutiny, he flashed a devilish grin and stood inches from me, looking down at me, intimidating me. He wasn't just tall; his toned limbs and muscles were on show through a snug fitting black t-shirt.

I forced myself to look up into his eyes, which caught me off guard. What I thought had been light blue from a distance was an unusual silver grey I'd never seen before. They were captivating.

"Look. I'm not telling anyone about tonight, I just want what you owe me."

"Why do I owe you?"

I clenched my fists as his question set my blood boiling. Someone at least owed me a car.

"Your idiot goon ran me off the road, on your say so, and hurt Connie!" I gestured behind me at Suits, Gio, and the woman still sitting on the other sofa covered her mouth to stifle a laugh.

"I apologise for my goon's behaviour." His silver eyes flicked over my shoulder momentarily, a sly smile playing on his lips. "I wasn't informed of any casualties. Is she hurt badly?"

"I think so, but I'm not a mechanic."

There was an uncomfortable silence as everyone worked out what I'd said. Silver Eyes rubbed a hand through his hair.

"Wait, Connie's a car? You named it Connie?"

"Well... yeah. She's a Corsa." He was struggling to keep a straight face, but the man and woman on the sofa couldn't contain themselves, erupting into a fit of giggles. I took a deep breath and mentally counted to ten. "I won't go through the insurance, and I won't report you to the police, so you can carry on with your gun wielding and personal strip shows. Just write me a cheque for a few hundred, I doubt she was worth more than that, and I will leave you to your business."

He eyed me, pondering, a thumb under his chin with his forefinger rubbing the stubble there. I wondered what it would be like to hold his face in my hands, to feel his smooth tanned skin beneath my fingers and explore the shadow of his beard. Did it feel rough?

Whoa! Where had those thoughts come from?

My eyes widened, and I gave a nervous cough, quickly looking to the ground as I knew full well he could tell in which direction my thoughts had travelled.

"Let's start this again. I'm Rafael, you've already met Gio." He gestured behind me and then turned to the man and woman on the sofa. "Those two over there are Sadie and Hunter."

Hunter lifted a hand in a wave and Sadie nodded. They shared similar red hair and a lighter hue to their skin, which meant they had to be related.

I returned my gaze to Rafael, who stood eagerly awaiting my introduction.

"Fine!" I huffed, straightening my shoulders. "I'm Avery, and I'm not an alcoholic."

Hunter and Sadie laughed again. Gio remained quiet. At least if I kept them entertained I wouldn't die tonight, right?

"Well, I can't say the same for the rest of us." Rafael smirked, raking a hand through his dark mane. I longed to reach out and do the same, to feel his silky hair between my fingers.

Avery! What is wrong with you today?

I mentally kicked myself. Maybe it was everything that had happened in the last twenty-four hours. Yes, that was bound to have an effect on anyone.

"Look, it's been a long ass day. I'm tired, my head hurts, and now I've got to look for a new car with next to no sleep." My voice came out in a quiet sigh. I couldn't keep up the fight any longer. I hadn't realised how tired I'd become, the adrenaline keeping me going quickly evaporating out of my system. "Please? Just let me go home and I'll forget everything."

"No." Rafael's immediate answer had my stomach plummeting. With the introductions he seemed to have lightened up. I thought we were getting somewhere.

My expression must have given my feelings away and Rafael abruptly changed stance, crossing his arms and returning to business.

"You will sleep here, and I will have a doctor come see you in the morning. If she gives you the all clear, we will run through the night's events to see if you can help us further with our enquiries."

"But..." I began, my throat drying up. "I don't know you. How do I know you're not going to kill me while I sleep?"

"You don't." He responded matter-of-factly, showing he didn't care whether I trusted him or not. "Sadie will show you to your room and bring you more comfortable attire. Hunter, take watch. We wouldn't want her leaving before Doc comes to check on her."

I looked at Rafael in disbelief. Calvin had accosted me at The Strip, I'd been in a car chase and accident, held at gunpoint, kidnapped and now held as a prisoner!

Hunter and Sadie stalked towards me, their movements light and fluid, somewhat surprising considering Hunter looked like he spent his spare time on a rugby pitch.

"Gio, we need words." Rafael snapped looking past me, eyes darkening like a stormy sky. I heard the door click and footsteps retreat into the hall.

"Oh, and Avery..." Rafael stepped forward until we were inches apart, his warmth radiating across my skin, the air between us charged with static. He leant down and whispered in my ear, his breath ruffling my hair and sending a shiver down my spine. "Sweet dreams."

More to come...

Tangles of Desire by Karen Nappa

A Blue-Collar Doms Short Story

Disclaimer

This is a short romance story and not meant as a how-to on BDSM practice.

BDSM Play should always be safe. I also want to promote safe sex. If people in my books have intercourse without a condom, they have been tested and have discussed birth control or pregnancy (whether it's mentioned in the book or not).

The story, all names, characters, and incidents portrayed in this production are used in a fictitious manner. No identification with actual persons (living or deceased), places, buildings, or products is intended or should be inferred.

One

Elena Mercer's fingers traced the delicate lace of a scarlet corset. Outside, the budding spring in Missoula coaxed blossoms into life, the air tinged with new beginnings.

She straightened the display of luxurious fabrics in her boutique when a familiar voice cut through the silence, pulling her attention away from the delicate arrangement. "That's a beautiful color,"

Elena spun around and her face brightened upon seeing the figure before her. "Emma! How good to see you!" she exclaimed, stepping forward to wrap her blonde friend in a gentle embrace. After Emma returned the hug, Elena stepped back and studied the woman who was about ten years her junior. "Married life agrees with you. You look radiant."

Emma gave her a shy smile and thanked her for the compliment.

As they settled into comfortable chatter, the conversation drifted to Emma's honeymoon and the wedding that had been the talk of their circle for weeks. Emma's eyes shone with happiness as she recounted the adventures and the undeniable romance of her newlywed life. Elena soaked in every detail with avid interest.

The moment the topic of the honeymoon waned, Elena's gaze caught a glimpse of a deep turquoise corset displayed amongst her collection. "This would complement your eyes," she commented.

Emma's gaze followed Elena's to the corset in question.

Emma cheeks tinted with a blush. "I *was* thinking of buying a silk nightgown as a surprise for Dan," she confessed, "but you're right. This corset is perfect." A mischievous sparkle appeared, making her look younger.

Elena's response was a blend of encouragement and teasing. "Oh, I agree!" she laughed, pulling the corset from the rack and leading Emma to the fitting room.

With a blend of giggles and hushed voices, Elena helped Emma into the corset, adjusting the laces to accentuate her friend's figure.

"It feels like a firm hug," Emma remarked when Elena tightened the laces for the third time.

"Only a woman who has experienced and enjoys bondage would think that."

Their laughter rang clear and light in the privacy of the fitting room. The atmosphere was charged with a blend of camaraderie and the thrill of a shared secret, a moment of pure, unadulterated fun between friends.

When the corset fit like a second skin, Emma admired her reflection, her confidence soaring.

"Dan won't know what hit him," Elena quipped, helping Emma out of the corset with the same care and attention as before.

Emma's decision was made the moment she saw herself in the mirror, and the transaction was swift, a mere formality between the excitement of the fitting and the anticipation of the surprise. Elena took extra care in packaging the corset, wrapping it in paper that crackled with potential. Just before sealing the package, she gave it a small spritz of perfume. She handed Emma the discreetly bagged corset, their eyes meeting in a silent promise of future tales to be shared.

Emma, now holding her new treasure, left the boutique with a spring in her step.

After Emma left, Elena relished a few minutes of quiet as she started to unpack new arrivals before the doorbell jingled again.

The new arrivals were young. Or was she getting old? With her trained eye, Elena could tell they were newbies in the world of sensual and erotic exploration, so she gave them a friendly greeting and allowed them to explore the boutique. "I'll be with you in a minute, feel free to look around and let me know if you have any questions."

Elena finished unpacking the box, before she approached the nervous young couple eyeing the toys. "Considering new experiences?" she asked, her voice a soothing melody of understanding. The woman's blush deepened, and the man shifted. "It's all about open communication," Elena continued, her tone warm, not overbearing. "Discussing limits, desires, fears—it strengthens your bond." The couple exchanged a look, comforted and encouraged.

As they absorbed her advice, the bell jingled. A broad-shouldered man stepped in, his form casting a brief shadow across the room, the scent of fresh grass and sawdust trailing behind him. The spring sun peeked around him, giving the boutique a warm glow.

Elena turned to identify the source. "Jack!"

"Jacques!" The way Elena pronounced his name betrayed her French roots and added an exotic flair that amused and delighted him. Jack closed the door behind him, workday residue of dust and the scent of timber clinging to his jeans. He ignored the couple, their presence fading into the background as he enveloped Elena in a passionate embrace.

Their familiar dance of lips and longing spoke of a day's worth of missed connections.

As they broke apart, Elena's animated chatter about Emma filled the space. Jack pictured Emma, the transformation from single to married life illuminating her. "I saw Dan today," he chimed in, recalling the brief sighting on the construction site east of town. The image of his friend, hard hat in place, crossed his mind, but their paths hadn't crossed long enough for conversation. "Didn't get the chance to catch up but I'll see him tonight in the gym."

"Your women's self-defense course tonight?" Elena asked, a hint of teasing in her voice. Jack nodded, his mind wandering to the gym's familiar scent of sweat and determination.

"Are you joining us?" he asked, half-hoping she'd say yes. The thought of Elena, fierce and empowered, throwing punches was a vision he found both endearing and attractive.

"Me? In a gym? Boxing?" Elena laughed; her disbelief clear. "Get real."

Jack's response was instant, the playful dominance in their relationship slipping into his voice. "Get real, Sir!" he corrected her, a grin spreading across his face. His eyes sparkled with the challenge, the unspoken dance of their love always a step away from playful banter.

In those moments, the boutique around them, with its whispers of desire and the soft rustle of silk, seemed to fade. It was just Jack and Elena, navigating the ebb and flow of their relationship, one conversation, one kiss at a time.

Two

Jack's footsteps echoed against the streets of Missoula, each step a beat in the rhythm of his hopeful heart. The spring air, laced with the scent of blooming lilacs, filled his lungs with a sense of promise. As he left 'Eros' Essence,' the image of Elena, with her knowing smile and eyes that seemed to see right into his soul, lingered in his mind.

"See you at 8, at La Petite Bistro?" he had asked, his voice betraying a hint of the butterflies dancing in his stomach. Her smile, warm and reassuring, was all the confirmation he needed. It wasn't just any dinner; it was the night he would ask her to be his forever.

He strolled, hands in pockets, through Missoula's bustling streets, pausing now and then to gaze at the Montana sky. It mirrored the expanse of his feelings, the depth of his desire to take this next step. People around him moved in their busy lives, but Jack was in a world of his own, contemplating the future he yearned to build with Elena.

Emma and Dan had paved the way, their love story unfolding in a connection that refused to wait. Jack and Elena had met shortly after, their bond a slow burn that now blazed with an intensity he could no longer contain.

His heart fluttered with every thought of Elena. The familiar storefronts passed in a blur as his mind played over the moment he would ask, the moment their lives would change. His decision felt right, like a path clearing in the wilderness, leading him to where he was always meant to be.

With a deep, steadying breath, Jack pushed open the door, the tinkling bell announcing his arrival. The shopkeeper, recognizing the look of a man on a mission, greeted him with a knowing nod.

Jack's eyes were drawn to a ring, its simplicity a reflection of Elena's elegance, its sparkle a match for the light she brought into his life. He knew it was the one the moment he saw it.

With the purchased ring tucked in his pocket, Jack stepped out of the shop, his step lighter, his resolve firmer. Tonight, he would ask Elena to join him on this journey,to intertwine her life with his. The Montana sky stretched above him, an endless canvas of possibilities. Tonight, under the soft glow of candles, he would offer her his heart, his hope, his all.

Three

Evening draped Missoula in gentle twilight as Elena and Jack entered the quaint bistro, the warm glow of the lights inside spilling onto the cobbled street. The familiar jingle of the bell greeted them, mingling with the comforting aromas of cured meats and fresh bread. Jack's hand was a reassuring presence at the small of Elena's back, guiding her through the cozy hustle of the deli.

They found a quiet corner table, the lively evening atmosphere buzzing around them. The glass case filled with culinary treasures reflected the flickering candle on their table, setting a romantic ambiance. Elena's heart beat a nervous rhythm, overshadowed by the memory of Jack's eyes, so full of love and certainty, the night before.

As they sat, Jack's gaze was tender yet anxious. The sounds surrounding them seemed to fade into the background as he reached across the table, taking Elena's hand in his. "Elena, being with you, it's changed me," he began, his voice a soft murmur amid the distant clatter of dishes and the hum of private conversations. The earnestness in his eyes was a mirror of his words, and as he paused, the weight of the moment hung between them.

From his pocket, he produced the small velvet box, laying it on the table. Elena's breath caught, her pulse racing. Time seemed to slow as Jack opened it, revealing a ring that glittered in the candlelight. "Will you marry me?" he asked, his voice steady but laden with emotion.

Elena froze, the world narrowing to the ring, a symbol of a future filled with love but also echoing the pain of her past. Memories of her lost husband and child crashed over her like a tidal wave, leaving her speechless. The joyous laughter from a nearby table, the clinking of glasses, the murmur of conversations around them – it all faded into a blur. Words eluded her, trapped in the chasm between her love for Jack and the paralyzing fear of reliving past heartbreaks. Her hand trembled in his, the unspoken answer lingering in the air, heavy with unshed tears and unvoiced fears.

The bistro continued its lively dance around them, unaware of the poignant scene unfolding in its corner. Jack's hand tightened around hers, a silent plea for a response, any response. But Elena remained locked in her internal struggle, caught in the shadows of her heart, unable to step into the light of a new beginning.

VARIOUS AUTHORS

Four

Jack opened the door to their home, the familiar warmth offering no solace for Elena. Her usual vibrancy seemed to have evaporated, leaving behind the shell of the woman he adored. The well-spoken, passionate Elena he knew was shrouded in a cloud of doubts and fears, her silence a stark contrast to the lively debate and laughter that usually filled their space.

As they entered, he removed her jacket, her movements mechanical, unresisting. Slipping off her shoes, he noticed the absence of her usual grace, the absence of her. Lifting her into his arms, he carried her through the entryway to the living room, her body light but her spirit seemingly heavy. He sank onto the sofa, Elena nestled in his lap, her presence more ghostlike than ever.

Jack's heart ached at her condition. He knew the depths to which a submissive could fall; he had navigated the turbulent waters of sub-drop before. But this was different, this was Elena lost in the maze of her past, trapped by a fear he couldn't fight with a safe word or a reassuring command.

Cradling her cold hand between his, he rubbed warmth back into her skin. He watched, patient and tender, as the slightest twitch of her fingers signaled a return to the present. Repeating the process with her other hand, he felt the ice of her shock melting under his touch.

"You don't have to answer now," he whispered, his voice a soft caress against the silence. "I can wait, Elena. No pressure." His words flowed, a stream of love and assurance. "I love you. I will always love you. With or without a ring, nothing changes for me."

Elena's rigid form began to soften against him, her body yielding to the warmth of his. She tucked her head under his chin, her breath a shuddering sigh that spoke volumes. The heaviness in the air lifted fractionally, replaced by the unspoken bond of their love, a connection that no fear or doubt could sever.

Jack held her close, his heart echoing his words, a silent vow to stand by her through the shadows and the light. In his embrace, Elena found a place where her fears could be voiced, and her doubts would be met with unwavering love and patience.

Five

Jack woke to the discomfort of a numb arm, the result of holding Elena close all through the night. As his eyes adjusted to the morning light filtering through the curtains, he saw her curled up beside him, her body folded into a tight ball. She looked small, almost fragile, trying to occupy as little space as possible. The sight tugged at his heart. She was still reeling from his proposal, the shock of it casting a shadow over her vibrant spirit.

He hated seeing her like this – shaken, disturbed. He had known his proposal would be a big step for Elena, but he hadn't anticipated this depth of retreat. With the care he always took with her, he extricated himself from the bed, leaving her undisturbed in her cocoon of blankets.

Padding on bare feet to the bathroom, Jack carried the weight of the previous night with him. The memory of Elena's pale, unresponsive face haunted him. The lively, confident, and sensual woman he loved seemed buried under layers of uncertainty and fear.

He perched on the closed toilet seat, his movements automatic as he pulled out his phone. Dialing Dan's number was a reflex, a need for a sounding board, for someone who might understand. The phone rang twice before Dan's gruff, alert voice answered.

"What's wrong?" Dan's directness was expected, a comfort in its familiarity.

"Good morning to you, too," Jack attempted a light tone, but it fell flat even to his own ears.

"Cut the bullshit, Grayson. You calling me this early on a Saturday is *not* to wish me a good morning. What's going on?"

Jack sighed, the weight of the situation pressing down on him. He leaned back against the cold tiles, the hardness a sharp contrast to the turmoil inside him.

He recounted the previous evening, the candlelit dinner, the moment he presented the ring, and Elena's reaction. He spoke of her silence, her distant gaze, how she seemed to retreat into herself, leaving him helpless on the other side of an invisible barrier.

Dan listened, his occasional grunts an affirmation that he was processing every word. "Fears don't have to be rational, man," he said. "Elena lost her husband and child out of the blue. One day they were there, and the next, she had cops at her door. That's not something you just get over."

Jack knew this. He knew her history, the wounds that time had healed but not erased. What he struggled with was the balance between giving her the space she needed and the urge to pull her out of her shell.

"She's my sub, Dan. She's holding back a part of herself. That's not how this works," Jack's voice was a mix of frustration and concern.

Dan's response was thoughtful. "No, it isn't. But how are things otherwise between you two?"

Jack's eyes drifted, focusing on the patterns of the bathroom tiles. "Great! We love living together. She fits right in with my friends and family. Our chemistry is off the charts. She trusts me, Dan. With her body, at least."

There was a pause before Dan spoke again, his voice firmer. "If she trusts you that way, start there. Use what you have. Peel back her defenses physically, and the emotional barriers will follow. That's your way in, Jack."

Jack let out a long breath, absorbing the advice. "Thanks, Dan. I'll let you know how it goes."

"Good luck, man. And hey," Dan added, "after this, I expect to be best man at the wedding."

The wedding. The word hung in the air even after Jack ended the call. Jack stood up, stretching the stiffness from his body, and approached the sink. The reflection in the mirror showed a man determined yet filled with a tumult of emotions. Brushing his teeth, he focused on the mundane task, allowing his thoughts to settle.

Lathering his face with shaving cream, he took up the razor, its sharp edge gliding over his skin. As he removed the stubble, an idea began to form, taking shape with each stroke of the blade. Elena's trust in him was profound, yet there was a barricade around her heart, one that he hadn't been able to breach.

He rinsed his face, the cool water a balm to his skin and his racing thoughts. He could use their physical connection, the deep trust she placed in him as her Dominant, to help her confront and peel away the layers of fear and pain that held her back.

Jack dried his face, his resolve solidifying. He couldn't push Elena, but he could guide her, show her that their love was a safe harbor, a place where she could face her fears without losing herself.

Exiting the bathroom, he looked towards the bedroom, where Elena still lay curled up, a small figure bearing the weight of her past. A surge of protectiveness and love washed over him.

Elena needed him, not just as her lover but as her Dominant, to guide her through this. He would be patient, yet persistent, helping her navigate her fears and doubts, showing her that their love was strong enough to weather any storm.

Six

The aroma of fresh croissants filled the room as Jack entered, bearing a tray laden with Elena's breakfast favorites. Orange juice glimmered in the morning light seeping through the curtains, coffee steamed, but Elena's eyes lingered on Jack. "*Merde*," she thought, her love for him undeniable. Yet, accepting his proposal felt like navigating through a dense fog.

After placing the tray on the nightstand, Jack opened the curtains and let the soft light of the morning envelop the room.

On his nightstand the elegant velvet box glared at her. She could visualize the ring inside without any problem. The gemstones it featured were a bit of a mystery. The ring didn't show the traditional diamond she might have expected from Jack, a man of conventional tastes. It held four shining stones, each a different hue. What did they symbolize? Why those stones?

Her mind buzzed with questions, but the words refused to form. Speaking them aloud felt like stepping into a void, so she remained silent.

"Eat," Jack invited.

Elena picked at her croissant, her appetite a casualty of her conflicted emotions. All she wanted was to dissolve into Jack's embrace, to say 'yes' with every fiber of her being. But fear held her tongue, a frustrating disconnect between heart and mind.

"Finished?" Jack's voice was gentle, his touch on her cheek a balm to her restless soul. She leaned into his warmth, a small island of comfort in her sea of doubt.

"Yes, *mon amour*," she replied, forcing a smile. "Thank you, it was lovely."

Jack's eyes softened. "You didn't eat much last night, so I figured you would be hungry." He took the tray, only to return with another, this one carrying a bowl of steaming water and various items she couldn't place.

Elena's brow furrowed as she eyed the new tray. The items on it were familiar, but out of place in their bedroom. What was Jack planning? The uncertainty added another layer to her already jumbled thoughts, leaving her more puzzled than before.

Seven

Elena watched, her curiosity piqued, as Jack set the new tray on the nightstand. The morning sun filled the room. Jack's movements were precise, each action deliberate, yet she couldn't discern his intentions.

"Please rise from the bed a moment," he said, his tone gentle but firm. Elena complied, the sheets slipping away from her as she stood, a shiver running down her spine and not from the morning air.

Her gaze followed Jack's hands as he spread a plastic sheet over the mattress, covering it with towels. The room felt like a stage for an unknown play, leaving her with a sense of anticipation mixed with uncertainty.

Her brow furrowed, a silent question forming. Jack's next words, however, redirected her thoughts. "Strip and lay down here, please." His voice was calm, offering a strange comfort amidst the swirling confusion in her mind.

Elena's heart quickened. The request, so direct and yet so out of the ordinary, heightened her senses. She felt a rush of vulnerability, coupled with a deep-seated trust in Jack. She began to undress, the rustle of her clothing the only sound between them.

As she lay down on the prepared bed, the towels soft and warm beneath her, she felt exposed yet safe under Jack's attentive gaze.

She didn't flinch or stiffen when Jack produced a handful of ropes. "What's your safeword, Elena?"

The question affirmed their dynamic was about to shift.

The sunshine played across his face, casting him in a glow that felt both intimate and surreal.

Elena's eyes drifted closed. *Mais oui, yes, this is what I need. To give over control and let Jack lead.*

"Red to stop, yellow to slow down, and green to continue, Sir." In this moment, stripped of barriers, both physical and emotional, she awaited Jack's next move, her heart a tumult of apprehension and anticipation.

Eight

Jack took the cotton rope, its deep blood-red hue striking against Elena's pale skin. His fingers weaved the rope around her in intricate patterns. Each knot he tied was precise, snug but careful not to constrict her circulation. He paused occasionally, his fingers lingering on her skin, ensuring each binding was just right.

Once finished, he stepped back to admire his work. Elena, bound and vulnerable, was a breathtaking sight. "You're beautiful, you know that?" he said, his voice filled with admiration and a hint of awe.

He rolled up his sleeves, his movements slow and deliberate. Watching him, Elena's body relaxed and surrendered. Her trust in him complete in this moment of total vulnerability.

Jack then began the delicate task of shaving her pussy. He moved with utmost care, his hands steady and sure. The sound of the razor gliding over her skin was almost meditative, the ritual an intimate dance of trust between them. Elena lay still, her breathing steady, the tension in her body ebbing away with each careful stroke.

This act, so personal and tender, was more than just physical care; it showcased their connection and Jack's commitment to her well-being and safety. It demonstrated the deep trust and understanding that lay at the heart of their relationship, a silent communication that spoke volumes more than words ever could.

Nine

After completing his task, Jack leaned back to survey his handiwork with a sense of accomplishment. His gaze lingered over Elena, bound and exposed before him. He leaned in and pressed a chaste kiss to her upper thigh, eliciting an involuntary twitch from her. The small reaction brought a satisfied grin to his face. He reveled in these moments, where he held her at his mercy, yet always with a foundation of deep trust and care.

"Thank you for your trust, sweetheart," he murmured unwilling to speak the words loud enough to break the peace and tranquility of the moment.

"I trust you, Jacques," Elena whispered.

Jack paused, his eyes narrowing as he regarded her. "Do you?" The question, though gentle, carried a weight, echoing the uncertainty that lingered between them. His gaze roamed her face and body. He didn't want just her verbal response but also the truth that lay in her eyes. He wanted to read the subtle language of her body.

"*Mais Oui*. Of course."

"You trust me with your body, but not with your fears or your heart."

Elena stilled and blinked.

A lone tear trickled down the side of her face. Elena's bound form quivered. Her voice, when it came, was a whisper.

"The day I lost them," she started, her voice catching, "it was like my whole world just stopped." Her eyes, brimming with unshed tears, met Jack's, conveying the depth of her anguish.

"I couldn't eat, Jack. I couldn't even get out of bed," she continued, the words flowing now, unstoppable. "I was there, but not. It was like living in a nightmare I couldn't wake up from."

Jack listened, his heart aching with every word, as he worked on loosening the ropes.

"I shut down completely," Elena's voice broke, the dam of her emotions giving way. "I felt dead inside, just going through the motions. But not really living. Not really feeling."

Her body shuddered with the force of her confession, the chains of her past loosened with each word spoken and the ropes fell away one by one. Jack pulled a sobbing Elena against him, weathering the storm with her.

When she quieted, she stared up into his eyes. "It's hard, Jack. To let someone in again," she admitted, her voice a mix of vulnerability and strength. "I'm scared of losing again, of feeling that pain again."

Jack understood her struggle and the complexity of her fear and love. "I'm here, Elena. I'm not going anywhere. You can trust me with your heart, just as you do with your body. Like I said last night, a ring doesn't change anything. Would I like you to wear it? Of course I would. But I know you love me, with or without the visual confirmation."

Her eyes locked onto his, a silent plea for understanding, for assurance. In that moment, bound not by ropes but by the raw honesty of her heart, Elena allowed herself to be seen, to be vulnerable. It was a turning point, a step towards healing, towards a future where love and trust could flourish once again.

She inhaled deeply. "Yes, Jacques, I will marry you!"

Ten

Elena's heart raced as she uttered the words that would change her future.

Jack's body tense against her, a palpable shock running through him. "You do, you will?" His voice was a mix of disbelief and hope.

Her laughter, bright and clear despite her tears, filled the room. "Yes, silly," she said, reaching for the ring box on the nightstand. Her fingers trembled with excitement as she presented it to him. "I want to wear this. To show the world I'm yours, and you're mine."

She opened the lid, the four stones glittering under the soft light. "Will you put it on?" She wiggled her fingers, balancing the box in her other hand.

Jack took the ring, his eyes not leaving hers. As he slid the jewelry onto the third finger of her left hand, he explained the meaning of each stone. "The Rhodonite, for healing from your past and symbolizing the connection with your late husband," he began, his voice steady. "The Rose Quartz, to honor the love for your child. Malachite, for transformation and growth, and Aventurine, for the luck and prosperity in our future together."

Elena listened, each word resonating deep within her. Tears streamed down her face, not just from sorrow but from a profound sense of being seen. Jack understood her better than she comprehended herself.

He slipped the ring onto her finger. Elena looked at the ring, then at Jack, her heart full. "*Je t'aime*. I love you, Jack Grayson," she whispered.

Jack pulled Elena into a tender and passionate embrace, and it ignited a fire deep within her. His hands roamed over her body, finding every sensitive spot and sending shivers down her spine.

He knew every inch of her, every curve and contour. Every touch of his fingertips felt like an electric current, awakening desire and igniting passion within her.

As his fingers danced across her sensitive skin, Elena's breath hitched. His touch was intoxicating, sending a wave of heat through her veins. She couldn't contain the sensations that coursed through her body, and pleasure stirred deep within her.

The first orgasm came upon her like a spring rain. It started as a gentle drizzle, gradually intensifying until it washed over her in a wave of pure bliss. The ripples of pleasure slowly faded, leaving her breathless and satisfied.

Jack settled between her legs, his hard cock pressing against her folds. His voice was deep and commanding. "Look at me, Elena."

His blue-grey gaze was more compelling than the heart of a flame, burning with an intensity that consumed her.

He gripped her hands and pressed them against the mattress, their fingers intertwined. With a powerful thrust, he entered her, breaching the barriers of their bodies and connecting them on a deeper level.

"Elena Mercier-Grayson." His voice was filled with reverence. "It has a nice ring to it."

He rocked in and out of her, each motion creating a symphony that reverberated through their bodies. His words echoed in her mind. Elena Mercier-Grayson. Her name, entwined with his.

As he continued to move within her, her eyes started to flutter closed, overwhelmed by the sheer intensity of it all.

"Look. At. Me."

She obeyed.

"Better."

Once again, their eyes locked and their bodies moved together. The world outside ceased to exist, and all that mattered was the connection between them. They were two souls bound by love.

With every thrust, Jack spoke her name. With each utterance, she became Elena Mercier-Grayson, the woman destined to be his wife. And as they continued their dance, she knew that there was no other place in the world she would rather be.

THE END

Yours in the Next Life by Laura Rush

Letters From the Heart Series

One

Hadley Jones ~ 16 years old
- Party and bullshit -

The music blasts through the speakers, the lights turned down low but bright enough to see plenty of teenagers dancing on tables with plastic red cups in their hands and making out with each other.

It's loud and depressing—a typical high school house party. Girls in skintight, short dresses giggling over the boys on the football team who stand around in groups with a smug *I'm above all of you* and *I get what I want* aura about them.

The others mingle about, laughing and cheering, dancing, or playing beer pong. I wouldn't usually be seen dead at these kinds of things, it's not my vibe. Give me peace and quiet, rainy days on the sofa under a blanket with a hot chocolate in hand.

Unfortunately for me, my best friend threatened to burn my entire book collection to dust if I didn't come with her tonight, and she's not exactly the person to back down on a threat. So, I begrudgingly agreed, *just this once.*

I push my way through the crowd and head into the kitchen. Lilly sits on the counter, waving her hands about, talking to Duncan Valero—another football goofball— who laughs along to whatever she's saying.

"Hads," Lilly calls out, "you're finally here, come say hi to Duncan!" *Urgh, do I have to.*

"Lilly." I smile and side-hug her. "Duncan." My tone is flat, and I scowl at him.

He must think Lilly's stupid, and me, for that matter. He's not the type of guy to talk to her in school or settle down. "Any hole's a go" is his motto; I'm sure of it. Valero here wants a quick bang, and he will soon move on to the next girl in line. I'll be damned if I let my best friend lose her virginity to this prick. She deserves way more than what he can give. Call me Cupid for believing your first time should be special, not at a house party with some guy who's a whore.

"She's not interested," I whisper into his ear, "now fuck off." I gently tap his cheek twice and grab Lilly's hand, pulling her away from him.

"Wait!" I halt on the spot.

"What?" I ask, folding my arms across my chest.

"You're wearing a dress." Her smile is wide, and I bite the inside of cheek to stop myself from smiling back at her.

I look down at my short black sequin dress. It's my sister's. I'd panicked earlier searching through my wardrobe when I found nothing to wear. After cursing my way to her room, I begged her to borrow one. Being the same size has its perks, but it's a shame she doesn't have my taste in clothing.

"Yeah, it's Margo's. I had nothing fit for a party." I shrug.

"Well, I think it's suits you." She smiles, linking her arm through mine and pulling me back through to the living room. Lilly's been my best friend, my only friend, my whole life. She's been there for every big moment. She's sweet and innocent but bites when she needs to. We are yin and yang—in a way.

We dance and sing along to the songs, drinking punch for the next hour like it's going out of fashion. I tell Lilly I need to go to the toilet, then stumble my way around people, feeling the effects of the vodka Red Bull kicking in, and head up the stairs toward the restroom.

Washing my hands in the basin, I glance up at my reflection, my long black hair is wild, and my mascara has smudged under my eyes. I'm drunk but look more like I've been royally fucked. *Welcome to my life.*

I wipe my eyes and smooth my long black hair, so it doesn't look like I fell out of a tree and hit every branch on the way down. Then I make my way down the stairs, gripping the banister to steady myself and thanking God I'm wearing my Converse and not heels. I'd have tripped long ago and found myself in the hospital if I had.

Searching for Lilly, I come up empty, and nausea rises inside me while trying to find her. Tapping on some random person's arm, I smile.

"Have you seen Lilly?" I ask.

"Urgh, yeah." He points upstairs. "Ssshe went up therrre with..." He snaps his fingers. "Some guy. I-I can't..."

Not waiting for him to finish, worry settles in. *She's way more drunk than me. What if someone takes advantage* of her. I make my way upstairs, then open the doors to see if I can find her.

When I reach the last room, I slowly open the door. My heart racing.

Lilly's red dress lies on the floor, and she moans. I glance up toward the bed and find Lilly on her back, legs spread wide. My vision doubles, and I take in the guy between her legs, eating her out as if it's his last meal. Everything slows in those few seconds, and time moves like eternity as I force myself to look away. Of all people. She knows how I feel about him. Hate burns through my veins, and I let out a scream. Lilly's fearful eyes meet my teary ones. She calls my name, and I run down the hallway.

Rushing through my parent's living room with tears streaming down my cheeks, I sprint to my bedroom, ignoring my family's concern. Then I dive under my covers, clutching the teddy bear I've had since I was four years old tight into my chest, and sob loudly.

Luke, of all people, it had to be Luke.

I've been in love with Luke Stevens for as long as I can remember. We grew up neighbours. Both have one sibling, same age as one another, and even share the same birthday: September 23rd. However, we never hung out in school or shared the same group of friends.

We would always spend time with each other on the weekends or school holidays on Mr. Trevor's farm. I started helping out soon after

Trevor's wife, Darlene, passed away two years ago. He'd stopped by one summer afternoon and asked my mum and dad if I'd like to earn money taking care of his horses.

He didn't want me to do much with them, only give them a brush and clean out the stables, and maybe take them for a ride if the weather was okay.

Trevor had known my love for his horses. When I was a younger, I used to beg Dad most weekends to go feed them apples after I did my chores for the day. Trevor told my parents there was no one else he'd trust more with his horses than me.

Luke had been helping out on the farm for a few months prior to when I started. He'd help Trevor out in the corn fields most days. In the afternoons, Luke and I would sit on the porch with Trevor and watch the sunset. Luke had always been nice to me. If he had a break on the farm, he would come down to the stables and help me out.

One morning when I was cleaning out the barn, he came by, and I was sitting on a pile of hay I had swept up. He sat with me in silence as we watched Trevor saddle up Buck, his favourite horse, before taking him out on a run.

"I think when you die, you're going to come back as a horse," Luke said as he glanced down at me before wiping the sweat from his brows with the back of his forearm.

Giggling, I said, "Yeah, sounds about right, what do you think you would come back as?"

"I don't know, but I'd like to come back as a pair of glasses." His cheeks pinked, and I raised a brow at him. "You know, so I could see life again but through someone else's eyes." He rubbed the back of his neck before jumping up and grabbing my broom to sweep the rest of the hay out of the stable.

"I think that's cool!" *Cool? Urgh!* He turned to look at me, and I snatched brush from him. "I mean, it's a good idea, wait not an idea, I-I mean." The corners of his mouth twitched up into a full-blown smile, and he laughed.

"What? Why are you laughing at me?" His laugh was contagious, and I joined him.

"You. You're so cute when you trip over your words, Tigger." He winked at me, and I smiled. His boyish charm glinted through his bright-green eyes. "It's okay, I know what you meant."

Tigger, his nickname just for me. I think it's sweet. Though, I don't really know why he calls me it, guess I'm scared it might be something bad, so I don't ask.

I stared at him for way too long, unsure what to say. He was wearing a tight white T-shirt that hugged his broad frame perfectly, clinging to each muscle in his arms. His dark-brown wavy hair was a perfect mess on top of his head, and it took almost every cell in me not to lift my hand and brush my fingers through it.

Turning away from me, he bent down to grab my water bottle, giving me the best view of his ass in those tight blue jeans.

"You get a good look, Miss Jones?" His tone was playful before he turned to face me. I bit my lower lip, and his eyes dropped to my mouth.

"Yep." I admitted, not at all embarrassed. That's one thing I didn't need to hide. He knew I liked him, I've told him, probably too many times, but Luke knew I wanted him.

"I'm gonna get you some water." He waved my empty bottle at me, then walked out of the barn.

My stomach dropped, and I huffed out a sad sigh. *Always eager.* My mother voice comes through to the front of my mind. Yeah, that's me. I had no chance with Luke. It's when I was around him, I couldn't help but try.

I wasn't like the other girls I'd seen him with in school. They were beautiful with perfect hair, makeup, and nails. Cheerleaders with a huge friend circle. The popular ones. They all looked like they fell out of a *Vogue* magazine.

Then there's me: curvy, short, and a tomboy. My wild black hair was never styled or straight, my clothes have a rip in them somewhere, if you look close enough. I read way too many books, and if you asked most people to describe me, they would tell you my fuse is non-existent, and my temper is unpredictable.

In another life, I wouldn't want to be a horse, I'd want to be his girl.

It wasn't too much to ask for, was it?

My mattress dips slightly to one side. "You want to talk about it, kiddo," my dad whispers as he pulls back the covers.

I sniffle and snap out, "No!"

"Okay, then, you want some ice cream?" *Mmm, ice cream sounds good, but* "No thanks."

"But it's your favourite, mint choc chip." *That is my favourite.*

I pull the covers the rest of the way off and rub my face, removing the last of my tears.

"That's my girl. Come on, I'll get the sprinkles, you can get the scoop." Dad doesn't wait for me reply, he just leaves my room.

―――

Two

Hadley ~ 16 years old

- Horses make me happy -

The first day back in school after spending the weekend crying over my so-called best friend and the love of my life hooking up at the party on Friday night, has filled me with so much anxiety. I didn't go to the farm either. I got Dad to call Trevor and explain I was ill. Dad knew it was a lie but didn't push me on it. It's affected me so much this time. I've seen Luke with girls; I've seen him kiss girls. But *she's my best friend.*

Lilly will hunt me down today, no doubt, and want to talk. She tuned up at my house on Sunday, but Margo got to the door before MUM and Dad and told her to go.

Luke and Lilly tried to call me over the weekend, and I ignored both. I blocked Lilly to make sure she got the message that I don't want to talk.

Margo seems to think it was revenge on Lilly's part because I'd cockblocked her so many times. I'd tried to explain to my sister that I pulled her away from guys because I knew one day she would regret it. I just wanted what was best for her.

Maybe that was the reason. Maybe it wasn't. But I'm not ready to find out her reason.

Making it through half of the school day was easy. I hadn't bumped into either of them. Luke did text me a *"are you okay?"* message during my first lesson, but I left him on read and turned my phone off.

"Hey, you coming to sit with me or you gonna stand there staring into your pie all day?" Margo asks as she bumps my shoulder on the way past with hers.

Shaking my head, I nod. "Yes, please." It's almost a whisper, but Margo hears me and gives me a sympathetic smile.

We take a seat at a free table in the lunch hall, and I do a quick scan of the room, hoping I don't see Lilly or Luke. I note the exit as well, just in case I need to do a quick getaway.

"So, I have something you might want to hear," Margo says just before talking a huge bite of her sandwich.

"If it's about Friday night, I don't wanna hear it."

"Yeah, thought that might be the case but—" Luke drops down into the seat in front of me. I stare at him for a beat before dropping my head down to the table. I've barely eaten all weekend and the pie did look appealing until he joined us at the table.

"Are you feeling better, I tried to call you." I whip my head up and stare him down. He seems taken back; his brows drawn together. "Trevor said you were sick this weekend."

Is he this dumb?

"I'm fine, you can leave now," I say, stabbing the fork into the centre of my pie.

"Are you mad at me? Did I do something wrong?"

Only devoured my so-called best friend's pussy a few nights ago. I'm tempted to say, but I keep my response simple.

"No."

"Tigger, look at me." His finger comes into view, and he pushes my chin up with it.

His expression is a mixture of confusion and hurt.

Tears brim my eyes, and I bite my lip. "What did I do wrong?"

Just when I thought my day couldn't get any worse, Lilly chooses this exact moment to appear. She stands to my side, as if waiting for permission to sit down. "Hads, can we talk, please?" Her voice is needy and grating every single nerve I have left.

Memories of Friday night flood back, and my heart rate picks up, so I stand abruptly, needing fresh air and to get the hell away from them both. I knock over my glass of water in the process, and it spills all over Margo's food, and she shouts. "Fucking hell, Hadley!" at the top of her lungs, making everyone in the hall turn in our direction. Panic rises again, and I rush out of the lunch hall and dart around students to get outside.

"Hey Tigger, wait up, for fuck's sake," Luke calls out, but I sprint out of the school gates before he can catch up to me.

Funny thing about emotions, in the moment, you forget about the consequences of what you're doing. Then, later on, when the rational part of your brain kicks in, you're met with the error of your ways, and my error was leaving school. When I got home, I received a lecture of a lifetime from Mum and Dad about leaving school without informing anyone. The *you could have been kidnapped or died* conversation.

I decide to take a nap in the hopes it will regulate my emotions somewhat, but just as I'm on the brink of a wonderful slumber, Dad comes into my room.

"Trevor called; wants to know how you're doing?" His voice is gruff, no doubt from all the shouting at me earlier on.

I roll over to face him. "What did you say?"

"Told him you where okay and you would be going over to the farm tonight to help out for a few hours." He has a smile plastered across his face.

"You did what?!"

"Look, kid, you are much more fun to be around when you're doing something you like. Working on the farm is good for you. So, you're going to go over there and de-stress, okay?"

I can tell this isn't up for discussion, and knowing my dad, he will have a plan B up his sleeve to make me go. Luckily for me, Luke doesn't work during the week. Going to help out tonight means I won't have to see him.

"Fine, you're right, horses make me happy," I grumble my way to my wardrobe, pulling out some black leggings and an oversized hoodie to put on. Dad sits on my bed for a moment before he announces he will let Trevor know I'm en route to the farm.

Please don't be there, Luke.

Three

Hadley ~ 16 years old

- You can leave your hat on -

Trevor's farm is set on the outskirts of Harpsden in Oxfordshire, it's picturesque, unique, and stinks of old money. The main barn where Trev keeps his horses sits in one of his large fields and is about a five-minute walk from the main house. It's large and painted bright red with white beams, but oddly enough, it doesn't ruin the natural beauty of the surrounding views. Trevor's home is charming with pretty brick and flint exterior, wall-climbing flowers decorate the outside, giving it a period home feeling. It's a dream home you'd imagine a princess living in.

I arrive a little past six in the evening. The sun is setting, and the dark sky is taking over. I head straight to the barn to avoid Trevor, but as I get closer, I notice him brushing Buck's coat.

He must hear me coming, as he looks up, giving me a smile and wave. "Hey Hadley."

"Hey, Trev, what you are doing?"

"Ugh, well, I took Buck for a run earlier." He pauses, placing his hands on his back as he slowly gets up off the ground, grunting every so often and giving me a lopsided smile. "Anyway, he went straight through a mud puddle, so I gave him a wash down."

I giggle. "Oh dear, well, I can take over now." I point to the brush on the floor. "You go rest up."

"Ahh, okay, if you insist." He holds his hands up in surrender.

"I do, now go," I say, placing both hands on my hips. He chuckles, then leaves the barn to head back up to the main house.

I kneel on the ground and pick up the brush to work on Buck but stop when my peripheral vision catches some large freestanding speakers in the corner of the barn. "Why are those in here?" I mutter to myself.

Turning back to my work, I make a mental note to ask Trev about it later.

Tonight, has tired me out. Though, I feel more like myself now than I have in the last few days. Going through my mental checklist, I note I've brushed Buck down, cleaned out each stable, and fed all four horses. I'm finishing up putting the brushes away before I head home when Luke appears at the barn doors. Jumping back, I gasp.

"Sorry, didn't mean to scare you," he says.

"You didn't?" I snort. *Liar.*

I turn away from him and place the broom in the corner, then grab my coat and put it on.

Facing him again, he looks at me in deep thought. His hands are in his pockets, and his head rests on one of the beams of the barn.

"It was Liam with Lilly on Friday, not me . . ." *His twin? Oh shit! How did not even think of that?*

I open my mouth but close it again when I can't find the words, and his mouth quirks into a smile.

"I asked Margo and Lilly what the hell happened at lunch, and Margo told me about Friday night." He moves closer, taking each step forward painfully slowly. I'm rooted to the spot as he comes to a stop in front of me. "You should know me well enough by now, Tigger"—his tone deep and dark— "I don't do parties."

I'm even more lost for words as he cups my cheek. The coolness of his breath hits my face, and his clean, crisp, woody scent fills my nose. With his lip's inches from mine, my heart begins to beat erratically. He stares into my eyes, and my mind chants over and over for him to *kiss me.*

Licking his lips, he leans in closer, our lips touch, then, for a few seconds, we are frozen, waiting to see what the other will do. It's all I've ever wanted, so I wrap my hand around his neck, pulling him closer and sealing our kiss. Our tongues dance and our hands fumble to feel each other's skin. We pant between kisses, trying to catch our breaths but fail before one of us pulls the other in again.

Luke steps back, brushing his thumb over my bottom lip and smirking before he pulls his phone from his pocket and hits a few apps on his screen. Then the speaker in the corner plays out a song I recognize.

"You Can Leave Your Hat On by Joe Cocker"

I roll my lips together as Luke flashes me a toothy grin. He rolls his shoulders back and removes his T-shirt. I let out a giggle, and he winks. It's not the first time I've seen Luke shirtless, but each time I do, the desire to touch each muscle on his stomach becomes harder to fight. A pool of need swirls around my belly as butterflies erupt inside me. I bite my lip to stop from drooling all over him or attacking him back into a kissing battle.

Luke grabs Trevor's cowboy hat from on a hook near the barn door, then drops it on his head before grabbing my hands and pulling me into his bare chest. The beat of the music is fast, too fast for a slow dance, yet neither of us care as we sway in sync from side to side. I lay my head near his heart with a hand wrapped around each other's backs and our other hands clasped together.

"I'm sorry." I finally gather the courage to utter. "I didn't think about it possibly being Liam, I just thought for sure it was you, and I know I have no right to act like that, you're not mine." My mind whispers, *you never will be,* and for a moment, I close my eyes and pray that's not the case.

Glancing up at him through my eyelashes, I notice his eyebrows are drawn together. "I shouldn't have snapped and ignored you, so I'm sorry again, really, I am."

Nestling my head into his chest, I hold back tears welling in my eyes. *I just want him to want me.* Luke lets go of my hand and wraps both arms around my shoulders, holding me close as I wrap my arms around his back. It weirdly feels like a goodbye hug, and I don't want it to end. *Maybe this time I have pushed him too much.*

"Tigger—" His voice breaks. "I-I. . . my dad has a job offer in London, and we have to move." I pull back from him, and the tears are now streaming down my face. "We won't be moving back."

"No, no, you can't" is all I can sob. My heart feels broken. I force myself back into his arms and hold him as tight as I can.

"We leave tomorrow. I've been trying to find a way to tell you for weeks, I'm sorry, Hadley."

"No, Luke, you can move in with my family. We have a spare room; my parents won't care." I beg, and he shakes his head.

"What about Trevor? I'm sure he would let you stay."

"I'm so sorry." Pulling back, he holds my head in his hands and tells me seven words I wish he hadn't: "I prayed we could be more too." Then he kisses my forehead and walks out of the barn and my life for good.

Crumbling to the floor, I cry out for him.

To be continued . . .

Author Note

Yours in the Next Life will be a full novel in the Letters From the Heart series.

I aim to have this book out by January 2025. But for now, catch up on the rest of the series.

Book 1 – Yours Truly available now.

Want to know more about Hadley's sister, Margo? Yours Impatiently is our Margo's story and is out June 3rd, 2024.

Hidden Identity (ClubHS #3) by Lisa M. Miller

Blurb

Max

I'm not a man easily distracted, but the moment I saw her dance, I was caught in her spell. She occupies my every waking moment, consuming my every thought. But she is more than my biggest temptation. She could be my greatest mistake because Sophie Kent isn't just a fantasy I want my fill. She's also my best friend's little sister.

Sophie

Hidden Secrets is where the elite pay for a good time–my time. The night Max Steele becomes my client my eyes are opened in a whole new way. Max is handsome, smart, rich, and only wants me. Behind the club doors is where this secret needs to stay hidden, especially from my brother. But how much longer can this last when I'm falling in love with my brother's best friend?

One ~ Max

I come out of the doors at Gatwick Airport. It's early morning, and I worked the entire flight home. I'm looking forward to spending a couple of days at home before another business trip later in the week. Alistair, my driver, is waiting for me. I head over to him with my luggage, suit bag, and laptop thrown over my shoulder.

"Mr. Steele," he says, taking my bags from me.

"Alistair." I nod, getting in the back seat and pulling my phone out of my inside pocket.

He closes the door behind me, while he sorts out my things before getting in the driver's seat.

"Are we heading straight to the office or your apartment, sir?"

"The office, please, Alistair. I won't be doing a full day."

"I understand," he replies before the privacy screen rises between us.

Alistair has been my driver since I moved to London nearly a decade ago. Now, I split my time between London and New York, but my *home* is my house–an old farmhouse–just outside London. That home has been in my family for decades. My mother loved the house and lived in it until the day she died–almost fifteen years ago. When my parents split, I was just about to hit my awkward teenage years, so the trans-Atlantic flight is one I'm used to taking after being shipped backward and forwards between my parents. My mother was a British society girl and model, and my dad was the stereotypical business executive. I'm my father's son through and through; something I'm not always happy about.

I work my way through my email inbox on the drive, noticing the red and orange leaves are covering the trees, and it feels colder than it did even a week ago before my trip to Milan. At least, that's how it felt when I got off the plane.

I look up to see we're approaching Tower Bridge. We're nearly there. My office has an amazing view of the bridge.

I press the button next to me for the intercom. "Alistair, once you've dropped me at the office, can you take my things back to the apartment?".

"Of course, sir." His voice comes through the speaker system.

"I'm hoping to be leaving by two o'clock."

"I'll be ready, sir."

Our car pulls up behind a car I recognize. Alistair gets out and opens the door, and I see my oldest friend–and business partner Daniel standing there smiling as I get out.

"I knew you'd head straight here from the airport," he says, slapping me on the shoulder as we walk into our building and take the elevator to the top floor. "Glad to be back in cold, wet England?" he laughs.

"Like you wouldn't believe. We finally got everything sorted out late last night." We make our way over to the elevator; Daniel presses the button to our floor. The elevator pings, and we step out. "I'll swing by your office in an hour or so. I think Amanda will have my balls if I don't check in with her first."

Daniel mumbles something I can't hear before heading down the opposite hallway to mine to his office, laughing to himself as he goes.

I head straight toward Amanda's desk. I smile down at the best executive assistant I've ever had. Finding her three years ago was the best thing I ever did, and my office wouldn't run the way it does without her.

"Max." She smiles warmly, standing. "How was the flight?"

"I worked most of it." I run my hand through my hair. I should have stopped by the apartment first. I still have that grimy feel from traveling. I should have asked the pilot to change the flight time home, but I wanted to get back. Being away all week, I knew my desk would be a chaotic mess.

"You look shattered. You don't have any in-person meetings today. I wasn't sure what your plans were." Amanda says, following me into my office, stopping in front of my desk. She takes a seat in the chair opposite and like every morning.

"Thanks." I pull my chair back from my desk and crash down onto it. "I'll be leaving in a couple of hours."

I work on the liquor side of the business. Gin is my current obsession. Daniel is the money man, our CFO, and I'm more hands-on with the clients. We've recently moved into the gin market. That was part of the reason for my trip to Milan. We offer some limited-release bottles.

"The Italians sent over the contract during your flight. They liked you," Amanda says. She puts her hair behind her ears, her pause making me nervous.

"What is it, Amanda?" I'm more gruff than intended, but I've been awake since yesterday morning.

"Daniel has asked that you go to his office."

"I saw him on my way in."

"Okay." She has Post-it notes in both hands. "This is the important pile." She hands them over, and there must be ten or more names and companies there.

"Thanks. Do I even want to see the other pile?"

"Probably not, but you're the boss." She gives me a weak smile before leaving.

I wish Amanda would use the inter-office message app. She's the only person who insists on giving me these Post-it notes. I look at some of the names and Mike Dawson is on my list. I have a meeting with him in New York on Friday. Mike owns a members-only club both here in London and New York. I've been trying to get him to hold one of our limited bottles in his clubs.

His number is already saved in my phone, so I scroll through my contacts and hit call.

"Hello," he says drowsily down the line.

"Hey, Mike, sorry to wake you," I say, genuinely when I realize what I've done.

"It's Max," I hear him whisper to someone else before there is movement and rustling in the background, followed by the sound of a door opening and closing.

"Mike?"

"Give me a second," he says. "Thanks for getting back to me. Kate and I flew into London yesterday. I was wondering if we could bring forward our meeting?"

"Yeah, I don't see why not. I'm free today if you are?"

"Perfect. Shall we say two o'clock at the club?"

"Sounds great. I've not seen the place since the refurb."

"Okay, see you then," Mike says before ending the call.

I put my phone in my pocket, log in to my computer and work on the emails that have flooded my inbox since I last looked.

Two ~ Sophie

The noise outside my apartment has been driving me insane for the last two hours. Not all of us work nine-to-five hours, assholes. My internal clock hasn't gotten used to working crazy hours yet. Last night was a late one. I've been working at Hidden Secrets for a month now, and I love it. We had VIP clients in until four this morning. Last night was the first time I met the owners; they were not what I expected. I pull my phone out from under the covers and see I've missed a couple of texts from my brother.

Daniel: Hey Soph, where are you this month? I hope the show is going well.

Daniel: When is your next trip to London?

Daniel: I'll pay your train fare.

Daniel: Soph. Get in touch with me!

Daniel doesn't know that I lost my job six months ago, on a popular touring show. I should have told him. I know I should have, but I didn't want him to cause trouble. One of the Producers on the show had been hitting on me ever since our first stop on the tour; things escalated though when we got to Edinburgh. He threatened to fire me if I didn't sleep with him. So I walked out. Why didn't I say anything? Because he's the money man, and a lot of people from the cast to the people who work behind the scenes rely on this job. It would also be my word against his; he made sure all of his advances were away from other people. My friend, who I was in a show with a million years ago, heard about what happened and got me a job at a club she's been working at. It's recently got new owners, who Rachel said are even better than the last. So I've been a cage dancer for the last month.

The club is fantastic, and the clients are much the same. Hidden Secrets is a kink club. Rachel is a waitress and dancer like myself, but the club also offers in-house entertainment. I'm not gonna lie; I've been tempted to ask the manager about that. The place is elite. During my first week working there, we had movie and TV star Reid Taylor with his partners. Yes, I said partners, plural.

I'm making more money here, and our benefits are excellent, too. Mike and Kate know how to look after their employees. We get paid extra for the extra services we offer, but everything is our choice. Like everything, nobody in this place does anything they're uncomfortable with. Kate said she wants to see me before my shift today, and I'm hoping she will let me move away from just being one of the cage girls.

I walk up the steps from the tube station, my bag with my 'uniform' over my shoulder. Looking at my watch, I see I'm cutting it a little too close for my liking. I hope Kate doesn't get mad at me. I'm the biggest people pleaser on the planet (or so my brother says), so I spend a huge chunk of my time worrying about what other people think.

Rachel is standing just outside the big glass doors, talking to the security guy she's had a crush on since he started a couple of weeks ago. They both nod at me as I walk through the glass doors and past the desk in the foyer. To the outside world and anyone who just so happens to wander in off the street, this place looks like a hotel or something. But they'd be wrong. Pure sin happens in this building, and I'm glad I get to work here. It's way more fun than I thought it was going to be. What I envisioned is totally different. This place is high class.

I press my employee key card against the lift's card pad and feel it jerk before moving upwards. I look at my reflection in the mirror and run my finger under my bottom lip, rubbing away a bit of red lipstick that must have gotten there in my rush to get ready. The doors open into the corridor of the changing rooms on the employee floor.

I nod at a couple of people. Only some people who work at the club are performers, some are front and back of house staff. I walk to my locker and see Kate standing, talking to one of the girls from behind the bar.

"Mike and I have a meeting with a potential new supplier. He's a club member here and in New York, but I don't think he's spent much time at this place," Kate says.

"Okay," I said, not knowing where she was coming from with this information.

"So I need to push our meeting back. I'll come and grab you after." Kate says; she looks at her reflection and then leaves.

"Okay," I shout to Kate, putting lip gloss on in the mirror. She nods her head making her way out of the changing room.

I grab the wig from my locker and go to the mirror to do my thing. I thought my wig-wearing days were behind me when I stopped touring. When I started working here, I was worried about somebody noticing me, so the wig was my way of protecting myself. A couple of the other girls do too. But now! I don't know; I'm not sure if I need to hide who I am now. I'm confident enough in my own skin.

I put on my barely there jeweled bikini top and black hot pants. Ready to start another night. God, I love my job here!

Three ~ Max
MOVEMENT: HOZIER

Mike and Kate meet me at the reception desk at the entrance to the building. The security guard returns my membership card as I walk over to the pair.

"Max, good to see you again," Mike says, his hand held out.

"You too," I smile. "Kate," I nod at her.

"Your assistant said you've been out of the country."

"Yeah, I got back from Milan this morning."

Mike and Kate share a look. "Oh really? Mike recently found out he has family there."

Mike says something under his breath that I can't quite make out, but Kate shakes her head as she presses the button on the elevator, the members-only discreetly above the opening doors.

"You've not been here since the refurb, right?" Mike asks.

"No, business has been crazy. I've not been to the house in the country for over a month either."

Mike raises his eyebrows at me. He knows how important the house was to me growing up, and it's the place I truly think of as home. I hope to spend some time there when I return from New York next week.

The doors open onto the open-plan playroom and bar; it's not as quiet as you'd think for the middle of the day but also not as busy as the evening. Not all of the cages are being used, but a couple of dancers are in them. A red glow is over the room as the mood and look of the room give *Moulin Rouge* vibes. I watch them as we walk through the area. The seating in this place is all dark red velvet and leather. The tables are all solid. I'm confident there is a good reason for that. I'm a guy who likes to observe; I'm a voyeur at heart. A dancer in the middle cage captures my attention; she's in the zone and sexy as hell. She moves to the music like she was born to be a performer a natural, moving to the beat of the music. The song has a slow beat that draws you in but is perfect at the same time. I'm aware I've been watching her for longer than I should. She seems so confident with her sexuality. It really is something special to see. I keep her in my line of sight as I sit at one of the tables Kate and Mike are sitting at.

"Someone has you distracted," Mike laughs as he sips his drink.

"Leave him alone," Kate says, poking him in the side.

"You two already act like an old married couple, you know that."

"Yeah, so we keep being told..." Mike mumbles, not looking impressed with the comment. "We didn't call you here for chit-chat about *our* love life."

Kate and I both laugh. I'm not sure what part she's laughing at, but I'm laughing at his use of the word *'love life'*; never in a million years did I think I'd see the day.

"You're dicks, the pair of you," Mike says.

"Hey, is that any way to talk to a client?" I argue.

"You're right."

"We want an exclusive bottle unique to the club as a brand," Kate says, with all the power I've heard and come to expect. She is an absolute boss bitch–and I mean that as a total compliment. If Mike hadn't taken her off the market, a million guys would have taken his place. But for years, nobody has so much as whiffed in her direction. It was obvious to everyone–except Mike until earlier this year–that she was off-limits.

"Everything okay now?" I ask, realizing I've not seen Kate since the day before her accident.

"Yeah, it takes more than a fender-bender to knock me down."

Mike turns to look at her. "It was way more serious than that, and Max knows it."

"I know, I was there." Kate glares back at him. Something tells me this is a conversation they've had before.

"Back to this exclusive bottle," I say, trying to get the topic of conversation back on track. I don't want to get in the middle of the current domestic situation these two are obviously in.

"You know we have big plans for this brand, Max we've started that with the addition of the clubs, and we have plans in place for more."

I knew Mike had deep pockets, and given the amount I spent on my membership, I should have thought of the elite private club scene.

"We're flying out to Milan tomorrow, but if you can get the team working on something," Kate says, and I give her credit for trying to steer this ship. I've not seen Mike this grumpy since his pining over Kate years.

I pull out my phone and open my diary app to see when I'm next stateside. "I'm in New York again in about a month. I could extend the stay and catch a flight over to L.A."

"E-mail over the dates, and we'll see. Kate and I usually take a trip to New York once a month, six weeks at the latest." I notice Kate fighting back a smile as Mike talks. I'd heard rumors from the club scene but thought it was just gossip. Mike didn't take me as the kind of guy who liked to share his toys.

I look at the dancer in the cage again and how she moves. "Is this a club-specific bottle you want or for your whole brand?" I ask, already the cogs turning in my mind on this.

"Just the club-specific currently," Kate smiles. "It was my idea to do something special for the clubs. I thought it would be a fun thing to add. What's the point in having an elite-members-only club and not going all in? Eventually, I'd like each club to have their own bottle."

She's right, and I love seeing her business mind at work. Kate is way more than someone who covered for Mike. I can see why he jumped at the chance to go into business with her.

"I look forward to working with you both."

"You staying?" Mike asks.

"Yeah," I say as I watch her again.

Kate and Mike leave me at the table we've been sitting at, and the next thing I know, a drink is put down in front of me, and I take in the view. It's good to be back in the London club. It's been too long. Mike and Kate really classed this place up when they bought out the last owner and expanded the club.

Four ~ Sophie

I could feel the guy's eyes watching me the whole time he was sitting and talking to Kate and Mike. Not in a creepy way–at least, I hope not. No, the guy seemed normal enough. He looked hot from a distance in the club's lighting. I wonder what he looks like up close?

Kate signals me from across the room. I wait until the song ends before getting out of the cage I've been dancing in since the start of my shift. I walk over to Kate, who is standing laughing with Mike and one of the guys from behind the bar.

"Sophie," she smiles at me. She motions to the table she was sitting at earlier with the hot guy. "Let's go and have a chat."

I know I knew this meeting would happen, but it didn't help that feeling in the pit of my stomach, that feeling of being sent to the headmaster's office. She sits on the couch and pats the seat next to her. So I follow and sit next to her. I hope the fact that this meeting is happening out in the open means I'm not about to be let go. This isn't a power move on Kate's part to fire me in front of everyone. I need to get out of my head.

"So Sophie, you've been with us a while now. I know you originally came to us…"

I stop Kate before she can say anymore. "I want to stay. If possible, I want to do more."

The smile on Kate's face gets brighter, and I know we're on the same page now.

"Well, that's good then. Everyone here speaks highly of you, and I know we've not had much chance to talk and get to know each other, but Mike and I are updated with everything. So you said you had some ideas?" She sounds hopeful and genuinely wants to hear what I have to say.

"How do you feel about something like a burlesque show a couple of times a week?"

I thought Kate's smile couldn't get any bigger, but I was wrong. "I love that idea. I was thinking something similar, but your idea is so much better."

I love how candid she's being with me; everything I've heard about Kate is true. She's the boss, but she's fair and takes on ideas from people. I feel a sense of pride over me as I tell her more about my ideas. Fun little things where we could utilize things already in the space. Take the stage, for example, that's mainly used for showcasing stuff we offer; a dancer could use that stage to perform.

Mike comes over to the table and places a drink in front of us both.

"Sophie is on the same page, but she had a better idea than I did," Kate says, beaming with excitement.

"Oh," Mike says, his eyebrows raising as he looks at us both.

"Yes. A burlesque show a couple of times a week."

I look at Kate, I'm buzzing with excitement then I move my attention to Mike who looks like he's playing the idea around in his head.

"I like it," he says finally. "We were gonna ask if you'd mind getting some of the dancers together once a month to do a show, but it looks like Kate likes your idea better." He laughs. "How do you feel about a promotion?" Mike smiles at Kate this time, and I know a million words are being conveyed to each other in that smile.

Pinch me!

When I lay in bed this morning, I was nervous that Kate may not want to keep me on. Now, she is offering me a promotion—a big promotion at that.

"Rachel mentioned you wanted to do more, maybe be added to the 'play' side of things?" Mike asked, "Is that still the case?"

"Yeah, I filled out all the paperwork last week."

"Great, I think you're going to be popular with some of the regulars." Kate puts her hand on my arm and gives me a reassuring squeeze.

"I have one question, though," I ask. I know at this point I should quit while I'm ahead.

Kate takes a sip of her drink.

"I still like performing in the cage..." I know with my promotion, they're going to need to hire someone new.

"You can still do that if you want. We don't have any rules that say you must do one or the other. Most people prefer one or the other, but we can work around you."

Mike gets Caroline's attention from the bar–my manager. "Caroline was aware we wanted to talk to you, but since she runs the place, I think we should bring her in on this chat now."

The next hour is way more than I bargained for, and I notice Rachel trying to look at what is going on from her position at the bar. I'm well aware she will be grilling me about this later. As I finish filling in my likes and dislikes on the iPad on the form that all members (and I guess staff) who want to 'interact' have to fill out. This is a detailed list of stuff I'd only read in romance books. I love to read in my spare time; of course, I've not had much of that lately. I've been pulling extra hours here, hoping to make a good impression on everyone.

Kate and Mike are gone from the table when I look up, sitting at the bar deep in conversation with the bar staff currently working.

I wrap my scarf around my neck as I approach the glass door, ready to face the cold. The weather has been typically British all week. Cold and gloomy. It feels like only last week, we were all in sundresses and sitting outside. Even for late September, it's cold. I walk towards the tube station and see my breath in front of me. I jump about from side to side, trying to avoid the puddles in front of me.

I pull out my phone and see Daniel messaging me again while I was at work. Thank god he's used to my schedule. I need to tell him I'm back in the City. Especially since I'm starting to make roots here and am not planning on leaving Hidden Secrets any time soon.

Daniel: CALL ME BACK!!!

Sophie: Will you chill! I've been busy.

Sophie: I know you're used to people dropping everything for you.

Sophie: News flash, I'm not on your payroll.

Daniel: A simple message would have been nice. I'll message you later.

Sophie: Point taken.

Daniel: Are you okay? Do you need me to send you some more money?

It makes me smile. He's always looking out for me. My brother and his best friend own a million-dollar company and have offices all over the world. But he's always looking out for me. If Daniel knew I was staying in some crappy apartment and not in the city. He'd have me move into his building in no time. I promised myself I would stand on my own two feet from now on.

Sophie: I'm good. I'm actually in the City.

Daniel: Why didn't you tell me sooner?

Sophie: I'm free tomorrow. We could have lunch.

Daniel: I'd like that. I'll get my assistant to confirm in the morning.

Sophie: Okay. I've missed you too, Dan.

Daniel: See you tomorrow, you pain in the arse. (smile emoji)

I put my phone back in my bag as the tube pulls up to the station. 'Stay strong, Soph', I say like a mantra in my head.

Author Note

I hope you have enjoyed these opening couple of chapters from my next release. Hidden Identity: ClubHS #3 is going to be available August 2024.

Dealer's Arrival by Liz Cain

A Dealer's Choice Short Story

One

I nodded to myself, looking around the apartment above the garage I had just purchased.

They all looked the same; the places I always ended up in. Four walls, a bed, and a kitchen I would use to store clothes and booze rather than cooking meals. I twisted a strand of my red curly hair around my finger and smiled at my home.

Five hundred years and it was getting easier to find comfortable living, especially in the last few decades. I only needed a bed and some place dry and warm to sleep but living conditions had improved over the centuries. It was easy enough for a siren to get the best deals when I really needed to. Not that I risked using my powers too much, when I did, I risked being found by my ex boss.

The one I managed to escape.

A new place, a new life and a fresh start. No need to dwell on the past.

The garage downstairs was a new development in my choice of home. Normally I found jobs at retail stores and as a waitress but I got bored easily and wasn't great at customer service.

As vehicles had evolved I had found myself drawn to the ever changing technology. Being able to fix cars and motorcycles was a useful skill, especially on the less than legal side. This time I had decided to make a business out of it and work for myself. Be my own boss. I wasn't sure why I hadn't done it before.

Now it was time to explore my new neighborhood. Before I left my apartment I looked down to make sure my clothes were at least clean. Not that I cared much.

My favorite leather jacket fit me perfectly, a souvenir from a fight with a biker chick in the eighties. It was nice to see this style coming back into fashion. My jeans had a small hole near the knee but not big enough for anyone to notice and my biker boots completed my look. It would do.

I would need to walk for now, until I could get my bike out of storage. That was a challenge in itself, making sure that it wasn't traced from my old life to my new life. I would have to fudge some paperwork and then "steal" it from a storage facility in Canada. Didn't want to make it too easy for my stalkers to find me.

My fingers trailed down the wall as I left the apartment and took the stairs down to the garage floor. The room was huge and lined with shelves. An empty shell, ready for me to make it my own.

My lips curved up into a smile as I looked at the closed shutters. I imagined working with them open, the noise from the city becoming the playlist for my new life.

It was always exciting coming to a new town and Chicago was the perfect fresh start for me. I never managed to settle anywhere for too long, always chased away from my homes by an assassin sent by the devil to find me.

The actual devil.

You should be careful making a deal with the devil; you never get what you expect.

That had been true in my case. I had sold my soul to Alaric to save the man I loved and you know what? He hadn't deserved it. I should have let my husband die.

Alaric had since become so powerful that he took the title of The Devil. He wasn't truly Satan, no one knew what had become of Lucifer, but the devil did run Hell or a realm that everyone thought was Hell.

I pushed the memories of my past away. I had escaped my deal but been on the run for centuries. The less I thought about it the better my life was. I hoped to get a few years here before Alaric's lapdog found me. A shadow assassin who had become legendary for his brutality. A shudder spread through me as I remembered the last time he had come close to finding me. I had lost a friend. I didn't know what he looked like, he took the shadow side of his job literally and surrounded himself in darkness.

Turns out when you manage to escape the deal you made and run off with his favorite sword your boss ends up a little pissed. Instinctively, I reached behind my back, the magic in place making my palm tingle but I resisted the urge to pull my sword from the in-between realm I kept it in. A witch had owed me a favor and after years of worrying about whether the sword would be recognized, we had come up with a spell that would hide it in another realm until I needed it. All I needed to do was reach behind me and pull it from the other realm when I needed it.

I rubbed my hands together. "Right," I said to the empty garage. "Time to find my new favorite bar."

Because every girl needed a place to hang out and chill at the end of a long day. I could never work in a bar, the amount I drank on shift ended up being docked from my wages the only time I tried. I usually owed more than I earned.

The night air drifted around my head, cooling my skin and the scent of the nearby lake reached me. My breath caught as an overwhelming urge to run to the water nearly overcame me. This was the risk of settling in Chicago. I pushed away the urge to walk straight to the lake and headed in the other direction.

I normally avoided cities close to the water but for some reason I couldn't resist this time. This was the closest I had lived to water in centuries, not daring to come within a mile in case I was overcome with the urge to use my magic.

Using my power would make me too easy to find. I had to resist the temptation in case those who hunted me found me sooner.

Though, really, it was only a matter of time. I usually managed a few years before the assassin found me and tried to drag me back to Alaric. He had come close but hadn't managed yet.

In the distance I could hear a rhythmic thudding, indicating there was a bar nearby. I wrinkled my nose, my mouth twisting into a grimace.

Too loud.

The next block was quiet, with no sign of a place where I could buy a drink and hang out. As I continued to walk my heart sank. I didn't like to be too far from a decent place to drink. I maybe should have thought about that before I bought the garage.

But the place had been too perfect.

It wasn't until I passed an alley and saw the flickering sign that I found what I was looking for. Set back from the street and further down the alley was a pink, neon sign with the word "Gamer's" illuminating the surrounding area.

It was quiet, dirty and set back out of the way.

"Perfect," I muttered, striding confidently toward the front door. The alley opened up near the entrance, with two more alleys leading away. It looked like it shouldn't have been there.

A black kitten slinked across the entrance, scampering away before I could stop it. I cocked my head and waited to see if it returned but it seemed to have found something to chase.

Part of me hesitated, wondering if I should hang around. The creature had been so small, though it seemed like it could take care of itself. I would keep an eye out for it.

My hand flattened against the wood of the door while I made my decision, a small vibration coming through and a low murmur of voices reaching my ears.

I coughed to clear my throat. "Let's see what you have to offer, Chicago."

I pushed the door open.

Two

The bar fell silent as I entered. Everyone turned to stare at me.

There were not many women here, that was for sure. I spotted two ladies having cocktails in one corner and looking out of place in their sparkly dresses. Tourists probably.

My heavy boots made a clomping sound as I took my first steps into the room. I inhaled deeply, the smell of stale beer familiar and comforting.

My eyes scanned the room, searching for those that would be the biggest threat. There was a group of men in the corner wearing similar colored jackets and with some gang tattoos. I smirked at one of them, giving him a little wave.

This was going to be fun.

Most women learned to fear groups of men like this, especially when alone. I welcomed their attention and if one of them was stupid enough to want to get to know me better, then it would make for an interesting evening.

The brown skinned man behind the bar gave me a wary nod, wiping a hand over his bald head and continued to clean the glass in his hand as I approached. With broad shoulders and a muscular build he looked like he could handle himself.

"Whiskey, please," I said, placing my hand flat on the bar and spreading my fingers. I hopped onto the bar stool, wishing as I always did that I had a few more inches in height.

At five foot five I had been tall for the sixteenth century but in this modern era I was considered short.

Didn't make much difference, in fact I had more fun when everyone underestimated me, but it sure would be nice if I could get onto a bar stool with a little grace.

I sighed. "Suits me really," I muttered, clumsily righting myself before I fell off the other side. Elegant and grace were not words I would use to describe my personality.

"What was that?" The giant behind the bar asked, sliding a glass of whiskey toward me.

"Nothing," I said, throwing it back in one swig. I welcomed the burn.

"You're new to the area," he said, picking the clean glass back up to continue to wipe it.

I smiled, gesturing for another drink. "That obvious?"

The bartender grunted and shrugged one shoulder. "Never seen you here before."

I looked around the bar, my eyes roaming over the jukebox playing rock music but not so loud that you couldn't talk to each other. I took a smaller swig of whiskey.

"I like it here," I announced. "You'll probably be seeing a lot of me."

Another grunt from the bartender. When I asked for another he gave me a surprised look. "Maybe you should slow down."

I chuckled. "I'll be okay." My supernatural metabolism meant that I could drink a fair bit of human liquor before I felt the effects. The only way I could get drunk was by drinking demon whiskey and I didn't want to draw their attention so that wasn't an option. Any demon who saw me would run back to Alaric to tattle on me. Demon bars were out of the question.

The bartender pursed his lips but poured me another. "I'm Terry," he offered. "This is my place."

"Nice to meet you Terry, I'm Morgan." I took a small sip so as not to worry him about my state of inebriation.

"What brings you to Chicago?" Terry asked.

"This and that. I travel around a lot. Just bought a garage here so I might stick around." I offered him a smile. "What's the gossip around here? Anyone I need to avoid?"

He shook his head. "Fairly quiet, just don't get on the wrong side of Hadrian and you'll be golden. He runs the streets around here and doesn't suffer fools."

"Fools?" I snorted a laugh. "Another gang leader who thinks he's in the mafia. I've seen his kind before."

Terry shook his head. "He's good people. Looks after those who can't look after themselves and yeah, what he does might be in a gray area but he doesn't tolerate drugs or picking on the weak."

"Sure," I said, rolling my eyes. I drummed my fingers on the bar, cocking my head. "How would he feel about you telling his life story?"

"Everyone knows Hadrian, he's one of the nicer criminals so the cops don't bug him too much." Terry gave me a reassuring smile.

"They part of his crew over there?" I jerked my head toward a group of men in their twenties. They were sitting in a corner and harassing the two girls in sparkly dresses trying to drink in one of the booths. A brunette and a blonde who were dressed to the nines and looked out of place here.

I had been watching the group while talking to Terry and didn't like how they were looking at the two ladies.

"Yeah," Terry said, his eyes narrowed and his hands stilled. "You're not going to make trouble are you?"

"Not at all," I said, my eyes wide and giving him an innocent look. I drained my whiskey and gave him a wink.

"Morgan," he said slowly. "You seem like a nice girl –"

I laughed. "Nice?"

He ran his hand over his head, which I now realized was a nervous habit. "Okay, you seem alright. But don't start trouble. I'll have none of that in my bar."

I waved a hand at him. "I won't destroy your bar, don't worry." I slid off the stool and strode over to the four guys drinking beer in one corner.

"Hello, boys." I sat down next to one of them. "I'm new to the neighborhood."

They all stopped talking and looked at me. The guy next to me sneered and I jostled him.

One of them snorted, lifting a tattoo covered arm to sip his beer. "You looking for trouble? We are busy." His attention was back on the two girls and I could see them shifting uncomfortably in the booth at the attention.

"Brody," one of the others nudged him with an elbow. "Which one are you taking home?"

"Neither," I interrupted, keeping my tone light. "They aren't interested."

Brody turned back and scrutinized me. "You offering to take their place? You're not bad looking."

I snorted. "I'm out of your league. I'm gorgeous and you know it."

His friends guffawed, one of them slapping him on the back. I noticed the two ladies slide out of the booth while they were distracted, and made their exit while the group's attention was on me. The blonde turned before closing the door, hesitating before leaving. I nodded to her, letting her know I was okay. She gave me a grateful smile and left.

I grabbed one of the beers on the table in front of me and took a swig.

"Hey, that's mine." A guy wearing a baseball cap said, snatching his drink off me. It was then that Brody noticed the girls had gone.

"Now look what you've done," he snapped.

I grinned. "What are you going to do about it?"

Three

"Chill bro," the guy in the baseball cap said and grabbed Brody's arm.

He shrugged it off. "She chased them away, Sean," he said, scowling at me. "Least she could do is take their place."

One side of my mouth lifted into a smile. "I prefer men to boys," I quipped.

He pushed a chair coming around to face me and I stood up, though it didn't make much difference.

Brody's eyes were full of anger as he stared down at me. "Why'd you come over here? We weren't hurting them."

"No but you were making them uncomfortable," I said, my fingers curling into fists. Just in case. "You should be more of a gentleman."

"Leave it," Sean said. "Let's get out of here. Hadrian wants to see us all later."

Brody squared his shoulders, looking down on me. I lifted my chin, ready in case he decided to take action. Most men I encountered didn't hit women but as I stared up into his face I could tell he would have no qualms about it. This Hadrian guy needed to get better men. Terry had said he was a good guy but I had to say I wasn't impressed if this was the caliber of men in his crew.

I waved my fingers. "Run along," I said, making my tone as condescending as I could. "You couldn't handle me anyway."

Brody huffed in frustration but let his friend pull him away. The two other men followed, barely registering my presence. By the set of their shoulders I could tell the exchange had made them uncomfortable. Maybe they weren't such bad guys but their choice of friend said a lot. They hadn't done anything to stop Brody leering at the two ladies.

When I returned to the bar Terry gave me a hard look. "You're chasing away my customers."

"Who them?" I said, jerking a thumb at the corner where the gang members had been. "They'll be back."

Terry's face relaxed into a smile. "I meant the ladies but it wasn't their scene anyway. I don't think they got what they expected when they came in."

I shrugged. "Your bar is set off from the main street, not sure what they were doing here. Maybe they fancied a walk on the wild side."

"My bar is usually quieter, I sometimes get tourists in but not often." Terry pushed another whiskey at me. "On the house."

"Thanks," I said, giving him a bright smile. Terry left to serve someone at the other end of the bar and I looked around.

"Yes, this will do nicely." I enjoyed the quiet while I finished my drink. Even though it was early for me, I figured I should get to know my new neighborhood so I settled my tab.

"See you tomorrow, Terry." I wondered if I could open a weekly tab instead of having to carry cash.

"Nice to meet you, Morgan." He didn't look my way but I could tell he liked me. "Don't make trouble," he added before I left.

"Never," I said, my tone was sarcastic as I gave him a wave.

A breeze caressed my face as I left and I was happy to see the black kitten scurrying off with a mouse in its mouth.

A thrill of excitement started in my chest and spread through me, giving me a pleasant hum in my chest. It was a feeling I was unused to, a contentment at my surroundings, as if the city was calling to me.

Home.

I hadn't had one before, not really. Yet a building expectation that this place was where I would settle.

I shook my head, knowing that it was a fantasy. While I was running I could never stay anywhere too long.

And yet I let myself hope.

My head and my heart were always pulling me in different directions but for the moment I let my heart feel what it wanted. I wanted to savor the welcome of the city before I let my reality sneak back in.

I spotted a pier and headed toward it, unable to resist the draw of the water for much longer. One peek wouldn't hurt.

My deep inhale was a sweet release after years away from water. My power surged in my core, uncoiling and begging me to jump in. To give in to the pull. Water droplets on the wooden walkway started to rise around me like raindrops hovering in the air.

My control nearly slipped but I managed to step away from the edge and let the water fall back to the ground. The surface shimmered and I watched it sparkle in the light of the city. I studied the pier and the large ferris wheel. It would be hard to stay away, to not give in to temptation but I would remain strong.

Otherwise he would find me. The assassin always found me eventually but I didn't want to make it easy.

Reluctantly, I turned away. Just in time to see two figures heading toward me.

"Here she is," Brody called. "Thought you could sneak off, you little bitch."

"Aw," I said, putting my hand on my hip. "You missed me."

"You think I won't hit a girl but you're wrong," Brody yelled, striding forward. He gave me a malicious smile but I lifted my chin and didn't back away.

He reached to grab my hair but I slapped his hand away.

Sean laughed. "Kitty has claws."

"You have no idea," I said, unable to hide my smile. This was just what I needed, and with the water so close, my power hummed under my skin, lending me strength. Not that I needed it.

When Brody reached for me again I let him pull me forward, his head dipped close to mine in a skewed reflection of a lover leaning in. "Let's have some fun," he murmured when I didn't resist.

Before he could react I hooked my foot around his leg, planting my heel next to his and pushed gently. His body reeled backward, his arms windmilling as he tripped.

"Oops," I said, leaning down over him. "Did you fall? My bad."

Sean stopped laughing as Brody scrambled to his feet.

"Now you've done it," Sean snarled. "Time to teach you a lesson."

Both men charged at me.

Four

A laugh burst from my chest, long and almost maniacal as I sidestepped. Brody crashed into Sean as they ran to the spot I had been standing. I managed to trip Sean and used my momentum to send a fist crashing into Brody's head. His face slackened and, in slow motion, his face planted at the end of the pier.

Sean lurched to his feet, stumbling. "What the hell?" He cried, managing to support himself on a nearby fence.

"You shouldn't judge someone by their size," I said, dancing away as he blindly struck out. I blocked each punch he threw at me, his steps awkward and putting his body off balance.

I ducked and dodged, cackling as he grew more frustrated. I saw Brody come to and push himself to his feet behind Sean. "Nice of you to join us," I called over my shoulder as I dodged another punch.

"Stand still," Sean ground out.

I scoffed. "I'm not going to stand still and let you hit me." What was I? An idiot?

Brody's face was swollen, his left eye half closed. "Bitch," he yelled, his arm coiled back ready to punch. I bent backward as he threw the punch and it connected with Sean's face. The man screamed in pain and I added my own strike. He dropped into a crumpled heap and it was Brody's turn to stare at me with a confused expression.

"But you're just a girl," he said, grabbing me.

He jerked me forward, my jacket in his fists.

"Nothing wrong with being "just" a girl." I grabbed his shirt and lifted him over my head with a strength a woman of my size should not possess. He landed in a heap on top of Sean who had just come to and started to rise.

I clapped my hands together, brushing away any dirt and staring at my handy work.

"Let's get me a drink," I said, grabbing the back of their shirts and dragging them with me. Fortunately, the streets were quiet and I didn't see anyone as I headed to Terry's bar.

Gamer's I think it was called.

By the time I pushed open the door and dumped them in the middle of the bar it was gone midnight.

"Brought you a present," I said, jumping up onto the stool. "Thirsty work, do you mind?"

Terry stared at me when I gestured to the whiskey behind the bar. His eyes flicked to the two men unconscious in the middle of the floor.

The one other patron finished his drink and left in a hurry. "What did you do?" Terry said, gaping.

"They started it," I hugged. "Tell this Hadrian guy that his men suck."

"Morgan," Terry said, his mouth slack. "They attacked you?"

"Yeah, no big deal. I can handle myself. Now about that drink." I leaned over and snatched a bottle of whiskey.

Terry rubbed a hand over his head, pressing his lips together. "I can't vouch for you, I wasn't there."

"I don't care," I said, swigging from the bottle. I dropped a fifty on the bar. "For the whiskey and the mess. Keep the change."

"You can't leave them here," Terry said as I walked to the door.

"I don't know where Hadrian is or would have taken them there," I said. "Next time. Send him my regards."

I left Terry standing over the two men, and looked forward to seeing how their boss would react.

Five

When I finished tightening the final bolt on the undercarriage of the car I was working on, I pulled myself out from under the vehicle, wiping my hands on a rag and coming to a sitting position on the creeper I used to work under the cars.

My garage was popular and I had chosen my location well. There hadn't been a day in the month since I opened where someone hadn't come in.

I spent my days working and my nights at Gamer's. After that first night Terry had been wary of me but my stool was always left open.

Hadrian's men had continued to harass me, not liking the punishment I had doled out on Sean and Brody. I loved the challenge though and had sent most of them packing. Some even ended up in the ER.

I heard footsteps approach the large opening at the front of my garage. Large metal shutters could be closed at night but during the day I liked to keep them open. I pushed my hair out of my face and stood, waiting for my visitor to approach.

A large man with an air of danger around him was standing and looking around with interest at my shop.

"Can I help you?" I asked, picking up a rag to clean my greasy hands.

"Yes," he said curtly. "I believe you can."

I waited, watching his carefully blank face as he studied me. Eventually he nodded.

"Terry told me about you, said I should give you a chance," he spoke slowly, as if he didn't really believe that.

I cocked my head. "Did he now?"

"I heard my boys were giving you trouble, but it seems you can handle yourself. The medical bills I have been getting have been interesting to say the least." He put his hands behind his back and wandered a few paces closer.

"You're the infamous Hadrian," I said, giving him a wide smile. "I heard you were "good people", are you here to prove Terry wrong?"

"Not at all," he said. "I think we can help each other."

"I'm listening," I said, taking slow steps. We were two predators prowling each other and waiting for one of us to strike.

"Terry vouched for you and I've been watching you work. You're quick, efficient and fair. I would like to send some work your way and I'll pay you well." He stopped walking, turning to face me. I hid my surprise that Terry had vouched for me after saying he wouldn't. Hadrian gave me a hard look. "Stop putting my men in the hospital and stop making trouble. Then we can do business."

I tapped my chin with my finger, pretending to think. "Promise to stop your "boys" harassing women and picking on people who don't deserve it and I'll think about it." It was usually what set me off, if they were fair and stopped being dicks then I might stop starting fights with them.

Hadrian grimaced. "They have been disciplined, I have become lax and I thank you for bringing it to my attention."

"If they start it then they're fair game," I said. I didn't want to stop all my fun after all.

"If they start it," Hadrian agreed, holding out his hand. It engulfed mine as we shook on it.

"Glad we could work it out," he said. "I look forward to working with you, Morgan."

I watched as he walked away and smirked.

I was definitely going to like it here.

Did you enjoy Morgan's arrival in Chicago?
You can follow her story in the Dealer's Choice series

A Hard Sell by Lucy Felthouse

Rowan shook hands with each of the three people who had come from Flynn and Bussel to meet with him. He'd given them his best sales pitch, had pulled out all the stops, determined to get their not-inconsiderable business. But still they were holding out on him. *Shit.*

Keeping a firm grip on his confidence, he gave a wide smile as the trio got into the lift. "I look forward to hearing from you. Thanks again."

The smile remained on his face even as the steel doors closed and the car began ferrying its passengers to the underground car park. In fact, it stayed put all the way along the corridor, through the open plan office with its many cubicles, and right into his own glass box in the corner.

After closing the door behind him, Rowan shut all the blinds and headed to his desk. Slumping heavily into his luxurious leather chair, he finally let his true feelings show. He dropped his head into his hands and let out a growl, followed by a stream of expletives.

"Um, boss?"

Rowan snapped his head up to see one of his staff, Mitchell, standing there holding a sheaf of paper. He'd been so deep inside his own turmoil he hadn't heard the knock, or the door opening. "Yes?" he barked.

Mitchell's eyes widened, and he took a step back. "I-I'll come back later."

Sighing, Rowan beckoned. "No, it's all right. Come on in. I'm sorry, I didn't mean to bite your head off."

Mitchell pulled the door closed, then walked across to Rowan's desk, where he placed the documents down in front of his boss. "You know," he said, "stress can be incredibly bad for your health."

Rowan stared at the dark-haired man incredulously. "And what the hell would you know about stress?"

"You'd be surprised," Mitchell shot back. "It's not just a thing people say they have when there's a lot going on in their lives. It can have physical manifestations, too, if you don't manage it. Very serious ones."

"Why don't you just mind your own business? I didn't ask for your opinion." His pulse raced. God, who did this guy think he was? He was a good member of the team with lots of promise, but he had no right to be lecturing him like this.

"And I'm not giving you my *opinion*," Mitchell said coolly, his blue eyes glacial behind his thick-rimmed glasses, his mop of black hair bouncing slightly as he tossed his head. "I'm giving you facts, out of concern for your health. Pardon me for giving a shit."

Rowan was too stunned to formulate a reply. He didn't think he'd ever heard quiet, mousy Mitchell say a harsh word to anyone in the time he'd been here, let alone raise his voice. And now he was standing in his office, letting loose on *him*.

After several long moments of silence, Rowan finally said, "There's nothing wrong with my health, thank you very much. I just had a difficult meeting with some clients. They're proving tough nuts to crack. I'll get there, though, and I'll manage perfectly well without you bossing me around."

Mitchell snorted, seemingly not giving a shit who he was talking to. "You just don't get it, do you? I'm not bossing you around, I'm genuinely concerned that you're well on the way to burnout. You work a lot of hours. You're in early, leave late, barely have lunch breaks... and as for time off, well, when was the last time you took a holiday?" His hands were on his hips now, and he stared at his superior accusingly, refusing to back down.

All set to shoot back an argumentative comment, Rowan suddenly clamped his mouth shut as the cogs in his brain turned. Shit, Mitchell was right! About all of it. He didn't feel any different physically, but his mood certainly wasn't the best. He'd lose his temper at the drop of a hat, felt fractious pretty much all the time, had trouble sleeping... damn, maybe he really was close to snapping.

He snatched up the glass of water on his desk, drained it, then pressed the cool surface against each of his heated cheeks in turn. "Sorry," he choked out, putting the glass down. "I'm sorry, okay? I'd say I don't know where that came from, but I'd be lying. It seems you struck a nerve and made me realise something I didn't have a clue about. Stress hadn't even occurred to me. You know what this working environment is like, Mitchell, you've been here long enough. It's busy, fast-paced, and sometimes it takes a hard sell to get clients to fork out their cash. I guess I'm so used to it being like this that I didn't stop and think what a knock-on effect it could have. Sit down, please." He gestured to the chair opposite him.

"I don't think I will, thanks. I'll just leave those documents with you—plans for adverts that I need you to check over and sign off—and come back for them later."

Mitchell spun on his heel and headed for the door, his movements surprisingly quick and graceful for such a tall man.

Before he knew it, Rowan was out of his chair, across the room and had his hand on top of Mitchell's, stopping him from twisting the door handle.

The dark-haired man peered down, unimpressed, at where their bodies touched.

Rowan snatched his hand away. "Sorry. Again. Please, don't go. Let's talk about this."

"What's there to talk about?" Mitchell raised an eyebrow.

"Me being out of line. You being right."

"Humph. Well, okay then."

"Great. Please sit down." Rowan watched as Mitchell crossed the room and sat in the visitor chair. Then, hardly knowing what he was doing or why, he locked the door.

After striding over and taking his own seat, Rowan leaned his elbows on the desk, steepled his fingers and rested his chin on top of them. Looking enquiringly at his employee, he said, "So, am I forgiven then?"

The other man snorted. "You're joking, aren't you? You're far from forgiven. All I was doing was showing care and concern, trying to help, and you bit my fucking head off. Without even thinking about it, I might add. You've now clearly realised there is a problem. But the question is, will you do something about it?"

Rowan ran his hands through his hair with a sigh. "I can't apologise enough, seriously. I really am sorry." He paused. "In terms of doing something about it, I'm not sure what I *can* do. My job is my job. It's hard work, but it pays well, so it's worth my while. And, difficult clients aside, I enjoy it."

"Well, you could start by relinquishing some responsibility. Instead of taking all the pressure upon yourself, all the work, you need to learn to delegate. You've got enough staff to do that, more than enough. And they're good, too."

Needing something to fiddle with, to occupy his hands, Rowan grabbed a pen. He started to play with it, slipping it between his fingers, twirling it around. He concentrated hard on what he was doing, so as not to have to look at Mitchell.

"Rowan." A single word, said firmly but quietly, commanded attention.

He dragged his gaze away from his hands and looked at his employee. A chill ran across his skin, leaving goosebumps in its wake. Christ, how had he not noticed just how... how... *dominant* Mitchell was? He'd always been kind of wimpy—or so Rowan had thought, anyway. He supposed that was just how people behaved with their boss, afraid of saying something wrong. Times were hard following the pandemic and subsequent cost of living crisis, so it was understandable workers would do anything they could to keep hold of their jobs.

But now, for some reason, Mitchell had changed. Become braver, more assertive. Rowan didn't know if it was just because he was trying to get this particular point across, or whether it was a permanent transformation. Either way, he was having an unexpected reaction to this new, bossy Mitchell. He thought it was *hot*.

"Y-yes?" It took a great deal of effort to choke out the word, as his mouth had gone dry.

"Did you hear what I said?"

"Y-yes," he said again. "Just... thirsty."

Mitchell rolled his eyes, then grabbed Rowan's glass, strode over to the water cooler at the side of the office and refilled it. He returned to the desk, put it down in front of his boss, then resumed his seat.

"Th-thanks." Rowan gulped at least half the contents of the glass down, shivering at the chilly sensation in his throat and stomach.

Putting the glass down, he glanced across at Mitchell, who was watching him, eyebrows raised. "Well?"

Pulling in a deep breath, Rowan tried to steady his racing pulse. Why the fuck was he reacting to the other man this way? He liked him as a person, thought he was a good addition to the team, but had never once found himself sexually attracted to him. Why now? Why the sudden change of heart?

Rowan forced himself to say, "Again, you're right. I've got a damn good team out there, and I should give them more responsibility. Learn to let go a bit."

"Excellent." Mitchell gave a curt nod, and a tiny smile flirted with the corners of his lips.

Rowan felt like a schoolchild being praised by his teacher. Except he didn't feel childish, exactly. Not when blood was rushing to his crotch and making his cock ache. Surreptitiously, he dropped his hand to his lap and pushed at his burgeoning erection, willing it to go away. This was neither the time, nor the place.

"Feels good, doesn't it?" Mitchell said, smiling widely now.

Gasping, Rowan snatched his hand away from his dick and smacked it on the underside of the desk, then let out a yowl as pain blossomed across his knuckles. "W-what?" he said quickly. "What feels good?"

The younger man's expression went from amused to surprised, then after a beat, sly. "Well, I actually meant letting go of some responsibility. But hey, touching your own cock feels pretty damn good, too."

"I wasn't!" *Oh God, this is going to be a HR nightmare.*

Mitchell shook his head. "For Christ's sake, Rowan, you can't fool me. I'm right fucking here, and I *know* what you were doing. Tell me," he moved his chair right up to the desk and leaned his elbows on it, before resting his face in his hands and smirking at his boss, "what exactly got you going? Was it the thought of passing some work on, lightening your load? Or were you thinking about some natural stress relief?"

"I-I don't know what you mean."

"You know damn well what I mean. The doctors, the scientists, whatever—they're always saying orgasm is a natural stress reliever. It's meant to be good for all sorts. Getting rid of headaches, any other aches and pains, lifting the mood. Magical, really. And on top of all that, it feels fucking *amazing*." He drew the last word out, curling it off his tongue and finishing up wearing a Cheshire Cat like grin.

Rowan cleared his throat. "Yes, um, well, it does. Of course it does."

"Glad we're agreed. So that'll be a big part of your treatment."

"My treatment?" He creased his brow.

"Yes." Mitchell tutted. "God, you're playing really dumb today, aren't you, boss? You've admitted you're stressed and need to do something about it. So I prescribe some treatment."

"What are you, a doctor all of a sudden?"

"Now, now, no need to be like that. I'm trying to help, remember? Now shut up and listen."

Rowan fell silent, and blood filled his cock once more at the other man's forceful words.

"I propose you hand off some work to the team. Also, and perhaps more importantly, we'll launch a two-pronged attack on your stress levels. Part of this will be ensuring you get *release,* and another part will be handing over control to someone else. That someone," he added with a smirk, "being me."

"Are you after my job, Mitchell?"

The younger man snorted. "Hardly. I don't want to end up in the state you're in right now, thank you very much. No, I don't want control of your workload, Rowan. I want control of your *body.*"

Rowan was suddenly very glad he was sitting down, because if he wasn't, he'd have ended up falling on his arse with shock. He'd begun to wonder whether he'd fallen asleep after the gruelling meeting and was now having some trippy dream. A sharp pinch of his arm confirmed it was, in fact, his reality. "Ouch."

"Not exactly the response I was going for."

"I don't get it."

Folding his arms, Mitchell looked irritated. "What's not to get? I become your Dom, you hand over control to me, sexually. I give you release, give you peace. You'll feel better in no time, I guarantee it."

Rowan frowned. "Where's all this come from? I mean, one minute you're my employee, and the next minute you're saying you want to... be my Dom. Fuck me."

"I never said I wanted to fuck you." Mitchell gave a predatory smile. "You're making assumptions. Maybe I want you to fuck *me*."

"But wouldn't that make *me* the Dom?"

Mitchell slapped the desk and jumped up out of his seat. "Not necessarily. Not if I *told* you to fuck me. It's all about who's in control, not who's doing what." He rounded the desk, stepped behind Rowan's chair and put his hands on the back of it, before pulling it downwards. "What do you know about domination and submission?"

After struggling with the imbalance of his seat for a moment, Rowan made himself relax and let gravity do its work. He was tilted farther and farther back, until he was looking up into Mitchell's striking face. Fuck, but he was sexy. Those enviable cheekbones, those lips with their deep Cupid's bow, designed for sin.

He gulped, then shrugged. "I know it's not black and white. There's no right and wrong. It's different for everyone."

"Correct," Mitchell purred, leaning over and pressing an upside-down kiss to Rowan's lips, which was over all too soon. Then he suddenly moved back and released the chair. Rowan's heart pounded as momentum flung him forwards, and he grabbed the edge of the desk to stop him bouncing around or being flipped right out of his seat.

His employee appeared at his side, then bent down and whispered in his ear, "I'm glad you're so well informed. It's certainly going to make my job a hell of a lot easier."

"Y-your job?" He still wasn't entirely sure what Mitchell was proposing.

But it was too late. The dark-haired man had crossed the room, unlocked the door and left, closing the door behind him with a gentle click.

Rowan was left astounded, open-mouthed, and with the most painful hard-on he'd ever experienced.

What the fuck was he supposed to do now?

Trepidation plagued Rowan when he arrived at the office the following day. He was tired, too, as his sleep—when it had eventually come—had been punctuated by dreams about Mitchell. Mitchell dominating him, to be precise. Standing tall, fully clothed, while Rowan knelt naked, listening to and obeying every command he was given.

The lurid sleep-fantasies had included everything from being ordered to crawl around his office floor, cleaning Mitchell's shoes with his tongue, to being slapped in the face and fucked up the arse. There had been a great deal in between, too, and Rowan was surprised his brain hadn't exploded from all the activity. Never mind his cock, which seemed as though it had been rigid all night. He'd even woken up a couple of times to find himself tossing off, on the verge of orgasm with barely enough time to grab a tissue before his bedclothes got awfully sticky.

Wrung out, Rowan exited the lift and headed for his office, wondering what the day had in store. Would Mitchell come and see him, order him about some more? Or would he act as though nothing had happened? Rowan wasn't sure which of those options he preferred.

Greeting the people he passed on the way to his glass box, Rowan smiled so much his face began to hurt. He wasn't used to getting to the office after anyone else—he was always in first, but his terrible night had made dragging his arse out of bed a real chore. He was glad to let the facade crumble away when he was by himself once more, firing up his computer and sipping at the takeaway coffee he'd grabbed en route to work.

Soon, his machine was busily downloading emails. They were a mixture of junk, general memos, queries from staff members, messages from clients, and so on. Nothing was marked urgent, so Rowan would work through them in the order they'd been received, as he usually did.

He'd just reached for the mouse when another message arrived, its subject commanding him to *Read Me First*. It was from Mitchell.

Rowan's heart rate kicked up several notches, and he swallowed in an attempt to combat the sudden dryness of his mouth. Pulling in a deep breath, he clicked to open the message.

Good morning. I hope you had a good evening and are well rested.

I've taken the liberty of organising some of the things we discussed yesterday, including the delegation of some of your workload. All you have to do is read through what I propose and say yes or no. Preferably yes.

If you have any questions, you know where I am.

Mitchell

By the time Rowan finished reading, his eyebrows had almost disappeared into his hairline. So he hadn't hallucinated the entire thing then, and Mitchell was, as promised, taking control.

Christ. All he had to do was approve his employee's list, and a bunch of stuff would be taken care of for him. It was tempting, incredibly tempting, and somehow he knew if he ignored the digital missive, Mitchell would chase it up until he got the desired result. That worried him more than he was willing to admit, even to himself.

After reading through the proposal, Rowan figured it made perfect sense, so he composed an email giving his approval and sent it, wondering what the hell was going to happen next. Delegation was only supposed to be part of his treatment, after all. It was the rest he was truly concerned about.

He was on tenterhooks for the entire morning, waiting for Mitchell to come in and start throwing commands around. He was glad some of his tasks had been passed on, because he was slower than normal due to being distracted. But he did manage to cross a few things off his list that had been dropped down and down the priority order due to his previous overload. As a result of chasing clients up, he scored a couple more contracts—including the one from Flynn and Bussel.

At around half past twelve, he began to consider lunch. What could he order in, or have one of the staff fetch for him?

An incoming email interrupted his thought process. It was from Mitchell, with the subject line *Take a lunch break*.

Rowan clicked to open it.

Go out and take a proper lunch break. I don't want to see you back in the office before your hour is up.

Releasing a choked sound, Rowan dared a glance out of the glass wall of his office and in the direction of Mitchell's desk. The man in question was sitting there, staring straight back at him, his expression unreadable.

Rowan felt pinned in place by the younger man's blue gaze. Trying hard to get a grip, to dilute the reaction his body was having, he gave a nod to indicate he'd read and agreed with the email.

The gap between the rim of Mitchell's glasses and his eyebrows increased slowly, then he jerked his head in the direction of the door.

"All right, all right," Rowan grumbled, breaking their eye contact. "I'm going. Oh… in a minute." At some point, his cock had awoken and he was sporting a semi. There was no way he was going to walk through the office in that state, so he dragged out the process of getting ready to leave. Essentially, all he needed to do was retrieve his wallet from the top drawer of his desk. But in order to buy himself some time, he grabbed his computer mouse once more and made a few clicks, putting the machine into sleep mode—something he never normally bothered with as it happened automatically after several minutes of no activity—then opened the drawer containing his wallet and riffled through it for several seconds, pretending the item in question wasn't sitting right there on top.

Fortunately, his delay tactics worked and he was able to go out on his commanded lunch break without embarrassing himself in front of his employees.

Exactly one hour later he returned to the office, and quickly came to the conclusion his having a proper break hadn't had an adverse effect on the business. The building was still standing, the phones weren't ringing off the hook, and, when he clicked his computer out of sleep mode, he had a reasonable amount of emails to attend to.

Heaving a sigh of relief, Rowan left his glass box for long enough to make himself a coffee, then got to work. He wasn't sure where Mitchell had gotten to, and he found he wasn't too worried, either. The younger man would no doubt show up when he was least expected, and when he did, he'd find his boss was already more chilled out, that his unorthodox plan was working.

Rowan cracked on, ramping up his productivity considerably since that morning, as the memories of his dreams had faded somewhat, and the food and time out he'd had at lunchtime had given him an energy boost. Happily, he checked some more items off his to-do list, replied to a bunch of emails, signed off a load of artwork and design stuff from his employees.

He even managed to make small talk with the couple of staff members who popped into his office—something he didn't normally do. It was due to lack of time rather than rudeness, but, since things weren't quite as urgent as before, it felt good to take the time for a little personal conversation. Just a word here and there, a query, a comment, would perk up moods, boost morale. And, given several of them had been handed extra responsibility, he needed them on his side more than ever. They were a team, he reminded himself, and the better they worked together, the more successful the business would be.

Five-thirty was upon him before he knew it, and instead of panicking when he noticed the time, he actually started to wind down. He wouldn't be dashing out of the door on the dot of the end of the working day—he just wasn't that kind of person—but he'd finish up his current task and go home. Cook a leisurely dinner, perhaps, instead of a ready meal, then chill out in front of the TV.

He waved cheerfully at the staff who said goodnight to him as they left, then shut down all his programmes, followed by the operating system, then waited until it was safe to power the device off properly.

He started when the silence was broken by the closing of his door.

Mitchell stood there, looking gorgeous, unruffled, even a little dangerous. Without saying a word, he locked the door and closed all the blinds. There was nobody left, but it wouldn't do to risk anyone coming back, having forgotten something, or the cleaners coming in and catching them up to... whatever they were about to get up to. It looked like his leisurely dinner and chilling out in front of the TV wasn't going to happen.

Rowan struggled to swallow, suddenly feeling as though a ping pong ball had jammed in his throat. He waited in silence for Mitchell's next move, resisting the temptation to tap his fingers on the desk. That probably wouldn't do him any favours.

Mitchell crossed the room and stood beside his chair. Then, after seeing Rowan's machine was powered down, said, "You did well today. Didn't come in ridiculously early, let me sort out the delegation of work, took a proper lunch break, and, if I'm not mistaken, you were just about to head home."

Rowan nodded. "I was..." He tailed off, with no idea what to say next. How did this work? Was he supposed to call Mitchell 'sir', or 'master'? He hoped not—he was already unsure how he was going to react to this weird new set up, and that might be taking it one step too far, pushing it past the bounds of realism.

"Good. Well, since you've had such a successful day, I'm not going to be too hard on you. Have you remembered the other parts of your treatment?"

Rowan stifled a snort. As if he could forget. He'd been dreaming about it all fucking night. "Yes, I have. They're release, and handing over control."

"Excellent. You've already done the latter to a degree, but I'm going to take it further, and, if you're up to scratch, you'll be allowed your release. Understood?"

"Yes." He bowed his head, hoping that would be showing enough subservience for Mitchell's needs.

"Well then, let's get started. First, I'd like you to remove all of your clothes. I've been wanting to see you naked since the first time we met. I admit I'm looking forward to the opportunity."

His comment came as a surprise to Rowan. Not the part about removing his clothes, but about Mitchell wanting to see him naked since they'd met. Until yesterday, Rowan hadn't even had a clue Mitchell was gay, never mind that he'd been lusting after him. Maybe that was why he hadn't found him sexually attractive—he didn't usually look twice at straight guys. Why worry about someone you could never have? But now things were different, and his cock was already responding.

He toed off his shoes, then bent to remove his socks. That done, he straightened, undid the buttons of his shirt, and shrugged it off. With the flip of a belt, pop of a button and tug of a zip, his trousers were gone.

Mitchell let out a low whistle, and Rowan followed the younger man's gaze to his own crotch. His cock stood proud, pushing insistently against his black boxer shorts. It clearly wanted out, and was ready for whatever games they were going to play, even if Rowan wasn't.

"Nice," Mitchell said, grinning. "Let's see it."

Heart pounding, Rowan wiped his sweaty palms down the sides of his boxers. Refusing wasn't an option, but that didn't stop his nerves trying to get the better of him. He hooked his thumbs into the waistband of his underwear and slowly pushed them down, let them drop to his ankles, then stepped free.

"Very, *very* nice," Mitchell purred, his gaze raking up and down Rowan's naked form.

Each second his eyes lingered, Rowan's blood pumped faster and his cock throbbed harder. He wanted to do something, anything that would get him off, but he knew if he disobeyed, he'd be tortured all the more, made to wait, or possibly even denied altogether. The sooner he came, the better. So he'd behave, do as commanded, if only for the sake of his dick.

Mitchell leaned against Rowan's desk, then reached down and pressed a palm to his own crotch. "I've been thinking about this since yesterday, you know. My imagination's been going wild. So many possibilities. But because we're just getting started, I'll break you in gently. So how about this?"

He undid his fly and manoeuvred his cock out through the gap. It was hard, thick, long and mouth-watering. Rowan suspected he knew what was coming next, but resisted the temptation to do something without being told.

"Suck me, Rowan. Make me come."

Nodding profusely, Rowan dropped to his knees and shuffled into position, ignoring the rasp of carpet fibres against his skin. The musky scent of Mitchell hit his nostrils, sending a fresh bolt of lust through his veins and making his cock lurch. Tentatively, he reached out and grasped

Mitchell's shaft, pumped it a couple of times, getting a feel for him, for what he liked. He might be new to BDSM, but he *wasn't* new to cock.

A moan from above his head indicated he'd made a damn good start. Pleased, he licked his lips, getting them nice and moist, then closed them over the delectable cock in front of him, greedily gathering up the pre-cum he found there before sinking further down, taking as much in as possible. After savouring the sensation for a couple of seconds, he began to suck and lick Mitchell in earnest.

"Oh... yeah!" Mitchell groaned, then tangled his hands in Rowan's hair before gripping tightly and forcing him to bob up and down his dick faster with rough pushes and pulls.

Rowan complied eagerly, making sure plenty of saliva coated the younger man's shaft as he teased it, flicked his tongue around, hitting all the most sensitive parts, while concentrating on maintaining a good amount of suction. It was difficult when his head was being manoeuvred for him, but he did his best.

Soon, even that choice, that control, was taken from him. Either Mitchell was getting ready to come or was asserting his authority, or both, as he held tighter to Rowan's hair and began to fuck his mouth furiously. Rowan could not move, could not introduce any finesse, any skill to giving his employee head. All he could do was kneel there, having his mouth pounded.

He reached around Mitchell's hips and gripped the edges of his desk to help keep his balance. It had taken him a while to figure out how he felt about what was happening, and now he had, he'd surprised himself. Far from feeling used and abused, violated in any way, he felt... free. Free from choice, from worrying about whether he was doing it right, whether Mitchell was close to coming.

The stunning realisation quickly followed that this was the whole point of Mitchell's "treatment" idea. When every ounce of control was stripped away from him, he had nothing. Nothing except freedom.

And it was bliss.

Rowan emptied his mind, allowed himself to get truly lost in the moment. His only focus was the cock in his mouth and the man it belonged to. The hardness thrusting in and out, scraping against his teeth, bruising his lips, pummelling his throat. Nothing else mattered.

Mitchell's grip on his hair increased, sending sparks of pain blooming across his scalp. His own cock felt like it would burst without even being touched. But he couldn't think about that, couldn't think about his own pleasure while Mitchell was taking his. And his climax was close; he could feel it.

"Unh…" Mitchell groaned, his thrusts growing shallower, jerkier. "I'm gonna… come!" A series of frantic movements were followed by one deep, hard shove, and Mitchell's cock twitched on his tongue. Spunk jetted from the younger man's balls, coating Rowan's taste buds momentarily before he eagerly swallowed it.

Heaven. That's what it was. Having such a gorgeous man fuck his mouth, take his pleasure from him without the promise of giving anything back was perfection. No complications, no confusion… it was just simple.

And, as Mitchell pulled out of his mouth and tucked his cock away with a satisfied grin, Rowan realised it was also incredibly addictive. Their encounter was barely over and already he wanted more. More cocksucking, more attention, more *anything*. Whatever Mitchell wanted was fine with him, any "treatment" he saw fit.

If this was submission, he was already hooked. It was indeed the perfect stress relief, even without his own climax. It seemed, though, as Mitchell set about stripping off, that giving his employee a blowjob wasn't the end. There was more to come, much more, and he could hardly wait. Mitchell knew what Rowan needed more than he did himself, and if that was Mitchell's domination, then so be it.

He'd soon forget how he ever lived without it.

Champion by M.F. Moody

An Altered Shifters Universe Story

Author's Note

Champion is a bonus story which takes place during the events of both *Mythic* and *Feral*, the third and fourth books in my *Altered Shifters Universe* series. To best understand the events related in this story, please read the series, starting with *Altered: Part One*.

However, if you don't wish to go back and read them, there should be enough context clues provided to help you navigate this short story. This story contains spoilers for both my *Altered* duet and *Mythic*.

Dedication

To all of the readers, both old and new, who have discovered the world that is my Altered Shifters Universe... and demanded more Doris. Here you go.

One ~ Doris

Night fell quite some time ago, but I ignore the late hour along with the exhaustion tugging at both my body and soul. I'd refused the kind offer of the Shifter Council to stay the night in one of the hotels they'd booked for those involved in the tribunal for Odette Muette and Icahn Koch. I didn't care how long it would take for me to get back home to Denver, I never *could* sleep properly if I wasn't wrapped in my mate's arms.

The beacon of our porch light shines through the darkness, calling me home. Most of our neighbors are already in bed and asleep by now, but the single bulb illuminating my front door tells me that my household—otherwise known as my husband and mate—is still awake. Our neighborhood is filled with families, and it is only those who work late or—like my Faris—have some reason to stay up that are still awake this close to midnight.

I don't even brush the handle before the front door swings open, the beloved, smiling face of my husband and mate of the past forty-plus years standing in the doorway. While he's obviously no longer in the springtime of his youth, his back is still straight, his shoulders are strong, and his skin is still relatively smooth. It's only the creases around his eyes that give any indication of his mature age, and they're the consequence of years of laughter, smiles, and happiness.

His lips part in a broad smile, teeth gleaming in the dim light, his joy at my return warming my soul.

"There she is, my beautiful, strong Champion!" Faris tugs me into his arms, his own personal scent of dried grass, seaweed, pine, and rain enveloping me along with his arms. I snuggle into his chest, feeling all the tension and worry of today's events sloughing away as I breathe him deep into my lungs.

He smells perfect.

He smells like *home*.

"Ah, what is the matter, *mutiara cilik*[1]? You smell... troubled...?" Faris' brow furrows as he pulls back to look at me.

I groan, tamping down on our bond to prevent my emotions from bombarding him before I'm ready to face it all. I'm dreading the conversation to come, just wanting to put it off for another few minutes so I can cuddle with my mate.

"Come inside, you go sit while I make you some *bandrek*. I think I've got some *batagor* and *lemper* left over, and if not, I'm sure we've got something in the freezer I can cook. The kids love their Dino nuggies and potato smiles, so I know we have plenty of those on hand."

I allow my mate to lead me inside, kicking off my shoes and leaving my bags at the front door. His concern and fussing is sweet and comforting, and before long I'm settled into a recliner, the footrest extended and my feet bare while my man flits around in the kitchen making my favorite Javanese comfort foods.

Now that my body is at rest, the mental exhaustion and physical fatigue I've been determinedly ignoring comes crashing down like a rogue wave at the beach. I've never felt so old or fragile in my life.

As a shifter woman in her fifties—alright, I'm actually sixty-four, but in this day and age who's keeping count?—I am essentially in my prime. Shifters tend to live quite a bit longer than humans do, something to do with the healing abilities of our animal half. While we're not immune to illnesses such as cancer, most human ailments don't affect us in any discernible way. In fact, with the advent of modern medicine and similar interventions, the life-spans for shifters have grown exponentially. It's becoming more common for us to live well into our hundred and twenties or thirties, something that has been a rarity for the majority of us until now.

Unlike tortoises and Greenland sharks. Fuck those geriatric assholes. Who wants to live to two or three, or even four hundred years of age, anyway? Smug bastards get *all* the time to finish their TBR piles.

Two ~ Faris

Puttering around in the kitchen, I mentally hurrying the oil heating on the stove top. I can feel Doris holding back from me, blocking what she's endured today at the tribunal.

I haven't said a word, knowing that she'll tell me when she's ready. However, I think I've hidden my concerns well, pretending that my stomach isn't roiling constantly ever since we got that foreboding phone call a couple of months ago.

"Hello?" I invite, cutting off the trill of the phone as I answer our landline.

"Uh, hello, is that Mr. Kennedy?" returns the young man on the other end of the line, and I smile. I know this voice, know it quite well in fact from all the times I visited my kinasih[2] at her work at Pred Academy.

"Ah, Master Simon, how are you today?" I kick off the requisite pleasantries while knowing full-well that Simon Gatto hasn't called our home for a friendly chat. No, he's probably got a question or request for my mate, Doris.

I grin slyly as he responds in kind, enjoying my little prank as I wander through the house looking for my wife. I find her in the laundry, folding clothes.

I eventually have mercy on the lion and hand the receiver over to Doris. My body rocks with silent laughter and I shake my head as I wander back to where I was preparing dinner.

Simon Gatto is a young lion shifter who attended Praedonius Felidae Academy before leaving to go to college in San Francisco. While neither myself nor my mate are big cat shifters, Doris has worked there for years. She is considered not only a senior member of staff, but has also developed a grandmotherly relationship with many of the students.

It had rocked her to her core when Simon had—rather cruelly and stupidly—allowed his peers to pressure and influence him into publicly rejecting his fated mate. While I had no doubt he was not the instigator of the entire fraças, he bore the full responsibility of shattering the poor snow leopard's life on his shoulders.

As one half of a fated pairing, Doris had come home in tears when she'd discovered Simon's cruelty that day. It was a side of him she'd never imagined possible, and it had damaged their relationship for some time. But my wife is rather soft-hearted, despite her intimidating demeanor. So when Simon's father had approached us both to help him redirect his son onto a straighter path, we had eventually agreed.

Michael Gatto is a good lion, an even better Leo, and a loving father. In the years since Simon detonated his future with a single action, we have become rather close. In fact, Michael and his wife Stella both leaned rather *heavily on Doris and me after Simon's bonds were stripped from him, and we opened our extended family to them all. While Simon is only an occasional visitor due to his removal to the Reficio Establishment in Wyoming, his younger siblings Lily and Ryan quickly glommed onto our older grandchildren. Holidays are now a combined affair, and it is highly amusing to watch lion cubs romping with otter pups in their shifted forms.*

Light footsteps down the hallway precede the appearance of my Doris, and I tilt my head in silent inquiry as she puts the receiver back on the station.

"That was Simon," *she begins, rolling her eyes as I smile broadly at her statement.*

"Cyril is currently visiting him at Reficio, and brought along a letter. It was from the Council concerning the tribunal for Odette Muette and Icahn Koch."

I wait patiently as my tresna[3] *pauses to gather her thoughts, my hands work on instinct preparing our dinner of* siomay, *slicing the potatoes and rolled cabbage to go with the steamed dumplings.*

"Essentially, Simon has been instructed to find a Champion to face Odette Muette in his stead. The Council prefer shifters of the same clade and gender to combat one another, and the only other Aves shifter he and Cyril could think of besides me was Greta Romero, and she's ineligible as she's a Councilor herself. So, they wanted to know if I would stand up and fight Odette Muette to her death."

My stomach plummets, but I keep my face calm. I know my wife. I know and love her sense of justice and righteousness. She is not the type to turn a blind eye to someone in need, nor will she stand by and allow wrongdoing to go unheeded.

I already know her answer.

"When and where is the tribunal set for?" *I ask calmly, stomping down my unease so it doesn't affect our bond. But my Doris knows me all too well.*

"I told them that I needed to discuss things with you first, atiku[4]. That I wouldn't make such a drastic decision without your input. I won't lie, my first instinct is to tell Simon that I'll be there, but this will impact our family. If I decide to accept the position, I'll need to fly down to Sacramento.*

Then, depending on how the fight goes, I may even end up with injuries that will need tending."

I snort at that. My wife has oft been described as a "prehistoric murder chicken in disguise," and while her heart may be soft, she's a being of pure vengeful fury when her ire is stoked.

"My love," I sigh, moving away from the food to wash and dry my hands before gathering her into my arms, "I know you. You will not find peace or contentment unless you accept, because it is who you are. You will call Simon back and tell him that you'll be there for him, just as you've been there for him and Sila both over these past years. They are family, no matter what they may shift into, and we never turn our backs on our family. **Especially** when they need us."

Doris snuggles into my embrace, her shoulders still tense. There's something else playing on her mind, but I only need to be patient. She'll tell me when she's ready.

There are no secrets between us.

"I don't want you there." Her words are quiet, almost mumbled under her breath.

I bite back my instinctual denial, and instead wait for her to finish.

"I know it's going to be vicious, and bloody. I also know that no matter what, you'll still love me. I just... I just don't want you there, to see me like that. I want to compartmentalize that day, leave it behind me once it's done and then come home to you. I don't want that memory between us. Is that selfish of me?"

She looks up at me from behind her long, silky lashes, teardrops glistening on the fine hairs. While my animal is yipping at me, **demanding** that I accompany her so I can protect her back if needed, the human part of me understands her request.

"If that is what you need, kinasih, then I will stay here and keep the home fires burning. But I **insist** that you return home straight after. If you're injured, I'm to be contacted **immediately**, so I can be by your side. I won't watch you end that shifter's life, but I **will** be here for you afterward, to be your support and your sanctuary. Those are my conditions to you going alone."

She smiles tremulously up at me, and I see the sweet girl I fell head-over-paws in love with all those years ago. I brush my thumbs along her cheekbones, gently swiping away the remnants of her tears.

"Come, tresnaku[5]. *I wish to feast on my wife until the only tears falling from her eyes are from an abundance of pleasure.*"

I turn my back on the discarded vegetables littering the counter and lead my mate to our bedroom.

Dinner can wait.

The hiss and spit of the hot oil rouses me from my reverie, and I quickly get to work dropping the *batagor* into the oil, frying them until they're perfectly golden. My hands move deftly, scooping the dumplings from the oil and onto a plate, the peanut, soy, and chili sauce already decanted and warmed, just waiting to be poured over the sliced morsels.

I had feared the violence my *kinasih* would be forced to inflict would cause her grief. Now I need to find out just how deeply the damage has cut into her soul.

Three ~ Doris

The slight rattle of ceramic against wood drags me from my reverie and I twist in my seat. Faris' gait is graceful and smooth as he carries a tray laden with heaping bowls of *batagor*, a tower of *lemper*, and two mugs full of steaming, fragrant *bandrek* garnished with green shafts of flavorful pandan leaves. Indonesian dishes, especially the recipes native to Faris' home island of Java, are my comfort food.

Neither of us speak as he sets the tray on the coffee table in front of my chair, nor do we say a word as Faris hands me a bowl of sauce-slathered *batagor* and a fork. Silence reigns supreme as we both dig into the fragrant and delicious food, only the sounds of clinking cutlery, the rustle of unwrapping banana leaves, and the soft grunts and moans of contentment as we devour the food on the tray.

It's not until Faris hands me my mug of *bandrek* that I speak, the calming scent of ginger, lemongrass, cinnamon, star anise, and cloves wafting from the vessel.

"It was a literal bloodbath," I begin haltingly, pausing to take a sip of my drink.

"Odette Muette continued to protest her innocence, despite the overwhelming evidence and testimony that had been gathered over the years proving her otherwise. She forced the Council to call in witnesses to testify once more, including two other Councilors who were present when she destroyed Simon's bonds. She tried to run and escape. At no point during the proceedings did she take ownership of her actions."

Guilt assails me as I remember how, in my fury at her refusal to take responsibility and face the consequences of her actions, I taunted and derided the swan.

"The words I said to her, Faris. I was so cold to her, callous in my fury, that I became cruel. I'm not a cruel person, but to see her sitting there in her robe after being found guilty not once, but *twice*, and then for her to claim that she rejected the judgments and if she didn't shift, then we couldn't fight? It broke something in me. I felt no mercy for her."

Tears streak down my cheeks as I continue to share the burden of my emotions with my mate.

"President Brenin ended up forcing Odette to shift into her swan. Instead of going down fighting, of dying with honor, she shamed herself and her family. She shamed *me*, Faris. I turned from acting as Champion, to becoming her executioner. There was no redemption for her, no attempts at wiping away the smears that her actions placed against her name, and the name of her victim. It was pathetic, one-sided, and everything that it *shouldn't* have been. I felt so ashamed of her that I was brutal, Faris. I used her as a football, and then when she was so broken that she couldn't even stand, I tore her apart."

Faris hugs me, his arms warm and secure as they gather me tightly to his chest, the steady beat of his heart strong against my cheek.

"This Odette Muette. How long did she know she was being investigated? How much evidence did the Council have against her? Did she receive a fair trial? Was there anything that President Brenin or the

Council did that could be construed as illegal or perjures?" Faris mumbles into my ear.

"No, they did everything by the book. They arrested her only a day or so after she'd shredded Simon's bonds, and that was because both Councilors Saputra and Romero reported her. She even *admitted* to doing it while being questioned, to making it hurt, and she was *proud* of her actions! She felt that she had every right to do what she did, because Simon had rejected Sila. She even said so during her trial, despite her lawyer's obvious instructions to the contrary. She simply didn't believe she deserved to die."

Faris hums at my response, the vibrations moving through my body and making my core tingle and clench.

Not now, you needy hussy! I mentally hiss at myself, although being held like this by my mate generally cranks my libido to eleven. But now is not the time, not while I still have the echoes of Odette's swan's pitiful honks as she died by my feet and claws rolling around in my head.

"So Odette's only true objection to today's tribunal was that she didn't wish to die? Even after she almost killed Simon Gatto and caused irreparable harm to him, his family, and those he'd had close fraternal bonds with? You have no reason to feel guilt or shame, my *prajurit galak*[6]. You did what you were asked. You stood up for Simon when he could not do so himself. Did anybody lambaste you for your actions after? Did they call you cruel or merciless?" Faris peers down at me, and at my responding shake of my head, he continues on, smugness radiating from him.

"Of course they didn't, because they knew you had been the hand—or in your cassowary's particular instance—feet and beak of justice. Were your actions a polar opposite of your usual nature? Most likely. But you had not been appointed as Champion to be your usual self. You were ordained to bestow justice—and that is not always the cleanest or prettiest of roles. Odette had shown no mercy or kindness in her actions and had reveled in her brutality. Therefore, it is only justice that she was shown no mercy or kindness, and only brutality at her end. Her refusal to take accountability meant that you had to force it on her in the only way she'd accept."

Faris' words are all well and good, except that he doesn't know about my final act as Simon's Champion. The guilt and shame turns my stomach to acid, and the confession bursts from my lips like a bird from its cage to freedom:

"But I shat over her bloody corpse!"

Four ~ Faris

I can't contain my chuckles at my mate's forlorn wail.

Doris may be many things, but she's never been the type of shifter to glorify in stating her emotional stance or marking her territory in such a way. It's likely that her final act, of evacuating her bowels over the remains of her opponent, is the true issue here.

"Again, *tresnaku*, did anyone shame or rebuke you for that action?" I rumble, stifling the chuckle threatening to rise.

"No... but—" she whimpers, and I cut her off before she can self-flagellate any further.

"But nothing. We've already established that you were not your normal self. You outrage, your fury, and the adrenaline of the fight against Odette—no matter *how* one-sided it ended up being—it all had to come out of you somehow. Had Odette fought you, had she tried to salvage some of her dignity and reputation, I have no doubt that your actions would have differed. But she metaphorically shat over the entire proceedings with her refusal to accept the judgment, so as Champion of justice, you shat over her. There is nothing for you to be ashamed of. In fact, I wish I had been there to see it. I'm sure you were absolutely *glorious* in all of your feathered fury."

My libido rallies as my imagination runs wild at the thought of my *kinasih* in her shifted state, as her nobility and majestic cassowary.

When shifted, Doris stands at almost eight feet—much taller than wild cassowaries who rarely exceed six feet—in height from the tip of her regal casque to her lethally clawed toes. Dense, hair-like feathers cover her body, the iridescent black quills contrasting stunningly with the brilliant blue and turquoise skin of her neck and face. As a southern or double-wattled cassowary, the skin of her long neck descends into feathers, and where they merge both her skin and plumage are offset by the magenta wattles dangling at her throat.

She is a distinct contrast to my own shifted form. As an Asian small-clawed otter, I can't reach the lowest of her torso feathers even if I'm standing on my hind paws and stretching upward. I don't mind, though. I know I make her happy, and that's what really counts.

Doris' soft, sad whisper cuts through my musings, and my arms tighten around her in response to the sorrow in her voice.

"Something else happened after my fight with Odette, Faris."

I pull back and look down into the deep hazel-brown eyes of my mate. They swim with tears, and she finally opens up to me, her fear and worry flooding through our bond and crashing into me as her words strike a devastating blow.

"Simon disappeared after my fight with Odette. I didn't find out until later. It wasn't by choice, either. Nox almost went feral when he felt their bond go dark, and apparently Sila had to be restrained. There's no trace of him, and the Council are also looking for Chadwick Corbin, Brantley Lönnberg, and Catherine Lönnberg. They also disappeared around the same time as Simon, and nobody knows if they left under duress or willingly. There is talk that the two events are connected, but there's no evidence—as of yet—to point one way or the other."

My stomach drops at her words. For a shifter who has trouble believing he's worthy of love and acceptance after what he did as a youth, Simon is surrounded by people who care deeply about him and his circumstances.

"I'll call Michael and Stella in the morning. We'll invite them and the children over for a visit and call in the troops to help keep them occupied until there is news." I look at my mate, desperate to alleviate the anxiety churning through our bond. "What can I do to help keep *your* mind off these events, *karepe atiku*[7]?"

"Hold me," comes her murmured response. My arms tighten like bands of steel around Doris' shoulders and back, pulling her hard against my torso, crushing her chest to my own.

Like clockwork, arousal thrums through me. Since the moment our eyes met all those years ago, I only need to be in close proximity to my mate for my libido to rouse, and when we're *this* close together, it's impossible to stifle my need and desire for her.

"Mmmm," she hums, wriggling slightly and making my cock ache, "you smell *delicious*. Like a warm day at the beach after a thunderstorm has rolled through, washing away the previous day's scents."

I inhale her own personal perfume, tasting her on my tongue and taking her scent deep into my lungs. Damp earth, sweet fruits and citrus, with after-notes of fresh camphor, dry sand and salt-laden air.

"And you, my *ratu galak*[8], you smell like a picnic surrounded by the tropical rainforests back home. All ripe and lush and absolutely *edible*. Hmmm, that's an idea..." I nuzzle at the soft skin of her neck behind her ear, grazing it with my lips.

"How about I have *you* for my dessert? After all, I've been starved of your presence all day, and now I'm *famished*."

Doris lets out a watery giggle and wiggles some more. I slide one arm down her back to her hips, pressing them into the rigid flesh straining against my trousers.

"Is that a yes, *mutiara cilik?*" I ask.

"That's a most *definite* yes," comes her emphatic response.

Ignoring the dirty dishes from our impromptu meal, I scoop my mate into my arms and carry her back down the hallway to our bedroom.

The dishes can wait.

Making love to my mate can't.

Five ~ Doris

Faris sets me down on our bed, the covers already pulled back and ready. He takes his time with me, undressing me piece-by-piece. His fingers are gentle as they stroke over my body, soothing away the marks left by my bra straps, massaging my feet and legs as he positions me to his satisfaction.

By the time he's done, I'm sprawled back on the mattress, my head and shoulders propped up on pillows with my legs splayed and open, baring my naked pussy to his gaze.

My skin is pale and bears the marks of my age. The occasional age spot dots my hands and arms, and silvery stretch marks litter my wide hips, thighs, and stomach. I wear them with pride, as each and every one of them is the mark of motherhood, physical proof of the love and devotion I share with my mate. While I might have some wrinkles and my hair is mostly silver nowadays, I am still strong, fit, and young where it counts.

And it most *definitely* counts in the bedroom.

Faris' fingers trail up over my knees and thighs, stroking lightly back and forth across the crease at my hip. His touch is teasing, as is his smile as I shift in an attempt to align his fingers where I want them—*need* them—the most.

At my core.

His other hand is busy unbuttoning his shirt, tugging it out of the waistband of his trousers. The warm sand colored skin of his chest is still smooth over his muscles, strands of dark hair dusting around his dark nipples and then again below his navel down to his waistband. I know what lies beneath his trousers and boxers, and my mouth salivates as I imagine how it will feel moving inside of me.

I don't have to wait long.

Faris finally uses both of his hands to finish removing his clothes, and I greedily devour the sight of him as he prowls back to the bed.

Muscles ripple and flex as he moves, his gait causing his cock to bob and sway with each step. That beautifully hard shaft of his is standing proudly erect, rising up with a slight curve from the nest of mostly dark hair at his groin and up toward his abdomen. The smooth stretch of his foreskin covers all but the tip of his cock, the crown of the mushroom-shaped head peeking out from its snug casing.

My delicious view is blocked when Faris kneels on the bed and crawls over to me. I haven't moved an inch since he arranged me thusly, and he slowly moves between my spread legs until he's braced over my body.

"My beautiful woman, so luscious and ripe for me. All these curves, all this skin... all for *me!*"

Faris drops to his elbows, his chest pressing against breasts, his cock rubbing over my stomach as he settles once more. His lips descend to mine, at first sipping and tasting my mouth before crushing against mine and devouring me like a man starved.

I hitch my hips, trapping Faris' cock between our bodies as I move, the silky slide of his foreskin gliding over my flesh sending goosebumps rippling over me. I'm drowning in his kisses, but my body is thirsty, demanding more, more, *more!*

"Faris!" I gasp, tearing my mouth from his. "Please, I need you!"

He doesn't answer me with words. No, instead he reaches down, stroking over my drenched slit, gently flicking at my clit before moving his hand to his cock. He notches it to my slick opening, the delicious pressure as it parts my pussy and fills me, eliciting a groan from my kiss-swollen lips.

Oh, the bliss of having my mate fill me is like no other. If I could spend the rest of my life with him inside me, I would. The sensation goes beyond the pleasure of sex between two people who know each other's bodies so well. It's a connection so basic, so elemental and deep that mere physical intimacy can't even compare. It's the bond between two fated mates, a connection forged through time and experience, with love and devotion. Our bond forms the roots of our tree of life, extending through the lives of those closest to us. One that echoes through the branches of the family it's formed, reinforcing the tethers binding us all into a cohesive, tight-knit community.

I feel like I'm overflowing with pleasure at having Faris buried deep inside me.

And then he moves.

My mate twists his hips, the motion practiced and perfect. It has the desired effect, pressing the curved head of his baculum up and into the spongy walls of my g-spot.

Pleasure rushes through me in a torrent, and my walls clench around his rigid flesh.

"That's one, *tresnaku*. I want at least two more, three if you're up for it, before I flood your sweet *weteng*[9] with my seed. Who knows, perhaps we can breed another whelp. I love seeing you round and fecund, growing my pups in your belly." Faris growls in my ear, my pussy gushing with desire as he thrusts deep inside.

Each stroke, each movement only sends me spiraling higher, and I'm lost to my rapture as his hips writhe and twist, my legs wrapped around his waist and locked together at my crossed ankles.

My cries echo through the room, as does the slap of our flesh as Faris drives me up and over the crest of ecstasy again and again. His movements become more fervent and wild as he draws close to his own precipice, and I claw my way back to the edge of my own.

Time ceases to exist as we both explode together, his cock pulsing and erupting as warm spurts of his cum floods my insides.

We float together on clouds of bliss until the cooling sweat slicking our skin draws us back to the here and now. My nerve endings sizzle and sing, and I clutch at Faris' back, reluctant to let go of this moment.

Alas, all too soon my regular aches and pains make themselves known, and I release my mate. He levers his body up and away from mine with a groan, his now flaccid cock slipping free from my core as he moves.

"Do you want me to run you a bath, *kinasih*? We'll both have a quick shower and then you can relax while I clean up from supper. Then it's bed for us both, yes?"

I sigh and lift my hand to Faris. He pulls me upright from the bed, and I ignore the trickle of cooling cum on my thighs. "That sounds wonderful. These old bones are tired and sore after today, so a lovely long sleep sounds like perfection."

"Old? Who are you calling old? You're still dusted with the blush of youth, don't you know that?" he retorts, and I chuckle.

"You're such a liar, Faris. And what was all that about earlier, with the dirty talk about breeding me? Have you been reading my smut books again, you lecherous old coot?"

"I repeat," Faris snarks at me while slapping my bare ass, "who are you calling old?"

We giggle and banter back and forth as Faris runs me a bath before leading me over to the shower stall. He refuses to let me wash myself, instead holding onto my soapy sponge as he cleans our combined sweat and his seed from my body. Only then does he help me into the tub.

I lounge in the warm water, watching as he wraps a towel around his hips and exits the bathroom. I loll and linger, the heat of the water seeping into my aching muscles and loosening the tension that has been locked there since I entered the arena in Sacramento.

Eventually, the bath water cools and I stir. Faris is there within moments, a huge, fluffy towel held in his outstretched hands. I gratefully accept his assistance as I step up out of the bath, and allow him to dry me off.

My eyelids are heavy as he bundles me into our straightened bed, and I'm already floating toward sleep as he finishes with our towels and climbs in beside me.

His chest warms my back as he tucks our naked bodies together and I drift off, cocooned in his strong embrace.

He is my heart.

He is my home.

He is my forever.

Acknowledgements

My thanks go to Sarah Michelle Lynch for organising this anthology. I find it fitting that the charity is the RSPCA, and my offering deals with people who can shift into animals.

To my PA, Kayleigh Reid. Thank you for being that leather-clad, whip-cracking Domme I need standing over me. I feel more prolific already.

VARIOUS AUTHORS

To Becky and her Babes, thank you for helping me choose which ASU story I needed to write. Everyone loves a prehistoric murder chicken in disguise.

Also to Dakota Brown, Rachelle Hobbs, Aeryn Havens, and R. Knight. Thank you for all you have done in helping me get my words out. I wouldn't have this wonderful series if it wasn't for your help and support.

And to my hubby.

I hope that we're just like Doris and Faris in another thirty years.

Forged by Shadows by Maddison Cole

Shadowed Souls - Book One

Disclaimer

This piece is the first look at a brand-new StepBrother, Why Choose romance in a university setting that I'm currently working on! The themes of the full-length story are dark, twisted and deliciously taboo. Please be aware, each character has a tragic backstory which causes them to have particular fetishes and quirks. They will find solace in each other, and I sincerely hope you fall in love with them as much as I have.

Happy reading.

Prologue ~ Avery

Breathe. Don't forget to breathe. Stop wringing the hem of your dress. Sit up straighter. Face forward. Don't appear irritated by whoever dared to laugh at the back of the room. Ignore the flash of cameras. Remember who you were raised to be.

Despite my inner chastising, each inhale coincides with a stabbing pain in my chest. If I weren't surrounded by the judgiest type of people on Earth, I'd give into the urges rising within. To scream, lash out and smash a whole bunch of shit. Not the appropriate response in front of the press and celebrities streaming into the room at their leisure. The service is only twenty-three minutes late so far, and apparently I'm the only one blood counting.

From my seat in the front row, I watch those shuffling forward to pay their respects to the open casket. I listen to their wishes for eternal peace, and nod politely when they offer me rehearsed condolences. The question in their gazes bounces off the practiced mask I keep firmly in place.

What's going to happen to you now? Where are the rest of your family?

Sighing, I stare longingly at the huge portrait at the front of the room. Usually, the conservatory is my favorite place to be. Filled with light and the scent of freshly cut grass drifting in from the rolling gardens. But not today. Today, the plush cream sofa, hanging plants and rows of bookcases have been removed. Instead, chairs dressed with teal bows divide the guests into two clear categories either side of the walkway. Those who knew my mom personally, and those who wish they had.

A hushed silence settles behind me, the low click of the rear doors being closed exploding within my head. I quickly glance at the wall of glass before me, dampening the impulse to vault over my mom's casket, use my body to smash through and run until I collapse. The press, who have permission to be here, would have a field day. My lips part, precious air slipping inside.

Don't freak out. Don't make a scene.

A body rushes into the seat next to mine, grabbing my hands. I flinch at the sting, only now realizing my nails were embedded into my palms.

"Shit, Avery. I'm so, so sorry I'm late." Meg whispers as my adoptive father walks down the aisle. "The security outside is unreal." Using my shoulder to sweep her brunette hair aside, Meg's head nestles in the croak of my neck. My best friend's presence is a balm, settling over me like a weighted blanket.

Fuck, I hadn't even considered that she might have been stuck at the gates, no doubt with many others trying to get into this funeral as if it's a red carpet event. To be fair, I haven't considered anything in the past few weeks I've spent laying in bed.

Tears gather in my eyes, the finality of what's about to happen making me dizzy. I watch the tired, well-dressed man take his place beside his wife's body without really taking notice. Her portrait stares at him, a humble smile on her perfectly painted face. Jade colored eyes glimmer out from the canvas with incredible accuracy to their unique brightness.

She is stunning. *Was* stunning. With love in his wrinkling features, Nixon addresses his audience with more composure than I could have managed.

"Thank you all for coming. Today, we gather to remember a remarkable woman whose radiant spirit illuminated the lives of all fortunate enough to know her. My beloved Catherine. Her infectious laughter has echoed through every room in this house, and her love, compassion and understanding made it a home for our two beautiful children." Nixon smiles towards me kindly, ignoring the obvious, which everyone else has noticed. My eyes drag to the empty seat at my side. "I hope you will join me in celebrating her life and giving her the send-off she deserves."

Nixon continues to deliver a flawless eulogy which drifts between heartfelt and poetic, enthralling those watching within the room and down the camera lens. To me, she was the woman who saved me from the depraved life I was born into. The woman who showed me love, and would snuggle under a duvet and read with me whenever she could.

Her death has affected so many others who loved her. It wasn't the movies she starred in, or the prestigious awards she won. No, Catherine Hughes will be remembered for the endless charity work she funded and partook in, saving countless lives. Including mine.

The rest of the ceremony passes in a blur of camera flashes and repetitive eulogies from actors who barely knew her. By the time the service comes to an end, the only thing distracting me from my itchy eyes is the growling in my stomach. I can't remember the last time I ate, as if surviving today was all I could focus on and didn't spare a thought for what happens now.

Nixon rises from the seat he took beside me, holding out his hand. His peppered dark hair has been styled back from his handsome yet weary face, an impeccably crisp navy suit clinging to his frame that seems at odds with the stubble lining his jaw. Blue eyes settle on me, a look of adoration passing through his features.

Inhaling my first full breath since I heard the news of her crash, I interlock our fingers and rise to my feet. We approach the casket, taking turns to place one last kiss onto her forehead. Long eyelashes fan her rosy painted cheeks, her chocolate brown hair pooling around her favorite chiffon dress.

"Thank you for showing me how to love," I breathe. Nixon catches the tear that leaks from my eye with the back of his hand before it can land, pulling me into his side for a hug. His strong heartbeat and gentle scent of cigar allow me to briefly hide from the imposing stares and cameras.

Turning to the central aisle, bright flashes assault us as we push our way, arm in arm, through the crowd waiting to offer their support. Meg steps into my other side, creating a wall which sees us to the rear doors. The crowd falls behind, hands patting our backs and stroking my long, blonde hair. Shrugging them off, I blink several times to banish the sparks from my vision. Intense emerald green eyes hit me with the weight of a dumpster truck. I recoil on instinct, before the anger breaks through.

"Wyatt." Nixon nods in greeting, not seeming at all pissed his son missed a majority of his own mother's funeral. I reckon Nixon expected nothing less. Wyatt's attention stays focused on me, a scowl forcing his sharp jaw to appear deadly. Dark curls fall into his face; the scruffy skater boy look not matching up with the suit and tie sitting lazily on his muscled frame. Leaving the top few buttons of his white shirt undone, the edges of black ink linger just beneath. I purse my lips, refusing to let him intimidate me.

As soon as the hired staff open the doors at his back, I shove past Wyatt. My shoulder connects with his ribs, hurting at least one of us, and I drag Meg with me. I desperately shove aside the awareness of his body, firm and unmovable. The smell of his expensive cologne, the way his green eyes drag over me like prey. Fuck, I really try, and fail miserably. The cameras follow, constantly snapping, waiting for the moment I snap and give them a real headline. It's only that thought which keeps me from flipping out. Entering the kitchen, I find a moment of privacy as the caterers usher everyone else away until they're ready. Meg and I slip behind the door, slumping against wallpaper flaked with real gold.

"Psst," Cook ducks her head around the corner. "We'll direct the guests into the ballroom. Grab what you need and escape while you still can." I smile at Cook's wink, her hair escaping its black net. The staff here are like extended family, since I rarely leave the mansion. There's been no need. My tutors come Monday to Friday, Meg is here more than she's home and the dance studio is my safe haven. Meg doesn't waste a second, grabbing a bottle of champagne from an ice bucket and an entire tray of canapes before we rush upstairs to my bedroom.

Slamming the door shut with her back, my bestie hands me the bottle so she can fan herself. "How does Wyatt get hotter every time he comes home?" My mouth drops open and I stumble while kicking off my heels. Landing on the bed, Meg dives in next to me a moment later, her smile too mischievous.

"That's seriously not the first thing you're going to say after I just said goodbye to my mom," I scoff, turning my attention to the bottle's cork. I probably shouldn't drink before the burial, due to take place in the gardens in an hour, but I don't know if I have the energy to leave this room again. I've already put myself through a whole morning of being ogled at.

"Oh, please. You were totally thinking it." She forces a laugh from me. A stab of guilt quickly accompanies it. I shouldn't enjoy any part of today–not even the distractions Meg is trying to provide and especially not at Wyatt's expense. The cork pops with a dramatic flow of bubbles, which Meg rushes to catch in her mouth. I call her a few choice words, taking a swig from the bottle myself. Sinking against my headboard, we sigh in unison.

"He won't stay," I comment into the quiet which settles. "He never does." Describing mine and Wyatt's relationship as love/hate is putting it mildly. As long as I'm around, he refuses to spend a single night in his own home, preferring to hide in his fancy boarding school. And in the summers, if all other options fail, he stays in the pool house. Anything to avoid seeing me.

"It's not your fault, Aves. None of it," Meg says, picking at the tray of canapes. I lean into her, nodding absentmindedly. I hear her words, I understand their truth, but it doesn't matter. If I wasn't around, Catherine would have spent more time staring at her son's face in real life, rather than the photographs lining her dresser. I prefer the photos personally; they are the only way I know what Wyatt's smile looks like.

True to my word, I don't resurface for the rest of the day. Meg and I eventually shed our black, tight-fitting dresses and replace them with sweatpants and hoodies. The afternoon is lost to snacking like only the rich can and binging a new series on my flatscreen TV. I barely take any of it in, but the background noise helps to block out the burial happening beyond my balcony. My mom would understand. I've never been one for living in the spotlight. I will grieve on my own terms, in my own time. At some point, I dozed off, only to be woken by Meg sneaking back into bed with a tub of ice cream and two spoons.

It's Friday, and it seems we're reverting back to our usual arrangement. Meg will stay here until Sunday. Her mum, Elena, is a single mom who lives on the border of Brookhaven, working as a therapist to the rich and famous – myself included. It's how Meg and I met, back when I was first adopted as a shy child with a dark past I couldn't understand. I barely spoke back then, but Meg has always been able to pull me from my shell.

Once we hit our teenage years, Elena started attending various workshops on the weekends, amongst her many flings which never work out. She seems happy enough, living the quality of life she would have had if not becoming pregnant with Meg at seventeen. There's no resentment there; the pair are more like sisters than mother-daughter.

Orange tones begin to bleed into the sky through the windows. Car engines signal the departure of guests until the noise on the floor below has decreased significantly. With every muffled goodbye, my heart eases slightly knowing this difficult day is nearly over. I'm practically a puddle of relief when my door abruptly flies open loudly, the intrusion of muscle making me screech.

"Dad's office. Now." Wyatt's deep voice commands our attention, despite speaking fairly quietly. The death glare in his green eyes leave no room for negotiation, so I jump down from my high bed and gesture for him to lead the way. Three steps out of the door, I stumble and crash into Wyatt's back. He steps aside, watching me fall ass over tit onto the floor.

"You're fucking wasted," he growls in the base of his throat. "Today of all days." Striding away, Wyatt's dress shoes click on the marble staircase until he's out of sight. Meg slides her arms beneath mine, helping me to stand. Her wobbly smile and unfocused eyes aren't any better than mine, as I spy the several wine bottles littering my bedroom floor. Fuck, I didn't even notice her sneaking them in, or that I was drinking all day on effectively an empty stomach.

"You've got this," Meg tries to bolster me. It doesn't help much when I have to hug the railing down the stairs and slide one fluffy sock in front of the other to reach Nixon's office. The door is open, two figures shrouded in the fireplace's glow waiting for me.

"Come on in, sweetheart," Nixon coaxes. I manage to reach the high back armchair and settle myself down, keeping my gaze on the man across the mahogany desk. "Ironic, isn't it?" He chuckles to himself. "The one thing Cathy wanted, and it's finally happened when she's no longer here to see it." There's no need to ask what *it* is. Wyatt and I haven't willingly been in the same room in years.

Holding a glass of bourbon in his hand, Nixon seems to have given up on his appearance for today. His hair is disheveled, the plum-colored tie hanging uselessly under open buttons to reveal his graying chest hair. Not even the sharp jawline and high cheekbones he and Wyatt share can stop him from appearing defeated in the fire's flickering.

I dare to steal a glance at Wyatt, but he keeps his face forward. A tick beats in his clenched jaw, waiting for Nixon to continue.

"We could have been a proper family. A complete one." I look away, tears blurring in my eyes. If Nixon cracks now, there's no hope for me. Mom was taken so suddenly, so viciously. The morticians are miracle workers for the way mom appeared today, not a single scratch visible of the car wreckage she was pulled from, killed on impact.

Nixon chuckles to himself again, but his pale eyes look blank and glazed. Throwing the rest of his bourbon back, Wyatt's scowl only deepens in my peripheral vision while I fiddle uncomfortably with the hem of my hoodie.

"Things change, today." Nixon seems to sober slightly, staring intently at Wyatt as if I'm not in the room. "I must return to my business in New York tomorrow evening. It is imperative that Avery is cared for." I chew on the inside of my cheek. I've been left alone many times before, under the supervision of my tutors and the house staff. Elena has upped my therapy sessions to twice a week for the time being, and I have a ballet exam fast approaching. Plenty to keep my mind busy. Nixon thinks carefully over his next words and delivers them with brutal confidence.

"This year's semester is only a few weeks in. I've spoken to Dean O'Sullivan, and Avery starts at Waversea on Monday morning. I've set her up with a dorm in your building, and you, Wyatt, will look out for her."

The silence which follows is filled with tension; a physical pressure I can feel pushing onto my chest. Wyatt's lack of reaction scares me more than if he'd flipped the table, his eyes turning murderous. More than that, the sinking ball of dread in my stomach explodes, my thoughts racing. I...I can't leave. I rarely ever leave the mansion. It's my home, a safety barrier between me and the world. And Nixon intends to drop me into university, in Wyatt's dorm building and expect him not to kill me in my sleep? I'm hyperventilating before Wyatt's even blinked.

"Please Nixon," I breathe, layering on the sweet and innocent appeal he usually caves for. "That's really not necessary. I'm happy here on my own. Even if I wasn't turning twenty-one next month, I have everything I need to look after myself. Let me stay," I flutter my lashes for good measure. Nixon's blue eyes soften. Hook, line and sinker. Nixon may be ruthless with everyone else, his son included, but he has always been softer with me. Reaching over, he takes my hand over the desk, stroking the back with his thumb. Wyatt growls once again.

"Seems I'm not needed, as usual. I need to get going. Thanks for the party." Wyatt rises from his chair and walks towards the door too damn casually. As if the entire world owes him a favor. Immediately, Nixon drops my hand, his posture strengthening. The emotions so recently swimming in his eyes disappear.

"Don't take another step!" I flinch at the sudden roar, twisting my face away. It's involuntary, but seems to irritate Wyatt further as he tuts. My nostrils flare in irritation. If he'd let me handle this situation delicately, if he'd just kept his mouth shut, Nixon wouldn't now be using his closed fists on the desk to push himself upright. Struggling to calm his voice, Nixon's eyes shoot daggers at Wyatt, still braced by the door.

"You will clear your schedule to show Avery around campus. You will make sure she settles into her new room. You will ensure no one bothers or distracts her from her studies. And so help me, if you want to continue living with my financial support, you will be a suitable guardian to your sister."

"She's not my fucking sister!" Wyatt shouts back and suddenly I'm transported back ten years in my mind. To a long summer in a new house with a spoiled little shit glaring at me. Even back then, his perfectly styled ash brown hair and taste for expensive clothing enhanced the brat he was, thinking he deserved whatever he wanted without ever having to work for it.

It was explained to me that Wyatt had no prior knowledge of my arrival. The Hughes weren't in the market to adopt until a small, filthy child stumbled into the road in front of their car. I understood, and I was just so thankful to know where my next meal was coming from. So, for years, I tried to find common ground with Wyatt. I gave him the space and patience I hoped he deserved. But he preferred boarding schools to his own home, and soon enough he stopped coming back during the holidays. Wyatt made himself a ghost, only his memory left within these walls. And I stopped giving a fuck.

Blinking back to the present, I balk to find Nixon has moved. A harsh crack reverberates from behind, silhouettes bouncing around the exposed wooden panels of the room. I spin in my seat, gripping the armrest. Wherever Nixon hit Wyatt, it's not apparent. The two are locked in a stare-off, but it's Wyatt who bravely closes the gap to bump his father's chest.

"You can give her our last name, give her half of the inheritance, parade her around like your perfect angel. But she is not, nor ever will be, my sister."

And there's the truth.

Fury bleeds through Nixon's features, the strain of the day becoming even more evident. He grabs Wyatt's collar in both fists. Standing nose to nose, Nixon's tone lowers to a threatening level I've never heard before.

"Avery has been more a part of this family for the past ten years than you have. I buried my fucking wife today. It's all of our responsibility to see Avery is safe, and time for you to step up. Don't push me, Wyatt." He shoves his son backwards.

Refuse, I beg inside my head. *Keep refusing until Nixon lets me stay.*

With a lasting death glare at me, Wyatt leaves, making sure to slam the door harshly. Foreboding settles over me. On top of everything I've lost today, the lifestyle I love has just been snatched away and I'm due to be left in Wyatt's care. Something tells me, my big brother will do everything in his power to ensure I'm the very opposite of 'safe'.

One ~ Avery

The BMW rumbles to a stop in front of a gigantic building of brick and light. Every window is illuminated against the fall of evening, figures moving within cramped dorms. My stomach turns to lead as Meg switches off her sickly-pink monstrosity, a pair of fluffy dice swinging from the rear-view mirror. We remain there, locked in place until various sources of music and chatter mingle with the balmy air leaking through our open windows.

"It could be fun," Meg offers for the hundredth time. I can't spare her a look of bravery, my mind reeling that there is nothing fun about the building before me. Forced social interaction, the onslaught of noise, being forced to share my space with a complete stranger. And somewhere within those walls is a fake brother who hates my guts. This is my new hell.

"You would fit in here much easier than I ever could," I sigh. I wish Meg was coming with me, but her athletic scholarship is at a state school miles away. Lacrosse is her speciality, becoming the first junior captain, whilst juggling the swim team, business studies and debate club. It's no wonder she hides at the Hughes mansion on weekends, needing to escape it all. Everything Meg has in this life, she's had to work for. But at least she has teams of friends and an incredible amount of group chats to fall back on. Without my tutors, dance coach, therapist...I have no one.

I take a deep breath, hoping my fear is masked from a bunch of basketball guys who wander past. Their jerseys are black with yellow trims, baggy around thickly-corded muscles coated in sweat. One looks back, throwing a wink at me before he empties his water bottle over his lengthy blonde hair and shakes it out. I sink back in my seat, flinching as Meg rests a hand on my arm.

"You'll be fine," she promises, leaning across the console to press a kiss to my cheek. I know I'm keeping her from the long drive she has to make back, but Meg refused to let one of the chauffeurs bring me.

Nodding, I pretend to find my resolve as I exit the car and grab my bags from the trunk. One medium-sized case for my clothes, a smaller one for my make-up, toiletries and shoes, and a backpack with my laptop, notepads-essentially everything I'll use for class. *Class*. I shudder to myself. Leaning through the driver side window, Meg returns my hug with equal vigor and pulls away to smooth the two tendrils of long hair out of my face. Her pale blue eyes appear gray, swimming with unshed tears.

"You've never needed Wyatt before. Don't give him that power over you now." Meg whispers in my ear. I know she's right, but her words almost cause me to break. Waving goodbye from the curb, I hold the tears back.

The night air grows heavy, my feet barely cooperating as I make my way to the building entrance and duck inside. Voices echo through the halls, doors slamming shut, laughter ringing out. I keep my head down, tackling the staircases with quiet resolve. Something I can attribute to my ballet; upholding stamina in the shittiest of situations.

Reaching the fourth floor, I enter a network of cramped hallways, tracking the numbers on closed doors for the one I've been allocated. Nixon forwarded on all of the emails from the Dean, including my dorm room, directions, a campus map and my class schedule. Music blasts from the doors left wide open, and I peer into each one, wondering if Wyatt will be on this floor too. I hope not.

I spot my dorm up ahead, the last one on the end. A group of girls huddle in the doorway, their brows raised when they see my approach. In a flurry, they rush past me, their giggles filling the air. My stomach cramps tightly but I refuse to let it show. Straightening my spine, I step into the room I'll be spending my foreseeable future in.

The room is small, two twin-sized beds against opposite walls. Separating them are a desk and a dresser for each. On one desk, beside a pot of brightly coloured highlighters and post-it notes, a strongly-scented candle flickers.

"What is that?" I inhale deeply. "Gingerbread? Maple syrup?"

"Cinnamon apple," a fiery redhead replies without looking up from her phone. She's lying on the bed closest to the window, scrolling endlessly and tapping her foot to a song in her head. I inhale again, deciding it's a pleasant smell despite originally being overwhelming.

Entering the room, I ditch my cases by the foot of the empty bed and sink on the mattress. It's not as giving as what I'm used to, but the stiffness in my limbs will take what it can get. Eventually, my roommate glances up, her eyes studying me for a moment before she speaks.

"You must be Avery," she comments. She doesn't smile nor grimace, as if she doesn't know what to make of me quite yet. I nod, pulling my hair free of its ponytail before a tension headache sets in. "Welcome to Waversea, I guess. Everyone is super excited for your arrival."

"They are?" I balk. There goes my careful constructed plan of laying low. The redhead hums, sitting upright.

"Oh yeah. You've been the hot topic all weekend. I gave up closing the door, bored of the insistent knocking and questions I couldn't answer. Now you're here, you can answer them yourself."

"What...what kind of questions?" My shoulders sag inward, a feeble attempt to protect myself. This is what I was afraid of. A strange unknown place, surrounded by people eager to know every shred of my business. The tabloids are the worst for it, but at least they weren't in my personal space everyday. I could block them out, locked away in my tower like Rapunzel. The redhead shrugs.

"Many of them are about your brother. What he likes, how he smells up close. If you've ever walked in on him in the shower, if his dick is really as big as they say. Things like that." My jaw drops, flames heating my cheeks. She laughs, waving my embarrassment off.

"I'm McKayla, by the way," she fills the silence. "Just Kay is fine, and I've got track at the buttcrack of dawn. Lock the door before you turn in." This time, Kay does roll over, pulling the covers up to her vibrant red hair. My eyes flicker to the doorway, noting the shuffle of steps and whispers nearing. I move in a flash, shutting and locking the door before my shadow has a chance to grace the grubby hallway carpet.

My hands are shaking as I silently unpack my clothes into the dresser and change out the bed sheets for a fresh set. Tomorrow will be a full-on day indeed, but not one I will be tackling without the right mindset. Starting with banishing the rumors I have no doubt Wyatt helped to create.

When Kay said she was leaving early, she wasn't kidding. I glance across the enclosed space, finding her bed empty and neatly made. Daring a glance at my phone, it's just past half five. I groan, pulling the covers over my head to block out warm rays of sunrise leaking through paper thin curtains.

After years of watching Wyatt sneer in the face of being ridiculously spoiled, I've tried my best to not follow suit. I don't ask for much beyond my means, working each Christmas in soup kitchens and asking for birthday gifts to be donated rather than receive them myself. But to a certain degree, it's impossible not to miss the blackout curtains, plush duvet and deep memory foam mattress I've become accustomed to.

Thinking ahead, I start to mentally play out the day, pre-empting and preparing. The cafeteria food won't be what I'm used to, the on-campus supermarket probably stocking brands I've never heard of. Then there's the thought of communal showers, which I'm dreading. It'll be an adjustment, but I haven't always lived this life. I once ate whatever crumbs were left behind and washed with the last drop of hand soap I could conjure from an almost empty pot.

I slip into a half-dazed state where the two versions of my life bleed together and somewhere along the way, I fail to remember which girl I am. The timid one sporting bruises, or the untouchable heiress who locks herself away. When I stir once more, it's with a dull headache starting to throb behind my eyes. Pulling the covers back on a sigh, the light is temporarily shrouded by a large silhouette looming over me.

"Ahh!" I scream, throwing a fist wildly. It connects, but doesn't pack half the punch my self-defense teacher taught me. A deep chuckle rumbles through the room.

"Oh, you're going to be fun," the figure muses and steps back. Watching me for a moment longer, while I clutch the cover to my heaving chest, he wanders towards the doorway.

"Who the hell are you?!" I find my voice. When he twists the latch from inside, my eyes widen. "And how the fuck did you get in here?!"

"Tsk, tsk, Peach. Do you kiss Nixon with that dirty mouth?" he chuckles again. I'm stunned, desperately trying to take in the stranger's features. Floppy brown hair flicks in all directions, as if it's been styled to look like he's just rolled out of bed. There's nothing to note about his clothing; sweatpants covering his lean legs and a pair of Air Jordan's on his feet. From the short sleeves of his t-shirt to his knuckles, he's coated in ink. A colorful mismatch of images that don't merge together, but rather tell individual stories. Secrets ready to be cracked open, but not by me. Definitely not by me.

I don't know this man, and I'm certain he doesn't know me. Upon opening the door to leave, another body suddenly appears and crowds him back inside. This is turning into an early morning circus and I'm the only spectator.

"Fuck's sake, Garrett," the man growls. His hair is trimmed short, causing the sharpness of his jawline and cheekbones to appear razor-cut in the artificial light streaming from the hallway. Slapping Garrett on the back of his head, he also turns to assess me too closely. I fight against the urge to shrink back under his all-seeing gaze. "Wyatt told us to watch her from a distance," he grumbles, his words not meant for me. Garrett is stroking his head, a wide smirk on his face.

"I just wanted a closer look. Besides, someone needs to give her an official tour."

"And you thought you were the best man for the job? I just watched you scale the drain pipes and climb through her bedroom window." My eyes widen. Note to self - replace all of the locks pronto.

The new man doesn't take his eyes off me, standing shoulder to shoulder with Garrett at the foot of my bed. The pair seem to draw the air from the room, making it hard to breathe, let alone scream at them to get lost. All of my training, every scenario of my past I've replayed in my head, pinpointing where I could have fought back or been stronger. Gone. I'm still just as easy to trap, and that drives more of a knife through my chest than the two seizing me up in my pajamas.

"Dammit, Garrett. You never do as you're told," the sterner one sighs. Then he snaps an order intended for me. "Get yourself sorted. We leave in ten minutes."

"Erm," my mind trips over itself. "Thanks but...no thanks. I have a map, I'm sure I'll be just fine." They give me matching condescending smirks, but I hold my ground. It's my first day, the first chance to make a new impression. I'm sure as shit not going to be caught trailing the babysitters Wyatt has ordered to 'watch me from a distance'. Garrett breaks his stare first, placing a hand on his friend's arm and giving me a pleasing eye flutter.

"See, she's so cute and naïve," he pouts. "I reckon we could keep her, just for a little while." My brows furrow but Axel sighs, stretching out his neck.

"Ten minutes." The pair retreat, leaving me alone with my heart pounding in my chest. I stare around the room, hunting for a means to escape. How close are drain pipes beyond the window?

"I don't hear any movement in there, Peach," Garrett calls back. "I can always come and give you a hand if needed." There's a swift 'oomph' where I imagine Axel has hit him again, but I don't wait around to see if he'll deliver on that promise. He's already climbed through my window once this morning.

Afterword

Thank you for reading the first snippet of 'Forged by Shadows.' Hopefully I've wet your whistle and now you're shaking with desire for the rest of the book! This step-brother, reverse harem college romance is due to rapid release along with its two sequels in Summer 2024. Make sure to pre-order, save the date and follow my socials for updates.

VARIOUS AUTHORS

With love, Maddison x

The Creaking Bough by Marie Anne Cope

'It was so long ago.' I ease myself out of the chair, pull the cardigan close around my bony frame and shuffle to the window. I shudder as I peek through the grimy glass; glass that once shone bright and clean. I reach my hand out, my forefinger uncurling against the gnarled joints and press my fingertip against the dirt, willing my movements to stay calm as I clear my view. I draw closer, peering through my peephole into the world I have occupied for two decades. Of course, all is calm now, the tree still, the swing unmoved. But then... well, that's what they are here to find out.

'But do you remember what happened?'

I turn, wincing against the unfamiliar movement, and look at the group before me. They aren't the first and they won't be the last, although they will be for me; I can feel it inside. My time is near and then it will start again; it has to. I've held it back for as long as I can, but I am only human, almost, and the vessel that contains me—correction, contains us—is worn thin.

'Will you tell us then?' the only young man in the group urges.

'Why do you want to know?' I always ask this question, but they rarely have an answer other than...

'Well, because it's kind of unbelievable,' the young man says.

'And scary, John, don't forget that. *That* is why we're here,' the young woman holding the camera says.

'You like to be scared, do you?' I ask as I stare into the lens. I smile as they look away, as they fiddle with whatever they are holding, as they clear their throats and shuffle their feet. Of course they do; it's human nature. But being scared by a retelling is far different than by reality.

'W-well, y-yes. That is why we're here.'

I look at the red-headed woman who has spoken and nod. It *is* why they're here, partly anyway.

'Very well.' I shuffle back to my chair by the fire and lower myself, resting my head against its back and closing my eyes. 'Please add some logs to the fire.' I listen as one of them does as I've asked and try to assemble my thoughts. Where to start? Where all stories start, of course, at the beginning...

'Time to wake up, Abs, we're here,' my mother's voice injected itself into my dream and I fought to push it away. Her warm hand curling around my balled fist dragged me from the sunshine and into the gloom. That's the only way I knew how to describe it—dark and gloomy. Even when my parents had shared the sales blurb with me, I'd wrinkled my nose and pushed it away.

'It looks sad and lonely,' I'd said.

'I know, darling, but we can brighten it up, can't we? You and me? What do you say?'

I hadn't said anything, just shrugged and walked away. I don't know why they'd involved me; it's not like my opinion had held any sway. I had to go where they went, end of story. I'd heard them arguing later, though—my father insisting they tell me the truth, my mother flat out refusing.

'Why this house? Really? There were so ma—' I asked as I stared through the window at the looming façade.

'Because it's all we could afford.'

'Ben!'

'Well, she needs to know. She's going to the high school, and she needs to know there will be no fancy clothes, no school trips, no—'

'Ben, that's enough!'

As always, my mother's stern words pushed my father back into his shell.

'Mum, why can't you just get a...' I didn't finish, catching my father's imperceptible shake of his weary head.

'So, why's it so cheap then?' I changed tactic, hoping my mother's flushed state would urge her to spill.

'Well, because—'

'Nat, don't!'

Even I was taken aback by my father's tone. I'd never heard him speak so sharply to my mother.

'What? So, it's okay for her to know why we're broke, but it's not okay for her to know the house she now has to live in is haunted?'

'Haunted? By what?'

'By nothing. This house is not haunted, Abs, I promise you. Isn't that right, Nat?'

I watched as my father took my mother's hand. I saw her flinch at the pressure as she glared at him.

'No, of course it isn't,' she finally said, turning to smile at me; a smile which didn't reach her eyes.

'Right, well, the moving van is here, so let's get in and unpacked before we lose the light.' My father patted my mother's knee, his voice light again, before he jumped out of the car. I watched my mother massaging her hand, flexing her fingers as she did so before she followed suit.

I stayed where I was, gazing through the window at the enormous tree in the front garden, a swing dangling from a bough almost as wide as the trunk. I allowed my gaze to sweep the front of the house, drifting over the peeling paint and rotted frames, settling on the second-floor window with the best view of the tree.

My room, I decided, before rolling out of the car.

I heard it that first night. At first, I thought it was part of my dream; I always had such vivid dreams that it was difficult to discern reality. But, as with all real things, the sound won through in the end.

I opened my eyes and lay staring, watching the shadows dance across the ceiling, my imagination conjuring dragons and brave knights, helpless maidens and endless slumber. As I drifted off, I heard it again, and my heart lurched, the hairs rising in waves across my body. I held my breath, listening, focusing, waiting. Sure enough, the metronomic sound returned, and with it an image that sent me lurching back against the headboard, my knees tight against my chest, the duvet swathing me.

My breathing was ragged now, my heart thumping so loudly I was convinced my parents would hear it, but there was no movement elsewhere in the house. My gaze swept my room, trying to assimilate objects with the sound, the window drawing my attention over and over. When no possession claimed what I could hear, I settled on the window, my need to correlate my senses pulling me forward.

Clutching the duvet as tight as I could around me, I tiptoed over. I rested against the wall and closed my eyes, willing my body to calm, knowing it wouldn't until I knew. Taking a breath, I peered around the edge, my chosen view perfect, but my answer absent.

I stared down at the tree—oak, I think—imagining it holding our house in the ball of its roots. Its branches were still, its leaves in repose. The night was calm and yet the noise persisted, the sound of creaking wood under load. I looked at the swing, its wooden seat suspended between two fraying lengths of rope, and my breath caught. Not that the swing was moving, because it wasn't... well... not entirely. One stretch of rope swayed as though suspending something heavy, yet the seat remained immobile.

How?

My curiosity overriding my fear, I flung off the duvet, pulled on a jumper and made my way down the stairs, treading to the sides of the steps so as not to awaken the wood and disturb my parents.

Outside, the elements remained still, their breath held, waiting to see what I would do. The rope continued its monotony, alone in its remembrance. I studied this phenomenon—what else could I call it?—for a while, but I couldn't work out how this was possible. The seat remained untethered, the rope bore no other weight, and yet that aching sound was definitely coming from that almost weightless rope.

I reached out to touch it, hesitating only briefly, before wrapping my hand around the coarse fibres...

When I awoke, dawn was breaking, and the rope was still.

'Abs, do you feel okay?'

'Mmmm?' I glanced away from my plate, my fork pausing its stabbing of the yolks.

'Your eggs? You usually wolf them down.'

I followed the woman's movements as she pushed away from the table and walked around to my side, placing her icy hand against my forehead.

'Jeez, you're burning up. Let's get you upstairs and into a cold bath.'

'Get your hands off me! I feel fine! I don't need a bath, especially not a cold one!'

'Abigail Collins. Do not speak to your mother like that?'

I turned my head to look at the man who'd spoken. I could feel my forehead furrowing, my jaw clenching, my chin dipping. I looked up at him as I spoke, the voice that emerged hoarse from disuse: 'I'll speak how I damn well please. This is my house!'

I slammed my fist onto the table, my plate bouncing to the floor, painting the quarry tiles in ochre.

'Abs, what on earth has got into you?' I heard the break in the woman's voice, and I turned to look at her, saw the tears brimming in her baby blue eyes. I felt my top lip curl and a sound like a growl emerge before I balled the saliva in my mouth and hurled it her way, smirking at the horror on her face as it made its mark.

The slap snapped my head to one side, but there was no sting; there was no feeling at all.

'Get out of my sight! I don't want to see you again until you are ready to apologise.'

'Don't hold your breath,' I growled as I glanced at their pathetic expressions. I kicked the chair out of my path, sending it hurtling into the dresser. 'Bullseye!' I fist-pumped the air as the contents crashed to the floor and shattered.

'Abigail!'

I didn't look back as I left the kitchen, just flipped them the bird.

I could hear them talking about me. The floors in this place were a single plank. There was no privacy; there never had been. Perhaps if I'd listened more closely, I could have stopped them. Perhaps not.

They always visited, my parents. Well, it was the least they could do after condemning me to this place, and for what? Because I didn't behave in the "proper" manner. What's the proper manner? Everyone I'd met in here was different. Maybe that's the point. They always left again, though, my parents, left me in the hands of people who could "make me" behave. No, they couldn't. No one could make someone do something against their will, not really.

I sat down at the small table they'd provided; a place to think and write letters home. I glanced up and paused on my reflection. I looked different, fresher somehow, a little younger maybe. I cast my mind back but drew a blank as to why.

Abigail? My name is Emily.

Oh, don't get me wrong, the dark circles were still there, the sunken eyes, the shaved head, the scorch marks at my brow, but they weren't the eyes I looked through yesterday, nor the face I saw either. I shrugged. Maybe I *was* losing my mind, rather than finding my senses.

I pushed away from the table, my interest gone, and climbed into bed. Might as well sleep; they never found an issue with that.

I jolted awake. The house was in darkness, my curtains rippling on the breeze from the open window. I shivered and rubbed my bare arms, tuning in to the rain drumming on the roof. A flash of lightning illuminated the room, and I saw the tray upended on the floor, the door ajar, food splattered up the wall. The sound was out of me before I could stop it. A growl.

What the hell?

I clamped my hand over my mouth, but I felt a weight pushing down on my forehead, making me frown as a dark filter washed across my eyes. It had to be the shadows. The lightning, the rain; it played havoc with my senses at the best of times.

I closed my eyes and shook my head. When I opened them again, the filter had gone.

'Mum! Dad!' I yelled as I jumped off the bed and raced for the door, slipping in the water pooled beneath the window, landing hard on the wooden floor. I lay there for a moment, winded, my head smarting from the blow. I listened. The house was silent.

'Mum? Dad?' I called again, thunder punctuating my request, but there was no response. They couldn't have gone out, surely, not in this.

They haven't left me, have they?

I eased myself onto my elbows and gripped the windowsill, hauling myself to my knees. Squinting through the slanting rain, I saw the car still sitting in the driveway where we'd left it. I rested my forehead on the windowsill and that's when I heard it—the same creaking noise as the previous night.

I lifted my head and look down at the tree, and my heart juddered to a halt.

'Nooooooo!' I screamed, shoving myself to my feet and racing from the room.

The rain plastered my hair to my face as I ran outside, the veil of water making it impossible to see clearly, and yet I would never unsee it, not as long as I lived.

'What did you see?'

I turn to glance at the red-headed woman before looking down at my liver-spotted hands. 'I saw myself.'

'But how, when you were in the house?'

'I saw myself standing before that tree, staring at the ropes as they swung back and forth, each bearing a load—'

'But I thought only one of them moved?' the young man interrupts.

'It did that first night.'

'So, what changed?' he continues.

'Never mind that. She said each rope bore a load. What kind of load?' the red-headed woman pushes.

I close my eyes again and rest my head against my chair.

'I think what we need to know is how she could have been in two places at once,' the woman holding the camera says.

I nod.

'Get away from them!' I screamed through the rain, sliding in the mud as I fought to get to the person heaving on the ropes, the tree creaking as it braced against the weight.

I hurled myself forward and landed hard in the mud, my right arm cracking on impact, my palms raging. Howling in pain, I rolled over, pulling my wounded arm to my chest, yelping as my palm made contact. I looked down at my good hand, the angry welts clear against my pallid skin, their ruts mirrored on my other palm.

I turned to look at the tree.

The swing was no longer there, its ropes secured—pristine and strong—its weights countering each other.

'Nooooooo!!' I screamed as the vacant eyes of my parents stared back at me, their faces forever reflecting what I'd done.

'So, you *did* kill them then?' the young man asks, a look of disdain clear on his face.

I smile slightly at his disappointment.

I wait.

This is the time people usually pick up and leave, dissatisfied the story doesn't live up to the hype.

'You didn't, did you, Abigail?' the red-headed woman asks.

I close my eyes again and dip my chin.

Finally.

Finally, someone has realised.

'But she must have. Who else could it have been?'

I let his question hang. If they've listened, and I mean really listened, then they will know.

I can feel her movement now. Her need is more than I can suppress. Her rage too much for my vessel to hold. I may be thirty-three, but my body is so much older. She's done that to me—Emily.

My time is near, and I know I should give them a chance to leave, but I can't, not anymore. Emily is stronger than me, she always has been. I've done my best, though, to keep her at bay.

I feel the shift in my body and go with it, opening my eyes to see the dark filter blurring my vision once more. I feel her pressure from within, feel her frown developing as she glares.

I can just about see the penny drop, sense them trying to pull away. They won't get far. She won't let them.

I didn't leave.

The authorities ruled I couldn't possibly have done that to my parents; I was a child, a thirteen-year-old girl. Where could I have got the strength?

I didn't leave because I knew that if I did, she would do it again to the next family who, having fallen on hard times, could afford nothing other than her house.

I can feel her shrugging away from me, and I sigh.

'A-Abigail? Are you all right?' I hear the red-headed woman say; the woman whose husband is so disbelieving; the woman whose child is asleep on the bed.

'Who's Abigail?' Emily growls as she leaves me to rest in peace.

THE END

Two Days by Marie Anne Cope

'Goodbye, my love, my dear Katharine. One day, I will see you again. Until that day, I will carry your love and this image of you in my heart. It will sustain me in the hard days ahead; I know it will. I have to believe it will. I have to.'

Katharine raised her hand to stroke the two-day-old growth on her husband's cheek. Two days was all they'd been allowed. Two days to consummate their love. Two days to build a lifetime of memories. Two days to sustain them through the days, weeks, months, years or even an eternity apart.

She traced his strong jawline and hooked her index finger under his chin, tilting his face upwards, forcing him to look at her with those liquid brown eyes she'd fallen in love with.

She scoured his face, devouring every inch of him. Her finger traced the hook shaped scar under his left eye; a memento from a teenage "duel"; although it had actually been more of a scuffle. She smiled to herself as she was pulled back to that field, over a decade ago, such a long time ago now.

'This is a matter of ownership, Kathy,' Jared said, brandishing his homemade sword in the general direction of his opponent.

'But, Jar, this is silly. It doesn't matter,' she said, positioning herself between Jared and his much larger adversary; an adversary who had somehow come into possession of a rather lethal looking bayonet; the potential damage from which was more than a little alarming to Katharine.

'C'mon then, Kent, let's settle this,' his opponent said.

'Please step out of the way, Kathy. I don't want you to get hurt.' Her protests were futile; she knew this and, as such, she dutifully gave in.

The future soldier and his foe faced each other, counted to ten and then advanced; Jared with his wooden sword and William with his bayonet.

That neither had ever fought before soon became obvious, and Katharine, terrified they might seriously injure each other, did the only thing she knew how to do.

'What, in God's holy name, is going on here?' John Rigby said as he stomped into the clearing, his daughter Katharine running to keep up. She halted at the sight before her. Jared had William by the throat, his wooden sword pressed under the other boy's chin, blood running down his own cheek from a gash under his left eye.

'William tried to steal a chicken, sir,' Jared said, pushing his shoulders back and puffing his chest out as best he could; given his position. 'I stopped him.'

'William was not stealing anything. Now let him go,' John said, glaring at Jared.

'But...'

'No buts, release him. Do not make me tell you again, boy.'

Jared let go and William nodded his head at John. 'Thank you, sir,' he said.

'Now, go take that chicken to your mama, like you were supposed to, and no more fighting.'

'Yes, sir. Thank you, sir,' William said and nodded once again. He grabbed the peacefully grazing chicken and, carrying his bayonet in his other hand, disappeared into the woods.

'You get yourself home. Now!' John said to a scarlet faced Jared.

※

Katharine smiled and looked back at that same scar now, all these years later. She wanted to absorb every line, every mark and every feature. The full, sensuous lips that had sent her pulse racing over these last two days. The dark brown, almost ebony hair that fell over his forehead and curled at his collar in that tousled, just woken up way. The weathered skin, hued brown by the years working outdoors in the fields, his father having refused to own slaves. In their county, Elijah Kent had stood alone on this point and it had been no secret that he'd struggled financially because of his stance.

If only we had more time, she thought. If only the war hadn't forced them apart; forced them into livings neither of them wanted. She dropped her hand and leaned her head against his chest. If they'd had a little more time, they could have sat for a photograph, and then she wouldn't have to try to remember. She would have something real; something to hold; something to look at. She would be able to pick it up and see him, clear as he was today, instead of the faint fuzzy image her mind would no doubt retain.

It worried her; the thought of not being able to remember him; of not being able to recall his face in the detail she was now trying to commit to memory. Yet, why should it? She could, after all, remember the first day they'd met, as if it had been yesterday. She'd been seven years old.

As a child, Katharine loved to play hide and seek in the cotton fields. She had no-one to play with as her sister, Izzy, considered such pursuits "too babyish". As such, Katharine had no choice but to play by herself, spending hours and hours running in and out of the rows of cotton, pretending she was being chased and hiding from her imaginary pursuers. Her day's labour done, she used to retire to her den.

Her den was, basically, a flattened area of the cotton field, which she'd painstakingly lined with balls of cotton. Here, she'd lie and gaze up at the china blue sky. On cloudy days, she would imagine that the clouds were dragons, with fearless knights coming to slay them and rescue the princess. On clear days, she would use the cotton to recreate her dragon slaying.

One day, though, as she'd hurtled into the field, all set for another boisterous day, the sound of voices had stopped her. She'd tiptoed through the cotton, in the general direction of the voices, and was horrified to find them coming from her den. She crept as close as she dared and could see the owner of one of the voices—a tall man, dressed in britches and a shirt; sleeves rolled up, revealing strong tanned forearms. He had large hands, but she couldn't see his face as it was hidden beneath the shade of his hat. She guessed he looked pretty mad, given he was shouting and gesturing with his enormous hands. She couldn't see who else was with him.

'I can't believe this! Who the hell would do this? Everyone knows how precious the crop is this year!' the man said.

'Look, Pa, will you just calm down?'

'Calm down! You listen to me, boy, and you listen good. We need to find who did this and we need to punish them. Someone has to pay for this!'

'It's probably just a kid—'

'I don't give a damn who it is. They need to be punished.'

'C'mon, Pa, it's not the end of the world—'

Katharine saw the man lash out and heard a loud "thwack". She gasped and stumbled backwards, stepping on the hem of her dress and falling onto her back, emitting a small scream.

'Who's there?' the man said.

'I'll go, Pa. You go back to the house.'

'See that you do and bring whoever it is to me. I'll soon make them regret what they've done.'

Katharine heard footsteps heading in her direction and curled herself into a ball and started whimpering. Her pa would be so angry with her; this was why she wasn't allowed to play in his field.

'Hey there,' the boy said and reached out to touch her shoulder. She screamed again.

'It's okay; I'm not going to hurt you.' His voice was so gentle that it soothed Katharine and she uncurled herself and sat up, hugging her knees tight into her chest as tears streamed down her cheeks.

'I'm s-sorry,' she said between sobs. 'I-I d-didn't m-mean any h-harm.'

'I know, I know, it's okay. I won't tell anyone, but you can't play here anymore, understand?'

She stared into his brown eyes and nodded.

'Hey, what's your name?' he asked, extending a hand to her. She reached out and took hold of it, and he pulled her to her feet.

'K-Katharine,' she said as she stared up at him.

'I'm Jared. It was very nice to meet you, Kathy. Now, off you go and maybe I'll see you again, someplace else; someplace safe.' He leaned down and planted a kiss on her forehead, before winking at her and disappearing into the cotton.

She stood there for a while, her heart pounding, her skin on fire where his lips had touched her. She fell in love with Jared Kent right there and then.

Jared pulled her to him, and she inhaled the damp mustiness of his uniform; not the clean, soapy smell she was used to. This wasn't the memory she wanted to retain. Katharine closed her eyes and buried her face against his chest, unable to feel the contours of his toned torso through the thickness of his horsehair coat. He held her tightly, as though his life depended on it, and maybe it did. She had to believe the feel of her, the smell of her, the taste of her, the image of her would sustain him, just as this moment would have to sustain her.

She heard the stomp of hooves and the impatient snort of horses not twenty feet away.

'I have to go, my love.'

Katharine nodded and bit down on her lip to stop the tears from falling, but it didn't work.

Jared tilted her chin up and brushed his thumb across her cheek, wiping away a stray tear. He brought his lips down to meet hers and she felt her heart would break as he kissed her, the memories of two days of kisses re-awakening the longing deep inside her.

A sudden cough from behind Jared broke her reverie, and she opened her eyes to look up at him.

'I'm sorry, sir, but we need to leave,' the owner of the cough said. Jared nodded, his eyes never leaving hers.

'I love you, my dear sweet Katharine. I will come back to you. I promise.'

Tears flooded her eyes, and she pressed her lips together, unable to speak. She watched, a sob finally escaping her throat, as he turned away from her and finally joined his men.

※

Katharine felt a pair of gentle hands on her shoulders. She closed her eyes and turned into the embrace, finally giving in to the emotions overtaking her.

'Now, now, dearie. There are plenty more where he came from. We can't have you getting like this every time now, can we?'

No one here would ever know what they were to each other because no one would ever understand; not in these times. Everyone knew what the war had done to her. Everyone knew what she'd lost, or they thought they did. They knew Union soldiers had taken her house. They knew every single one of those soldiers had raped her, over and over, week after week, until they'd got fed up with her and had thrown her out.

Penniless and homeless, Katharine had been taken in by a local trader, Bill Matheson, who'd found her collapsed in a ditch. Bill had tasked his wife, Mary, with nursing her back to health. They'd been so kind to her and had promised to provide a roof over her head and food in her stomach, as long as she earned her keep. Katharine, so grateful for their kindness, had accepted without a second thought.

Jared didn't know; nor could he ever know. Good, sweet, kind Jared. He'd believed what she'd told him. He'd always believed what she'd told him. He could never know the real impact of what this war had done to her; the truth would kill him.

Katharine let herself be propelled back towards her shelter, pulling the shawl tightly around her naked shoulders.

Why?

She had no idea. She would have to relinquish it soon enough. Still, for a moment, she could pretend to be who she wanted to be—the desolate wife, devastated at sending her husband back to this God-awful war, rather than who she was forced to be—a whore.

'I did warn you, dearie. You can't allow yourself to care. Now, get a smile on that pretty face and get back in there and earn your keep.'

She took a deep breath, raised her chin high, and hardened her heart as she threw off the shawl and strutted into the saloon.

'Hello boys,' she said, hands planted firmly on her shapely, scantily clad hips; exposing herself for all to see. 'Who's next?'

THE END

Falling for the Scammer by Martina Dale

One ~ Emily

It all started when my friend Jess suggested I start dating again. It's been five years since my husband passed, and I still don't feel ready. James was the love of my life, and although we never got around to having children, I know he would have been an amazing father. James was kind, caring, and wouldn't hurt a fly. He wasn't the type of guy to go out and look for trouble, but on New Year's Eve five years ago, trouble found him. We were spending the evening at home. Everywhere was so busy and expensive, it just made sense to spend the evening with the person we loved.

James was late coming home, and when he didn't arrive by 8:00 p.m., I called his cell. A strange voice answered and then proceeded to tell me my soulmate had been shot in an armed robbery in a convenience store.

He'd gone to buy me wine on his way home from the office.

I rushed to the hospital and arrived just in time to say goodbye. They had managed to keep him alive for longer than they expected. I guess he just wanted to be with me one more time.

I grieved and grieved, and I'm still grieving. No man will ever come close to him. There just isn't a man alive that could make me feel loved and cherished like James did.

As I click the submit button on my dating profile, a lump forms in my throat. *Urgh, what the hell have I done?* I consider deleting it straight away, but Jess takes my phone out of my hand and stops me.

"Jess, I'm really not sure!" I say, unsure of what I've just done.

"I am. You need to get out and get laid. You're young, beautiful, and successful, and you deserve to add happy to that list."

"But what if I get a weirdo or a crank?"

"Then you swipe left. If you like them, then you can swipe—" She's interrupted by a dinging sound coming from my phone. "Shit, you've matched already. That was quick! What did you put? That you're a stripper who only wants one-night stands?"

"No! And . . . I don't even want to know. That type of man must be sat around waiting for women to prey on."

"It doesn't work like that," Jess says, rolling her eyes.

Jess met her now husband on a dating app, and she thinks that it's an amazing way to meet your next beau. I don't. The whole thing makes me wary.

"Fine, what does he look like, and more importantly . . . what does his profile say?" I ask, not able to look myself. The knot in my stomach is getting bigger by the minute.

"So . . . Oh wow, you've matched with five. Hellfire, Em, this is crazy," she says, smiling as she flicks through the matches.

"No, no, no, possible, and *hello*," she says as she swipes across the screen.

"Now what?" I ask, my hands trembling.

"You start to chat. If you click, chat some more. But don't agree to meet or give your phone number or address. Don't even tell them what state you live in."

"Okay, but what if he asks? It'd be rude to say 'I'm not telling you.'"

"You need to be a thousand percent sure before you tell them anything real. Just get to know him first. Talk about pets or what interests you have."

"This is too scary, Jess. I don't think I can do it. I'd rather go and hook up in a bar and have a one-night stand than go through this," I reply, thinking about deleting the app again.

I watch as Jess does something on my phone and then smiles. "It looks like his name is Christopher, as his profile says. I've just done a reverse look up on the internet, so at least we know his profile pic is right."

"What does it say about him?" I ask, knowing I'm being dragged down a rabbit hole.

"He's rich, a CEO of an investment banking company. He's single and a total hottie."

"So, why is he on a cheap and nasty dating site?"

"Only one way to find out, Em. You talk to him, and when the time is right, ask him. He could be just like one of those guys you read about in your romance books. Sick of the entitled princesses and looking for a real woman."

"He'd have to be. I'm nowhere near supermodel stature."

"You are beautiful. Stop putting yourself down."

"Really? Then why am I on a dating site and not turning men away from my door?"

"You want the truth?" Jess asks, chewing her cheek.

"Yeah, of course I do."

"You're a little intimidating. Obviously, I don't see you that way, but some people . . . are a little scared."

"What? Why?"

"Because you are a fucking kickass bitch. The only time I've seen you upset was when James was killed."

"Well, it's all about how you manage the situation, but I'm not intimidating . . . am I?" I ask, feeling the hurt.

She nods slowly. "I'm sorry, I don't see you that way. Fuck, look who's in charge here," she says with a slight laugh.

"I don't really care what anyone else thinks," I say honestly. It's been a shit five years, and Jess has been with me nearly every day. I trust her more than I trust myself.

I take the phone and exchange a few messages with Christopher. He seems nice and isn't asking any red flag questions. When I said I was going to sleep, he simply said good night and that he'd message again soon.

So, I was surprised when I woke and found a "Good morning" message. It gave my heart a little flutter, which I quickly chastised myself for.

Don't be stupid, Emily. It's a good morning, not I love you.

I reply with a "Good Morning" and a sunshine emoji, and within minutes, he replies.

Christopher: Did you sleep well?

Emily: Yes, thank you, you?

Christopher: I did. Our chat last night really helped. Thank you.

Our chat? What the hell does he mean? We exchanged pleasantries.

Emily: That's okay. I enjoyed the few messages, too. I need to get ready for work now. Maybe I'll catch you later.

I drop my phone into my bag out of sight and get ready for the day ahead. As the head of HR for a multimillion-dollar manufacturing company, I have to be on my game. I've two big meetings, a restructure of the company to work through, and three disciplinaries to sit in on.

By the time 6:00 p.m. comes around, I am completely beat. All I want is a hot bath, a glass of wine, and a takeout. In that order. That's the routine I've had now since James. Cooking for one? Not my thing. Drinking alone? Definitely my thing.

I don't check my phone until I go to order my takeout, and I notice a notification on the dating app. I feel the little flutter of excitement when I open it up to see Christopher's profile picture and three unread messages.

10:00 a.m. Christopher: Hope your day is going well.

2:00 p.m. Christopher: You must be really busy. You should take a break.

4:00 p.m. Christopher: Sorry, but I thought we'd connected. I won't message you again until you message me. If I don't hear from you, it was really good to chat. C x

Oh god, he thinks I've been ignoring him. I don't want to come across as rude as a first impression.

Emily: Sorry, I have had a day from hell and only just looked at my phone.

Christopher: Hey, that's fine. I was just making sure I hadn't misread the situation. I get that you are busy. Honestly, I am, too, but I just couldn't get you out of my head today.

Emily: I wish I had had time to breathe today. I didn't even get a break for lunch.

I send off the message and then open up the takeout delivery app and order my usual for a Monday night.

The message icon flashes, and I open it up.

Christopher: You need to take better care of yourself. I don't want you wasting away before we've had a chance to get to know each other.

I read the message and try to think of a reply. He seems really sweet, but I'm still not sure about him. He's a little pushy, and I'm not used to anyone caring about my wellbeing.

Emily: Thanks. I'm having dinner now, so I think I'll survive.

Christopher: What's on the menu?

Emily: Chicken spring rolls and chicken chow mein.

Christopher: So, you like chicken? Good to know. I like a woman who is a meat eater.

I blush instantly. Is that an innuendo? Or is he just saying he doesn't like vegetarians?

Two glasses of wine later, I reply.

Emily: Yes, I like meat. I like it a lot.

I press send and blush again and regret it instantly. *What the hell am I doing?* Another glass of wine down, and I'm starting to feel even more reckless with my messages. Christopher doesn't seem to mind. In fact, he is throwing those innuendos and slightly sexy comments around like confetti.

Christopher: So, do you like big sausages?

Emily: Of course. A chipolata doesn't fill a hole, does it?

I'm crying laughing at my own childish responses. I haven't laughed like this in years, and at the same time, I'm starting to like this guy. Maybe I should give him some of my attention after all.

Sunday comes around again, and Jess arrives for our weekly catch up. We talk and laugh, and I show her some of the message exchanges between me and Christopher. Things seem to be progressing nicely. He doesn't seem to be a creep, and the night we spent sending innuendos back and forth has now matured into what I can only call a friendship. He makes me laugh, and I think I do the same to him. So much so, that a few messages in the evening have turned into full-on message marathons every night, sometimes until the early hours.

"Has he asked to call you or where you live?" Jess asks, her eyes sceptically looking at the messages.

"No, we haven't really talked about our private lives as such. I did tell him I worked in HR, and he told me he was in investment, which checks out from our internet search."

"Good, don't tell him anything else. Not for a long time. He seems nice enough, but scammers know how to play the game."

"How did you know that Lewis wasn't a scammer?"

"He told me his favourite sandwich and where he buys it from. I took his profile into the deli and asked the lady behind the counter. She said he was a really nice guy and wished me luck."

"Oh yeah, I remember. But what if Christopher doesn't live around here? How can I check and make sure?"

"Just run a mile if he asks to borrow money or has a bad accident and needs you to pay his medical bills."

"Well, duh, yeah. I'm not that stupid. But what if he has a wife and kids, and he doesn't have that on his wiki page?"

"I'm sure someone who is as rich as he is would make sure that his wiki page is up to date. Just don't do anything without telling me first."

I nod and smile. Jess is my best friend, and I know she'll have my back and make sure I don't fall into anything stupid.

Two months later...

Christopher: I don't know about you, but it does worry me a bit that other people can read our messages. I know we haven't exchanged anything too personal, but when you are in my position, it's a little risky. Would you mind if we took this off here and text in private?"

We've chatted every day. He's not shown any red flags, and I get why he doesn't want other people having access to our conversations. So, I take a deep breath and reply.

Emily: I understand, but I'm not sure about giving out my number. Can we exchange emails instead?

There is a long silence before he replies.

Christopher: I'd rather text. I only have one email address, and it's my business one. I can't manage more than one. I'm a man, after all.

I laugh at that, although one email address does worry me, so I call Jess. I did promise after all.

I explain what he's asked for and his excuse for not using email, and she thinks about it for a minute.

"Go buy a burner phone and only give him the number," she says.

"Why? I don't understand what protection that will give me?"

"If you get sick of him or he gets weird, you can just chop up the SIM card."

"Oh yeah, good plan. That way, I don't have to get a new number if things go bad."

"Exactly . . . Em?" She stops talking and waits for me to respond.

"Yeah?"

"Thanks for talking to me. I know you like this guy, but you still need to be careful. It's early days, and although I don't get a bad feeling, it's no excuse to be careless."

"I know, and I promised I would talk things through with you, and I will. Stop worrying. You'll know before I do anything."

"Good, cos I don't fancy spending a few years behind bars for kicking ass."

My phone is beeping with messages, and I hear Jess giggle. "Go and speak with your man. Have fun, but be careful."

"Night, Jess, and thanks."

I end the call and click on the messages.

Christopher: I don't want to scare you off. We can stay chatting like this.

Shit, how do I tell him that I'll give him my number tomorrow?

Emily: Let me think about it, and I'll let you know tomorrow.

Christopher: Take your time, and don't worry if you don't want to. I just want to be able to share more of me with you, and I don't want others having access. You understand, don't you?"

Emily: I do. Till tomorrow. Good night, Christopher.

I let out the breath that I didn't know I was holding in. My heart races, and my palms are sweaty. I hope to god I'm doing the right thing. I open up my shopping app and order a cheap smartphone and SIM card to be delivered to my office tomorrow.

With the order placed, I finish off my glass of wine and climb into bed. Since starting to chat with Christopher, my sleep pattern has been turned upside down. A good night's sleep will do me the world of good.

That is until I get a notification of a message and then another one and another one. I look at the clock. It's 3:00 a.m. My eyes are burning as I squint to read the message.

Christopher: I'm sorry. I don't mean to push you.

Christopher: I wish we could talk, like, *really* talk.

Christopher: Emily, I'm sorry. I know it's late, but I can't get you out of my mind.

He will know I've seen the messages, but sending them at 3:00 a.m.? Really? I turn my phone to silent, put it back on the charging block, and close my eyes. People at work have already noticed how tired I am during the day. I need a good night's sleep before I end up losing my job.

The new phone arrives, and I set it up and send Christopher the number. He very quickly sends me his, and we begin chatting as we were before.

Christopher: Now we are away from prying eyes, are you going to come off the dating site?

Emily: Yes, I've not been talking to anyone else, anyway. How about you?

I reply as my stomach churns. What if he doesn't want to stop, or he's talking to more women?

My new phone chimes.

Christopher: I deleted my profile the minute you sent me your number, and I've cancelled my subscription.

Relief floods through me, and it scares me at the same time that I wanted him to say exactly that.

Before I close my account, I check that he's no longer searchable. He's gone, and when I try to send a message, it sends a reply that the account is closed. I click on the cancel subscription button and pick up my new phone.

Emily: Me, too.

Christopher: So, does this mean we're exclusive? Only talking to each other, and no one else?

Oh shit . . . exclusive? Well, why not? I'm not actually talking to anyone else anyway.

Emily: I think it does.

Christopher: Think????

Emily: Yes, it does.

Christopher: Good, and thank you, beautiful.

Did he just call me beautiful? I read the text again and, yes, he did. Maybe now we are in a private chat, things are developing.

Emily: What for?

Christopher: Trusting me.

My little heart thumps hard. I do trust him. He hasn't been demanding, and at no point has he asked me for any sort of help. He doesn't need it, anyway. He owns a huge corporation. He has people who manage almost everything for him and more money than the national reserve.

Each day, our texts become more and more intimate. We begin to share more and more about ourselves and our lives. Each message we exchange makes me want to see him, to be with him and be able to touch him. Maybe it's time we video call and have a real conversation.

Emily: I know I've been the one who has been cautious, but I think it's time we speak. Can we do a video call? I really want to see you.

Christopher: Oh, darling, I would love that, but I want the first time we see each other to be in person. How about we take it back a step? We've not even talked on the phone yet.

My heart sinks a little, but I get what he's saying and why. I feel a little deflated that he didn't jump at the chance of taking our relationship to the next level, but at least he's said he wants to meet me in person.

Biting my lip, I press the call button on Christopher's name. It rings and rings, and then after what feels like forever, he answers. My stomach is in knots, and my heart is racing . . .

"Christopher?" I ask warily.

"Emily . . ." he replies softly. His deep voice is different from what I'd imagined in my dreams.

"I'm sorry, maybe I should have asked first, but I wanted to speak, to hear your voice."

"I'm really pleased you did. I just needed to step out of the boardroom."

"Oh, I should let you go. I'm sorry," I reply, my hands shaking and my heart thumping hard.

"No, it was boring, anyway. I made an investment for a friend, and it's just made him a very rich man."

"Really? Oh wow, that's really cool. I bet your friend is over the moon."

"You could say that. It means he can send his kids to college now and buy a nicer house. His wife is disabled, so he'll be able to provide better care for her, too."

"That's amazing. You must really know what you're doing."

"I didn't make it to where I am today without learning a thing or two. It's the same with you and employment law: you'll have picked up a few tricks of the trade along the way."

His office is in New York and not that far from me in Boston, so when he speaks, I'm a little taken back.

"Thank you. I have to say, you sound a little different to how I imagined. I don't really know how to describe it, but you don't have the New York accent I was expecting."

He laughs hard, and the sound makes me smile. "I lived all over America when I was a child, and my family came to the States from Italy when I was a baby. My parents still speak Italian more than English, so I have a slightly mixed-up accent. I do make an effort to lose the idiosyncrasies when delivering speeches, but I feel like I can be myself with you, Emily."

Butterflies explode in my tummy as a knock on my office door sounds.

"Sorry, Christopher, I have to go, someone wants to see me."

"I wish I could see you, too. I'll call you later, after work?"

"That would be lovely. After work!" I reply, smiling like a crazy woman as my boss opens the door wide and walks in.

"Morning, Em," Sarah, the CEO, says as she takes a seat opposite me.

"Morning. Everything okay?" Sarah doesn't often come to my office to see me; it's usually the other way around.

"Not really. We've noticed that your mind has been elsewhere recently, and I wanted to ask if everything was okay. It's not like you to drop the ball, but you've been preoccupied for a while."

"Dropping the ball? I didn't know I had. Have you any examples?"

"Your report of the sexual harassment claim was what I'd have expected from a junior head of the department. I asked you to deal with it personally, as we wanted to avoid going to court. Guess what arrived this morning." She slaps a brown envelope down on the desk.

"No, I don't believe it. They agreed on a settlement."

"Yeah, well, that's changed. Emily, you need to sort your head out. We can't afford any more mess ups like this. I know you've had a hard time over the years, but even after James's death, you weren't this distracted."

"I'm sorry, I'll work harder. I've just had a few personal things going on."

"Sort them out and get back in the game. I don't want to fire you, but any more of this, and you won't leave me any option." She stands and heads for the door. "You've got two weeks. Turn it around, Em," she says before closing it behind her.

Two weeks . . . I didn't even know I'd done anything wrong. It's not my fault Suzi Trafford decided to actually take Peter Jenkinson to court. Maybe this wasn't about the money for her. Maybe she wanted justice.

In all my working life, I've never been in trouble, never even had a warning, and now I'm at risk of losing my job.

I pick up my phone that I've ridiculously named 'Lover' and hover my finger over Christopher's name. I've only just spoken to him, and he was busy in the boardroom, but I desperately need to talk to him.

The call rings out for a while and then I cut the call. He's obviously busy and taking his business far more seriously than I have been doing. I need to put some distance between us and concentrate on my job. There's no way I'm letting them fire me.

I've no sooner decided to cool things down when Lover rings. I grab at it as if it's a lifeline and answer so quickly, it doesn't even get a chance to ring twice.

"Emily? Is everything okay?"

"Yeah, no. My boss is threatening to fire me because I've been so distracted recently. I wish I could just tell them to shove their job where the sun doesn't shine, but I can't. I couldn't live off my savings forever if they fire me. I'm sorry . . . I'm sorry . . . I think we should—"

"Emily!" he interrupts me in a stern tone. "Don't you dare think about ending things. We have something good, something amazing. If they fire you, don't worry. I'll look after you."

"I can't let you do that."

"I didn't mean send you money. I can help you be financially independent. I can tell you what to invest in and how to make money fast. I've just made my friend over a million dollars in less than two weeks."

"You can really do that?" I ask, my chest tightening as I think of my little pot of savings.

"Yeah. Of course, it all depends on what you put in to start with, but I can double your money in no time at all."

"I don't have that much. I don't think it would be worth it."

"How much? How much can you safely invest without leaving you without a safety net?"

"I've got James's life insurance. It's only $125,000."

"Imagine if I can turn that into half a million. It would take a little longer than a few weeks, but investment is the best way to make a small amount grow."

"I don't know. I'll think about it, but thank you, Christopher. I really do appreciate it."

"Emily . . . I was going to save this until tonight, but I can't hold it in anymore. I think I'm falling for you. I think we need to meet. I want to hold you and keep you safe. I want to see if your skin is as soft as it looks in your picture."

"Oh, Christopher, I want that, too. But I need to get back to work. I'll call you when I get home, is that okay?"

"You can call me anytime, day or night, you know that, don't you?"

"I do. Speak soon."

For the next week, we talk almost constantly. The worry of me losing my job is becoming less of a worry and more of an irritation. Every time I look at Sarah, I want to tell her to fuck off. How dare she be like this with me? Christopher has made me see things more clearly: I'm just a number to the board of directors. They don't care that I've given the last ten years to this company, and it makes me even more eager to get the hell out.

I've spoken with Christopher either by message, text, or phone for over three months now, and I've even checked him out online. A few articles about him being here and there match up with what he tells me. I feel bad for checking, but Jess still isn't convinced. I am though. I have fallen for Christopher and fallen hard. He listens, understands, and offers really good advice, which is why I've decided to let him invest my savings.

I send over the bank transfer to his company account. Not the one for Integral Investments Global but for his private fund that he works with for his friends.

My phone pings with a message.

Christopher: Thank you. I'll be in touch soon with an update. I'm just in an important meeting.

It's more formal than normal, and my heart begins to race.

Emily: Can you ring me? I'm feeling a little weird.

Christopher: Later. I'm busy.

What? He knows how important this is to me. He knows it's my life savings.

Emily: Why are you being like this?

I wait for a reply, but I get nothing, and as the hours pass and I don't get a reply, my heart begins to race, and my stomach threatens to twist itself into a huge knot.

Sitting on my sofa, I know there is only one thing to do. I send a text to Sarah saying I won't be in tomorrow as I have a stomach bug, and then I book a flight to New York with the last of my savings.

The flight leaves in four hours, so I pack a bag, call an uber, and race off to the airport.

Luckily, the flight is short. I'm holding down vomit the whole time. My nails are now a mess from biting and chewing them. My face is pale, as if I've just had the flu, and my whole body can't stop shaking.

As I reach the airport doors, I look around for a taxi, and my heart stops dead. There he is. Christopher. In the flesh. He's surrounded by other men in suits and heading for the departures area. He never said anything about travelling.

Fuck it . . .

"Christopher! Christopher!" I yell as loud as I can.

He turns to look at me and then looks away.

"Christopher . . . Wait! Christopher, it's me, Emily!" I yell again as I run to catch up with him.

As I reach his side, I reach out for his arm, but I'm moved back by two of the men around him.

"I'm sorry, miss, please step back."

What? Why is he doing this? "Christopher, please, just talk to me. Please. You're scaring me."

He stops and turns around and looks at me with an intensity that nearly sets me on fire.

"I'm sorry, but have we met? Do I know you?"

To be continued...

A Night to Remember by Mia Kun

~ Matt ~

I was nervous as hell as I fixed my suit jacket. My hand was missing a drink to calm my jitteriness, but I knew better than to fall into that trap. Tonight had to be perfect. It was our chance to start over, to enjoy ourselves and leave all the craziness behind.

It was a new beginning.

"Ready?" Axel asked as he knotted his tie with simple moves and smoothed his hair back, making sure the gel didn't allow it to move.

I left mine untamed, knowing Kiki loved pushing her fingers through my curly strains and playing with them.

"Everything is taken care of," my cousin said, glancing at his phone. "We should get going, picking up the girls."

Contrary to any other dance before, Essie wanted to do this the right way. She hid Kiki from me as they were getting ready in her apartment and like the good boyfriends, we were we had to go pick them up.

A loud exhale left me, and I nodded. "I'm ready."

"Dude, this is just a dance, not your wedding," Axel joked, looking at my suffering face.

"I think this is more important to Kiki then a wedding."

"You underestimate that girl. I'm sure she has a wedding Pinterest board already," he joked, making me grin. That sounded like my girlfriend.

I knew how much Prom meant to her. When we were freshman she told me she wanted to go with me, because she was sure we were going to last. She told me the exact flower corsage she wanted, the one mixed with white peonies and roses, and she confessed her dream of being Prom Queen. She added, of course, that she knew Essie would win, just because of who she was, and it was impossible for anyone else to win it. She didn't realize I remembered everything and made sure tonight went down exactly how she imagined it.

It was my gift to her, for waiting on me and for seeking the help she needed. For giving us a second chance, and for never giving up on us.

She deserved the world, but if a stupid title was all she craved, I could make that happen.

Toying with my tie one last time, before my cousin beat my hand away, I confessed.

"I'm nervous."

"No shit," Axel grinned. "You're going to do just fine. It's a high school dance, no booze is allowed anyway."

I rolled my eyes. For the first time, I wasn't worried about temptation suffocating me and my throat burning from the need to drink. I was more worried about dancing all night long in an environment where everyone was going to stare at us. Dancing at The Playroom was one thing, but in the indoor ballroom specifically built for dances with thousand lights shining was a whole different thing. It wasn't intimate at all.

"I'm not worried about that."

"I can write right and left on your hands if you need reminder how to slow dance," my cousin teased me.

Axel picked up an annoying habit of trying to be a jokester, but his jokes sucked big time. His moody personality was not meant for going around cracking jokes. Even if he only did it with me.

"Come on," he clamped me on the shoulder. "It's time we get this party moving. The sooner we get there, the sooner we can leave with our girls, and get a better kind of dancing started."

I still didn't get over the warmth in my chest every time Axel said 'our girls'. I couldn't believe I've gotten this far, having my girl by my side. The one that was always meant to be. Despite all the toxicity in our relationship, we managed to stand our ground. And that was a real accomplishment.

By the time we made it into the limo, and we were on our short drive over to Essie's place, my phone was blowing up with the girls getting impatient with every passing second. They were hundred percent taking advantage over this situation.

"I told Essie we are doing this now, and not even our wedding is going to be this flashy," Axel muttered looking cool, but his bouncing knee gave him away.

It wasn't just my first dance with my girl, it was his as well. They never got to go to Homecoming as it was cancelled last semester.

"Come on, you need to make your wedding over the top as well," I grinned, already imagining his miserable face from all the attention. I was half convinced he only helped me in my mission to crown myself as Prom King so he would get out of the spotlight. There weren't many things Axel hated more than attention. While he was dating the most attention seeking person ever.

"Nope. I don't even want a wedding," he chuckled. "It's something that Essie knew since we were little. Does she still hope I will change my mind? Sure. Does that mean I will do it for her? I'm not convinced. I'm sure you will get married before us… and when you do, I'll kick your ass because it will open Pandora's box for me. So, if you ever want to propose you need my permission."

"And you promise to give your blessing?" I wiggled my brows as he grimaced.

"Let's not push it," Axel muttered as we pulled in front of the building. The limo parked in the drop-off bay, allowing us to jump out and make our way to the lobby. Axel mumbled something along the way of how unnecessarily stupid this was as he called the elevator and swiping his card, it took us all the way to the penthouse.

"Hi, are you girls ready?" I shouted in the empty foyer as I walked across the marble floor into the living room admiring the Manhattan skyline. "Kiki? Essie?"

Axel groaned as he dropped himself on the sofa. This was particularly his second home, but I rarely spent time here. We either hung at my or Axel's place if not the CHM offices.

The sound of high heels clicking on the floor echoed through the empty flat and my attention was directed towards the descending girls. In particular my girl. She looked like she's walked off the pages of Vogue, wearing a silky emerald dress with an elegant V-neck cut, making her long neck seem infinite and hugging her breast in the right way. The dress itself was A-lined and floor length not showing off any of her newfound curves that I loved on her body. But with each step she took, the slit on the side revealed her long, toned legs.

Emotions clogged my throat and I was at loss of words.

She looked like a dream come true, and I was tempted to pinch myself to see if it was reality.

Our eyes connected, and time slowed. I watched her lashes bet over her uncertain eyes, as she scanned my face for a reaction. I pulled my lips into a small smile, and she mirrored it immediately. Our bodies were connected, just like we were.

Stepping to the bottom of the stairs, I extended my arm to her. "You look beautiful."

Beautiful sounded wrong, as she was much more than that, but Kiki seemed to be content with my choice of words. She ducked her head as her cheeks flushed.

"Thank you," she muttered as she placed her hand in mine, giving it a small squeeze.

I twirled her around to admire her fiery red hair flying together with her silk dress, before I wrapped my arms around her and pulled her into my chest.

"You are the most beautiful girl, I've ever seen," I muttered into her ear, making her chuckle.

Our lips found each other without further delay, and I hoped my kisses could convey all my feeling that words couldn't express. How lucky I was to have her by my side and how much I appreciated her every single day. The hunger inside me grew with every caressed of a tongue, and sinking my fingers into her hair, I pulled her closer, deepening the kiss, owning every inch of her mouth with my tongue. Kiki opened up to me with a small moan, her body stuck to mine, teasing my erection.

"If you keep this up, we won't be going anywhere," she said when she pulled away her forehead resting on mine.

My hand cupped her chin, and I rubbed my thumb over swollen lips, needing to bite them and suck on them just couple of minutes longer.

"That's why I told you not to put lipstick," Essie's voice broke me out of my happy bubble, and I lifted my eyes to see her in Axel's arms. I gave her a quick once over taking in her black dress. It seemed to be the same silky material as Kiki's but her was more bodycon, hugging her body tighter and with the same big slit on the side, showing off her legs. Axel's hand rested on her exposed thigh.

"Maybe you girls should find a brand that has long lasting lipsticks."

"That's none existing... there are couple that are okay-ish, but you have the talent to remove them all," Kiki muttered reminding me of our date when she was wearing red lipstick that didn't move from her lips all through dinner, but the moment I decided to kiss her was all over me. She burst out laughing saying I reminded her of the Joker. That's what every guy wanted to hear on his date.

Flashing her a smile, instead of rolling my eyes, I wrapped my arms around her neck and pulled her closer, kissing the top of her head. "You can go without lipstick."

Kiki gasped, and gently pushing on my chest, she shook her head. "That's a crime."

"No one's going to alert the fashion police," I joked with a resigned sight, as I watched her pull out the same burning red lipstick that I had my uncomfortable encounter with.

She opened her little mirror and without even asking me if I wanted to kiss her more, she applied a thick coat of make-up on her plump lips. I watched in awe, as she pressed the stick to her lips outlining them over and over, wishing it was my tongue or at least my finger doing it.

My expression must have given me away, as she reached up and planted a big kiss on my cheek. "You will have your opportunity to kiss me."

"Is that a promise?" I arched a brow.

Kiki's eyes glimmered with mischief and happiness as she nodded. "Yes, it is."

"Good," I grinned, before rubbing my cheek. "Now please make sure I don't have red on my cheeks."

"Relax, my love, you're perfect," she giggled looping her arm with mine. "Ready to go?"

"As ready as I'll ever be."

The ride to our school was short, in all fairness we could have walked, but since it was Prom we wanted the full package. Minus the annoying picture taking part which the parents did in movies. We took a group photo and one picture of each couple that we sent to our respective families and that was all. There was no need for tears and bullshit like that. I knew, my mom would never forgive me for taking this away from her, but Kiki didn't need additional reminders of how screwed up her family was. If I could shelter her from that feeling for a night, I wanted to do it.

By the time the limo pulled up in front of Eastview High there were several cars in the parking lot and several other limos and town cars dropping off students.

"...Gabriel must have been pissed," I heard Essie finish taking, snapping me back into the conversation.

"What happened?" I asked already thinking of the worse. My brother and Essie's were in the final stages of buying the Casino that was located in our newly opened hotel, but the previous owner was dragging it out, making us all anxious.

"Natalie pulled a page from Bianca's playbook and petitioned to get Gabriel removed as coach," Kiki filled me in on the gossip, since being back with me officially has gained her untouchable position back. It also meant she was our eyes and ears. She had an ear for gossip.

I let out a low whistle. As far as I knew Gabriel was determined to stay coach for the next year as he needed it for his double degree. There was no way Natalie was successful in kicking him off. Which only meant she succeeded of making an even bigger enemy out of him.

Resisting the urge to text her and scold her, I squeezed Kiki's hand and stared out the window.

"Doubt she will come. Prom is not her scene. Plus, she told me as soon as school's out she is hopping on a flight to Barcelona and not coming back until end of summer."

Would have liked to think she wasn't going to leave without a goodbye.

"Let's go," Axel muttered as our limo pulled to a stop and opening the door, he stepped and reached his hand to help Essie out.

Planting a small kiss on Kiki's flushed cheeks, I offered her a small smile. "Did I tell you, you look beautiful?"

She chuckled. "Only hundred times."

"That means not nearly enough times." With my free hand, I touched her exposed silky skin under the slit. "You will drive me crazy tonight. It will be your fault if they catch me with an erection."

Kiki laughed and slipping into my lap with one smooth move, she pushed her nose to mine, her red lips teasing me. "You know I really want you to kiss me... but you shouldn't risk ruining my lipstick."

My hands fisted over her hips and I pushed my fingertips into her flesh, breathing in her sweet scent through my nose. "The moment they announce Prom King and Queen I'm ruining that pretty lipstick of yours."

"That's going to be a long night then," she smiled her hips rolling over my erection.

A low groan escaped me. "If you play with fire, you might get burned. And I'm fighting with everything inside me to not rip your dress open and fuck you in the back of a limo before you even had a chance to enjoy your prom."

"I'm just helping you build up resistance."

"I have resistance to many things... not for you," I muttered through clenched teeth.

Kiki threw her head back in a laughter, her Hollywood curls staying in perfect place just the way she styled them. I resisted the urge to touch them, worried they were probably half as soft as I liked them from all the hairspray.

Spanking her butt gently I nodded towards the door. "Come on."

Kiki nuzzled her nose to mine ne last time, a sexy smirk sitting on her lips, before she slid out of my lap and out of the limo leaving me with my throbbing erection.

Throwing my head against a headrest I took a long breath in to calm myself.

This was going to be the longest and most painful night of my life. I already knew that.

―――

Once we made it inside, we moved around the grand ballroom that looked like it was one of our father's hotel ballrooms instead of a high school ballroom. The room was dressed in dim lighting and different colors bounced off the walls illuminating the dancing couples. Catering of canapes and drinks was set up along the wall and tall rounded tables accompanied them for resting. Axel took up residence at one of the central high tables, his elbow casually leaning on it as he held a Coke in his hand, while Essie wrapped her arms around his neck and was most likely talking his ear off and convincing him to dance.

Instead of joining my cousin, I secured my arm around Kiki's waist and guided her to the dancefloor. Grabbing her hand, I twirled her under our locked hands and pulled her to me.

"Who could have guessed that you are a charmer?" she teased me with a light smile on her plumping lips.

"Don't fool yourself, my love," I grinned. "You knew this all along. That's why you fell for me."

"Falling for you wasn't a choice," Kiki said. "It was an unintentional misstep yet the best mistake I've ever made."

"You are the only girl who calls me a mistake and gets away with it."

Kiki chuckled. "I'm the one, remember."

Something tugged on my heartstrings from her words, and I flashed her a sweet smile. She was the one. Undyingly. People twice our age didn't go through the shit we went through in so little time. We were a turmoil of emotions and despite what she tried telling me, she and I... we kept choosing each other every step of the way.

We might have fallen in love by chance, but it was a conscious decision to keep fighting to each other instead of giving up and moving on.

As we swayed to the slow, classical music playing in the background, our bodies flashed together, I kept reminding myself this night is for her. It's not for me. I had to ignore the painful throbbing in my pants, and the need burning thorough my veins. I could never get enough of her. She was my new addiction. A year ago, I would have said she was a more dangerous addiction than alcohol, but now I knew she was the best kind of addiction I could have.

She wrapped her arms around my neck and rested her chin on my shoulders. "You smell nice."

"Thanks," I chuckled, happy she noticed the new cologne I tried on.

"This isn't your usual. It's not One Million." She sniffed me some more.

"It's Bad Boy from Carolina Herrera," I helped her out with a grin. I got it because I liked the lightening shape of the bottle, and the smell was good enough. I wanted to switch up my signature scent as it reminded me of a dark period in my life.

"I would have thought you are more like a Dior Savage kind of guy."

I gagged. "I'm basic, but not that basic."

Kiki laughed, throwing her hair back, and exposing her long, kissable neckline. "Sorry, I forgot about that."

I shook my head, as my eyes ate up the length of her neck, before dropping to her cleavage.

How the hell was I supposed to get through the night without ripping her clothes off? My hand gripped her hips tighter, fisting the soft material of the dress. Whoever decided couples needed to get ready separate, so guys could suffer through the night, was a real asshole.

Song after song, we remained glued together, our bodies moving as one as we danced between the sea of people.

I didn't care about anyone approaching me or wanting to say hi to Kiki. We didn't even notice anyone else existing in that room. It was just the two of us and our joined heartbeat drumming in our chest.

With every sway and every new step we took, I was falling deeper and deeper in love with her. If it was physically possible.

The music suddenly changed and a more upbeat song blasted through the speakers, bursting out happy little bubble. Kiki let out a low giggle and turning her back to me, she moved against me, her hips circling in seductive motion. Her arm came around my neck as she laid her head on my shoulder.

My hand fisted as I grabbed her holding her in place.

"If you keep that up, we are leaving."

"They will announce Prom King and Queen now anyway," she turned, our bodies completely flat against each other. My erection branched out between us making her laugh.

"Are you that horny?" she teased into my ear, her tongue daring out to lick my neck. "We can leave..."

"I'm not horny," I corrected her, as I relaxed my hold on her. "I'm affected by your beauty, your smell, your adorable smile and the happiness in your eyes."

Kiki melted in my arms, her mouth pulling into a shocked little 'o' before she captured my lips with hers and kissed me with such and passion that I have rarely seen from her. Her tongue entangled with mine, and we both forgot about the lipstick that was going to be all over me. Our bodies flashed against each other, our limbs entangled and in that moment I forgot about everyone and everything around us. Nothing mattered just her lips on mine and my hand that was teasing her skin through the slit.

It would have been so easy. Slipping my hand up her dress, finding her panties and fingering her in the crowded dance floor.

Kiki pulled away, and I almost protested before she touched her lips to mine and spoke in hushed voice. "I'm not wearing underwear."

If I was going crazy before, those four little words drove me to the edge. I grabbed her hand and without a word started walking towards the exit.

"Hey, you can't..." someone tried stopping me, but I pushed the person out of my way and almost dragged Kiki out of the crowded fake ballroom all the way to the nearest bathroom, locking the door behind us.

"What if someone has to come in?" she asked glancing at the door.

She was very mistaken if she thought I was going to let anyone hear the noises she made when she came. Those sounds belonged to me.

"Don't care," I muttered as my hands found her hips and I pulled her to me.

Kiki pouted at me as I sat her between the two sinks and caught a reflection in the mirror. My face was full of red lipstick smudges.

"I lost the bet..."

"What?" I dragged my eyes away from the mirror and to her adorable fake-sad face.

"Essie told me you will snap before they announce prom king and queen," she muttered her fingers hooking into my shirt and pulling me closer. "I told her you wouldn't make it out of the limo."

I let out a low, strained laugh. "You would have won... if it wasn't for me wanting to give you a special night..."

"But now you decided that your dick was special enough?" she teased me as she unbuckled my belt and undid my dress pants. "Are you going to fuck me?"

"You are begging for it," I muttered over her lips before I kissed her deeply. My hands found her dress and I dragged it up until she sat bare in front of me, her legs falling open. Two of my fingers teased her clit before I dipped them inside her, her wetness immediately coating them.

A loud moan escaped her and her head fell back. "Yeah... I am... fuck me."

She didn't need to beg me or ask me twice. Pulling out my fingers, I slammed into her without thinking twice. She was on the pill so there was nothing for me to worry about as I claimed her.

My fast-paced thrusts intensified with every moan and groan leaving her as she clung onto me. Lifting her off the sink, I squeezed her ass cheeks as I bounced her on my dick. Kiki's arms circled my neck and with every deep thrust her breath hitched more.

"Tell me, you're close," I begged her, barely containing myself.

"I am... I'm going to come, just keep going," she moaned, her eyes squeezing tight as I turned her to push her against the wall finding a deeper, better angle for my final thrusts.

Within seconds, she screamed as her orgasm claimed her and I followed her with a loud grunt, almost collapsing against the wall.

I didn't realize how much I needed to empty my sack and how crazy this girl was driving me.

"I love you," I muttered into her hair as I hinted kisses along her cheeks, neck, and collarbone to contrast my possessive and asshole fuck-boy behavior.

Kiki chuckled and her green eyes remained hidden behind her closed eyelids. "I love it when you lose control and fuck me like you're not scared of breaking me."

Silence followed her confession because most of the times we still tiptoed around each other. I still through she was made of glass, and she still thought of me as an addict who was going to relapse any moment. But times like this, when we could shed the past and allow our instincts to take over made everything so much sweeter.

"We are working on it," I kissed my way up to her lips and smiled. "We are on the right path."

"Definitely, and I love all the bumps in the road," she winked, making me chuckle.

A loud bang sounded on the door and we both glanced towards it.

"It's occupied," I shouted unsure which idiot didn't get the memo of a locked door.

"Get the fuck out of there. They are announcing the winners." Axel's voice came from the other side and I groaned.

Of course, it was going to be my stupid cousin. No one else would have dared to interrupt.

"Fun time's over," I put Kiki on the floor and fixed her dress.

"Until later, right?" she wiggled her brows suggestively. "You totally owe me a bath after you left you cum spilling down my leg."

I grinned and my primal part felt proud swelling inside of me. "I'll clean you up after... until than I want to make sure everyone knows you belong to me."

"Everyone always knew that," she smiled, lacing her fingers with mine after I adjusted my pants. "No one ever dared to take me away from you, even when I wasn't yours."

A groan escaped me as I turned her to face me before we exited the bathroom. "You were always mine."

AATA 2024: THE ANNUAL

We made it just in time for the announcement. I needed to take an extra minute to wipe off all the lipstick from my face before re-emerging in public. Drumroll echoed through the crowd as we stepped next to Essie and Axel. Kiki squeezed Essie's arm as the student body president made a show of opening up an envelope. It was funny to see how she thought Essie was going to be announced.

"And your Prom Queen is... Katherine Madden."

I watched as Kiki continued clapping as the words didn't immediately register with her. Her facial expression changed, completely falling and freezing before her eyes widened and she met my gaze.

I nodded. "You heard that right, my love."

She swallowed hard, as tears misted her eyes, and she quickly blinked them away as I nudged her towards the stage.

"Go," I kissed her forehead as I pushed her, and I watched with pride and happiness as the crowd parted for her and she made her way up onto the stage.

Her cheeks were flushed, and her smile stretched from ear-to-ear.

She was given her crown and a stash before the student president reached for the other envelop.

"And joining us as Prom King is... Matthew Hayes."

I didn't even try to act surprised or fake it as all I wanted was to be by Kiki's side and hold her. She clapped her me, slightly shaking her head in disbelief as I quickly climbed the steps to accept my crown and stash before I reached for her hand and squeezed it.

"And now their first official dance," the student body president announced, vacating the stage for us and all the lights dimmed once again.

It felt like it was just me and her in the whole universe.

"I can't believe you remembered," Kiki whispered as I pulled her into my arms for a slow dance. She rested her head on my shoulder and it never ceased to amaze me how perfectly she fit into my arms. She was made for me.

"I told you I was going to make all your dreams come true, love," I muttered into her ears as we swayed to the slow classical music. "Every single one of them, for the rest of my life, or as long as you have me. I messed up once, but I'm never planning on repeating that mistake again. You and I... we were meant to be. And our road might not have been the smoothest one, but I would go through all this hardship again and again if it leads me back to you. Because you're the real deal, Kiki. You're the love of my life. And that's one thing that will never change, no matter what happens in my life. I love you, and I'm sorry it took me so long to figure it out and come back to you."

Tears spilled from her eyes and rolled down her cheek as she gulped down the knot of emotions clogging her throat. A small sniffle left her as she nodded, tears spilling from both eyes.

"You're my family."

And that one sentence meant more than any long love declaration as it meant she has finally forgiven me fully.

The End

Thank you for reading!

If you enjoyed Matt and Kiki's story and you want to know everything that happened before they got together make sure to check out **Buy-In (Elites of Eastview High #2)**

For Axel and Essie's story ready **High Roller (Elites of Eastview High #1)** and for Natalie and Gabriel's check out **Double or Nothing (Elites of Eastview High #3)**

Raven Seer Beginnings by Paula Acton

Ilyanna watched as the Dragon rose into the sky and began its flight. Her brother and Antonio quickly became little more than specks on the horizon as they disappeared. Turning back to Isha she tried to hide the fear on her face.

"A few days ago, I never even knew I had a brother now everything is changed."

"Change is necessary both personally and for the good of the kingdom." Isha motioned for Ilyanna to join her back in the seating area. "I won't say it's easy or without pain. But if you are brave enough the rewards are more than worth the sacrifice."

"Was it for you? You said you were a fae before you became the Raven Seer, was it worth giving up your freedom to be trapped here in this tower."

"You misunderstand the situation. I am still fae, but I am also more. While it is true I am tethered to this tower and my powers weaken if I stay away too long, I have more freedom now than I have ever had before."

"But you can't leave here. You can't decide to go live somewhere else in the kingdom."

"That is true, but it is also true that I am here because I chose to be. We have a little time while the men undertake their quest, I would like to share my story with you. That is if you would like to hear it?"

"Please. Will you tell me about you and Antonio as well?"

"He is as much a part of my story as I am. He likes to act all gruff and badly treated but as you will hear, he knew exactly what he was getting into. He will be miserable when he eventually joins me here, not that he would ever admit it. Antonio was born and trained to be a warrior, not to sit on a throne and watch others fight his battles."

"What about you? What were you born to do?" Ilyanna pulled her feet up under her, getting comfortable for the story to come.

"I was born as a fae, but I was always destined to be right here, it just took a while for me to learn that. You remember me telling you that there had been another seer who became disenchanted with eternity?"

"Yes, but you never said what became of her."

"I lived in her lands. She has her own isolated island much like my own."

"Has? You mean she is still alive."

"Oh yes, she is immortal. She is happier now she no longer has to concern herself with the lives of others. But that is where my story begins. She was known as The Dream Seer, the Book of Dreams was originally hers. I have no idea where the magic came from that created the book, but she created her island as a paradise, a place of peace and beauty."

"Your land is beautiful too. But how can you not know the source of your power? Surely you must have some idea?"

"I believe it comes from the land itself, you will understand why I think that soon but as I say she created her land and for the longest time the kingdoms lived in peace. She held court on her island, both mortals and fae would mingle, everyone lived in harmony until one day they didn't."

"What changed?"

"Nothing changed and everything changed."

"Do you always talk in contradictions?" Ilyanna looked puzzled.

"No, what I mean is that mortal nature never changed, there will always be some who want more, some willing to take it by force if necessary. What changes is the mortals themselves, they die, others take their places. She was too complacent in the peace she had achieved to notice that some of the people visiting were no longer as happy to accept their place in the bigger picture. They wanted more."

"Like the current lords who rule now?"

"They were not as bad at first. It began with petty border disputes, sheep that wandered onto another's land being claimed by another. By the time she noticed it had begun to evolve into something more. Then there was a murder."

"What?"

"A young lord got into an argument with another while on her island. It was over a woman, the father of the woman believed that the man had insulted his daughter, he had the wrong man but by the time his daughter convinced him it was too late, and the young lord lay slain by his hand."

"But why didn't she see this coming in the book?" Ilyanna leant towards Isha. "How did she not see this coming?"

"Because she thought she had everything under control. She believed her own powers were greater than those of the book. Her own sense of importance had clouded her judgement but that day it all began to crumble. Innocent blood spilled in her own lands poisoned the earth itself. A darkness descended and rather than fight it she withdrew to her tower. Without her light that divides between the kingdom deepened, generation by generation mortals grew greedier, and fought more. Still, she did nothing, until one day in despair she threw the Book Of Dreams out of the tower."

"And you found it?"

"No, not I personally but one of my kind. You see while the mortals fought each other we had done nothing, maybe we were as much to blame as she was for the blight on the kingdoms. We tried our best to heal the earth, but our magic was no match for the evil that rules. We created pockets of land where crops thrived, but no sooner did we manage it that the areas were plundered by others."

"That's terrible, but I have seen so little of the outside world I can hardly imagine it."

"I hope you won't need to, though there will be death and destruction before peace can be restored. However, I jump ahead of myself. The book was found, and the elders gathered together to examine it. Fae are not true immortals. We live many hundreds of years but not forever as such. It is said we fade into the fabric of the kingdom, become part of the magic, even I am not sure where we go eventually but that is a conversation for another day.

At first, they could not make out what was written in the book, the pages were blurred as if the book itself could not see a solution to the problems of the world. I was a young, and foolhardy fae. Far too curious. My parents were two of the elders called upon to examine it and I accompanied them. They placed the book on a table while they sat around talking about it. I swear it called to me. I couldn't help myself, I was drawn to it. I wanted to see what they were all talking about but also, I felt like I had to see it, to touch it."

"And you did?"

"Yes, and the minute I touched the page I was changed. It was like my soul was on fire. I remember seeing light, so bright, blinding. Then, I remember nothing else until I awoke two days later. When I came to everyone was hovering around the edges of the room, only my parents dared to approach me." Isha paused as if it were painful to recall what had happened.

"Were you alright? Had something happened when you touched the book?"

"No one would tell me at first, every time I asked what happened they changed to subject. The first few days after I woke, I still felt tired, but it was a strange feeling, now I know it was my body changing, but at the time I didn't understand. The other thing I remember from those first days was the hum of the book calling to me. I would be talking to my parents, or eating, then, all of a sudden, I would feel it summon me."

"Did you tell anyone?" Concern laced through Ilyanna's voice.

"I told my parents the first few times but the looks of terror on their faces soon silenced me. They weren't scared of me. They were scared for me. Eventually, I was taken back to the room with the book. They all stood around watching as I walked towards it. The pages changed from grey blurs to flights of ravens soaring across the pages. I remember reaching out to touch the book again and my mother stopping my hand. She turned to me and asked if I was sure, that once I touched the book there was no turning back. I don't need to tell you the choice I made."

"You touched the book, but did you pass out again?"

"No. This time the energy flowed into me showing me my destiny with almost complete clarity."

"Almost?"

"Even in the face of magic and destiny we have free will. Antonio is my choice. I loved my family, but I could not remain amongst them. A seer must have space and tranquillity to understand all the messages given to them."

"Who gives you the messages? Where does the power come from?" Ilyanna interjected.

"I cannot tell you. I have my theories, I believe it comes from the very earth itself, but that is not the point of this story. I made the choice to become what I am. I left my home, found this island, created the tower, and the grounds around us. I worked on restoring the balance in the world one village, one field, one tree at a time. Then the book showed me a woman who must live. I had no idea why. I only knew that, somehow, she was linked to the future. I should have used magic to intervene, now I would have, but back then, I was still so new to it all and had yet to learn my limitations."

"Was it my mother?"

"No, but you are correct that you were descended from her. It was your mother's grandmother. She was ill and too poor to buy even the most basic herbs from the apothecary. I went to her bedside and nursed her back to health, but I was fascinated by her. I wanted to understand what possible place this woman could have in destiny."

"Was she special?"

"I wish I could tell you she was remarkable, but she was normal. She was pretty but not beautiful, she was kind but nothing out of the ordinary. Once she was well, she began to question who I was, I told her a story about simply being a traveller who has come upon her cottage while she was ill, and I took my leave from her. But I had stayed away from my tower too long. I did not have the strength to transform and use my powers to return."

"How did you get back?"

"I could still summon my birds. They made sure I was travelling in the right direction. They ensured I had nourishment, in the cold of night they covered me cloaking me with their wings, our body heat sustaining each other. It was during the day that the men found me. They saw a woman alone in the forest miles away from anyone and thought they would have sport at my expense."

"And Antonio came to your rescue?"

Isha laughed. "I have never needed anyone to come to my rescue. When Antonio came upon the scene the birds were feasting upon the carrion. Not just my ravens, but eagles, crows, any bird that ate flesh. Antonio came rushing into the clearing thinking he needed to save the men from this hideous fate. By the time he arrived there was little left, and I was sat on a log watching."

"Didn't that horrify him?"

"If it did, he hid it well." Isha smiled at the remembrance of Antonio discovering her. "He rushed over to me, trying to shield me from the sight, not realising I had enjoyed it. That is another difference between us, one he struggles to understand."

"What do you mean?" Ilyanna pulled her legs up underneath her body. She was both fascinated and a little fearful at where this story was going. It struck her she was alone her with this creature who was speaking so openly about killing others.

"Antonio values life above all else, he would never kill without what he considers a justified cause. He fights for honour and right."

"And you?"

"I see a bigger picture, one where sacrifice is required at times. It doesn't mean I like it. He thinks I do because I do it without a second thought but that is not true, I just don't show my emotions to others. He wears his heart on his sleeve, at least away from the battlefield but I don't have that luxury. This is something you too will learn to understand, for a woman to be seen as strong we can never show weakness, a man can show his compassion without it being to his detriment."

"So, you are saying that I must appear to not care to be seen as strong?" Illyana shifted uncomfortably.

"You have the benefit that you will rule along side your brother, as long as you balance each other out it won't matter as long as you are seen as just and compassionate between you. I don't have that option. I stand alone. I have to make choices not just about what is happening now, but also what will be in years to come."

"So, if the book had told you that either I or my brother must die? You would have sent Antonio to do that? And he would have followed your orders?"

"That upsets you. If the book had showed me the reasons why you must die, and I believed it was for the good of the kingdom as a whole, then, yes. Antonio would have done as I asked, but only because he knows me and trusts me to do the best for the land as a whole, but he wouldn't liked doing it. He would have fought me over it, and trust me we have had so many fights through the years."

"And he always does as you ask?"

"No, not always. There have been the rare occasions where he has begged for time for someone, where he had pled their case. Only once did it ever change anything."

"What happened there?"

"There was a child, destined to become evil. He would become cruel and unfeeling because of the circumstances of his birth. Well, obviously I could not change who his parents were, but something else changed the circumstances. There was a blight on crops, people starved. Even those in the palace he lived in suffered, he would go out to hunt in an attempt to put more food on the table. You see while his father ate his fill, the boy watched his mother go hungry so he could eat. He was around ten summers old at the time, he failed catching anything, but he met a man in the woods, a man who befriended him and helped him. The man taught him to catch food, but the more he took home the more his father ate. He even watched his father feed his dogs rather than let his mother eat."

"That's awful. Why didn't the man teach him to hide the food and take it to his mother directly?"

"Because Antonio could not grasp the nature of such a man, he could not imagine letting the mother of his children starve."

"So, what happened? Did the child learn to be a better man from Antonio?"

"No, the father demanded to know where the child was getting the food. When he refused to say the father killed him and fed him to his dogs."

The colour drained from Illyana's face.

"Antonio swore he would never question my judgement again. The result may have been the same, but I would have made sure it was swift and painless. The father tortured his son first and made the boys mother watch it all. I would never order the death of anyone on a whim, I only ever do so after carefully studying all the variables and potential outcomes. I do not like the things I send Antonio to do but watching his heart break over that boy brought out the worst in me. It is one of the few times I have acted with pure vengeance. I burnt the castle to the ground with everyone in it."

"Including the mother?"

"No, she had passed before I took out my anger on them." Isha's eyes burnt with fury as though she were relieving the events. "He questions my love for him but he has no need, I love him more than any other being in this realm."

"How did he end up falling in love with you if you met under such gruesome circumstances?"

"I was still weak and needed to get back here as quickly as possible. He had no idea what I was or what I was capable of, and I was not honest with him. I am ashamed of that, even though he knows it all now and has forgiven me. I allowed him to gather me in his arms and place me on his horse. I rode cuddled against his chest, I can't explain it to someone who has never loved or felt the chemistry, but I knew that very first day that I would never be able to let him go."

"But you don't use magic to keep him with you?"

"No, I have never needed to. He felt the same way I did, each time we made contact, skin to skin, it was like a fire coursing through my veins. It wasn't until we returned here that anything really happened between us. I still remember that first kiss. I had ordered a meal for us and we had talked, I mean really talked. I had told him what I was, we drank some wine, and then we laid under the stars and talked some more. At some point he leaned over and as his lips touched mine the world fell away."

"And you knew you knew you loved him?"

"I knew I wanted him; love came a little later. We should rest now; I will tell you more of the story tomorrow."

Monstrous Grave by Rainelyn

A Dark Forbidden Taboo Romance

Prologue
Arcane, 20 Years Old

The night sky looms ominously overhead, shrouded in darkness and devoid of stars—a foreboding shadow cast over this sinister mansion.

I wonder if you have felt it—the tug-of-war between the realms of goodness and evil, balancing on that line between right and wrong, knowing that one misstep could plunge you into a horror so profound, it threatens to corrupt you.

I know you have, my dear brother.

It's there, isn't it? That festering darkness staining your soul, tearing away at its flesh piece by piece. It's why you seek solace in my darkness. We're two halves of a shattered mirror, bound by the agony of our shared existence. You slice into my skin with every glance, only to leave me bleeding in your aftermath.

Another sound shatters the stillness, and I snap to attention, the peaceful rhythm of my heart transforming into a wild one against the cage of my ribs—almost as if I can feel it beating outside my chest. With fists closing around the duvet, I wait, terror thrumming through my veins. My gaze fixates on the balcony perched on the second floor of this sprawling mansion.

Is it an intruder? If it is, the guards patrolling the perimeters would take care of it. But my foster parents have never cared, especially not my father.

Tonight, even the moon's light fails to calm me, knowing that someone dangerous is waiting outside on my balcony. Like a warning alarm, every nerve ending in my body buzzes with apprehension.

I glimpse a shadowed figure standing motionless, a silent sentinel with a menacing aura. With wide-open eyes, I stare at him, afraid that if I blink, I'll miss his actions. A force thrashes against the confines of my ribcage, desperate to break free, while I anticipate his strike.

I know it's him, he's always entering my room uninvited.

Yet, his presence offers a sense of protection, knowing I'm secure in a world filled with predators. Even with how much I want to deny it, he makes me feel safe in a way no one else can, though we're both corrupted. It's sick, wrong, twisted—are siblings supposed to act like this?

Is it wrong to seek solace in each other after fourteen years of living under the same roof, even if he's only my foster brother?

The shadowy presence now observes me, his gaze piercing through the sheets surrounding my resting frame, and I instinctively pull the duvet tighter around me.

A silent presence in the night, he stands there, merely waiting, watching, observing.

He's lingering outside, not only protecting me but also anticipating the moment when terror will strike me. Then, he will pounce without hesitation.

He wasn't always like this—he used to be kind, with a smile that could shatter your heart with the beauty of it, like a rainbow splitting the sky. Now, his demeanor has grown colder, marked by broken bones and bruises. His once warm manners are replaced by a chilling one, giving way to an unwavering intensity. He's dangerous. Our father changed him with the family's shady business. Dealings I'm not privy to know about. But, in the dead of the night is where he thrives, and that's when he can truly be himself.

He craves the fear he instills in me. His predatory smirk makes beastly insects fly around my stomach like a crush I can't have on my own fucking brother, and tingling sensations between my legs. I wish there was some way to cut the emotions out, leaving me bleeding dry so I wouldn't feel safe with this predator.

"We're going to play a little game, you and I," he had whispered earlier in the morning, his words laced with mystery.

He refused to elaborate more and left me both intrigued and hesitant, never knowing the true extent of his intentions.

Ever since we met at the orphanage when I was seven and he was nine, there has been an enigmatic force around him that slithered its way into my soul, gripping my heart and refusing to let go of his claws.

Our foster parents, who adopted us two years later, remain oblivious to the intricate threads that bind us together. They will never understand the connection we share, nor the despair of being homeless with no one to care for you or keep you safe. They see us simply as two children they took in, expecting our close bond will be severed now that we're adults.

My brother's warnings about our foster parents rang true the moment we first stepped foot into the manor and I saw everyone discreetly wearing guns for the first time. I instantly knew something was off. Our new father's eyes glinted with malice, his jaw ticking with an unrelenting anger. Within a month of arriving, my brother's demeanor shifted, and he became more lethal and aggressive; the hidden traits of his personality filtering through the facade he constructed around me. Other times, he accompanied our father at the shooting range. I never understood the reason for it until years later.

They had shattered his innocence, replacing it with something far more lethal. Days would pass, and I'd catch glimpses of bruises littering his skin, serving as haunting reminders of how much my life had changed since living at the orphanage. We were thrust into a treacherous world, forced to navigate a place where enemies lurked in every corner we hid.

Now, as the years have unfolded, the opulent manor we inhabit is secured by a plethora of guards scattered across the perimeters of our lawn. I find myself sheltered, a pawn in a game much bigger than I will ever be able to comprehend. All the while my brother is condemned to endure all the horrors that come with living here.

My eyes land on the figure outside once more, his head tipped back, allowing half of his face to become bathed in the glowing moonlight. His sharp cheekbones emerge, tracing a confident path against his face—a magnificent masculine elegance.

He observes me the same way I've observed him for the past few weeks, with a sense of foreboding hanging thick in the atmosphere, an intensity that could slice through the air like a sharp knife, and a lethal curiosity.

He watches me with those deep brown eyes that see through the depths of my soul, able to tell my own emotions even when I cannot decipher them myself.

After what feels like an eternity, the balcony door eventually creaks open. The sound echoes within my mind, my heart a madman inside my chest. I can't breathe, the anticipation of what's going to happen wreaks havoc inside of me.

As the door opens all the way, he slips through the opening and steps into my room without making a sound.

Like a dangerous shadow, he pauses on the threshold with a reluctance that makes his shoulders tense. He knows this is wrong, entering my room at night when everyone is none the wiser. None of that deters my brother, though, as he takes another step, the balcony door left open behind him. It allows the wind to graze its chilling touch over my bare arms, freezing me underneath the blanket. My breath hitches as he comes forward.

Closer.

Even closer.

Until he stands right by the side of the bed, his brown eyes filled with so much intensity and depth as he takes in my appearance. It's as if the darkness of the room obscures the color, making them look all black. One eye is swollen, yet another bruise forming that has me swallowing a lump in my throat, especially as it colors him purple and black.

It's a strange combination of hues, and I despise seeing him hurt, nausea churning me from the inside out.

I observe his chest rising and falling, compelled to reach out and touch his cheek, an irresistible urge to draw closer. Worry glazes over me as I notice his slight wince before my hand even makes contact. He's quicker than me, capturing my wrist in his large palm and holding it in a tight grip.

The firm shake of his head causes his hair to fall over his eyes, and a look of warning crosses his face.

Don't touch me, he mouths.

I inhale sharply, tension building in my throat as I fixate on his eyes, nearly covered by long, black lashes that used to make me jealous while growing up. All the girls in school were prettier than me, though my brother always told me I was the prettiest. He never looked at them the way he looked at me, with equal amounts of adoration and a need to protect.

We were each other's, and no one else had the chance to even get close to us.

Now, though, all I wish is for him to let me touch him because I can tell that something is wrong and not only is it the bruise forming on his eye. There's an urgency in his voice, one that jolts through my body in an electric current and causes goosebumps to skitter across my skin.

I allow my gaze to shift to where his hand grips my wrist, still as tightly as before, and then I meet his eyes again, evidently darkening with intensity.

"A game, remember?" he whispers, his voice piercing through the silence that has descended over the room.

An odd sensation takes over me on the inside, like a vise gripping my heart in its hold before squeezing the life out of me. Confusion laces all of my actions and makes me unable to utter a word. I merely stare at him. Meanwhile, he cocks an eyebrow, waiting for me to reply.

I know he's always loved hearing me talk, wanting me to read him bedtime stories even when he's the older one, but now I won't give him the satisfaction of it. He doesn't deserve to hear the sound of my voice when he won't elaborate on what's going on.

It feels like minutes pass when the only thing occupying the room is an intense and uncomfortable silence full of emotions I cannot put into words. My eyes flicker to the world outside the window and how the trees move in the harsh breeze, gently lit by the still-glowing moonlight.

The grip on my wrist hardens, and I do my best not to let out a yelp from the slight burn of pain. That would only make him even more satisfied. Eventually, I'm forced to obey him when the grip never relents, his nails only digging deeper into my skin.

"What kind of game?"

With defiance, I stare into his eyes, although I don't feel nearly as daring as I try to sound. My voice is a hoarse whisper after a night of sleeping, and I'm definitely not as composed as he is right now.

His demeanor is always posed with a lethal calm that could make the strongest enemy relent, a trait I'm sure he acquired once we were adopted into the Grimaldi family.

The corners of his thick lips twitch into a cryptic smile that gives way for nothing else. "A game of survival."

My eyebrows must be scrunching in confusion because those lips of his curl further, staring down at me with a look that has me shuddering, not knowing if I should be afraid or feel safe in his presence.

"You will see. But it's a game that requires you to be observant. Trust no one but yourself and always keep an eye on your surroundings." His voice is low and demanding, making chills dance across my body while I listen intently, clinging to every word he utters. "Don't crash into the waves."

His last sentence rings out in my head like a repeating echo, words I've heard many times before when I've needed reassurance from the cruel world we live in.

"Trust no one but you, right?"

An audible sigh slips from his lips as he looks down at me, and I observe the subtle tightening of his jaw, a habitual gesture he often displays.

His head tilts to the side, but I cannot tell what it's for. Every action he makes stirs confusion within me, creating a vortex of uncertainty and leaving me slightly rattled. A creeping sense of terror slowly comes into my subconscious, telling me that something might be amiss yet again.

"Can you do that for me?" His words are laced with a serious tone that takes me aback.

Despite that, I nod my head, still unsure of what his intentions are as my mind races with apprehension.

He has always been a mystery; a puzzle to be solved where I was the only one who had the key to open up these puzzle pieces. Yet, at this moment, it's as if I've lost that key temporarily, unable to understand him.

"Your words, please."

It's the first time I've heard him ask for something.

The sense of urgency emanating from him sparks a desperate impulse in me, an overwhelming desire to claw at his hand and keep him close to me forever. As if I could anchor him to my side by sheer force.

Somewhere deep within my subconscious is a voice telling me this is it, this is goodbye.

And that makes me want to scream my throat out until nothing is left within me to fight for.

This is all too cryptic; my throat is clogged with untold emotions that feel like a tumultuous sea, and I am a boat fighting to stay afloat against the lethal waves of death.

I swallow. "Yes."

He nods his head, accepting my words for what they are, meanwhile, his fists clench. "Close your eyes," his request is barely a whisper, yet it commands compliance, and I obey.

With my eyes closed tightly shut, my heart pounds hard within me; each thud mirroring the seconds that slowly pass. With a pulse spiking into unnatural heights, it's as if I'm going to pass out at any moment from anticipation poised with unease. The unmistakable scent of his sandalwood cologne along with leather—coming from the glove he uses to cover his scarred hand—permeates my nostrils.

Nervousity taking over, I glance at the clock standing on my nightstand beside him, noticing that it's eleven fifty-nine p.m.

In my periphery, I sense him drawing nearer, and my breath quickens at his closeness. The clock ticks, signaling the start of a new day at midnight.

"Happy birthday, Arcane," he whispers in a hoarse voice that sends butterflies slicing up my insides.

It's a strange concoction of emotions; one entirely unwelcome, with dread seeping through to my marrow, and the other inciting a flutter of beastly insects within me, akin to a teenage crush.

Without a second to comprehend what's happening, the warmth of his minty brushes against my lips. My heart combusts as he presses his lips against mine, bruising and punishing in its hold. It's intimate, stirring a storm deep within me.

I lose myself in the kiss as his tongue prods my lips, pushing inside and tangling with my own. He's brutal in his kiss, demanding and pushing, never leaving me time to breathe. One hand slides to my throat, encircling it with a pressure that tightens with each passing second, silently demanding my submission. He restricts the air entering my lungs, and a whimper escapes me.

It's a bruising kiss made of lies and deceit.

My eyes close automatically, wanting to savor the feel of his lips on mine. Then, he slips away, his hand leaving my throat and lips leaving mine, and I don't open my eyes. Even long after I hear the balcony door closing and his fragrance subtly fading away from my room, I cannot bring myself to re-open them.

For a short moment after, I find myself smiling, until his strange composure comes back to me, and the weight of that small kiss sends a jolt of despair through my entire being, akin to what I imagine being infected with a flawed vaccine.

It was a wordless and bittersweet farewell etched with tenderness and cruelty as he took my heart in his hold, along with my soul, shredding it apart with his bare hands.

And as dawn breaks, the painful truth hits hard like an unrelenting storm, mercilessly tearing through my fragile peace of mind. The word 'dead' lingers in the air, heavy and suffocating, spoken from my foster parents' mouths.

A train wreck.

He steered me away from an impending crash against the cliffs and the tempting waves that whispered promises of a tranquil descent. In doing so, he spared me from the suffocating yet alluring embrace that could have plunged everything into a serene silence. Ironically, he never followed his own path of advice.

And now, he is gone.

AATA 2024: THE ANNUAL

The full book will be released on 10th July

The Betrayal by Ruby Bloom

Dear reader

This is a snippet from my upcoming dark mafia romance book, the second in the Zakarian Syndicate Series. The Betrayal follows the youngest Zakarian sister, Arpina, and the Zakarian family consigliere, Ardian, who is tasked with chaperoning her in Las Vegas for six months as she courts her fiancé before an arranged marriage.

For the first instalment, read book one, The Vow. For further history read my MC romance crossover series, The Black Coyotes MC. More books in both series are coming soon!

Tropes and triggers: Enemies to lovers, dark romance, some physicality, threat of harm, arranged marriage themes, mental health battle.

~ Arpina ~

The night was all going swimmingly until she was violently grabbed from behind.

Dragged roughly backwards, by a strong, hard hand around her stomach. Quick as lightning. Too quick to scream, too quick to breathe.

Her back slammed into a hard body behind her, and another hand clamped over her mouth.

Like whiplash down her spine, she felt sick at the rate with which she was yanked into the dark alleyway, away from the streetlights and the people. Away from the night she had planned. The life that was laid out at her feet. She wanted to marry Tigran, the casino owner, the eldest son to the second largest Armenian mafia family in the Southwest. She wanted to be bought pretty things and dress up for the evening and look like a Rolex watch on his wrist. Like something he wanted to show off, something that sparkled under the lights and then was put away in a soft, velvet cushioned box at the end of the day. She wanted softness and a plush, easy, happy life. Didn't she?

She kicked. She struggled and flailed with her arms. Her flimsy sequinned dress rucked up at the hem and pulled down at the neckline, she felt the hot night air of Vegas on newly exposed skin. She squeezed her eyes shut and whimpered. What was she to be the victim of? She accepted her fate, she felt her dreams wash away from her, like a pebble being dragged back into the sea, powerless against the inevitable pull of the tide.

Her heart was banging fast against her ribs, adrenaline flooding her bloodstream. She couldn't grip the floor, her stiletto strap-on sandals were useless. Pretty, elegant shoes for strutting about the casino like the owner's fiancée she was. Not the kind of shoes you want to get kidnapped in.

Fuck fuck fuck. She was in trouble. She was pinned against her kidnapper's chest now. He was pulling her against him. A hard chest, a warm chest. A male chest. No, she didn't want this. She didn't want it taken from her, by him, like this. She prayed silently for help. For absolution. Was he going to take her away? Mistreat her? Manhandle her? Demand a ransom? Was she now in for a rough ride? The trappings of her safe, little, glitzy, soft life melted away in front of her. This was going to hurt.

The panic was bubbling up inside her now. Suffocating. What was happening? Where was she being taken? Who by?

Where was Ardian? Her boring, stoic, follow-the-rules bodyguard? Her father's consigliere, tasked with chaperoning her around Vegas for a six-month engagement with her fiancé? She had told Ardian to fuck off earlier that night, that's where he was. He was constantly cramping her style, constantly no, she couldn't go there, couldn't do this, couldn't dress like that. And he clearly looked down his nose at her, held her in such contempt, like she wasn't worth his time, and that fucking irked her because everyone else worshipped the ground she walked on.

She'd told him to disappear, so he had. And now, fuck, he was right. She should have paid attention to his warnings. He always said, if she wasn't careful, something bad would happen. She was as good as royalty. He treated her like she was first in line to the throne, anyway. Youngest daughter of the most powerful Armenian crime family in the Southwest states. The Zakarian Syndicate held respect, fear, love, power, and she was the pretty, sparkly jewel in the middle of the crown.

She hadn't been careful; she hadn't heeded his warnings. She had wanted to go and party with the others and now...

She tried to force her mouth open. Her kidnapper's hands were strong, clamped on her jawbone. Her lipstick would be smudging, she knew it, she wanted to get her teeth free. She tried to bite, to lick. Not that a lick would put off some hardened kidnapper, but still.

She snorted air through her half-exposed nose and managed to issue a little shriek, pulling her head away, and she felt his hand loosen a little. He put his finger in her mouth, squashing her tongue. She found herself sucking and biting his finger. He didn't budge. She let out a louder muffled yell. She wanted to fight further. He was big and tall and strong, and he could take her anywhere, do anything he wanted with her.

It terrified her. Her life, unravelling in an instant.

It thrilled her. It freed her.

She felt his face next to her cheek now. Stubble. His chin pressing into her cheek, every muscle in his body trying to hold her back. But she felt something stirring at this proximity to him. His obvious maleness. Everything about him, the tension humming through his body. She was so aware of how big and strong and hard he was, and how small she felt in his arms. She wanted things that she knew she shouldn't. And here she was, in the arms of a stranger.

"Quiet!" he hissed. She couldn't hear properly. The blood pounded in her ears too loudly. His voice was deep and urgent and rough. Her heartbeat quickened.

His body enveloped her from behind. Such heat. Such strength. She pushed against it, pushed and pulled with all her might. He shook her, pulling her back into him, almost shushing her.

His face was still on her cheek. His mouth right next to her earlobe. She felt his breath, and she was surprised. It humanized him. He was panting too. His breath was shallow, skittering across her face, carrying a few strands of her flyaway hair. Was he nervous? Was he a seasoned kidnapper, or was this his first time?

Everything was getting tangled and confused now. She knew she should want to escape. And yet she had never felt safer. Her brain was telling her to run back to the light, but her body wanted to stay warm, right here. She had been so sure she was on the right path, and now she wanted to walk right off into the wilderness. Hot skin and muscles pulling, pushing, straining. Tiring. Fast breath, was it his or hers? She panted, he panted. She gasped, he gasped. What was it she was wanting to escape from? Who was it she was wanting to escape from? Him? Or herself?

She yanked her head free and took a gasp of air. "Please!" she managed to yell out. "Please!" she didn't know what she was begging for. She didn't know what she was praying for anymore.

Her body hurt from fighting, the lactic acid, the lack of oxygen and the spike of adrenaline in her blood taking its toll. Wanting payback. She felt his immutable strength and she sagged a little into his arms, a little mewl escaping her now-husky throat.

Into his chest. Into his warmth. Into him. What did he want from her? What did the universe want from her? She was meant to play the part of the mafia wife. Wasn't she? She was meant to be the demanding princess; she was meant to be paired off with her eligible bachelor-mobster casino-owning fiancé. He was meant to buy her pretty things and keep her as a trophy wife. They were meant to look good together at parties. That was what she thought the universe wanted from her. That was the part she had been playing, the part she had wanted to play. Wasn't it?

And now, she felt the pull of something else. Something more. Something warmer. Not the shimmer of the diamonds, not the smell of the new designer handbags and the plush interior of a sports car. Not the soft feather trim of her silk dressing gown and the real fur coating of her kitten heel slippers. Something raw and rough and alive and infinite.

The man around her. The sheer heat from his body. Not just heat, there was something else. And it engulfed her and flowed into her too. She realized she wasn't fighting him, they were locked together in a spiral, in a tornado, they were both spinning wildly around, blown by forces they didn't understand, clinging onto each other.

"Please, please," they were both breathing it together.

She felt his hand on her throat, his arm around her stomach, his hand clasping her hip. She leant her head back into the crook of his chest and gasped up to the night sky.

And he gasped too, right beside her, and the arm on her stomach, pushed differently now. It ground her butt into his crotch. And she arched her back slightly to get more. To feel more. To give more.

She raised her arm up, using her hand to feel for him. She felt his head, his hair, her hand trailed down, she needed to hold, to grip onto something. She felt a slight stubble of his cheeks, his jaw. It humanized him further. He wasn't a monster; he was a man.

Her other hand found his thigh, his butt. Hard as iron underneath whatever pants he was wearing. She rubbed her body backwards harder, and... there it was. Something she hadn't felt before. Something else hard. His cock. The boys she'd dated kissed her from arms reach. They bought her pretty, expensive things and linked arms with her, held their fancy car doors open for her. Held her hand and stroked her cheek. They didn't let her anywhere near their hard-on's. They worried her dad would chop it off if he found out his precious youngest daughter had been anywhere near their cocks.

"Fuck," she heard him mutter. She heard it through the ear pressed to his chest, through his skin and bone, through her skin and bone. "Fucking...hell, this isn't what should be happening...oh my fucking god... this is too fucking good..."

She wanted him to stop talking, and yet, she wanted him to talk to her like this forever. Soft whispers in the darkness. This close to him, so close that she could feel his heart beating in his warm chest. She could smell him, his aftershave yes, but even the soap he used in the shower, the laundry detergent to wash his clothes. She could smell his skin.

But this man... he didn't seem to care who her daddy was in that moment. He used her hip to grind his cock into her butt harder. She felt alive and free, and she wanted to push it further.

She closed her eyes, tilted her head up, opened her lips, and kissed him.

He stopped talking and froze. His lips were warm and soft. Softer than she could have imagined. She crushed her lips against his, harder, committed now. Invested. Kissing her kidnapper. The ball of twine that had been her life's plan was unravelled now in a heap on the floor. What more could a few extra tugs to the ruined reel do?

He almost pulled away. She felt a moment of hesitation at her escalation. So, she pulled back. Pulled on his neck and his thigh, pushed her lips into his.

And his opened. His tongue flicked out and lathed the inside of her mouth. She gasped, and returned, hungry, oh so hungry for more. She shouldn't be doing this; she couldn't stop herself though. She kissed more, licking at his tongue and the inside of his mouth, feeling the heat, the wetness.

She heard him groan. And shiver. The hand on her hip moved from her hip. It moved under her dress. Between her legs.

She gasped now and shivered. His fingers went low, straight away feeling his way into her. There was no hesitation in the way he moved. No pawing about. Straight there, pushing his fingers into the untouched, burning place she barely knew about herself. A part aching, longing to be touched, to be relieved of the heaviness she felt there.

She was shaking now. She felt it, but she kept going, kissing him through the thunderstorm inside her. His fingers thrust in and out, mercilessly, repetitively. He was fucking her. That's what this was, she hadn't imagined it could be like this. But that is what he was doing. And she could barely breathe. The pressure within her, it hurt. And he was both multiplying it and easing it, all in one go.

His fingers dipped out for a moment. Her eyelids flew open, and she heard herself scream softly. But his hand only dipped long enough for his fingers to find her clit. Which he immediately massaged. A fast, hard, circular rub.

Oh God he knew what he was doing. Oh God it was too much, it was too good. Too wild. Too hot. Too wet. All of it. Too much. She pulled her mouth away from his lips, squeezed her eyes tightly shut and screamed. Loudly.

Howled.

And trembled.

And came. A hard, snapping, hungry orgasm. Her core clenching and pulsing again and again, as she shook in his arms. Shook to a new beat, one that she knew in that moment, she'd be seeking and craving and wanting for the rest of her life. One that she would be hungry for, forever.

This man was no kidnapper. He was no threat. He was her rescuer, her redeemer, the answer to her prayers.

He let out a muffled moan, releasing his hold on her a second.

It was all she needed. She took the opportunity, wrenching herself from his arms, breaking the connection. Breaking the spell. Breaking the faith.

She turned and stared through the low light into the man's face.

Her heart dropped out of her body. Spluttering in a messy heap on the floor, trying to keep beating. Flailing. Failing. Sickeningly instant, warm, sticky feelings exploded within her.

"Ardian!" she gasped.

~ Ardian ~

Holy fuck. He hated her. He hated how she had scowled and shook off his arm and stomped away from him in the club earlier. He hated how he was having to baby-sit her for this farce of a courtship in sweaty stinking Vegas. He hated how she was an absolute brat and looked down on him like he was dirt on her little designer shoes. But most of all right now, he hated how she made him feel.

Because in that moment, he felt like he was about to explode. The pressure in his cock was unbearable. The pressure in his chest was something else. He couldn't breathe. He was that suffocated with how he felt in that moment, that he simply couldn't breathe. Couldn't function. It was a miracle he was still standing because she was honestly bringing him to his knees with desire.

He had never felt desire for her. He'd never felt anything other than pure annoyance. And impatience. She wasn't his kind of woman. She was an 18-year-old spoiled brat. She's been misbehaving the whole time they were in Vegas. And she'd fucking pushed him over the edge earlier that night.

Ardian thought back to earlier. She disappeared in the casino night club. They were all in there, her fiancée, Tigran. His harem of beautiful, vacuous women who he was clearly rotating round in his bed every night. And he had the fucking gall to drag Pina out to sit alongside them all. His meathead friends and bodyguards too. All quaffing vodka and champagne like it was heading for extinction. He stalked to the bar but one glance around in the flashing blue and purple lights told him that she wasn't there.

A high-pitched giggle from the smoking area had caught his attention over the thump of the base of the music playing loudly. He had prowled over there ready to sink his claws into her when he eventually found her. She didn't smoke, she shouldn't be hanging around breathing second hand smoke-

But there she was, with a few of the girls from Tigran's harem. She was trailing after those girls like a fucking lost puppy, determined to prove herself, determined to keep up with them. Ardian tutted, didn't she see, she was who they should be following, not the other way round?

Ardian had marched all the way up to her, grabbed her elbow and hissed in her ear. "Pina, what the fuck do you think you are doing?"

She turned to him, surprise on her pretty face. Her dark hair was straight and up in a ponytail that flicked him as she turned her head to him. Her perfume wafted into his nostrils. Ardian let go of her bare arm. She was wearing a barely-there dress of creamy lace and sequins that Ardian thought belonged in the bedroom rather than as a going-out dress, but what the fuck did he know about fashion? Fuck all. He did know about basic personal safety though. And right now, Pina Zakarian was flaunting her blatant disregard for her own safety in his face. And as her bodyguard and chaperone, Ardian would be left to pick up the pieces if it all went to shit.

Pina rolled her eyes theatrically. "Ardian, I'm just talking to these charming men, Derek and…" she giggled drunkenly and tottered on her heels a little. Ardian narrowed his eyes. How much had she had to drink? The other man, the one whose name she had forgotten, reached out to catch her. He put his hand on her back. But then it lingered and slipped down unnecessarily low. Ardian almost growled.

"The other girls are going," she grabbed Ardian's forearm, and hissed to Ardian crossly under her breath. Ah, so she did know what she was doing, huh? Tigran's harem of beautiful party girls were just that. Girls who looked sparkly under the neon lights of the bar for one night, who you could be entertained by shoving your cock down their throat and snorting cocaine off their fake tits, but that was all they were. One-nighters. Tigran kept them around him because he was incapable of entertaining himself. He needed babysitting. But look closely and they rotated. Frequently. It would be Jolana and Arabell for the first week. Then it was Heidi, Lula and Frankie for the second week. Ardian pretty sure their make-up was flaky; their dresses were cheap, and they had as much depth as the stingy martini's they clung to.

Ardian shook his head. "Yes, but you aren't the other girls-"

"Ardian, I'm just having some fun, Tigran said I can have some fun-"

"He didn't say go make a fool out of yourself-"

She immediately pouted and frowned, pushing her hand off his arm like she had been burnt by it.

He'd gone too far; she'd go wild now just to annoy him. Just to retaliate for that comment. Fuck.

Ardian pursed his lips. "I've told you before, you are going to be Tigran's wife, head of the family, you should behave differently, with decorum-"

One of the girls lurched over. "We're all going back to Derek's hotel suit; they are having a party-"

Ardian answered for Pina, "there is no way she is going-"

"Sure!" Pina talked over Ardian, "I'd love to go!"

Ardian's heart sunk in his chest.

She'd shaken him off and he'd lost his patience and stormed back to the car, slammed the door shut behind him and pounded his fists into the steering wheel. But fuck it, he felt guilty. He was being paid to protect her. She was a brat, yes, but she was his brat, his ward. She was his.

It was only meant to be a silly stunt to scare her. He'd gone back for her, of course, as he did, as he always would. He saw her tottering along in her barely there dress and her high heels, giggling with the other girls. Heading off to someone's hotel suite to party. Well, he'd have her home by midnight, tucked up safe and sound and no longer his problem. Even if he had to pick her up and carry her away. That would result in a terse call from her Daddy, but Ardian was past the point of caring for the old man's opinions by now. Ardian would probably find himself with a bullet in his back by sunup too, but at least it would say on his tombstone that he was loyal to the end.

So, he'd crept up behind, any self-respecting mafia man knows the basics of stalking up and grabbing someone from behind, after all. He wasn't being too rough, but he wanted to hold her firm. He wanted to scare her a little. Unsettle her. Show her how easy it was for someone to harm her if she wasn't paying attention and following his security advice.

And it had been going fine. He could tell she was scared. She was genuinely trying to fight him off. He was subduing her, he felt nothing but annoyance that once again Arpina Zakarian had pushed him to take extreme, ridiculous measures to keep her safe from her own stupidity.

She was writhing about all over the place, trying to push him off. He pressed himself into her, to try to get her to keep still. He'd planned on spinning her round and revealing himself, teaching her a lesson. She'd stomp and huff about it but hopefully it would show the kind of danger she put herself under when she didn't listen to him.

However, he hadn't bargained on how rapidly her surprised shriek would kick a hard-on into his pants. How aware he'd be of her soft mouth underneath his palm. How her lips and tongue would feel under his fingers. How much he wanted her to fight it, fight him. But how much he wanted to win. To overpower her. To possess her. She was his.

Fuck.

He liked to be rough with women in bed, he knew that. He made it clear that's what it involved if any woman wanted to be with him.

But this was next level. This was starting an ache within him that he knew he wouldn't be able to relieve. It was exciting him.

And then she had done something that had completely knocked him down. She had reached a hand up, stroked him, sighed wantonly in his arms, then kissed him.

And his world had spiralled out of its axis, and he'd found himself kissing her back. Touching her. Reaching down into her little panties and finding her core.

And fuck him, if she wasn't all wet and ready for him. And he'd pushed, giving to her, revelling in giving, in her melting more and more into him, becoming a part of him, attaching herself to his heart and soul. Fuck it. And he'd pushed until she'd exploded.

He was right along with her, her spasming and gasping in his arms, he was so close, he was about to follow her into the cosmos, he was-

"Ardian!" She had spun around, gasped, and unmasked him.

And that was when something inside him snapped. He felt it. Something moved, and it could never move back again. He wasn't sure yet if it was good or bad, but it was profound.

He cleared his throat. Unsure what to say, what to do. She continued to stare. Wide eyed, panting still after her orgasm. Hair all over the place.

He panted too, his hard-on refusing to bow out of the occasion, even though it was obvious relief would not be coming his way anytime soon. Fuck, the hard-on she's been grinding her tight little butt into seconds ago. The hard-on he had wanted to slip inside that hot, warm little cunt of hers and pound her into the next fucking galaxy-

"Ardian, I... it's, just I..." She stuttered, biting her lip, searching his face for an answer.

He didn't have one. Fuck it, he had nothing. No explanation of that, no warning, no clue what had happened or what was coming next.

"Hreshtak," he said with a hoarse voice. He called her the Armenian name for angel. It had started as a joke, it was meant to be ironic, because she wasn't an angel, she was a bratty terror and Ardian was constantly tasked with cleaning up the maelstrom she left in her wake. But in that moment, it felt like she could be an angel, for him. He felt a funny, silly, almost drunk hope bubble up in him. His angel. She could be his angel. She was his.

But no, she could never be his. He was a low born servant to her family, basically. And he'd just betrayed them.

He was nothing and she was everything. He couldn't ever let himself slip like that again. He would fight it, he would deny it, he felt the walls closing in. Even though they were outside, that panic welled up in him again. His breath whooshed out of his lungs as his panic attack took hold.

He tried to hide it, he turned away, head down, hiding in his head in his arms. He gasped for air; he was drowning in it all. The betrayal. He was such a traitor. He betrayed his family; he shot his own brother. He betrayed the Zakarian's, the family that his father and his father before that had worked for.

And now he'd done something he shouldn't have with the youngest daughter. He'd felt things he shouldn't have. He'd touched her where he shouldn't have. He'd let her in where he shouldn't have. He hated himself. He didn't hate her, he hated himself for letting her get to him, in whatever way she now had.

He was spiralling out of control, and he had no idea how to pull up, how to manoeuvre out of the tailspin he was in. The nosedive. He gasped and gasped, and faced away from Pina and couldn't bring himself to look at her, to imagine what she would be thinking.

Deep breaths. Deep. In and hold. And out. And in again. And hold again. And out. Slowly.

He did that again. Each breath lasted a second and a century at the same time. He felt the night return to him, the noises of people passing by further away, and cars, and music. He saw the streetlights now. He felt her. Watching him. Her face, unreadable.

"I'm taking you back home, Pina," was all he managed to croak out of his sore throat.

But there was no coming back from this. He knew that. He would fight it, of course. Life was a fight and Ardian had always faced odds stacked against him. He couldn't let any of this happen again. The panic attack, the kiss, fuck, the explosion of aches in his chest that he felt she left him with in her wake. None of it. And yet, he already knew, things couldn't go back. He hated that he no longer hated her. He hated that she could never be his.

Notorious Legacy #1 by Sophie Dyer

This is a snippet of an upcoming project that will be the next generation of The Notorious Five.

~ Alanis ~

Love doesn't come easy when your family leads one of the notorious organized crime gangs of New York City. Life isn't easy when you're battling morals, jobs, and broken promises. There's also a razor thin line between love and hate, and I tread so close to it that sometimes I struggle to discern the difference.

I know, because I *love* hating Roman Genovese. And I *hate* that once upon a time, I may have loved him. It's funny what the young mind can perceive as love; how naïve we can be when we're too immature to know any better. But I know now. It wasn't love I felt—it was lust. Obscene lust that blinded me, and Roman took full advantage of that, like the manipulative bastard he is.

That's what fuels the burning sense of loathing in the pit of my stomach. Anger is the first emotion I feel when I think of him, quickly followed by the desire to drive a knife through his stupidly pretty face.

I'd never do it. It'd cause a war between families, and the alliance we have forged has done ridiculously well in this city. My father makes up just one of The Notorious Five. Axel Bonanno is the founder of the organization; the one everyone fears, respects, and bows to. He inherited the position from my great uncle, a man who betrayed his family just to gain a sliver of power over the city. It's one of the reasons my father built his legacy the way he did; not just for the Bonanno name, but for his brother's bound by loyalty: Colombo, Lucchese, Gambino, and Genovese. Together, they're the five pillars that became the leading crime syndicate in New York City, and now my father is handing his legacy down to the next heir, my twin brother Alvaro.

Tonight, we're celebrating his new title as leader of the Bonanno family. A while back, my father decided it was finally time to step down and let my twin take the reins, so he's been preparing for retirement, making plans with my mom to spend more quality time together. Of course, Alvaro can't wait to prove himself to Dad. *Not that he has to.* My dad thinks the sun pretty much shines out of every orifice when it comes to my brother. He can't do anything wrong in his eyes, even when he fucks up.

Unfortunately, it's a different story for me entirely. I'm not exactly daughter of the year—or the past five years, for that matter—since I declared that I didn't want to be a part of the family business. It's not that I don't agree with what our families do, it's just that my passions lie elsewhere. Mom's totally on my side, and so is my Aunt Lexie, but Dad's still on the fence about setting me free. Actually, he's more on the other side of the fence, giving me the evil eye from afar. Even tonight my father stands across the room, seemingly in deep conversation with Uncle Noah, but I know his attention is firmly on me. Too bad the intensity of his glare only encourages me to act out. Nothing I do is ever good enough, so defying him has become a talent I've honed.

My gaze bounces through the crowd, taking in the groups of friends and family clinking glasses and laughing over the music. Everyone's here tonight; the Gambinos, Luccheses... even the O'Sullivans have made an appearance. Roman's parents are around here somewhere, and I've already seen Aunt Lexie—though I don't want to revisit that memory because I'm almost certain I caught her and Uncle Trigger fucking in the bathroom—and the DJ is in the far corner, blaring the playlist Haldon Gambino curated for his best friend's ascension to leadership.

The beat travels through the room, the bass thumping through my chest. It's no surprise that Haldon's talent is in music, since his father owns half the clubs in Hell's Kitchen. Haldon follows in his father's footsteps, the looks, the lines, the leadership. The Five is slowly handing the mantel down to the next generation. We're all in line to take something from this, but the biggest shoes to fill belong to my father.

I return my attention to my mortal enemy, Roman Genovese, as he makes his rounds through the crowded room. His tattooed hands clutch other people's, shaking them with graceful conviction, feigning smiles I'm all too familiar with. His entire presence grabs the attention of everyone in the room, even me, and I hate it.

You might think that with our parents being best friends, their kids would follow in their footsteps.

Not. A. Chance.

We're enemies. Our hatred towards one another is built on the plight of our past. Our history forged our emotions, and now every time I look at the jerk, I want to rip his tongue out and shove it up his ass. The only thing stopping me right now is the room full of people I'm standing in.

I can't deny that the man is poised to go far in this world. He's in line to take over for his father, too. Not in the immediate future, but judging by the way he holds himself, it won't be too long before he's commanding others to do his dirty work. And I can't wait for the day. He'll demolish everything in his wake, just like he did to me, and I'll revel in that moment. Until then, I'll just stick to the shadows, keep my distance, and pretend that I actually want to be here.

"If you keep glaring like that, he might combust," my brother comments from beside me.

"I wish," I mutter, grabbing an open champagne bottle from the nearest waiter's tray.

Alvaro chuckles, shaking his head. Despite this being *his* party, he's kept me in his line of sight the entire evening—just like our father. Considering he's the favorite, he spends every moment he can ensuring I'm not left out. It's been like that since we were kids. It's what I love about him; his ability to remind me I am a part of this family, even when I don't feel like I am.

"Just make sure nobody else gets caught up in the fire," he remarks.

Rolling my eyes, I continue surveying Roman from afar. I haven't seen him in a year. He spends all his time in California now and it's evident from the sun-kissed glow that it's not been strictly business.

Since The Five branched out to the West Coast, Roman has been helping his father and the O'Sullivans out there. The rest of The Five stayed here to run their outfit, which is probably a good thing. It means I don't have to see the asshole as much.

"Are you ever going to tell me what happened between you two?" Alvaro asks, arching an inquisitive brow.

No. Not in a million years.

I could never admit that Roman Genovese, one of my brother's best friends, stole my heart, and then shattered it into a trillion, irreparable pieces. We were close until we weren't, and that's what hurts the most. That's what I refuse to talk about, refuse to address—because the hatred spurs me on, drives me to never let my guard down for anyone, and pushes me to focus on the more meaningful things in my life.

There's also the fact I don't want to burst my brother's bubble. Even though we've all grown up together, Haldon, Roman and Alvaro have always been inseparable. But my brother is also super protective of me, and I him. If he knew what Roman did, there wouldn't be a friendship between them anymore, that's for sure. There'd be bloodied fists, black eyes, and maybe even a gun pulled. What Roman did is between me and him, and I plan to keep it that way.

"Are you ever going to go mingle with your minions?" I retort, just loud enough for my twin to hear. I take a long pull off the champagne bottle, the bubbles fizzing down my throat as my eyes narrow on the tall blonde weaving through the throngs of people. His hair is brushed back, loose strands falling over his eyes and shining every time he passes beneath a strategically placed light. I remember all the times I used to run my fingers through those strands, tug on them while... *fuck*... I need to stop letting my thoughts run free.

"I came to check up on you," my brother says sweetly, resting a hand on my arm.

"I'm fine," I snap.

"Look, I don't know what happened, but you can't continue to bottle that shit up."

Swallowing another mouthful of the bubbly liquid, I slide my anger-filled gaze to my brother, my knuckles whitening as I grip the neck of the bottle. "Some things are better left in the past."

Alvaro retracts his hand, returning his attention to Roman, who is heading straight towards us. "Keep telling yourself that, sis. Maybe one of these days you'll believe it."

"Varo," Roman nods at my brother as he reaches us. Then he scours those bright blue eyes over my body, and every inch of my skin responds with a betraying burn, a desire that I try to push as far away from my consciousness as possible. "Lani," he smirks.

My back stiffens. "*Alanis*," I correct through gritted teeth.

With an awkward nod, my brother retreats. His expensive shoes clip the hardwood floor as he heads towards the bar, unable to leave the toxic tension quick enough.

I gulp back my vexed frustration. The urge to slam the damn champagne bottle over Roman's head just so I can get away from him is too strong to ignore. Sure, it's violent, but the damage it'd inflict would be nothing compared to how he left me.

Roman clearly has other ideas, though. He circles my figure with his own like I'm prey. His vibrant irises darken as they tour my neck, my chest. As his footsteps prowl behind me, I feel his hand drag down my waist, his touch leaving a path of scalding desire burning down my side. "Have I ever told you red looks good on you, Presh?"

I wince at the nickname, closing my eyes as his manly scent surrounds me. "Fuck off, Roman."

Hot breaths suddenly kiss my ear. Roman's proximity is deliciously suffocating; a confusing storm of lust and loathing that spins me around until I'm dizzy. It doesn't help that beneath that cocky, disgustingly confident and nauseating mask, is a man who's fucking *great* in bed. I just have to remember why I need to steer clear.

He doesn't love you.

"You know how much I love it when you talk dirty," Roman whispers before sliding his hot tongue behind my ear.

I suppress the shiver that crawls up my spine, the hairs on my arms refusing to obey my demand not to react. With my body standing rigid and resolute, I grit my teeth and reply over my shoulder, "Go bother someone else."

"Why would I do that, Presh?" His fingertips gently caress my bare arm, starting from my shoulder and coaxing every hair to stand to attention as his touch descends to my wrist. When he reaches my palm, his little finger links with mine; a sharp reminder of our past. "You're the sexiest girl in the room," he purrs.

I snatch my hand away, feeling the frigid ache of his vanishing touch. I'm not about to let him get close again. I can't afford to.

Never again.

"Want to know a secret?" Roman rasps against my ear as he leers over my shoulder from behind. His hand squeezes my hip, before dropping down the curve of my ass.

Yes. "No."

"I enjoy bothering you the most."

I suck in a breath when his palm tours my thigh, landing on the one thing I never leave home without.

"How the hell did you get this in here?" he tuts, fingers thrumming against the piece holstered to my thigh.

I swing my arm around, hand clutching his wrist as I yank it away and twist it back. He winces slightly, but that's about as much emotion as this asshole will ever show, so I go for the jugular, reminding him just how much I hate him.

"Call it a present. You can take it and use it on yourself."

"So hostile," he breathes out heavily, his other hand planting firmly on my ass and pulling me close to him. "You know I enjoy your fight."

I do. I also know how much he enjoys fucking everything up, taking whatever he wants and leaving me with nothing. I'm all too familiar with how much enjoyment he takes from obliterating everything good.

"Go fight someone else," I grit out.

"I don't want to fight. I want to dance," he winks.

I shove him away with as much force as I can muster without causing a scene. "In your fucking dreams," I hiss.

With only two steps, Roman presses his chest flush with mine, his forehead pushing against my own and our lips so close to one another's that any sudden move could result in catastrophe. A surge of panic blended with excitement pools in my stomach, dropping to the throbbing pulse between my legs.

I hate how responsive I am to him, even after everything he did. It's like I can't stay away—no matter how broken he left me, I'm always craving more. My body betrays me, my brain doesn't know what to do anymore, especially when Roman leans forward to press his lips to my cheek, searing his promise into my skin.

"You're always in them," he whispers. Confidence fixes his posture as he moves away from me, and his smile stretches those detestably perfect lips. Another wink makes my heart skip a beat before he glides past me and towards my brother, who's now throwing back shots with Haldon at the bar.

There is no way I can stand to be here anymore, not while Roman is on the prowl, not while I'm in his line of sight. Not when I know he will make every effort to piss me off tonight, just like he does every time I see him.

"Why is it always the good-looking ones who are assholes?" A head rests on my shoulder as I watch Roman leave. I know it's Haven Gambino from the signature perfume she always wears, and it makes me smile.

I sigh, spinning around and handing the half-drunk bottle of champagne to my best friend. She takes a swig from the bottle before handing it back to me, wiping her mouth with the back of her hand.

"Beats me."

"What's he doing here, anyway?" She frowns.

"The same thing everyone else is. Celebrating my brother's succession."

"I meant *here*. What did he want this time?"

"Haven," I warn.

"Lani," she mirrors back, punching a fist on her hip for emphasis.

I groan, knowing there's no fighting her stubbornness. We've been best friends for so long that she knows me inside and out. She's also the only one who knows what happened between Roman and I, and how much I detest talking about it, but that doesn't stop her from pushing my buttons to get what she wants.

She's been by my side throughout. "*If you hate him, so do I.*" That's what she said to me five years ago, and that's what makes Haven one of my bestest friends because even though we should all be close, the rift between Roman and I stretched to Haven too.

"I guess he wanted to torment me some more. Don't worry, I told him where to stick it."

Haven casts an inquisitive glare over my shoulder. "Hmm... whatever you said didn't work. He's still got his eye on you."

I refrain from turning around, knowing that if he *is* looking in this direction, he'll know we're talking about him. I don't want to give him that satisfaction.

"I'm not even surprised," I scoff. Nothing seems to affect the guy, no matter how nice or brutal I am about things. Roman Genovese has no feelings; no heart. I'd do well to remember that. "Wanna get out of here?"

Haven nods, beaming a bright Hollywood smile at me.

Looping her arm through mine, we turn together and head towards the patio doors lining the back of the room.

As soon as the fresh air hits me, I tuck around the corner and lean against the cool brick wall. The cool air wraps around me, soothing the heat crawling up my neck. Haven joins me, throwing her head back and letting her long brown hair brush up against the brickwork.

"How are things with your dad?" she asks me.

I close my eyes, pushing away my resurfacing anger. "Still rough," I answer, handing her the champagne bottle. Things have been worse than that, but I don't elaborate.

"I'm sorry, Lani. But great news about the academy!" She takes three large gulps, finishing the bottle off before waving it in the air. She's the only person I've told about my acceptance into the force. Telling my dad would result in more arguments, and I'm just not ready for that.

As for my brother, this is *his* night. I refuse to steal Alvaro's spotlight from him, even though I know he'd be stoked for me. If I told him, I'd have to tell everyone else, so this secret between Haven and I has to stay just that.

"What do you say we drink to that instead?" she suggests.

My heart grows three sizes for my best friend. She never fails to cheer me up, even when I don't feel like I deserve it. We're here for my brother, not for me, but I'd be a liar if I didn't admit that a small part of me is hurting that I haven't had a chance to celebrate my own achievement.

I give her the most sincere and appreciative smile, eyes burning up slightly. "I won't say no."

As soon as the door closes behind me, I sink back against it and kick my heels off, brushing off the sound of them clattering against my apartment floor. My exhale invades the silence and I smile to myself as I relax in my own space. Well, technically it's mine now. I inherited it from my Aunt Lexie when I told her I wanted to move out. I don't know why she held onto this apartment for so long, but I'm glad she did.

The apartment still needs a bit of work since it's over twenty years old, but it's home for me. I've made it my own and decorated it how I like, but my favorite part about this place is the peace and quiet.

My mother understands, but my father, not so much. He still thinks my moving out was an act of rebellion, and while he's partially right, it's really because I just need my own space. Dad insisted I live with my brother if not at home, saying I needed the protection, but that didn't appeal to me. Especially with how close Alvaro is to Roman. So, naturally, I defied him and wound up here.

Just being around Roman tonight was exhausting. I don't even want to think about what it would be like living with my twin brother and having to deal with his best friend on a regular basis. I'm hardly able to avoid Roman in public settings, let alone in the confines of my brother's apartment. I can barely stand looking at the man. All I can think about when my eyes land on him is what he did; and it's not just the bitter taste the memories leave on my tongue, but the scars he left on my young, naïve heart.

It's the scars you don't see that hurt the most, and Roman brings out the worst in me. He makes me mad, manic, a complete idiot filled with anger and hatred. Yet I'm so utterly tethered to him that I hate not only him, but myself, too. I try to avoid him as much as possible—though he always seems intent on finding me. There's just something about him I'm always drawn to. Even tonight, I couldn't take my eyes off him, as much as I wanted to. I might hate the asshole, but there are moments when he's not around that I find myself remembering what it was like when we were kids; the good times before everything fell apart. *Before I fell apart.*

Making my way to the bedroom, I push those irritating thoughts out of my mind and shrug out of my dress. I let the satin material slip down my body, pooling at my feet in a puddle of red fabric. I step out of it and run through the motions of getting ready for bed, throwing on an old t-shirt and unclipping my gun from its holster on my thigh before sliding it under my pillow.

It's the only protection I need.

As I slide into bed, *my* mind is still reeling over tonight's events.

The way Roman's eyes never left me all night.

The way my body betrayed me when he ran his hands over my skin.

I hate that I can't control myself around him, no matter how hard I try. It doesn't matter that our past is fractured, barely glued back together by my own attempt to heal. Somehow, Roman has stolen a fragment of my shattered heart, and no matter what I do, I haven't found a way to reclaim it.

I shake my head, grumbling to myself as I cocoon beneath the covers and pull them up to my chin. It's only midnight, but with all the dancing Haven and I were doing earlier, my body is aching for sleep. Though with the way my mind won't quiet, I doubt I'll be getting much. Still, I close my eyes and try to lose myself to the blanket of darkness.

I inhale deeply, letting my body sink into the mattress. I exhale loudly, finally letting my exhaustion wrap around me. And just when I feel like the world is falling away, I hear it.

It's just a creak of the floorboards, a potentially innocent sound in the dead of night. But as soon as I hear the telltale sound of my bedroom door opening, I slide my hand under my pillow until I feel the brush of cold metal on my fingertips.

The bed dips and a familiar scent reaches me, hitting me like a freight train. I roll over swiftly, swinging my leg over for momentum and pinning my assailant beneath me. My legs straddle his waist as I thrust the barrel of my gun under his chin, but there's no fear in his eyes, just smug satisfaction.

"Is that anyway to greet me, Presh?" Roman tuts, hands immediately cupping my bare ass and giving it a squeeze. It's a test, an inquisitive touch. When he realizes I'm not wearing panties, his grin stretches further. Even in the dead of night, I can see his piercing blue eyes, the menacing way his lips curl up to expose his straight white teeth. I'd love to knock a few loose right now, but I refrain, purely because right now he looks so infuriatingly beautiful looming over me in the darkness that I lose focus for a second.

In one fluid movement, he seizes control back and rolls me over, leaning his weight into the weapon. I should have known that any threat like this would be met with his obnoxious brand of unwavering confidence. He leans over me, blanketing me in an intoxicating blend of his aftershave and tequila. His warm breath skates over my lips, an embarrassing moan escaping my own as my grip slips and the gun presses against his temple.

"*Do it*," he whispers, forcing my stubbornness to the recesses of my mind.

My eyes blow wide. Heat crawls up my spine, expanding in my chest until I'm suddenly breaking out in a sweat. Yet again, my body is defying my brain, my inner strength giving out. *Shit*. He knows that I'd never do it. I've never pulled my gun on someone I didn't intend to harm, and that thought causes my mask to slip.

That's what Roman does to me. He makes me do crazy shit, my anger driving my actions instead of thinking clearly.

With my legs wrapped around his waist, Roman circles his hips, his excitement at the turn of events evident in the way his hard length presses into me. My traitorous pussy is so damn eager that I can't ignore the needy pulse throbbing between my legs.

He hitches forward, the heat of his body covering mine as he runs his nose along my own. "Pull-" his tongue traces a wet path along my neck, "The-" he nips my jawline, "Trigger."

Our lips brush, the magnetizing tension between us ramping up. I've lost my fight to ignore the attraction between us. Once again, the need to *hate* him is overshadowed by the need to *have* him.

When I don't respond, his lips curl into a smug grin like he knows he's won. Roman yanks the gun from my hand, sitting back on his haunches to slide the barrel over my chest, tracing the cold metal over my hardened nipples. The thin cotton barely conceals how reactive I am to him, and Roman laps it up. He rolls my nipple under the metal, his rushed breaths mingling with mine. He widens my thighs with his own, dragging the weapon over my stomach until he reaches my bare pussy.

"You knew I'd be coming tonight," he comments, and I know he means it in more ways than one. Rubbing the cold metal against the sensitive pulse of my clit, Roman then guides the weapon between my pussy lips, coating it in my juices.

I won't lie that the danger lacing this moment has me on edge, but it's also heightened my senses. My nerves are frayed, and my brain is misfiring, unable to decipher what should be perceived as pain versus pleasure.

"I hate you," I grit out, though my words are a direct contradiction to how my body is responding to his ministrations.

"Keep telling yourself that, Presh. But we both know it's a lie." He works the weapon faster over my clit, my toes curling as I throw my head back.

My back arches off the mattress as I'm lost in the dangerous sensations he's evoking from me. I bite down on my lip, desperate to suppress the sounds he's coaxing out, but his assault is so intense that I'm unable to keep it in. My thighs shake as his movements quicken, the weight of the gun putting more pressure on my pussy until I'm throbbing with need.

"And if you're going to threaten me, at least be sure that you're going to pull the trigger."

Roman drops his head to my chest and latches his teeth around my nipple through my shirt, tugging until I'm whining and writhing. As usual, he doesn't soothe the pain coursing through me—he just moves to my other nipple, offering it the same assault, like I should be grateful for the attention.

I roll my eyes, but that only goads him further. He wraps his hand around my throat, essentially pinning me to my mattress. It's not hard enough to cut any circulation, but it restricts my air enough to cause spots to dance in front of my eyes. And the most sickening part is that even after everything, I still trust him. I still love what he does to me. There's a look of dangerous intent in his eyes, blended with the familiar desire that he reserves only for me, and I know he'd never offer me the pleasure of dying under his hand.

As he rubs the gun harder against my clit, a needy whimper escapes me. It's like that sound is his undoing, because Roman dives in to swallow it, his lips sliding against mine, hungry and harsh. His tongue tastes mine, the familiar pull that I've tried so hard to ignore threatens to drag me into its void. But it's too late. It's too late to fight it. The only thing I can do is give in, allow myself to ride the wave.

And I do.

I pull Roman closer, the kiss deepening until all the breath is knocked out of me and all I feel is dirty and lost. Lost in Roman. Lost in the enemy that has warped my sensibility once again.

It's like my body remembers *everything*. Roman's touch, Roman's kiss, Roman's ability to make me come so violently that it almost becomes an out of body experience.

I shudder beneath him, unable to fight the warmth coursing through my veins, or the ball of pleasure unraveling like yarn deep in my belly. And then it hits me, like a wave crashing into cliffs. I fall over the blissful peak of an orgasm, shattering under the assault of my own gun, screaming out in ecstasy. My harsh, panted breaths rattle in my chest as my heart pounds against my ribcage. The dizzying sparks exploding through my extremities momentarily obliterate my anger for the devil hovering above me.

Roman pulls away to run his tongue along the barrel of the gun, groaning with eyes closed as he laps up my release. "How do you taste better than the last time?"

Shame pours over me, and all I can think about is how I let my guard down once again. I let Roman in when I swore I wouldn't. But yet again, I've found myself caught up in our chaotic attraction.

Roman leans down to capture my lips once more. I can taste myself; my arousal tainted with the bitter blend of betrayal. Shame coats my skin in a thin sheen of sweat, my breath slowly steadying. His chest presses against mine, but he makes no attempt to push this moment further.

That's the thing about Roman; he can read me like a book. And right now I feel like a children's book with pretty pictures and simple words, but there's so much more beneath the surface that I'm battling. As if he knows what I'm thinking, he pulls away, rolling to the edge of the bed.

"Don't act so guilty, Presh." He rests my gun on the bedside table, looking over at me. The gentle glow of the moon through the window behind me cascades over him, bathing him in ethereal light. It juxtaposes everything about the man standing before me. Not one bone in the asshole's body is good, and the sooner my own body gets the message, the better off I'll be. But I don't know how long that will take, and with Roman's constant intrusion in my life, he's not making it easy. He never does. He always finds a way to reassert his ownership over my body. It's not like I need the reminder, but every moment spent beneath his touch sends me spiraling into darker madness. Just when I think I'm finally over him, he reappears, locking his deviant blue eyes with mine and reminding me of *everything*.

"How long are you in the city?" I find myself asking as I push up onto my hands, clutching the covers against my chest like that will somehow protect me. I watch him as he stands up, silence following him as he heads towards the door. His retreating footsteps only make the weight of my own guilt sit heavier on my chest.

Just when I don't think I'm going to get another word out of him, he freezes in the doorway, resting his hand on the frame as he glances over his shoulder at me. "However long you want me here."

The smugness is back, coaxing back my temporarily retreating hatred.

"I don't want you here."

Shaking his head, he locks eyes with me. "When are you going to stop lying to yourself?"

"The day you leave this earth," I retort. "This can't happen again."

He spins around, chuckling to himself. I don't need to see his face to know he's smirking at the ridiculousness of my words. Even I hear the way they sound; so repetitive, *lies*. "Now where have I heard that before?"

Secret Project by Stephanie Hurst (Title TBA)

I stare at the two-story colonial building, a knot in my stomach. My brother, Obsidian, has repainted the stone to hide the deterioration, and a delicate iron bench replaces the usual clutter that used to inhabit the front porch. I've not returned since my mother's death. The abuse she inflicted was just another reason to stay away.

"I'll pick you up at eight," Selene says as I exit the car.

I nod, my voice trapped by my nerves and apprehension. I've spent the past three years ignoring the pain and suffering this town brought me, and for the most part, it worked. The people of Crimson Ridge made it clear I never belonged, and coming back here is opening that wound.

Grabbing my bag from the trunk, I turn to what was once my family home and head up the steps. The unease grows the closer I get. My mother doesn't dwell on this earth any longer, but Obsidian turned his back on me long before she passed away.

The overwhelming familiarity catches me off guard as the door swings open. My heart quickens, and a shiver runs down my spine as I step back into my childhood. I expect a change in the interior, but it's still a homage to our late mother. The summer green and white walls look tired and worn, and the brown and gold rug covering the walkway from the door to the kitchen is old-fashioned.

The unmistakable aroma of spaghetti and meatballs wafts down the hall, instantly transporting me back to countless family dinners. I follow the scent to the kitchen, where I find my brother, Sid, wrestling with a pot of red sauce. He curses when the sauce spits at him, and the sight of him struggling brings a smile to my face despite the circumstances.

"You have the heat too high," I remark, rushing to his side and adjusting the stove.

"Raven, your home! I've missed you so much." Obsidian drops the wooden spoon before wrapping me in a hug, pinning my arms to my side.

"Lovely to see you too, Sid." Sarcasm drips from my words as I strain against the bear hug.

"Shit, sorry, sis." He drops his arms and steps back with a sheepish look.

Sid practically buffed out overnight when he turned sixteen. He never did learn to control his strength around me and even accidentally broke my arm when I challenged him to arm wrestle. Not long after, he abandoned me, leaving me to our mother's wrath.

I look up at him while battling the warring emotions. His warm greeting catches me off guard, stirring up a whirlwind of old memories. We'd been close growing up. Sid took great pride in being my older brother, a job he did exceptionally well. When he abandoned me, he broke my heart and the remaining pieces were eventually torn out by his best friend, Slade.

"I was twelve years old the last time you showed an ounce of affection. What gives?"

Guilt flashes across Sid's face, and he drops his eyes to the ground. If Sid wants to step back into the big brother role, he better have a damn good reason why he stepped out in the first place. I could appease him. Pretend it doesn't matter and enjoy having my family back, but it does.

"Raven, listen, there are things you don't understand. I know I've been an asshole, but please trust me when I say I had my reasons."

Our blue eyes connected for the first time in years. I love my brother, and those feelings don't just go away because he's a dick, but I've constructed a wall. It protects me from the hurt he could so easily inflict.

So, you're ready to explain what happened to our father?" I demand, "Or your fucked up choice to embarrass me on my eighteenth birthday? Or why our mother was so broken? Or what happe—"

"Raven, stop!" Sid shouts, an unnatural growl coming from deep within his throat.

Fear shoots through me, but anger quickly replaces it. "Fuck you, you don't get to tell me what to do anymore."

"I know none of it makes sense. Jesus, the last ten years almost killed me, but it's nearly over," he pleads, moisture pooling in his eyes.

I've never seen my brother cry. I presumed he was incapable of genuine emotion, and the realisation he actually has a fucking heart is jarring. He wipes his eyes and leans back on the counter, defeated.

"What do you mean, nearly over?" I ask.

"It doesn't matter."

I turn to leave as frustration pricks my eyes. Just when I think I'm finally getting somewhere, the cryptic talking that plagued this house returns. They treated me differently. I can't forget all the times the hushed whispers between Mum, Dad, and Sid ended the moment I walked into the room. I don't belong in Crimson Ridge. I never did.

"Raven, wait." I pause but refuse to give him my full attention as I prepare myself for further disappointment. "I promise you'll have all the answers and more in five days."

My eyebrows furrow, and I spin to face him. "What the fuck has my twenty-first got to do with anything?"

Sid steps forward, "Please, can you trust me? Can we go back to the way it used to be? I promise you'll understand everything in five days. I've never asked you for anything. Just give me this."

I mull over his proposal. I could tell him where to shove his promises and walk away, but where would that get me? All my life, something was hidden from me. A secret everyone in this town knew, yet I was blissfully unaware of. It wasn't blissful, though; *I thought I was crazy*. Now, he's offering me a reason —a secret lurking beneath.

Walking away now would be an injustice. It would torment me, keep me awake at night, and eventually destroy me. Five days. My birthday is in five days, which apparently means I get answers. "You promise to tell me everything I want to know?"

"Everything."

He could be lying, trying to appease me, but that would be a mistake. I'll give my brother the time, but if he doesn't give me what I want, I'll leave him behind and never look back. He'll lose me forever.

"Fine, you've got five days."

The water cascades over my flesh, urging my muscles to relax. After our intense start, Sid and I spent nearly an hour talking and attempting to eat his disastrous meal. I don't know how he's so buff when he messes up a simple meal like spaghetti and meatballs.

It was peculiar yet cathartic to finally be in my brother's presence and talk like we used to. He listened intently to my stories from living in New Galha, all of which revolved around my work at the coffee shop. Being at odds with Sid weighed me down, something I didn't realise until I felt the release. I'm finally ready to leave the shadows of my past and move into a bright new future.

Wrapping a towel around me, I gaze into the mirror. My long, black hair hangs over my shoulders, dripping water onto the tiled floor, and my deep blue eyes stare back, filled with curiosity. I don't appear any different, but the changes inside are immense. Thanks to the reconciliation with my brother and the promise of answers, I've finally got something worth celebrating.

I dry my hair into soft waves and apply makeup before dressing in a white off-the-shoulder top, light blue skinny jeans, and cute white flats. Admittedly, a small part of me hopes a certain someone will be in attendance tonight because, with my newfound confidence, I want to show him exactly what he's missed.

The front door opens, and Selene yells, "Raven, are you ready?"

"Selene, you look gorgeous," I say as I descend the stairs.

Her curly auburn locks compliment her turquoise lace T-shirt that stops above her belly button, a white bra visible beneath. Her creamy skin shows through ripped, high-rise white skinny jeans, and on her feet, turquoise kitten heels finish her outfit perfectly. To put it simply, she looks crazy hot.

"Thank you. I love your sexy, casual look. The men will fall over themselves to get a piece of you, so don't break all their hearts at once."

I scoff at her comment. Ironically, the last party I attended in Crimson Ridge left *me* with a broken heart. If the opportunity presented itself, then payback is a bitch.

"I'm leaving my car here for the weekend. I won't need it tomorrow, so feel free to use it," Selene says, passing me the keys.

I trace my finger over the silver wolf keyring with red crystal eyes. "Are you going to be wrapped up with this wedding all weekend?"

It hurts that I didn't receive an invite. In my opinion, being friends with the bride or groom is a ridiculous stipulation. Have they never heard of plus-ones?

"We have tonight and Sunday."

"And tomorrow?" I say hopefully.

"No. Tomorrow will be an all-day and night affair, finishing when the moon is at its highest. There's a beautiful clearing in the middle of the forest, and when the moon casts its glow over the happy couple, it's a sign of blessing."

"It sounds like a cult ritual. Are they anointed with the blood of a wolf first?" I laugh but quickly shut my mouth when Selene glares at me.

"And you wonder why you're not invited," she mutters.

The comment stings, but I know she's only lashing out because I hurt her first. "I'm sorry."

Selene's brown eyes soften, and she hugs me, "No, I'm sorry. I shouldn't have said that. I know how hard it is for you to return here, but I didn't want to be without my best friend this weekend. Did you speak to Obsidian?"

"Yeah," I say as we leave the house. It's a warm night, the slight breeze keeping the temperature bearable as we set off toward the abandoned mansion.

"How did it go?" From the sound of her voice, she doesn't expect much.

"Surprisingly well. It almost felt like I had my brother back," I say.

"Well, I didn't expect that. So, you don't think he's hiding anything anymore?" Selene is the only person I confessed my suspicions to. She tried to talk me out of them but eventually gave up. Nothing she said made me think my brother had a reason to destroy our relationship or that my father's death was an accident.

"Oh, I'm more certain than ever that he's hiding something. He practically admitted it," I laugh.

Selene's body tenses as her eyes dart around the empty street. "What did he tell you?" She's on the verge of a panic attack.

"Calm down. He promised to tell me everything after my birthday. Which proves he *does* have something to tell me." I can't take my eyes off Selene. She's acting strange. Only moments earlier, she was terrified, but now she looks perplexed.

"That doesn't make sense unless..." Her eyes bulge as they dart to me.

"What?"

Does she know something? Selene turned twenty-one a few months back, so maybe she knows the truth. It sounds ridiculous, like a conspiracy theory, but after my chat with Sid, I know this town is hiding something.

Selene smiles and shrugs. "Nothing. I'm just a little surprised and confused. Will you let me know what he tells you?" I can't take my eyes off her as she returns to her usual self, which sets me on edge. I presumed my best friend would never lie to me, but now I'm unsure.

"If he answers my questions, of course you'll be the first to know," I say, laying it on thick, but it's valid. I've never lied to Selene.

Okay, I didn't tell her about my feelings for Slade, but that wasn't a lie. It was an omission.

"You may be attracted to someone at the party tonight. If you are, tell me straight away," Selene blurts out as we near our destination.

Shit!

"Yeah, of course." I swallow the lump in my throat.

So, I never lied to Selene until now, but she lied first.

"We're going to have so much fun tonight," Selene says, her excitement for this party increasing exponentially after her previous statement.

Does she think I'll meet the love of my life tonight and live happily ever after? Newsflash: I thought I did, and he rejected me on my eighteenth. But there's no point telling her about Slade. It's been three years, and even if he changed his mind now, I don't want him.

Now I'm lying to myself. Of course, I still want him. Slade has set up residence inside my heart, and I've tried countless times to evict him to no avail.

"You are nothing but a child, Raven. I formed our friendship because I felt sorry for you after your father died. Get over your little infatuation and grow up." I hear his cruel words echoing in my head. I want to hate him, but my heart refuses to listen.

Up ahead, our destination comes into view. The eerie abandoned colonial building sits on the hill overlooking the town. Ivy winds around the six enormous pillars that stretch up two floors, a sign of deterioration.

The house is owned by a corporation that rents it out, but the last wealthy family that lived there disappeared overnight, and it's remained empty ever since.

The residents petitioned multiple times, requesting that the house be returned to town ownership. Even though the corporation doesn't maintain it, it ensures all taxes and paperwork are kept up to date, so there's nothing the politicians can do.

The people of Crimson Ridge hit back the only way they knew how: by using the property without permission. If there's a college party or drinking session, this is the place to host it. The sheriff is more than willing to look the other way as long as the party remains within the mansion grounds.

The corporation cut off the electricity to deter the squatters, but that didn't stop the Crimson Ridge youth. After tearing down the back wall, they brought in a generator, hung fairy lights, installed a sound system, and spray-painted the old furniture left by the previous tenants, giving it a new lease of life. The mix-match of colours turned the mansion into a work of art.

As we make our way up the gravel pathway, the thrum of music pours into the night air, the bass vibrating the ground. The cheers and chatter grow louder when we step over the threshold.

"Drinks?" Selene questions, and I nod, my racing heart beating in time with the music.

We head to the kitchen, waving and smiling to the people we recognise. Selene knows everyone, but that's no surprise. I, on the other hand, pretend their acknowledgements are also for me because the alternative is what kept me away for so long.

I don't belong here.

The kitchen, now an empty shell, sits at the rear of the property. The cabinet fronts are long gone, but the remaining marble surface holds an astounding array of beverages and mixers. Selene grabs two plastic cups while I methodically survey the room hoping to see a certain someone. Even now, after everything he's done, I hope to experience the comfort his presence once filled me with.

"Hay Raven, long time no see," Logan stands to my right, a grin on his face and arms stretched out.

Urgh.

"Hi, Logan. How've you been?" I attempt a friendly half-hug with one arm, but he wraps his arms around me, pulling me into him. His manly scent envelopes me, and my hands skim over his massive arm muscles.

To be fair, this town is filled with ripped men and women. Something I'm only now realising after living in a city filled with different shapes and sizes. Maybe there's something in the water because there's no gym in Crimson Ridge.

"I'm good. I work at the garage now." His eyes unashamedly trail down my body.

"I'll be back soon." Selene passes me a drink with a knowing smile before rushing away.

No, Selene, this definitely isn't the guy.

Logan stares at me like I'm his next meal, and the uncomfortable reality sets in.

"How's Stacey?" I ask, hoping to remind him of his girlfriend—no such luck.

"We broke up, but now you're here." He licks his lips, and I battle the urge to roll my eyes.

Logan is still the ultimate jock. He and Stacey were together throughout high school, even with rumours flying around that both were continuously unfaithful. Logan hit on me several times, but I always found ways to dodge the bullet.

"So, how long are you back in town for?" Logan moves closer, and I immediately step back.

"Just the weekend. Selene has a wedding to attend." My eyes dart around the room with unease, and my stomach flips when they fall on *him* sitting in an old armchair in the corner.

He hasn't changed, and it seems neither has my attraction. He's a God among men, with light brown shoulder-length hair, trimmed beard, and a black T-shirt straining against broad shoulders. My eyes wander over the tattoo that begins on both his wrists, the tribal lines disappearing underneath the fabric before reappearing on his neck. I've spent many hours imagining the hidden aspects of the design.

Slade sits on his throne, king of the world, his hazel eyes fixed on me.

"Raven, did you hear me?" My gaze flicks back to Logan.

"Sorry, what?" Blood pounds in my ears as Slade's intense stare burns my flesh.

"I said, if you're not doing anything tomorrow, I want to take you out?" Logan offers, taking yet another step forward. I'm too distracted and fail to retreat in time, allowing Logan to snake his arm around my waist. My focus shifts as Slade stands, anger twisting his beautiful features.

"Or we can forget about tomorrow, and I can take you home tonight," Logan murmurs, snapping me out of my daze.

His arousal presses against my stomach, and I push down the need to vomit. "I'm sorry, Logan, some other time."

I attempt to remove his arm, but Logan doesn't budge. "Come on, Raven, I know you want it." His lips brush against my ear, causing me to flinch away.

"As I said, Logan, not now." I place my arms on his chest, trying to keep some distance between us, but he refuses to take the hint. His other arm slips around my back before he pulls me to him, crushing my arms between us.

"And as I said, I know you want it." He runs his nose along my neck, and I shiver in disgust.

Panic wells in my chest, but I refuse to be a willing victim. I shift my leg and prepare for my knee to make acquaintance with his balls. Before I can strike, Logan is dragged off me and thrown across the room.

What I'm seeing doesn't make sense. One minute, Logan is holding me, and the next, he crashes against the far wall as Slade stalks toward him. The whole room goes quiet when Slade grabs Logan by the collar of his shirt and lifts him into the air like he weighs nothing.

Slamming Logan into the wall, Slade growls, "She is mine! Look at her again, and I'll rip out your eyes and feed them to you. Do I make myself clear?"

Slade's deep, commanding voice shakes the house. The music cuts away, and the other guests bow their heads.

What the fuck!?

Logan cowers, his eyes trained on the floor. "Yes, Alpha." He says before tilting his head to the side to reveal his neck.

Seriously, what the fuck?

Slade releases his grip, sending Logan crashing to the ground. Slade then turns in my direction, and my throat tightens with a scream. His hazel eyes shine unnaturally golden, while his face distorts as if something moves beneath the surface. The anger ripples from him, and the air around us thickens. Adrenaline surges through my body as my fight or flight kicks in.

I choose flight and bolt for the back door.

The warm air caresses my skin as I take a moment to fill my lungs with much-needed oxygen. I don't need to see who it is when I sense a presence behind me; there's always been an unexplainable connection between us, even if he denies it.

I immediately force my legs to move. After what I just witnessed, the last thing I want is to be near Slade. I can practically taste his anger.

"Raven," he growls in warning, but I refuse to stop, my eyes fixed on the broken wall ahead.

"Go back to the party, Slade. I don't want you here." I want to be angry, but my voice betrays me, revealing my fear.

He grabs my arm and pulls me back before my feet take me over the wall debris and past the mansion threshold. "It's not safe for you out there."

I spin around but refuse to look at his face, keeping my eyes fixed on his chest. "It's much safer than in there, especially with the people in attendance," I point, making it clear I mean him and Logan.

Slade places a finger under my chin and lifts my face, but I squeeze my eyes shut, terrified of what I'll see.

"Look at me," He commands, and an unexplainable internal pull stops me from refusing. My eyes snap open, but to my shock, Slade's face appears normal.

Of course it is. What were you expecting?

Had it been a trick of the lights? It would be easy to blame the alcohol, but my drink sits in the house, untouched. Slade's anger subsides. "Are you afraid of me?" He asks despondently.

Should I be? Everything tells me that what I saw wasn't natural, which means only one thing.

Jesus, I really am crazy.

"I didn't need or want your help. I had it handled." I pull my face from his grip and cross my arms over my chest to make a point and for protection. Am I afraid of him?

"Didn't seem that way to me." His arrogance only stokes my anger.

"What are you playing at Slade? You announce to a room full of people that I belong to you. The last time I checked, I'm not a possession," I seethe. I prod him in the chest. "I don't belong to anyone, *especially* not you."

With a deep growl, Slade stalks forward, and I instinctively back up but hit the tree behind me. I whimper when Slade places his hands on either side of me, trapping me between them.

"You *are* mine, Raven." The heat from his body engulfs me as I stare into his golden eyes. My fingers itch to reach up and pull at his chestnut hair, to have the harsh brush of his short beard against my face as his lips meet mine.

He only wants me now because someone else does.

"You had your chance. It's too late." I cast my eyes down, unable to meet his intense glare. My heart doesn't agree, and I don't want to risk Slade seeing.

"You don't mean that, Raven." His words are soft as his fingers brush against the right side of my face. I close my eyes, enjoying the flames that burn my skin from his touch. My heart skips in my chest, and I curse the disloyal organ.

I plan on hitting back with an intelligent retort, but my breath catches in my throat when our eyes connect, blue on hazel. His lips crash to mine, stealing my breath as his arms wrap around my waist, holding me in place.

When his tongue runs along the seam of my lips, begging for entrance, I'm lost. I should stop and deny him as he denied me, but who am I kidding?

I open my mouth and allow him to deepen the kiss. He claims me as he did in the room only moments earlier, but desperation replaces the viciousness.

Tasting him for the first time causes me to fall deeper into my obsession. My hands take what they crave, fisting his soft hair. Slade's grip around my waist tightens as he pulls me closer against his hard chest, and my nipples harden at the contact, hampered by the material between us. His familiar smell of leather and cedarwood fills my senses, and I ache for more.

"Slade! What the hell?" I pull away, gasping for air at my brother's voice.

Slade doesn't let go of me and rests his forehead against mine as he catches his breath, his eyes closed. His chest heaves up and down, his heart racing. Or is that my heart?

I dare a peek at Sid and instantly regret my decision; he is beyond pissed. His face contorted with pure rage, and I swear his eyes flash like Slade's.

Nope, I am not going there again. Crazy, remember?

"What the fuck do you want, Sid?" The challenging tone of Slade's voice makes my libido pulse with need. His chest vibrates, rubbing against my nipples and causing me to whimper with need. Slade's lips twitch with a smile, and I've never hated my brother as much as I do right now.

Cockblocker.

"Her birthday is five days away." Sid's teeth grind together as he clenches his fists. My eyebrows draw together, and my gaze flicks to Slade.

Sighing heavily, he releases his grip, not meeting my gaze. I shiver with the sudden loss of heat and narrow my eyes at Sid. "What has my fucking birthday got to do with this?"

Sid immediately drops his head when Slade turns to him with a growl, which increases my anger, dousing the flames of desire.

I wave my arms around for attention, "Hey, I am right here. Why did you mention my birthday, Sid?" All the ridiculous growling and unanswered questions are pissing me off.

"Sid is reminding me of a party I'm throwing for you," Slade responds, glaring at Sid. Sid glances up, momentarily meeting my eyes, before nodding his head. They're lying, and I've had my fill of it.

"Hell no, you don't get to do that. Do I look stupid to you both?" Slade snaps his head to me. His face tells me to drop the subject, but I'll be damned if I'm going to listen to anyone who can't be straight with me.

"I'm not going to be here on my birthday. I have plans, and after how my eighteenth turned out, I would rather walk over hot coals than have *you* ruin another one for me." Slade opens his mouth to speak, but I raise my hand and move on to my second target.

Narrowing my eyes at my brother, "You ask me to wait for my twenty-first before you can talk about mum and dad. Now you're telling me I have to wait for my birthday before I can even *kiss* Slade. What is going on?" I shake with rage as I've officially reached my bullshit quota.

"You promised to wait," Sid begs, his eyes fixed on the floor. His weak response confirms what I already knew. My thoughts and feelings don't matter. I shouldn't be surprised; Mum taught me this lesson at a young age. It only hurts so much now because it comes from my brother.

"You know what? Go to hell." I sob, a single tear falling from my eye. The irony isn't lost. I said the exact words to my brother on my eighteenth birthday.

"Where do you think you're going?" Slade demands as I make my way back to the house.

"I'm going home to New Galha. Thanks for reminding me why I shouldn't have come back here."

"Raven, what happened?" My head shoots up to find Selene, her focus on the people behind me. I follow her flustered gaze, looking back over my shoulder. My brother and Slade still stand in the same spot, their eyes trained on me.

"I want to go home," I demand.

"Of course." Selene's gaze flicks back behind me, and I almost lose it. Is she looking for their approval? With a huff, I storm past her and back into the mansion.

I bring the tension along with me as all eyes turn my way. The noise dies to an eerie silence, and my heart races at the unwanted attention. The girl closest to me tips her head to the side, revealing her neck, and a shiver runs down my spine. I remember Logan doing the same thing to Slade. I continue past her, heading for the exit while even more people show me their necks.

I fucking knew it. They are all part of some weird cult.

I regret coming to this stupid party. Hell, I regret ever coming back to Crimson Ridge. It all makes sense. At twenty-one, the town brings you into their little cult family, and everyone drinks the Kool-Aid. Fuck that shit. I'm out of here.

Selene shouts my name, but I ignore her as I exit the house and walk up the gravel path. The emotional rollercoaster has worn me down, and exhaustion creeps in. I desperately need to get home where I'm safe.

"Slow down," Selene calls as she struggles to keep up. "What happened in there?" I stop and face her when she gently touches my arm.

It's time to tell her everything.

"Honestly," I sigh. "I've had feelings for Slade for five years." Selene's mouth drops open, but I continue. "I kept it quiet because I never thought anything would happen. Then he started throwing me signals, so I confronted him on my eighteenth, but he rejected me. I tried to forget him when we moved to the city, but he's infected my soul."

Tonight, Logan tried it on with me. Slade threatened him and declared to everyone that I belonged to him. Mine! Fucking prick. Anyway, I stormed out, he followed, we kissed, and it was amazing." I suck in a much-needed breath. "*Then* my moronic brother turns up and starts spouting some crap about my birthday again."

Selene bends her head to the side, her hair falling away to reveal her neck before she catches herself and stops. "Shit."

"And then there's that! What the fuck is that, and why is everyone doing it?" I say, gesturing at her neck.

When she remains silent, my outrage drifts away, replaced by a dark pit of confusion and suspicion. "What do you know, Selene? You're already twenty-one, which is a huge deal in this town, so what am I missing?"

Selene looks away, and that action tells me everything. She's betrayed me. I turn away from her in disgust, pain tearing through my heart.

"You don't understand, Raven. I can't tell you anything." Tears prick her eyes when I look back, but the realisation that my best friend has been lying to me hurts more than Slade ever could.

"I'm going back to the city tonight without you," I whisper, unable to meet her eyes.

"I understand. Take my car, and I'll get a lift back." She's clearly in pain, and it tugs at my heartstrings, but I can't let this go. I'm confused, upset, exhausted, and need time away from everyone.

I built walls to protect myself from the men in my life. I never imagined I would need their protection from Selene. Her choked sob follows me as I walk away.

This was an excerpt from my upcoming dark, paranormal romance novel. The title and cover have yet to be announced, but I aim for an end-of-year release.

All my works promise a wild ride with plenty of twists and turns.

If you've enjoyed this and want to read more, start with my debut novel, Muse of Ruin.

The Viking City Murders by Marie Moore

A JAY CORRIGAN CRIME THRILLER

This short story is a first glimpse at a new collaboration between authors Steven Moore and Marie Anne Cope, writing together under the highly imaginative penname, Marie Moore. I know, we should be writers, right?

We're planning a 10-book series, which we are branding as crime thrillers. The series is set in the Puget Sound area of Washington State, in the US, and we think you're going to love it.

One

"Black hole sun, won't you come, da da da daaa ddaaaaa? Won't you commmme, won't you commmmeee." Jay Corrigan winced at the sound of his own voice, and the fact he couldn't quite recall the words to one of his favorite songs.

Better stick with the day job, *Corrigan*, he mused as he glanced at his dusty toolbox in the truck's passenger side footwell, and grinned.

What day job?

Gazing out the front window as traffic streamed across the highway from all directions except his, Jay caught himself tapping his fingers on the steering wheel as the next Soundgarden song, "Spoonman," spilled from the speakers. He wondered if his tapping was in time with the song beats or out of impatience at still being stuck at the lights when another realization hit him.

Holy shit, it's been twenty-three years since this came out. I was twelve!

With one elbow resting out the open window, Jay shook his head and willed himself to relax as he attempted a note way too high for a voice forged in the smoky halls of the sports bars of his youth. A swift glance to his right reminded him he was never meant to be a Chris Cornell impersonator as the female passenger in the adjacent vehicle confirmed it with an unsympathetic shake of her head, though her gaze lingered long enough for him to will the lights to hurry and change. When he got his wish, Jay shrugged at the woman, angled his modest yet spotless blue pickup off the highway, and turned into the parking lot of his home for the next several weeks—the convenient yet severely underwhelming Poulsbo Motel.

Jay pulled up in front of his room and stared through the windshield at the plate-glass window and flimsy chip-board door that hid his current home from the world. As he pushed open the truck door, Jay saw the net curtains shift in the end unit. He frowned. He didn't know the motel had a new guest.

No car, though, he thought abstractly, glancing at the space in front of the room.

He shrugged as he locked the truck and made his way toward the ageing hotel's reception.

"Hey, Shaun, who's staying—Oh, I'm sorry. I didn't mean to interrupt," Jay said as his gaze rested on the fiery young woman occupying the receptionist's attention.

"Just what I was about to ask," she said, turning her chocolate-brown gaze to Jay, a slow smile spreading across her plum-stained lips. "At least, I think I was... if you were inquiring about the end unit?"

She arched an eyebrow and Jay watched as the red corkscrew curl—the cause of his fiery assessment—bobbed in response, before settling amidst her shoulder-length dark curls. A diamanté nose stud, nestled against her coca skin, caught his eye as she turned her attention briefly to Shaun.

"Just a guy passing through. Needed a room for a couple nights."

"Yeah? I thought there was a problem with the plumbing?" the woman said.

"There is, but he isn't bothered. Gave him a discount, which he was happy with."

The woman nodded and turned her attention back to Jay, her gaze washing over him.

"Be my guest," she said, stepping back to allow him to talk to Shaun.

"What can I do for you, Mr Corrigan?" Shaun asked.

"Jay, please."

"Okay... Jay... what can I help you with?"

"Just wanted to let you know I won't actually be here most of the time... I'm renovating a houseboat at the marina. So could you shove any mail I get under my door? No doubt you'll have clocked off by the time I get back each day."

"Sure thing, Mr... Jay. No problem."

"Thanks."

As Jay turned to leave, the woman blocked his path.

"I know the marina. So, you're planning on living there?" she asked, looking up at him through thick eyelashes, rolling her shoulders back, emphasizing her assets.

"Hopefully, yes," he replied and smiled, attempting to get past her.

"You should pop into The Kraken for a drink after a hard day's toil. You'd brighten the place up... and my shift. I'm Jazz by the way."

"Hello, Jazz. I know The Kraken," Jay said, this time pushing past her.

This place is a dump! Jay thought, shaking his head as he stepped inside his room. The dated decor was in as much need of an overhaul as the houseboat he'd inherited several years ago, and which was to be his new home base down at the marina. The boxy TV on a dusty side table was a hangover from the 80s, and the tiny kettle-for-one took several hours to boil. In the cramped bathroom he'd been pleased to learn that at least the water pressure wasn't terrible, though it only turned hot at the same speed as the kettle.

He kicked off his shoes and sprawled on the bed, stretching out his long frame to its full six feet.

After some recent life-changing decisions—most notably to quit the Seattle Police Department after twelve years' service—Jay had come to the conclusion that he needed not only a new challenge, but a new place to live. For years he'd put off renovations on the houseboat, but with the expiration of the lease on his Tacoma apartment coinciding with his decision to leave the SPD, he felt the moment was right to take a pre-middle age sabbatical from the real world. He still had no solid idea what his next move was going to be, career or otherwise, but it didn't matter. He was okay for money and figured he'd spend the next few months fixing up and living on the houseboat while he pondered his next life choices.

"After all," Jay had said to his old friend Bill Clearwater back in Tacoma before he'd left the city, "living on the water in Poulsbo isn't the worst way to spend the late summer... fishing, hiking the nearby hills, supping icy craft beers at the Kraken." To his credit, Bill had agreed, albeit reluctantly, Jay had suspected.

And Jay was right. Poulsbo, a small Norwegian-themed town in the heart of the Puget Sound, was gorgeous all year round. It was especially alluring as summer drifted slowly into fall, and the long warm evenings promised the peace and tranquility Jay had been hankering after for years. His great aunt Mona had left him the houseboat in her will. The feisty Irish woman he'd adored, and whom he missed greatly, had been as damaged as the floating pile of timber she'd bequeathed to him. Jay had become fond of the town in his infrequent visits to check the potential deathtrap hadn't sunk.

He'd struck up some semblance of a friendship with Captain, the grizzled old Harbor Master at the marina, a man who had known Jay's aunt, though the details of their 'friendship' Jay didn't know and hadn't been inclined to ask about. The old sea-dog liked a drink—as had Mona to the point it had almost certainly hastened her demise—and Jay was sure Captain would be propping up the bar at The Kraken when he made his way down there later that evening.

It's good to be back, he thought as he closed his eyes and let his mind wander to all things boat repairs and marinas and what life might have to offer him in what the locals proudly called Viking City.

Two

"Local police are today on the hunt for disgraced MMA fighter Marcus Baker. Baker, 27, who was banned from the sport following a fatal brawl in a bar two years ago, has reportedly fled the scene of a triple homicide. Neighbors called in a domestic disturbance between Baker and his long-suffering girlfriend Charlotte Harris, 25. But when the police arrived on scene, they found Harris and two others dead. It's no secret that since the brawl Baker has been struggling with addiction to pain meds, and this addiction has led to multiple run-ins with police, called to his home by Harris, who later refused to press charges. Baker is said to be driving a late model..."

"Yeah, good luck finding that," Marcus Baker huffed as he muted the TV and returned to the window. He had never known a day last so long. He parted the curtains again and eyed the beaten-up Chevy he'd watched pull up outside a neighboring unit a short while before. If he stood any chance of reaching Ritchie's place in Canada, he needed transport, and the more inconspicuous, the better.

I could just wait for dark and then make a run for it, he mused as he eyed the car's slightly open window, which he could probably squeeze his arm through, his muscles not as hard as they once were. *But then what?* It's not like he could hot wire the thing. He was many things, but an accomplished car thief was not one of them.

"Maybe she's left the keys?" he muttered as he glanced back at the TV to see his picture front and center, his arm thrown around Charlotte's shoulders. Grins brightened their faces as they toasted the cameraman.

My last win. Happy times.

Marcus turned away and flexed his hands, his skin tingling as his high began its descent. All he'd wanted was for her to refill her prescription.

"I've told you before, baby, I'm not doing it," Charlotte had said as he'd bounced up and down on his toes, the yearning clawing at his insides, needing to be sated.

"But you know I'm in pain. My hand, baby... you know what the doctors said. That I've—"

"I know exactly what they said. I was there, remember?" She rounded on him, fire dancing in her gray eyes.

Marcus knew that look. He knew he stood no chance of getting her to help him. Yet...

"Last time, I promise, baby. Then I'll—"

"Then you'll what? Quit? Get help? I've heard it all before, Marcus, and your words mean shit."

Marcus could feel his dark shadow rising within him, the familiar persona that had helped him bring home title after title, that had ensured he won no matter the cost, that had made sure no one belittled him, whether in the ring or not. It settled its weight, his vision clouding as Charlotte continued her rant.

Marcus shook off the memory, or fragment of memory, as that's all it was. He'd needed his pills, and she'd stupidly stood in his way. She should have known better. He strode to the bed and dropped to his knees, rummaging under the mattress until his fingers settled on the object of his quest. Marcus slumped back against the wall, holding up the brown plastic bottle. The afternoon sunshine illuminated its contents. Four pills. Four. Nowhere near enough. But all she'd had.

He closed his eyes and watched himself ransacking her limp body, knowing she had some somewhere; she always did.

"What you done to that poor girl this time?"

Marcus had bristled at the sound of the old man's voice. Denzel Rodgers. Their neighbor. Their overly protective neighbor. Their neighbor that had the cops on speed dial.

"Fuck off, Rodgers, this is none of your damn business," he growled, continuing his search.

"Course it's my biznez. It always my biznez where that girl concerned. I told her I don' know how many times she can do better'n you!"

Marcus pulled the small bottle from Charlotte's body and stood, turning to loom over Rodgers.

"And don' you try all that intimidation crap on me. It won' work." The old man planted himself between Marcus and the exit and folded his arms.

"Have it your way." Marcus shrugged and launched himself forward, hurling Rodgers against the doorframe. The old man's spine had cracked upon impact.

"Shouldn't have got in my way," muttered Marcus as he refocused on the remaining pills. Just like the caretaker shouldn't have. He popped the cap and tipped out one of the pills, holding it between his thumb and forefinger, marveling at how something so small could make it all go away. *How could anyone say these things were bad?*

Marcus swallowed the oxy, washing it down with some water before lying on the rumpled bed to give the pill time to weave its spell. As he closed his eyes, musing about the Chevy outside, a thought took root: *Maybe she has some pills for me*? She certainly looked the sort.

With a smile on his face for the first time since ditching his car in Lake Tarboo, Marcus drifted into the comfort of numbness.

Three

When Marcus awoke, the shadows had lengthened, and the sun was taking its curtain call for the day. He jumped off the bed and raced to the window.

Good... still there.

With his hand on the doorknob, Marcus paused and took a breath. He could do without drawing attention to himself, especially given his mug shot was plastered all over the news. He was about to leave when a thought occurred to him, and he jogged to the non-functioning bathroom and grabbed one of the threadbare towels.

Just in case.

Marcus found the parking lot deserted as he wandered over to the old Chevy and issued up a prayer of thanks, one which was immediately denied as he stopped beside the car.

Shit! Must've come out while I was asleep.

He stood staring at the rolled-up window before checking the handle. He wasn't surprised to find it locked. Deserted or not, if he started jimmying the door open, someone was bound to see.

That's the problem with these nasty motels. Every window faces the lot.

He stepped away from the car and studied it, walking around to the back and trying the trunk. Locked.

"Can I help you?"

Marcus paused, hand on the driver's door handle this time. His mind raced for a plausible story.

"I thought I saw your window open and was just coming to check." He opted for the truth as he turned to see the owner of the Chevy bearing down on him, her frizzy hair bouncing in time with her swaying hips.

"Well, given I closed it a few hours ago, you can't have been paying that much attention, can you?" she said as she stopped, arms crossed under her breasts, accentuating her cleavage.

Marcus guessed that was a deliberate move on her part. He allowed his gaze to wander over her curvaceous hips, clad in spray-on black jeans, the studded belt peaking from beneath her enhanced band t-shirt, a perfect match for her Doc Marten boots; boots he had no doubt would cause some serious damage if she so chose.

His wandering gaze soon found her face as she stared up at him, arched eyebrows pulled higher by her quizzical look.

"Can't be too careful with the weather," Marcus said, shrugging. He pulled the towel off his shoulder and twisted it in his hands.

"What's with the towel? Going for a swim?"

A swim. I didn't think of that.

He almost nodded until he remembered he wasn't exactly dressed for the part. Marcus looked down at her, her curly hair seeming to fizz as she continued to stare at him.

"No water," he said, cocking his head back toward his room.

"I'd invite you to use my shower, but I'm heading out," she said and winked as she brushed past him. "There's no rest for the wicked, and someone's gotta keep the boozy punters in check."

As she lowered herself into the car, Marcus was unable to tear his gaze away from the view until she cleared her throat.

"I'll be back later though, if you fancy a nightcap?" She held his gaze for a moment before winking again.

Marcus didn't respond. Instead, he watched as she reversed the car, crunched the gears, and accelerated out of the parking lot.

Four

"Into the flood agaaaain... same old trip da daa daa, daaahhh. Da da dah a big mistaaake... da da daaa my waaaayyyy..."

Jay flicked off the radio, finishing the Chains' classic "Would?" in his mind as he eased his long legs out of his truck. He slammed the door and made his way toward his room before stopping, his shoulders slumping.

"Forget my damned head if it wasn't screwed on," he mumbled as he retraced his steps and yanked open the door. He reached across to the passenger seat and retrieved the six-pack he'd snagged from the store on the way home.

The night was cool but refreshing after what seemed like an eternity tucked inside the watery work in progress down at the marina, and Jay decided to crack the first of the beers right there in the parking lot outside his motel room. The desk chair he had pulled outside for his coffee that morning was still there and he slumped into it, sighing with pleasure as his ass connected with the soft seat.

He downed the first beer in six long gulps and immediately cracked the next. Negra Modelos weren't really for guzzling, but Jay was thirsty after spending the last dozen hours on a combination of his back, his knees, or on tiptoes as he peeled, painted, sanded, and scrubbed the houseboat, with what seemed like little or no progress.

One chore at a time, he thought as he swigged down half the second beer. Jay raised his free arm and sniffed.

"Hope there's hot water tonight…" he muttered. "Man do I need a shower."

He polished off the second beer and made his way inside the motel room and flicked on the TV. It was all garishly bad commercials and even worse news—*"Car pulled from Lake Tarboo belongs to wanted fugitive Marcus Baker"*—so he killed the TV and stripped off his clothes, folding them neatly, as was his compulsion, despite them being covered in paint and grease. Jay grinned. The clothes were in to their third day of use and ready for the landfill.

It's not like I'm trying to impress anyone, is it?

He stepped beneath the tepid water that did as little to replenish his energy as it did to clean his soiled skin.

Five minutes later, Jay felt just about fresh enough to put on some clean clothes, and then perched himself on the end of the bed. He laid back and promised himself he'd just close his eyes for five minutes before heading back to the marina, but to the Kraken this time, for food and a couple more well-earned beers.

He was asleep the moment his head hit the pillow.

Five

Marcus paced up and down the pokey room, his denim-clad leg making contact with the corner of the bed on each pass. He glanced at the TV, as he had a thousand times that day, and stopped, watching as a recovery vehicle hauled his truck from the lake.

Fuck! So much for a great hiding place.

That was the trouble in this day and age; big brother was always watching. No doubt some nerd had a drone flying overhead and spotted the car.

Whatever the reason, Marcus knew his time was running out. It had been a few hours since they'd found the truck, so it was only a matter of time before they found him; he was in no doubt about that. He had to move. But to move, he needed a vehicle, and the vehicle he wanted wasn't back yet.

He parted the curtains and scanned the dimly lit parking lot. Still no sign of her. He glanced at his watch. It was almost midnight. When she'd suggested a drink, he presumed she'd be back at a reasonable hour. Marcus grabbed the cigarette packet off the bed.

Time to loiter, he thought, but as he looked inside the packet, he shook his head. Something else he was running low on. If she didn't return soon, he'd have no excuse to be standing outside in the middle of the night.

One good thing about smoking bans everywhere, he mused as he ducked outside and lit up.

Ten minutes later, Marcus watched the Chevy swing into the lot and roll into its space in front of her room. She didn't look at him after she turned the engine off. She simply sat and stared through the windshield.

Tough, Marcus thought. *Shouldn't have flirted with me.*

He dropped his cigarette to the pitted asphalt and ground it out with his boot before sauntering over. His high was waning again, and it took all his willpower not to scratch the itch, but he needed to focus. Yes, he needed pills, but he needed to get to the border first.

Marcus rested his elbow on the roof of the Chevy and leaned down.

Ignoring me, hey?

He rapped on the window, prompting her to turn and look at him. Marcus watched as she graced him with a smile and a stretch before flopping back against the seat.

Nice try.

"Long night?" he asked as she finally opened the door. He stood back so she could get out.

"You could say that," she said, rolling her eyes as she exited the car. It wasn't lost on him how she pushed her tits out, probably hoping to distract him.

"Yeah, well, I have a little something that will help you unwind," he said and rested his hand on top of hers as she locked the ancient Chevy, hoping she wouldn't notice the growing tremor.

"Not tonight." She snatched her hand away and hugged it to her, the keys disappearing behind her purse as she did so.

Dammit!

"Don't tell me you're standing me up?" He threw up his hands in mock horror, bringing a smile to her face. It worked. She relaxed and dropped her hands by her sides. Her purse in one hand. The keys in the other.

"Not standing you up, I promise. But I am gonna ask for a rain check. Honestly, I had a helluva night." She tossed the words over her shoulder as she walked to her room. Marcus followed, his gaze riveted on the sway of her hips.

"Let me at least help you with something." He made a grab for her keys.

"What the fuck?" She shoved him away and backed toward her door, a frown marring her face. "Just leave it, okay, or there'll be no rain check." She turned her back on him and inserted her key in the door.

Marcus could only watch as she pushed open the door.

It's now or never. I can't wait.

In desperation, he lunged forward and grabbed hold of the keys dangling from her hand before he shoved her in the back, knocking her to the ground.

Six

Fucking old cars! Marcus thought as he fumbled with the keys. An animalistic roar interrupted him, and he turned in time to see the woman launch herself at him, wrapping her thighs around his waist as she grabbed him by the throat.

They tumbled to the ground; the woman cried out as their combined weights crushed her left leg. The car keys skidded out of reach. Her grip loosened enough for Marcus to get his arms between the two of them. He shoved her away and jumped to his feet.

He spotted the car keys and dove for them, but the woman grabbed his ankle and yanked herself toward him, sinking her teeth into his calf.

Marcus yelped and kicked out, his boot heel catching her chin, stunning her. But in moments, she was on her feet. She jumped at him again, but this time, Marcus was ready. He punched her in the face; the blow caught her right cheekbone. She grunted and staggered backward, righting herself in time to catch the roundhouse he aimed at her stomach, knocking her off her feet.

Marcus left her sprawled on the asphalt as he turned back to the car, cursing as he struggled to find the door key. Just as he reached the last key, the woman barreled into him and snatched the keys out of his hand before making a dash for her room.

Oh, no you don't!

Marcus lunged after her and grabbed a handful of cork-screw curls, yanking backward, almost pulling the woman off her feet.

"Hey! What the hell do you think you're doing?"

Marcus dragged the woman against him and wrapped his arms around her. "Not a fucking word," he hissed into her ear before turning to address the interloper.

"Nothing for you to be concerned about," Marcus barked at the man, watching him approach. He was Marcus's height and build, and from the look of the man's face, shadowed somewhat by the lights of the parking lot, he could clearly handle a fight.

Fuck!

He shoved the woman toward her room, hoping to get them inside before the man got to them, but she resisted his every effort. He released her with one hand and grabbed his gun from his waistband, where it had been hidden by his jacket. He rammed it into her back. She froze. "Move," he hissed again.

She relented and allowed him to propel her into her room, where he shoved her forward. She lost her balance and fell onto her hands and knees, crying out.

"I don't believe you," the man called, and Marcus turned to see him racing toward them. Not knowing what else to do, he slammed the door and pressed his back against it.

"Help me!" screamed the woman.

"Shut the fuck up!" he growled, pointing his gun at her.

Fuck! Fuck! Now what?

Seven

Jay reached the door just as it slammed shut. "Goddamitt!" he seethed, banging his fists against the wood.

Jay heard the woman screaming for help and cursed himself for not reacting sooner. He was unarmed—he owned a gun, but it was at the Airstream he kept out in the woods at Chilicum—and knew he couldn't just smash the door down and risk both his and the kidnapped woman's lives.

Jazz… is that her name?

With no better plan, Jay raced to reception.

"Put a call through to room thirteen. Do it now!" he demanded of Shaun.

But Shaun faltered, frowning.

"Forget it. I'll do it myself!" Jay snapped and reached over the counter for the phone.

"Okay, I've got it," Shaun cut in and placed the call. As it connected, he handed Jay the receiver.

The phone rang for a full twenty seconds before a gruff voice answered. "Who is it?"

"Never mind who I am," Jay stated. "Let me speak to the woman."

"No. This has nothing to do with you. I suggest you back off. This is my business."

"You treat all women like that? Like a coward? Way I see it, you've already made this my business."

"I said back the fuck off. I have a gun and this bitch means absolutely nothing to me. You hear me?"

Jay inhaled. He had to be careful. He had no idea who this prick was or what he was capable of.

"Alright… you have a name?"

The man didn't respond.

"Well, can I ask what you want?" Jay asked, trying to pacify the loose cannon he suspected might be on drugs. "Why are you holding that woman hostage?"

"I told you to back off!"

"Well, I can't very well do that when you have my friend held against her will at gunpoint, now, can I? So, how about you tell me what I can do to help you resolve this. No one needs to get hurt and we can all just—"

The phone went dead.

The prick cut the call! Well, that was smooth, Corrigan.

"Call the room again," he told Shaun. "Just do it!" he snapped as Shaun dithered a second too long.

This time, the phone rang unanswered.

Shit! What now?

His gaze narrowed in on a stack of line-drawn maps of the motel. "Are all the rooms the same layout?" he asked, his mind churning. "Beds, bathroom, windows etcetera all in the same place?"

Shaun nodded. "Identical, except every second room is in reverse."

"Understood." Jay nodded, making a decision. "Okay, call the police. Tell them there's a man with a gun holding a young woman hostage. Do it now!" Jay told Shaun over his shoulder as he hustled to the door.

Jay trotted back toward the room, slowing as he approached and ducking behind Jazz's car out front. From his vantage point, he noticed a sliver of light between the window frame and the curtains. He strode over to the wall, keeping his back to it as he slid closer.

He risked a quick peek inside, and saw Jazz sprawled face down on one of the beds as the man with the gun stood in the center of the room, his back to the window.

Jay leaned back against the exterior wall and pulled up a mental map of the room. Two large double beds to the left. Jazz lay on the bed farthest from the window, near the bathroom at the back. On the right, a chest of drawers, writing desk, chair, plus a small cabinet containing a minibar with a microwave on top. A couple of lamps on bedside tables, and a TV somewhere on the right. No other windows. No other way out or in except through the front door.

Jay was torn. He considered knocking on the door and trying to reason with the man. He also thought that if he kicked in the door and rushed him, he might be able to wrestle the gun from him before the bastard had a chance to react.

Too risky.

If the man was high on drugs, anything could happen.

"Help! Someone help me, for fuck's sake!" Jazz yelled, prompting Jay to look through the gap. She was on her knees on the bed, slapping wildly at the man who now held the gun to her head.

"Fucking stay down!" the man yelled, swinging the gun and pistol-whipping her. She collapsed onto the bed, clutching at her head and screaming. "I'll fucking shoot you, I swear to god," he growled. "Stay fucking quiet or I'll break that pretty head of yours."

Mother fucker!

Jay seethed but held still as he watched the man edge farther away from the bed, one hand clutching the back of his neck, his face contorted.

Jazz screamed again, and this time the man roared and fired a round into the roof. Jay grabbed a small rock from the ground and retreated behind Jazz's car before hefting the rock at the window. The large pane cracked but didn't break. A moment later, a series of rounds shattered the glass in an explosion of shards, destroying the window from the inside.

Jay sprinted to the room and launched himself through the near empty window frame, shards tearing at his skin. He barreled straight into the man, knocking him into the side of Jazz's bed before kneeing him in the jaw, sending him sprawling to the carpeted floor.

The man jumped to his feet and faced Jay, the gun still in his hand.

The man grinned, raised the gun, and pulled the trigger. Jay dove to the left between the two beds as the round just missed him, instead destroying the microwave in a blast of sparks. Jay leapt up and smashed his right hand into the gunman's neck with a tiger claw punch. The gun discharged again, the pillow behind Jazz exploding in a flurry of down feathers and scorched cloth.

Jazz scrambled off the bed and toward the sanctuary of the bathroom as Jay dropped onto the man, pinning him down.

"Get out of here, now!" Jay demanded but Jazz stopped and turned. "No!"

"Get the hell out of here—"

The man beneath him suddenly corkscrewed his body and aimed the weapon directly at Jay's head.

"I told you to back the fuck off," the man grunted and pulled the trigger just as Jazz kicked him in the head, her hefty Doc Marten boot knocking him out. The round zinged past Jay's ear and through the missing window into the night sky.

An hour later, after being checked over by a team of paramedics, Jay and Jazz sat at the end of Jazz's bed, each cradling a beer Jay had grabbed from his fridge.

"Helluva night," Jay said as he watched her fighting back the tears that threatened to spill.

The police had arrested Marcus Baker without further incident and he'd been led away by a team of police officers. The officer in charge of the arrest had informed them both of the three murders Baker was accused of committing, adding that they had done the Pacific North West a great service by taking the 'scumbag' down before he could harm anyone else.

Jay smiled at Jazz, which caused the dam to burst, and she flung her arms around his neck, half squeezing the air from his lungs.

"Thanks," she whispered in his ear. "I'm not sure what I'd have—"

"You're fine," Jay soothed. "It's over. You were amazing."

Stifling a sob, she muttered, "You too…"

Jazz pulled back and looked into his eyes, and for a fleeting moment, Jay had the uneasy feeling that she was about to kiss him.

"Hey, time for some rest, I think, don't you?" he said, easing out of her clutches and standing. "And how about you let me buy you a beer tomorrow, eh?"

Jazz wiped the tears from her eyes and nodded. "Deal," she said, smiling.

Jay nodded and turned to leave.

"Jay?"

Jay paused in the doorway and turned. "What is it? You doing okay?"

She shook her head, her wild hair jiggling. "Would you... you know, could you...?"

Jay thought he understood. "Would you like me to... stay—?"

"Yes, please," Jazz answered before Jay could fully finish his sentence. "Nothing like, you know... like that, obviously..."

"Obviously," Jay said. He turned and locked the door.

Jazz climbed onto her bed. "Thanks again, Jay Corrigan... my hero."

Epilogue

As Jazz led Jay into The Kraken the following evening, the crowd of locals that sat around the bar area all stood and, as one, erupted into a round of applause, some whooping and hollering as they approached the pair and greeted them like heroes, hugging Jazz and shaking Jay's hand.

"You've earned this, son," said a tall, bearded man as he thrust a beer into Jay's hand. "The name's Erik. Pleasure to meet you."

"Erik, this is Jay. Jay, Erik," Jazz said as she approached. "Until you showed up, Erik here was the local hero."

"Now now, young Jazz," Erik said, his voice deep and with a heavy accent. "Don't exaggerate."

"Great to meet you, Erik," Jay said. "But I'm no hero."

"Neither am I, kid," Erik said, shaking his head. "Neither am I."

A couple hours later, as the drinks continued to flow, Jay was getting acquainted with the locals and thinking that he would soon be a Poulsbo resident like them. In the corner, a band made up of shaggy-haired youngsters was blasting out a series of classic 90s grunge tunes that were released, Jay suspected, before they were even born.

Jay stepped out of the lively bar onto the back deck and gazed out across the passive surface of Poulsbo Marina, glimmering under a waxing moon. His gaze settled on his houseboat a few piers over and he inhaled, relishing the cool night air.

There could be worse places to live in the summer, he mused, remembering his words to his friend Bill before he'd left Tacoma. "Much worse places," he murmured, before singing along to the latest song from the band inside, or at least trying to.

"Black hole sun, da da dah, da da dah the raaaain? Black hole sun, da da dah, da da dah..."

THE END

The Waiter by Suzanne Lissaman

London
June 1991

Lisa hobbled out of the lift and into the hotel corridor. A few more steps to her hotel suite, and then she'd be able to take off these bloody boots. Why had she thought 4-inch heels were a good idea? They had felt like slippers in the shop, but after an hour at tonight's ceremony, she lost the feeling in her toes. Then she tripped as she walked on stage with the rest of the band to accept the Best Song Award. She would have fallen flat on her face if Pete hadn't grabbed her arm. Not the best way to get noticed on national television.

As she opened the door to the suite, she heard moaning. It must be coming from the room next door. She'd expected a 5-star hotel to have better soundproofing.

As she walked into the room, she noticed Pete's shirt casually discarded over the back of the sofa. Odd - he was usually annoyingly tidy. But it wasn't the only thing that wasn't where it should be. Her eyes automatically followed the trail of clothes leading across the sitting area to the open bedroom door, which perfectly framed a view of a naked Pete scrabbling to get under the covers on the king-size bed. Judging by the lumps in the bedding, someone was lying beside him. Lisa took a sharp intake of breath.

'Hi, darling,' Pete said in a cheery tone that didn't match the rabbit-in-the-headlights look in his eyes. 'I wasn't expecting you back yet.'

'No shit! Let me guess. You wanted a nap after downing all that booze earlier, and you needed someone to give you a massage to get you off, so to speak?' Lisa did her best to hold back her fury.

The lumps in the bedspread next to Pete moved slightly.

How dare Pete ruin what should have been a fabulous day. Lisa put her hands on her hips. 'Who is she?'

Pete looked like he had no idea what to say.

If Lisa had been a betting woman, she'd have put money on his lover being the pretty blonde photographer he'd been flirting with before the ceremony. Not that Pete flirting with the opposite sex was unusual. 'It doesn't mean anything - I just like having a laugh. There's no other woman for me but you,' he'd insisted when she'd challenged him about it early in their relationship.

And she believed him. Pete was always caring and attentive whenever the two of them were together, but he couldn't resist the temptation to flirt. It didn't matter what the women looked like or how old they were; he wanted all of them to love him.

The targets of his affections usually treated it all as a bit of fun, at least when Lisa was in the vicinity. But while the band was posing for photos this evening, Lisa could tell from the photographer's body language that this woman wanted to get to know Pete a whole lot better.

Ignoring the uncomfortable boots, Lisa strode purposefully to her side of the bed.

'Come out, you bitch.' She dragged the covers down before Pete could stop her. 'Fuck me!'

'I'd rather not. I prefer blokes, personally.' The voice was deep, with a strong South London accent. The head and body she'd revealed belonged to the male music journalist who'd interviewed them a few hours earlier. Andy someone - Lisa hadn't bothered to remember his full name. She'd complained to Pete afterwards that Andy had behaved like a sexist pig, ignoring her while hanging on Pete's every word. Pete was usually supportive when journos were dismissive of her, but today he'd been uncharacteristically noncommittal. Now it all made sense.

Lisa was speechless. She'd never felt this combination of rage, stupidity and confusion before. It was all too much to take in. She turned and marched out of the suite as fast as her painful feet would carry her.

What was she going to do now? Lisa needed somewhere quiet to think it all through. She took the stairs - less chance of running into someone else that way. She remembered the hotel had a balcony on the second floor. Fresh air would help. Well, as fresh as you could get in London on a warm summer evening.

She emerged from the stairwell into the plush carpeted second-floor landing. The balcony sign pointed to a glass door on the left. She peered through. No one was out there. Perfect.

She walked to the edge and stood gripping the ornate ironwork tightly as if it were the only thing stopping her from toppling off. She stared out at the lights across the square. The sound of lots of people having fun came from the ballroom behind her, but she tried to filter it out. She needed to concentrate on answering the key question going around in her head.

How had she missed that Pete was gay? She went back over their year-long relationship, looking for clues. He'd pursued her, confessing that he'd looked for excuses for them to be alone until he'd eventually made a move. And he'd been an enthusiastic lover - until recently, anyway. She'd put that down to being tired from the lengthy European tour they'd just completed. But perhaps he wasn't getting what he wanted. There'd been no hint of him being attracted to men, though. Maybe he'd been very good at hiding it, or he didn't want to admit it to himself.

Not that any of that mattered now. Pete had cheated on her. How could she carry on working with him after that? After the excitement of being presented with that iconic award less than an hour ago, Lisa's world felt like it was crumbling around her. And her boots weren't helping either. At least that problem was easily solved. She unzipped them and hurled them over the balcony into the garden. There was a shout from below.

She looked down into the street. Shit! They'd been more aerodynamic than she'd anticipated, overshooting the garden and narrowly missing a passerby. She watched the man's dog pick up one boot and run off. It was welcome to it. She started sobbing.

'You look like you could do with one of these.' The voice startled her. She looked over her shoulder to see a young waiter standing beside her, holding a silver tray containing a solitary glass. 'Champagne,' he said.

Her feet were still throbbing despite being free of their patent leather prison. A drink might help take the edge off the physical pain and possibly the emotional pain, too. There was one slight problem.

'I haven't got any money on me,' she said.

'It's on the house.' He smiled reassuringly. 'Congratulations on your award.'

He'd recognised her. She could see the headlines now. *Sapphire Satans' lead singer overwhelmed by fame.*

She looked at him pleadingly. 'Please don't say you've seen me like this.'

The waiter looked sympathetic. 'I won't - I promise. Can I get you anything else? Shoes, for instance?'

She looked self-consciously at her not-so-rockstar pink and white spotty socks peeking out from under her black silk and lace skirt. 'Thanks, I'll be fine. Honestly.'

He smiled. 'Find me if you need anything.'

'Thank you,' she called after him as he headed back into the ballroom.

The ballroom guests were spilling out onto the balcony to give the waiting staff space to clear away the tables. Judging by their well-cut tuxedos and expensive evening gowns, they were senior executives for some big corporate. They were going to wonder what a 20-year-old shoeless woman in a leather bodice was doing, gatecrashing their formal dinner dance. Time for Lisa to leave. She tipped back the champagne glass, the bubbles tickling her throat as she gulped it down.

Right. She'd made up her mind. Pete's infidelity wasn't going to ruin what should be the best evening of her life so far. She was going to go back downstairs to the after-party to bask in the glory of being a winner. But first, she needed to sort out some footwear.

She hoicked up her bodice and walked onto the landing with her head held high. The lift took her back to the fifth floor, where she marched into the suite unannounced. It was in darkness with no sign of Pete or Andy. The trail of clothes had disappeared, and the bed was made. There was a piece of hotel notepaper on her pillow: *I'm so sorry. We need to talk. I'll be back by midnight. P xxx*

She sighed. She wasn't looking forward to that conversation.

Lisa left the note where she'd found it. She had a shower, redid her makeup, dressed in a fresh shirt and jeans, and found her trusty old baseball boots. She could dance the rest of the night in those.

She went back to the lift. The doors opened as soon as she hit the down button. She walked inside and pressed G. It shuddered into life. She watched the numbers slowly count down until they stopped at 2. The lift doors opened to reveal a familiar middle-aged man who looked like his suit last properly fitted him when he was in his teens.

'Lisa!'

'Dougie!' Why did their bastard of a manager have to be catching the lift now? She did her best not to scowl at him. She could smell the alcohol and stale cigarette smoke on his breath as he lurched towards her, and planted a soggy, wet kiss on her cheek.

'Congratulations, bab!' he slurred.

Lisa recoiled in disgust and went to hit the door open button. But he knocked her hand away, before slipping his arm around her waist and pulling her to him, unsubtly staring down her cleavage. 'Why don't we discuss your solo career in my room?'

Without waiting for an answer, he forcibly kissed her hard on the lips, his tongue trying to probe her firmly shut mouth.

Could today get any worse? A proposition from a sleazy scumbag of a man with a hairdo and moustache that went out of fashion at least ten years ago hadn't been on her wish list. Dougie would sell his own grandmother to make a fast buck. Lisa would rather become a nun than allow his stubby, gold-ring-clad fingers to explore her body.

None of which she could say out loud because the lovely Dougie was in charge of the Sapphire Satans' money, and Lisa was 99% sure he'd already embezzled a significant chunk of their royalties. She needed to keep him onside until she'd got evidence, which meant even a swift knee to the groin was out of the question. She could've done with her stilettos to "accidentally" tread on his toes - damn those bloody boots again.

'I've promised an interview to the NME,' she said, hopeful that the prospect of more free publicity would make him give up on his plans for her tonight. Instead, he pulled her closer just as the lift doors opened again, revealing a familiar figure standing outside. The waiter.

Dougie turned to see who was interrupting his seduction routine, inadvertently loosening his grip as he did so.

Lisa took the chance to free herself and ran out of the lift. 'Could you show me where the after party is, please?' she asked, grabbing the waiter's arm. She knew exactly how to get there, but it was the best excuse she could think of on the fly.

'Of course, madam.' The waiter indicated the staircase. 'Shall I lead the way?'

She nodded and followed him, glancing back to see a fuming Dougie glowering at them.

As they arrived outside the function room, Lisa turned to her knight in shining armour. She looked at him properly for the first time. His name badge said NICK. Her best mate, Jen, would say he was exactly Lisa's type: tall and slim, just like Pete, but with piercing blue eyes and blonde hair. Nick looked concerned. 'Are you okay, now?'

She nodded. 'Thank you - again.'

He smiled. It was an appealing smile accompanied by a twinkle in his eyes. He looked like he'd be fun to spend time with. If she were single, she'd have flirted with him. *What do you mean if you were single? You're planning to be single very soon,* her inner voice pointed out.

Lisa heard herself saying, 'I owe you a drink. What time do you finish?'

In her head, her mother's voice admonished her, "Nice girls wait to be asked." But there was going to be no more nice Lisa. She was new, confident Lisa now, and new, confident Lisa called the shots.

'There's a bar on the street opposite,' Nick suggested. 'Not many mainstream music fans go there. It's called Jack's. Shall we meet there? I'll be finished here by 10.'

'Sounds perfect. I'll see you later.'

'I'll look forward to it.' He grinned and headed back up the stairs.

She watched him walk away, admiring the rear view as much as the front. Perhaps she could get her own back on Pete.

Lisa checked her watch. Ten o'clock already. She was going to be late. Hopefully, Nick was a patient man.

She'd played the part of "life and soul of the party", determined to network with the great and the good of the music industry to make the most of tonight's win. But now the effects of the champagne were wearing off, the introvert inside her was craving solitude. The idea of lying on a comfy bed to gather her thoughts and plan what to do next was so tempting. But that reminded her of what had been happening in that bed earlier. Besides, Nick didn't deserve to be stood up. Just one quick drink as a thank you, perhaps get his number if he was as lovely as he looked, and then she could return to the hotel.

Her fellow band members were busy or absent: Pete hadn't made an appearance, unsurprisingly, Simon was chatting up a famous DJ, and Tez had gone home to his girlfriend. Only drummer Ed was keeping Lisa company now.

'I feel like I'm getting a migraine. I need some peace and quiet,' she said, getting up.

'Yeah, alright. Do you want me to get you anything?' Despite his offer, Ed was mid-cigarette and didn't look as if he planned to leave the sofa he was lounging on.

'No!' Lisa said, a little too emphatically.

Ed looked affronted. She didn't need to fall out with anyone else this evening. Lisa gave him a peck on the cheek. 'I don't want you to miss out on the fun. See you tomorrow,' she said, waving as she made a beeline for the exit.

Jack's Bar was tucked away in the side street opposite the hotel, exactly where Nick had said it would be, with only a simple sign over a solid black door advertising its presence. Lisa would never have dared to go in there normally - probably wouldn't have even noticed it. She tentatively walked inside. There was a bare brick wall in front of her with a staircase to her right leading down into a basement. The entrance wasn't welcoming, but the sounds of talking, laughter and piano drifting up from the basement were.

Lisa headed down the stairs and into the bar. It was like stepping onto a film set of a 1920s New York speakeasy, except the extras were dressed in contemporary clothes. Her eyes naturally followed the long, shiny pewter counter to where Nick was sitting in a pool of light cast by an Art Deco glass lamp above his head.

He looked lost in his thoughts, staring into an empty pint glass, turning it around slowly on the counter. He was even more attractive now he'd replaced his waiter's white shirt and tie with a battered black leather jacket and a dark t-shirt. Nick must have sensed her looking at him as he raised his gaze towards her and beamed. That smile again. It sent a rush of warmth to all the right places. It had been a while since Pete had had the same effect on her.

Lisa made her way through the crowd towards him.

'I was beginning to think you weren't coming,' he said, turning on the bar stool to face her.

'I lost track of time - I'm sorry. Thank you for waiting.'

'What'll you have to drink?'

'G&T, lemon, no ice. What are you having? I'll get these.'

'No, you won't. You can get the next round,' he said, smiling.

Old school gentleman, then. Hardly surprising, considering how attentive he'd been earlier.

'I'm supposed to be buying you a drink to say thank you,' Lisa insisted.

'It's ok. I don't need a thank you.' He turned to the barman and placed their order. 'Shall we sit over there?' he asked, nodding towards an empty booth in the corner. 'We'll be less visible.'

'Ashamed to be seen with me?' Lisa joked as Nick picked up their drinks and led the way to the booth.

'No,' Nick laughed. 'I thought you'd appreciate some privacy, that's all.' He set their glasses down on the table.

'How did you know I was in the lift earlier?' Lisa asked as she slid onto the leather bench seat opposite him.

'I was walking past when that bloke went inside. I didn't like the look of him, so I pressed the lift button.'

'You're an excellent judge of character.' Lisa explained who Dougie was but left out her suspicions about his money-stealing tendencies.

'Has he tried that on before?'

'No, but I had a feeling he might. I've managed to avoid being alone with him until tonight.'

'So what are you going to do about it?'

'I don't know yet. I've got quite a few things to work out how to deal with after this evening's events.'

Why did you say that?! He's going to ask what else is bothering you now! Lisa changed the subject. 'You know a lot about me already. Tell me about you.'

Nick was studying drama in London and earning a few quid as a casual waiter to supplement his student loan. He'd moved from Birmingham last year.

'You don't sound very Brummy,' she said.

'Years of acting and elocution lessons removed all trace of my accent,' he said in a strong, Birmingham voice. She liked his sense of humour.

He was the fourth child of six. 'It was difficult getting attention at home, so I got it on stage.'

'I had too much attention.' She told him about being an only child and how music had been her escape from an unhappy life at home. It was a bit more than she'd intended to say, but the G&T was having a greater effect than usual after the champagne earlier. *Be careful not to reveal too much.* Lisa changed the subject to books and films.

They chatted easily for another ten minutes or so until she sensed people were looking at them, some more obviously than others. This was the downside of tonight's extra publicity.

A man approached their table, politely asking for Lisa's autograph. Nick was about to say something to him, but she raised her hand to stop him. 'Who's it for?' she asked and obligingly signed her name on the serviette he'd handed her.

Nick looked disappointed as the man walked away. 'You could have said no. You're entitled to privacy.'

'I wouldn't be here without people like him buying our records. Signing an autograph is the least I can do.'

He grinned at her again. 'I guess I'm going to have to get used to that.'

An interesting thing to say. 'Planning to be famous too?' she asked.

'Possibly, but that's not what I meant.'

She liked his confidence. It came across as reassuring rather than arrogant. 'Are we going to be doing this again, then?'

'I hope so.' Nick looked round at the rest of the customers. 'How do you fancy going to the cinema? People won't recognise you in the dark.'

'When? Tomorrow?'

'I meant now. There's a late-night cinema about ten minutes' walk away. They're showing *Bladerunner* tonight. I was planning to go before I met you.'

'But you said you'd seen *Bladerunner*.'

'I've watched the video, but I'd like to watch it on the big screen.'

Lisa wasn't ready to face Pete, and a couple of hours watching Harrison Ford might take her mind off everything else. 'OK then. You're on.'

They squeezed their way through the other customers and went outside. Nick took her hand to lead her across the road. He kept holding it as they walked together up the street. He didn't seem intimidated by her fame, unlike most of the new people she'd met in the last month or two, who fawned over her to embarrassing levels.

The cinema could be a ruse, and he's planning to drag you off into some dark alley. She could always rely on her inner voice to come up with a downside. She stopped walking.

'Are you ok?' he asked.

'I was just thinking you could be a psychopath.'

He nodded, looking serious. 'I could be, but I promise I'm not. Does this help?'

He pulled a folded-up cinema flyer out of his jacket pocket. 'See. Thursday 14th at 11.15 pm.'

Harrison Ford stared back at her.

Nick smiled reassuringly. 'The route's via busy roads. No dark alleys, I promise. I don't want to get mugged either.'

⚜

Lisa stood in the cinema foyer, admiring its ornate ceiling and the grand staircase leading up to the auditorium. Although it was tatty around the edges now, it was still popular, judging by the steady stream of people walking through the entrance.

Nick bought tickets in the middle of the second row from the back. 'Best view and best sound,' he said.

'It's busier than I expected,' Lisa whispered to him as they found their seats.

'This is quiet. The Friday and Saturday night late night showings are always packed out.'

The trailers were just finishing. The lights dimmed, the film rating card appeared on the screen, then the curtains drew back further.

Lisa shivered.

'Cold?' Nick whispered, slipping his arm around her shoulders.

It felt good. She snuggled in closer. 'Not any more,' she whispered in his ear.

He held her tighter. How could she feel so safe and relaxed with someone who'd been a complete stranger a few hours ago? It was like she'd known him forever. She pulled away slightly so she could see his expression. He was looking at her intently. She couldn't resist gently stroking her thumb across his full lips. He appeared to be deciding whether to kiss her or not. Lisa made the decision for him.

⚜

That first kiss had set Lisa alight like no kiss she'd experienced before. Her thoughts kept coming back to it as she walked in the cool early morning sunshine. *Stop thinking about Nick. Concentrate on Dougie and how to finish with Pete without breaking up the band.*

She'd woken up half an hour previously, thanks to the daylight streaming through the thin curtains in Nick's bedroom. She'd lay there momentarily, horrified to realise she'd spent the night with him. One-night stands were normally not her thing, especially now the tabloids would be very interested in any juicy gossip about her. She panicked and quietly sneaked out before she had to face him.

But why be afraid? She'd never felt so relaxed with anyone. Pete always seemed to be holding something back, and now she knew what. Nick, on the other hand, appeared to be an open book. She hoped her instincts were right and he wouldn't head off to Fleet Street later in search of a fat cheque in exchange for his story.

She blushed at the thought. Had last night just been a way to get her own back on Pete? She didn't think so. There had definitely been something more than pure lust between her and Nick.

Lisa could do with Jen's advice to make sense of it all. As for Dougie, she was due back in the studio with the rest of the band this afternoon. She'd mention her suspicions to them then. But first, she needed to check out of the hotel.

A few minutes later, she arrived at the main entrance. She greeted the doorman and headed inside. With a bit of luck, her hotel suite would be empty again, but when she let herself in, she could hear Pete gently snoring. At least he was alone this time.

He stirred when she opened the curtains, looking seriously hungover as he sat up. 'Where the hell have you been? I've been worried sick,' he said as he rubbed the sleep from his eyes.

'I spent the night shagging a waiter. And you?' *Why did you dismiss last night like that?* It sounded petulant and pathetic, as well as disloyal to Nick.

Pete looked stunned. 'I don't believe you.'

Lisa headed towards the bathroom. 'You can believe what you like. It's none of your business anymore.'

'Is that it, then? Are we over?' he called after her.

'Of course we are. I can't give you what you want, can I?' she said. 'We need to go back to being just friends again?'

'I guess so.' Pete looked bemused.

Part of her wanted him to argue, to declare his undying love for her. But that was just her ego talking.

When she emerged from the shower five minutes later, Pete was fully clothed and sitting on the end of the bed. 'I don't want to see Andy again, but ...'

She didn't let him finish. 'Let's pack up and check out, and I don't just mean the hotel. I'll move back in with Jen.'

Pete silently nodded.

Nick woke up in his bed alone. He rubbed his hands through his hair. He hadn't drunk much last night, but he had a headache. It must be a lack of sleep. He smiled, remembering why.

He headed out onto the landing. There was no sign of Lisa in the bathroom and none downstairs either.

Disappointing, but what did he expect? It was naive to expect her to stay for breakfast. She was used to luxury hotels, not this run-down Victorian terrace that shook every time a train went past the end of the backyard. As if on queue, the 7.30 am to Liverpool rumbled by.

He hadn't intended to ask Lisa back to his house share. Not that he was opposed to one-night stands, but there was something about her that was different, and it wasn't her terrible taste in socks or the fact that she was famous. He'd met celebrities before - some barely acknowledged his existence, others were polite. But Lisa had listened to him and seemed genuinely interested in what made him tick.

And then there was that kiss. He'd kissed loads of girls, but her soft lips on his had set his whole body on fire. After he'd rescued her from that incident with her manager, he'd planned to take it steady, but Lisa had other ideas. She hadn't wanted to go back to her hotel when they left the cinema. She'd invited herself back to his, and by the time they got to his room, they couldn't keep their hands off one another.

He put the kettle on and stood looking out of the kitchen window into the backyard, still replaying last night in his head. He'd recognised Lisa immediately when he first noticed her on the balcony, the fading light in the sky making a halo around her red hair. She was shorter in real life than she appeared on television, but no less striking. And when she'd smiled at him, it had made him catch his breath.

Come on, Nick. Don't give up that easily. She's worth seeing again.

Lisa had said something about going into the studio later. That must mean today, but he had no idea which studio. It would be simpler to go back to the hotel and leave a note at the Reception desk for her to collect when she checked out. He better get a move on.

He grabbed a pen and looked around for something to write on. Someone had left a chip paper on the work surface. That was no good - grease stains wouldn't exactly enhance his message. The final demand for the gas bill wouldn't do either. He ended up tearing off a sheet of his housemate's flowery shopping list paper from the notice board.

Nick got dressed and headed towards the nearest underground station. As soon as he walked onto the platform, he heard the rattle of an approaching train. Fate must be on his side. He grabbed a seat so he could compose the note on his knee as the carriage creaked and groaned its way to Leicester Square. Nothing gushy - he sensed Lisa wouldn't appreciate that.

Would love to see you again. Call me on this number at 6 pm tonight if you fancy another drink together.

He wrote the number of the phone box at the end of his street and signed his name. He hesitated for a moment before adding a couple of kisses. Then he folded the note and tucked it in on itself so no one could casually read it.

Five minutes later, Nick emerged from the tube station and walked the short distance up the side street towards the hotel. As he turned the corner, he saw a black cab parked in front of the hotel, with a doorman holding the back door open. A familiar woman walked out of the main entrance towards the cab. Lisa. He was going to be too late.

Nick was about to break into a run when he noticed a tall, dark-haired man following her - the keyboard player in her band. Nick heard Lisa say, 'Back to ours?' as Pete put his hand proprietorially on her waist.

VARIOUS AUTHORS

You bloody fool, Nick. Did you really think she was interested in you? He scrunched up the note in his pocket and quickly retraced his steps before anyone noticed him.

This short story is an extract from my new novel, The Waiter, which will be published in late 2024.

A Shot in Time by T.S. Simons

Blurb

What if a single day altered the trajectory of your entire life? After years studying art, Alexanne Fraser's dream is to open her own photographic gallery, not shoot formulaic, boring weddings. Demanding Bridezillas throwing their weight around are not her thing, but wedding photography pays the bills. Just when she thinks she has seen it all, a colleague asks for help to shoot the most harrowing ceremony possible, leaving Alexanne facing challenges that will change her life forever.

One

"Alexanne!"

Stephanie waved from under the red and white striped umbrella at our favorite table. She stood, pushing the sunglasses to the top of her head.

"It has been too long!" She shrieked as she wrapped her arms around me and pulled me in for a hug.

"Ally! You've lost weight," she said accusingly, pulling back and staring at my face as I sat down opposite her. "New man?"

"Sort of," I blushed, replacing my sunglasses to hide my reaction.

"You always lose weight when you have a new man. So predictable. Tell me everything."

"It has been a few months now," I admitted. "He is lovely."

"Ooh! About time! How someone as gorgeous and talented as you is still single is beyond me. Tell me everything. Name. What does he do?"

"His name is Hamish," I started cautiously. "He is 28."

"Ooh, a great age to settle down." Stephanie interrupted. "What does he do?"

"He is a software engineer for Barclays Bank, IT security for international financial systems, so he travels a lot."

"Professional. Well-traveled. Earns good money. Tick. What does he look like?"

I sighed dramatically. "He is perfect. Five foot eleven, brown hair, and the most gorgeous brown eyes you have ever seen. Not too thin, but not fat either. Loves cats, and doesn't smoke, but not one of those ridiculous fitness types either that makes you feel like a heifer. Super intelligent. Just... he is everything I want in a package."

"What about his family? Have you met them?"

"He is from Lewis, in the Outer Hebrides, moved here for boarding school, then university. Old money. His folks are retired and travel a lot. But I hope to meet them soon."

"So, when do I get to meet him?" Stephanie gushed. While we rarely saw each other now that she was following her dream of being a flight attendant jetting around the world, we had been best friends since high school, and I knew she would always have my back.

"Soon, I hope. We are looking at places in Dean Village. Then we will have a housewarming."

"Whaaat! That is serious! You have been holding out on me all this time? How did you meet?"

"I was photographing a wedding in St Andrews, and he was staying at the same hotel."

"A wedding guest?"

"No, he was there for work. They were closing the bank branch and facing technical issues, so he went there in person. We met at the hotel bar. By the time I managed to escape Bridezilla and her entourage, who I swear wanted a photograph in front of every rock in the castle, I was exhausted and just wanted something quick to eat before heading back to my room. The restaurant had closed, and I had ordered a meal of crisps and whisky."

"Classy. And?"

"Well, he teased me about my nutritious diet, and then the next thing I knew, we had whisked me off to a late-night French bistro, eating duck confit, drinking red wine, and exchanging life stories."

"Love at first sight," she sighed dramatically. Stephanie really should have stuck to her initial major of drama. Likely, first-class passengers didn't appreciate a flamboyant hostess.

"Not quite," I said coyly. "Oh, maybe. There was a definite connection. A spark. Oh, Stephanie, I think he might be the one. He said it, you know."

"It?"

I nodded.

"Who said the actual words first?" She grilled, her eyes narrowing.

"He did!"

"No way!" Her voice rose an octave, as it always did when she was excited. "Hold on, were you in bed? It doesn't count if he says it after sex. That is just oxytocin talking."

"No! We had been out to Glencoe for a hike. We were driving home, the song finished, and in the pause, he just turns to me and says, 'You know, I have never loved any woman as much as I love you.'"

"What did you say?"

"I admit, I froze, but I did it."

"I'm so proud of you! That must have been so hard." Stephanie squinted, studying me. "That's it! This is why you look different. He is your soulmate," she squealed. "I have never seen you so happy. You are positively glowing! Your skin is radiant, you look amazing. And I know how hard it is for you to say those words."

"Thanks. I truly think he is the one. I can't believe I am so happy," I admitted. "For the first time since Craig died, I am happy with a man and not scared that he will leave me."

"You deserve it. It has been nearly ten years. Do you think he will pop the question?"

"Probably not. He told me a few weeks ago that he has everything he needs with me. I am the most important person in his life, and we don't need a piece of paper to make it official."

"True enough. Now, tell me what else is going on with you."

"Work is good. My diary is booked every weekend. Finally, I am developing a reputation as a high-end wedding photographer. Then I get product work throughout the week to keep me busy. The occasional newborn or family shoot."

"You used to hate photographing weddings. Fake and pretentious, you used to call them. What happened to the girl who dreamed of opening her own gallery of artistic landscapes?"

"Bills need to be paid," I shrugged. "I guess I got real."

My bag hanging over the chair beside me vibrated, the sound resonating across the table. I sighed.

"Another Bridezilla?" Stephanie teased as I looked at the screen, screwing up my face at the name popping up. Airlie Jones, a rival wedding photographer with whom I had a chilled professional relationship. She was pretentious and arrogant, and not my style at all. She and I were in constant competition as the best wedding photographers in Edinburgh, often competing for the same high-end clients. Airlie's style was ostentatious and over the top, even her business name 'A Shot Above the Rest' screamed arrogant, whereas I preferred the classic 'let the bride shine and the photographer remains in the background' style. Regardless, we worked in the same limited space, and she could spread gossip throughout the industry, so I was always polite.

Making a face to keep Steph quiet, I politely answered the phone.

"Hello, Artful Lens Photography, Alexanne speaking."

Steph pulled silly faces at me over the table as I listened to Airlie's rambling. The server finally came over as I was speaking, and I pointed to the chicken caesar salad on the menu. Steph ignored me and ordered prawn risotto times two with a serving of garlic bread. I scowled at her as I tried to interject into the conversation in my ear.

"Thank you for thinking of me. I'm not...."

The irritating voice continued, and my head slumped.

"Fine. Where? I'll find it. What time? Sure. Can you email me the details? Do the couple know?"

More ranting in my ear as Steph continued to make faces.

"As long as she is alright with it. No one wants a grumpy bride on her big day. Thanks. Bye."

"You don't look terribly happy," Steph observed as I replaced the phone in my bag.

"I was actually looking forward to a weekend off," I admitted. "It has been months since I took a day off, and I need a rest. I'm shattered."

"A dirty weekend with Hamish?" Steph teased.

"No, he leaves tomorrow. He is working in the US for three weeks, and yes, I will miss him terribly, but we have plans to go away together when he returns. Wedding season is exhausting. I shoot every weekend, sometimes two in peak season. I was looking forward to a sleep-in, cooked breakfast, and a weekend of Netflix."

"So why did you say yes?"

"Because it pays well, and building a reputation in this business is important. Brides talk to each other, and wedding photography is a small and highly competitive market. If Airlie is referring clients to me, then she respects my work. She wouldn't tarnish her name by recommending someone sub-standard."

"Why did she ask you to do it?" Sara asked suspiciously.

"She is in the Royal Infirmary with a ruptured appendix and won't be able to walk by Saturday."

"Fair enough."

"Maybe I should send her flowers?" I mused.

"Let's not go too far. Didn't you say she was the competition?"

Saturday weddings were tough. Traffic to reach the venue was always worse, and there was a sense of pressure that I didn't find at Sunday weddings. Sunday brides were more relaxed somehow. The day was less about the ceremony and more about the guests.

After receiving the email from Airlie, I contacted the bride, Catherine, to ensure she was aware of the change. She was, but haughtily demanded my portfolio, which I happily provided a link to. It was a big day, and I fully understood the nerves associated with a last-minute change. I did my best to reassure her I was professional and produced quality work. She was terse, and I couldn't work out if it was nerves, or if she was going to be difficult. I sighed as I hung up the phone. Not that I didn't enjoy photographing weddings, I did. Traveling around the country and seeing the most spectacular sights and historical monuments were the best parts of my work. It was some people I struggled with. With increasing regularity, brides insisted I make them look like movie stars and ensure that every combination of family members was included, often in different arrangements so that they could cut them out of a photo if someone was exonerated from the family. Still, it was work, and I loved seeing the joy on their faces when they came back to see their portfolio of shots.

The wedding was scheduled for midday at Achnagairn Castle near Inverness, where the wedding party had booked the entire venue for the weekend. It was a new venue for me, so I researched it. When I saw the spread in Harper's Bazaar and googled the costs, my eyes popped. £30,000 for the venue alone! Who had that type of money? People who could afford privacy, a vaulted ballroom, and luxury hotel rooms to accommodate their family and friends for three nights evidently. I quickly reassessed my clothing choices. Usually, I wore black pants and a top, trying to remain discrete and in the background. But for my upmarket weddings, I tried to wear something comfortable but more elegant. Pulling out a simple but classic emerald silk dress that set off my green eyes and auburn hair, I paired it with some strappy low-heeled wedge sandals. Comfortable enough to walk in, but also not sink into the grass. At least I wouldn't look out of place. Hopefully.

It took me three hours to drive from Edinburgh to the venue, planning to arrive mid-morning so I could get the shots of the bridal party getting ready. The reception staff looked relieved to see me and showed me to the bride's quaint thatched whitewashed cottage where she and her eight bridesmaids were getting ready.

"Hi, I'm Alexanne, the photographer." I smiled as kindly as I could at the heavily made-up blonde woman wearing a dusty pink silk robe who answered the door. "Is Cathy here?"

Her eyes bolted open as she hissed, "No one calls her Cathy!"

"Sorry, it just slipped out," I whispered. "It is my sister's name."

"Who is it now?" The shrill, posh English-accented screech radiated from the back room. "Don't they know this is my day?"

"Photographer!" The woman called back. "I'm Elodie," she said, more quietly. "Come on in."

"Well, it's about time!" The huffy voice grunted. "I'm nearly ready. I was expecting her hours ago. That is what you get when you get a ring in at the last minute. As soon as I spoke to her, I knew she was going to ruin my day."

My face flushed, knowing instantly the type of bride she was. This was going to be a challenging one.

"Hi Catherine, I'm Alexanne. Do you mind if I start taking candids while you and your entourage get ready and then we can talk about planned shots? Airlie has provided a gull briefing on what you are looking for."

Catherine scowled at me but grunted consent. *Fabulous*, I thought. *I wonder how much of a demon the groom is.* While brides were usually worse, I had met some horrendous grooms while working in this industry.

"Then, while you relax, I can get some shots of the groom and his groomsmen," I continued, checking my sheet of planned shots.

"No! Who told you that? This day is about me!" She squawked haughtily, making me look at her in surprise.

"Don't you want photos of your husband getting ready for you?"

"There will be plenty of him later," she announced firmly. "This time is for *me*."

"Absolutely no problem," I assured her, recognizing how this would go. "It is my job to do whatever you want."

Over the next few hours, Catherine took my last statement literally, and put me through the ringer. Her bridesmaids, a mixture of family and friends, were either enablers of her appalling behavior or terrified of her, actively avoiding incurring her wrath. Coordinating shots where she was the center of attention took all my charm and resolve, but I finally managed to pull together what I hoped was a good spread, making her selfishness look as attractive as possible.

Catherine's father, a charming, handsome man in his sixties, wearing an expensive gray tailcoat, arrived to escort his spoiled daughter to the chapel. He was an utter gentleman, taking the time to check in and assist all the girls, but he was besotted with his daughter, who could do no wrong. She played up to it, simpering and looking angelic. Once again, I wondered what the groom was like. Women like this were the worst, using men as toys to get what they wanted.

Racing ahead so I could capture the bride coming down the aisle and get some early shots of the guests, I saw the groom and groomsmen enter from the side door. The four groomsmen flanked the groom, and for a moment, I wondered why she had eight bridesmaids. Usually, they matched up with numbers. Maybe there were more coming? Though it would be just like Catty Catherine to have double the number of bridesmaids to groomsmen.

The camera slipped from my hands and crashed to the floor, making my heart sink. While I had spares, that one was new and had cost me thousands. But it wasn't the damage that triggered the wave of nausea rising into my mouth. The groom had turned to face me, watching me intently, his eyes filled with horror. Unable to control the shock on my face, I knew my expression mirrored his. Hamish, *my* Hamish, stood at the altar waiting for another woman.

My eyes filled with tears as I hastily turned my back, checking on my equipment, but also trying desperately not to vomit across the altar. *How could it be? He was in America.* A peek at my camera with the viewfinder switched showed me he was most certainly not in New York, as he had told me. He was here, immaculately groomed, looking desperately handsome, and about to get married. *To another woman.*

Fighting my instincts to run, I forced myself to take deep breaths and coached myself to slow my heart rate. Catherine was the type of woman who would destroy my career and me personally if I ruined her big day. After all, as she had told me several times, it was all about *her*.

❦

Two

Eight excruciating hours of hell ensued. No, a spin class in hell wearing a fur jacket would be a cakewalk compared to this. My still-beating heart had been ripped from my chest, and now I needed to watch the man I truly thought was the love of my life marry another woman and capture it all on film.

After the ceremony, when we had taken the formal shots, Hamish had tried to make eye contact, pleading. But I had fake smiled through the photography, handily placing the camera in front of my face so he couldn't see my distress. Counting the hours until I could leave, I forced myself to snap away, smothering the pain that filled my chest. The worst part was that I needed to be in their faces, arranging them to show them to the best effect, to complement each other.

At several points, I prayed Airlie was in agony in her hospital bed, payback for the torture she had caused. Not that it was her fault. My heart was killing me, and I had a migraine from choking back the tears, forcing a smile as I impersonated the consummate professional, asking the happy couple to pose in all the classically cheesy poses. Feeding each other cake, the first kiss. The extended family photos. Hamish with his arm around her. Catherine tipped back, showing off her cleavage. My Hamish. Kissing that fake, pretentious blonde Barbie airhead who couldn't be more different from me if she tried. My head was pounding. When she left to change into her reception outfit, I slipped off to the loo for three minutes and swallowed some painkillers, praying I could make it through.

My brain was racing, biting back the desire to scream that he slept with me just two nights ago and made me orgasm. Twice. How we had laid in bed and made plans. Made a short list of houses to inspect when he returned from the US, discussed decorating, and what style we both liked in what he called our forever home.

As they cut their multi-layer wedding cake, I envisioned taking the sharp knife and imagined it embedded hilt-deep between his eyebrows, which had been neatly groomed for the occasion. His mother was lovely, elegant, and refined, and I nearly cried watching him treat her so tenderly, dancing with her. The way he had treated me. Like a gentleman. *The lying, cheating fucknuckle.*

Anger finally overtook the distress as I snapped away images of their guests dancing and enjoying the evening. *How dare he. Liar. Cheat.* I did my best to capture the look of fear in his eye every time I sweetly purred his name, making him terrified I would cause a scene.

Finally, a speck of rationality bubbled to the surface amidst the pain. What if I hadn't taken this job today? How much longer would he have strung me along? How would he have moved in with me and yet maintained a life with Catherine? Sleeping with both of us? What if we had started a family?

God, she was whining again. There was a wrinkle on her dress. I pretended to fiddle with the camera settings so she wouldn't ask me, yet again, to fix her appearance. She thought I was her personal dresser. Unable to catch my attention, she barked an order at one of her entourage. My heart went out to the poor girl, trembling as she helped the bitch queen.

As bitchface went off to change into her third outfit, her leaving outfit I hoped, I lingered in the back of the room, leaning against the wall. My head was throbbing, but I didn't dare take any more painkillers lest I fell asleep. Catherine would love to tell her guests and social set I was a druggie photographer. That would make a great story for the tabloid society pages.

"You need to eat."

Jolted out of my stupor, I stared blankly at the guest offering me a canape. Ordinarily, I would. I needed to eat something, but right now I couldn't. Some brides didn't like the photographer eating on the job, and I knew Catherine was one of those.

"I'm fine, thank you."

"I insist. He waved the plate in front of me. I have been watching and you haven't even had a sip of water all day. The bride may be a monster, but she won't want you fainting either. Then she won't get her precious photos of *me*!" He mimicked Catherine's rich English accent to perfection, and I let out a stifled giggle.

"I am so sorry," I blushed furiously. "That was not professional."

"You or me?"

"Me! I am so sorry. I should not have laughed."

"I'm just impressed that someone here at this stuck-up, pretentious boring as all fuck event, knows how to laugh. How boring were those speeches?"

Looking away, I had to agree. It was evident that Catherine had vetted all the speeches. Dull and repetitive, people yawned their way through. The entire day had been scripted and formulaic. Honestly, whilst one of the most expensive events I had attended, it was probably the most boring. One of the bridesmaids had whispered that Catherine's dress cost £6000, and I wondered for a second who had paid. Likely her father. It looked expensive too. Covered in pearls, antique lace, and bling, it was clearly pricey but ostentatious. I would never have worn a dress like that.

To marry who, Alexanne? I berated myself. *The fucking groom!*

Pain wracked me once more and my new friend watched as I winced from the lights.

"Are you ok?"

"Not really," I admitted. "Not feeling well. Migraine. But the show must go on. I can be sick later."

"Can I help in any way?" The concern was genuine in his voice.

"Not really," I admitted wanly as the aura from my pounding head blurred my vision. "Unless you can make the party end."

"Sadly, that is not within my power," he admitted. "But I can help you. Here, sip some water. Hydration always helps."

Handing him my camera, I downed the water in one chug,

"Sip, I said," he berated me as he filled the glass from the crystal decanter on the table behind us. "Now, eat."

The ten minutes I spent with James were the highlight of my day. Charming, witty, and a wonderful conversationalist, we struck up a conversation about the venue, the people, and the history of the place. Carefully, I kept the conversation on neutral topics and avoided the bridal party, but he didn't seem to have noticed. He was one of those relaxed, natural people who could hold a conversation about anything and anyone. I found myself relaxing, and enjoying myself for a moment.

"Ahh, she's back," James muttered, gesturing with his chin towards the side door.

"Shit," I muttered, grabbing my camera from the table. If I missed her third grand entrance, there would be hell to pay.

Catherine held court as the guests oohed and ahhed over her third dress, a sequined sea green dress that showed off her enhanced cleavage. What the hell did Hamish see in this woman? Bleached hair, evident facial work, fake boobs, and tan. Clearly, I didn't know him at all if this was what he wanted. Snapping away as each guest greeted her anew, I saw Hamish standing behind her, looking distracted. Like he didn't want to be here. But he was here. Now married. For the hundredth time, he tried to make eye contact. Pleading. But I refused. If I caught his eye, my heart would break, and I couldn't do that in public. I had a reputation to uphold.

My prayers were finally answered. It was over. The happy couple took one last dance, a long walk through the center of the room, and into a classic silver Aston Martin with bells attached to the back. Catherine made a great show of throwing her bouquet into the gaggle of women while Hamish stood back awkwardly. Being a gentleman, he helped her into the waiting vehicle and left, waving madly to the crowd. The guests dispersed slowly back inside, some staying for a cigar or to enjoy the cool night air. Many older guests started slipping off to their accommodation. The younger guests changed the music to modern songs and started drinking and dancing. Everyone was more relaxed. Snapping a few more shots, I breathed a sigh of relief. This was my cue. I could go. This nightmare day could finally end.

Packing up my bag on a side table, a warm hand touched my arm. I looked up into James' stunning blue eyes and smiled.

"Thank you for your kindness," I said sincerely. "It has been a long day, and I need to get home."

"Where is home?"

"Edinburgh."

"You can't possibly drive home tonight," he exclaimed. "It is a three-hour drive!"

"Yes, but..."

"But nothing. You are staying and that is the end of the matter."

Nothing in the history of the world could make me stay here. The place where the love of my life had married another. I would never return to this place again. I opened my mouth to argue, but nothing came out. Instead, the room began to spin and go black at the edges. I felt the arms come around me as the world went black.

Three

"Where am I?" I mumbled as shadows broke through my blurred vision.

"You are safe. Stay still."

My head was on a pillow, that became clear as my thoughts slowly returned. *A sofa? A bed?* My heart jolted.

"Where am I?" I repeated.

"One of the hotel suites. We are not discussing this. I took care of it. Now, when was your last meal?"

"Last night?" I slurred, my head still spinning.

"No breakfast?" James questioned.

"Just coffee."

"Lunch?"

"Too busy."

"So in the past twenty-four hours, you have had a coffee, a glass of water, and nothing else? No wonder your blood pressure is in the toilet, and you have a migraine. Can you sit?"

I reached for the proffered glass and sipped, feeling weak.

"Let me know when you can eat something. I have some crackers. Salt is good for you after a loss of consciousness."

Reaching for the cracker and nibbling cautiously, I started to feel better... and worse. "You didn't need to do this," I said, feeling immensely foolish. Memories flooded back of where I was. I needed to get out of here. "Who saw?"

"No one except me and two staff. You are fine. Most people were either dancing, hooking up, or had already gone to bed. Your timing was impeccable."

"I aim to please."

"Good, you are feeling better. Now, let's get some solid food into you. What do you like? Any allergies?"

"None, I eat and like everything."

"Ahh, a woman after my own heart." James picked up the phone and dialed, waiting for a moment, before using his impeccable English manners. "Room Service? Can I get... ahh, yes, I see. Yes, a cheese platter would be wonderful. Some fruit as well? For two please."

James turned his attention back to me as he replaced the receiver. "Well, I hope you like cheese."

"Cheese is a food group," I admitted. "Especially washed down with wine."

"Well, I am not convinced wine is a good choice right now," his eyebrows raised.

"Are you a doctor?"

"That obvious, am I?"

"Well, yes."

"Need to work on that."

"Not sure why. It isn't a problem, is it?"

James sighed. "No, except people always ask medical questions when they learn you are a doctor. You know, 'Oh, there is this spot I've been meaning to get checked out. Would you mind looking at it for me?' It becomes a bit tiresome."

"Kind of like an art historian," I said, then giggled. "Sorry, that is a stupid analogy. How would you know?"

"How is that?"

"As soon as people learn you studied art, they bring out a painting that was willed to them by their grandmother's cousin's neighbor and insist you appraise it."

"Were you an art major, then?"

"I was. Art history at the University of Edinburgh, and then art business from Sotheby's Institute of Art."

"Wow, that is impressive. So photography is your side business?"

"It was supposed to be. I wanted to be a museum curator, but there are so few jobs in Scotland. I lived in London for a time but hated it. So

I started wedding photography to pay the bills while I set up my own gallery. But it kind of took over."

"Well, Ms. Fraser, when are you opening your own gallery?"

I sighed, saved from answering as a knock sounded at the door with a thick Scottish accented, "Room service."

James leaped up from the chair and opened the door, politely ushering the tired-looking man to the table.

"Thank you," he said graciously as the server left and the door closed.

"Do you feel well enough to share this with me?" he asked with the utmost chivalry.

I nodded, and sat slowly, my head still spinning. James held out his arm for me to hold, and I swung my legs around, resting on the side of the bed. Smiling down at me, he waited until I was ready and escorted me to the brown leather Chesterfield sofa.

"You don't need to fuss, I am fine," I insisted as he arranged a cushion behind my back.

"Well, I want to. Now, eat."

Time flew as we ate cheese and drank wine. James finally relented and poured me a glass of the most superb red I had ever tasted. He was easy to talk to, and we spoke about art, history, university, travel, and our families. Finally, he asked me what had happened at the reception, and I paused, wondering if this was career suicide.

"Can you keep a secret?" I asked finally.

"On my honor, I can. Is it juicy?"

"The juiciest," I admitted, before proceeding to tell him about Hamish and me.

James' eyes popped with astonishment as I reached for my phone, scrolling through the images of Hamish and me, at my home or his, on trips we had taken.

"Shocked?" I finally asked, realizing that I was still speaking, and he was silent.

"Not really," he admitted. "I've known Hamish all my life, and I never understood what he saw in cold-blooded Catherine. You are his type, through and through. Beautiful, down to earth, intelligent, worldly, and independent."

The cheese blocked my windpipe. Not from the compliments, but from his description of Hamish.

"How do you know Hamish?" I asked, my voice quavering.

"He is my cousin. We are only 13 months apart in age. Our families are close. We grew up together."

My mouth dropped, and tears filled my eyes. "I am so sorry. I should never have told you."

"Why?"

"Because it will affect how you see him. I would never want that."

"That is where you are wrong. I always knew Hamish was a cad, and treated women with disrespect. Even when we were at Eton together, he had no sense of ethics. Nothing has changed. My father took a mistress, and it killed my mother. Literally. Upon learning about his affair, she took her own life. I was fifteen. Maybe that is why fidelity means everything to me. Had my father not cheated, my mother may still be alive."

"I'm so sorry." The words burst from my chest as a sob, suddenly feeling this was all my fault.

"Why are you sorry? You did nothing wrong." James' arms came around me, holding me against his chest. He smelled delicious, and I felt bad for dripping mascara tinted tears down his white shirt.

"Because I brought all this back for you."

James held me by the shoulders and pulled back slightly so he could study my face. "That was many years ago. Your trauma is fresh, yet you feel sorry for me? You are a good woman, Alexanne."

The tears rolled again at the mention of my trauma, and he pulled my face back into his shoulder, soothing me gently. His arms scooped me up like a rag doll and carefully carried me to the bed. Refusing to let me speak, he tucked me under the covers. I listened, exhausted and barely able to open my eyes as he bustled around the room, cleaning up, and turning off lights. I felt the warm body, still dressed, slip in behind me and hold me against him, comforting. Falling asleep, the last thing I remembered was the divine scent of his cologne, smelling like a pine forest after rain.

AATA 2024: THE ANNUAL

The pre-dawn light filtering past the curtains woke me with a start and I froze, sensing the warmth of the man in the bed behind me. As my memory returned, I felt and checked. I was clothed. A glance over my shoulder indicated he was also fully dressed.

Slipping out of bed as silently as I could, I collected my things and opened the door. Closing the door with a click, the bed creaked. Dashing down the corridor as I hastily slipped on my shoes, I clutched my camera bag to my side as tightly as I could and ran. Tossing my camera and lenses on the spare seat, I started my car and flew out of the carpark, not looking back until I hit the main road. Then the tears started, my heart shattering into a million pieces.

Want to know what happens next? *A Shot in Time* will be released as a full-length story in 2025.

Thank You for Reading

Your support means everything to the authors.
And to the charity benefiting from this book.
So please go to the sales channel you purchased from and add a review in the hope this collection gets the attention it deserves.
Many thanks x

---

[1] little pearl

[2] beloved

[3] love

[4] my heart

[5] my love

[6] fierce warrioress

[7] my heart's desire

[8] fierce queen

[9] womb

(FOOTNOTES FROM M.F. MOODY'S PIECE)

Printed in Great Britain
by Amazon